P9-DUQ-665

THE
EMPIRE
OF
GOLD

ALSO BY S. A. CHAKRABORTY

The City of Brass

The Kingdom of Copper

THE
EMPIRE
OF
GOLD

THE DAEVABAD TRILOGY, BOOK THREE

S. A. CHAKRABORTY

HARPER Voyager
An Imprint of HarperCollins Publishers

THE EMPIRE OF GOLD. Copyright © 2020 by Shannon Chakraborty. All rights reserved. Printed in the United States of America. No part of this book may be used or reproduced in any manner whatsoever without written permission except in the case of brief quotations embodied in critical articles and reviews. For information, address HarperCollins Publishers, 195 Broadway, New York, NY 10007.

HarperCollins books may be purchased for educational, business, or sales promotional use. For information, please email the Special Markets Department at SPsales@harpercollins.com.

Harper Voyager and design are trademarks of HarperCollins Publishers LLC.

FIRST EDITION

Designed by Paula Russell Szafranski

Maps by Virginia Norey
Title page art © Aza1976/Shutterstock
Half title and chapter opener art © AZDesign/Shutterstock

Library of Congress Cataloging-in-Publication Data has been applied for.

ISBN 978-0-06-267816-4 (hardcover)
ISBN 978-0-06-298836-2 (international edition)

20 21 22 23 24   LSC   10 9 8 7 6 5 4 3 2 1

FOR MY PARENTS, WHO WORKED SO HARD TO

MAKE SURE THEIR CHILDREN COULD DREAM,

AND WHO WERE ALWAYS THERE, NO MATTER

HOW LONG AND FAR MY WANDERINGS

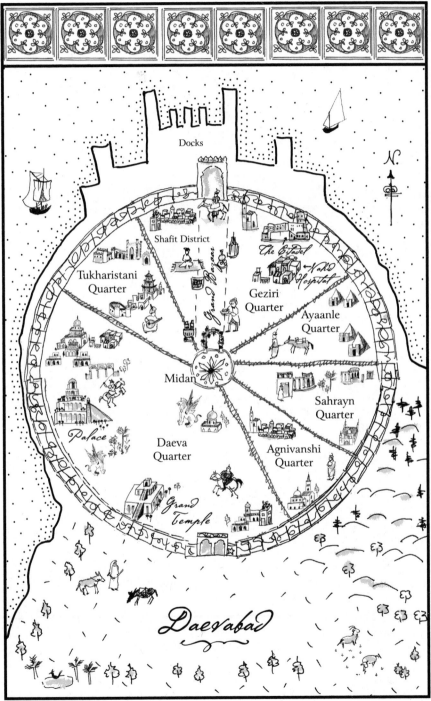

THE
EMPIRE
OF
GOLD

PROLOGUE

MANIZHEH

Behind the battlements of the palace that had always been hers, Banu Manizheh e-Nahid gazed at her family's city.

Bathed in starlight, Daevabad was beautiful—the jagged lines of towers and minarets, domes and pyramids—astonishing from this height, like a jumble of jeweled toys. Beyond the sliver of white beach, the dappled lake shimmered with movement against the black embrace of mountains.

She spread her hands on the stone parapet. This was not a view Manizheh had been permitted while a prisoner of the Qahtanis. Even as a child, her defiance had made them uneasy; the palace magic's public embrace of the young Nahid prodigy and her obvious talent curbing her life before she was old enough to realize the guards that surrounded her day and night weren't for her protection. The only other time she'd been up here had been as Ghassan's guest—a trip he'd arranged shortly after he became king.

Manizheh could still remember how he'd taken her hand as they'd gazed at the city their families had killed each other for, speaking dreamy words about uniting their peoples and putting the past behind them. About how he'd loved her since they were children, and about how sad and helpless *he'd* felt all those times his father had beaten and terrorized her and her brother. Surely she must have understood that Ghassan had had no choice but to stay silent.

In her mind's eye, Manizheh could still see his face that night, the moon shining upon his hopeful expression. They'd been younger; he'd been handsome. Charming. *What a match*, people would have said. Who wouldn't want to be the beloved queen of a powerful djinn king? And indeed, she'd laced her fingers between his and smiled—for she still wore such an expression in those days—her eyes locked on the mark of Suleiman's seal, new upon his face.

And then she'd closed off his throat.

It hadn't lasted. Ghassan had been quicker with the seal than she'd anticipated, and as her powers fell away, so did the pressure on his throat. He'd been enraged, his face red with betrayal and lack of air, and Manizheh remembered thinking that he would hit her. That he'd do worse. That it wouldn't matter if she screamed—for he was king now and no one would cross him.

But Ghassan hadn't done that. He hadn't needed to. Manizheh had gone for his heart and so Ghassan did the same with ruthless effectiveness: having Rustam beaten within a hair of his life as she was forced to watch, breaking her brother's bones, letting them heal and then doing it again, torturing him until Rustam was a howling mess and Manizheh had fallen to her knees, begging Ghassan for mercy.

When he finally granted it, he'd been even angrier at her tears than he'd been at her initial refusal. *I wanted things to be different between us*, he'd said accusingly. *You shouldn't have humiliated me.*

She took in a sharp breath at the memory. *He's dead*, she reminded herself. Manizheh had stared at Ghassan's bloody corpse, committing the sight to memory, trying to assure herself that her tormentor was truly gone. But she wouldn't have him burned, not yet. She intended to examine his body further, hoping for clues as to how he'd possessed Suleiman's seal. Manizheh hadn't missed that his heart had been removed—carved from his chest with surgical precision and making it clear who'd done the removing. Part of her was grateful. Despite what she'd told Nahri, Manizheh knew almost nothing about how the seal ring was passed to another.

And now, because of Nahri, Manizheh knew the first step after finding them would be to cut out the heart of Nahri's djinn prince.

Manizheh returned her gaze to the city. It was startlingly quiet, adding an eerie facade to the entire experience. Daevabad might have been a kingdom at peace in the dead of night, safe and still under the helm of its rightful guardians.

A lie a distant wail betrayed. The cries were otherwise fading, the violence of the night giving way to sheer shock and terror. Frightened people—hunted people—didn't scream. They hid, hunkering down with their loved ones in whatever shelter they could find, praying the darkness might pass them by. Everyone in Daevabad knew what happened when cities fell. They were raised on stories of vengeance and their enemy's rapacity; depending on their roots, they were told hair-raising tales of Zaydi al Qahtani's violent conquest of Daevabad, Darayavahoush e-Afshin's scourging of Qui-zi, or the innumerable sacks of human cities. No, there wouldn't be screaming. Daevabad's people would be hiding, weeping silently as they clutched their children close, the sudden loss of their magic only one more tragedy this night.

They are going to think another Suleiman has come. It was the conclusion any sensible person would arrive at. Had Suleiman's great judgment not started with the stripping of their ancestors' magic?

They probably expected to see their lives shattered and their families torn apart as they were forced to toil for another human master, powerless to fight back.

Powerless. Manizheh pressed her palms harder against the cold stone, aching to feel the palace's magic. To conjure dancing flames or the shimmer of smoke. It seemed impossible that her abilities were gone, and she could only imagine the injuries piling up in the infirmary, injuries she now couldn't heal. For a woman who'd endured the ripping away of everything she loved— the shy country noble she might have married, the dark-eyed infant whose weight in her arms she'd yearned to feel again, the brother she'd betrayed, her very dignity as she bowed before the Qahtanis year after year—the loss of her abilities was the worst. Her magic was her life, her soul—the power beneath the strength that had enabled her to survive everything else.

Perhaps an apt price to pay, then, for using healing magic to kill, a voice whispered in her head. Manizheh pushed it away. Such doubt wouldn't help her or her people right now. Instead she'd lean on anger, the fury that coursed in her when she watched years of planning be upended by a quick-fingered shafit girl.

Nahri. The defiance in her dark eyes. The slight, almost rueful shrug as she shoved their family's most cherished treasure onto the finger of an unworthy sand fly.

I would have given you everything, child. Everything you could have possibly wanted. Everything I never had.

"Enjoying your victory?"

Aeshma's mocking voice set her teeth on edge, but Manizheh didn't so much as twitch. She'd been dealing with the ifrit long enough to know how to handle him—how to handle everyone, really. You simply offered no target—no weaknesses, no doubt. No allies or loved ones. She kept her gaze forward as he joined her at the wall.

"A long time I've waited to look upon Anahid's city." There

was cruel triumph in his voice. "But it's not quite the paradise of the songs. Where are the shedu rumored to patrol the skies and the gardens of jeweled trees and rivers of wine? The fawning marid servants conjuring rainbows of waterfalls and a library teeming with the secrets of creation?"

Manizheh's stomach twisted. *Gone for centuries.* She'd immersed herself in the great stories of her ancestors, and they painted an utterly unfamiliar Daevabad from what she saw now. "We will bring them back."

A glance revealed cold pleasure rippling across Aeshma's fiery visage. "She loved this place," he continued. "A sanctuary for the people she dragged back together, her carefully tended paradise that allowed no sinners."

"You sound jealous."

"Jealous? Three thousand years I dwelled in the land of the two rivers with Anahid, watching the floods recede and the humans rise. We warred with the marid and traveled the desert winds together. All of that forgotten because of some human's ultimatum."

"You chose different paths in dealing with Suleiman."

"She *chose* to betray her people and closest friends."

She saved her people. I intend to do the same. "And here I thought we were finally setting that aside and making peace."

Aeshma scoffed. "How do you propose to do that, Banu Nahida? Do you think I don't know what's happened to your abilities? I doubt right now you could even summon a spark, let alone hope to fulfill your bargain with me." He raised a palm, a tendril of fire swirling between his fingers. "A shame your people haven't had three millennia to learn other ways of magic."

It took everything Manizheh had not to stare at the flame, hunger eating through her soul. "Then how fortunate I have you to teach me."

The ifrit laughed. "Why should I? I have been helping you for years already, and I've yet to gain a thing."

"You've gained a glimpse of Anahid's city."

Aeshma grinned. "There is that, I suppose." His smile widened, his razor-sharp teeth gleaming. "I could gain even more right now. I could throw you from this wall and kill her most promising descendant."

Manizheh didn't flinch; she was too accustomed to men threatening her. "You would never escape Darayavahoush. He would track down every ifrit left, torture and slaughter them before your eyes, and then spend a century killing you in the most painful way he could imagine. You would die at the hands of the magic you desire most."

That seemed to land, a scowl replacing Aeshma's mocking grin. It always did; Manizheh knew the ifrit's weaknesses as well as he knew her secrets.

"Your Afshin does not deserve such abilities," he snapped. "The first daeva freed from Suleiman's curse in thousands of years, and he's an ill-tempered, overly armed fool. You might as well have given such abilities to a rabid dog."

That wasn't an analogy Manizheh liked—there was already a bit too much defiance simmering below the absolute loyalty she typically enjoyed with Dara.

But she pressed on. "If you desire Dara's abilities, you should stop issuing worthless threats and help me get Suleiman's seal back. I cannot free you from the curse without it."

"How very convenient."

"Excuse me?"

He dropped his gaze to stare at her. "I said it is *convenient*," he repeated. "For decades now, I have been at your side, awaiting *your* help, and you keep coming up with excuses. It is all very distressing, Banu Nahida. It's making me wonder if you're even capable of freeing us from Suleiman's curse."

Manizheh kept her face carefully blank. "You were the one who came to me," she reminded him. "I've always made clear that

I would need the ring. And I would think you've seen enough to know what I'm capable of."

"Indeed I have. Enough that I'm not particularly eager to see you master my kind of magic as well. Especially for the mere promise of some future freedom. If you want me to teach you blood magic, I'm going to need something more tangible in return."

More tangible. Manizheh's stomach knotted. She had already lost so much. The little she had left was precious. "What do you want?"

The ifrit's cold smile curled again as his gaze drifted over Daevabad, the eagerness in it sending a hundred warnings through her mind. "I think of that morning every day, you know. That raw power scorching the air, screaming in my thoughts. I hadn't felt something like that since Anahid pulled this island from the lake." He ran his fingers along the parapet in a caress. "There's nothing quite like Nahid magic, is there? Nahid hands raised this city and have brought back untold masses from the brink of death. A mere drop of their blood is enough to kill an ifrit. A Nahid life . . . well, imagine all the things *that* could do." Aeshma twisted the knife deeper. "The things it already has done."

Now Manizheh did flinch. How quickly it all came back. The smell of burned flesh and the sticky blood coating her skin. The twinkling city seemed to disappear, replaced by a scorched plain and smoky sky—the dull color reflected in her brother's vacant, unseeing eyes. Rustam had died with an expression of faint shock on his face, and seeing that had broken what was left of Manizheh's heart, reminding her of the little boy he'd once been. The Nahid siblings who'd lost their innocence too soon, who'd stuck together through everything only to be ripped apart at the end.

"Speak plainly."

"I want your daughter." Aeshma was brusque now, any coyness gone. "And since she's proven herself a traitor, you need her gone."

A traitor. How simple it was for the ifrit to declare such a thing. He hadn't seen a trembling young woman in a torn, bloodied dress. He hadn't stared into frightened, achingly familiar eyes.

She betrayed you. Indeed, Nahri had done worse, tricking her with a sleight of hand more appropriate for a low-born shafit thief than a Nahid healer. But Manizheh could have forgiven that, *would* have forgiven that, had Nahri taken the ring for herself. Creator knew she could not judge another woman's ambitions.

But Nahri hadn't. No, she'd given it to—of all people—a Qahtani. To the son of the king who'd tormented her, the king who'd stolen any chance Manizheh had at a happy life and driven the final wedge between her and her brother.

Manizheh couldn't forgive that.

Aeshma spoke again, perhaps seeing the doubt in her long silence. "You need to make some choices, Manizheh," he warned, his voice dangerous and low. "Your Scourge is obsessed with that girl. If she was clever enough to deceive you, how do you imagine that lovesick fool would fare if she made a play for his heart? But the things I could teach you, that Vizaresh could teach you . . ." Aeshma leaned closer. "You would never again have to worry about Darayavahoush's loyalty. About *anyone's* loyalty.

"But only for a price."

A glimmer caught Manizheh's eye—a fiery shard of sun emerging from behind the eastern mountains, its brilliance taking her aback. Sunrise wasn't usually that bright in Daevabad, the protective magic veiling the city off from the true sky. But it wasn't just the sun's brightness that felt wrong.

It was the silence accompanying that brightness. There was no drumming from the Grand Temple or djinn adhan, and the quiet failure to welcome the sun's arrival sent more dread into her heart than all the blood that had dripped from her unhealed finger. Nothing stopped the drums and the call to prayer; they were part of the very fabric of time in Daevabad.

THE EMPIRE OF GOLD   ✧   9

Until Manizheh's conquest ripped that fabric to shreds. Daevabad was her home, her duty, and she'd torn out its heart. Which meant it was her responsibility to mend it.

No matter the cost.

She closed her eyes. Manizheh had not prayed since she'd watched two djinn scouts bleed out in the icy mud of northern Daevastana, dead at the hands of the poison she'd designed. She'd defended her plan to Dara; she'd gone forward with bringing an even worse wave of death to Daevabad. But she had not prayed through any of that. It felt like a link she had broken.

And she knew the Creator would not help her now. She saw no alternative, only the path she'd forged and had to keep walking—even if there was nothing left of her by the time she finished.

She made sure her voice was steady; Manizheh would not show the ifrit the wound he'd struck. "I can offer you her name. Her true one.

"The name her father gave her."

PART I

I

NAHRI

When Nahri was a very little girl, in the last orphans' home that would take her, she met a storyteller.

It had been Eid, a hot, chaotic day, but one of the few pleasant ones for children like her when Cairo's better off were most inclined to look after the orphans whose welfare their faith preached. After she had feasted on sweets and stuffed butter cookies in new clothes—a pretty dress embroidered with blue lilies—the storyteller had appeared in the haze of sugar crashes and afternoon heat, and it wasn't long before the children gathered around him had passed out, lulled into dreams of faraway lands and dashing adventures by his smooth voice.

Nahri had not been lulled, however; she had been mesmerized, for tales of magical kingdoms and lost royal heirs were the exact fragile hopes a young girl with no name and no family might nurse in the hiddenmost corner of her heart. But the way the storyteller phrased it was confusing. *Kan wa ma kan,* he kept repeating when describing fantastical cities, mysterious djinn, and clever heroines. *It was and it wasn't.* The tales seemed to exist between this world and another, between truth and lies, and it had driven Nahri mad with longing. She needed to know that they were real. To know that there might be a better place for her, a world in which the quiet things she did with her hands were normal.

And so, she had pressed him. *But was it real?* she demanded. *Did all that really happen?*

The storyteller had shrugged. Nahri could remember the rise of his shoulders, the twinkling of his eyes, no doubt amused by the young girl's pluck. *Maybe it was and maybe it wasn't.*

Nahri had persisted, reaching for the closest example she could find. *Is it like the thing in your chest, then? The thing that looks like a crab around your lungs, that's making you cough blood?*

His mouth had fallen open. *God preserve me,* he'd whispered in horror, while gasps rose from those who were listening. Tears filled his eyes. *You cannot know that.*

She hadn't been able to reply. The other adults had swiftly intervened, yanking her up by the arms so roughly they tore the sleeve of her new dress. It had been the last straw for the little girl who said such unnerving things, the girl who cried in her sleep in a language no one had ever heard and who showed no bruises or scrapes after being beaten by the other children. Nahri had been dragged out of the crumbling building still begging to know what she'd done wrong, stumbling to the dust in her holiday clothes and rising alone in the street as people celebrated with their families inside the kind of warm homes she'd never known.

When the orphans' home slammed its door behind her, Nahri had stopped believing in magic. Until years later, anyway, when a Daeva warrior came crashing to her feet among a tangle of tombs. But as Nahri stared now in utter incomprehension at Cairo's familiar skyline, the Arabic words ran back through her memory.

Kan wa ma kan.

It was and it wasn't.

The storybook world of Daevabad was gone, replaced, and Cairo's mosques and fortresses and old brick buildings were hazy in the distance, heat shimmering off the surrounding desert and flooded fields. She blinked and rubbed her eyes. The city was still there, as were the Pyramids, standing proud against the pale sky across the wide blue Nile.

Egypt. I'm in Egypt. Nahri found herself pressing her knuckles against her temple, hard enough to hurt. Was this a dream?

Or maybe Daevabad had been the dream. The nightmare. For surely it was more likely she was a human back in Cairo, a poor thief, a con artist taken in by her own scheme rather than someone who had lived the past six years as the future queen of a hidden kingdom of djinn.

And that might have been a possibility, were it not for the wheezing, sweating, and still slightly glowing prince who stepped between Nahri and her view of the countryside. Not a dream, then—not unless she'd brought a piece of it back with her.

"*Nahri,*" Ali whispered. His eyes were bloodshot and desperate, water beading down his face. "Nahri, please tell me I'm seeing things. Please tell me this isn't what it looks like."

Still numb, Nahri glanced past his shoulder. She couldn't look away from the Egyptian countryside, not after aching for it for so long. A warm breeze played through her hair, and a pair of sunbirds twittered as they climbed through a patch of thick brush that had swallowed a crumbling mudbrick building. It was flood season, a thing the inundated banks and water lapping at the roots of the palms made clear to any Egyptian in a moment.

"It looks like home." Her throat was horribly strained, her healing magic still blocked by Suleiman's seal blazing on Ali's cheek. "It looks like Egypt."

"We cannot be in Egypt!" Ali stepped back, falling heavily

against the minaret's crumbling inner wall. There was a feverish flush to his face, and hazy heat rose from his skin. "W-we were just in Daevabad. You pulled me off the wall . . . did you mean to—?"

"No! I just wanted to get away from Manizheh. You said the curse was off the lake. I figured we'd swim back to shore, not rematerialize on the other side of the world!"

"The other side of the world." Ali's voice was hollow. "Oh my God. *Oh my God*. We need to go back. We need to—" His words slipped into a pained hiss, one hand flying to his chest.

"Ali?" She grabbed him by the shoulder. Closer now, Nahri could see that he didn't just look upset—he looked *sick*, shivering and sweating more than a human in the death throes of tuberculosis.

Her training took over. "Sit," she ordered, helping him to the ground.

Ali squeezed his eyes shut, pressing the back of his head into the wall. It looked like it was taking all his strength not to scream. "I think it's the ring," he gasped, pressing a fist to his chest—or to his heart rather, where Suleiman's ring should now be resting, courtesy of Nahri's sleight of hand back in Daevabad. "It burns."

"Let me see." Nahri grabbed his hand—it was so hot it felt like plunging her own into a simmering kettle—and pried it away from his chest. The skin beneath looked completely normal. And without her magic, there was no examining further—Suleiman's eight-pointed mark still blazed on Ali's cheek, blocking her powers.

Nahri swallowed back her fear. "It's going to be okay," she insisted. "Lift the seal. I'll take the pain away and be able to better examine you."

Ali opened his eyes, bewilderment swirling into the pain in his expression. "Lift the seal?"

"Yes, the seal, Ali," Nahri repeated, fighting panic. "Suleiman's seal. I can't do any magic with it glowing on your face like that!"

He took a deep breath, looking worse by the minute. "I . . . okay." He glanced back at her, seeming to struggle to focus on her face. "How do I do that?"

Nahri stared at him. "What do you mean, *how*? Your family has held the seal for centuries. Don't you know?"

"No. Only the emir is allowed—" Fresh grief ripped across Ali's expression. "Oh God, *Dhiru* . . ."

"Ali, please."

But already dazed as he was, the reminder of his brother's death seemed too much. Ali slumped against the wall, weeping in Geziriyya. Tears rolled down his cheeks, cutting paths through the dust and dried blood on his skin.

The sound of birdsong came, a breeze rattling through the bristling palms towering over the broken mosque. Her own heart wanted to burst, the sweet relief of being home warring with the nightmarish events that had ended in the two of them appearing here.

She sat back on her heels. *Think, Nahri, think.* She had to have a plan.

But Nahri couldn't think. Not when she could still smell the poisoned edge of Muntadhir's blood and hear Manizheh cracking Ali's bones.

Not when she could see Dara's green gaze, pleading from across the ruined palace corridor.

Nahri took a deep breath. *Magic. Just get your magic back, and this will all be better.* She felt horribly vulnerable without her abilities, weak in a way she'd never been. Her entire body ached, the metallic smell of blood thick in her nose.

"Ali." She took his face in her hands, trying not to worry at the frighteningly unnatural—even for a djinn—heat in his clammy skin. She brushed the tears from his cheeks, forcing his bloodshot eyes to meet hers. "Just breathe. We'll grieve him, we'll grieve them all, I promise. But right now, we need to focus." The wind had picked up, whipping her hair into her face. "Muntadhir told me it could take a few days to recover from possessing the ring," she remembered. "Maybe this is normal."

Ali was shivering so hard it looked like he was seizing. His skin had taken on a grayish tone, his lips cracking. "I don't think this is normal." Steam was rising from his body in a humid cloud. "It *wants* you," he whispered. "I can feel it."

"I-I couldn't," she stammered. "I couldn't take it. You heard what Manizheh said about me being a shafit. If the ring had killed me, she would have murdered you and then taken it for herself. I couldn't risk that!"

As if in angry response, the seal blazed against his cheek. Where Ghassan's mark had resembled a tattoo, blacker than night against his skin, Ali's looked like it had been painted in quicksilver, the mercury color reflecting the sun's light.

He cried out as it flashed brighter. "Oh, God," he gasped, fumbling for the blades at his waist—miraculously, Ali's khanjar and zulfiqar had come through, belted at his stomach. "I need to get this out of me."

Nahri ripped the weapons away. "Are you mad? You can't cut into your heart!"

Ali didn't respond. He suddenly didn't look *capable* of responding. There was a vacant, lost glaze in his eyes that terrified her. It was a look Nahri associated with the infirmary, with patients brought to her too late.

"*Ali.*" It was killing Nahri not to be able to simply lay hands upon him and take away his pain. "Please," she begged. "Just try to lift the seal. I can't help you like this!"

His gaze briefly fixed on hers, and her heart dropped—Ali's eyes were now so dilated the pupils had nearly overtaken the gray.

He blinked, but there was nothing in his face that even indicated he'd understood her plea. God, why hadn't she asked Muntadhir more about the seal? All he'd said was that it had to be cut out of Ghassan's heart and burned, that it might take the new ring-bearer a couple of days to recover, and that . . .

And that it couldn't leave Daevabad.

Cold fear stole through her even as a hot breeze rushed across her skin. *No, please, no.* That couldn't be why this was happening. It *couldn't* be. Nahri hadn't even asked Ali's permission—he'd tried to jerk away, and she'd shoved the ring on his finger anyway. Too desperate to save him, she hadn't cared what he thought.

And now you might have killed him.

A scorching wind blew her hair straight back, sand whipping past her face. One of the swaying trees across from the ruined mosque suddenly crashed to the ground, and Nahri jumped, realizing only then that the air had grown hotter, the wind picking up to howl around her.

She glanced up.

In the desert beyond the Nile, orange and green clouds were roiling across the pale sky. As Nahri watched, the river's glistening brightness vanished, turning a dull gray as clouds overtook the gentle dawn. Sand swirled over the rocky ground, branches and leaves cartwheeling through the air.

It looked like the storm that brought Dara. Once, that might have given Nahri comfort. Now she was terrified, shaking as she rose to her feet, Ali's zulfiqar in her grip.

With a howl, the sandy wind rushed forward. Nahri cried out, raising an arm to protect her face. But she needn't have. Far from being lashed and torn to pieces, she blinked to find herself and Ali inside a churning funnel of sand, an eye of protection inside the storm.

They weren't alone.

A darker shadow lurked, vanishing and reappearing with the movement of the wind before it landed on the edge of the broken minaret, like a predator who'd caught a mouse in a hole. The creature came to her in unbelievable pieces. A tawny, lithe body, muscles rippling beneath amber fur. Clawed paws the size of her head and a tail that cut the air like a scythe. Silver eyes set in a leonine face.

And *wings*. Dazzling, iridescent wings in what seemed all the colors in the world. Nahri nearly dropped the zulfiqar, a startled gasp leaving her mouth. She'd seen renderings of the beast too many times to deny what was before her eyes.

It was a shedu. The near-mythical winged lion her ancestors were said to have ridden into battle against the ifrit, one that remained their symbol long after the mysterious creatures themselves had vanished.

Or so everyone thought. Because feline eyes were fixed on her now, seeming to search her face and size her up. She'd swear she saw a flicker of what might have been confusion. But also intelligence. Deep, undeniable intelligence.

"Help me," she begged, feeling half mad. "Please."

The shedu's eyes narrowed. They were a silver so pale it edged on clear—the color of glittering ice—and they traveled over Nahri's skin, taking in the zulfiqar in her hands and the injured prince at her feet. The mark on Ali's temple.

The creature ruffled its wings like a discontented bird, a rumbling growl coming from its throat.

Nahri instantly tightened her grip on the zulfiqar, not that it would do much to protect them against such a magnificent beast.

"Please," she tried again. "I'm a Nahid. My magic isn't working, and we need to get back to—"

The shedu lunged.

Nahri dropped to the ground, but the creature simply soared

over her, its dazzling wings throwing the minaret into shadow. "Wait!" she cried as it vanished into the golden wave of sand. The storm was pulling away, rolling into itself. *"Wait!"*

But it was already gone, dissipating like dust on the wind. In a moment, it was as if there had been no storm at all, the birds singing and the sky bright and blue.

Ali let out a single sigh—a hush of breath like it was his last—and then crumpled to the ground.

"Ali!" Nahri fell back to his side, shaking his shoulder. "Ali, wake up! Please wake up!" She checked his pulse, relief and despair warring inside her. He was still breathing, but the beat of his heart was wildly erratic.

This is your fault. You put that ring on his hand. You pulled him into the lake. Nahri swallowed a sob. "You don't get to die. Understand? I didn't save your life a dozen times so you could leave me here."

Silence met her angry words. Nahri could shout all she liked. She still had no magic and no idea what to do next. She didn't even know how they were *here.* Rising to her feet, she glanced at Cairo. She was no expert, but she'd guess it was a few hours distant by boat. Clustered closer to the city were more villages, surrounded by flooded fields and tiny boats gliding over the river.

Nahri looked again at the broken mosque and what appeared to be a scorched pigeon coop. Cracked foundation stones outlined what might once have been homes along a meandering, overgrown path that led to the river. As her eyes traced the ruined village, a strange sense of familiarity danced over the nape of her neck.

Her gaze settled on the swollen Nile, Cairo shimmering in the distance across from the mighty Pyramids. There was no trace of the shedu, no hint of magic. Not in the air, nor in her blood.

Its absence made her angry, and as she stared at the Pyramids—the mighty human monuments that had been ancient before

Daevabad was even a dream—her anger only burned hotter. She wasn't waiting around for the magical world to save her.

Nahri had another world.

ALI WAS EERILY LIGHT IN NAHRI'S ARMS, HIS SKIN scorching where it touched hers, as if half his presence had already burned away. It made it easier to drag the overly tall prince down from the minaret, but any relief Nahri might have felt was dashed by the awful suspicion that this was not a good sign.

She eased him to the ground once they were out, taking a moment to catch her breath. Sweat dampened her forehead, and she straightened up, her spine cracking.

Again came the unnerving sensation she'd been here before. Nahri glanced down the path, trying to let whatever teasing pieces of familiarity drifted through her mind settle, but they refused. The village looked like it had been razed and abandoned decades ago, the surrounding greenery well on its way to swallowing the buildings entirely.

I'm sure it's just a coincidence that of all the places in Egypt two fire-blooded djinn could have been magically whisked to, a creepy, burnt-down village was it.

Throughly unsettled, Nahri picked Ali back up, following the path to the river as though she'd walked it a hundred times. Once she was there, she laid him along the shallows.

The water instantly lapped forth, submerging the line of dried grass underneath Ali's unconscious body. Before she could react, tiny rivulets were creeping over his limbs, racing across his hot skin like watery fingers. Nahri moved to pull him away, but then Ali sighed in his sleep, some of the pain leaving his expression.

The marid did nothing to you, really? Nahri recalled Ali's zulfiqar flying to him on a wave and the way he'd controlled the waterfall in the library to bring down the zahhak. Just what secrets was he still harboring about the marid's possession?

And were they secrets that were dangerous now? A flying lion everyone believed long gone had just checked up on them. Were some river spirits next?

You do not have time to puzzle all this out. Ali was sick, Nahri was powerless, and if Manizheh somehow found a way to follow them, Nahri didn't intend to be an easily spotted target in an abandoned village.

She was ruthless in taking stock of their circumstances, banishing thoughts of Daevabad and slipping into the cold pragmatism that had always ruled her life. It almost felt good to do so. There was no conquered city, no calculating mother who should have been dead, no warrior with pleading green eyes. There was only surviving.

Their possessions were pathetic. Save for Ali's weapons, they had nothing but the tattered, blood-soaked clothes upon their backs. Nahri usually spent her days in Daevabad wearing jewelry that could have bought a kingdom but had been wearing none in deference to the traditions of the Navasatem parade, which dictated plain dress. She'd been taken from Cairo barefoot and dressed in rags and had returned the same—an irony that would have made her laugh if it didn't make her want to burst into tears.

Worse, she knew they looked like easy marks. Their clothing might be destroyed, but it was djinn cloth, strong and luxurious to any eye. Nahri and Ali were visibly well-nourished and groomed, and Ali's glimmering zulfiqar looked exactly like what it was: a stunningly crafted weapon more suited for a warrior from an ancient epic than anything a human traveler would be carrying. Ali and Nahri looked like the wealthy nobles they were, dragged through the mud but clearly no local peasants.

Considering her options, Nahri studied the river. No boats had come by and the nearest village was a smudge of buildings in the distance. She'd probably manage the walk in half a day, but there was no way she could carry Ali that far.

Unless she didn't walk. Nahri eyed the fallen palm, an idea forming in her head, and then she reached for Ali's khanjar, thinking it would be a more manageable blade than his zulfiqar.

Her hand stilled on the dagger's jeweled handle. This wasn't *Ali's* khanjar—it was his brother's. And like everything Muntadhir had fancied, it was beautiful and ridiculously expensive. The handle was white jade, banded with worked gold and inlaid with a floral pattern of tiny alternating sapphires, rubies, and emeralds. Nahri's breath caught as she mentally calculated the value of the khanjar, already separating out the valuable gems in her mind. She had no doubt Muntadhir had given this to his little brother as a remembrance. It was perhaps cruel to contemplate bartering bits away without Ali's permission.

But that wouldn't stop her. Nahri was a survivor, and it was time to get to work.

It took her the entire morning, the hours melting by in a haze of grief and determination, her tears flowing as readily as her blood did when she gashed her fingers and wrists trying to pull together a makeshift skiff of lashed branches. It was just enough to keep Ali's head and shoulders above the waist-high water, and then she waded in, mud sucking at her bare feet, the river pulling at her torn dress.

Her fingers were numb by midday, too useless to hold the raft. She used Ali's belt to tie it to her waist, earning new bruises and welts. Unused to such enduring physical pain, to injuries that didn't heal, her muscles burned, her entire body screaming at her to stop.

Nahri didn't stop. She made sure each step was steady. For if she paused, if she slipped and was submerged, she wasn't certain she'd have the strength to fight for another breath.

The sun was setting when she reached the first village, turning the Nile into a glistening crimson ribbon, the thick greenery at its banks a threatening cluster of spiky shadows. Nahri could only imagine how alarming she must appear, and it didn't surprise her in the least when two young men who'd been pulling in fishing nets jumped up with surprised yelps.

But Nahri wasn't after the help of men. Four women in black dresses were gathering water just beyond the boat, and she trudged straight for them.

"Peace be upon you, sisters," she wheezed. Her lips were cracked, the taste of blood thick upon her tongue. Nahri held out her hand, revealing three of the tiny emeralds she'd pried from Muntadhir's khanjar. "I need a ride to Cairo."

NAHRI STRUGGLED TO STAY AWAKE AS THE DONKEY cart made its rumbling way into the city, night falling swiftly and cloaking the outskirts of Cairo in darkness. It made the journey easier. Not only because the narrow streets were relatively empty—the locals busy with evening meals, prayers, and the settling down of children—but because right now Nahri wasn't sure her heart could take an unencumbered view of her old home, its familiar landmarks lit by the Egyptian sun. The entire experience was already surreal—the sweet smell of the sugarcane littering the floor of the cart and the snatches of Egyptian Arabic from passersby contrasting with the unconscious djinn prince burning in her arms.

Every bump sent a new jolt of pain into her bruised body, and Nahri could barely speak above a murmur when the cart's driver—the husband of one of the women at the river—asked where next. It was all she could do not to fall apart. To say this was a lean plan was an understatement. And if it failed, she had no idea where to turn next.

Fighting despair and exhaustion in equal measure, Nahri opened her palm. "Naar," she whispered to herself, hoping against hope as she said the word aloud, as Ali had once taught her. "*Naar.*"

There was not the slightest hint of heat, let alone the conjured flame she was aching to hold. Tears pricked her eyes, but she refused to let them fall.

They finally arrived, and Nahri shifted in the cart, her limbs protesting. "Can you help me carry him?" she asked.

The driver glanced back, looking confused. "Who?"

Nahri gestured in disbelief to Ali, less than an arm's length from the driver's face. "*Him.*"

The man jumped. "I . . . Weren't you alone? I could have sworn you were alone."

Apprehension darted down her spine. Nahri had been under the vague understanding that humans couldn't see most djinn—especially not pure-blooded ones like Ali. But this man had helped lift Ali's body into the cart when they'd started out. How could he have already forgotten that?

She fought for a response, not missing the fear blooming in his eyes. "No," she said quickly. "He's been here the entire time."

The man swore under his breath, sliding from the donkey's back. "I told my wife we had no business helping strangers coming from that accursed place, but did she listen?"

"The Nile is an accursed place now?"

He shot her a dark look. "You did not just come from the Nile, you came from the direction of . . . that ruin."

Nahri was too curious not to ask. "Are you talking about the village to your south? What happened there?"

He shuddered, pulling Ali from the cart. "It is better not to discuss such things." He hissed as his fingers brushed Ali's wrist. "This man is burning up. If you brought fever into our village—"

"You know what? I think I can actually carry him the rest of the way myself," Nahri said with false cheer. "Thanks!"

Grumbling, the driver dumped Ali into her arms and then turned away. Struggling to adjust to the weight of his body, Nahri managed to drape one of Ali's arms around her neck, then made her laborious way toward the small shop at the end of the dark alley—the small shop upon which she was pinning all her hopes.

The bells still rang when she opened the door, and the familiar sound as well as the aroma of herbs and tonics nearly made her double over with emotion.

"We're closed," came a gruff voice from the back, the old man not bothering to look up from the glass vial he was filling. "Come back tomorrow."

At his voice, Nahri promptly lost the battle with her tears.

"I'm sorry," she wept. "I didn't know where else to go."

The elderly pharmacist dropped the glass vial. It shattered on the floor, but he didn't appear to notice.

Yaqub stared back at her, his brown eyes wide with astonishment. "*Nahri?*"

2

DARA

It was shocking, truly, how easy it was to kill people.

Dara stared at the devastated Geziri camp before him. Spread across the manicured grounds of the palace's public garden, it had been a beautiful place, fit for the honored guests of a king. Towering date palms from their homeland were set in giant ceramic pots among the smaller fruit trees, and glittering mirrored lanterns hung over paths of amber pebbles. Though magic had been stripped from the camp like everywhere else in Daevabad, the silk tents gleamed in the sunlight, and the gentle burble of the water fountains carried through the silence. The aroma of flowers and frankincense contrasted sharply with the acrid smell of burnt coffee and sour meat, meals that had been ruined when the people eating them were all abruptly murdered. There was the heavier smell of blood, of course, clinging to the patches of copper vapor still lingering in the air.

But Dara was becoming so accustomed to the scent of blood that he'd stopped noticing it.

"How many?" he asked quietly.

The steward standing next to him was shaking so badly it was a miracle the man was still standing. "At least a thousand, m-my lord. They were travelers from southern Am Gezira, here for Navasatem."

Travelers. Dara's gaze dropped from the tents and the trees—the dreamy setting for a fairy-tale feast—to the carpets so soaked with blood it was running in tiny streams into the surrounding garden. The Geziri travelers—many of whom he assumed had never been to Daevabad, who must have so recently gazed upon the city's famed markets and palaces with wonder—had died swiftly but not instantly. There had been enough time for many to run, only to die clutching their heads on the pebbled paths. More had died holding each other, and dozens had died in what must have been a panicked stampede to escape a small plaza set up with handicrafts. The vapor Manizheh conjured had not discriminated between young and old, or woman from man, instead killing all with equal brusqueness. Young women with embroidery, old men stringing lutes, children holding sticky sweets.

"Burn them," Dara commanded, his voice low. He had not been able to raise his voice today, as though if he gave any opening to the part of him that wanted to scream, the part of him that wanted to throw himself in the lake, he would be undone. "Along with any other Geziri bodies found in the palace."

The steward hesitated. He was a Daeva man, a Creator-fearing one if the ash mark on his brow was anything to judge by. "Should we . . . should we make some effort to learn their identities? It doesn't seem right to—"

"No." At Dara's curt response, the steward flinched, and Dara tried to explain. "It is better if the true toll is not known in case we need to adjust the number."

The other man paled. "There are children."

Dara cleared his throat, swallowing the lump rising there. He looked directly at the steward, letting his eyes brook no further discussion. "Find one of their clerics and have him pray over them. Then *burn them*."

The steward swayed on his feet. "As you command." He bowed and then scurried away.

Dara let his gaze fall on the dead again. It was utterly silent in the bloody garden, the close air feeling like a tomb. The palace walls loomed high overhead, their height tripled by his magic. Dara had done the same for the entire Daeva Quarter, taking advantage of the pandemonium to thoroughly seal his tribe off from the rest of the city. He'd done more magic than he ever had before, not even caring he'd had to stay in his fiery form to conserve his strength.

And looking at the murdered Geziris, he was glad. For if their kin on the other side of the city had somehow survived the vapor, Dara doubted even the loss of magic would keep them from coming for vengeance.

Devil, a voice whispered in his mind as he returned to the palace. It sounded like Nahri. *Murderer.*

Scourge.

He shoved the voice away. Dara was the weapon of the Nahids, and weapons didn't have feelings.

The halls were desolate, his steps ringing on the ancient stones—many of which had cracked during the quake that had shaken the city when its magic was ripped away. The djinn who hadn't managed to escape the royal complex, along with any Daevas caught protecting them, had been rounded up and herded into the ruined library. Many were inconsequential—bloodied

scholars and civil servants, wailing harem companions, and terrified shafit servants—but among the mix, Kaveh had pointed out
a few dozen nobles: men and women who would make for useful
hostages, should their tribesmen start feeling mutinous. There
was also a handful of surviving Geziris, the few besides Muntadhir who'd managed to remove their relic in time.

Dara kept walking. *These are the corridors you said would be filled with
celebration, aren't they? Music and joy: the victory you promised your young warriors who now lie slaughtered on the beach, their bodies left to rot. The warriors who
trusted you.*

Dara squeezed his eyes shut, but he couldn't stop the heat
crackling down his limbs. He exhaled, smoky embers escaping
his mouth, and opened his eyes to see fire swirling in his palms.
Had the Qahtani emir not accused him of belonging to hell?
Perhaps his current appearance was an apt one.

He could hear the cries of the infirmary's injured long before
he passed through the thick wooden doors. Inside was organized
chaos. Manizheh might not have her healing magic, but she commanded a forceful presence and had pulled together a team to
help her, including the followers she'd brought from their camp
in northern Daevastana, servants who'd worked with Nahri in
the infirmary, a few seamstresses who were taking their talents to
flesh, and a midwife she'd plucked from the harem.

Dara spotted her across the room now, dismayed to see she'd
replaced the quilted armor he'd insisted she wear during the attack with lighter clothes she must have pillaged: a man's tunic
and a blood-soaked apron stuffed with tools. Her silvering black
hair was gathered in a hasty bun, strands of it falling in her face
as she bent over a crying Daeva girl.

Dara joined her, prostrating himself and pressing his brow
to the ground. The show of obedience was intentional. In the
face of an incomplete conquest and a frightened city stripped of

its magic, the strains in their relationship were petty concerns. He would not dare undermine her in public—people needed to believe her rule was absolute.

"Banu Nahida," he intoned.

"Afshin." There was relief in her voice. "Rise. I think we can put off the bowing for the time being."

He did as she commanded but kept his tone formal. "I have done what I can to seal off the Daeva Quarter and the palace from the rest of the city. I cannot imagine the djinn have the resources to scale such high walls anytime soon, and if they try, I have archers and Vizaresh awaiting them."

"Good." Her attention shifted to a man across the room. "Did you find the saw?" she called out.

The Daeva servant hurried over. "Yes, Banu Nahida."

"A saw?" Dara asked.

Manizheh inclined her head toward her patient. The girl was young, her eyes squeezed shut against the pain of her wound: a grisly bite in the meat of her arm. The surrounding flesh was crimson and badly engorged.

"She's a simurgh trainer in the royal menagerie," Manizheh explained softly. "When the firebirds panic, they emit a venom in their saliva. Apparently the arena's karkadann escaped when its magical gate fell away, and in the chaos, one of her birds bit her."

Dara's heart dropped. "What will you do?"

"If I had my abilities, I could draw the poison out before it reached her heart. Without magic, there's only one thing I can do."

The meaning of the saw became horribly clear, and whatever was between them, Manizheh seemed to have some mercy left for him. "She is the last patient I need to stabilize, and then I would like to catch up with you and Kaveh." She nodded to a pair of doors. "He's waiting in the other room."

Dara bowed haltingly. "Yes, Banu Nahida."

He weaved his way through the crowded infirmary. It was

packed with the injured, and Dara didn't miss that they were all Daevas. He doubted it meant casualties were confined to his tribe—on the contrary, he suspected that in the cold calculus of their world, it meant only after the Daevas were helped would Manizheh turn her attention to the rest of the djinn.

We are never going to have peace, he despaired as he pushed through the doors she had indicated. *Not after this.* Consumed by his thoughts, Dara only realized where Manizheh had sent him when the door fell shut behind him.

He was in Nahri's room.

Compared to the rest of the conquered palace, Nahri's room was quiet and untouched. Dara was alone, Kaveh nowhere to be seen. The apartment was pretty and well appointed and at first glance could have belonged to any Daeva noblewoman. A silver fire altar smoldered in a prayer niche, perfuming the air with cedar, and a pair of delicate gold earrings and a ruby ring had been left on a small painted table.

Looking closer, though, Dara saw signs of the woman he'd known, the woman he'd loved and betrayed. Books were stacked in a precarious tower beside the bed, and what appeared to be small, almost crude items—a reed bent to resemble a boat, a dried garland of jasmine blossoms, a carved wooden bangle—were set with reverence on the windowsill. An ivory hair comb and an abandoned cotton shawl lay on the table beside him, and it was everything Dara could do not to pick them up and touch the things Nahri had touched so recently, to see if her scent lingered.

She cannot be dead. She simply cannot be. Losing the battle with his aching heart, Dara ventured farther into the room, feeling like an intruder as he ran his fingers over the finely carved mahogany bedposts. He could still remember doing so six years ago. How full of himself he'd been that night, righteously indignant after learning the Qahtanis intended to force Nahri to marry Munta-dhir. Dara had not doubted for a moment when he had slipped

into her bedchamber that what he was doing was right, that Nahri
would greet him with a relieved smile, take his hand, and escape
Daevabad at his side. That he was saving her from a terrible fate
she could not possibly want.

He had been so entirely, utterly wrong.

In hindsight, it was obvious he'd lost her here, that night,
and Dara had no one but himself to blame. He had taken Nahri's choice away from her—from *her*, the only person who'd seen
something in him beyond the legendary Afshin, the abominable
Scourge, and might have loved him for it.

"Afshin?"

Dara straightened up at Kaveh's faint voice. The grand wazir
stood at the steps that led to the garden, looking pale as parchment and about as stable as the gauzy curtain dancing in the
breeze.

"Kaveh." Dara crossed the room, reaching out a hand to
steady the other man. "Are you all right?"

The grand wazir let himself be led to a cushion near the fire
altar. Despite the warm day, he was shivering. "No. I . . . Manizheh
said I should wait here, but I can't." His bloodshot gaze darted to
Dara's. "You've been all over the palace . . . is it true about the
Geziris?"

Dara nodded grimly. "A few survivors removed their relics in
time—the emir is one of them—but the rest are dead."

Kaveh jerked back, one hand going to his mouth in horror.
"Creator, no," he whispered. "The poison, the vapor . . . it wasn't
supposed to spread beyond the spot in which it was unleashed."

Dara went cold. "Manizheh told you that?"

Kaveh nodded, rocking back and forth. "H-how many . . ."

There was no point in pretending. Kaveh would learn the
truth either way. "At least a thousand. There were . . . travelers
staying in the garden that we didn't anticipate."

The grand wazir let out a strangled sound. "Oh my God, the

camp." He was pressing his fingers so hard against his skull it had to hurt. "There were children there," he wept. "I saw them playing. It wasn't supposed to happen like this. I only meant to kill Ghassan and his men!"

Dara didn't know what to say. Manizheh had known damn well the vapor would spread—she and Dara had fought bitterly about it. Why had she kept it from Kaveh? Was it because she feared the man she loved would protest? Or was it to spare him the shared guilt since she'd already made the decision to proceed?

She spared him nothing. Manizheh had made Kaveh into an instrument of mass murder, and for that, Dara had no reassuring platitudes. He knew the feeling all too well.

He tried to change the subject. "Is there any news of Jamshid?"

Kaveh wiped his eyes. "Ghassan only said he was holding him with people he trusted." He started to shake harder. "Afshin, if he was at the Citadel . . . if he died when we attacked it . . ."

"You have no reason to believe he was there." Dara knelt in front of the other man, gripping his arm. "Kaveh, you need to pull yourself together."

"You're not a father. You don't understand."

"I understand that there are thousands of Daevas who will be slaughtered for our actions if we lose control of this city. Manizheh is out there amputating limbs because she has no magic. She has the ifrit buzzing all around her, searching for a weakness. She needs you. *Daevabad* needs you. We will find Jamshid and Nahri. I pray as much as you do that the Creator has spared them. But we are helping neither if we don't secure this city."

The door opened and Manizheh stepped in. She took one look at them, and weariness creased her expression. "Well, don't you two look hopeful."

Dara stiffened. "I was updating Kaveh about the number of Geziri dead." He met her eyes. "It seems the vapor spread farther than anticipated. Nearly all the Geziris in the palace are dead."

He had to give her credit—Manizheh didn't so much as flinch. "A pity. But then I suppose war is often more violent than expected. Had their people ruled justly, we wouldn't have had to resort to such desperate means. But quite frankly, a few hundred dead djinn—"

"It is not a few hundred," he cut in. "It is at least a thousand, if not more."

Manizheh held his gaze, and though she did not directly rebuke him for interrupting her, Dara did not miss the warning in her eyes. "A thousand, then. They still aren't our most pressing issue. Not when compared with our loss of magic."

There was a moment of silence before Kaveh spoke. "Do you think it's a punishment?"

Dara frowned. "A *punishment*?"

"From the Creator," Kaveh whispered. "Because of what we did."

"No," Manizheh said flatly. "I don't think the Divine had anything to do with this. Quite frankly, I don't see the Divine anywhere in this awful city, and I refuse to believe Zaydi al Qahtani could have sacked the place and not suffered similar heavenly retribution if that were the case." She sat down, looking rueful. "Though I don't imagine you'll be the only person to leap to that conclusion."

Dara paced, too agitated to stay still. A thousand responsibilities pulled at him. "How do we rule a city with no magic? How do we *live* without magic?"

"We can't," Kaveh replied, dourer by the moment. "Our society, our economy, our *world* depends on magic. Half the goods traded in the city are conjured. People rely on enchantments to wake them up, to take them to work, to cook their food. I doubt one in twenty of us could even light a fire without magic."

"Then we need to get it back," Manizheh said. "As soon as possible."

Dara stopped pacing. "How? We don't even know why it's gone."

"We can make some guesses. You're both fretting, but we're not completely in the dark. You still have your magic, Afshin, as do the ifrit."

He scowled at the comparison. "Meaning?"

"Meaning the magic that vanished is that which Suleiman granted our ancestors *after* their penance," she explained. "You have yours because you're untouched by Suleiman's curse. The ifrit have their tricks because it is a different sort of magic, things they learned to *circumvent* his curse. It cannot be coincidence that our powers only vanished when Nahri and Alizayd took Suleiman's ring and jumped into the lake."

Dara paused, following her reasoning. "You are certain?"

"Quite," Manizheh replied, a trace of bitterness in her voice. "Nahri slipped it on his finger, they vanished into the lake, and moments later, the veil fell and my abilities were gone." She looked grim. "I watched the water. They didn't resurface."

"I checked the cliffs as well." It had nearly killed Dara to do so, the prospect of discovering Nahri dashed upon the rocks too awful to contemplate. "I found nothing. But the fall is not long. Perhaps they swam back, and I missed them. They could be hiding elsewhere on the island, Alizayd using the seal to stop magic."

Manizheh shook her head. "It was too sudden. Ghassan went into seclusion for days when he first took the seal and looked like he'd been on the wrong end of a plague when he returned. I do not think this could be Alizayd's doing."

Kaveh cleared his throat. "I will say what neither of you want to: they are just as likely dead. That *is* a fall that could kill a man. For all we know, they drowned, and their bodies sank beneath the water."

Dara's heart twisted, but Manizheh was already responding. "The ring-bearer being dead should not have affected magic like this. After all, how many hours did Ghassan lie slain with it?"

Dara pinched the bridge of his nose. "Nahri is not dead," he said stubbornly. "It is not possible. And I do not believe for one moment that the marid let their little pawn *drown*."

Kaveh looked confused. "Why would the marid care? From what Manizheh told me, I got the impression Alizayd was nothing to them, merely the first convenient body to jump in that night they cut you down."

"For someone who was merely convenient, he's certainly been well rewarded. That sand fly killed my men with water magic. Vizaresh said he found Alizayd controlling the lake as though he were marid himself."

"You might have mentioned that a bit sooner," Kaveh sputtered. "They jumped in a marid-cursed lake, Afshin! If Alizayd is under the protection of those creatures—"

"The marid told me they wouldn't interfere with us again," Dara argued. "I made clear the consequences."

"Enough." Manizheh raised a hand. "I cannot think with you two shouting like that." She pursed her lips, looking troubled. "What if he didn't need to be under their protection?"

"What do you mean?" Dara asked.

"I mean that it might not have been Alizayd," Manizheh suggested. "*We* were the ones who insisted the marid restore the lake's original enchantment, the one that let Nahids travel through the waters—it's how we returned to Daevabad. What if Nahri somehow used it to get them away?"

Kaveh opened his mouth, looking even paler. Dara was genuinely surprised he hadn't fainted yet.

"That . . . that could fit. Back at the camp, you both said there was no evidence Suleiman's seal had ever left Daevabad. Maybe *this* is why," Kaveh continued, gesticulating like an overexuberant lecturer. "Because if you remove the seal from Daevabad, everything falls apart. Does it otherwise not seem strange the Qahtanis never took the seal back to Am Gezira? That they wouldn't have tried to build an empire closer to their home and allies?"

"It's a theory," Manizheh said after a cautious silence. "One that might fit, but even so, if Nahri accessed that kind of magic, they could be anywhere. She would have merely needed to think of a place, and they'd be gone."

"Then I will go find them," Dara rushed, not caring how emotional he sounded. "Egypt. Am Gezira. Nahri and Alizayd are not fools. They'll go somewhere familiar and safe."

"Absolutely not." Kaveh's voice fell like a hammer. "You can't leave Daevabad, Afshin. Not for a single minute. Besides the ifrit, you're the only magic-user in the city. If the djinn and shafit thought you weren't here to protect us . . ." He began to shake again. "You didn't see what they did to the Navasatem parade. What they did to Nisreen. The dirt-bloods don't need magic. They have ghastly human weapons capable of blowing people to pieces. They have Rumi fire and rifles and—"

Manizheh's hand fell on Kaveh's wrist. "I think he understands." She glanced at Dara, resignation in her face. "I am desperate for my magic, Afshin, I am. But we took this city by blood, and now Daevabad comes first. We'll need to come up with another way to get the seal back."

If Dara had felt the weight of his duties before, it landed even more heavily now, tightening around his shoulders and throat like a barbed scarf. Manizheh wasn't manipulating him this time. Dara knew damn well the price his people would pay for the violence their invasion had wrought.

It was not a thing he would let happen. "Then what *do* we do?" he asked.

"We finish what we started: we put Daevabad—all of it—under our control. And while we'll need to find out if magic is gone beyond our borders, for now we keep news of what's happened under wraps. I won't have the shafit running off to bring magic to the human world or the djinn fleeing to their homelands. Have the ifrit burn any boats trying to cross the lake."

Kaveh visibly started at that. "But there will be travelers trying to come for Navasatem."

"Then we'll deal with them. And on a more personal note"— Manizheh took a deep breath—"is there any news of Jamshid?"

The grand wazir's face crumpled. "No, my lady. I'm sorry. All I know is that Ghassan said he was someplace secure. He might have been at the Citadel when it fell."

"Stop saying that," Dara demanded, seeing Manizheh pale for the first time. "Kaveh, you were the one who told me about Alizayd's rebellion. The Citadel was his when it fell—why would Ghassan have sent Jamshid there?"

Manizheh stepped closer to the mirrored table, picking up Nahri's hair comb. "There's someone else who might know where Ghassan would have kept Jamshid," she said, running her fingers over the ivory teeth. "Someone who might also be able to tell us about Suleiman's seal—and where his brother and wife would run if indeed they're still alive." She slipped the comb into one of her pockets. "I say it's time we pay a visit to our former emir."

3

NAHRI

Yaqub reentered the room, and dropped a shawl around her shoulders. "You look cold."

Nahri drew the shawl closer. "Thank you." It wasn't particularly chilly in the apothecary's cramped back storeroom—especially not at the side of a feverish, unconscious djinn—but Nahri hadn't been able to stop shivering.

She dipped her compress into a bowl of cool peppermint-scented water, squeezed it, and then laid it flat upon Ali's brow. He stirred but didn't open his eyes, the cloth steaming where it touched his hot skin.

Still standing, Yaqub spoke again. "How long has he had the fever?"

Nahri pressed her fingers against Ali's throat. His pulse was still too fast, though she'd swear it was a degree slower than it had been at the riverside. She prayed to God it was, anyway, clinging to Muntadhir's warning that it would take the new seal-bearer a few days to adjust to the ring's presence and praying this was all normal, not a consequence of taking the ring out of Daevabad.

"A day," she answered.

"And his head . . ." Yaqub's voice was uncertain. "You've bandaged it. Did he take a blow? If there's a wound and it turned septic—"

"It didn't." Nahri wasn't sure what a human would see if they looked at the glowing mark of Suleiman's seal on Ali's temple but had decided not to find out, ripping a strip from the bottom of her dress and tying it tight around his brow.

Gripping a new cane—it really had been a long time—Yaqub lowered himself to the ground beside her, carefully balancing another bowl. "I brought some broth from the butcher. He owed me a favor."

Guilt stabbed through her. "You didn't have to trade a favor for me."

"Nonsense. Help me raise your mysterious companion a bit. He's moving enough that you should try and get some liquid in him."

Nahri lifted Ali's shoulders, her arms still aching from the river. He mumbled something in his sleep, shivering like her, and her heart panged. *Please don't die,* she begged silently as Yaqub slid another cushion behind him.

Yaqub wordlessly took over, coaxing a couple of spoonfuls of broth into Ali's mouth and down his throat. "Not too much," he instructed. "You don't want him to choke." His voice was gentle, like a man trying not to spook a nervous animal, and it touched Nahri almost as much as it embarrassed her. If she had feared him turning her away at the door, such worry had been entirely unfounded—the old pharmacist had taken one look at her with a sick man in her arms and invited her in without question.

He sat back. "My mind or my eyes must be going. Every time I look at him, he seems to vanish."

"Odd," Nahri replied, her voice strained. "He looks normal to me."

Yaqub set down the bowl. "I always had the impression that you and normal did not quite fit. Now, I would ask if you'd like to get a proper doctor to see him and not just some batty old pharmacist, but I suspect that I already know the answer."

Nahri shook her head. No human doctor was going to be able to help Ali, and she didn't want either of them attracting undue attention. "No doctors."

"Of course not. Why do something that would make sense?"

Ah, there was the old business partner she remembered. "I don't want to get in trouble with anyone," she retorted. "I don't want *you* to get in trouble. It's best if we lie low for now. And I'm sorry, I shouldn't have intruded on you like this. I'll get the rest of this broth in him and then—"

"And then you'll what? Drag an unconscious body around Cairo?" Yaqub asked drily. "No, you will both be staying right—" He jumped, staring in bewilderment at Ali. "He did it again," he said. "I would swear he just vanished."

"It's your eyes. They start going at your age." When Yaqub gave her an incredulous look, Nahri forced a pained smile. "But thank you for your offer of hospitality."

Yaqub sighed. "You would return under such circumstances." He climbed heavily to his feet, motioning for her to follow. "Come. Let whoever this is rest. You need to eat, and *I* have some questions."

Apprehensive, Nahri nonetheless drew a light blanket over Ali and climbed to her feet. She straightened up, twisting her back to relieve her aching body. She felt so horribly frail.

It's only temporary. Ali would wake up and lift the seal, they'd get their magic back and then they'd sort everything out.

They had to.

Nahri's stomach grumbled as she passed through the door.

Yaqub was correct about her hunger. She hadn't eaten in a long time, her last meal spent in the hospital with Subha as they struggled to take care of the victims of the Navasatem attack.

By the Most High, was that only two days ago? A wave of fresh despair welled in Nahri's chest. What would happen to Subha, her family, and the rest of the shafit in a city controlled by Manizheh and Dara, especially when their new Daeva rulers learned of the Navasatem attack? Might the doctor be shown mercy for having saved Daeva lives? Executed for her brazenness?

"Are you coming?" Yaqub called.

"Yes." Nahri tried to distract herself from her fears, but being in Yaqub's shop only shook up her emotions more. The apothecary looked like it had been plucked from her memories, as messy and warm as always. There were the old wooden workbench and scattered pharmacy tools—many of which looked as old as Daevabad. The air was thick with the smell of spices and herbs, and barrels of dried chamomile flowers and gnarled gingerroot covered the dusty floor, with tins and glass vials of more precious ingredients perched upon the shelves.

She ran her hand over the worn table, her fingers brushing the various boxes and baubles. Nahri had spent countless hours in this cramped room, helping Yaqub with inventory and trying to pretend she wasn't hanging on every precious word he imparted about medicine. Back in Daevabad, she'd have done almost anything to return, to spend just one more day in Egypt, one more afternoon dicing herbs and pounding seeds in the sunlight streaming through the tall window as Yaqub droned on about treating stomach cramps and insect bites.

In none of those dreams had Nahri arrived fleeing Daevabad's violent conquest at the hands of people she'd thought dead, people who in another life she might have loved—nor did she imagine traveling with a man who by any right should be her enemy.

Yaqub snapped his fingers in front of her face and then gestured to an oil-splattered paper package. "Sambousek. Eat." He grunted, settling on a stool. "Were I smart, I would only give you one per question answered."

Nahri opened the package, her belly rumbling at the pile of sambousek, the smell of the fried dough making her light-headed. "But that would make you a terrible host. After all, you did call me a guest." She all but inhaled the first pastry, closing her eyes in delight at the taste of the salty cheese.

Yaqub smiled. "Still the little street girl. I remember the first time I fed you: I'd never seen a child eat so fast. I thought for sure you would choke."

"I was hardly a child," she complained. "I think I was fifteen when you and I started working together."

"You were a child," Yaqub corrected softly, remorse in his voice. "And clearly so very, very alone." He hesitated. "I . . . after you disappeared, I regretted that I had not done more to reach out to you. I should have invited you into my home, found you a proper husband . . ."

"I would have turned you away," Nahri said wistfully. "I would have thought it was a trick."

Yaqub looked surprised. "Did you not trust me even at the end?"

Nahri swallowed her last bite and wordlessly took the cup of water he offered. "It wasn't you. I didn't trust anyone," she said, realizing it as she spoke. "I was afraid to. It always felt like I was one mistake away from losing everything."

"You sound so much older."

She forced a shrug, dropping her gaze before he could see the emotions in her face. She'd started to trust people in Daevabad—at least as much as Nahri was capable of trusting anyone. She'd had friends and mentors—roots. Nisreen and Subha, Elashia and Razu, Jamshid and Ali—even Muntadhir and Zaynab in their own way.

At least she'd had roots until the first person she'd trusted—the first person she'd let into her heart—had ripped them out and set everything she'd built spectacularly ablaze.

"It's been a long few years." Nahri changed the subject, her appetite vanishing. "How have *you* been doing? You look pretty good. I wasn't sure you'd still be . . ."

"What? Alive?" Yaqub harrumphed. "I am not *that* old. The knee gives me trouble, and my eyes aren't as sharp as they once were—as you so kindly pointed out—but I'm still better than half my competition, out there mixing chalk and sugar syrup into their marked-up products."

"Have you considered taking on an apprentice?" She nodded to the untidy shop. "It's a lot of work."

He made a face. "I've tried a few sons-in-law and grandsons. The ones who weren't useless were lazy."

"And your daughters and granddaughters?"

"Are safer at home," he said firmly. "There has been too much war, too many of these foreign soldiers mucking about. French, British, Turkish—one can hardly keep track."

Nahri drew back, confused. "British and Turkish? But I thought . . . aren't we controlled by the French?"

Yaqub gave her a look like she'd lost her mind. "The French have been gone for years now." His face grew even more disbelieving. "Nahri, where have you been that you did not know about the war? They were battling on both sides of the Nile, through the streets of Cairo . . ." His voice grew bitter. "Foreigners, all of them. Bloodying our land; seizing our food, our palaces, all these treasures they were said to have dug out of the ground—and then claiming it was all done because each would be better at ruling us."

Her heart sank. "And now?"

"The Ottomans again. A new one. Says things will be different, that he wants to lead a modern and independent Egypt."

Yaqub let out a grumpy snort. "Plenty of people like him, like some of his ideas."

"But not you?"

"No. They say he is already turning on some of the Egyptian nobles and clerics who supported him." He shook his head. "I do not believe ambitious men who say the only route to peace and prosperity lies in giving them more power—particularly when they do it with lands and people who are not theirs. And those Europeans will be back. People do not cross a sea to fight without expecting some return on their investment."

At that, Nahri forced herself to eat another pastry. It seemed wherever she went, her people were being pushed down by foreign rulers and killed in wars over which they had no say. In Daevabad, at least, she'd had some power and had done her damnedest to set things on a different course—her marriage to Muntadhir, for starters, and the hospital. And still it had done nothing, her efforts at peace destroyed by violence again and again.

Yaqub leaned against his workbench. "So now that you have effectively diverted the conversation twice, let us return to those questions I have for you: What happened? And where have you been all these years?"

Nahri stared at him. She wasn't sure she could answer that for herself, let alone for a human who was supposed to have no inkling of the magical world.

A human. How quickly that word had risen unbidden in her mind. The realization threw her, making her fumble for an answer even more awkward. "It's sort of a long story—"

"Oh, have you somewhere to be? An appointment?" Yaqub wagged a trembling finger. "Child, you should be happy for all the wars. They distracted people from the rumors flying around after you disappeared."

"Rumors?"

His expression darkened. "A girl was found murdered in El

Arafa, surrounded by decaying bodies, ransacked tombs, broken graves—like the dead themselves awoke, God forbid. People said she was shot with an arrow that looked like it came from the time of the Prophet. Wild stories, including gossip that she'd taken part in a zar earlier in the evening. And that it was led by . . ."

"Me," Nahri finished. "Her name was Baseema. The girl, I mean."

She didn't miss the way he drew back ever so slightly. "You weren't actually involved in her death, were you?"

Creator, Nahri was so tired of lying to people she cared about. "Of course not," she said hoarsely.

"Then why did you vanish?" Yaqub sounded hurt. "I was very worried, Nahri. I know I'm not your family, but you might have sent word."

More guilt, but at least this Nahri could answer somewhat honestly. "I would have if I could, my friend. Believe me." She thought fast. "I was . . . taken—rescued. But the place I ended up, the people—they were on the controlling side," she explained, in what had to be the mildest assessment of Ghassan al Qahtani ever uttered. "In fact, that's why we're here. We're sort of . . . political exiles."

Yaqub's fuzzy gray brows had been rising higher in disbelief as she spoke, but now he just looked confused. "*We?*" he repeated.

"Me and him," Nahri replied, nodding at Ali, his sleeping form visible through the open door.

Yaqub glanced back and then jumped. "Oh, goodness, I'd completely forgotten about him!"

"Yes, he seems to have that effect." Not that Nahri was complaining. If Ali woke up in Cairo, it might be better for everyone that humans had trouble seeing—and perhaps more importantly, hearing—the djinn prince with the habit of saying exactly the wrong thing.

If he wakes up. Even thinking it made her want to rush back in and check on him.

Yaqub was still staring at Ali's feet, squinting as though that would keep him from popping out of view again. "And who exactly is 'he'?"

"A friend."

"A friend?" He clucked his tongue in disapproval. "What is a 'friend'? You are not married?"

Nahri's guilt left her in one fell swoop. "I vanish in a cemetery full of exhumed skeletons only to show up in your shop six years later, and your primary concern about the man you can barely see is whether or not he's my *husband*?"

Yaqub flushed but remained stubborn. "So you and your not-husband are political exiles, you said? From where?"

A magical court of djinn. "An island," she answered. "It's this tiny island kingdom. I doubt you've heard of it."

"An island where?"

Nahri swallowed. "Afghanistan?" she tried. "I mean, you know, in that general area."

Yaqub crossed his arms over his chest. "An island. In *Afghanistan*? Where? Near the endless desert steppe or the rocky mountains weeks from the sea?"

His sarcastic response only made Nahri more heartsick. How quickly they'd fallen back into their verbal sparring matches, the biting remarks she'd always trusted more than if Yaqub had treated her with pity.

And suddenly she wanted to tell him. Ali might be dying, the magic that had been part of her identity since she was a child was gone, and her world had been torn apart. She wanted someone to tell her it was all going to be okay, to hug her as she wept the tears she rarely let fall.

She looked at Yaqub, at the gentleness in his warm, human-brown eyes and the weary lines in his face. What horrors had he seen in the wars Nahri had missed? How had he survived, managing his shop and feeding his family in a city filled with hostile foreigners—a city where his faith marked him out as different and possibly suspicious, a sickening situation Nahri could empathize with all too well?

Nahri would not shake his world further. "Grandfather, you always made it clear you didn't want to know certain things about me. Trust that this isn't a tale you want to hear."

Yaqub's eyes dimmed, a quiet sadness crossing his face. "I see." There was tense silence for a moment, but when he spoke again, his voice was understanding. "Are you in trouble?"

Nahri had to bite back a hysterical laugh. She'd tricked Manizheh—a woman who controlled people's limbs with her mind and summoned back dead Afshin from ash—and stolen the seal ring her mother had been after for decades. Yes, Nahri would say she was in trouble.

She lied again. "I think I'm safe for now. For a little while, at least," she added, praying that part was true. Nahri didn't put tracking her and Ali out of Manizheh's skill set, but Daevabad was a world away and presumably consumed by utter chaos. Hopefully her mother would be too busy with her new throne to come hunting for them so soon.

But she would come eventually. Nahri hadn't missed the hunger in Manizheh's face when she spoke of Suleiman's seal.

Or maybe she'll send Dara. God forgive her, Nahri almost wanted to see him. She wanted to confront him, to understand how the man who'd escorted her to Daevabad, the charismatic warrior who teased her and conjured his mother's stew, had knowingly taken part in an assault meant to end with the murder of every Geziri man, woman, and child.

And then what? Will you kill him? Could she? Or would Dara simply sweep Nahri's opinions and pleas aside once again, rip Ali's heart from his chest, and then drag her back to face Manizheh?

"Nahri?" Yaqub was staring at her.

She glanced down, realizing she'd crushed the remaining pastry in her hand. "Sorry. Just lost in my thoughts."

"You look exhausted." Yaqub nodded to the storage room. "I have another blanket in there. Why don't you get some sleep? I'll head home and see if I can't find the two of you some clean clothes."

Shame blossomed through her once again. "I don't want to take advantage of your hospitality."

"Oh, stop." Yaqub was already rising to his feet. "You don't always have to do everything on your own." He waved her off. "Go rest."

Nahri found the second blanket upon a thin, rolled pad and spread them both on the floor. She grunted in relief as she collapsed. It felt heavenly to lie flat, a small mercy to her battered body. She reached out, finding Ali's wrist at her side and taking his pulse once more.

Slower. Only by a count or two, and his damp skin still burned—but it didn't scorch. He shifted in his sleep, murmuring under his breath.

She slipped her fingers through his. "A woman is sleeping beside you *and* holding your hand," she warned, her voice breaking. "Surely you need to wake up and immediately cease such forbidden behavior."

There was no response. Nahri hadn't expected one and yet still felt herself fighting an edge of grief.

"Don't die in my debt, al Qahtani. I'll come find you in Paradise, I swear, and they'll kick you out for associating with such a disrespectful thief." She squeezed his hand. "Please."

4

DARA

The twisting tunnel that led to the palace dungeons was as bleak as its end point, a narrow corridor that burrowed deep into the city's bedrock, lit only by the occasional torch and smelling of mildew and old blood. Ancient Divasti graffiti spoke to its origins in the time of the Nahid Council, but Dara had never been down here.

He'd heard stories, of course. Everyone had—that was the point. Rumors of bodies left to rot into a gruesome carpet of bones and decaying viscera, a cruel welcome to new inmates who might suddenly find confessing their crimes a better alternative. The torture was said to be worse—illusionists who could make you hallucinate the deaths of your loved ones and poisons that melted flesh. There was no light and little air, just tight cells of death where one would slowly go mad.

Had Zaydi al Qahtani succeeded in capturing him, Dara had no doubt that would have been his fate. What better propaganda than the last Afshin, the rebel Scourge, driven to insanity beneath the stolen shedu throne? Such punishment had still been on Dara's mind when he'd escorted Nahri to Daevabad, and it had taken every bit of courage and bluster he'd had to stare Ghassan al Qahtani in the eye while envisioning himself being dragged away to spend eternity in a dark stone cage.

Dara had never imagined, however, that the haughty emir at Ghassan's side, the heir apparent wrapped in every wealth and privilege, would be the one who ended up here instead.

Dara stepped closer to Manizheh as they turned the corner. "Did you know Muntadhir well when you lived in Daevabad?"

Manizheh shook her head. "He was barely out of boyhood when I left, and the djinn children of the harem believed me a witch who could break their bones with a single glance."

"But you *can* do that."

"Answers your question, doesn't it? But no, I didn't know Muntadhir well. He was precious to his mother, and she was careful to keep him away from me. He was young when she died, but Ghassan had him moved out of the harem and into the emir's quarters. And from what I've heard, he handled his abrupt transition into public adulthood by pouring everything he could down his throat and sleeping his way through the nobility."

There was no missing the disdain in her response, but Dara wasn't so ready to underestimate the son Ghassan had raised to rule a divided city.

"He's not a fool, Banu Nahida," he warned. "He's reckless and intemperate when drunk, but no fool—especially when it comes to politics."

"I believe you. Indeed, I'm relying on the fact that he's not a fool, because it would be quite foolish for him to decide not to talk to us."

Dara had little doubt what she was alluding to. "It does not work as well as you think," he said. When Manizheh glanced at him, questioning, Dara was blunter. "Torture. Hurt a man badly enough and he will say anything to make it stop, regardless of whether or not it is true."

"I trust you have the experience to make such a judgment." Manizheh's expression was contemplative. "So perhaps there's another way to reach him."

"Such as?"

"The truth. I'm hoping it's such an unexpected departure from the way our families typically deal with each other that it might startle him into some truths of his own."

Gushtap, one of Dara's surviving soldiers, stood beside a heavy iron door, a wall torch throwing blazing light on his harrowed face. He caught sight of them, jerking to attention and offering a shaky bow. "Banu Nahida."

"May the fires burn brightly for you," Manizheh greeted him. "How is our prisoner?"

"Quiet for now, but we had to chain him to the wall—he was smashing his head into the door."

Manizheh blanched, and Dara explained. "Muntadhir thinks I've returned from hell to avenge myself on his family. Killing himself before I can do it more painfully likely seems a sound plan."

Manizheh sighed. "Promising." She laid a hand on Gushtap's shoulder. "Go take some tea for yourself and send another to relieve you. No one should have to serve in this crypt long."

Relief lit the young man's face. "Thank you, Banu Nahida."

The door creaked when Dara pushed it open, the heavy wood scraping the floor. And though he trusted his men about the chains, he still found himself reaching for his knife before stepping into the black cell. The memory of the slaughtered Geziris was fresh in his mind, and Dara knew how he would react if he were suddenly face-to-face with the individuals who'd done that to his people.

The stench hit him first, blood, rot, and waste, so thick he covered his nose, trying not to gag. With a snap, Dara conjured a trio of fiery floating globes that filled the cell with golden light. It revealed what he'd dreaded all those years, though the remains of the infamous "carpet" looked nearly worn away, reduced to blackened bones and scraps of cloth.

Muntadhir was chained to the opposite wall, iron cuffs binding his wrists and ankles. Daevabad's once-dashing emir was still dressed in his ruined clothes from the night before, bloodstained trousers and a dishdasha so torn it hung around his neck like a scarf. A shallow gash stretched across his stomach, a nasty wound to be certain, but nothing like how it had looked before magic vanished: the skin flushed with the ominous green-black of the zulfiqar's poison, the steadily spreading tendrils of inescapable death.

Muntadhir jerked back against the sudden light, blinking. He met Dara's eyes, and hatred ripped across his face.

Then he noticed Manizheh.

Muntadhir's mouth fell open, a strangled sound leaving his throat. But then he laughed, a hysterical, bitter laugh. "Of course," he said. "Of course it was you. Who else would be capable of such a thing?"

Manizheh's tone was almost polite. "Hello, Emir."

Muntadhir shuddered. "I watched you burn on the funeral pyre." He glared at Dara. "I watched *you* turn to ash. What devil's deal did the two of you make to return and visit such slaughter on my people?"

Dara tensed, but Manizheh was implacable. "Nothing so dramatic, I assure you." She pointed at his wound. "May I check that? It should be cleaned and may require stitching."

"I would rather it kill me. Where is my brother?" Muntadhir's voice broke with worry. "Where is Nahri? What have you done with them?"

"I don't know," Manizheh replied. "The last I saw of them, Alizayd had seized Suleiman's seal ring, grabbed my daughter, and jumped into the lake. No one has heard from them since."

And here I thought we were trying the truth. Yet Dara would be lying if he said that wasn't a story he wished he could believe as well. It would be easier to have a new reason to hate Alizayd than confront the unsettling truth that Nahri had chosen another side.

"I don't believe you," Muntadhir retorted. "The lake kills anyone who goes in it. Ali would never—"

"Wouldn't he?" Manizheh countered. "Your brother has partnered with marid before. Maybe he thought they would help him."

Muntadhir's expression stayed flat. "I have no idea what you're talking about."

Dara spoke up. "Come on, al Qahtani. You've seen him use water magic. He did so right in front of us. And you were on the boat that night he fell in the lake, and they possessed him."

The emir didn't flinch. "Ali didn't fall in the lake," he said coolly, reciting the words with the ease of an often-told lie. "He was caught in the ship's netting and recovered in time to strike you down. God be praised for such a hero."

"Odd," Dara said, matching his chill. "Because I remember you wailing his name as he vanished beneath the surface." He stepped closer. "I've met the marid, Emir. You may think me a monster, but you have no idea what these creatures are. They use the rotting bodies of their murdered acolytes to communicate. They despise our kind. And do you know what they called your brother? A mistake. A mistake they were *very* angry about and one which delivered them into my debt. Now he has vanished into their domain with your wife and one of the most powerful magical objects in our world."

Muntadhir met his stare. "If they have escaped you, I don't care who helps them."

Manizheh cut in. "Where would they go, Muntadhir?"

"Why? So you can poison that place as well?" Muntadhir laughed. "Oh, right; you can't now, can you? Do you think I didn't notice? Except for your Scourge, magic is gone." He snorted. "Congratulations, Manizheh, you've done what no invader has accomplished before: you've broken Daevabad itself."

"We're not the ones who took the seal out of the city," Dara shot back. "That is why this happened to magic, is it not?"

Muntadhir's eyes went wide with feigned innocence. "Certainly seems like a strange coincidence."

"Then how do we restore it?" Manizheh asked. "How do we get our magic back?"

"I don't know." Muntadhir shrugged. "Perhaps you should go make friends with a human prophet. Best of luck, truly. I'm guessing you have about a week before Daevabad devolves into anarchy."

The emir's haughty sarcasm was grating on the last of Dara's nerves, but Manizheh still seemed unaffected. "You don't strike me as a man who would enjoy watching his home slip into anarchy. That doesn't fit the gentle boy I remember, the polite young prince who always joined his mother for breakfast in the harem. Poor Saffiyeh, taken so early—"

Muntadhir lunged against his chains. "You don't say her name," he seethed. "You murdered my mother. I know you stayed away on purpose when she was sick. You were jealous of her, jealous of all of us. You were probably scheming even then to slaughter all the djinn trying to be nice to you!"

"*Trying to be nice to me,*" she repeated faintly, sounding disappointed. "I had thought you cleverer than that. A shame that, for all the fondness you are said to have for the Daevas, you never saw through your father's lies."

Wildness twisted across Muntadhir's blood-streaked face. "Nothing he did deserved the kind of death you visited on my people."

"If you rule by violence, you should expect to be removed by violence." Manizheh was curter now. "But it need not continue. Help us, and I will grant mercy to those Geziris who survived."

"Fuck you."

Dara hissed, still deeply conditioned on behalf of the Nahids, but Manizheh waved him off, stepping closer to Muntadhir. Dara eyed the emir's shackles, not liking any of this.

"It isn't only your mother I remember you visiting," Manizheh continued. "For if I recall, you were always very polite to your stepmother, going so far as to shower her with gold when her first child was born. How sweet, the women said, the toy horse the emir brought his baby sister. The silly song he made up about teaching her to ride it one day . . ."

Muntadhir pulled at his chains. "Don't speak of my sister."

"Why not? Someone should. All these questions about your brother and wife and none for Zaynab? Are you not worried about her fate?"

A flicker of alarm, the first, crossed Muntadhir's face. "I sent her to Ta Ntry when my brother rebelled."

Manizheh smiled. "Odd. Her servants say she ran off with some Geziri warrior woman when the attack began."

"They're lying."

"Or you are. Still eager to watch Daevabad fall into anarchy if your sister is out there somewhere, defenseless and alone? Do you know what happens to women in cities swallowed by violence?" She glanced back, speaking to Dara for the first time since they entered the cell. "Why don't you tell him, Afshin? What happens to young girls who belong to families with so many enemies?"

The breath went entirely out of him. "What?" Dara whispered.

"What happened to your sister?" Manizheh pressed, not seeming to notice the raw anguish he felt stealing over his features. "What happened to Tamima when she was in the same position as Zaynab?"

Dara swayed on his feet. *Tamima.* His sister's bright, innocent smile and gruesome fate. "You—you know what happened," he stammered. Manizheh couldn't really mean to make him say it, to speak aloud the brutal way his little sister had been tortured to death.

"But does the emir?"

"*Yes.*" Dara's voice was savage now. He couldn't believe Manizheh was doing this, trying to twist the single worst tragedy in his life into a crude prod to goad a Qahtani into talking. But Muntadhir did know—he'd thrown Tamima's death into Dara's face that night on the boat.

Manizheh kept going. "And if you could do it all over again, would you not have done anything to save her? Even assisted your enemy?"

Dara's temper broke spectacularly. "I would have delivered every member of the Nahid Council to Zaydi al Qahtani myself if it meant saving Tamima."

That was clearly *not* the answer Manizheh wanted. Her eyes blazed as she said, "I see," with a new frost in her voice. But she turned back to Muntadhir. "Does that change your response, Emir? Are you willing to risk what befell the Afshin's sister happening to yours?"

"It won't," Muntadhir snapped. The goad hadn't even worked. "Zaynab isn't surrounded by enemies, and my people would never hurt her."

"Your people might feel differently if I offer her weight in gold to whoever brings me her head." Manizheh's flat tone didn't waver at the grisly threat, and Dara closed his eyes, wishing he were anywhere else. "But if you're not ready to discuss your sister's safety, then why don't we start with someone else?"

"If you think I'll tell you anything about Nahri—"

"Not Nahri. Jamshid e-Pramukh."

Dara jerked back to attention.

The emir's face was blank, his anger replaced by a mask of coolnesss. "Never heard of him."

Manizheh smiled and glanced at Dara. "Afshin, is your quiver close?"

He could barely look at her, much less respond, so instead he raised a hand. In a moment, a conjured quiver was there, twisting from a swirl of fire to reveal a glittering array of silver arrows.

"Excellent." Manizheh plucked free one of the arrows. "It would be twelve arrows, correct?" she asked Muntadhir. "If I wished you to take two for every one that ripped through Jamshid when he saved your life?"

Muntadhir gazed at her, arrogance filling his voice again. "Will you bend the bow yourself? Because your Afshin is looking rather mutinous."

"I don't need a bow."

Manizheh plunged the arrow into Muntadhir's thigh.

Dara instantly forgot their argument. "Banu Nahida!"

She ignored him, twisting the arrow as Muntadhir cried out in pain. "Do you remember him now, Emir?" she demanded, raising her voice over his groans.

Muntadhir was gasping for breath. "You crazy, murderous— Wait!" he yelped as Manizheh reached for another arrow. "My God, what do you even want with Kaveh's son? Someone else you can threaten into compliance?"

Manizheh released the arrow, and Muntadhir crumpled. "I want to grant him his birthright," she declared, gazing at the emir with the same contempt he'd shown her. "I would raise Jamshid to the station he deserves and one day see him on the throne of his ancestors."

Dara could not have described the look that came over Muntadhir's face for all the words in the world.

He blinked rapidly, his mouth opening and closing like a fish. "Wh-what station?" Muntadhir asked. "What do you mean, the *throne* of his ancestors?"

"Remove your head from the sand, al Qahtani, and try to recall the world doesn't revolve around your family. Do you really think I stayed in Zariaspa when you were a child, risking your father's wrath when he begged me to save his dying queen, merely to spite him? I stayed because I was pregnant, and I knew Ghassan would burn down my world if he found out."

Muntadhir was trembling. "That's not possible. He doesn't have healing abilities. Kaveh wouldn't have brought him to Daevabad. And Jamshid . . . Jamshid would have told me!"

"Ah, so we've gone from not knowing his name to the two of you being so close he would have shared his most dangerous secret?" Anger finally broke through Manizheh's cool facade. "Jamshid has no idea who he is. I had to bind his abilities and deny him his heritage to keep him from being enslaved in the infirmary like I was. I only tell *you* because you've just made very clear how much family means to you, and you should know there is nothing I won't do to keep my son safe."

Anguish twisted Muntadhir's face. "I don't know where Jamshid is. Wajed took him out of the city. He was to be some sort of hostage—"

"Some sort of hostage?" Manizheh cut in. "You let the man who saved your life be used as a *hostage*?"

Dara could barely look at Muntadhir—the bone-deep guilt radiating off the emir was too familiar.

"Yes," Muntadhir whispered, regret thick in his hoarse voice. "I went to my father, but I was too late. The poison had already killed him."

"And had the poison not taken Ghassan, then what?" Manizheh prodded. "What were you prepared to do?"

Muntadhir squeezed his eyes shut, seeming to breathe against the pain, his hands pressed around the arrowhead still buried in his leg. "I don't know. Ali had taken the Citadel. I thought I could try and reason with my father, insist he release Jamshid and Nahri . . ."

"And if he didn't?"

Wetness glistened in the other man's eyelashes. When he spoke again, his words were barely audible. "I was going to join Alizayd."

"I don't believe you," Manizheh challenged. "You, a good son of Am Gezira, were going to betray your own father to save the life of a Daeva man?"

Muntadhir opened his bloodshot eyes; they were full of pain. "Yes."

Manizheh stared at the emir. "You love him. Jamshid."

Dara felt the blood drain from his face.

Muntadhir looked shattered. His breath was coming faster, his shoulders shaking with the rise and fall. "Yes," he choked out again.

Manizheh sat back on her heels. Dara didn't move, shocked at the turn in the conversation. How in the Creator's name had Manizheh learned about Muntadhir and Jamshid? Not even Kaveh had wanted her to know!

She kept talking. "You and I both know how devoted Wajed was to your father. I've heard he all but raised Alizayd as his own son." She paused. "So what do you imagine Wajed and his men—his good Geziri soldiers—will do to Jamshid when they learn their king, their favorite prince, and all their kinsmen are supposedly dead at Kaveh's hands?"

For all the enmity between Dara and the Qahtanis, the slow, awful panic that rolled across Muntadhir's face made Dara sick to his stomach. He knew that feeling too well.

"I . . . I'll send word to Wajed." The emir had broken, and he didn't even realize it. "A letter! A letter with my mark ordering him not to hurt Jamshid."

"And how will we send word?" Manizheh asked. "We have no magic. No shapeshifters who can fly, no whispered enchantments to our birds. Nor would we even know where to send such word."

"Am Gezira," Muntadhir blurted out. "We have a fortress in the south. Or Ta Ntry! If Wajed finds out about my father, he may go to the queen."

Manizheh touched his knee. "I thank you for that information." She rose to her feet. "I only pray it's not too late."

It was Muntadhir who pursued her now. "Wait!" he cried, scrambling to stand and hissing as he shifted weight away from his injured leg.

Manizheh was already motioning for Dara to open the door. "Don't worry, I'm just getting some supplies to see to your wounds, and then I'll return." She glanced back. "Now that you're feeling more talkative, perhaps I'll bring the ifrit. I have a great many questions I would like to ask you about Suleiman's seal."

She stepped through the doorway, leaving Dara in her wake.

Muntadhir stared at him desperately from across the cell. "Afshin . . ."

He is your enemy. The man who pressured Nahri into his bed. But Dara could summon no anger, no hate—not even a flicker of triumph for finally defeating the family that had devastated his.

"I will let you know if we learn of Jamshid," he said softly. Then, leaving Muntadhir the floating globes of light as a small mercy, Dara left, shutting the door behind him.

Manizheh was already headed toward the corridor. "Zaynab al Qahtani is in the Geziri Quarter."

Dara frowned. "How do you know?"

"Because that man is not nearly as clever as he thinks. We need to get her out."

"The Geziri Quarter is fortified against us. Alizayd unified the Geziris and the shafit under his call and was preparing for a siege well before we arrived. If the princess is behind their lines, it is going to be hard to get her out."

"We have no choice. I need Zaynab in our custody, preferably before her mother gets wind of what happened here." Manizheh pressed her mouth in a grim line. "I had planned on Hatset being in Daevabad. We could have held her hostage to keep the Ayaanle in line. Instead, I have an angry widow with a sea to protect her and a mountain of gold to support her vengeance." She turned away, motioning him to follow. "Come."

Dara didn't move. "We are not done here."

She glanced back, looking incredulous. "Excuse me?"

He was trembling again. "You had no right. No right to use the memory of my sister like that."

"Did I not speak the truth? Zaynab al Qahtani is absolutely at risk running around Daevabad with no protection. Forget whatever noble Geziri warriors Muntadhir seems to think are going to protect her. Her father brutalized people in this city for decades, and there are plenty who would happily take advantage of the current situation to get some revenge."

"That's not . . ." Dara struggled for words, hating how easily she seemed to twist them against him. "*You know what I mean.* You should have told me in advance you planned to mention her."

"Oh, should I have?" Manizheh spun on him. "Why, so you could craft a better way to say you would have delivered my ancestors to the Qahtanis?"

"I was shocked!" Dara fought to check his temper, flames flickering from his hands. "We are supposed to be working together."

"And where was that sentiment when you and Kaveh were whispering behind my back about Jamshid and Muntadhir?" Her eyes flashed. "Did you not think *you should have told me in advance* that my son had been carrying on a decade-long affair with Ghassan's?"

"Are you spying on me now?" he stammered.

"Do I need to? Because I'd rather not waste our extremely limited resources, and I'd hope the safety of our people was enough to keep you in line."

The entire corridor shook with his frustration, the air sparking.

"Do not lecture me as to the safety of our people," Dara said through his teeth. "*Our* people would have been safer if we had not rushed this invasion and tried to annihilate the Geziris—as I advised!"

If he thought Manizheh would be taken aback by the show of magic, Dara had underestimated her. She didn't so much as twitch, the darkness in her black eyes suddenly deeper.

"You forget yourself, Afshin," she warned, and had he been another man, he might have fallen to his knees at the lethal edge in her voice. "And you are hardly innocent in our failure. Do you not think Vizaresh told me of your delays with Alizayd al Qahtani? Had you executed that bloody sand fly when you first laid hands on him, Nahri wouldn't have run off with him. She wouldn't have given him Suleiman's seal and fled from the city, ripping away our magic. Our invasion might have been a success!"

Dara bristled, but that was not a point he could refute. He might strangle the ifrit later for running his mouth, but not killing Alizayd had been a fatal error.

Manizheh seemed to recognize a hint of defeat. "Do not ever keep anything from me again, understand? I have an entire city to rule. I cannot do so while also worrying about what secrets the head of my security is harboring. I need my people *loyal*."

Dara glowered, crossing his arms and resisting the urge to

burn something. "What would you even have me do? We still have no idea where either of your children is, and you have made it clear I'm not allowed to risk our tribe's safety by leaving to go look for them."

"We don't need to go look for them," Manizheh said. "Not ourselves. Not if we send the right kind of message."

"The right kind of *message*?"

"Yes." She beckoned to him again. "Come, Afshin. It's time I address my new subjects."

5

ALI

From the time Alizayd al Qahtani was very small, he'd been blessed with the peculiar ability to instantly wake up.

It was an ability that used to unsettle others—nursemaids in the harem tiptoeing about when the little prince who'd been snoring abruptly spoke up, cheerfully greeting them; or his sister Zaynab, who'd go screeching to their mother when he snapped his eyes open, bellowing like the palace karkadann. That Ali slept so lightly had thoroughly pleased Wajed, who proudly declared his protégé rested like a warrior should, constantly alert. And indeed, Ali had seen firsthand what a blessing it was, saving his life the few times assassins came for him in the night during his exile in Am Gezira.

It wasn't a blessing now. Because when Ali finally opened his eyes, he had not the mercy of a single moment of forgetting his brother was dead.

He was flat on his back, a low, unfamiliar ceiling before him.

There must have been a window, for a few rays of sun pierced the warm air, dust motes dancing and sparkling before blinking out of existence. The grassy aroma of fresh-cut herbs, a steady rhythmic pounding, the clip of hooves, and the murmur of distant conversations were all signs indicating that Ali was no longer on an uninhabited bank of the Nile. He was cold, shivering under a thin blanket with the kind of clammy chill he associated with fever, and his body ached, weak in a way that should have concerned him.

It didn't. Far more troublesome was the fact that Ali had woken up at all.

Was it quick, akhi? Or did it take as long as everyone says? Did it burn? Did the Afshin find you, hurt you worse? Ali knew those weren't questions he should be asking. He knew, according to the religion he'd preached his entire life, that his brother was already at peace, a martyr in Paradise.

But the pious words he would have spoken to another in his place were ash in his mouth. Muntadhir wasn't supposed to be in Paradise. He was supposed to be grinning and alive and doing something vaguely scandalous. Not falling against Ali's chest, gasping as he took the zulfiqar strike meant for his little brother. Not touching Ali's face with bloody hands, failing to mask his own fear and pain as he ordered Ali to run.

We're okay, Zaydi. We're okay. All those months of their stupid feud, weeks and days Ali would never get back. Could they not have sat and hashed out their politics, their resentments? Had Ali ever made clear to Muntadhir how much he loved and admired him—how much he desperately wished he could have ended their estrangement?

And now he would never be able to. He'd never talk to any of his brothers again. Not Muntadhir, who if the zulfiqar's poison hadn't taken him first, had almost certainly been tortured by the

Afshin in his final moments. Not the men Ali had grown up with in the Royal Guard, now floating dead in Daevabad's lake. Nor Lubayd, his first friend in Am Gezira, a man who'd saved his life and left his peaceful home only to be murdered by the ifrit. Had Ali ever properly thanked him? Sat him down and cut through Lubayd's constant jesting to tell him how much his friendship meant?

Ali took a deep, rattling breath, but his eyes stayed dry. He wasn't sure he could weep. He didn't want to.

He wanted to scream.

To scream and scream until the awful crushing weight in his chest was gone. He understood now the grief that led people to pull out their hair, to tear at their skin and claw at the earth. More than scream, though, Ali wanted to be gone. It was selfish, it was contrary to his faith, but had he a blade at hand, he was not certain he could have stopped himself from carving out the ache in his heart.

Pull yourself together. You are a Geziri, a believer in the Most High.

Get up.

Still trembling and feverish, Ali forced himself into a sitting position, biting back a grunt of pain when every muscle in his body protested. He gripped his knees, black spots blossoming across his vision, and then touched his body, shocked by how frail he felt. His ruined dishdasha was gone, replaced with a soft cotton shawl that wrapped his shoulders and a waist cloth tied with what seemed like haste around his hips. He rubbed his eyes, trying to see straight.

The first person he spotted, lying unconscious on the floor, was Nahri.

Overwhelmed by worry, Ali lurched for her. He did so too quickly, nearly blacking out again as he crashed to his elbows next to her head. Closer now, he could see clearly the rise and fall of

Nahri's chest as she breathed. She murmured in her sleep, curling tighter into a ball.

Sleeping. She's just sleeping. Ali forced himself to relax. He wasn't helping either of them like this. He pushed himself back into a sitting position, taking a deep breath and closing his eyes until his head felt like it had mostly stopped spinning.

Better. So first, where were they? The last thing Ali remembered was feeling like he was about to die in a ruined mosque overlooking the Nile. Now they appeared to be in some sort of storeroom, an extremely disorganized one, packed with broken baskets and drying herbs.

Nahri must have gotten us here. He glanced again at the Banu Nahida. Her royal garments had been swapped for a worn black dress that looked several sizes too big, and the scarf tied around her head was doing little to contain her hair, the curls spilling out in an ebony halo. A few rays of dusty light striped her body, highlighting the curve of her hip and the delicate expanse of the inside of her wrist.

His heart skipped, and Ali was self-aware enough to recognize that it wasn't grief alone spiking through him. Clever, stubborn Nahri who'd somehow kept him alive and gotten them from the river to wherever this was. She'd saved his life again, another debt in the ledger he knew she never forgot. She looked beautiful, sleep easing her features into a peaceful expression Ali had never seen before.

Muntadhir's words from the arena stole through his mind. *Abba will make you emir; he'll give you Nahri. All the things you pretend you don't want.*

And now Ali had them, technically. All it had cost him was everything else he loved.

Ali swayed. *Don't do this. Not now.* He'd already had to pull himself together once.

But before he dropped his gaze, he noticed something else. Scratches marred Nahri's skin. Nothing serious, just the small gashes one might expect had they been dumped in a river and climbed through underbrush.

Except Nahri shouldn't have had scratches. She should have healed.

Suleiman's seal. Our magic. The memories tumbled through him again, and Ali instantly reached for his chest. The scorching, barbed pain that had driven him to his knees when they first arrived in Egypt was gone. Now Ali simply felt . . . nothing.

That can't be. He tried to focus, closing his eyes and searching for something that felt new. But if there was some connection he was supposed to pull on to lift Suleiman's seal, it was a power he couldn't sense. He snapped his fingers, attempting to conjure a flame. It was the simplest magic Ali knew, something he'd been doing since he was a child.

Nothing.

Ali went cold. "Burn," he whispered in Geziriyya, snapping his fingers again. *"Burn,"* he tried in Ntaran and then Djinnistani, raising his other hand.

None of it worked. There was not the slightest hint of heat, nor the shimmer of smoke.

My zulfiqar, my weapons. Ali looked wildly around the room, spotting the hilt of his sword poking out from a pile of filthy clothes. He lurched to his feet, stumbling across the room and reaching for his zulfiqar like a long-lost friend. His fingers closed around the hilt, and he desperately willed flames to rise from the blade he'd spent his life mastering—the blade tied so intimately to his identity.

It stayed cold in his hand, the copper surface dull in the dim light. It wasn't just Nahri's magic that was gone.

It was Ali's.

That's not possible. Ali had seen his father wield magic while using the seal to strip it from others. That was part of the ring's legend—making its bearer the most powerful person in the room.

Panic raced through him. Was this a normal part of taking the seal, or had they done something wrong? Was there an incantation, a gesture, *something* that Ali was supposed to know?

Muntadhir would have known. Muntadhir would have known what to do with the seal had you not gotten him murdered with this very blade.

Ali dropped the zulfiqar. He stepped back, stumbling on his discarded blanket, the fragile veneer of control he'd pieced together slipping away.

You were supposed to protect him. It should have been you who held off the Afshin, you who died at his hand. What kind of brother was Ali, what kind of *man,* to be hiding in a storage room half a world away from the palace in which his father and brother had been murdered and his tribesmen and friends slaughtered? Where his sister—his *sister*—was trapped in a conquered city and surrounded by enemies?

Nahri mumbled in her sleep again, and Ali jumped.

You failed her. You failed all of them. Nahri could have been back in Daevabad right now, with the world and a throne at her fingertips.

I have to get out of here. Ali had a sudden driving need to get out of this claustrophobic little room. To breathe fresh air and put space between himself, Nahri, and his awful, bloody memories. He crossed the room, reaching for the door and stumbling through. He caught a glimpse of crowded shelves, the scent of sesame oil . . .

Then Ali crashed directly into a small, elderly man. The man let out a surprised yelp and stepped back, nearly upsetting a tin tray of carefully heaped powders.

"I'm sorry," Ali rushed to say, speaking in Djinnistani before thinking. "I didn't mean to . . . oh, my God, *you're a human.*"

"Oh!" The man put down the knife, setting it next to the bright bed of herbs he'd been cutting. "Forgive me," he said in Arabic. "I don't think I quite understood that. But you're still here—and awake. Nahri will be so pleased!" His fuzzy brows drew together. "I keep forgetting you exist." He shook his head, looking oddly undisturbed by such alarming words. "But I am forgetting my manners. Peace be upon you."

Ali swiftly pulled the door closed, not wanting to wake Nahri, and then stared at the man in open astonishment. Ali couldn't have said what set him so immediately apart; after all, he'd met plenty of shafit with rounded ears, dull, earthy skin, and warm brown eyes like the man before him. But there was something entirely too real and too solid, too . . . *rooted* about this man. As though Ali had stepped into a dream, or a curtain had been drawn back he'd never realized was there.

"I, er . . . upon you peace," he stammered back.

The man's gaze traced across Ali's face. "It is like the more I try to look at you, the harder it is. How bizarre." He frowned. "Is that a tattoo on your cheek?"

Ali's hand shot up to cover Suleiman's mark. He had no idea how to interact with this man—despite his fascination with the human world, he had never imagined actually *speaking* with a human. By all accounts, the man shouldn't have been able to see him at all.

What in the name of God has happened to magic? "Birthmark," Ali managed, his voice pitched. "Completely natural. Since birth."

"Ah," the man marveled. "Well, would you like some tea? You must be hungry." He beckoned Ali to follow him deeper into the shop. "I am Yaqub, by the way."

Yaqub. Nahri's stories of her human life came back to him. So they really were in Cairo—with the old man she said had been her only friend.

Ali swallowed, trying to get his bearings straight. "You are

Nahri's friend. The pharmacist she worked with." He glanced down at the small man, Yaqub's head barely reaching Ali's chest. "She always spoke most highly of you."

Yaqub blushed. "That was too kind of her. But my mind must be going with age. I cannot seem to recall her mentioning your name."

Ali hesitated, torn between politeness and caution—the last time a non-djinn asked for his name, it had not gone well. "Ali," he answered, keeping it simple.

"Ali? Are you a Muslim, then?"

The human word, a sacred word his people rarely voiced, tumbled Ali's emotions further. "Yes," he said hoarsely.

"And your kingdom?" Yaqub ventured. "Your Arabic . . . I've never heard an accent like that. Where is your family from?"

Ali grasped for an answer, trying to piece together what he knew of the human world and match it to his djinn geography. "The Kingdom of Saba?" When Yaqub merely looked more perplexed, he tried again. "Yemen? Is it the Yemen?"

"Yemen." The old man pursed his lips. "The Yemen and Afghanistan," he muttered under his breath. "Of course, the most natural of neighbors."

But questions about Ali's family had sent darkness rushing forward again, despair unfurling and creeping through him like vines that couldn't be beaten back. If he stayed here and tried to make small talk with this curious human, he was going to slip up and unravel whatever story Nahri had already spun. The apothecary walls suddenly felt close, too close. Ali needed air, the sky. A moment alone.

"Does that lead outside?" Ali asked, raising a trembling finger at a door on the other side of the shop.

"Yes, but you've been bedridden for days. I'm not sure you should be out and about."

Ali was already crossing the apothecary. "I'll be fine."

"Wait!" Yaqub protested. "What should I tell Nahri if she wakes before you return?"

Ali hesitated, his hand on the door. Forget whatever was going on with Suleiman's seal and magic; it was hard not to feel like the kindest thing he could do for Nahri would be to never return. That if Ali truly cared for her—loved her as Muntadhir had accused—he'd leave and let her go back to the human world she'd never stopped missing, without needing to worry about the useless djinn prince she kept having to save.

Ali pulled open the door. "Tell her I'm sorry."

ALI HAD SPENT HIS ENTIRE LIFE DREAMING OF THE human world. He'd devoured accounts of their monuments and marketplaces, envisioning himself in the holy city of Mecca and wandering the ports of great ships that crossed oceans. Exploring markets packed with new foods and inventions that had not yet made their way to Daevabad. And libraries . . . oh, the libraries.

None of those fantasies had included being nearly run down by a cart.

Ali jerked out of the path of the snub-nosed donkey and its driver and then ducked to avoid a mountain of sugarcane heaped on the back. The motion sent him crashing into a veiled woman lugging a basket of vivid purple eggplant.

"Forgive me!" he said quickly, but the woman was already brushing by as if Ali were an invisible irritant. A pair of chatting men in clerical robes parted like a human wave as they passed him, not even pausing in their conversation, and then he was almost knocked to the ground by a man balancing a large board of bread on his head.

Ali lurched out of the way, stumbling as he walked. It was too bright, too busy. Everywhere he looked was sky, a more vibrant, sunnier blue than he ever saw in Daevabad. The buildings were low, none more than a few stories tall, and far more spread out than they would have been in his packed island city. Beyond were glimpses of golden desert and rocky hills.

Ali might have craved open sky and fresh air, but in his dazed grief, the bustling human world was suddenly too much; too different and too similar all at once. The heavy, dry heat felt like an oven compared to the misty chill of his kingdom, the rich scent of fried meat and spices as thick in the air as it was in Daevabad's bazaars, but the notes unfamiliar.

"Allahu akbar! Allahu akbar!"

Ali jumped at the adhan. Even the call to prayer sounded strange, the human intonation falling on different beats. He felt like he was dreaming, as if the awful circumstances to which he'd awoken weren't real.

It's real, all of it. Your brother is dead. Your father is dead. Your friends, your family, your home. You left them when they needed you most.

Ali clutched at his head but started walking faster, following the sound of the nearest muezzin through the winding streets like a man bewitched. This was something he knew, and all Ali wanted to do right now was pray, to cry out to God and beg Him to make this right.

He fell in with a crowd of men streaming into an enormous mosque, one of the largest Ali had ever seen. He didn't have shoes to kick off, as he was already barefoot, but he paused as he entered anyway, his mouth falling open at the vast courtyard. The interior lay exposed to the sky, surrounded by four covered halls held up by hundreds of richly decorated stone arches. The skill and devotion displayed in the intricate patterns and soaring domes—done with painstaking effort by human hands, not by the simple snap of a djinn's fingers—stunned him, briefly pulling Ali from his grief. Then the glisten and splash of water caught his eye: an ablution fountain.

Water.

A worshipper shouldered roughly past, but Ali didn't care.

He stared at the fountain like a man dying of thirst. But it wasn't hydration he craved; it was something deeper. The strength that had run through his blood on Daevabad's beach when he'd commanded the lake's waves. The peace that had eased him when he'd coaxed springs out of Bir Nabat's rocky cliffs.

The magic that the marid's possession—the possession that had ruined and saved his life—had granted him.

Ali stepped up to the fountain, his heart in his throat. He was surrounded by humans, and this would be a violation of every interpretation of Suleiman's law his people had, but he needed to know. Ali extended a hand just above the water. He called to it with his mind.

A ribbon of liquid leapt onto his palm.

Tears stung his eyes and then Ali faltered, a spasm stabbing through his chest. The pain wasn't awful, but it was enough to break his concentration. The water fell away, streaming through his fingers.

But he had done it. His water abilities might be weakened, but they were there, unlike his djinn magic.

Ali wasn't sure what that meant. Dazed, he went through his ablutions. Then Ali stepped back, letting the crowd sweep him away as he surrendered to the familiar rhythm and movement of prayer.

It was like slipping into oblivion, into bliss, muscle memory and the murmured song of sacred revelation relaxing his tightly wound emotions and offering a brief escape. Ali could not begin to imagine how the two men he stood between—an elder in a crisp galabiyya and a pale, jittery boy—would react if they knew their arms were brushing those of a djinn. This was probably another violation of Suleiman's law, and yet Ali found it impossible to care, aching only to call out to his Creator, whom he so obviously shared with the worshippers around him.

Tears were brimming in his eyes by the time he finished. Ali stayed kneeling in numb silence as the other worshippers slowly left. He stared at his hands, the scarred outline of a hook marking one palm.

We're okay, Zaydi. The poisoned lines creeping over his brother's stomach and the pain Muntadhir couldn't hide in his last smile as he reassured Ali. *We're okay.*

Ali promptly lost the battle with his tears. He fell forward, biting his fist in a poor effort to contain his wail.

Dhiru, I'm sorry! I'm so sorry! Ali was crying so hard now that his entire body shook. To his ears, his sobs rang out across the vast space, echoing off the lofty walls, but none of the humans seemed to hear him at all. He was utterly alone here, in a world he was not only forbidden to be in, but one that seemed to deny his very existence. And wasn't that what he deserved for failing his people?

The salty taste of blood burst in his mouth. Ali dropped his hand away, fighting the mad desire to do something reckless and destructive. To hurl himself back into the Nile. To climb these high walls and jump off. Anything that would allow him to escape the grief tearing him open.

Instead, he pressed his face into his hands and rocked back and forth. *Merciful One, please help me. Please take this from me. I can't survive this. I can't.*

Hours passed. Ali stayed rooted to the spot he'd claimed, falling apart in his grief in a span of time that felt endless. His voice faded as his throat grew sore, and his tears dried up, his head pounding with dehydration. Numb, he was barely aware of the humans bustling around him, but he pulled himself from the ground each time they came to pray. It was a tether, a fragile line anchoring him from complete loss.

When night fell, Ali climbed the steps that spiraled around the minaret, feeling like the restless creature he'd heard humans believed djinn to be—the unseen spirits who haunted ruins and crept through graveyards. He pulled himself onto the small, ornate roof and then finally slept, tucked between the cold stones beneath the stars.

He woke just before dawn to the sounds of the muezzin shuffling up the steps. Ali froze, not wanting to frighten the man, and then listened quietly as the call to fajr rose in waves across the city. From this height, Ali could see much of Cairo: a labyrinth of pale brown buildings nestled between hills in the east and the winding dark Nile in the west. It was larger than Daevabad, sprawling across a land so very different from his fog-wreathed island, and though it was dazzling, it made Ali feel very small and very, very homesick.

Is this how Nahri felt? Ali recalled his friend on the night before everything had gone so terribly wrong. The longing in her voice contrasting with the sounds of celebration as they sat together in the hospital and spoke of Egypt. The night she'd touched his face and urged him to find a happier life.

The night Ali realized too late that his heart and his head might be taking different paths when it came to the clever, beautiful Banu Nahida. And though he was not arrogant enough to believe his world had been punished for the beginnings of a forbidden attraction he would never have acted on, it didn't help his guilt.

You shouldn't have left her at Yaqub's like that. Ali might have been senseless with grief, but it had been cruel and selfish to have vanished without a word. Nahri probably would be better off without him, but that was still her decision to make.

So he'd make sure she could.

IT TOOK ALI MOST OF THE MORNING TO RETRACE HIS steps, an effort that sent him down several wrong streets and made him briefly fear that he was lost for good. Finally, he found the twisting lane he half remembered and followed it to its end.

Nahri was outside the apothecary, perched on a stool in a

patch of sun. Though she'd veiled her face, Ali would have known her anywhere. There was a basket in her lap, and she was sorting through a pile of leafy twigs, separating out the green leaves like she'd been doing it for years. She seemed at peace, already back in the rhythms of her old life.

Then she glanced up. Relief rushed into her eyes, and Nahri shot to her feet, knocking over the bowl.

Ali crossed the street with equal haste. "I'm sorry," he blurted out. "I woke up, and I just needed to get away." He dropped to his knees, trying to pick up the leaves she'd scattered. "I didn't mean to startle you—"

Nahri grabbed his hands. "You didn't startle me. I've been waiting out here, hoping you'd come back!"

Ali met her gaze over the overturned basket. "Oh."

Nahri quickly let him go, averting her eyes as she knelt and stuffed the leafy twigs back into the basket. "I . . . when I woke up and you were gone, I wanted to go after you, but I wasn't sure you'd want to see me. I figured I'd wait a day, but then I was worried if I wasn't outside, you'd never find the apothecary again . . ." She trailed off, stammering in a very un-Nahri-like way.

It wasn't close to the anger Ali had been expecting to be greeted with. "Why wouldn't I want to see you?"

Nahri was trembling. "I put that ring on your hand. I took you away from your family, your home." He heard her voice catch. "When you left, I thought it might have been because you hated me."

"Oh, God, Nahri—" Ali took the basket out of her hands, setting it aside and rising as he helped her to her feet. "No. *Never*. I was at the palace with you; I saw the same things. I don't blame you for *anything* that happened that night. And I could never hate you," he insisted, shocked that she could think so. "Not in a thousand years. By the Most High, I actually thought you might be happier if I stayed gone."

It was her turn to look confused. "Why?"

"You're free of us," he said. "My family, the magical world. I thought . . . I thought if I was a good friend, it would be better to let you return to your life. Your human one."

She rolled her eyes. "I dragged your burning body through the Nile for a whole damn day. Trust that I wouldn't have done so if I wanted to get rid of you."

Shame rushed through him. "You shouldn't have had to. You shouldn't have to keep saving me like this."

Nahri stepped closer. She touched his hand, and Ali felt all the walls he'd bricked up around his broken spirit crash to the ground. "Ali . . . I thought I made very clear to you I never intended to let you out of my debt."

Ali choked, a sound that might have been a sob or a laugh. But it was tears that pricked his eyes. "I don't think I can do this." Ali couldn't even say what "this" was. The enormity of how thoroughly his world had just been broken, the danger his loved ones were in, the impossibility of ever fixing it all . . . he knew no words to convey it.

"I know." And indeed, there was no mistaking a wet glimmer in her eyes as well. Nahri dropped her hand. "Why don't we take a walk? There's a place I'd like to show you."

6

NAHRI

"It's the first thing I remember," Nahri said softly, her eyes on the coursing river. "Like my life started the day I was lifted out of the Nile. The fishermen pounding my back to get the water out of my lungs, asking me what happened, who I was . . ." She wrapped her arms around herself, shivering despite the warm air. "Nothing. But I remember the sunlight on the water, the Pyramids against the sky, and the smell of mud like it was yesterday."

They had returned to the Nile, walking its bank as fishermen and sailors brought their boats and nets ashore. After a while, the two of them had settled at the base of a towering palm tree, which was when Nahri had started talking, sharing stories about her old life.

Next to her, Ali was tracing patterns in the dust. He had barely spoken, a quiet shadow at her side.

"That's the first thing you remember?" he asked now. "How old were you?"

Nahri shrugged. "Five? Six? I don't really know. I had issues with speech—all the languages in my head." Nostalgia swept her. "The little river girl, they called me."

"Bint el nahr." They'd been switching between Djinnistani and Arabic, but he said the words in Arabic, glancing up at her. "Nahri."

"Nahri," she repeated. "One of the few things I could decide for myself. Everyone was always trying to stick proper names on me. Never fit. I've always liked choosing my own path."

"That must have been hard in Daevabad."

A half-dozen sarcastic responses hovered at her lips. But the devastation still felt too close. "Yes," she said simply.

Ali was silent for a long moment before speaking again. "Can I ask you something?"

"That depends on what it is."

He looked at her again. Creator, it was hard to hold his gaze. Ali had always been an open book, and the achingly raw grief in his bloodshot eyes was nothing like the reckless, know-it-all prince she'd unwittingly befriended. "Were you ever happy there? In Daevabad, I mean."

Nahri sucked in her breath, not expecting that question. "I . . . yes," she replied, realizing it was the truth as she said it. "Sometimes. I liked being a Nahid healer. I liked the purpose it gave me, the respect. I liked being part of the Daevas and being able to fill my mind with books and new skills rather than fretting over where to find my next meal." She paused, her throat hitching. "I liked the hospital a lot. It made me feel hopeful for the first time. I think . . ." She dropped her gaze. "I think I would have been happy working there."

"Until my father found a way to crush it."

"Yes, admittedly, the constant fear your father would murder someone I loved and being forced to marry a man who hated me were less than ideal." She stared at her hands. "But I've got a lot of experience finding slivers of light to cherish when life gets more miserable than usual."

"You shouldn't have to." Ali sighed. "My Divasti is, well, pretty awful, but I heard some of what Manizheh was saying to you that night. She wanted you to join them, didn't she?"

Nahri hesitated, wondering how to respond. Ali was a Qahtani, she was a Nahid, and their peoples were at war. It seemed foolish to point out that she had a foot in each camp.

But right now, Ali didn't look like her enemy. He looked like a man grieving for his dead, like the optimist she knew had desperately wanted a better world for all of them—and then had seen his hopes destroyed.

Nahri could relate. "Yes, Manizheh wanted me to join them." Alone by the river, she'd removed her veil, and she worried it between her hands now. "Dara too." Her voice, which had been steady, trembled at Dara's name. "He said he was sorry, that I was supposed to be in the infirmary with Nisreen and . . . oh. *Oh.*"

"What?" Ali immediately moved closer, sounding worried. "What is it?"

But Nahri couldn't speak. *I was supposed to be with Nisreen the night of the attack.* Nisreen's comments about future training, her determined assistance in preventing Nahri from having a child with Muntadhir . . .

Just get through Navasatem, Nisreen had urged their last night together, as they drank soma and made peace after months of estrangement. *I promise you, things are going to be very different soon.*

Nisreen had known about Manizheh.

The mentor who'd been like a mother, who'd died in Nahri's arms, had known. Along with Kaveh. Dara. Who else among the Daevas, among the people Nahri had thought she could trust, had quietly plotted the slaughter of the djinn they lived among? Who else had let Nahri dream, knowing it was just that—a dream?

"Nahri?" Ali started to reach for her shoulder and then stopped. "Are you okay?"

She shook her head. She felt like she was going to throw up. "I think Nisreen knew about Manizheh."

"*Nisreen?*" Ali's eyes widened. "So, if Nisreen knew, and Kaveh knew, you don't think Jamshid—"

"No." But Jamshid . . . her brother's name was another knife through her heart, one Nahri did not feel remotely capable of extracting right now. "Jamshid would never have taken part in such a thing. I don't think either of us was supposed to be involved. I guess they figured if they swept in, killed your father, seized the throne, and disposed of the bloody evidence, we'd just be happy to be saved." The words were bitter in her mouth.

Ali looked sick. "Every time I think there's no lower our world can sink, we all plunge deeper."

"Some of us rise," she countered. "What Muntadhir did . . . that was one of the bravest things I've ever seen."

"It was brave, wasn't it?" Ali hastily wiped his eyes, doing a poor job of hiding his tears. "I can't stop thinking about him, Nahri. I feel like I'm losing my mind. I can't stop wondering how long it took, how much pain he was in, if he blamed me at the end—"

"Don't. Ali, don't do that. There's no way Muntadhir blamed you, and he wouldn't want you killing yourself thinking that."

Ali was shaking. "It should have been me. I still don't understand what happened, why I couldn't fight Darayavahoush . . ."

Another subject Nahri wasn't ready to discuss. "I can't—I can't talk about him right now. Please."

Ali blinked at her, his eyes wet and uncertain. He managed a nod. "All right."

But the silence that stretched between them didn't last long. Because no matter how much Nahri didn't want to talk about

Dara, she remembered the rage of the woman who commanded him, and right now Nahri and Ali were powerless.

"Have you had any luck lifting the seal?" she asked, trying to keep the hope from her voice.

Ali's expression was not inspiring. "No. The ring has mostly stopped feeling like it's going to explode in my heart, but I can't detect anything of its magic."

"Muntadhir said it might take a couple of days."

"It's been a couple of days."

Nahri toyed with her veil. "Well, there was one other thing."

"What *one other thing*?"

"Muntadhir said the seal ring wasn't supposed to leave Daevabad."

Ali jerked upright. "Why didn't you say something earlier?" He gestured wildly at the Nile. "We are very much not in Daevabad!"

"I didn't want you to overreact! Like you're doing right now," Nahri said when Ali groaned and dropped his head into his hands.

"God forgive me," he muttered through his fingers. "We broke a prophet's ring."

"We didn't break a prophet's ring! At least, not intentionally," she amended. "And we're getting ahead of ourselves. It's only been two days. We'll keep trying."

Ali lifted his head. "So if I don't have magic, and you don't have magic . . ." Alarm rose in his voice. "What if no one does?"

"What do you mean?"

"I mean, what if *no one* does, Nahri. Did any of your powers return while I was gone?" When she shook her head, he explained. "My father couldn't strip magic from that far a distance. When he used the seal, it was only on those in his presence. What if we *did* break a prophet's ring?"

Oh. Nahri's mouth went dry. She hadn't quite considered all that.

"We'll fix it," she replied, trying to sound more confident than she felt. "Though I cannot help but point out that it would slightly even the odds between us and Manizheh if we were all powerless."

"About that . . ." A little shame crept into Ali's voice. "I'm not entirely powerless. I still have this." He made a beckoning motion at the river.

Water leapt into his hand. A tiny liquid tendril spun there like a miniature cyclone before Ali twitched as though in pain, and the water spout collapsed.

"Ah," she said acidly. "That. One of the many secrets you swore you didn't have."

"There might be a few secrets," Ali confessed. "About me, about the marid, the war. I don't even know where to start."

Had a Daevabadi royal wanted to spill secrets last week, Nahri would have been eager to listen. But right now she wasn't ready to hear about some new horror of the magical world.

"Why don't you not start? Not today anyway." When Ali frowned, looking confused, Nahri tried a different tack. "I asked Subha once how she kept herself from being crushed by healing, by the weight of her responsibilities and the bleakness of the work." Thinking about Subha hurt; it made Nahri sick with fear to imagine how terrified her shafit friends might be right now. "Do you know what she told me?"

"That depends on how early in your relationship it was. As I recall, the first few weeks were rather barbed."

Nahri gave him an imperious look. "She *told* me to keep myself whole. That there wasn't any shame in taking care of yourself in order to help those who needed you."

Ali shifted. "What are you suggesting?"

"That we table discussions of secrets for a few days. We go back to the apothecary. We eat. I introduce you properly to Yaqub and maybe get you some clothes that aren't . . . this." She gestured to his ragged shawl.

"And then?"

She took his hand. "Ali, we're spent. You couldn't fight Dara, I couldn't fight Manizheh. Now we're halfway around the world in even worse straits with no clue how to get back." Her voice grew gentler. "I know you want to rush home. To save your sister, save your people, and avenge Muntadhir. But we're not ready. Let's take a couple of days to recover and see if anything changes with the seal."

Reluctance crossed Ali's face, warring with the logic she'd laid out. "I suppose you're right." He took a deep breath and then, quick as a bird, squeezed and released her hand.

Nahri climbed to her feet, catching sight of a pack of giggling girls approaching the river with laundry. In the dying afternoon light, the Nile blazed, the familiar buzz of insects washing over her. Farther ahead, the streets leading back into Cairo were bustling with people headed home, ducking out of shops and setting up tables for coffee and backgammon.

Ali had stood as well, looking a little better. Some of his old determination settled over his features, and then he spoke. "I know things look bad, but I'll get us back to Daevabad, I promise. We'll find a way home."

Nahri's gaze was still on the Egyptian street. "Home," she repeated. "Of course."

7

DARA

Aeshma clucked his tongue, gazing upon Dara's creation with open admiration. "Now this is a thing worthy of a true daeva." He gave Dara a grin of gleaming fangs. "See what happens when you embrace your magic instead of sulking?"

Dara threw him an annoyed look, but he had to force it. For what the ifrit had helped him conjure was indeed magnificent.

It was a blood beast, shaped from Dara's own smoke and life-blood to resemble a massive shedu. Its hide was a rich amber and its glittering wings a rainbow of jewel-bright colors. Bound to his mind, the shedu was pacing, the ground shaking with the impact of its chariot-wheel-size paws.

Dara ran his fingers through its mane, and a burst of fiery sparks erupted from the dark locks. "Is it supposed to be so *big*?"

"I've killed larger," Aeshma replied, supportive as usual. "It was always a delight to see their Nahid riders smash against the ground. I suppose they couldn't heal from that."

"You look like each other," Vizaresh added. "The hair. Maybe if she lives, your Nahri could ride it."

The ifrit's tone was as lecherous as it came, and Dara took a deep breath, reminding himself that Manizheh still needed these cretins—which meant that he was not yet allowed to remove Vizaresh's head from his neck.

Instead, he glared. "Such a sharp tongue when you're not running away from djinn boys a fraction your age."

Vizaresh snorted. "I did not survive this many centuries by picking fights with creatures I don't understand, and your oil-eyed 'djinn boy' who was using water currents like a whip is one of them." He leaned back, reclining against the base of an apricot tree. "Though I do regret not staying to see your lover bring the ceiling down on your head. That would have been most entertaining."

"Coward. I suppose that is why you scurried straight to Banu Manizheh and told her I tried to enslave him. Curious that you left out your involvement."

"I did not wish to get in trouble. Besides . . ." Vizaresh shrugged, glancing at Aeshma. "I would never do *anything* to jeopardize our alliance with the Banu Nahida." He pressed a clawed hand to his heart. "I am ever so loyal."

"Is this a joke to you?" Dara demanded. "People are dead, and my home is broken."

Resentment swirled into Vizaresh's fiery eyes. "You're not the only one who's seen your world broken, Afshin. Nor the only one who grieves for their dead. You don't think I mourn my brother, the daeva your blood-poisoning little Nahid murdered at the Gozan?"

"No," Dara shot back. "I doubt you demons are capable of any real affection. And you are not daevas, you are ifrit."

"We called ourselves *daevas* millennia before you were even born. Before Anahid betrayed us and—"

"Vizaresh." Aeshma's voice was thick with warning. "That is enough." He jerked his head toward the palace. "Go."

The smaller ifrit stalked off but not before shooting Dara another hate-filled scowl.

Aeshma looked equally annoyed. "You are *impossible,* do you know that?"

Dara wasn't in the mood to hear comments about his character. "Why are you here?"

"What are you talking about?"

"Why are you *here*? Why are you helping Banu Manizheh if your people hate the Nahids?"

"Oh, are you asking questions now? I thought that part of your mind was removed during training."

"*Why are you here?*" Dara snarled a third time, baring his fangs. "If I need to repeat myself again, I will drop *you* from the sky."

The ifrit's eyes danced with malice. "Maybe I want to be like you. Maybe after ten thousand years, I'm dying and would settle for peace and a taste of my old magic. Or maybe I simply find your Manizheh amusing and novel and enjoy the entertainment."

"That does not answer my—"

"I do not answer to you." The jest was gone from Aeshma's voice. "My alliance is with your master, not her dog."

Rage boiled down Dara's arms, flames twisting through his hands. "I have no master," he snapped. "I am a slave no longer."

"No?" Aeshma nodded to the emerald gleaming on Dara's finger. "Then why do you still wear that ring? Because it's pretty? Or because you're too frightened to try and remove it?"

"I could kill you," Dara said, stepping closer. "It would be nothing."

Aeshma laughed. "You're not going to kill me. You don't have it in you to defy your Banu Nahida, and she's made it clear we're not to be harmed."

"She will not always need you."

The slow, vicious smile that spread across Aeshma's face sent a thousand warnings screaming through Dara's mind. "But she will. Because I can give her magic she can wield herself instead of power she can only watch you wield in her name." Aeshma stepped back, gesturing to the shedu. "Which I believe is what you're meant to be doing now, yes?" He clucked his tongue. "Best hurry, Afshin. You wouldn't want to make your betters angry."

Dara reached for his magic, sweeping it over his body. The fiery flush vanished from his skin as he shifted to his mortal form, his plain tunic and trousers transforming into a brilliant crimson and black uniform. Glittering scaled armor crawled into place, and then Dara spread his hands. A magnificent silver bow appeared before them, flashing in the sun.

"You still cannot do this," he said coldly. "And you never will. Bluster and puff all you want, Aeshma, for when the day finally comes that you cross a line and threaten my Banu Nahida, I will be there to deal with you."

"Odd," Aeshma replied as Dara turned and walked away, retrieving the quiver of arrows he'd prepared before returning to the shedu's side. "For I told her much the same about you."

Dara stilled for a moment, his back to the ifrit. But it was only for a moment—he was not letting Aeshma toy with him any longer.

Instead, he considered the shedu before him. Dara was an accomplished rider, but horses and flying lions were rather different beasts—particularly since this shedu was no true animal, but rather an extension of his own magic, a feeling more akin to a limb.

A very *new* limb. Gripping its mane, Dara pulled himself onto the shedu's hazy back. A thrill raced down his spine. His circumstances might have been bleak, but part of Dara felt like a giddy little boy, the child who'd grown up listening to the hair-raising legends of the Afshins of old and their mighty Nahids.

With but a thought, the creature shot into the sky, and Dara gasped, seizing its mane as its wings whipped overheard. The palace shrank beneath him, a tiny jeweled toy, and he could not help but laugh, an uncharacteristically nervous sound, before gaining some semblance of control. He could see everything from this distance: the midnight lake and lush forests, the neatly terraced fields beyond the walls, and intricate Daevabad, a miniature of twisting streets and stone towers.

But it was the mountains that called to him, the wide world beyond. A smarter man would fly for them, would take the opportunity to flee the madness below and start anew, rather than be the cause of more violence.

And then every Daeva in the city would die. With a twinge of regret, Dara urged the shedu to dive, pulling free one of his arrows. There were five he'd prepared specially—one for each of the djinn tribes, binding a scroll to the shaft with a strip torn from Ghassan's bloodstained turban. Upon the scroll was a short message demanding immediate surrender. It had been three days since they'd taken the throne, and there hadn't been a word from the other tribes. No ambassadors demanding to know what had happened, no worried relatives of the government officials unfortunate enough to have been in the palace that night—there wasn't even the vengeful, suicidal charge he expected from whatever Geziri survivors were holed up with the princess. Instead, they all seemed to have retreated to their respective quarters and barricaded themselves away with whatever nonmagical means they could muster, awaiting the explosion they must fear would come.

An explosion neither Dara nor Manizheh wanted to see—one he hoped the djinn would have the wisdom to avoid.

The Agnivanshi were first. Though Dara knew he had only minutes before being spotted—his was a presence meant to terrorize, not hide—he quickly studied the fortifications they'd made, having bricked up their pretty sandstone gate and sent a handful of men with bows, swords, and ladders to guard the walls. They were likely civilians, as Dara knew the only djinn allowed military training in Daevabad were those in the Royal Guard—the Royal Guard whose Citadel his forces had already annihilated.

Just past the gate, a pile of bulging sacks was stacked on a wooden platform. A crowd had gathered, waiting with baskets and jars. Dara flew nearer, watching as grain was distributed to the waiting djinn. Armed men and nervous faces aside, it all looked rather orderly.

But there would be no order in Daevabad unless it came from Banu Manizheh.

With a snap of his fingers, the sacks burst into flame. The handlers cried out in alarm but moved swiftly to try and beat out the fire. Dara coaxed the flames higher, sending the djinn running. Finally, one of the women glanced up.

"The Scourge!"

His conjured shedu dived as the djinn started shouting in panic, fleeing in all directions. Dara drew back his bow, not missing that one of the Agnivanshi guards was doing the same.

Dara was faster. He shot the other archer through the chest. The man collapsed, the bloody silk binding the scroll to Dara's arrow fluttering like a downed flag on a battlefield. Dara flew on, leaving screams in his wake.

Let them scream. Better submission than a civil war, he tried to tell himself. Better that the Agnivanshi open their gate and cut a deal with Manizheh that kept grain flowing to *all* of Daevabad rather than one tribe hoarding more food than it could eat. Dara was sorry for the djinn, he was. He had no desire to shed more blood and sow more fear.

But he'd be damned if they would lose Daevabad now.

Dara set fire to the manicured vineyard in the heart of the Sahrayn market flush with grapes, and then burned the grand caravanserai in the Ayaanle Quarter to the ground, aiming to inflict a far more costly wound to the Geziris' closest allies. He hadn't the heart to burn anything that belonged to the Tukharistanis, and yet he knew the location of his scroll—shot into a wreath of blossoms adorning a memorial to the victims of Qui-zi—was message enough.

He studied every bit of ground he could, taking note of the magical buildings that had collapsed and the evidence of fires that had raged. There were enormous cracks in the ground from where the earth had split during the brief quake that had accompanied magic's disappearance, a quake that had felled even more buildings. Twisted piping and broken bricks littered the streets, water pumps still spraying wildly. He gagged on the smell of waste as he flew over the disinterred remains of a public latrine.

There will be disease, Dara thought, as he gazed upon his shattered city. *Famine and panic and death.*

And it will be because we chose to come here.

It was not a good state of mind to be in as he approached the Geziri Quarter, the section of the city he was most dreading, and the number of alarming things he saw didn't help his disquiet. First, judging from the hive of activity in the streets, the sand flies were very much not exterminated. Whether it had been Zaynab al Qahtani or not, clearly someone had succeeded in warning the rest of the Geziris about the vapor that had killed their kinsmen in the palace.

Second, they'd been *busy.* The wall that once separated the Geziri and shafit neighborhoods had been torn down, the bricks redistributed to fortify the boundaries and gates that separated them from the rest of the city. The Citadel lay in ruins like an ugly wound, but the bodies must have been removed, likely with whatever blades, bows, and spears could be scavenged from the armory.

Dara swore. So the Geziris and the shafit had indeed united. The tribe they'd tried to annihilate and the human-blooded people who knew best how to survive without magic. If there were remnants of the Royal Guard, they would be there. If there were those damnable dirt-blood weapons that had wreaked havoc during the Navasatem procession, they would be there as well.

And Dara could not imagine any way such a stand-off ended in peace. Manizheh had included a note to Zaynab in the scroll meant for the Geziris, entreating her to consider Muntadhir's fate, but he wasn't sure a single princess would be able to convince thousands of angry, grieving djinn. And why would they surrender? The Geziris knew Manizheh had intended to wipe them out, and the shafit knew Dara's reputation as the Scourge. Either group would be fools to trust them.

Uneasy, Dara flew closer, searching for a place to leave his message. But he'd no sooner passed the first neighborhood than a terrible clanging sound rang out, like someone was smashing a shop full of porcelain while also playing the tambourine.

What in the name of the Creator is that awful racket?

He spotted the source of the sound. A wire had been strung across the wide street, copper pots hanging from it in bunches and crashing into one another as a man pulled it back and forth with a long, crooked cane.

A man who was looking straight at Dara.

Before Dara could react, a woman down the street followed suit with a similar setup of steel dishes, the noise carrying through the neighborhood as more and more posts took up the alarm, a signal fire of broken crockery and metal pans. Below, people raced away, but not with the disorganized panic of the other tribes. Geziri and shafit civilians—mostly men, but also a smattering of women and children—vanished into whatever building was nearest as though they were expected guests, doors flying open.

An explosion cut through the air. Dara spun as a projectile zipped past his face, smelling rankly of iron and close enough to

singe his hair. He cursed, tightening his knees around the conjured shedu as he doubled back, searching wildly for what had
targeted him. He traced a glimpse of white smoke to a balcony on
a multistoried stone building near the Grand Bazaar. Two shafit
men were wrestling with a long metal barrel.

A gun, he recognized. Like the one Kaveh said had been used
to slaughter their people during the Navasatem attacks. Perhaps
the very same one. For as Dara soared over the main avenue, he
finally spotted what remained of one of his people's most cherished traditions.

The enormous chariots of the Navasatem parade lay where
they'd been attacked, many reduced to half-burned husks. Broken brass horses, shattered mirror-and-glass ornaments, and
the twisted remnants of a traveling grove of jeweled cherry trees,
most of their gems and golden bark stripped away, littered the
dusty ground. Food carts festooned with dirty streamers were
abandoned, children's toys spilling from a turned-over wagon.

Rage scorched through him—the hatred Dara carried for
the djinn and shafit stoked so fast it was as though someone had
thrown oil upon smoldering coals. The bodies of the murdered
Daevas were gone, but Dara could still see shoes and blood-
soaked patches where they'd been cut down as they celebrated
their youth, parading merrily through the streets of their sacred
city.

Cut down by weapons like the one the shafit had just tried to
use on him.

In truth, Dara knew very little about guns. There had been
nothing like them in the world during his mortal life, and he'd
rarely crossed humans since he was resurrected, catching sight only
once of a human hunter bringing down a tiger in the mountains.
He'd been shocked by the damage the gun had done, disgusted to
see it happen in what seemed like some type of competition.

Perhaps Dara should have been frightened by such astonishing technology. By a weapon whose implication he could scarcely grasp.

But Dara had never frightened easily, and as he watched the shafit who'd tried to shoot him attempt to load their weapon again, fumbling and shouting at one another as he flew at them, it was not fear he felt. What a shame their guns took so much time and effort. Not enough time to keep dozens of his Daevas from being murdered, but still.

Dara didn't need time. Roaring as magic boiled in his veins and crackled through his fingers, he raised his hand and then clenched it into a fist.

The entire building crumbled to the ground.

Dara collapsed nearly as fast, the power exhausting him. That wasn't magic he should have done in his mortal form, and it took every bit of strength he had to urge the shedu to keep flying. Breathing heavily, he glanced back. Dust rose from a new hole in the skyline.

His stomach twisted. There had probably been innocent people in that building too.

But there were going to be a lot more innocent people dead before this was over, and not just at Dara's hands. The Creator only knew how many human weapons had been smuggled into Daevabad over the years. There might be things worse than guns, weapons his Daevas—with their careful segregation from anything human—would have no clue how to counter. And as the full danger took shape before him, the cold realization he'd had while watching Manizheh's copper vapor creep over the frozen ground of northern Daevastana returned to him.

We will never have peace with them. And if Manizheh's forces weren't going to have peace with the Geziris and shafit, then they would remain a threat. And Manizheh clearly dealt with threats the same way the Geziri kings who'd ruined her life had.

She eliminated them.

But she can't. Not without her abilities. There would be no magical plagues striking down djinn in Daevabad while Suleiman's seal rested in the heart of a ring-bearer possibly on the other side of the world. Trepidation stole over Dara, the shedu slowing in response. For the next part of his mission was meant to put them on the road to recovering that very seal.

You are the weapon of the Nahids, Dara reminded himself at last. *The protector of the Daevas.*

And a good Afshin obeyed.

IT TOOK A LONG TIME TO CROSS THE LAKE, THE WATER vast and glimmering. No longer a deathly still pane of liquid glass, now currents danced and whirled over the surface, the water lapping thirstily at the shore like a parched dog. Dara eyed it with apprehension as he flew overhead, keeping his distance. The marid might have claimed they wanted nothing more to do with the Daevas after they aided Manizheh in her conquest, but Dara strongly suspected the Daevas had not seen the last of them.

But thoughts of the marid ebbed away as Dara passed the lake, flying out over the mountains. The mist that had once shrouded them was gone, the trees ending abruptly in a sandy waste, and where the threshold had stood was a stand of dying forest. Rot crept up the trees, bulbous growths swelling their papery, flaking bark. Dara breathed deep, tasting decay on the air.

He kept flying, soaring over the rushing Gozan, and then he saw them camped out on the dusty plain above the river: the travelers Kaveh said would be heading to Daevabad for Navasatem. The tourists and traders who but for a quirk of timing had been on the other side of the veil when magic fell. The travelers on whom so much hung in the balance right now.

Dara had his answer the moment he settled his gaze upon them.

They had no magic.

A crashed Sahrayn sandship lay on its side, its massive sails repurposed into a crude tent. There were no pavilions of enchanted silk or floating lanterns. Instead, the travelers had made a circle of their wagons, palanquins and chariots shoved together to create a wall. Dozens of animals—camels and horses, but also simurgh and a rare tame zahhak—were gathered in the strangest herd Dara had ever seen, the lean ground stripped of grass.

There must have been a hundred travelers, but none were studying the sky. They looked miserable, cold and disheveled, with no flames to warm them or cook their food. Kaveh had been right: with no magic, few people knew how to build a fire. But they had otherwise banded together. Among the drawn faces, Dara saw men, women, and children from all six of the tribes passing around cold food and talking. About a dozen children were playing on the downed ship, climbing over the sewn hull—Daevas and Geziris among them.

Dara steeled himself, hardening his heart once again. Because he was about to undo such intertribal camaraderie.

He slammed to the ground, landing the shedu with a thud that shook the earth. There were cries of alarm, people scrambling to their feet, but he ignored them, drawing up to survey the crowd with every ounce of arrogance he possessed. He tossed his hair back, letting his hands rest on the hilts of his swords. Dara wore no helmet, nothing to obscure the tattoo and emerald-bright eyes he knew shouted his identity to the world, and he could only imagine the spectacle he presented—indeed, that was the point. He was to be the Afshin from legend, the dashing war god of a bygone era.

Unsurprisingly, it was a Daeva man who reacted first. "By the Creator . . . ," he choked out. "Are you—" His eyes widened on the conjured shedu. "Is *that*—"

"Rejoice!" Dara commanded. "For I bring glad tidings." The words sounded false in his mouth, no matter how many times Manizheh, Kaveh, and he had practiced them. "The usurper Ghassan al Qahtani is dead!"

There were a couple of gasps, and then a pair of Geziri men who'd been cleaning saddles jumped up.

"What do you mean, he is dead?" the younger one demanded. "Is this some sort of trick? Who do you think you are?"

"You know who I am," Dara said. "And I do not mean to waste words." He drew his second sword—Ghassan's own zulfiqar—and threw it to the ground, the rest of the king's bloody turban knotted around the hilt. "Your sand fly king is gone to hell with the rest of his kin, and should you not wish to join them, you will listen."

More of the djinn were pushing to their feet now, a mix of incredulity and fear on their faces.

"Liar," the Geziri man shot back, drawing his khanjar. "This is some fire-worshipper nonsense."

With a burst of heat, Dara commanded the blade to melt. The Geziri man shrieked, dropping his dagger as the molten metal dripped down his skin. The nearest djinn, a Sahrayn woman, started to run to him.

Dara held up a hand. "Don't," he warned, and the woman froze. "Touch another weapon, and what I do next will make that look like a kindness."

The Daeva man who'd spoken up, an older man with silver in his beard and an ash mark on his brow, carefully edged in front of the group. "We will raise no weapons," he said, his gaze darting to the angry djinn. "But please tell us what happened. How is it you still have magic?"

"Because I serve the Creator's chosen. The rightful and most blessed Banu Manizheh e-Nahid, who has taken back the city of her ancestors and now rules as was intended."

The Daeva man's mouth fell open. "Manizheh? Banu Manizheh? But she's dead. You're both supposed to be dead!"

"I assure you we are not. Daevabad belongs to us again, and should you wish to save the lives of your loved ones, you will carry our words." Dara looked past the Daeva man. He appreciated the courage it must have taken for his tribesman to put himself between the Afshin and the djinn, but this message was not for him. "Those of you from the djinn tribes will not be permitted to continue into the city. You are to return to your lands."

That provoked another outcry. "But we cannot return!" a woman declared. "We have no supplies, no magic—"

"Silence! You will return to your lands with our mercy, but there will be no magic restored to you yet." He glared at the djinn in the crowd. "Your ancestors strayed from the right path, and for that there is a cost. You will return to your lands, gather whatever councils you use to govern yourselves, and send your leaders and their families back to Daevabad with tribute and word of immediate fealty."

There was bristling in the crowd, but Dara wasn't done. "As for your magic, you have one man to blame: the traitor Alizayd al Qahtani." He all but hissed the words, letting his anger show—finally something that didn't feel like an act. "He is a liar and an abomination, a crocodile who sold his soul to the marid and took advantage of the chaos to steal Suleiman's seal and kidnap Banu Manizheh's daughter."

It was an Ayaanle woman who stood now, an elder with flashing eyes. "You are the liar, fiend. And more a monster than any marid from legend."

"So ignore me. Perhaps the Ayaanle do not wish to see their magic return, but surely not all of you feel the same. For those, Banu Manizheh offers a deal. Alizayd al Qahtani has fled, slipping through the lake as his marid masters have taught him, to hide in your lands. Find the traitor and Banu Nahri both, return them—*alive*—and your tribe shall see its magic returned.

"Else, perhaps you best go beg the humans of whom you are so fond to show you how to live."

Dara could see unease rippling across the djinn, straining whatever new and fragile bonds had started to knit them together.

The Ayaanle woman was still glaring at him. "And our kin inside the city?"

"No one leaves Daevabad until the Banu Nahida has her daughter back. And she is not the only one to be returned un-harmed." He turned to the Geziris. "You look like soldiers, so let us see if you cannot convey a warning to your Qaid. Should he take vengeance on Jamshid e-Pramukh, we will release a poison into your land that will kill every Geziri within a day."

The Geziri man recoiled. "You have no such power. Nor does the witch who commands you. That is magic beyond—"

"Sand fly," Dara interrupted, "how do you think we took the city?"

The man instantly drew back, horror in his gray eyes. "No," he whispered. "That cannot be . . . There were *thousands* of us in Daeva—"

"There were. And there are yet more of you in Am Gezira." Dara glanced again at the crowd. "Our world is returning to the way things should have been, and I pray this time, your people show the sense your ancestors never did. Surrender."

Some of the djinn were already edging away, parents grab-bing children and people eyeing the supplies as though wonder-ing what they could seize.

But with threats and violence, there would also be mercy, a hint of the pleasures that awaited them if they obeyed. "You need not fear your journey," Dara declared. "As promised, it will be provided for."

He spread his hands, concentrating on the sandship. With a burst of magic, it divided into a half dozen smaller ships, silver sails swelling with air, each marked with a different tribal emblem. His head throbbed, but Dara pressed on, visualizing holds filled with food and drink.

He fought the instinct to shape-shift, his body aching to burst into the fiery form that allowed such power. "Go," he growled, his hands clenching into fists as flames danced through his fingers. He exhaled, heat scorching the air. "*Now.*"

Dara didn't need to repeat himself. The djinn fled, clearly too frightened to bid farewell to their companions across tribal lines. Or perhaps they were already cutting those ties, eager to get home and make sure their people were the ones who found and returned Alizayd and Nahri.

Let them be divided. Let them return to their homes with tales of horror and a magic they couldn't fight. Let everyone know peace was only possible under Banu Manizheh.

But as Dara saw the Daevas retreating with the same speed, he spoke up, his voice still ragged. "Wait," he called, flagging them down. "You needn't leave. You are welcome to enter the city."

That was met with hesitant silence, the other Daevas glancing uncertainly at one another.

Finally, one of the men replied. "Is that an order?"

Dara was taken aback by the question. "Of course not. But we control Daevabad again," he assured them, baffled by their attitude. "It is ours. We did this for you."

One of the Daeva children, a little girl, began to cry. A woman quickly picked her up, shushing her with obvious fear.

The grandstanding he'd shown with the djinn went out of Dara in one breath. The last time he'd been among Daeva children, they'd been cheering him as a hero, pushing to show off their little muscles.

"I—I mean you no harm," he stammered. "I promise."

The Daeva man seemed to be struggling to conceal his misgivings. "All the same, I think we would like to leave."

Dara forced a smile. "Then go with my blessings. May the fires burn brightly for you."

No one replied in kind.

The other djinn ships were already sailing away. He watched as the Daevas did the same, sickness rising in his heart. Only when the horizon was clear did Dara exhale, letting his fiery form sweep over him. The scorching pain vanished as did his exhaustion, a cruel reminder once again that this was what Dara truly was now. And considering how his own people had just fled from him, perhaps he should keep this visage. He certainly felt like a monster.

Dara strode back to his conjured shedu, his warm breath coming in a steamy hush. His boots crunched on the ground. He frowned at the sound and then glanced down.

Fine crystals were racing across the churned earth.

Ice. Dara suddenly realized everything had gone quiet. Cold. The stillness to the chill air was utterly unnatural, as though the wind itself were holding its breath.

Dread rising in his core, Dara moved fast, closing the distance between himself and his winged creation. He reached for its mane.

The wind exhaled.

A blast of frigid air hit him so hard that Dara stumbled back from the shedu, falling to the frozen earth. He covered his head as the remains of the travelers' camp went hurtling by, flung across the landscape by the howling wind. The shedu disintegrated in a puff of smoke that was gone on the next breeze, the air churning so violently Dara felt as though an invisible assailant were pummeling him.

The storm vanished nearly as soon as it came, leaving behind barely a breeze. The entire landscape had been iced over, glittering in the dying sun.

Dara was shaking, breathing fast. What in Suleiman's eye had just happened?

But the answer was already coming to him on the stinging breeze. Not fire nor water nor earth.

Air.

The peris.

He shivered again. But of course—this was where Khayzur had been slaughtered by his own people, doomed for the "crime" of saving Dara's and Nahri's lives. Because it hadn't just been the marid who'd toyed with Dara. No, it had been Qahtanis and Nahids, marid and peris.

Anger roiled through him. The accusations he hadn't been able to shout at Manizheh, Khayzur's gentle last words, and Nahri's betrayed eyes. Dara was so sick of despairing over his fate, of guilt eating him alive. Now he was just furious. Furious at being used, at *letting* himself be used again and again.

These creatures did not get to make him feel worse.

"Where were you when *my* people were slaughtered?" he howled into the wind. "I thought the mighty peris did not interfere, did not care what the lowly daevas did to each other?" He threw out his fists, fire bursting from his hands. "Go on! Break your rules, and I will return to destroy you as I did the marid! I have flown to your realms—I will do so again and set fire to your skies. I will leave you nothing but smoke to choke on!"

The chill immediately left the air, the ground beneath him warming. Dara shoved himself to his feet. He would not be intimidated by a damn breeze.

But it pulled at him even as he stalked away, the wind flowing through his hair and tugging at his clothes. It felt like a warning, and when combined with the sight of the diseased trees across the Gozan, the mountains concealing an even more broken city, it created a ripple of undeniable fear that crept down Dara's back. The peris didn't interfere. It was their most sacred code.

So what did it mean when they sent a warning?

8

NAHRI

The reeds tore at Nahri's legs as they hurried through the flooded marsh. She burst into fresh tears, burying her face in the warm neck of the woman carrying her.

"Shush, little love," the woman whispered. "Not so loud."

They climbed down into the narrow canal that watered the fields. Nahri peeked up as they passed the shadoof, the wooden beams of the irrigation tool jutting up against the night sky like massive claws. The air was thick with the smoke and screams of the burning village behind them, the curtain of papyrus doing nothing to conceal the horror they'd narrowly escaped. All she could see of their village now was the shattered top of the mosque's minaret above a sea of sugarcane.

She dug her small fingers into the woman's robe, clutching her closer. The smoke burned Nahri's lungs, nothing like the pleasantly clean scent of the tiny flames she liked to sing into creation. "I'm scared," she whimpered.

"I know." A hand rubbed her back. "But we just need to get to the river. El Nil. Do you see it?"

Nahri saw it. The Nile, flowing fast and dark ahead. But they'd only just crashed *into its shallows when she heard the voice again—the stranger who'd arrived speaking the musical language Nahri was never permitted to use outside their small home, the words that whispered and burned in her mind when her scraped knees healed and when she breathed life anew into the tiny kitten crushed by a reckless trader's cart.*

"Duriya!" the stranger yelled.

The woman wasn't listening. Transferring Nahri to her hip with one arm, she bit deep into her other hand until it bled and then thrust it into the water.

"I CALL YOU!" she cried. "Sobek, you promised!"

A heavy stillness stole across the air, silencing the dying cries of Nahri's blazing village and freezing the tears rolling down her cheeks. Her skin prickled, the hair on the back of her neck standing up as though in the presence of a predator.

On the opposite bank, a shadowy form slipped into the water.

Nahri tried to jerk back, but the arms around her were strong, pushing her into the river.

There was arguing. "I will get you your blood!" A brow pressed against hers, a pair of warm brown eyes, flecked with gold, locking on Nahri's eyes, the eyes neighbors whispered were too dark. A kiss upon her nose.

"God will protect you," the woman whispered. "You are brave, you are strong, and you will survive this, my darling, I swear. I love you. I always will." The next words came in a blur, the woman weeping as her gaze turned to the water. "Take this night from her. Let her start anew."

Teeth clamped around Nahri's ankle, and then, before she could scream, she was dragged under the water.

"Nahri?" A hand shook her shoulder. "*Nahri.*"

Nahri started awake, blinking in the dark storeroom. "Ali?" she murmured, thrown from the nightmare. She sat up, rubbing the sleep from her eyes. Her cheeks were wet, streaked with tears.

Ali was crouched next to her, looking worried. "I'm sorry. I heard you crying, and you sounded so upset . . ."

"It's all right," she said, shucking her blanket free. It had twisted around her body like she'd been fighting it. Nahri was drenched in sweat, her gown sticking to her skin and her hair plastered to her neck. "I was having a nightmare . . . about that village, I think." The details were already drifting away in the fog of waking. "There was a woman . . ."

"A woman? Who?"

"I don't know. It was just a dream."

Ali looked unconvinced. "Last time I had 'just a dream,' it was the marid putting visions in my head two days before the lake rose up to tear down the Citadel."

Fair point. She wiped her face with her sleeve. "What are you doing up? You should be resting."

He shook his head. "I'm tired of resting. And of having nightmares as well."

Nahri gave him a sympathetic look—she'd heard Ali screaming Muntadhir's name in his sleep just the other night. "It'll get easier."

Another time, she knew he would have nodded with genuine earnestness—or, more likely, Ali would have been the one telling Nahri it was going to get better.

Now he did neither. Instead, he pressed his lips in a obviously forced expression of agreement and said, "Of course." The lie seemed to age him, the optimistic prince she'd known gone. He rose to his feet. "If you're not going back to sleep, I made some tea."

"I didn't know you knew how to make tea."

"I didn't say it was good tea."

Nahri couldn't help but smile. "I'll take a glass of not-very-good tea over returning to nightmares." She reached for her shawl, draping it around her shoulders to fight the chill, and followed him.

She blinked in surprise when she entered the apothecary. The tins and glass vials on the shelves had been neatly reorganized and dusted and the floor freshly swept. The braids of garlic, herbs, and roots Yaqub stuffed into the ceiling to dry had all been moved to some apparatus Ali appeared to have constructed from the broken baskets the old pharmacist had been saying he'd mend since before Nahri left for Daevabad.

"Well," she started. "You've certainly been doing more than brewing tea."

Ali rubbed the back of his neck, looking sheepish. "Yaqub's been so kind. I wanted to be useful."

"Yaqub's never going to let you leave. I didn't even realize there was this much room in here." She perched on the workbench. "You must have been up all night."

Ali poured a glass of tea from a copper pot set over the fire and handed it to her. "It's been easier to keep busy. If I'm doing things—fixing things, working, cleaning—it keeps my mind from everything else, though that's probably a cowardly thing to admit."

"Not wanting to be destroyed by despair doesn't make you a coward, Ali. It makes you a survivor."

"I guess."

But again, Nahri could see her words had failed to pierce the haunted expression in his gray eyes.

It made her physically ache to look at him. "Let's go to Khan el-Khalili tomorrow," she offered. "It's the biggest bazaar in the city, and if trawling through human goods won't keep your mind occupied, I don't know what will." She took a sip of her tea and then coughed. "Oh. Oh, that's awful. I didn't think you could ruin tea. You do know you're supposed to take the leaves out, right? Not let them steep until it tastes like metal."

The insult seemed to work better than kindness, bringing a glint of amusement to Ali's face. "Maybe you like weak tea."

"How dare you." But before Nahri could expand on her offense, she heard shuffling outside the apothecary door—followed by voices.

"I am telling you she returned." It was a woman. "The pharmacist says she's a servant, a peasant from the south, but Umm

Sara says she has the same black eyes as the girl who used to work for him."

Nahri instantly reached for Yaqub's paring knife.

Ali gave her a bewildered look. "What are you doing?"

"Protecting myself." She tensed, gripping the knife. It was astonishing how quickly it all came back. The constant worry a mark would return with soldiers, accusing her of theft. The fear that one wrong move would lead to a mob calling her a witch.

There was a knock at the door, rough and insistent. "Please!" the woman called. "We need help!"

Nahri hissed a warning under her breath when Ali moved for the door. "Don't."

"They said they needed help."

"People say a lot of things!"

Ali reached out and gently lowered her hand. "No one's going to hurt you," he assured her. "I don't know humans well, but I'm fairly certain if I make all the liquids in here explode, they're not going to stick around."

Nahri glowered. "I'm not putting down the knife." But she didn't stop him when Ali opened the door.

An older woman in a worn black dress pushed her way inside.

"Where is she? The girl who works with the pharmacist?" Their new arrival had a markedly southern accent and, from a glimpse at her unveiled, sun-beaten face, looked like she'd lived a hard life.

"That's me," Nahri said coarsely, the knife still in her hand. "What do you want?"

The woman lifted her palms beseechingly. "Please, I need your help. My son, he fell from a roof last week . . ." She gestured behind her and two men entered, carrying an unconscious boy in a sling. "We paid a doctor to come out who said he just needed to rest, but tonight he started vomiting and now he won't wake . . ."

She stumbled on, sounding desperate. "There are rumors about you. People say you're the girl from the Nile. The one who used to heal people."

The woman's words struck a little too close: the one who *used* to heal people. "I'm not a doctor," Nahri replied, hating the admission. "Where's the physician you originally saw?"

"He won't come again. He says we cannot afford him."

Nahri finally put down the knife. "There's nothing I can do."

"You could look at him," the woman persisted. "Please just look at him."

The pleading in her eyes nagged at Nahri. "I . . . oh, all right. Ali, clear the table. You"—she nodded at the men carrying the boy—"bring him over here."

They laid the boy out upon his sheet. He couldn't have been older than ten, a wiry youth with close-cropped black curls and a wide, innocent face. He was unconscious, yet his arms looked oddly extended at his sides, his hands flared outward.

Nahri took his pulse. It was thready and far too slow. "He won't wake up?"

"No, sayyida," the older man answered. "He's been sleepy all week, complaining his head still hurt and speaking little."

"And he fell from a roof?" Nahri asked, carefully unwrapping the bandage around his bruised skull. "Is that what caused this injury?"

"Yes," the man replied urgently.

Nahri continued her examination. She lifted one eyelid.

Dread rushed over her. His pupil was widely dilated, the black nearly overtaking the brown.

And immediately Nahri was back in Daevabad, trailing Subha as she went through the tools she'd brought to the hospital. *But how did you know?* she'd pestered, harassing Subha into the details of the patient Nahri had spotted in her garden.

Subha had scoffed. *A blow to the head a few days back and a dilated pupil? There's blood building in the skull, no doubt about it. And it's deadly if not released— it's only a matter of time.*

Nahri kept her voice controlled. "He needs a surgeon. Immediately."

One of the men shook his head. "We're Sa'idi migrants. No surgeon is going to help us. Not unless we pay upfront with money we don't have."

The woman looked at her again, her gaze brimming with a hope that tore Nahri to shreds. "Could you not . . . lay your hands on him and wish him well? My neighbors say that's what you used to do."

There it was again. What she used to do. What, deep in her heart, Nahri feared she might never do again.

She stared at the boy. "I'm going to need boiling water and lots of clean rags. And I want one of you to go to the pharmacist's home. Tell him to bring any tools he has from his grandfather."

The woman frowned. "You need all that to lay hands upon him?"

"No, I need all that because I'm going to open his skull."

TYING BACK HER HAIR, NAHRI STUDIED THE INSTRUments that Yaqub had brought, thanking the Creator when she recognized the small circular trephine among his great-grandfather's old tools.

"This is it," she said, plucking the drill free. "How fortunate you're descended from a surgeon."

Yaqub shook his head fiercely. "You've lost your mind. That thing is a hundred years old. You're going to kill that boy and get us all arrested for murder."

"No, I'm going to save his life." She beckoned to Ali and then handed him the drill. "Al Qahtani, you owe me. Go boil this and get me the scalpel already in the water."

"Nahri, are you—"

She was already turning Ali around, pushing him in the direction of the cauldron. "Less talking, more helping."

Yaqub stepped in front of her. "Nahri, in all the time I've known you, you've never done anything like this. What you're talking about is surgery that people train for years to master."

Nahri hesitated. She actually agreed with him—she'd practiced on some coconuts and melons with Subha, but that was it. Contrary to the pandemonium that characterized the rest of her life, she was typically cautious with healing, and her years in the infirmary had only made her more careful. It was a responsibility and a privilege to be entrusted with a patient's life, not a thing she took lightly.

But Nahri also knew the disregard with which people like this family were treated. Peasants and migrants, girls with no name and parents with no coin to convince a reluctant doctor.

"They don't have time to go around Cairo begging for a surgeon to take pity on them, Yaqub. This boy could be dead by dawn. I know enough to try and help."

"And if you fail?" He moved closer, lowering his voice. "Nahri, you know how things are here. Something happens to that boy in my shop and his neighbors will come for my family. They'll run us out of this neighborhood."

That stopped her. Nahri *did* know how things were—it was the same fear that had haunted her back in Daevabad. When emotions got high, the lines that divided their communities grew deadly.

She met his gaze. "Yaqub, if you refuse, I'll understand, and I won't do this. But that child will die."

Emotion swept his lined face. The boy's parents had taken up a vigil on either side of their child, his mother clutching one of his hands to her tearstained cheek.

Yaqub stared at them, indecision warring in his expression. "You chose a very inconvenient time to develop a conscience."

"Is that a yes?"

He grimaced. "Don't kill him."

"I'll try my best." Still seeing reluctance in his eyes, Nahri added, "Would you mind making some tea for his parents and keeping them back? They don't want to see this."

She scrubbed up with soap. Ali had returned and laid her tools out on a clean cloth.

"Go wash your hands," Nahri ordered.

Ali gave her an alarmed glance. "Why?"

"Because you're helping me. The drill takes some strong-arming. Go." As he walked away, muttering under his breath, she called, "And use plenty of soap."

Straining to recall everything Subha had taught her, Nahri measured a spot about a hand's breadth behind the boy's brow and then carefully shaved his hair, scrubbing the skin with more soap before making a precise cut in the scalp. Dabbing away the blood that instantly blossomed from the cut, she pinned back the small flap of skin, revealing the bone underneath.

Back at her side, Ali rocked slightly. "Oh. That's what that looks like."

"Hand me another cloth," Nahri replied, swapping out the blood-soaked one. "Now the drill."

His hands were shaking when he gave it to her, and as the weight of the drill fell into hers, so did the staggering prospect of what she was about to do. *Was* Nahri mad? Who was she to take this boy's life in her hands and drill a hole into his head? She was a thief, a con artist.

No, you're the Banu Nahida.

When Nahri placed the drill against his skull, her hands had stopped trembling.

Later, she could not say when the eerie hush of calm descended, a feeling like what she'd been told proper prayer was supposed to invoke. There was the steady grinding of the drill and the wet, chalky smell of bone dust and blood. When her hands and wrists began to throb, she carefully coached Ali through a few rounds, sweat beading on her skin. She stopped him as soon as she saw the last bit of bone begin to give way. Nahri took over, her heart nearly stopping as she carefully withdrew the drill, removing a bloody coin of bone.

She stared at her work, too awed to speak. She'd just *put a hole in a skull.* Excitement buzzed beneath her skin, layering in with fear and anxiety.

Breathe, she reminded herself, Subha's words coming back to her. *There's a membrane just below the skull. Beneath is where the blood builds. That is what you must puncture.*

Nahri picked up her scalpel. The silence of the room was smothering, her heart beating so fast it felt ready to burst. She took a deep breath, offering a prayer to the Creator, Anahid, and anyone else willing to help tip the scales in her favor.

Then she pierced the membrane. Blood sprayed directly into her face. It was thick and dark, purple, with an oily cast.

That caught the other woman's attention. "What have you done?" the boy's mother cried, lunging up from where she'd been sitting with Yaqub.

Ali stepped between them, catching her before she could grab Nahri. Nahri had frozen, staring at the bloody incision. As the dark fluid dribbled out, she could see the pinkish-yellow brain beyond begin to pulsate with the boy's heartbeat.

He stirred.

It wasn't much, just a sigh and a slight twitch of one hand.

But then there was movement beneath his closed eyes. The boy mumbled in his sleep, and Nahri let out a choked breath, fighting not to collapse.

She glanced back. Every eye in the room was on her, staring with a mix of horror and awe.

Nahri grinned. "Would someone hand me my sutures?"

IT TOOK THE REST OF THE NIGHT TO STITCH HIM UP. Nahri waited until the boy opened his eyes, and then another relative came by with a board to move him. His home was only down the block and Nahri gave his parents thorough instructions on how to care for him, assuring them she'd come by around noon for a checkup.

His father was an apologetic, grateful mess when he left. "May God shower you with blessings," he gushed. "We'll find a way to pay you, I promise."

Nahri shook her head, watching as the mother cradled her son. "You don't need to pay me," she said, holding open the door. "I was happy to help."

She watched them depart as dawn softened the sky. It was quiet save for the song of birds, a breeze bringing the scent of the Nile. Nahri took a deep breath, feeling a sense of peace and purpose she hadn't felt since the morning of the Navasatem parade.

She still had it. Her magic might be gone, but Nahri had just saved a life, doing a procedure she suspected trained physicians would be lucky to pull off. She leaned against the apothecary door, trembling as the buzz of anxiety and excitement drained from her body, and then she wiped her eyes, embarrassed to find them wet.

I am who I always wanted to be. Forget Daevabad's politics or the lack of whatever certificates the human world would never grant a woman like her. Nahri *was* a healer, and no one could take that away from her.

She went back inside. Ali and Yaqub were sitting across from each other, both looking stunned amidst the bloody tools and rags.

No, not just stunned—Ali looked as close to vomiting as she'd ever seen him. Nahri had to bite back a smile. "You're the last person I'd think squeamish."

"I'm not squeamish," he said defensively. He raised a shaking finger at the drill. "I do not *ever* want to touch that thing again, but I'm not squeamish."

Trying not to laugh, she laid a hand on his shoulder. "Why don't you get some sleep while I clean up? I'm far too jumpy."

Relief lit his face. "God bless you." Ali was gone the next moment, lighting out of there like he was being chased by a karkadann.

"Let me help you," Yaqub offered. "I don't think I'll be able to sleep after watching brain surgery being performed in my apothecary."

They got to work, Nahri piling the bloody rags in a sack to be washed, and Yaqub wiping down his instruments.

Nahri rolled up the cloth she'd used to cover the table. "I'm sorry for not asking your permission first. I shouldn't have put you in that position."

Yaqub clucked his tongue. "First she takes a risk for a stranger, now she apologizes. Where is the rude girl who tried to swindle me so many years ago?"

Gone, for a long time now. "I can steal those instruments if you'd like to feel nostalgic."

He shook his head, clearly not buying it. "You've changed for the better, whether or not you want to admit it." He hesitated before meeting her gaze. "You did it somehow, didn't you? You went and trained as a doctor."

"You could say that."

His eyes didn't leave hers. "Where were you, Nahri? Really?"

A dozen excuses ran through her head, but God forgive her, she was so tired of lying.

Nahri took a deep breath. "Would you believe me if I said I came from a long line of djinn healers and was being held captive in a hidden magical kingdom on the other side of the world?"

Yaqub snorted. "Not even you could sell that story."

Nahri forced a nervous laugh, the blood leaving her face. "Of course not," she said, fighting disappointment. "Who would believe such a crazy tale?"

Yaqub set a kettle over the fire again. "It was an astonishing feat wherever you learned it," he said, spooning tea leaves into two glass cups. "You'll have stories spreading about you."

"Especially since I didn't make them pay."

"That does sweeten the pot."

Nahri dried the instruments, wrapping them in clean cloth, and then Yaqub motioned for her to sit. "You have ruined my night, so now take some tea with me," he ordered, handing her a glass. "I would talk to you."

She was instantly anxious. "If this is about us moving on, I can find other lodgings—"

He shushed her. "I'm not asking you to leave. I'm asking the opposite. I want you to stay."

Nahri frowned. "What do you mean?"

He blew on his tea. "It's hardly a secret that I'm getting old—you yourself have made any number of obnoxious comments to that effect—and no one in my family is equipped to take over the apothecary. My wife and I had discussed selling it, but I wonder if you and your friend would be interested in staying on and taking over."

She stared at him in astonishment. That was frankly the *last* thing she'd expected Yaqub to say. "I haven't trained as an apothecarist," she sputtered.

"You haven't trained as an apothecarist . . . for God's sake, you just did brain surgery on the table! You could build your own sort of practice here and let your reputation speak for itself. And if you're so concerned, I'm not yet ready to retire. I'd be perfectly happy to take the two of you on as apprentices for a few years."

The offer was so kind and perfect that all Nahri could do was find reasons to push it away. "I'm a woman. No one will take me seriously as an apothecarist, let alone as a doctor."

"Then to hell with them. You know perfectly well there are women practicing in the city, particularly on female patients."

"Rich women. Daughters and wives of doctors who work alongside them."

"So *lie*." Some of the tea sloshed out of Yaqub's glass at his exuberance. "Every other word out of your mouth used to be a lie to further your ambitions. Surely you can craft a suitable background for yourself. Claim you studied medicine in whatever mysterious island kingdom your not-husband is from."

Nahri sat back. Before she could stop herself, she could see such a future spinning out before her. She *was* a good healer. Maybe rich nobles and fancy foreigners would turn up their noses at a so-called female doctor with no degree, but people like that boy's family? Like the people she'd grown up among? Someone like Nahri would be a blessing. And who cared if they couldn't pay much? She'd have the apothecary, and she'd always been good at finding ways to hustle. Ali was clever with numbers. They'd make enough to have a comfortable life.

Except . . .

Except the future Yaqub was offering was the one she'd wanted growing up in Egypt. She had new responsibilities now and people back in Daevabad waiting for her. And while Nahri felt the thrill of having saved that little boy, that wasn't all the power at her disposal. She could save so many more with her magic, and until they found a way to restore it, she'd never truly be who she felt herself capable of being.

Yaqub must have seen the emotion in her eyes. He set down his tea and reached for her hand. "Nahri, child, I don't know what the two of you are running from. I don't know what you're planning next. But you could have a life here. A good one."

Taking a shaky breath, Nahri squeezed his hand. "That is . . . an incredibly kind offer. I need to think about it."

"Take the time you need," Yaqub said warmly. "Talk to your friend." He smiled. "But I think Cairo could use someone like you."

Nahri didn't disagree.

But she wondered if Daevabad might need her more.

9

ALI

Ali would be having nightmares about open skulls for months, but the marvelous market Nahri took him to the next day more than made up for it. It was the human bazaar of his dreams, and Ali wandered through with open delight, grateful that humans seemed inclined not to see him because he wasn't even trying to check his curiosity. Instead, he raced from shop to shop, stall to stall, touching everything he could get his hands on and examining embroidered tapestries, carpentry tools, mirrored lanterns, glass spectacles, and shoes with unbridled enthusiasm.

"Oh," he gushed, catching a glint of metal in the distance. "*Swords.*"

"*No,*" Nahri said, tugging on the sleeve of the extremely ill-fitting galabiyya he'd borrowed from Yaqub. "I almost lost you to toy chickens. We're not going to look at swords. We'll never leave."

"Those 'toy chickens' were marvels of mechanical ingenuity," Ali defended himself, relishing his memory of the captivating device that had made a pair of tin chickens bob their heads when he pulled a hammer, appearing to "eat" grains of painted glass. He had desperately wanted it, aching to take the device apart and see how it worked.

"Yes. Marvels of mechanical ingenuity . . . for children."

"I refuse to believe you weren't equally enchanted by your first encounter with Daevabad's bazaar."

Nahri gave him a small, confessional smile that made Ali feel warm all over. "Maybe a bit. *But*"—she pulled the coffeepot he had been examining from his hands before dragging him away—"I have something better to show you."

The next alley was covered, the narrow path snaking under a ceiling carved into a geometrical honeycomb. They turned a corner, and there, spread upon rugs and chests, was a sea of books and scrolls.

"*Oh*," Ali said again. "Yes. Yes, this is better than swords." He immediately went for the first shop, his eyes going wide as he took everything in. Besides books, there were rows and rows of maps and what appeared to be nautical scrolls laid out on blue velvet.

Ali knelt to examine them. The maps were beautiful, richly illustrated with miniature cities and tiny boats. He traced the bright blue line of a river, studying hand-drawn hills and a trio of islands.

"Is this Cairo?" he asked.

Nahri peered over his shoulder. "Maybe? I'm not very good with geography."

He stared at the map, tugging absentmindedly at his beard. "How far south does the Nile go?"

"Pretty far, I suppose. I had the impression the southern parts ran through Ta Ntry."

"Interesting," he said softly.

"Why?"

Ali didn't miss the guarded tone in her voice. "Just thinking," he murmured, scanning the maps to see what else was available.

"Well, you can stay here and ponder rivers. I remember a man who used to sell medical texts down a ways. Catch up when you can."

He muttered an assent, rifling through the pile of maps. Here was another showing the Nile. Ali traced the southern reaches, studying where the river branched and trying to make out what he could of the Arabic notes, most of the names unfamiliar.

But the land beyond . . . that he'd heard plenty about. The lush mountains and hidden castles built among human ruins, the desert peninsula seeming to nearly kiss Am Gezira and the humid, monsoon coast Ali had grown up listening to stories of at his mother's knee.

Ta Ntry.

Amma.

Hatset would be home by now, right? It seemed so impossibly far, but . . . Ali brushed his thumb over the painted lands, his mind spinning with possibility. He was still struggling with his grief, but he hadn't stopped quietly contemplating ways to return to Daevabad, turning their circumstances over like a puzzle in his mind.

And here was a new piece.

Ali rose to his feet, still holding the maps. A glance revealed Nahri several stalls down, immersed in her own perusing. He opened his mouth to call her name, then stopped.

No, let her be, he told himself, a rush of tenderness stealing through him at the sight of his friend. He wouldn't get her hopes up, not yet. On the surface, Nahri seemed to be doing better than he was, but Ali wasn't sure he believed it. Ali's pain was bone-deep, but simply rooted: his loved ones had been murdered and his home conquered. Nahri had had her entire world turned upside down for the second time in six years, betrayed by seemingly everyone close to her, including the mother and Afshin she'd believed dead.

Besides, surely Ali could do this part on his own. He approached the bookseller.

"Peace be upon you. . . . *Peace be upon*—excuse me!" Ali shouted, snapping his fingers in front of the human's face.

The man blinked, a dazed look slipping across his features as he tilted his head. "Hello?" he said, sounding uncertain of the word.

"I would like to buy these," Ali announced. He fumbled in his bag for the coins Yaqub had given him this morning. The apothecarist had wept, admiring his newly polished workbench. "*You are a blessing. You . . . whatever your name is again,*" he'd added, because every night he seemed to forget anew Ali's name and, on occasion—his very existence.

Ali held out the coins. "Is this enough?"

The bookseller glanced down at the coins and abruptly blinked again. "Yes," he said, sweeping them from Ali's hands. "The exact amount, yes."

"Oh," Ali replied, not missing the glee with which the merchant shut his money away in a small chest. He knew it was frowned upon to assume the worst of others, but he was pretty sure he'd just been cheated.

"What are you doing?"

Ali jumped at Nahri's voice. "Nothing!" he said swiftly, turning around and hoping she wouldn't figure out how easily he'd just been swindled. "So where to next?"

"Lunch. It's time I repaid you for the feteer you brought me back in Daevabad with a proper Egyptian meal."

NAHRI

Nahri lay back on the roof beside Ali, the remains of their feast surrounding them. "I concede defeat," he admitted. "Human food is better."

"Told you," she replied, finishing the last slice of watermelon and tossing the rind aside. "Conjured spices have nothing on fried street dough."

"And yet the place you've chosen to enjoy our meal is very djinn of you," he teased, gesturing to the crumbling building they'd climbed. It looked like it had been a khanqah, a Sufi lodge, abandoned as the city's heart shifted away. "Humans believe we haunt ruins, don't they?"

"Exactly. It was a great place to hide when I was younger, and it has an excellent view," she said, gazing at the spread of brown domes and minarets set against the glint of the Nile.

Ali pushed himself into a sitting position. "It does." But then sorrow swept his face, obliterating the brief levity he had seemed to be enjoying. "There was a view of Daevabad like this from the Citadel tower," he said softly, running his fingers over the broken bricks. "It's still hard to believe it's gone. The Citadel was my home for so long, the other soldiers like my family."

His words struck close. "That's how I felt about the infirmary and Nisreen. Jamshid too," she added, guilt clawing through her. Jamshid *was* family, and Nahri couldn't help but recall that one of the last things she'd done in Daevabad was refuse Ghassan's attempt to use her brother's life to blackmail her. Had Ghassan lived a few hours more, he might have taken it—killed Jamshid before Nahri's very eyes.

And she'd been ready to let it happen: all to save the life of the man sitting next to her now in the hopes he'd take down his father. Not that she dared tell Ali any of this yet. Nahri didn't think they were ready for that conversation.

"Kaveh might be a traitorous snake, but I'm sure he had a plan to keep his son safe." Ali's face fell. "Though when Jamshid finds out about Muntadhir . . . they were so close."

Please tell him I loved him. Tell him I'm sorry I didn't stand up for him sooner. Nahri squeezed her eyes shut. She didn't want to talk about any of this. She survived trauma by suppressing it, by shoving back the grief and rage that would otherwise swallow her whole.

She was saved from having to respond by the sudden bang of a large drum. Ali jumped, reaching for the khanjar at his waist.

"Relax," she said, easing his hand down. The strains of singing were already following. "It's probably a wedding." She peered over the wall, searching the maze of lanes below. "A decade ago, I'd have hunted it down and pretended to be a guest for the food."

"Believe it or not, back in Bir Nabat, we did the same. We used to stalk human festivals and bring back their scraps. People skilled at the magic can re-create the whole feast." Disappointment colored Ali's voice. "Well, others went. I was never allowed. No one thought I could be discreet."

Nahri grinned. "You, not discreet around humans? I could never imagine it." She paused, feeling another question build in her. "But you liked it there. Living something like a normal life."

"I loved it." Ali leaned on his elbows, staring out at Cairo. "It got a little lonely on occasion, and I didn't completely fit in. But I liked feeling useful, you know? Like I could do some good." He sighed. "It was so much easier to do that in Bir Nabat than in Daevabad."

"Yes," she muttered. "I think I know how that feels."

Ali turned to face her. "How is your patient doing, by the way?"

"Good, thank God." Nahri had checked on the boy this morning. His incision looked great, and though he had some weakness on the left side of his body, he'd survived. "His mother wouldn't stop crying and kissing me."

"I thought the cookies you brought back were damp." But there was a seriousness in Ali's eyes that the jest didn't touch. "I'm glad to hear he's going to be okay. Because we need to talk."

"About what?"

"About Suleiman's seal and the fact that our magic isn't returning."

Nahri was already shaking her head. "Muntadhir said it could take a couple of days—"

"It's been five. And Nahri, nothing's changed. I don't feel anything of my djinn abilities, or of the seal." Ali touched his chest. "There's pain in my heart when I call upon my water magic, but that's it. Unless you've . . ."

"No." Nahri woke every morning reaching for her healing magic, aching for its return.

"Then I think we need a new plan." Ali reached for the bag he'd been carrying. "Maybe Manizheh and Dara have been stripped of their magic, maybe everyone has, but we don't know for sure, and we can't just wait here. It's not safe for us or any of the humans we associate with. We need to find a place where we can reconnect with our people and start building alliances, an army . . ."

Alliances. An army. A buzz was growing in Nahri's mind. She cleared her throat, suddenly finding it difficult to speak. "Where?" she managed.

"Ta Ntry." Ali pulled a bundle of papers from his bag—no, not papers, maps.

"That's why you were looking at maps?"

"Yes. And look—" He gestured to a spot on the map, somewhere in the golden lands beyond the Sea of Reeds. "Am Gezira is close, but I don't think we should risk Manizheh bringing her plague to any more Geziris in case she still has her powers. But if we were to go south . . ." He ran his index finger much farther down, tracing the coast along the ocean. "My mother is from Shefala—here." Ali tapped an invisible point. "She should be home. Ta Ntry is a power in its own right; it has money, warriors, enough resources to be largely self-sufficient."

Ta Ntry. Nahri blinked, trying to take that all in. Her rocky relationship with the queen aside, Nahri could not deny the wisdom in going to Hatset—the cunning matriarch seemed a natural match for Manizheh.

But leaving Cairo . . . "Would we even be welcome in Ta Ntry?" Nahri asked. "Muntadhir always made it sound like the Ayaanle were plotting against us."

"There might be something to that." When Nahri lifted an eyebrow, Ali swiftly added, "But the library at Shefala is said to be extraordinary. They have a lot of texts taken from Daevabad during the original conquest, and we might find something about Suleiman's seal in those books. Maybe there's a part we're missing, a way to fix all this and restore our magic."

Creator, Nahri wanted her magic back. But another meddling court of djinn—who apparently had kept her family's stolen archives—ruled by a sovereign she didn't trust . . . "We can't. We have no way to get there."

"We do." Ali again gestured to the map. "We sail."

Nahri gave him a skeptical look. "You know how to sail?"

"I know a bit. But more importantly, I can do this." Ali leaned over the balustrade, gesturing to a fallen palm tree drifting in the river's languid current. It abruptly stilled and then reversed course as if being pulled by an underwater chain, moving toward Ali's hand. He let it go, and it continued spinning away.

He grimaced, rubbing his chest. "It's not going to be painless." He glanced at Nahri, and for the first time since Daevabad fell, she saw hope in his eyes. "But I think it could work."

Nahri stared at him, trying to act like a cage wasn't closing around her. "It's too dangerous. It's too far. We're all but powerless, and you want to set off on some trek through deserts and jungle because you can make a log go upriver?"

Ali deflated. "Then what would you suggest?"

Nahri hesitated but only for a moment. "That we consider staying longer." She held his gaze, feeling more vulnerable than she liked. "Yaqub wants me to take over the apothecary."

"*Take over the apothecary?*" Ali repeated, sounding bewildered. "What do you mean?"

"He's offered to train us as apprentices," Nahri explained. "We'd inherit it when he retires, and I could see patients there as well. I could be a doctor, or something like one, treating people who can't afford anyone else."

Ali was visibly shocked. "You're not talking about staying in Cairo *longer*. You're talking about staying permanently."

"And if I am? Would it be so bad? We could have a good life here. We could help people!"

"Nahri." Ali was already shaking his head and rising to his feet.

"Would you just consider it?" She followed him, hating the plea in her voice. "We could just be *us*: Nahri and Ali. Not Nahid and Qahtani, locked in some murderous feud." Feeling desperate, she continued, "You like it here, don't you? You'd get to ogle all the human toys you want; you could clean Yaqub's shop and play accountant with his books—all with the added benefit of not being killed in some reckless plot. We could be *happy*."

"We can't stay here. We *can't*—" Ali repeated when Nahri turned away, hating the pity in his eyes. "I'm sorry. I wish we could, but Manizheh is going to come for the seal. You know it. I know it. It's only a matter of time."

"We don't know it," Nahri countered fiercely. "For all we know, she thinks we drowned in the lake. And even if she has magic, so what? Will she search the whole world?"

"She doesn't need to search the whole world." Ali hesitated. "You didn't hide your love for your human home. Surely if asked, Darayavahoush would—"

"Dara doesn't know *anything* about me."

A tense silence followed that. Ali paced away, linking his hands behind his head, but Nahri didn't budge from her spot on the roof. If she could have, she would have rooted herself there.

Breathing hard, she fought for control of her churning emotions. Nahri had always done best when she was cold. Pragmatic. "Maybe it won't be forever," she said, trying to find a compromise. "If magic comes back, wonderful. We'll consider going to Ta Ntry then. But if it doesn't? We have a backup plan, a safe life here."

"We will never be safe here and neither will anyone around us." Ali tapped the mark on his brow. "Not with this. For all we know, she'll send the ifrit after us. After Yaqub. And I don't *want* to be safe. Not if my people aren't. Not if my sister isn't."

"Then what? We go to Ta Ntry and build an army so we can fight in another pointless war?" She threw up her hands. "Ali, they turned the lake into a beast and designed a plague capable of killing thousands of djinn in a single night. She's allied with the ifrit. There's nothing she won't do to win."

"Then we'll find a way to fight back!"

"Like you fought back?" Ali spun at the challenge in her voice, but Nahri pressed on. She needed to make him see. "How many Daevas did you kill that night?"

A hint of anger blossomed in his face. "The Daevas I killed were soldiers. Soldiers who invaded my home, killed my friends, and meant to slaughter my entire tribe."

Nahri gave him an even look. "Change 'Daevas' to 'djinn,' and I bet that's just what Dara said to himself."

Ali stepped back like she'd slapped him. "I am *nothing* like him. I would take a blade to my throat before I'd do the things he's done." He blinked, hurt replacing the anger in his eyes. "He killed my brother. How could you say such a thing to me?"

"Because I don't want that for you!" Nahri exploded. "I don't want that for *me*! You looked like him that night on the palace roof and I . . ." A sick feeling rose in her. "I helped you. I helped you kill three Daevas. And when I cut into your father's chest, Ali? It felt good. I felt *satisfied*."

Shaking, Ali turned away again, crossing the roof as if to put space between them.

She followed, growing more frantic. "But don't you see? We don't have to go to war. Let them think we drowned. You and I, we tried, okay? We tried more than most. We built the hospital, and look what happened. The Daevas attacked the shafit, the shafit attacked the Daevas, and your father was ready to start slaughtering people before my mother killed him. Daevabad is a death trap. It corrupts and ruins everyone who tries to fix it. And we could be free of it. *Both* of us. We could have a life here together. A good one."

Ali stopped at the roof's edge, breathing hard. And then

Nahri saw it, a flicker of longing in his face. She knew that longing. She was used to spotting it in others and then closing in, using the desire her mark was too foolish to conceal. A half dozen
responses hovered at her lips, ways to convince him to stay, to
force him to agree.

But Ali wasn't supposed to be a mark anymore; he was supposed to be her friend.

He turned back around, the ache gone from his expression.
No, not just gone—Ali was focused on *her* like he was about to read
a mark himself, and Nahri didn't like it one bit.

"I need to say something no Qahtani has a right to tell you,
but it needs to be said and there's no one else," he began. "Even
if Manizheh doesn't hunt us, even if we don't get our magic back,
we can't stay here. We have a duty to go back, no matter the consequences. Our families caused this mess, but they're not the only
ones who are going to pay. There are tens of thousands of innocent civilians who are going to pay. And you and I don't get to
look away from that, no matter how tempting."

Nahri could have punched him in the face. "You're correct,
you don't have the right to say that to me. *Tempting?* So I'm selfish for not wanting to die in Daevabad when I could help people
here?"

"I didn't say you were *selfish*—"

"You might as well have." Fury rose in her, at herself as well
as at Ali. Why was Nahri wasting air trying to convince some
stubborn djinn prince to stay at her side?

Because you want him to stay at your side. Because Nahri didn't want
to be a lonely, selfless doctor in the human world. She wanted to
drink bad tea and browse books with someone who knew her. She
wanted a life, a friend.

Nahri didn't need Ali. She wanted him.

And that made him a weakness. Nahri could hear the word

in Nisreen's voice, in Ghassan's voice, in Manizheh's. That's what Ali was, what all of them were—the whole of Daevabad. She should have continued to live the way she had in Egypt. No attachments, no dreaming of a hospital or a better future. Just survival.

The sky abruptly darkened, the sun sinking behind the Pyramids. The murmur of river traffic and the bustling city pulled at her soul. It all suddenly felt so fragile that she wanted to clutch Cairo to her chest and never let it go.

"Forget it," she declared. "I'm not going to waste my breath trying to save you from yourself again. You want to go die in Daevabad? Fine. But you'll be doing it alone."

Nahri turned away, meaning to leave him on the roof, but he was already pursuing her.

"Nahri, she's going to come for the seal."

She glanced back. It was a mistake. Because the beseeching look in Ali's eyes tugged on a part of her heart Nahri wanted to crush out.

So she crushed him instead. "Then I'm glad I gave it to you."

NAHRI SHOOK WITH ANGER AS SHE STORMED AWAY from the khanqah. To hell with Alizayd al Qahtani and his idealism. To hell with *Daevabad*, the doomed, poisoned city she'd tried to help. The Grand Temple had enough shrines to Nahids who'd martyred themselves. Nahri wasn't planning on joining them.

She didn't go back to the apothecary. Let Ali go back first, collect his things, and take off on his ludicrous Nile adventure. Maybe when he was starving and lost on some backwater stream, he'd realize he should have listened to her.

Instead, she walked. Not along the riverbank, but deeper into Cairo itself, through the crowded streets that led toward the hills and past neighborhoods of new migrants. Nahri didn't want the quiet peace of the flooded Nile, one that invited contemplation.

She wanted distraction, noisy human life and activities: children playing and neighbors gossiping. The normal life she should have been living for the last half decade instead of getting pulled into the deadly politics of a bunch of vengeful, warring djinn. She walked without paying attention to where her feet took her, part of her hoping she'd get so lost that by the time she made it back to Yaqub's, Ali would be gone, and she'd be free of her last tie to the magical world.

Yet, despite her desire to wrench it all away, Nahri was not surprised when she ended up in the neighborhood where it had all begun.

The empty lot where she'd performed the zar was eerily untouched, though the neighborhood had grown busier, extra floors built on the surrounding tenements and huts constructed against the walls. Yaqub had said that people were hopeful things were changing in Egypt. The French occupation had been defeated, and their new foreign ruler was promising reforms. More people were moving to the city, looking for opportunities.

She wanted to tell them not to. It hurt worse to see your dreams destroyed than to never have them at all.

It didn't seem anyone had dared hope for this lot, however. The plain square of dust was filled with rubbish, an orange cat cleaning its whiskers the only occupant.

Not for the first time, she thought of Baseema. Had they removed Dara's arrow from her throat before bringing the girl's body to her grieving mother, the mother who'd kissed Nahri's cheeks and blessed her the night before? Had Baseema's fingers started to char from the ifrit's possession, her final moments spent in agony all because Nahri had, on an utter whim, decided to sing in Divasti?

You're as responsible for that girl's death as Dara and Vizaresh. It had been unspeakably arrogant of Nahri to dabble in traditions she hadn't understood, twisting abilities that were meant to heal into a way to deceive innocent people.

The sky was darkening, maghrib prayer already called. Nahri probably should have been concerned, a young woman alone, but strangely enough, though her magic was gone, she felt little fear from the humans around her. Her time in Daevabad had changed her, setting her apart from the people she once considered her own.

They'll be my own again. The future she'd always wanted was finally in her hands, and Nahri wasn't going to lose it.

But that night tugged at her like a string, bringing her to El Arafa once again, the vast cemetery looking just as Nahri remembered it, the jumble of tombs and mausoleums an eerie landscape of the dead she knew didn't always slumber peacefully. She made her way inside, following the meandering alleys of her memory, and sat upon a crumbling stone pillar, half-bathed in moonlight.

And then—and only then, in the place where he'd arrived in a storm of sand and fire—did Nahri finally and fully let Dara back into her thoughts.

You weren't supposed to see it. You were supposed to be safe. Nahri pressed her hands against her temples, remembering the anguish on his handsome face as he stammered those words, his bright eyes begging for understanding.

How could you do that, Dara? How could you have done any of this?

For Nahri could no longer deny that Dara was guilty of the whispered crimes that clung to his name. He'd carried out the slaughter of innocent shafit at Qui-zi, a crime so brutal it still scarred their world. He'd then done something equally heinous: knowingly abetting her mother in the attempted annihilation of Daevabad's Geziri population.

And she'd fallen for him. No, she had *loved* him; she might as well admit it to herself. Maybe it had been the rush of adventure and sweeping excitement, the almost embarrassingly inevitable and clearly doomed romance that resulted between dashing warriors and wide-eyed young women. Had Muntadhir not accused her of living in a fairy tale, unable to tell the difference between its hero and its monster? Nahri, who always read her mark, who'd called out a djinn king. How had she not seen the darkness lurking in Dara?

Because you *were the mark,* she thought bitterly. *And you think to go back to Daevabad, to proclaim yourself a leader capable of outwitting Manizheh?* Her mother had taken one look at Nahri and seen straight through to her weaknesses. Her shafit heritage and her stupid fondness for an idiot prince. The darker resentments about being crushed by the djinn. The twinge of pleasure when she'd burned Ghassan's heart.

Maybe that was how it started. Nahri wondered what might have happened if the invasion had gone according to Manizheh's plan. If she'd been kept safe and in the dark by Nisreen and then woken to a world in which Ghassan was dead, the Daevas were free, and Nahri was reunited with her family and the man she loved. Might it have been easier to believe whatever lies they spun to justify it? To quietly choose to look ahead instead of at the bodies and blood propping up their new world?

Did Dara do that? Nahri tried to imagine him as a young man, as someone brimming with adoration for the Nahids and committed to protecting his people—someone who could have been convinced the shafit of Qui-zi were an existential threat and chosen to follow an order that must have seemed shocking. How many of those choices had led to Dara bowing before Manizheh, standing at her side while she committed genocide?

I don't want to think about this. Nahri had made her choice. She wrapped her shivering arms around her knees and squeezed her eyes shut against the tears she refused to let flow, taking refuge in the darkness of her closed lids.

And then she saw them. Subha in the infirmary they'd rebuilt, forcing a cup of tea on her as Nahri tried to hold herself together for her injured tribesmen. Jamshid laughing in the infirmary on his steed of cushions. The shafit children in the school at the workcamp. The Daeva children grinning at her in the Temple.

The Geziri children who died with sparklers in their hands. The people who, like Ali had irritatingly pointed out, did not have their choice.

Nahri swore, loud and profuse enough to startle a pigeon that had been resting in the eaves of the nearest mausoleum. Then she rose to her feet and returned to Yaqub's, praying she wasn't too late.

THEY WERE WAITING FOR HER OUTSIDE THE APOTH-ecary. Yaqub was dressed in the shawl he wore on his walks home, visibly fretting as he passed his cane from hand to hand. At his side, Ali was somber, looking even more isolated than usual from the humans passing by.

Yaqub clucked his tongue as he caught sight of her. "You are terrible for the nerves, do you know that?"

"I didn't mean to worry you," Nahri apologized. "I just . . . I needed some space to think." She kept her attention fixed on Yaqub, not unaware of the weight of Ali's gaze.

The pharmacist looked unconvinced. "Young women should do their thinking in their homes," he grumbled, adjusting his shawl. "It is safer." He nodded at the door. "I left you beans and bread."

Nahri let the "young women" comment slide for now. "Thank you, grandfather," she said simply. "Give my blessings to your family."

Ali stepped toward her the moment Yaqub was gone. "Nahri, I'm sorry. You're right; I had no business—"

"You're going to tell me everything," she cut in. "What the marid did to you, whatever lore and history you've been hiding about the war, about the seal—everything, understand? No more secrets."

He blinked. "I mean, of course—"

Nahri held up a hand. "I'm not done. If we're going to do this, you need to listen to me. We need to be *careful*. No reckless plans of self-sacrifice and spouting off things that will get us killed. I'm not going near Banu 'I control people's limbs with my mind' until we have a plan that I—not you—believe solid."

Ali brightened. "Wait, you're going to come with me to Ta Ntry? You don't want to stay in Cairo?"

"Of course I want to stay in Cairo! And if Daevabad wasn't in the hands of a murderous Nahid who makes your father's body count look like child's play, I would. But it's like you said," she explained begrudgingly. "We have people there relying on us."

His eyes were shining with pride. God, Nahri wanted to stab him.

He touched his heart. "It would be my greatest honor to fight at your—"

Nahri let out an exasperated hiss to shut him up. Better rudeness than letting slip how relieved she was that he hadn't already left. "No. None of that. I'm not even committing to anything, understand?" she warned, jabbing a finger in Ali's face. "I haven't had the greatest experience showing up unexpectedly at magical courts of bickering djinn who warred against my ancestors. If things go to hell in Ta Ntry, I'm gone."

The ghost of what might have once been a smile curved his lips. "Then there's no one I'd rather be abandoned by." Ali's expression softened. "And thank you, Nahri. I don't think I could get through all this without you."

She grumbled, fighting the emotions eating at her heart. "You're not so bad yourself."

Now Ali did smile, the first time she'd seen him do so since the attack. "Then what do we do next, as it seems you're in charge?"

Nahri nodded at Muntadhir's khanjar. "We go buy a boat."

DARA

Dara grimaced, watching as the line of young men before him shot arrows into the trees, into the grass, into a distant tent . . . really, anywhere that wasn't their target.

"Are they getting any *better*?" he finally asked.

Noshrad, one of his original warriors, looked discouraged. "They have generally started shooting in a forward direction instead of at each other."

Dara pinched his brow. "I do not understand. Our people are renowned at the bow. Navasatem was to be occurring. Where are all the Daeva archers who would have competed?"

"Since your death, the only Daevas permitted to own a bow have been noblemen sworn to the Qahtanis. Kaveh warned me many were the boon companions of Emir Muntadhir and advised we weed them out of potential recruits until things are . . . less tense."

The news that there was a whole group of skilled Daeva

archers—the exact kind of people Daevabad needed—unavailable because of their ties to Muntadhir al Qahtani filled Dara with a new desire to strangle the former emir.

He cracked his knuckles, forcing himself to remain calm. "There must be more Daeva men willing to protect their city."

"We've already posted everyone with any fighting experience." Noshrad hesitated. "But we haven't been as successful with recruitment as we'd hoped. People are too afraid. With magic gone, everyone's just waiting for the next catastrophe."

Waiting for the next catastrophe seemed an entirely too-apt description of their current circumstances. Dara gazed at the field his men had turned into a training yard. With the rest of the city walled off, the Daevas had opened the gate that led from their quarters into the hills, forests, and farms that dominated the rest of the island—a gate and an option no other tribe had. Most of the land was owned by the city's oldest Daeva families—or at least had been until Manizheh declared everything under her control. The city had been well stocked for Navasatem, but between the huge number of tourists and the fact that no ships or caravans were coming in, it was only a matter of time until food became an issue, so they intended to make sure what had yet to be harvested remained in their hands.

Food wasn't technically Dara's problem; only security and military affairs were. Yet it wasn't easy to divest himself of the day-to-day issues of running the city. It had been two weeks since they'd taken the palace, and Manizheh was still attempting to piece together a government—if by government, one meant a dozen cowed ministers of extremely varying levels of experience ruled by an increasingly exhausted and exasperated Kaveh e-Pramukh. Despite Manizheh's ultimatum and the havoc Dara had unleashed while delivering said ultimatum, none of the djinn had surrendered. The Agnivanshi had sent over a cautiously worded letter that could have been interpreted a dozen different ways, the Tukharistanis a far blunter missive suggesting the Scourge of Qui-zi go burn in hell, and the Sahrayn an *actually* burning barrel of dung. From the Ayaanle and Geziris was silence, though Dara supposed silence was what happened when someone was actively conspiring to bring you down.

And there was nothing he could do about it besides train more warriors. "Keep at it," he told Noshrad. "I shall see if I can't rustle up more recruits."

Dara took the main avenue back to the palace, steeling himself for the mixed reactions his presence provoked. When he'd first returned to Daevabad, he'd been treated like a hero by the Daevas, the legendary Darayavahoush e-Afshin brought back to life to escort the even more miraculous and mysterious Banu Nahri e-Nahid. It made for a fantastic story, truly—Dara had once seen it performed by some sort of street puppets while walking with Jamshid in more peaceful times. He was also not unaware of the *other* angle people brought into it: Nahri was a beautiful woman, Dara a handsome warrior, and the Qahtanis made for excellent villains. He'd heard the sighs as he bowed before Nahri in the Grand Temple, not missing the admiring whispers, longing looks, and overly excited children eager to show him the Afshin marks they'd drawn on their cheeks.

No one wore Afshin marks now.

Oh, there were plenty of Daevas who'd greeted their conquest with grateful tears and flocked to see Manizheh during her rare public appearances. But like Noshrad said, most of their people just seemed wary. Resigned, traumatized, and as intimidated by Manizheh and Dara as they had been by Ghassan. And Dara couldn't blame them. They'd been stripped of their magic, and ifrit strolled the streets. Ghassan might have been a tyrant, but Dara suspected the brutal way the Geziris had been slaughtered— the Nahid magic his people revered as sacred twisted to deliver a gruesome death—was simply too much to accept. Dara kept his eyes down as he walked, aware of the conversations that abruptly ended when he drew near, and the whispers that picked up in his wake. There were almost no women and children out, and the markets and cafés were empty, litter and weeds beginning to overtake the cobbled streets.

It was no easier to enter the palace grounds, for Dara walked straight through the scoured dirt field where the doomed Geziri traveling camp had been. It stood out like a wound against the rest of the lush garden; no one had yet the stomach to do anything about it.

Nor did Dara. Because every time he looked at this field, it was impossible to deny that what was left of his soul screamed this was wrong.

It could have been worse, he tried to tell himself. The palace had been just as blood soaked the last time Daevabad was conquered— and that time it had been *his* people slaughtered. The Daevas cowering in their homes should count themselves lucky to still be cowering. His family never had that chance.

But the justifications were getting harder to swallow. Dara continued to the massive throne room. This place too still smelled like blood. They'd removed the bodies of the dozen Geziris they'd found here, and Dara had ordered the room cleaned, first by servants and then by his own magic, but the pungent aroma lingered.

Without it, the throne room would have dazzled. Knowing this would be the place where Manizheh greeted her subjects, Dara had not held back from returning it to its former glory. He'd stripped the age from the enormous columns with a snap of his fingers, restoring the lustrous shine of the sandstone walls and the bright paints of the original Daeva ornaments. A thick conjured carpet ran the entire length of the audience hall, the luminous threads depicting dancers and animals and feasts, the patterns he remembered from his youth. Two large fire altars had been brought in, filling the room with cedar incense. And yet beneath that holy fragrance . . . still blood.

The room has always demanded a cost. Dara could still remember the first time he'd set foot in here. Suleiman's eye, he'd been young. Eighteen, nineteen? Still in training, since he'd been taken directly from the sparring yard by an impatient steward in royal colors who said Dara had been summoned by the Nahid Council.

Summoned by the Nahid Council.

The five words that changed the entire course of his life.

AT FIRST DARA THOUGHT IT WAS A MISTAKE. WHEN IT became clear it wasn't, he was both thrilled and panicked. Afshin minors did not get *summoned by the Nahid Council.* Dara knew he was favored—though he came from a talented generation of Afshins, he was head and shoulders above his cousins when it came to military skills. Considered a prodigy with the bow, he'd been taken for specialized training two years earlier, a decision that had quietly irked his father. *Zaydi al Qahtani takes votes with his generals and sends their sons to rebuild villages we have destroyed,* he recalled his father complain to his mother in a whispered conversation, *while we make assassins out of warriors we should be training to lead.*

Indeed, his father, Artash, was there when Dara arrived, kneeling before the shedu throne, his helmet at his side. Yet everything about the set of his features was wrong. Everyone bowed before the Nahids, but there was a simmering despair under his father's carefully neutral expression Dara had never seen before. His own heart was pounding so hard he could hear it in his ears, more embarrassing because he knew the healers could detect it as well.

Almost too nervous to proceed, Dara prostrated himself before he even neared the throne, dropping to the ground to press his face into the carpet.

A chuckle broke the tense silence. "Come forward, young

warrior," a Baga Nahid teased. "We can hardly converse when you're all the way back there."

His gaze lowered and his face burning, Dara approached, taking the cushion beside his father, aching to ask him what was going on. Artash was a hard but loving man, both Dara's commander and his father. Dara never disobeyed him, had always looked to his father first, and seeing him suddenly bowed in grim silence was a disorienting experience.

"Look up, boy. Let us see you."

Dara glanced up. The throne catching in the sunlight was blinding and he blinked, the Blessed Nahids coming to him as indistinct shapes in their blue-and-white regalia, their faces veiled. Five sat there, one on the throne and the others on jeweled stools. He'd heard they took turns sitting on the throne and possessing Suleiman's seal. None but members of their family knew who ruled and when.

He'd also heard that the Council had once been thirteen—before that even more. People whispered the Nahids were turning on themselves, relatives who quietly dissented being exiled, and those who openly criticized being found dead. But those were rumors, blasphemous gossip that good Daevas—Daevas like Dara—didn't listen to.

There was a smile in the Nahid's voice. "A handsome young man," he remarked. "You must be so proud, Artash, to have raised such a diligent warrior, one praised by his instructors for his skill. For his obedience."

His father's voice was halting. "He is my life."

Worried, Dara snuck a glance at his father, surprised to find him unarmed, the iron knife he wore at his waist missing. A trickle of fear stole through him. What could have reduced his towering father to such a state?

"Good." The Baga Nahid's clipped voice brought Dara back to attention. "For we are sorely in need of such a man for a very important mission. A difficult one, but perhaps the most crucial we've faced in a long time." He stared at Dara over his veil. "We believe you are he."

Startled by the pronouncement, Dara nearly broke protocol, his mouth falling open to protest. Surely this was a mistake. He was skilled, but he was a minor, still years away from his first quarter century. The Afshins held themselves to notoriously strict standards, particularly when it came to training the next generation. Their warriors did not go near a battlefield until their majority; leading a mission was unheard of.

But there was no questioning a Nahid—a good Afshin obeyed—so Dara said the only thing he could. "I am here to serve."

He remembered the Baga Nahid's eyes crinkling, his smile hidden beneath his veil. "See how easy that is, Artash?" he remarked before returning his attention to Dara. "There is a city called Qui-zi . . ."

The rest was a blur. Dire warnings that shafit had infiltrated and corrupted a Tukharistani merchant city. That the fanatic Zaydi al Qahtani, desperate and losing, schemed to so brazenly flout Suleiman's law that he'd trigger another cataclysm. That to save their people, this all needed to be stopped.

Their orders. So specific that Dara, who had spoken out of turn not once, drew in a sharp, shocked breath and glanced again at his father, an act that prompted the Nahids to start fretting about what might happen should another Suleiman return. How they'd all be stripped of their magic, their names, their family, their very identity—pressed into human service for untold centuries. How his mother and little sister might suffer in such a disaster.

So Dara again said the only thing he could. "I am here to serve."

And once again the Baga Nahid seemed pleased. "Then take your father's helmet. He will not need it. He has another task."

Dara did so numbly, too overwhelmed by the warning and his orders—by the shock of being in such a holy presence—to understand the despair in his father's eyes, to realize his father's "task" was to be sent to the front lines as fodder.

He couldn't know that, though, so Dara obeyed. Or, at least, he tried to. He left the next day and served the Nahids, clinging to their assurance that the shafit who screamed and begged for mercy at Qui-zi were not real people: they were invaders, soulless deceptions plotting the destruction of *his* people. His family. It became easier to believe as the bodies piled up. For it had to be the truth.

If it wasn't the truth, Dara was a monster, a murderer.

And Dara wasn't a monster. Monsters were the ifrit, the treacherous Zaydi al Qahtani who'd murdered his garrison commander and loosed shafit hordes on Daeva civilians. Dara was a good man, a good son who would return to parents who loved him. Who'd tease his young sister as they sat for dinner. The kind of upstanding youth anyone would be proud of.

He was only following orders.

But on one order Dara failed. He'd been told to leave no survivors. The Nahids had spoken in the language of healers, and one did not leave an infection to spread. But in telling him how to so brutally isolate those who had human blood—with the scourge he'd be tied to for the rest of his life—they had ensured that Dara knew just how many women and children were not shafit. The weeping survivors who screamed for husbands, for sons, for fathers. They were not soulless deceptions, and when his men barred the gates of Qui-zi and left it to burn, Dara could not bear to shut them inside. Instead he'd brought them back to Daevabad.

And they rightfully, justifiably, told the world he was a monster.

The Nahid Council was furious, the story it had wanted to

tell torn from its members' tongues. Dara was home only a week—his mother unable to look him in the eye—when they decided to banish him. The Scourging of Qui-zi had been meant to end the war, and instead it had done the opposite, pushing the surviving Tukharistani clans into the welcoming embrace of Zaydi al Qahtani, who already counted the Ayaanle and Sahrayn as allies. The Agnivanshi retreated, their traders and scholars quietly disappearing one by one, and then the Daevas were left isolated, alone in their slowly starving city with the thousands of shafit they'd forced to live in squalor.

And five years after Dara burned their city and killed their kin, the Tukharistanis—no doubt led by some of the survivors he'd spared—entered the city at Zaydi al Qahtani's side. They sacked the Daeva Quarter. They hunted through the streets until they found his family's home.

They got the revenge that would haunt him through all his resurrections . . .

RAISED VOICES FROM THE OTHER SIDE OF THE CHAMber caught Dara's ear, pulling him from his memories.

"—if the djinn want their kin returned, they can come to *me* and surrender," Manizheh said, her voice lifting in anger. "The Grand Temple had no business interfering!"

"They are afraid of you," he heard a familiar voice plead. "Banu Manizheh, they are terrified. The rumors they came to me with . . . they think your Afshin is drinking blood and eating the hearts of his enemies. They think you're giving over anyone who opposes you to the ifrit to be enslaved!"

Dara flinched at the words from Kartir, the Daeva high priest—he could see the back of Kartir's peaked azure cap and crimson robe. Dara moved closer but stayed out of sight. Before the conquest, he would have never contemplated so blatantly spying on his Banu Nahida. But Manizheh had proved at least one of the secrets she held—the poison that had killed the Geziris—was deadly, and while Dara believed she was still working for the good of their people, it seemed wise not to allow himself to be kept completely in the dark.

"And if they came to me directly, they'd learn such things were ridiculous." Manizheh was seated on the throne, dressed in a gown of indigo and gold, her chador hanging lightly from a braided crown. Kaveh was at her side, as usual, watching the exchange with concern.

"They're not going to come to you. Not after what happened to the Geziris. That poison was a cruel act, my lady. People are saying it's the reason magic is gone, that you twisted your Nahid abilities, and the Creator punished you."

Manizheh drew up. "And is that what the high priests believe as well? Have you been wringing your hands in the temple *my* ancestors built, taking meetings with djinn and undermining me with our people? You might remember it is my family that our creed elevates—it's we who are to lead *you,* not the other way around."

"You are to be stewards," Kartir corrected, and Dara couldn't help but respect the man's courage, even as his words stirred an unease that had been growing in Dara's soul. "The Nahids were tasked with caring for this city and its people, all of them. It's a responsibility, Banu Nahida. Not a right. I beg you, turn back from this violence. Let the djinn being held hostage in the palace go home."

Kaveh spoke up, perhaps seeing the fury burning in Manizheh's eyes. "That's not possible, Kartir, and respectfully, you are out of your element. This is a political matter. Everyone holds hostages, and right now, they're one of the most powerful cards we have."

"That was how Ghassan ruled," Kartir rebuked him. He'd crossed the room to service one of the fire altars, swapping the low-burning incense for fresh cedar. His voice was soft, but Dara did not miss his next words, for they went to his heart like a lance. "How the last Nahid Council ruled as well . . . and then lost the support of its people."

"Blasphemy," Kaveh spat, true anger in his face. There was no quicker way to shed Kaveh's political pragmatism than to criticize the woman he loved. It was worrying Dara more and more—Manizheh needed advisors who didn't always tell her what she wanted to hear. "The last Nahid Council didn't lose the support of its people, it was slaughtered by a bunch of dirt-blood obsessed sand flies."

No, Dara wanted to say, his heart aching with the memory of Qui-zi. *The Nahids had started to go astray, we just didn't know until it was too late.*

"Dirt-blood," Kartir repeated. He was staring at the fire altar. "This is not ours, did you know that?"

Manizheh was still glowering. "What are you talking about?"

"Our fire altars. We were not the ones who invented them. Humans did. If you travel to southern Daevastana, you will find the remains of them in buildings that look like ours but were built long before this city was erected. The humans used them in their rites. Our fire temples, our buildings, our food, the very cut of our clothes . . ." Kartir turned around, his gaze falling on Kaveh. "Your title, Grand Wazir. Our government. Do you think our ancestors before Suleiman built grand palaces of mudbrick and discussed financial policy when they lived on the winds and took sustenance from wildfires? We owe our survival to humans. We built our entire civilization off theirs, and now we act as if the greatest contamination in our world is a drop of their blood."

Manizheh shook her head. "What you're talking about happened thousands of years ago. It isn't relevant anymore."

"Isn't it? For much of my life, I thought the same. I taught the same. And yet I wonder if we've been blind to the lessons of

Anahid's own life. Did she not build a city, a palace, a temple with human architecture and fill it with human innovations? Was her closest companion not a human prophet?" Kartir drew nearer to the throne. "Anahid embraced all that humanity could teach her; she designed a capital not just for the Daevas, but with room for all. And I fear that's an inheritance and debt our tribe has forgotten, sealing itself off from the world that gave us so much."

Kaveh eyed the other man with skepticism. "You have been listening too closely to Banu Nahri."

The priest flushed. "I did not agree with her ideas originally, but I have been to her hospital and seen Daevas and djinn and shafit caring for one another."

"And was this before or after shafit attacked the Navasatem procession?" Kaveh provoked him. "Before the dirt-bloods she was helping returned her kindness by trying to assassinate her and my son? Did you give this lecture to the hundred murdered Daevas during their last rites? To Nisreen?"

"Kaveh." Manizheh laid a hand on his wrist. She returned her gaze to the priest, looking more exasperated than angry now. "Kartir, I am given to understand my daughter can be very convincing, but I wouldn't let her sway your opinion on the shafit. She has been under the influence of Geziris and humans for far too long and does not know of what she speaks."

"I don't believe that," Kartir replied, sounding offended. "I know Banu Nahri. She has her own mind."

"Her own mind led her to commit treason," Manizheh argued. "I don't think we should let her opinions influence the direction of our faith."

The priest paled. "Treason? But you said Alizayd kidnapped her."

"I lied. The truth is that Nahri gave Alizayd the seal and fled at his side. I'd like to get her back and believe it best if her treachery is concealed for now." Manizheh's voice grew delicate. "It's so hard for young women to recover their reputations. I don't want our tribe to turn on her forever just because she lost her head for some silver-tongued prince."

Kartir rocked back on his heels. "You're surely not suggesting . . ." He trailed off, his cheeks going red. "I don't believe it."

Dara felt like a rug had been pulled out from underneath him. What *was* Manizheh suggesting?

And then he saw Nahri again, her eyes blazing as she stood before him and the Qahtani brothers and brought the ceiling down on Dara's head. As she tackled him to the ground when Vizaresh had been trying to enslave the djinn prince. The affection between the pair that Dara himself had used six years ago to put a blade to Alizayd's throat and force Nahri's hand.

Dara could not put a word to the emotion that twisted through him. It wasn't quite jealousy, nor was it guilt. He realized it wasn't friendship Manizheh was suggesting had moved her daughter's actions, but he also knew he'd long ago lost the right to plumb the depths of Nahri's heart.

However that didn't mean he had to stand by while Manizheh spread such damaging gossip. "May the fires burn brightly for you all," he greeted them loudly, striding out from the columns as though he'd just arrived. "Something I've missed?"

"Not at all," Manizheh replied calmly, as though she hadn't been slandering her daughter as a treasonous adulterer. She smiled at Kartir. "I thank you for your counsel. Please be assured I will consider it. Indeed, perhaps I could oversee sunrise ceremonies tomorrow and meet with the rest of the priests and Daeva dignitaries? I understand this turn of events is shocking and frightening, but I do believe we can overcome things if we band together."

She might as well have physically tossed Kartir out. The priest looked a little lost, his earlier drive gone.

"Of course," he stammered. "We look forward to welcoming you." His eyes briefly flickered to Dara, but he said nothing, making his way out.

The silence that fell over the three of them was heavy, the weight of the magnificent chamber eerie without a full crowd. Manizheh watched the priest retreat beyond the doors.

"I want him gone." Her cold voice sliced through the warm air.

"It will be difficult," Kaveh warned. "Kartir has held the position for a long time and is highly respected."

"More reason to get rid of him. I don't need him teaching heresy to his flock, and I'm sure there are plenty of senior priests who prefer the old ways. Find one and replace him." Her gaze shifted to Dara. "I hope you bring better news."

Dara took a moment to set aside everything he'd overheard—it would not do to reveal he'd been eavesdropping. "Regretfully, no. We have too few volunteers and even fewer with military skills. We're managing to protect the Daeva Quarter, but I fear effective offensive action is out of the question. We don't have the numbers."

"Any idea how to get them?"

"We could offer an increased stipend," he suggested. "I do not like the idea of needing to bribe men to protect their own people, but it's an option."

"It's not," Kaveh said. "I wish it was, but the Treasury cannot accommodate such a thing right now. The more we dig into Ghassan's finances, the more trouble we find. The Ayaanle had been working to pay their back taxes but stopped when Queen Hatset was banished. The Treasury was overspending in the hopes of making it back during the Navasatem celebrations, but without that income, funds are very low. We're already having enough problems paying the Daeva noble families whose lands and harvests we commandeered."

"Those families should be happy for the opportunity to play their part," Manizheh retorted. "I doubt they fared well under Ghassan."

"They fared better than you might imagine," Kaveh said. "They're the oldest and wealthiest houses in the city, and they got that way by learning when to get in bed with the Qahtanis."

"I take it the skilled archers I am not permitted to use in the city's defense are also from these families?" Dara asked, scowling.

"Yes. I've already had two of them thrown in the dungeon for inquiring a bit too aggressively about Muntadhir's fate."

"That won't do," Manizheh said. "We have enough djinn conspiring outside our walls. I will not brook disloyalty from our people as well. Get them in line."

Before Kaveh could respond, Dara drew up. There was the sound of marching coming from the garden. Faint and uneven—but getting louder very quickly.

"Stay behind me." Without another word of explanation, Dara seized Kaveh by the collar, yanking him behind the throne as he moved between the entrance and Manizheh. A conjured bow was in his hands the next moment, an arrow aimed at the figure dashing up the path.

It was a Daeva servant. The man fell to his knees. "My lady, I tried to stop her, but she insisted on coming straight to you. She claims she has a message from Ghassan's daugh—"

"Ghassan's daughter has a name," a rude, thickly accented voice interrupted, the new arrival striding into the chamber.

It took Dara a moment to recognize the armed Geziri warrior before him as a woman. She was dressed in a motley assortment of men's clothing: a black tunic that might have been taken from a member of the Royal Guard and loose, fraying trousers. Dark braids spilled from a crimson turban, framing a severe face. A sword and khanjar were belted at her waist, her bare arms corded with muscle and scars.

Woman or not, she looked capable of taking down all his new recruits with her bare hands, and so Dara refocused his arrow. "Stop where you are."

The warrior halted and gave him an openly appraising look, her gray, unimpressed eyes sweeping Dara from his boots to his face.

"*You're* the Scourge? You look like you spend more time combing your hair than wielding a whip." Her gaze narrowed on Manizheh, her expression curdling. "I suppose that makes you the Nahid."

"You suppose correctly," Manizheh said coolly. "And you are?"

"A messenger. Her Royal Highness, Princess Zaynab al Qahtani, has returned your people." The warrior stepped aside and whistled, beckoning to the garden.

Dozens of Daevas—scores, the crowd he had heard marching—filed into the throne room. They were also dressed in a miscellaneous assortment of clothing—hand-me-downs and garments stained with old blood. There were men and women, young and old, nearly all wounded, sporting bandaged heads and splinted limbs.

"They were in the hospital after the Navasatem attack and got trapped behind our lines," the warrior explained. "Our doctor has been caring for them."

"Your *doctor*?" Manizheh repeated.

"Our doctor. Ah, that's right. If your magic is gone, I suppose you can't heal anyone anymore. How fortunate these people were on our side," she added with a mocking smirk of concern.

An expression of pure wrath blazed across Manizheh's face, and Dara found himself thinking the other woman was indeed fortunate the Banu Nahida's magic was gone.

"Kaveh," Manizheh said, her voice low and deadly as she continued in Divasti, "*who is this woman?*"

Kaveh was staring at the Geziri warrior like he'd drunk rotten milk. "One of Alizayd's . . . companions. He arrived with two of them, barbarians from northern Am Gezira."

"And is what she says true? You mentioned you feared some

Daevas might have been trapped on the other side, but you've barely discussed this supposed hospital, let alone another doctor."

"Because I did not think much of either, my lady. The hospital was some vanity project Banu Nahri worked on with Alizayd, and this so-called doctor is a shafit. You know what they say about human medicine." Kaveh shivered. "It is little more than the hacking off of limbs and superstitious ritual."

Manizheh pursed her lips and then spoke again in Djinnistani. "We sent a message to Ghassan's daughter demanding her surrender." She swept her hand over the group. "I don't see anyone who appears to be her."

"Princess Zaynab doesn't intend to surrender herself to the people who stole the throne, murdered her father, and arranged the slaughter of her tribe. Her Highness has released these Daevas not as a favor to you, but because they requested to be freed, and she is ever merciful to her family's subjects."

"Your princess has a skewed view of the concept if she thinks her father and grandfather ever showed mercy to their subjects." Manizheh switched to Divasti again. "Kaveh, see that these people are catered to. Food, money, their every whim granted. I will not have them return to our quarter speaking of the *mercy* of a Qahtani." She raised her voice, speaking more warmly to the Daevas. "Thank the Creator for returning you. My grand wazir will see to your needs and make sure you are reunited with your loved ones."

Dara held his tongue, not taking his eyes off the Geziri warrior as Kaveh led the other Daevas out. The woman was openly studying the room, looking a bit too much like she planned on taking it back.

Manizheh waited until the two of them were alone with the warrior before speaking again. "I made it clear to Ghassan's daughter what would happen to her brother if the Geziris didn't surrender."

The warrior scoffed. "You've given her no proof he's still

alive, and strangely enough, the thousands of Geziris and shafit under her protection don't want to submit to people who planned to massacre them. Which is why she offers *you* an alternative way to prove your good intent. And to save another Daeva as well."

Suspicious, Dara spoke up. "What Daeva?"

"An injured warrior we found on the beach. An archer, judging from the grips she wore."

An archer. *Irtemiz.* Dara's protégé, who'd been among the warriors he'd sent to the beach—the ones he'd believed had been slaughtered by Alizayd.

"Were there any others?" Dara asked urgently. He didn't miss the annoyed look Manizheh shot him, but he pressed on. "How badly is she hurt?"

Triumph glittered in the woman's gray gaze. "How fortunate you are so concerned, Afshin, for the deal Zaynab offers involves you." Her attention shifted back to Manizheh. "Her Highness understands how desperate you must have been to ally with the ifrit and the Scourge of Qui-zi, for it's clearly not the act of a rational mind, certainly not a mind anyone could trust to rule."

Magic or not, Dara would swear the entire chamber shivered when Manizheh narrowed her eyes. "Get to the point, sand fly."

"Get rid of your ifrit, fire worshipper. And hand over your Afshin. He'll be the one held responsible for the massacre and executed accordingly. Then we'll return your warrior and open negotiations."

Dara's stomach dropped. Again, they wanted him to take the blame for the decision of a Nahid.

Manizheh stood up. "It was *I* who killed your king," she declared, venom in every word. "And it was *I* who would have seen my city emptied of your people, a future that sounds more promising with each minute you remain in my presence. Tell your so-called princess that. Tell her the day my Afshin is in your company, it won't be tears of victory you're weeping."

"A shame," the warrior replied, looking at Dara again. "Your soldier spoke so fiercely in your defense." She turned away, striding through the doors as if she didn't have an arrow locked on her neck.

Dara lowered his bow. "You didn't give me up."

Manizheh glared at him. "Of course I didn't give you up! Though I appreciate learning just how much you trust me."

"They have Irtemiz," he whispered. "I thought she was dead. I thought they all were."

"She is just as likely dead," Manizheh warned. "That sand fly was testing you, and you blundered right into it."

Dara shook his head. "She is one of mine. I have a duty to try and get her back."

"You certainly do not." Manizheh's eyes were wide with disbelief. "By the Creator, theirs isn't even a clever trap. They're trying to divide us—to get *rid* of you." She must have seen the rebellion brewing in his face. "Afshin, this is not a matter on which there is any negotiation. I mourn the girl, I do, but there are thousands of Daeva girls like Irtemiz who'll be at risk if you're killed."

"But it isn't right that she suffer in my place. This is maddening, Banu Nahida. I cannot go after Irtemiz, I cannot go after Nahri—"

"It has only been two *weeks*, Dara. You must be patient. Give us time to secure the city, for the djinn to turn over Nahri and Alizayd as they've been warned. There is no other way. They are waiting for us to stumble, to make a mistake."

"But—"

"Am I interrupting something?"

At the sound of Aeshma's coy, mocking voice, Dara abruptly lost the battle he was waging with his emotions. Thunder cracked across the throne room, the air growing hot.

"What do you want?" he hissed.

"To relieve the Banu Nahida of your ever-pleasant company." Aeshma turned his attention to Manizheh, bowing slightly. "You are ready?"

Manizheh sighed. "Yes." She glanced at Dara. "I will find a way to send proof of Muntadhir's life," she assured him. "Hopefully that will convince this princess to spare Irtemiz, especially since she has already given up her other Daeva hostages—a mistake I will not be making on our part. You are not to engage with them further, understand?"

Dara grunted assent, still glowering at the ifrit. "What does Aeshma want with you?"

Manizheh's eyes dimmed. "It's complicated." She turned to follow the ifrit but then stopped, glancing back once more. "And, Afshin?"

"Yes?"

Manizheh nodded toward the direction in which the Geziri warrior had departed. "Start training more women."

That he agreed to more readily. "Understood." Dara watched her leave with Aeshma, not missing how she'd dodged his question.

Fine. Manizheh wanted to keep her secrets?

She wasn't the only one who had them. And there was one in particular Dara had been aching to try again.

12

ALI

"I just don't understand why you had to be so *mean*," Ali complained, setting down a basket of oranges next to a sack of dried beans. "Surely there are ways of commerce that don't involve insulting everyone around you."

Nahri handed him a tin of dates. "I didn't say anything untrue."

"You said his mother must have dropped him on his head as an infant!"

"Did you hear his asking price? And for *this*?" Nahri gestured at their new acquisition: a small, ramshackle felucca that looked like someone had tried to dress up a larger version of the hand canoes Ali had seen children zooming about the waterfront on. "He should be happy we're taking it off his hands." She shoved a box in his arms. "That's the last of our supplies."

Ali inhaled, smelling sugar and aniseed. "I don't remember buying this."

"A sweet-seller looked at me too long, so I relieved him of his goods."

The meaning behind her words took a moment to land, and then he groaned. "This is going to end with us in prison, isn't it?"

"You wanted to leave Cairo. No better motivation than being chased."

A cough drew his attention. Yaqub was making his way down the bank, his arms wrapped around an enormous basket.

"Healing herbs," he explained, wheezing. "Some tonics, gauze, and a good supply of anything you might need should either of you fall sick or get injured."

"That wasn't necessary," Nahri protested. "You've already done enough."

"Let someone help you, for the love of God, child," the apothecarist said, shoving the basket in her arms. He eyed their boat with open concern. "Is the sail supposed to look like that?"

"Of course." Nahri passed the basket to Ali. "Haven't you heard? My friend here is an expert sailor. Ali, tell Yaqub why the sail looks like that."

Yaqub's questioning gaze slid to him. Ali fought to appear knowledgeable. "It's . . . resting."

"*Resting?*"

"Yes," he lied. "It rests and then it . . . it goes." Ali attempted to make a sailing motion with his hand.

The apothecarist turned back to Nahri. "Are you sure you don't want to stay?"

She sighed. "I'm sorry, old friend. I wish I could, but we have people relying on us back home."

We could have a life here together, a good one. Ali fumbled the knot he'd started to untie, a stab of uncertainty going through him. He wondered if Nahri had known just how tempted he'd been. How deep the vision of them, together—Nahri taking care of patients, Ali handling the books—had struck.

But Daevabad came first. His father's mantra, the duty that strangled them. Even Nahri had called it "home."

Shoving aside his doubts, Ali jumped from the boat, splashing into the ankle-high water as he crossed to join them on the riverbank.

"But God bless you, uncle," he said. "Truly. We would have been lost without your assistance."

The old man blinked brightly, the slightly vacant daze sliding across his face as it usually did when Ali drew closer. "You're very welcome, Ahmad." He shook his head as if to clear it and then slid a black bag from his shoulder. "I brought something else," he added, handing the bag to Nahri.

Nahri had no sooner peeked inside the bag than she tried to give it back. "I can't take these instruments, Yaqub! They belong to your family."

Yaqub held up his hands. "I'd rather they be with someone who can put them to use." He smiled at her. "Nahri, child, I don't know where you came from. I don't know where you're going. But I saw what you did for that boy. You're a healer by any name."

Ali watched Nahri bite her lower lip, looking like she wanted to object. But then she threw her arms around Yaqub in a tight hug. "God be with you, my friend. I left something for you as well. Back in the shop. In the box where you keep sweets."

Yaqub looked puzzled. "What?"

Nahri wiped her eyes. "A token of my affection." She pushed him away. "Now go. Don't be wasting a business day on me."

"Take care of yourself," Yaqub called after her. Ali didn't miss the sorrow in his voice. "*Please.*"

We could have a life here together, a good one. Ali swallowed the lump in his throat as Nahri brushed past him. "What did you leave him?"

Nahri shoved Muntadhir's khanjar into his hands. They'd used several of the gemstones to buy the boat, and now only one—a tiny ruby—remained. "He helped us, so I helped him. I don't like being in debt."

Ali ran his thumb over the hilt. "Not everything has to be a transaction, Nahri."

"It should be. It's easier." She pulled herself aboard, ignoring his hand.

Knowing how Nahri felt about the audacity of having, let alone sharing, emotions, Ali held his tongue, pushing the boat into the river as mud sucked at his feet. He climbed aboard, using a pole and then the oars to make their way deeper into the water.

"So what now?" Nahri prodded. "Because forgive me . . . but we seem to be going in the opposite direction of what you wanted."

"Would you give me a minute?" Ali closed his eyes, trying to call to the water sloshing against the boat. It resisted, shying away from the edge of his magic.

Annoyed, he leaned over the side and slipped his hand beneath the surface, letting the current stream through his fingers. He could almost taste it, the scent of brine and mud on his tongue. *Come on,* he urged, envisioning the river pushing against the boat.

"Your expression is not bolstering my confidence."

Ali scowled. "I know what I'm doing."

"Of course you do. You have an intimate understanding of the *resting* habits of sails." He opened his eyes to see her idly lounging against a cushion, one of the stolen sweets already at hand. "You've really got to find a way not to look like a startled pigeon every time you lie."

"I do not look like a *startled—*"

The boat surged forward, the marid magic hungrily lapping at the annoyance in his chest.

Nahri flashed him a triumphant, lovely grin. "Someone once told me a little emotion helps."

A lash of pain went straight through Ali's heart. He gasped, nearly losing his grip on the magic.

Nahri was instantly at his side. "What's wrong?"

Ali pressed a hand against his chest, trying to catch his breath. "I don't think the ring likes me doing marid magic."

"We're relying on marid magic to get us to Ta Ntry."

He waved her off, dodging back before she could touch him. "I know. And I'm fine; the pain is already gone." It wasn't entirely, but Ali wasn't risking anything that would have Nahri insisting they stay in Cairo longer.

"If you say so." She didn't sound convinced, but at least the boat was going fast. Perhaps a little too fast, the water racing with his heart. "No, this doesn't look suspicious at all."

"We'll be using the sail as well, so it doesn't just look like we're zooming upriver with nothing powering us." Or rather, they'd be *trying* to use the sail—Ali hadn't told Nahri that the total of his sailing experience was a couple of weeks with the Royal Guard and a few hours spying on Nile boatmen.

He was, however, not unaware of her watching him struggle. Finally, after driving them into sandbanks twice, Ali was able to tack the sail into the wind properly, and they started moving south even faster. Had he been alone, he might have wept with gratitude. Instead, out of breath, his body aching in all sorts of new ways, he let himself collapse, lying prone on the flat deck.

"Things seem to be going well," Nahri said drily.

"I think," Ali panted, kneading his chest as his heart sparked in pain. "I may have underestimated how difficult this would be."

"I'm glad you're learning that lesson early in our quest." A cup pressed against his lips. "Drink."

Still dizzy, Ali obeyed, pushing himself up to sit beside her. Now that it was settled and packed with supplies, he realized just how small the boat was, and a new kind of anxiety swept through him. He hadn't thought through the logistics of spending every moment—day *and* night—at Nahri's side. Ali wasn't even sure there was enough room for them both to lie flat to sleep.

"At least eat something, doctor's orders." She opened the tin of stolen pastries and handed one to him. "Trust me, the illicitness makes them taste sweeter."

Nahri's fingers brushed his at the exact moment she said it, and though Ali knew there was no way she meant it like *that,* a bolt of nervous energy barreled through his body. "Oh," he managed. "Does it?"

Nahri winked and sat back to open Yaqub's bag. She sighed in open pleasure and then began laying out the medical instruments like they were prized jewels.

Spotting the trephine drill and still feeling queasy, Ali looked away as he ate, gazing at the river. They continued in silence for a bit longer, and a rare peace settled over him. The sensation that he had a vise in his chest aside, this was a pleasant way to travel. The gentle rocking of the boat, the spread of the glistening water, and the warm breeze . . . it was almost hypnotic. He finished his pastry—and Nahri was right, it was pretty good—and then bent low, trailing a hand through the river again.

Ease swept over him so fast Ali exhaled aloud, the pain in his heart lessening as if a cool compress had been laid upon it. Water rippled up his wrist, tracing the path of his scars, as his reflection came to him in shimmering undulations. It was probably a trick of the light, but his eyes looked strange, not his usual warm gray, but rather deep, fathomless pools of obsidian even darker than Nahri's.

It would feel so good to swim. The prospect of submerging, of the world going quiet and still as the Nile closed over his head, suddenly felt irresistible. Tendrils of water wrapped around his arm, gripping tight, and mildly—as though half awake—Ali realized he had not summoned them.

"I think that's where we woke up."

Ali started, pulled from his daze. The water fled from his fingers. "What?"

Nahri pointed. On the distant shore, a cracked minaret stood among tangled greenery, the crumbling remains of what might have been a small village becoming clearer as they drew near. "Do you remember anything of it?" she asked.

"Not really."

Nahri's gaze was locked on the village. "Can we get closer?"

Ali nodded, moving to adjust the rudder and steering them toward the flooded shore. "Do you think this was it?"

"Yes." She shivered. "It's strange, but the place felt so familiar. The path to the river, the lay of some of the ruins . . ."

"And this is the village you've been having nightmares about?"

"I think so, not that I can recall anything when I wake up." She let out a frustrated sound, putting down the scalpel she'd been admiring. "It's like something won't *let* me remember, like the dream is yanked away the moment I open my eyes."

"Like how you also don't remember anything of your childhood before Cairo?"

Nahri looked uncertain. "A bit like that, yes."

"This village isn't far from the city, and there were scorch marks inside the minaret. Do you think—"

"That I was there when it was destroyed?" Nahri was trembling. "Maybe. I don't know. I don't think I want to know."

"It could be important."

"Ali, it's only been two weeks since I watched my mother's poison tear through the palace. I'm not ready to uncover some new horror from my childhood. Not yet."

He swallowed back his questions. "All right." He turned around, adjusting the rudder again.

"But I did see a shedu."

Ali jolted the rudder, nearly steering them off course. "You saw a *what*?"

"A shedu. Just before you passed out. There was a sandstorm, and then this creature . . . It looked at me, looked . . . *through* me like it was unimpressed, and then vanished. It all happened so fast that I'm not sure I wasn't hallucinating."

Ali wasn't sure what to say. "I didn't think the shedu still existed. Honestly, I thought they might have just been a legend in the first place."

"That's what I used to think about djinn."

It's what I used to think about marid. Ali wasn't sure he was ready to see any more legends come to life, at least not without being better prepared. "I hope the library at Shefala is as grand as my mother always claimed. I suspect you and I have a lot to read up on."

"I'm surprised you don't know for certain. I'd think you'd be begging your mother for tales of some massive library."

Regret peppered him. "I wasn't always open to tales of Ta Ntry as a child," Ali confessed. "Once I was sent to the Citadel, I found I fit in better with the other Geziris if I ignored my Ayaanle side. It also made things easier with my father." He ran his hands over his knees. "Not that it matters. He died thinking me a traitor anyway."

"You did the right thing." Nahri's voice was unexpectedly fierce. "Your father needed to be stopped."

"I know." And he did—his father's last act would have slaughtered hundreds of innocent shafit if Ali hadn't taken the Citadel. But that didn't erase his sorrow. There would be no explanations, no apologies, no chance to make things right. Ghassan was dead, and he'd left Daevabad in no less a brutal fashion than he had ruled it. All Ali could do now was pray the Almighty had more mercy on his father than Ghassan had shown his subjects. At least with Muntadhir, he had the slight solace of knowing his brother died a hero, of having a moment to say good-bye.

We're okay, akhi. We're okay. Ali steeled himself for the grief, for the clawed beast that erupted from his chest when he thought of

Muntadhir, but it didn't feel as vicious as it usually did. Ali was no longer uselessly wringing his hands in Cairo; he'd taken a small step on his path to avenge his brother and save their people, and even his broken heart seemed to recognize it.

He turned back around. Nahri was no longer looking at him; instead she was leaning against a cushion, her attention focused on cleaning and admiring her new medical tools, a far happier expression on her face. She'd removed her scarf, and her hair fell to her waist in a thick halo of black curls.

The sight stole his breath. Forget the royal finery she'd worn as Daevabad's next queen. Sailing down the Nile in a dull second-hand dress with the Egyptian sun shining on her face, deadly medical tools in her hands, Nahri was radiant. What Ali would do to sink his fingers into her hair, to pull her close . . .

Shame on you. She makes herself comfortable and you betray her trust by ogling her? Ali dropped his gaze, heat creeping up his neck. His friend—his brother's widow, no less—and here he was, fantasizing about her.

A bead of water blossomed on his forehead as if to mock his control. Ali could lower his gaze all he liked—he had plenty of experience doing that.

But he had absolutely no experience doing battle with the barbed, bladed, and wildly irresponsible notions in his heart that seemed to be gaining strength with each additional day he spent in Nahri's company. Ali had never felt this way about someone before—he wasn't even sure *what* he felt. This . . . this *tangle* of tenderness and longing, of sheer terror and unexpected light, the certainty that he could have blissfully spent the rest of his life with her hand brushing his wrist as they perused books and argued about food in a Cairo ruin, the sensation like he'd been shoved off a cliff each time she grinned . . . Ali didn't know how to fight that.

He didn't know if he wanted to.

You are becoming the lovesick fool you always denied being. And Ali didn't have time for that. They had a very long journey on a *very* small boat to navigate—and then a war to fight.

"Is the pastry not agreeing with you?"

Ali jumped back to attention. "What?"

"You look like you're about to throw up." Nahri frowned, setting aside the instruments. "I knew you shouldn't be using all this weird water magic. Let me examine you."

Yes! Part of him cheered, thrilled at the prospect of her hands on his body. "No," Ali said just as swiftly, cursing the entire concept of love. "I was just thinking . . . you wanted to know about the marid," he blurted out. "About all the secrets I was keeping from you."

Surprised pleasure lit Nahri's expression. "I assumed I'd have to pry them from you."

Oh, God, even for Ali this was a new low in putting his foot in his mouth. "I agreed there would be no more secrets," he said faintly.

"Well, then." Nahri straightened, packing up the instruments and turning to face him with a feline grace. Like a lion might calmly assess a trapped antelope. "Let's get started with '*the marid didn't do anything to me, Nahri,*'" she said, doing a poor impersonation of his voice. "'I just conjure waterfalls in the library and send boats shooting up the Nile for no reason.'"

Right to it. Ali tried to refocus. "The marid did something to me."

"Yes, I think that's been established. What did they do to you?"

"I'm honestly not certain," he admitted. "But what I do know is that after they possessed me on the lake, it was as if I had the same affinity with water as I do with fire. I could sense it, summon it, control it. In Am Gezira, it was a blessing: I was able to find springs and cisterns, to draw them up through the sand

and turn Bir Nabat green. But when I returned to Daevabad . . ." Ali shivered. "The magic was too much. It was getting stronger, harder to conceal and control. I was hearing voices in my head, seeing things in my dreams—I was terrified that I was going to get caught."

"Caught?"

"You know what people say about the marid. They're demons, tricksters. My mother says they lure djinn in Ta Ntry to the water to drown them and drain their blood. Issa was ready to throw me before the ulema and denounce me as a heretic just for asking questions."

"People are often afraid of what they don't understand." Fortunately, Nahri looked neither repulsed nor afraid—merely thoughtful, as though she was puzzling all this out. "Did the marid who possessed you *say* anything? Explain why they were giving you such power?"

Ali thought back to that awful night. To the way the marid had seized upon everything—every*one*—precious in Ali's memories and then tortured him, making him watch the most brutal of deaths. The way it had grabbed him with tentacles and teeth and shaken him like a dog to drag him from death's embrace.

His mouth went dry. Ironic. "No," he whispered, realizing it for the first time. "I don't think they meant to give me these powers. Quite frankly, I don't think they gave much thought at all to me. I think they saw a tool they could use to suit their purposes and changed me into what they needed." Hatset's stories of the demons who stalked Ntaran waterways and Ghassan's recollection of the effort it took to recover Ali after the possession came back to him. "And I don't know that I was meant to survive it."

Silence fell between them, and when Nahri finally spoke again, her voice was uncharacteristically subdued. "I'm sorry, Ali. I know a lot happened between us that night, a lot I'm still angry about. But I also know you wouldn't have gone into the water if it weren't for him." She didn't have to say Darayavahoush's name—the two of them danced around the topic of the Afshin like he was a pot of Rumi fire. "And for that I'm sorry."

"You don't have to be," he muttered. "I don't think either of us wanted things to go the way they did."

She met his gaze again, and Ali felt something soften between them, a jumble of unspoken resentments and shattered hopes. They'd both had their lives ruined and shoved off course. But they were still here.

It was unfortunate, then, that Ali had far worse secrets to reveal. "I did learn something after the possession," he continued. "Something I think you should know that might help us piece together the marid's role in all this."

"What?"

By the Most High, how should he say this? Ali adjusted the rudder, fighting for time. The secret he'd kept from his mother, the one that risked undermining his people's own understanding of their history and his family's reign.

But there was no moving forward without addressing what had gone so terribly wrong in the past.

"When I first woke up after the marid possessed me, I was with my father." Ali's heart twisted with the memory, for it had been one of the few times in his life Ghassan had been a father first, fiercely protective and unusually gentle as he assured Ali that everything would be okay. "He was the one to suggest that the marid had possessed me. I didn't believe him. I said the marid were gone, that they hadn't been seen for thousands of years. He told me that I was wrong. That the marid *had* been seen—they'd been seen at the side of Zaydi al Qahtani's Ayaanle ally during the invasion of Daevabad."

Nahri blinked. "Zaydi al Qahtani worked with the *marid*? Are you sure? Because I've never heard of anything like that, and let me tell you, you have no idea how much Daeva history I've had crammed down my throat in the past few years."

Ali forgot sometimes that for all Nahri's cleverness, she was still fairly new to their world. "It wouldn't be in any Daeva history books, Nahri. No matter how much our tribes bicker and war, we're supposed to be fire-bloods first. To betray that, to use the marid against each other, that would be a scandal. One my ancestors wouldn't risk. Zaydi al Qahtani broke the order that had ruled our world for centuries. It would have to look as . . . clean, as noble as possible."

Nahri stared at him, some of the friendliness going out of her eyes. "Ah."

And just like that, he felt the old divide between them, between their families and their peoples, rise up.

"I'm sorry," he said. "I—"

"Stop." Nahri didn't sound angry, merely tired. "Just stop. If you and I have to apologize for everything our families did to each other, we'll never get off this boat. And you might have forgotten, but believe me when I say that I know how the old Nahid Council felt about shafit. How many Daevas still feel."

Another topic they'd been avoiding. "Is it true what your mother said, then?" Ali ventured. "About you being shafit?"

Her eyes narrowed. "Yes. But we're not talking about my secrets today. So the marid helped Zaydi overthrow the Nahid Council. Did your father say anything else?"

"Not much. He said until that night he thought it was just a legend to explain the warning Qahtani kings passed to their emirs."

"What warning?"

"Don't cross the Ayaanle."

"*That's* the warning? I thought your tribes were allies!"

"We are . . . sometimes," Ali said, thinking back to the various coups, religious revolutions, and tax delays his relatives in Ta Ntry had instigated. "But it wasn't meant as a threat. Zaydi's Ayaanle ally apparently paid a terrible price for his connection to the marid. We were never to betray their people."

"What price?"

"I don't know. My mother caught me out about the marid when I first returned to Daevabad and convinced Ustadh Issa to help us try and learn more. But neither of them seemed to know anything about the marid being involved in the war, and I wasn't inclined to tell them. Instead, Issa was looking into an old family connection my mother believed we had with the marid."

Nahri nodded slowly. "That's right, people say the Ayaanle worshipped the marid centuries ago, don't they?"

"A lie," Ali replied, trying to keep the defensiveness from his voice. "Issa told me that the marid used to trick people into making ghastly pacts, convincing them to kill innocents for riches and give up their life's blood. I wouldn't call that worship."

"Sounds like just the kind of creatures you should take as military allies." Nahri leaned back on her cushion again. "But what I don't understand is *why*. Why are a bunch of overpowered water demons so determined to come after us? To trick people in Ta Ntry and overthrow the Nahid Council? To kill Dara?"

"If I had to guess, I don't think they were as eager to hand over their sacred lake and serve Anahid as Daeva legend would suggest."

"And revenge was handing their sacred lake over to a *different* group of fire-bloods?" Nahri groaned, pinching the bridge of her nose. "Creator, every time I think I've found the bottom in all of this, I get some new story of murder and vengeance." She sighed, pushing back the midnight locks that had fallen in her face. "Any more gruesome family secrets?"

She'd asked it mockingly—as if Nahri didn't think Ali had anything else equally ghastly—and he'd been so busy trying to *not* follow the movement of her fingers through her hair that the question threw him. "No. I mean, yes. There's . . . well, there's a crypt beneath the palace."

"A crypt?"

"Yes."

Nahri stared at him. *"Who's in the crypt, Ali?"*

"Your relatives," he confessed softly. "All the Nahids who've died since the war."

Genuine shock swept her face. "That's not possible. We keep their ashes in our shrines."

"I don't know whose ashes are in your shrines, but I've seen the bodies myself."

"Why? Why has your family been hoarding the bodies of my ancestors in some crypt beneath the palace?"

"I don't know. I got the impression no one does anymore. The crypt looks ancient, and there are all sorts of wild stories about the earliest Nahids. Legends claiming they could resurrect the dead, trade bodies. Maybe . . ." Heat crept up his neck in shame. "Maybe it made my relatives rest easier."

Nahri glared at him. "Oh, how reassuring for them."

Ali dropped his gaze. This conversation was about to get so much worse. "Nahri, that's not all that's in the crypt. I don't know how, I don't know why, but Darayavahoush's relic is also down there."

She sat up so fast that she rocked the boat. "Excuse me?"

"His relic," Ali repeated, feeling sick. "What we think is his relic. And if it's truly his, it's probably the one he was wearing when he was killed during the war."

"When he was enslaved by the ifrit, you mean," she corrected coldly. "Does that mean it was the Qahtanis who gave him up?"

Ali looked at her beseechingly. "I don't know. This was centuries before you and I were born. My father didn't know. My grandfather likely didn't know. I'm not excusing it, I'm not justifying it, but I can't offer explanations I don't have."

Nahri dropped back down, still looking enraged. "Do you know how long he was a slave? Do you know how *Manizheh* is going to react if she learns her brother and parents are rotting beneath the palace?"

Ali tried to offer some hope. "The crypt is well hidden. Maybe they won't find it?"

"'Well hidden.'" She let out an exasperated sound. "Ali, what if this is beyond us?"

"What do you mean?"

"I mean Dara and Zaydi al Qahtani were seasoned military commanders. Manizheh is considered the most powerful Nahid healer in centuries. My ancestors, your father, they ruled tens of thousands and ran governments. And they *still* failed to fix all of this. Everything they did only caused more violence. If they couldn't make peace, how in God's name are you and I going to?"

Ali wished he had an answer for her. "I don't know, Nahri. I don't think there's going to be a simple fix. It might be a lifetime of work. It might be a peace we don't live long enough to see."

"That's your inspirational rallying speech?" Her expression grew darker when he had no response. "Then do me a favor."

"What?"

"Learn how to lie by the time we get to Ta Ntry."

13

DARA

Dara's promise to Manizheh about Irtemiz did not last a day.

He examined the weapons in his chest, selecting knives and a sword and securing them to his waist. His bow and quiver went next. Dara could always conjure arms, but considering he was jumping directly into a trap designed to kill him, he figured he might as well take the extra precaution.

Yes, you would not want Manizheh to be denied the chance to murder you herself when she learns you disobeyed her direct order.

But he wasn't leaving Irtemiz with his enemies. Not Irtemiz, the spirited country girl he'd shaped into a talented archer, the one who reminded him of the little sister he hadn't been able to save. And Dara had a trick up his sleeve not even Manizheh, let alone some wretched sand flies and dirt-bloods, knew.

The old daeva wind magic.

Dara hadn't used it since the night before Navasatem, when he'd become formless to fly over the icy mountains and cold lakes of northern Daevastana. For one, he hadn't had a spare moment since they took the palace—revolution, it turned out, was time-consuming. But more than that, Dara didn't trust himself with the temptation. The wind magic had been intoxicating, offering a thrilling escape from all this madness, one that tugged nearly as hard on his heart as did his duty to his people.

Now, however, he would use it to achieve both.

It took a few moments to recall how to summon the magic, and then he was gone, his body vanishing from the balcony of his small room in a swirl of dead leaves. In another moment, the city was below him, around him, part of him.

And had he lungs, Dara would have choked on the miasma of rot that clung to the island. Everything was dulled, as if he'd submerged in a murky pool. It was nothing like his previous experience in which he could taste a buzz on the air, molten energy in the warm earth, and life in the inviting, mysterious waters.

He floated farther, Daevabad dark and unmoving below him. Though Dara remembered its nights being livelier, he supposed cities embroiled in civil strife shut down the moment the shadows grew deeper, if people dared creep about at all. Beyond, he spotted the gleaming desert past the threshold, bright with starlight and life.

Daevabad is sick, he realized, dread sinking deeper into his soul. The island and its lake stood out like a festering wound on the world, as though a vital piece had been stolen away. The loss of Suleiman's seal—it had to be.

By the Creator, Nahri, please be alive. Please bring it back. Dara couldn't imagine any way Nahri and the current holder of Suleiman's seal could return to Daevabad that didn't end with one of them dead, but the true toll of all this was suddenly so clear. They'd broken their world, and now their home—the home of tens of thousands—was dying.

Awful as that thought was, Dara could do nothing to save

Daevabad tonight. But he could save the life of someone who'd trusted him.

Fixing the hospital in his mind, Dara found himself there in the next moment, spinning down and landing on the roof, light as a bird. It was a disorienting experience; there was the ghost of stone beneath what might have been his feet—except glancing down, he didn't *see* his feet. Trying to pull himself back into the material world, he cloaked himself in shadows and crept to the roof's edge.

Nostalgia swept him. The hospital looked different, but the bones of the old institution were still there. In his youth, Dara had spent plenty of time in the hospital—most warriors-in-training did—and his memories returned to him, of Nahid healers in facemasks and aprons forcing foul potions down his throat and resetting snapped bones.

It was quiet now, the breeze rustling the trees in the courtyard the only sound. An arcaded corridor surrounded the garden, and in the eastern corner, he noticed the flicker of firelight beyond the pale bricks.

This is a trap. It had been there in every goading, mocking line of that Geziri woman's speech. The djinn wanted him dead. A smart man wouldn't take this risk—one didn't risk catastrophe for a single life, and until recently, Dara himself would have made the same cruel calculus.

But there was another part of the equation worth examining: *They have never beaten me.*

Dara had been cut down only twice—by the ifrit when he was enslaved and then by Alizayd and his marid masters, fiends who couldn't touch him now. And that was before he'd awoken with the incredible abilities of an original daeva. There was no one below but ordinary djinn soldiers and shafit servants. Trap or not, they were no match for him.

Dara vanished again, letting himself become immaterial, but

it was a struggle to hold, an ill-timed reminder that his magic and strength were finite, no matter what he wanted to believe. He slipped from the roof and then into the hospital's murky heart. He was not entirely silent—he might be invisible, but the curtains shivered when he passed, and the torches blossomed, their fire growing wild in his presence. As he went deeper, it became clear the place wasn't completely asleep. A yawning shafit servant, her arms filled with linens, passed in the corridor, and there were murmured whispers behind doors. Farther away, someone moaned in pain, and a child whimpered.

He drifted around the next corner and then stilled. Two Geziri men stood at attention beside a closed door, light playing below the doorjamb. The men weren't in uniform, and one looked barely older than a boy, but the elder wore a zulfiqar and the other a straight sword, their posture indicating training.

Dara considered his options. With corridors snaking in three different directions, he knew a single cry would carry, alerting the rest of the hospital. But he wasn't sure he could pass by like this. The djinn might not know the extent of his abilities, but wild gossip would have carried of his fiery form and the lake that had risen like a beast. They were probably on guard for the slightest hint of magic, and he didn't need the wall torches next to the guards' heads flaring and giving him away.

He studied the door, letting himself reach out. The wooden particles were old and dry, insubstantial, really. Beyond, he could sense a vacuum of air, a single hot presence and beating heart. Acting on instinct, Dara willed himself inside.

He stumbled, falling to his knees as he abruptly rematerialized—thankfully *inside* the dark room. He was out of breath and exhausted, his magic nearly spent, but he had just enough to pull his mortal form over his body, masking his fiery skin. By the Creator, maybe he should have taken to interrogating the ifrit more often about their ancient abilities. From the stories they'd shared, it seemed they'd been able to stay formless for years on end—and not end up an exhausted mess once they returned to the earth.

A problem for another time.

Staying as still as possible, Dara checked to make sure his weapons had come through and then straightened up.

He breathed a sigh of relief. Irtemiz.

The young archer was asleep on a straw mat, her breath rising and falling in the beams of moonlight that streamed in from a barred window near the ceiling. A skin of water rested at her side, and if she was disheveled—her black hair knotted and wild, her clothes threadbare—she'd at least been treated for her injuries. Her left arm and leg rested in splints, her body mottled with old bruises. Her right ankle was shackled, an iron chain leading to a pipe that ran vertically through the room.

Dara's heart sank. The shackle he could deal with. How to silently escape a guarded room with a badly injured woman was another story.

He carefully crept forward, lowering himself to her ear. "Irtemiz," he whispered.

Her eyes shot open, but she was too well trained to shout. Her gaze darted to his.

There was no relief. "You shouldn't be here, Afshin," she said, her voice barely audible. "They're expecting you. They mean to kill you."

"A lot of people have already failed at that," he said, trying for a reassuring smile. He nodded at her leg. "Can you walk?"

Despair grew in her face. "No. I can't even put weight on it. A wave smashed me into the remains of the Citadel. Their doctor says it's shattered." Her voice trembled. "My arm too. I'll probably never hold a bow again. I'm useless, but you're not. You need to get out of here."

"You're not useless," Dara said fiercely. "And I don't intend to leave you, so you might as well help me." He gestured to the room. "Are there any other ways out of here?"

"I don't know. They blindfold me whenever I'm moved and only speak in human languages. They had a Daeva man, a patient, here to translate, but I haven't seen him in days."

Dara took all that in, considering his options. He'd planned on flying out, but there were two of them now, and his magic was still recovering. Could he really burst through these doors, navigate back through the maze of corridors, and take to the air without getting them killed?

He glanced again at the window. It was small . . . but perhaps not too small. Quietly pulling over a wooden stool, he climbed up to examine it. The bars were metal and new, their welding still gleaming. The construction looked flimsy—maybe the bars would keep Irtemiz in, but not Dara. Beyond the window, the midnight sky beckoned. It would be a tight fit, but it was better than going through the door.

Dara climbed back down. "I'm going to need to change to my other form," he warned. "I'll help you through the window, but it might hurt."

She still looked uncertain but gave a shaky nod.

He released his mortal guise, fire sweeping over his limbs. The relief was immediate. Not all his magic returned right away, but Dara could already breathe more easily. With a flick of his hand, Irtemiz's mat floated up from the ground.

"Wait one moment." He climbed back up on the stool and then grabbed the bars with his scorching hands. He popped the entire metal frame out of the window with little effort and then looked for a spot to set it down.

Weak-blooded fools. Had their builders proper magic, they would have had stone mages shape the window bars out of the bricks itself and had blacksmiths temper them with fiery hands. Kaveh had called the hospital a vanity project with shafit labor; small wonder they had resorted to inferior human techniques.

Movement drew Dara's eye. A skinny length of cord that must have been held in place by the frame jerked swiftly out of sight. Odd.

He'd only just stepped back when there was an explosion outside the window.

Dara stumbled, shielding his eyes against the sudden flare of light, the stool tilting and falling with his movement, depositing him ungracefully on the ground. There was the acrid aroma of gunpowder.

Ah. The trap.

Another blast and a metal ball the size of his fist shot through the window he'd been hoping to fly through, smashing into the opposite wall and raining dust over his head. Irtemiz yelped, ducking beneath her uninjured arm.

The door to the room burst open. The two Geziri guards stood there, outlined in the blazing light of the corridor's torches.

Dara felt a moment of sorrow looking into their doomed faces. He'd been a soldier and knew the feeling of being thrust into a battle you had no choice in fighting.

They'd taken his warrior, though, and made a snare of her. So his sorrow was short-lived.

He lunged forward, drawing his knives before the men could take a breath. They were dead in the next moment, falling to the ground while clutching the throats he'd opened. It didn't matter—shouts and the sound of pounding feet were already drawing nearer.

A second shot came through the window, ending any hopes of escaping that way. Dara spun back on Irtemiz, tossing her a knife.

"Run," she begged him. "Leave me, please."

"Not happening, little one. Hold tight." With a knife in one hand and his ax in the other, he charged out the door, beckoning for her mat to float after him.

A volley of arrows and bolts greeted his emergence, but Dara had been expecting the attack and froze them in the air.

Over a dozen warriors blocked them in, arrayed across the three corridors. The majority were Geziris, some still wearing tattered uniforms from the Royal Guard.

"It's an ifrit!" one of the soldiers cried, aiming a crossbow.

An older man snarled. A nasty gash split his face, a wound Dara suspected would never heal. "That's not an ifrit," the man said. "It's the bloody Scourge. He takes the demon's form now."

Dara stared at them, almost pleading. He didn't want to kill more men. Creator, he wanted to stop being the Scourge that destroyed lives, the cursed enemy in the hearts of more children of murdered fathers. "Let us leave. I do not wish to kill you."

"You had no problem butchering our brothers in the Citadel."

"You cannot defeat me," Dara said plainly. "You will all die, and it will be for nothing."

The man lifted his zulfiqar, the copper blade looking diminished without its flames. "No one is letting you leave, and you might find we've our own tricks now."

Dara's heart sank. Resolve was growing in their faces, as the shock of confronting a monster from legend became the urge to revenge themselves on the very real man who'd murdered so many of their friends.

"So be it," Dara said quietly. He snapped his fingers.

Their arrows and bolts—still hanging in the air—hurtled back at them.

The majority were prepared, raising shields or ducking, but a handful fell. Dara didn't wait, hurling himself on the rest and cutting through their line with ease. They were simply not as fast, not as strong. They were good, well trained, and brave.

But they weren't him, and so he slaughtered them.

He returned to Irtemiz, stepping past the steaming corpses. He could already hear more men coming. "Let's go," he said, hopping on the front edge of the floating mat like he might have on a horse cart. "Hold on to my belt. I'm going to need my hands free."

The mat shot forward on the air. They zoomed through the corridor, dipping and diving around corners and over the heads of more warriors. Too busy trying to fly and steer, Dara didn't have enough strength to freeze the arrows that zipped by, so he drew his bow, shooting anyone and anything that moved.

Finally, a square of trees and dark night: the courtyard open to the sky. Dara urged the mat faster, cutting through the air.

They had no sooner escaped the cramped corridor than he heard a shout and the scrape of metal.

Acting on instinct, Dara threw himself over Irtemiz, provoking a pained gasp from his wounded friend. A moment later, a heavy net landed on them both, and it was his turn to scream. Fitted with iron studs—broken nails, barbed clippings, and scavenged razors—the burning metal pierced his skin, the fire flickering out where it touched.

They crashed to the ground, and Irtemiz groaned, crying out as her broken body took the jolt. Dara tried to free himself, but the motion only pushed the iron studs deeper into his body.

An arrow tore past his shoulder, another barely missing Irtemiz's head. There was a blast of a rifle and an explosion as its projectile shattered the tile near his foot.

Trapped. The real trap. And now he was about to have warriors shooting at him with everything they had, desperate to take him out before he could murder them all.

Dara met Irtemiz's frightened eyes. He'd failed her and her fellows before, sending them alone into battle during an invasion he knew was rushed.

He wouldn't fail her again. He threw himself off Irtemiz, rolling away, the net tangling his limbs as more barbs pierced his skin. Dara reached for his magic, commanding the mat beneath her to rise. *The palace. Manizheh.*

"Afshin, no!" Irtemiz cried, but she was already gone, the mat soaring up and away.

Dara got no reprieve, nor did he care. Irtemiz was safe.

Which was good—because everyone else here was going to die.

Dara ripped the net away with his bare hands, the links melting and snapping. He bellowed in pain—Creator, it hurt, tearing out flesh and blood—but there was relief the moment the net was gone. His bow flew to his hand, and then he was firing arrows faster than an eye would have been able to track, the motion between plucking and drawing and releasing a blur of muscle memory.

That took care of the fools shooting from an upper story—the man holding the rifle first and foremost—but then their fellows charged him, wielding maces, zulfiqars, and lengths of pipe. There were shafit among them, which seemed fitting. The kin and people of all his victims, come to finally try and cut him down.

But no one was cutting Dara down. He shoved his sword through the throat of the nearest sand fly, ripping it out to decapitate the dirt-blood next to him.

"*COME!*" he roared. Any inklings he'd had of mercy were gone. The Geziris and shafit thought to kill him *here*—here at this hospital where so many of their forebearers had slaughtered his Nahids and kicked off the violent sack of his city that had ended with the deaths of his mother and little sister?

Dara would bathe it in their blood.

He tore through them, crimson and black gore coating his hands, his wrists, his face. He was a weapon again and he acted accordingly, not hearing their screams, their gurgles, their dying cries for their mothers. It was a relief, who he was meant to be.

"Aqisa, no!"

The female voice caught him off guard, jerking him from his bloodlust, and then a warrior did—Aqisa, the Geziri woman who'd delivered Zaynab al Qahtani's threat. She swung her zulfiqar at his neck in a motion that would have left a slower man headless, but Dara ducked back in time. He forced her against the fountain, raising his sword.

"Stop!" Another woman rushed out from beneath the shadowed arcade. She was armed as well, but it wasn't her blade that caught Dara's attention.

It was her gray-gold eyes and the instantly familiar set of her face.

The princess. Between her eyes and the striking resemblance to Alizayd, she had to be. Manizheh's enemy, the key his Banu Nahida needed to force the Ayaanle and Geziris to back down.

Dara didn't hesitate. "Do not move!" he boomed to the soldiers as he lunged for the princess, seizing her arm. "Drop your weapons, or—"

A fierce thrust punched through his shoulder, stealing his next words. There was the sharp smell of gunpowder and iron.

Then a white-hot blast of the worst pain he'd ever felt, in all his lives, exploded through his body.

Dara cried out, his sword dipping as he stumbled. Aqisa pulled Zaynab from his grip as he tried to recover, but it was as if someone had shoved poison into a gaping wound and set the entire thing ablaze. Spots blossomed across his eyes and Dara bit his tongue so hard he tasted blood.

Gunpowder. He could smell it, the iron scorching his flesh. They'd *shot* him. Some filthy dirt-blood had actually *shot* him with one of their wretched human weapons.

And by the Creator, were they going to pay. A burst of magic and his sword split into a dozen barbed strands, the handle transforming in his hand.

His scourge. Dara drew it back and whirled around. He would shred the man who had dared . . .

He froze. It wasn't a man. It was a woman, standing not five paces away, the smoking pistol still in her hands.

She was shafit, brown visible in her tin-toned eyes, her skin a human matte in the darkness. She was breathing hard and was dressed in a bloodstained smock, small metal weapons poking out of the pockets. No, not weapons. A scalpel and small hammer, a roll of bandage cloth.

The shafit doctor Aqisa had mentioned.

The princess gasped. "Subha, run!"

But the doctor didn't run. Instead, she stood tall, glaring at Dara with all the hate someone like her was right to hold. Creator, how he must look, wild and gruesome, his infamous scourge in one fiery hand.

He should have struck her down. He'd just killed dozens. What was another life—particularly when it belonged to a woman holding one of the few weapons that could kill him?

A shafit woman and the metallic smell of human blood. Somewhere a baby cried, but Dara did not move, the hospital suddenly feeling very far away in the fog of pain racking his body. It wasn't the raging courtyard battle he saw, but a plaza in a bustling merchant city, lanterns hanging from pretty, tiled buildings and stalls packed with bolts of silk in all the colors of the world. They'd burned so fast, so violently, snapping and cracking in the heat, delicate embers floating in the air.

The doctor raised the pistol, leveling it at his head. Wouldn't this be justice? The Scourge of Qui-zi killed by some shafit civilian, taken down with a weapon from the human world. He thought of just closing his eyes, giving in.

But Dara didn't close his eyes.

Instead, he dropped his scourge and ran.

Surprised shouts followed as he threw himself into the maze

of corridors leading off from the courtyard. Dara took the turns at random, but he was in so much pain, he was staggering more than sprinting. Black spots exploded before his vision, blood in his mouth. All that compelled him forward was the wild desire to escape, to live.

He could hear them hunting him. There were a few cries of triumph, but not many. The warriors after him now were professionals, and the tide had turned. A good story this would make for the djinn and shafit, the cruel Darayavahoush chased down like a wounded animal. The torture probably wouldn't be long—they wouldn't risk the opportunity to put him down for good—but it would be vicious. They'd probably hack him apart and put his head on a spike, a present for Manizheh when their forces broke into the Daeva Quarter.

Not like this. Creator, please . . . not like this.

The fire was steadily leaving his skin and with it the embrace of magic. The icy pain of the iron projectile in his shoulder pulsed harder with each breath, leaving him weak and rasping for air. Dara tripped, falling to his knees.

He blinked, dazed to find himself in a narrow hall, pitch-black save for the soft glow still emanating from his skin. The ghostly light danced upon wall paintings of sandships and seabirds, a narrow pocket of beauty and silence in the last moments before his horrific end.

And then Dara spotted his ring, the emerald gleaming in the darkness.

Everything went very still. The last time he'd been separated from his ring, he'd died. His body had turned to ash, his soul fleeing to the garden of shade and cypresses where his sister waited. Maybe he could go there again.

You will not go back to Tamima. Not this time. If there is any justice in this world, you will suffer for a thousand more years.

The ring seemed to brighten slightly, the halo of light spread-

ing. And there before him, a miracle he didn't deserve . . . a
door.

Weeping with pain, with loss, Dara forced himself back to
his feet, leaning heavily against the wall. He could still hear the
approaching mob, but maybe there would be a window, another
way out.

Maybe this was not the night he died yet again. Dara eased the
door open and slipped inside. The room was small and messy,
covered with lengths of canvas, pots of paint, brushes, and half-
completed portraits.

And a single Sahrayn woman with brilliant green eyes.

The breath went out of him. The woman had wedged herself
into a corner and was holding some sort of paint-covered metal
prod in her shaking hands. She stared in shock at him, her emerald eyes wide and startled. They were as green as his—the first
time in his life he'd come face-to-face with another victim of ifrit
slavery.

"Down here!" Shouts in Djinnistani and Geziriyya beyond
the closed door, his pursuers catching up when there was nowhere else to run. Dara was caught.

But in the blink of an eye, the woman dashed to his side. She
grabbed him by his collar and yanked him forward, surprisingly
strong for her size. Stunned by the resulting burst of pain, Dara
let himself be dragged toward a large ebony chest set against the
wall.

She threw open the top and pointed.

Any other time, he might have hesitated. But about to pass out
and with running footsteps closing in, Dara fell into the chest.
She shut it, throwing him into darkness.

The smells of linseed oil and chalk were so thick he struggled
not to cough. Paintbrushes were poking into him, his injured
shoulder throbbing, but a small crack in the wood let in a fraction of light. Dara pressed an eye to it, glimpsing the Sahrayn

woman covering a patch of blood on the floor with an old rug. He shifted, trying to get a better look as the footsteps stopped outside the door.

The movement cost him. A wave of fresh pain stabbed through his shoulder, and Dara's vision blurred. He fell back against the chest's interior.

There was an impatient knock, followed by the sound of the door scraping open. A man barking in Djinnistani, the words weaving in and out. *Scourge. Escaped. Elashia.* The Sahrayn woman didn't seem to be saying anything.

And then Aqisa's rough voice. "She's shaking her head. That means she knows nothing, so you can stop badgering her."

There was a protest and then the rather distinct thud of something—someone—being shoved into a wall.

"—and I said let her be," Aqisa snapped. "Let's move on. He's probably hiding down the other way."

Darkness was shutting in, hot blood running down his arm. Wetness on his cheeks that could have been tears or more blood.

Dara closed his eyes and let the blackness take him.

THE CHEST ABRUPTLY OPENED, PULLING DARA FROM unconsciousness. Two faces swam before him, both with emerald eyes. One belonged to his Sahrayn savior and the other to an older Tukharistani woman.

Half dead, insensible with pain, and sitting in a pool of his own blood mixed with paint cleaner, all Dara could think to do was croak a greeting. "May the fires burn brightly for you."

The Tukharistani woman groaned. "This was not the sort of surprise I was hoping you had for me in your studio."

The woman named Elashia gave her an imploring look, gesturing between the three of them.

"He's *not* one of us," the Tukharistani woman said fiercely. "Being enslaved by the ifrit is no justification for what he and

Manizheh have done." She touched Elashia's face. "My love, what were you thinking? I know you have a tender heart, but these people have allowed us to stay here in peace and protected us, and now you hide their enemy?"

Dara tried to sit up, wheezing out a plume of smoke. "I mean you no trouble. I can leave," he added, gripping the edge of the chest with his good hand.

The Tukharistani woman kicked the chest, sending a ricochet of pain through his body. Dara gasped, falling back.

"You can stay put," she warned. "I won't have you leaving a trail of blood back to us."

Blazing pinpricks of light danced before his eyes. "Yes," he agreed weakly.

She sighed. "Fire or water?"

"What?"

"Fire or water," she repeated, as if speaking to a dense child. "What revives you?"

He squeezed his eyes shut against the new throbbing in his shoulder. "Fire," he rasped. "But it does not matter. They shot me with some sort of iron projectile—"

"A bullet. Come now. I've got a millennium on you, and I keep up with the modern words."

Dara gritted his teeth. "The *bullet* is still in my shoulder. It is interfering with my magic and keeping me in this form."

The woman regarded him. "And if I removed it from your shoulder, do you think you could escape?"

Dara stared at her in shock. "You would help me?"

"That depends. Did you kill them?"

"You need to be more specific."

Her expression grew hard. "Banu Nahri and Prince Alizayd."

Dara's mouth fell open. "*No.* I would never harm Nahri. I was trying to save her."

"Then what happened?" the woman demanded. "And don't

give me this nonsense about Ali kidnapping her. That's not them."

"I do not know," Dara confessed. "They jumped in the lake with Suleiman's seal. We think they were trying to get away, but they vanished."

Anger crept into the woman's gaze. "I am very fond of that girl, Afshin. If what happened in the palace was enough to convince her that jumping in a cursed lake was safer than staying with you, I'd say you've done quite a bit of harm."

"I know." Dara's voice broke. "I know I have wronged her, but I was trying to set things right. Manizheh had a plan—"

"To rule over a city of corpses? How was killing more people going to help Nahri?"

"I serve the Nahids," he whispered. "The Daevas. I wanted them to be free."

There was a long moment of silence before she spoke again. "Baga Rustam used to whisper of freedom too. But only when he was young." She poked him, and Dara winced. "You still have your magic, and people say there are times you look like an ifrit, that you can shape smoke into living beasts. You are not like Elashia and me, are you?"

Dara shook his head. "I was before. Closer, anyway."

"And Manizheh did this to you?"

There was a knowing in her voice that sent ice racing down his spine. "Did she not free you as well?"

"Baga Rustam freed me." She met his gaze, a careful look in her eyes. "He told me once that he did not trust his sister with the freeing of slaves. She had ambitions that worried him."

"What sort of ambitions?"

She ignored the question, crossing her arms and continuing her own interrogation. "Does your bond still exist?"

"My *bond*?"

The two women exchanged a glance. "Nahids use some of

their own blood to conjure our new bodies," she explained. "It creates a bond. A strong one. You should be able to sense Manizheh's presence, to hear if she calls for you."

I have only ever heard one Nahid call for me. A song that had dragged him across the world to a human cemetery on a long-ago night. Not for the first time, Dara was struck by how very little he knew about his own existence.

"I don't know," he finally replied. "I don't know anything of this."

"Then you're not very useful, are you?" But she beckoned him forward. "Sit up. Let me see your shoulder."

Dara obeyed, grunting as a new burst of pain stabbed through his arm. "Blasted human weapons."

"Ah, yes, it must be terrible to briefly feel powerless." She tore his blood-soaked shirt at the gash, peeling it away from the wound. "They won't forget its effect on you."

With every press of her fingers, Dara was fighting not to pass out again. "I won't either."

She sat back on her heels. "The bullet isn't deep. I can get a tool to cut it out. It will be crude and painful, but you'll be able to escape, and then you can get Manizheh to properly care for you."

"Again, why would you help me?"

"Because *you're* going to help me." She rose to her feet and then shoved his head back down. "Stay."

She slammed the chest shut.

DARA FAINTED, DRIFTING IN AND OUT OF CONSCIOUSness as he slowly continued bleeding to death. That fact—and the pain—had started to bother Dara less and less as he lost feeling in the limbs jammed into the abominably small chest. He was dimly aware of the passage of time, of arguing voices.

And then the lid was flung open again. Light blinded him, the flare of a blazing candelabra and two torches.

There was yet another djinn in the room with bright emerald eyes.

"Suleiman's eye," Dara wheezed, embers falling from his lips. "How many of you are there?"

The new djinn—an elderly Ayaanle man with wild, overgrown eyebrows—reared back like Dara was a rukh.

"No," the man said, shaking badly and attempting to back away. He brandished the candelabra like a weapon, which seemed unnecessary given Dara's actively dying state. "I will not go with him, Razu. I will not!"

"*Issa.*" The Tukharistani woman—Razu—stepped into view, pulling the candelabra from his hands. "We've discussed this. You need to leave, my friend." Her voice softened. "I know how frightened you are of the ifrit, and it is tearing me apart to see you suffer. Let the Afshin send you home."

Let the Afshin do what? Dara opened his mouth, trying to object, but the only sound that emerged from his throat was a rattle. There were suddenly six freed djinn with green eyes, the original trio having sprouted twins.

No, not twins. He was seeing double. His head lolled back, his vision blurring.

Razu snapped her fingers in front of his face. "Pay attention. I have a deal for you." She gestured to Issa. "I'm going to save your life and get you back to Manizheh. In exchange, you're going to send *him* to Ta Ntry. That is your specialty, no? Flying rugs and conjured winged horses? Make him one and send him home."

Dara squeezed his eyes shut, trying to summon what remained of his strength. "I . . . cannot. Banu Manizheh does not wish news to leave."

"And I do not wish to fly one of his contraptions!" Issa protested.

Razu made a hissing noise, silencing both men. "Elashia,

help Issa pack. Make sure he takes food, not just books and explosives."

Dara heard the door open and close, the Ayaanle elder still rambling.

Razu sighed. "You're not dead yet, are you?"

He managed a slight shake of his head.

"Good." There was a moment of silence. "Banu Nahri planned out every detail of that courtyard. The tiles on the fountain, the trees overlooking the walking paths. She wanted it to be a place of healing for her patients, and you turned it into a slaughterhouse."

Dara pressed the back of his skull into the wood. "They took my warrior."

"Then why did you stop?" He opened his eyes, meeting Razu's jewel-like gaze. She continued. "If you were justified in killing them, why did you stop when Doctor Sen shot you? They say you dropped your scourge and fled like a child."

Humiliation and anger boiled in his veins, giving Dara a bit more life. "I did not wish to kill a woman."

"I am Tukharistani, Afshin. I may have lived and died before Qui-zi rose, but I know your reputation. You've killed plenty of women."

Dara didn't know how to respond to that. "I did not wish to kill more," he finally managed. "I was looking at her, and it all came back and I—I could not do it again."

"I see." Razu seemed to stare right through him. "Elashia thinks we should have a bond with you, she and Issa and I. I don't know how I feel yet about you, but I do care about Issa. His grasp on reality was shaky before the invasion, and it has vanished entirely with the knowledge that ifrit are walking the streets. He spends his days talking to himself and his nights locked in closets with weapons. He nearly impaled himself just the other morning. You are going to send him home."

"I cannot—"

Razu took Dara's chin in one hand, forcing him to look at her. "You *can*. It is what Nahri would want," she added, the words a sharp thrust to his heart. "You don't seem like an evil man, Afshin, but you have a lot of blood on your hands. Do this small kindness, mercy for a man who has suffered at the hands of the same creatures as you, and maybe a drop or two can be washed away."

Warnings were running through Dara's mind, but Creator, he was torn. These people—closer to him in many ways than his own tribe—had already suffered so much. Could he not show mercy to a harmless old man?

Razu was waiting for a response, a tense, long silence stretching on the close air. The bloody courtyard—Nahri's courtyard—came back to him, and Dara realized he had likely slain dozens of men in the same time it was taking him to contemplate granting mercy to just one.

"I will help you," he finally whispered, feeling as uncertain as a new bridegroom, as though he were embarking on an unknown and dangerous journey. "I will need you to get the bullet out of my shoulder first, but then I will help you, I swear."

Pleasure creased Razu's face. "Good." She rose to her feet.

"Wait," Dara croaked. "Where are you going?"

"To get you a strong drink and something to bite." She twirled the scalpel. "This is definitely going to hurt."

TWO DAYS AFTER HE'D TAKEN TO THE WIND TO RESCUE Irtemiz, Dara limped into the Daeva Quarter.

Battered and covered in blood, he was a far cry from the arrogant immortal who'd sliced a path of death through the hospital. His shirt was gone, cut away so Razu could extract the iron bullet lodged in his shoulder—an experience that had made every other injury, including actual death, seem painless in comparison. Dara had been able to revert to his fiery form—but only just, pulling on enough magic to send Issa off in a giant cauldron enchanted to zip him to Ta Ntry and then collapsing yet again.

His frailty had surprised Razu. "My grandparents were from the generation Suleiman punished," she explained. "They spent the rest of their lives grieving for the abilities taken from them and spoke of their magic at length. They could have leveled the hospital with a snap of their fingers and flown to Ta Ntry and back in a single night. You do not have their strength."

Dara had been too foggy-headed to guard his words. "Then what in the name of the Creator am I?"

"A mess," she'd assessed bluntly, before forcing him into the cart she wheeled around to sell some sort of self-brewed liquor called soma. It had not only gotten them out of the hospital, it got them out of the shafit district entirely, the Tukharistanis calling welcome to her in their language as Dara hid beneath boxes of tinkling glass bottles. Razu had ducked into an empty alley long enough for him to slip out, and then he'd waited in a trash heap until it was dark enough to climb the wall.

Smelling of garbage, Dara was in an exceedingly foul mood even before the first person he saw was Vizaresh.

"Afshin," Vizaresh greeted him, bouncing in excitement. "Oh, you are in *so* much trouble."

IT WASN'T THE INFIRMARY DARA WAS LED TO, BUT rather a small room nearby. Manizheh and Kaveh were waiting for him, the Banu Nahida dressed in a plain linen smock and standing beside a tray of healing supplies.

Kaveh lost his composure the moment Dara was through the door.

"You selfish, arrogant, *witless* bastard," the grand wazir accused. "Do you have any idea the risk you took? We were ready to start evacuating women and children to the hills!"

"I miscalculated the odds," Dara muttered, falling upon a glass pitcher next to a platter of fruit. Wine, thank the Creator.

"You *miscalculated the—*"

"Kaveh, please leave," Manizheh interrupted. "I can handle this."

Kaveh threw up his hands, glaring at Dara as he shoved past. "You have learned *nothing.* You're still the same blundering fool who rushed off to save Nahri and got dozens of Daevas killed."

Dara abruptly smashed the wine pitcher, wiping the liquid from his mouth with the back of his hand. "Not Daevas. Not this time." He let out a hysterical laugh, whirling to face the angry minister. "Sand flies and dirt-bloods, Grand Wazir. Dozens. Scores! Should that not please you? Were you not the one who declared killing people was the reason I was brought back to life?"

"Enough." Manizheh's voice was as curt as a whip. "Kaveh, go. Afshin, *sit.*"

Dara sat, ignoring the furious look Kaveh shot him as he left. Let him be furious—he had nothing on Dara's rage.

"Where is Irtemiz?" he demanded hoarsely. Dara knew he shouldn't be demanding anything. If he had any sense and training left, he would have greeted Manizheh with his face in the dust. But with the blood of more victims thick on his skin, the memory of their hatred and how close he'd come to being torn apart by their hands, he found his composure was long gone.

"Resting." Manizheh stepped behind him and then gasped at the sight of his wound. "Did they *shoot* you?"

"With an iron bullet. Else I would have returned sooner."

There was a long moment of silence. "I see." She pressed a soaking compress to his skin, and Dara flinched at the cool liquid. "I'll clean and stitch it. Hopefully your magic will allow you to recover more thoroughly."

He said nothing, and she set to work. Manizheh was as precise and professional as always, which made it harder. Had she been openly mad or treated him with rough impatience, it would have been easier to stay angry. But she was gentle and careful as she tended his wound, healer first.

"I am sorry," Dara finally apologized as she tied off a stitch. "I had to get Irtemiz out of there, but I did not realize the extent of their weapons."

Manizheh pierced his skin once more with her needle and pulled the wound closed. "I'm certain you didn't." She laid a bandage over the stitches. "Lift your arm so I can wrap this in place."

Dara obeyed, trying to catch her eye as she wound a length of gauze around his shoulder and torso. "It will not happen again," he added.

"No, it won't." Manizheh stepped back. "Confine yourself to your quarters for at least three days. No heavy lifting, no training, and absolutely no archery. Rest."

"Understood," Dara said, trying for more deference. "I will have Noshrad take over in my place during that time."

"Is he your best?"

Dara nodded. "He has a half century on his fellows, and they respect him. Irtemiz and Gushtap are the better warriors, but Noshrad is a more experienced leader and can stand in for me at court."

"Then he will be doing that from today on."

"You mean, until I recover?"

Manizheh leveled her gaze on him. "No, I mean from today on. You are my Afshin and you will continue to lead my army, but I will require neither your council nor your presence at court."

Dara stared at her in shock. "Banu Manizheh—"

She held up a hand. "You disobeyed a direct order, put your life—and thus the lives of all your fellow Daevas—at risk, and

showed our enemy the best way to take you down. I have been willing to indulge your temper because I care for you, Afshin, and I
know how much you've suffered, but I won't abide disloyalty. I want
to trust you, I do," she added, a flicker of emotion in her eyes.
"But if I can't, I need to find other ways to keep our city safe."

He opened and closed his mouth, struggling for a response.
"I have only ever tried to serve my people."

"That's just it, Afshin. I don't need you to serve the Daevas. I
need you to serve me so that I may *lead* the Daevas. I have plenty of
councilors, and I don't need another arguing voice. I need someone to carry out my commands."

"You need a weapon." This time there was no keeping the bitterness from his voice.

"There is honor in being a weapon. Your family believed that
once." She picked up her tray and began putting away her supplies. "Did you at least learn anything useful nearly getting yourself killed?"

The blunt question took him aback, as did the immediate
answer rising to his mind. Dara had indeed learned something
useful—he'd learned where Zaynab al Qahtani was hiding. And
had he succeeded in capturing her, he knew Manizheh would have
greeted him with gratitude and praise rather than a demotion.

He started to reply . . . and then Razu's words returned to him.

What would happen to the hospital he'd already ravaged if
Manizheh learned the princess was there? Dara suddenly envisioned her ordering the ifrit to charge in, Aeshma and Vizaresh
laughing as they slaughtered women and children and hunted
down Elashia and Razu.

Zaynab has probably already fled. The princess was clearly no fool
and it would have been suicidal to stay in a place her enemies had
spotted her.

"No," Dara replied, the deception settling over him. It was
different from flouting Manizheh's orders to rescue Irtemiz.

This was an open lie, the kind of treason that in another life he might have had his tongue plucked out for. "I saw nothing."

Manizheh looked at him for a very long moment. "That's unfortunate." She turned for the door. "Rest, Afshin. We wouldn't want anything else to happen to you."

PART II

14

NAHRI

Nahri teased aside the tissue-thin pomegranate skin with her scalpel, revealing a section of ruby clusters. Holding the splayed fruit between her knees, she set down the scalpel and picked up her needle. She pierced the skin, drawing a section of thread through the rind to stitch it in place. She'd piled her hair into a bun on the top of her head, and the sun beat on the back of her neck, pleasantly warm.

It was an idyllic scene. They'd pulled the boat alongside a jumble of ruins, and Nahri sat on a downed column carved with pictograms that jutted out of the water. Ali was gone, swimming in the river, and so Nahri was alone with her instruments and the quiet. A breeze played over her face, smelling of wildflowers, and above, birds twittered sweetly as they built a nest in the remains of the monument's pockmarked ceiling.

She finished another stitch, admiring the neat row she'd

made so far. The pomegranate tissue was even more delicate than flesh, and yet her sutures were perfect.

Nahri clearly wasn't the only one who thought so.

"That looks very impressive," enthused a male voice just past her ear.

Nahri jumped, letting out a yelp of surprise as she nearly stabbed herself with the needle. "Ali, *for the love of God*—I thought you were swimming!"

"I was." Ali nodded to where his footprints still gleamed wetly across the stone. "I am done."

"Then can you practice making some *noise* when you move?" She stared unhappily at her fruit. She'd torn through the skin when she jumped. "You killed my patient."

"Does that mean we can eat it?"

"No, it means you can get me another before I start getting a feel for my instruments on *you*."

Ali rolled his eyes but headed back toward their boat, water streaming down his legs. Ever prim, Ali kept a dry shawl within arm's reach of the river when he swam, but he was still soaked to the bone, the glistening water droplets clinging to his bare skin twinkling in the sun.

"There are no more pomegranates," he called back, rooting through the basket where they kept their fruit. "Will an orange do?"

Nahri didn't respond right away. The shawl had slipped from Ali's back while he searched, creating a rather distracting effect. The waist cloth he wore when swimming was tied tight around his hips. Very tight. And it too was still wet, leaving perhaps less to the imagination than its wearer intended.

Well, aren't you looking fully recovered? Nahri forced herself to look away, self-aware enough to know staring at Ali's backside was of little diagnostic value. "What?" she asked distractedly.

He turned around, holding up two oranges. "An acceptable offering?"

"Sure."

Ali rejoined her. "I'm sorry for startling you." He stretched his neck, rolling one shoulder. "It feels good to swim, though. I was so *weak* after taking the seal. I think a child could have beat me up."

Nahri gave him an incredulous look, taking in his overly lithe form as he dropped to the ground. Forget where her thoughts had been a minute ago; even now Ali might have passed for some sort of fabled river spirit, a guardian of the water trickling down his arms. "You're out of your mind. God knows I saw enough of you when you were sick, and you looked fine then too."

Ali froze, the orange dangling from his fingertips. "What do you mean, you saw *enough of me?*"

"I mean . . ." Heat rushed into her cheeks. "You were unconscious for a couple of days. Who do you think took care of you? Yaqub? The man could barely see you."

Horror swept his face. "But I had been bathed. I had been *changed.*"

Nahri tried to calm him. "Listen, it's a very normal part of my job—" When Ali only appeared more panic-stricken, his eyes going very wide, her patience vanished. "Creator, why do you always make things so awkward? I'm a healer, I see people—men!—all the time. And it's not like you have anything to be embarrassed about!"

Ali opened and closed his mouth. "Why don't I have anything to be embarrassed about?"

Nahri was very much not expecting that question. Before she could stop herself, her mind flashed back to his wet waist cloth, and it was her turn to grow flustered. "You're a warrior. You've clearly spent a lot of time training, and you're, you know . . ." She fought for an appropriate word, cursing the embarrassed heat in her cheeks. ". . . well-formed."

It was not an appropriate word.

Nahri swore she heard an insect sneeze in the excruciating silence that sprawled between them.

"I think that was a compliment," Ali said finally, his gaze firmly on the ground. "So thank you. I'm going to change the subject now, yes?"

"I beg you."

When he looked up again, his expression was politely blank. "These ruins," he started. "All the carvings, they're interesting, aren't they?"

Nahri jumped into the topic with enthusiasm. "They're fascinating!" They were, actually, an easy topic for two overly curious djinn to get distracted by. She nodded toward the larger pictograms dominating the fallen structure, the majority depicting a muscled man with the head of a crocodile. Faded paint still clung to it in pieces. "Considering half of them are carved with crocodiles though, maybe you should rethink all the swimming."

"I'll be careful." Ali tossed her one of the oranges and set to peeling the other. "Do you know anything about the people who built these places?"

"Not really. I spent most of my childhood breaking laws, not learning history." Nahri traced the figure of a woman carrying a platter of grain. "Maybe this was a temple. They'd have to be offering people paradise to spend all this time carving rocks."

"You are aware there are similarly grand carvings of your ancestors on the walls surrounding Daevabad?"

"I'm very aware. Why do you think I used my religious clout to convince people to build a hospital? At least it's useful."

That brought a more genuine smile to Ali's face, relaxing the mood. "Don't you sound like quite the revolutionary? People would call me a fanatic if I said that."

"To be fair, people call you a fanatic for a lot of reasons."

"One should not concern oneself with gossip." Ali handed

her half the peeled orange. "Do you know that if you try to chisel down the Nahid reliefs, you dissolve into a puddle of brass?"

"You *what?*"

"Do you really think my ancestors would otherwise have left them up?"

Nahri groaned. "Tell me again why we're not settling into peaceful lives in Cairo?"

"It's the right thing to do?"

"It's the life-shortening thing to do."

"One step at a time," Ali assured her. "First Ta Ntry."

"Ah, yes, another mysterious magical court where I'll arrive powerless with nothing but the clothes on my back and an assortment of people who want me dead." Nahri shuddered. "What do you think would be worse: everyone's magic failing the moment we get close with the seal, or their abilities already being gone?"

"I don't imagine either option leaves us popular. But if my mother is back, we should be okay." His face fell. "I wonder if they've heard any news by now. She might think I'm dead."

We would probably be safest if everyone thought us dead.

"Put down the fruit," Nahri said, coming to a decision and setting aside her own tools. "We're practicing with the seal."

Ali sighed. "We've not had any luck, Nahri. I think it's clear Suleiman's seal ring wasn't meant to leave Daevabad. For all we know, we broke some sacred promise Anahid made thousands of years ago."

"I'm not ready to give up yet." Nahri racked her mind, trying to think of any possibilities they hadn't explored.

She frowned. "Where does it hurt?" she asked. "When you use your water magic, where exactly?"

"My heart, I suppose," he said, touching the striped fabric of his shawl where it crossed his chest.

"Let me see."

Ali looked embarrassed again, but obeyed, drawing down just enough of the shawl to reveal his heart.

You are a doctor, Nahri told herself, thoroughly annoyed by the effect that following the beat of Ali's heart—along his very firm chest—was having on her. Creator damn all that sparring. She didn't miss Ali shiver at her touch, his pulse picking up, but Nahri dismissed it. Well-formed or not, Alizayd al Qahtani had probably never allowed himself an impure thought.

A shame. Now Nahri did flush, fighting the urge to slap some sense into herself. No more journeying with attractive warriors on dangerous quests after this. She clearly had a problem.

"Is something wrong?"

"Yes, you're talking and distracting me." Nahri pressed her fingers closer, probing the muscle. "I feel like I'm examining you with my eyes closed," she complained. "If my magic comes back, I'm never taking it for granted again."

"Am I allowed to respond?"

"No. I want you to try a little water magic. Just enough to trigger some pain."

Ali made an exaggerated show of obedience and then beckoned toward the river. A tendril of water had no sooner flown to his hand than he flinched, the muscles seizing under her fingers.

"Hmm," she murmured, pulling her hand back. "I don't—"

"Wait," Ali grabbed her hand, pressing it hard against his chest. He'd closed his eyes and they were darting beneath his lids like he was dreaming. "There's something—I think if I . . ."

The seal blazed on his face and then flushed out, the light vanishing to leave the eight-pointed ebony star stark and dull against the warmer hue of his black skin. Power surged through Nahri, so fast it left her breathless. The steady beat of her heart and the faster one of Ali's. The rushing of blood through veins and air through throats.

Her *magic.*

After so many weeks, even a hint of it felt like Nahri had drunk too much wine, a heady sensation of strength and invulnerability. Her aching muscles and scratches vanished.

Ali gasped, his eyes shooting open.

Nahri dropped her hand. Her magic instantly fell away, but she was encouraged. "It worked!"

"Wow," he whispered, his shoulders dropping. Sweat broke out across his brow.

Her glee faded a bit. "Are you okay?"

"I think so." He rubbed the spot over his heart and then raised his palm, snapping his fingers as though to conjure a flame. "It didn't last."

"It's a start."

Ali reached for her hand, looking drained but no less determined. "Let's try again."

"If you insist." Nahri touched his chest, and the seal fell even faster this time. She inhaled, welcoming the embrace of her magic.

Ali grimaced. "Still burns when I use my water abilities."

"Just hold it another second," she urged, trying to calm the spikes of pain radiating through his body. "I want to examine your heart."

She closed her eyes, letting her abilities envelop her. It was as if she'd been too long underwater, surfacing in a world whose sensations overwhelmed her. Before her, Ali was a maze of muscle and tissue, coursing blood and churning fluid.

And something very wrong.

"The ring," Nahri whispered, stunned. She could sense its hard contours just below the surface of his heart, so close it seemed almost possible to pluck it free. Nahri wasn't sure what she'd expected, but it wasn't that. She hadn't sensed the ring in Ghassan's body and thought perhaps it was meant to bond with one's heart in some sort of formless state, reappearing only when the organ was burned.

She opened her eyes to find Ali gazing at her with a strange expression. "What?" she asked.

"I . . . your face. I think I'm seeing how you look without the marid's curse on your appearance." Ali seemed stunned. "So that's how he knew. You have Suleiman's seal marked on your face."

Ghassan's words from that night came back to her. *They all bear it. Every single Nahid.* "Your father said that to me once. He claimed all Nahids had it."

Including Jamshid. But Nahri didn't mention her brother. No matter her and Ali's growing closeness, Jamshid's identity wasn't her secret to divulge.

Ali fell back against the column, visibly worn out. "I didn't know that." He rubbed his chest. "By the Most High, it feels like a city worth's of magic just burned through me."

Nahri hesitated, torn between wanting to know more and wanting to change the subject. "What else did you see?"

"What do you mean?"

Was there anything this man wasn't obtuse about? "The *curse*, Ali, the one that makes me appear human. How do I look without it?"

He inclined his head. "I think you had the glow to your skin, but I was more focused on Suleiman's mark." He must have picked up on her disappointment. "Don't tell me that's something you fret over."

She was immediately annoyed. "Maybe it seems shallow to a pureblood prince, but you might have noticed the rest of our world is obsessed with whether or not one looks shafit. I had an entire fleet of servants whose job was to cover me in magical powders. Yes, I *fret* over it."

Ali winced. "I'm sorry." He glanced around and then nodded at the water. "Tomorrow when the light is better, let's try this again in a place where you can see your reflection."

"I don't need you to do that."

"Who says you need anything? Maybe I want to study my own reflection. After all, I hear I'm *well-formed*."

Equal parts embarrassment and warmth stole through her. "Did you just make a joke? Surely you would have needed the permission of at least three clerics."

Ali smiled. "I'll be sure to check with the appropriate authorities when we get to Ta Ntry." But then he flinched, again, kneading the spot over his heart. "I wish I could cut this out of me."

Nahri bit her lip, recalling her own impression. "I'm not sure the ring bonded with you the same way it did with your father. Muntadhir said the heart needs to be burned, and the ring reforms from the ash, but I'm telling you, I can sense that thing intact and clear as day, just below the heart muscle."

"But you put it on my finger before we left Daevabad. Why wouldn't it have bonded?"

"I don't know." Nahri found herself drawn to the spot on his chest, an ache in her own heart. "It feels like it's *right* there. Like I could just pluck it out."

"Want to try?" Ali nodded at the ruined pomegranate. "I promise I'll be a better patient." Despite the jest, there was a genuine plea in his voice.

"No," Nahri said, aghast. "I'd have to cut into your heart."

"You cut into a child's skull."

"That was different!"

But Ali looked grim. "I feel like I'm not meant to have this. I remember the way my father's heart burned in your hands. I can feel *mine* burning when you touch me. It wants you."

"It doesn't want anything. It's a ring. And we've already discussed this. You know what Manizheh said about my being a shafit. If I took the seal, it would have killed me."

"She was *lying,* Nahri. She was trying to get under your skin." His expression softened. "Listen, I can't imagine how difficult—"

"No, you can't." Nahri rose to her feet, stalking into the shadows of the ruin.

There was a moment of silence before Ali spoke again. "Then tell me. God knows you've listened to enough of my family's problems. Let me return the favor."

"I wouldn't know what to tell you. No one bothers to keep me in the loop. They didn't even tell me my own mother was alive."

"Do you have any idea who your father might be?"

"No," Nahri replied, checking the ache in her voice. "And I can't imagine the kind of man Manizheh would have fallen for. He probably murders kittens to relax. Not that it matters. If he's shafit, that's all the Daevas are going to care about."

"You don't know that," Ali argued. "I've seen you with your people. They love you. If you told people who you really were—"

"They would turn on me."

"Or maybe you'd bring everyone together. In a way no one else can."

For a moment, Nahri imagined it. Declaring her true identity to the world, finding peace with both her communities, defiant proof a shafit could be anything, even a Nahid healer.

And then it was gone. That kind of optimism had been beaten out of Nahri a long time ago.

"I envy you sometimes," she said softly. "I wish I had your faith in people's goodness." And then before she could see the pity she'd hate in his eyes, Nahri turned and walked away.

NAHRI DIDN'T RETURN UNTIL SUNDOWN, AND AFTER A tense meal of stale bread and dates—they'd learned to mutual chagrin early in their journey that each assumed the other had more cooking experience—they went back to the boat, sailing until the day's light was gone before dropping anchor. Ali fell asleep fast, the pain from his marid magic taking a visible toll.

Nahri should have found a way to keep herself awake. Ever

the soldier, Ali had suggested they trade shifts. But it had been a long day, and she found it impossible to keep her eyes open as the warm velvet of the darkening sky and gentle rock of the boat lulled her into a drowsy spell.

The sounds of distant sobbing pulled her back to consciousness. Nahri blinked, momentarily forgetting where she was, and then another wail came. It sounded like a woman, somewhere upriver, ending in weeping that carried along the water.

A finger of ice brushed down Nahri's spine, adrenaline banishing the remnants of her stupor. She must have been sleeping for some time, because it was now pitch-black, so dark she could barely see her own hands. And utterly, unnaturally silent, the usual drone of insects and the creak of frogs gone.

The weeping came again. Nahri sat up and then tumbled as the boat lurched in the water, rocking as though the sail had caught. Which was impossible because the sail was tied back and the anchor let out.

I don't think I've ever seen a night like this. She crept forward. The moon was a bare sickle, its weak light scattered on the flowing water, and the scrubby trees and reeds on either bank were impossibly black, the kind that seemed capable of swallowing one whole.

Her bearings lost, she stumbled directly into Ali's sleeping body. He popped upright like he was on a spring, the gleam of his khanjar already in hand. She opened her mouth to explain, but then the weeping came again, the plaintive cry nearly musical.

"Is that someone *singing*?" Ali asked.

"I don't know," Nahri whispered back. The woman did seem to be singing now, though not in any language Nahri had ever heard. It cut through her, bone-deep, and goose bumps erupted over her arms. "It sounds like a funeral dirge."

The glint of the khanjar disappeared as Ali resheathed it. "Maybe she needs help."

"That's unfortunate for her." When Ali glanced at her, disapproval in his glimmering eyes, Nahri spoke more firmly. "I don't know what stories you heard growing up, but I'm not hunting after some mystery voice in the middle of the night."

Light suddenly burst before them, fire flaring so brightly that Nahri held a hand over her eyes. The scene came to her in starry pieces: the large, pale lumps scattered across the choppy water, the rocky riverbank and spiky brush jutting up like teeth.

The woman swaying on the bank, fire gushing from her outstretched hands.

The burning singer before them was definitely not some lost farm girl. Her skin was pale—too pale, the color of bone—and her black hair was uncovered, falling in glossy waves past her ankles to pool in the shallows at her feet. She was dressed simply and sparsely in a thin shift that clung wetly to her body, leaving little of its curves hidden.

Not to mention the *fire*. Nahri instinctively stood, the healer in her mind going to burns and salves . . . until she realized the woman wasn't burning, not quite. Tendrils of flames caressed her wrists and danced through her fingers, but her skin wasn't blackened, nor did the air smell of charred flesh.

And when she met Nahri's gaze, there was no pain in it. There was *delight*. The delight of one genuinely and wonderfully surprised.

"Oh, but you are the last person I expected in my net." The woman grinned, her teeth gleaming in the firelight. "What a lovely gift."

Nahri gaped at her. There was something about the woman's leering smile and voice that she would swear . . .

Her stomach dropped. "Qandisha."

The ifrit laughed. "Clever girl." She snapped her fingers, and the fire rushed to embrace her, the human appearance vanishing. "You'll forgive the disguise. The fiery skin doesn't lend itself to hunting."

At the word "hunting," Ali edged in front of Nahri. The ifrit's gleaming orange eyes locked on the prince, and her lips twisted into a snarl.

"Suleiman's mark," Qandisha sneered. "Are you that djinn king, then?" She regarded them with a hungry, amused curiosity, like how a cat might watch an insect. "Oh, Aeshma . . ." She chuckled. "Whatever has gone wrong with your grand plan?"

Ali drew his zulfiqar. "And what plan would that be?"

"One that should have ended with both of you dead." Qandisha's voice turned alluring. "There's not much you can do with that blade all the way out there, little mortal. Why don't you come closer? I have been *aching* for some company."

Nahri stepped back, dread crawling up her chest. "Ali, I don't care what magic you have to use. Get us out of here."

"I wouldn't do that," Qandisha warned. "We've not yet finished our conversation." She snapped her fingers, making a beckoning motion at the water. "My friends will find you rude." She spread her hands, illuminating the river.

Nahri let out a strangled gasp.

The pale humps floating in the water were not rocks. They were *bodies,* at least a score of them, in various states of decay. Slain human men who abruptly raised their heads from the water and stared at her with sightless eyes.

Qandisha dropped her hands, and the bodies fell back into the water with a sickening unified splash. "Your countrymen are so welcoming," she goaded. "'Ya, sayyida, do you need help?'" she mocked in Egyptian Arabic. "And so very eager to share their whispers of a boat reputed to fly across the Nile as though enchanted." She tsked. "I've been roaming these lands for thousands of years in search of djinn slaves. You really should have taken better care to mask your presence."

Nahri swore under her breath, cursing herself for her misstep. That it was Qandisha who'd caught them made it worse.

Nahri still remembered how easily Qandisha had overpowered Dara at the Gozan, nearly drowning him before the marid made the river rise. She and Ali might have been safe with the thick band of the Nile separating them from the ifrit, but Nahri didn't like their odds should a mob of ghouls swarm the boat.

And they weren't just ghouls. They were her countrymen. Innocent humans, Egyptians who shared her tongue and her land, killed to slake an ifrit's curiosity.

Hatred rushed through her. "I take it Aeshma left you out of his plan if you're out here murdering defenseless humans. Was your company so unbearable?"

The ifrit shrugged. "A concession to your Afshin. It's a shame he's so disinterested in recovering his memories of our time together. He was glorious." Cruelty flickered in her eyes. "He must be crushed to have lost you again. You were the first one he begged for, you know. No sooner dragged back to life than he was weeping, 'Nahri! Where's Nahri?'"

The words had been meant to cut deep, and they did, memories of Dara's pleas tumbling through her. Nahri fought for a response, angry denial coming first. "Dara serves my mother now. He's a murderer. They both are."

The ifrit laughed, but there was a new coldness in it. "So are you, but no matter. Darayavahoush clearly meant just as little to your ancestors. A shame, truly, to waste such loyalty . . . and talent."

Qandisha licked her lips as she said it, but Nahri refused to indulge that line of provocation. "I'm no murderer," she said instead.

"No? You killed Sakhr in cold blood." When Nahri frowned, the name confusing her, genuine anger flashed in Qandisha's eyes. "You don't even remember his name, do you? A man you blood-poisoned and left for his brother to find."

Blood-poisoned. Sakhr, the ifrit who'd attacked her at the Gozan, of course—years ago.

Nahri shook her head, still defiant. "He was no man, he was an ifrit. A monster."

Qandisha growled. "Who are you to decide who is a monster? You are a slip of time, a little mortal girl foul with the taint of humanity and descended from a traitor. Sakhr was worshipped as a god. He battled with prophets and roamed the northern winds. He was my *friend*," she snapped, all trace of humor gone. "A companion during these long centuries."

"Nahri . . ." Ali moved toward her, a warning in his voice.

"Interrupt again, djinn, and I will have you dragged beneath the waves." Qandisha's gaze was for Nahri alone. "How very Nahid of you to flit between djinn and Daeva, disregarding your allies and friends however the winds blow. A shame your poor Dara had to learn that lesson again."

Nahri picked up the remaining oar. She was not going to wait around and let this creature bait her. For all they knew, Qandisha was stalling while she worked some unseen magic to call the other ifrit. "Get us out of here, Ali," Nahri said, hefting the oar like a baton. "I'd rather take my chances with ghouls than listen to her lies."

"No lies, Nahid. I had hoped to take a djinn soul for company tonight, but I don't go near Nahid blood, and I suspect Suleiman's accursed seal will make any efforts toward your newest consort useless.

"So it will be vengeance for Sakhr instead."

Qandisha had no sooner spoken than a boulder rose in the air, dripping with mud. She threw out her hand, and it flew toward them.

And then, even faster, a glistening wave erupted from the Nile like a wet shield. The momentum of the water was enough to slow the boulder, and it landed in the river before it could smash their boat, the splash drenching them.

Ali.

The djinn prince held out his hands. He was gasping, his face pained with the effort the marid magic must have cost him.

"You talk too much," he grunted, and then, sweating and shivering, he jerked his hands down. The water around the ifrit's ankles dashed up, pulling her into the shallows. Ali hissed, clutching his chest, but their boat was already moving.

Qandisha recovered more quickly than Nahri would have expected, however, climbing back to her feet and looking as angry as a wet cat.

"Another time that might've intrigued me," the ifrit said, fire rasping in her mouth. "But I did warn you not to interfere."

Qandisha snapped her fingers, and the sail burst into flames, fire rushing down the mast with malicious speed.

The bodies in the river jerked back to life.

If Nahri thought Vizaresh's control of ghouls was powerful, the other ifrit had nothing on Qandisha. The murdered human men, their eyes veiled in ashen gray, moved in fast, spasmodic motions, swarming the boat in seconds. But they didn't go for Nahri.

They went for Ali, mobbing him so thoroughly that he'd barely managed a cry before he vanished beneath the mass of hungry dead flesh.

Nahri lunged for him, but the burning mast cracked before she could take two steps. The weight of the sail dragged it down, smashing the deck and ripping their boat open.

In an instant the water was at her chest, ropes tangling around her legs. Nahri wrenched them away, kicking madly as the felucca fell apart beneath her. Debris snagged the bottom of her dress, dragging her under the water.

She ripped it away and resurfaced. "Ali!" Nahri screamed his name, but she could see nothing except fiery debris and choking smoke. There was no response from Ali save the wet grunting of ghouls and a horrible, awful crunching.

No, Creator, no. Nahri scrambled at the remains of the boat. *"Ali!"*

"Oh, wouldn't Anahid be proud of your spirit." Qandisha laughed. "But she chose mortality for you all, and well, that only ends one way."

From the haze obscuring the river came three murky shapes, bloated and gray.

Ghouls.

Nahri didn't even get a last gulp of air. The ghouls seized her and pulled her down, the river closing over her head again.

NO. She fought wildly, kicking and scratching at dead flesh, writhing against their arms. It made no difference. In seconds, they were at the bottom, Nahri pinned against the murky mud and terrified out of her wits. Her chest throbbed, aching for air.

Focus, Nahri! She was the con artist of Cairo, the stealthy thief. This couldn't be how things ended for her, drowned beneath the Nile. She had to have a plan, a quick turn of hand.

But this time, Nahri had nothing.

This is how Dara died. Dara's memories, shared so long ago, surged back into her mind. Thrown down a well by a laughing Qandisha. His desperate struggle, the panic and despair when he realized he couldn't escape the dark water . . .

She was losing her ability to fight, her strength leaving her in waves. Daevabad flashed before her eyes and, with it, all the people Nahri had failed. The hospital courtyard filled with her celebrating friends. Nisreen guiding her hands through a new procedure. Ali coaching her through reading a sentence in the magnificent palace library. Jamshid and Subha's cautious first meeting.

A warrior pulling himself upon the stage of a crumbling amphitheater, his green eyes blazing.

Darayavahoush! Darayavahoush e-Afshin is my name.

Darkness beckoned at the edges of Nahri's vision. *My name.* A sunlit room in a small mudbrick home, a name she couldn't remember called aloud. Warm brown eyes and a blanket tucked around her shoulders. A kiss on her nose.

A boat of fishermen, pulling her aboard with strong hands. *What is your name?*

And then the water surged past her lips, and Nahri remembered no more.

15

ALI

Ali thrashed against the ghouls, kicking and cutting and smashing his head into the press of dead flesh and sharp nails. He gagged on the aroma of rot, desperate to free himself. To stop moving would be to die; to be still for even a second would give the ghouls that same second to tear him apart. Ali clutched his khanjar and zulfiqar so tight it hurt. If he lost his blades, he was finished.

A bony wrist shoved against his throat, cutting off his air and silencing his grunts. Beyond, Nahri was screaming his name.

Ali choked, trying to call out to her. There was the sound of splintering wood, crashing, the sensation of falling. The ifrit was laughing, but her words were drowned out by the blood pumping in his ears and the moans of the ghouls.

Nails ripped at his stomach, blunt teeth gnawing at his shoulder. Abruptly aware he was moments away from being eaten alive, he welcomed the cold touch of water at his ankles like the hand of a savior. To hell with this; his heart exploding would at least be a quicker way to die than being torn apart by the dead.

Ali called to the river with everything he had.

The water leapt to his aid and then Ali howled, the scorching lash in his chest causing him to nearly black out. The river reared up like a beast, hungry devouring tongues of water ripping the ghouls from his body. Ali screamed, his body seizing . . .

His grip on the marid magic shattered, and then it was over. Ali lay on broken pieces of floating wood, senseless with pain. His weapons hung in his hands, his clenched fingers locked about their hilts.

Coming back to himself, Ali glanced blankly around. He could smell his blood on the wet air, a new throb coming with every beat of his heart. He rubbed his eyes, trying to make sense of his surroundings. Their boat was destroyed, nothing but fiery debris bobbing on the coursing river.

And Nahri was gone.

Panic rushed through him, and Ali pushed himself up into a sitting position. Blood filled his mouth, dripping past his lips when he spoke. "Nahri . . ."

A chuckle drew his attention to the riverbank, Qandisha standing in the haze of oily smoke. She inclined her head toward the dark water. "Too late."

The meaning of her words took a moment to land.

The river. Nahri.

Ali plunged into the Nile.

The cool liquid was a balm against his skin. Ali sheathed his blades, summoning the last bit of his strength to swim, but relief vanished the moment he called on his marid powers again. The magic was so hard to hold, the very thing he needed to find Nahri sending spikes of pain stabbing through his chest.

No matter. Ali forced himself to swim deeper, his limbs protesting, blood streaming from his wounds. He expanded his powers, searching farther, but the drifting bodies of the ghouls confused his senses, and the fire burning on the surface sent jagged, unreliable light flickering through the murky water in a way that made him feel like he was trapped in a muck-covered madhouse of glass and mirrors. Then . . .

There!

A spark of warmth, swiftly growing colder. Ali raced along the bottom, spotting the serrated outline of the broken boat where ghouls had pinned Nahri to the riverbed. Her eyes were closed, her dress drifting around her motionless body.

Ali was there the next moment, ripping away the ghouls and pulling her into his arms. He shot to the surface, kicking hard.

"Nahri, breathe," he gasped as they broke through into the air. "*Breathe!*"

Nothing. Nahri remained limp in his arms, silent and unresponsive. Frantic, Ali pushed the strands of wet hair away from her face. Her eyes were closed, her lips tinged with blue.

No. God, no. PLEASE. Hugging her to his chest, Ali staggered toward the shallows and laid her on the muddy bank.

"Nahri, please," he begged, clapping her back. "*Please!*"

Qandisha strode forward. Muscles rippled below her fiery skin, light gleaming on the metal in her braids and the knife-sharp gems of her chest plate.

She loomed over him. "You should have stayed in the water." Hunger filled her eyes. "I wonder what would happen if I cut the seal from your face, if your soul would be open for me to steal." She reached out, her claws glittering. "I think I shall try it . . ."

She hadn't even grazed Ali's cheek when everything went very, very cold.

The water lapping at his feet grew chilled, the air turning so icy that Ali's ragged breaths became steam and goose bumps broke across Nahri's bare arms. He whirled around, watching in bewilderment as great clouds of mist billowed from the Nile, extinguishing the fires dotting its churning surface with an angry hiss.

The unnatural darkness that had accompanied Qandisha vanished next, beams of moonlight breaking through the cloudless night and the sounds of life returning—insects and frogs and the wind through the reeds, so loud it was like a chorus.

Something moved in the black water. Ali grabbed Nahri, pulling her away as a muscled tail lashed his legs with a swipe of scaled flesh.

Then the largest crocodile he'd ever seen burst from the Nile.

The creature let out a bellow that sliced through the night, shaking the trees and silencing the frogs. Its roar cut through Ali, sending a surge of deep primal fear galloping through his body. With a wet snap, the enormous crocodile transformed, rearing up on its back legs as its reptilian form gave way to that of a man. His body was slender and wiry, his skin an unnatural dark green that spread in a pattern of leathery scales down lanky limbs. Stubby reptilian claws crowned long webbed fingers, bony ridges running down a bare scalp.

Ali did not consider himself a coward. He had dueled with the greatest warrior of his people, faced down a mob of ghouls, and had an ifrit run claws over his throat. But staring at the creature that charged out of the misty Nile, the very land and river gone still in submission, he had never felt so utterly small.

The marid—for Ali knew the very moment the water magic stilled in his blood what he was looking at—studied them all with the cool regard of an uncaring predator. He moved like a reptile, shoulders and neck swaying and twisting as yellow-and-black-dappled eyes shifted between Qandisha and Ali before fixing on the ghouls.

They immediately stilled. The gray veneer of magic vanished from the faces of the slain men, replaced by masks of peace. And then, with murmured sighs, they sank below the water.

The marid hissed, turning back. "*Qatesh.*"

Qandisha stepped away, shocked fear crossing her face. "Sobek," she whispered.

The marid—Sobek, she had called him—took a halting step in the ifrit's direction. "You took life in my waters," he accused her, gesturing to where the ghouls had slipped away.

Qandisha was still backing up. Ali hadn't known she could look so afraid. "I did not know you were here. They said you were gone. Killed by—"

"*GET OUT OF MY LAND.*"

Ali would have been on the other side of the continent, had the marid bellowed that at him, but Qandisha held her ground.

"The daevas are fire-born," she argued. "You have no right to them."

"I have every right to them. Leave."

Flames twisted through her hands. "You cannot hurt me. I am an ally of the daeva Darayavahoush, the one who commands you."

Sobek's eyes flashed. "No daeva commands me, and you are alone." Hunger laced into his voice. "It has been an age since I devoured one of your kind. You have already transgressed; declare yourself equal and I am within my rights."

"You will regret this."

"I will regret not tasting your heart in my teeth. *LEAVE.*"

She was gone the next moment in a whirl of sand and smoke, thunder breaking the air.

Ali, though, was rooted in place. There was no point in running. The river had surged behind him and Nahri, cutting through the rocky bank like a scythe.

Sobek towered over them, blocking out the rest of the world. His scaled skin glittered in the starlight, dazzling. Breathtaking. His visage flickered, a dozen forms shifting in the fog, though the yellow-black eyes stayed fixed.

Ali inhaled, fighting a tremble. The marid was so utterly beyond him, beyond anything he knew. He suddenly had no doubt Sobek was among the creatures painted and carved in the ruins he and Nahri had wandered through, a lost god from an ancient world. Unbidden, the declaration of faith rose to his lips, and he honestly wasn't sure if he said it as a reminder or in preparation for his imminent death.

The marid. The creatures who had toyed with him, changed him, ruined him, and saved him. The ones who terrorized his people in Ta Ntry and dragged the Citadel into the lake. One was now so close Ali could smell his silty breath.

Sobek studied him with an open, merciless appraisal, his eerie eyes tracing the seal marked on Ali's cheek and the blood running down his arms. His gaze shifted to Nahri, and then Sobek tilted his head, glancing at Ali with expectation in his cold expression.

And all of Issa's words rushed back into his head.

The marid can give you almost anything you desire. The pacts djinn and humans made with these evil creatures for power, for wealth. For love. Pacts sealed in blood and death and the damnation of their souls. Pacts Ali would never in a thousand years contemplate.

Until Nahri was lying too still in his arms.

Ali gazed up at the marid, blinking back tears. He couldn't not know. "What is your price?" he asked hoarsely.

The marid regarded him with those unfeeling, alien eyes. "You have taken the ring of Anahid the Conqueror from the city of fire?"

Still dizzy, Ali fought for a response. "The ring of Anahid the Conqueror? You mean, Suleiman's seal? I . . . yes," he managed. "But—"

"Then the price has been paid."

Before Ali could react, the marid was kneeling at his side. He took Nahri from Ali's arms as though she weighed nothing and laid her on the riverbank between them.

Fresh grief stabbed through Ali at the sight of his friend so unresponsive. At any moment, Ali expected to see Nahri's dark eyes open, rolling with sarcasm. The thought of her not waking was unbearable.

"Give me your hands," Sobek demanded.

"My hands?"

"It is against my nature to restore a drowned one. I will need to use you."

Ali held out his hands, trying to still their trembling and failing the moment the marid's scaled fingers slid over his. His heart hammered as Sobek pressed his hands down, one over Nahri's heart and the other upon her mouth.

He extended his claws, and Ali gasped as they pierced his skin.

But a far worse violation waited. Because with a wave of icy magic, the riverbank vanished, and then Sobek was in his head.

The intrusive presence was so horribly familiar that Ali tried to jerk back, thrown into his memories of the marid's torture on Daevabad's lake. It was too late: Sobek was already leafing through his mind. The harem garden back in Daevabad's palace materialized before Ali's eyes. The willow tree he and Zaynab used to hide under as small children, the canal . . .

"Look what I can do!" Zaynab wiggled her fingers over a glass bowl of water. The liquid inside rose to dance in the air, following the movement as they giggled together—

Ali shoved wildly at the presence in his head. "Get out of my mind," he choked out. "You don't get to see that."

Sobek sank his claws deeper, both in Ali's hands and in his mind. When he spoke, it was not aloud. *This is how you save her.*

Shaking, Ali tried to back down.

He was suddenly older. Still a child, but in the striped gray waist cloth of a Royal Guard cadet. He was again in the harem, but this time with his mother, learning to swim.

Hatset held him by his skinny waist. "Straighten your legs, Alu. You cannot swim crumpled up like a ball."

"But why do I need to learn how to swim?" he'd asked, his child's voice high and plaintive. "None of the other boys do. They make fun of me, Amma. They call me a crocodile."

His mother had taken his chin in one hand. "Then you tell them crocodiles snap up boys like them every day and drown them in the river. You are my blood, and this is what we do."

The garden vanished again, and then pain tore through his body, teeth and scales and claws. His possession on Daevabad's lake. Ali screamed his own name and then was racing through the water. "Kill the daeva, kill the daeva—"

The flooded fields of Bir Nabat, rich mud squelching between his toes, springs bursting through rock to dance through his fingers. Daevabad again—the Citadel on that awful night, the lake looming up through the window . . .

"Please," Ali begged. "Not that."

The corridor outside his father's office. Darayavahoush charged him, and Ali swung his zulfiqar, but it was like an invisible hand seized it, flinging him back. The Afshin ripped the blade from his hands, the flames soaring as he brought it back down. Muntadhir moved, shoving himself between them . . .

There was no fighting it. Ali's hands were pinned to Nahri's body; while magic burned through his blood, and Sobek rummaged through his mind, it was hard enough to remain conscious. So instead, he felt Muntadhir fall heavily against him again and heard the gasp that left his brother's lips. Tears ran down Ali's face, sparks bursting before his eyes . . .

And then Daevabad was gone.

He rested alongside his waters, sunning himself on a warm rock. It was a bliss-fully pleasant afternoon, the humans downriver bustling about their temples, men in pale waist cloths quarrying stone. His likeness was everywhere, on the shiny limestone pillars and carved statues, and it pleased him. He was sated with their worship and with the bloody gristle still staining his teeth, the remains of the young woman he'd lured into his shallows.

Ali gagged, but beneath his hands, Nahri stirred. Water gushed from her mouth as though he had summoned it, and then she was choking, coughing, fighting for air.

"*Nahri.*" Barely aware of Sobek removing his hands, Ali raised Nahri to a sitting position, helping her onto her knees as she threw up. "Breathe," he whispered, rubbing her back as she sucked for air. "Just breathe. It's all right; you're all right."

She put her head back against Ali's chest, her skin still icy. The blue tinge had yet to leave her lips, but then her eyes found his, and Ali was so relieved he had to resist the urge to clutch her close.

"Ali?" Nahri's voice was hoarse. Her gaze drifted past his shoulder.

Sobek laid a hand on her brow, and her eyes shuttered.

Ali whirled on the marid as Nahri slumped in his arms. "What did you do?" he cried.

Sobek rose to his feet. "She merely sleeps, daeva, do not fear. She is not to see me."

Ali was still shaking, trying to understand everything that had just happened. "Why not?"

"I made a promise."

That answered nothing. Ali held Nahri tight, trying to take reassurance from the steady beat of her heart.

Sobek was still studying him, his lambent eyes seeming to peel Ali apart layer by layer. He bent down, and Ali stilled as a webbed hand grasped his chin, a stubby claw brushing the seal marked on his face. It was everything he could do not to rock back in revulsion. Who knew how many people had died under these claws? How many more had been slaughtered in Sobek's name?

The marid spoke again, his voice like water tumbling over rocks. "You are the daeva they took, the one they used to kill the Nahid's champion."

It was not a question. *The Nahid's champion.* "Do you mean the Afshin?" Ali asked. "Yes."

Sobek pursed gray lips. For a second, Ali saw rows of teeth like broken arrows jutting in every direction.

"A moment of hesitation," the marid murmured. "A moment to taste the flavors of your blood, and all this might have been avoided." Regret filled his voice, the first emotion besides anger that he betrayed. "They must have been so desperate." His claw pressed harder against the seal mark, enough that the skin began to tear. "It was not your choice to take Anahid's ring and bring it to my waters?"

Ali shivered. Just how much had Sobek seen? "No," he replied.

Sobek's eyes gleamed, and Ali had to fight not to jump as the pupils turned to vertical slits like a lizard's. "So you do not know who I am?"

There was weight behind that question, the humid air heavy with tension. "No," he said again, for it seemed impossible to lie to the creature before him. "I don't know who you are."

Sobek drew back like a whip. "Then you should leave, both of you. Qatesh spoke truthfully about the Nahid's champion. My people owe him a blood debt; we cannot harm him, and I will not be able to protect you if she brings him."

The Nahid's champion. For a moment, the image of Darayavahoush danced before Ali. The zulfiqar ripped from his hand, Muntadhir's blood on his face.

Let his brother's murderer come. Ali would welcome it. Let the two of them finish this.

You'll finish nothing. You couldn't even raise a blade to him. The bitter truth crushed him, making Ali feel small and useless. If Qandisha returned with Darayavahoush, Ali was dead—the Afshin would not make the mistake of delaying his death again.

And then Nahri and Suleiman's seal would be returned to Manizheh.

Ali exhaled, glancing at the river. His heart dropped. Their boat was destroyed, the pieces and supplies that hadn't sunk smoldering. Their food, their possessions. Ali had his weapons, but they were otherwise right back where they'd been weeks ago, all their work for nothing. Worse—now there was no city, no village or farmland. Nothing indicating a nearby human presence where they could barter for a new boat or buy supplies. There was nothing but dark desert, untouched by djinn fires or human lamplight.

"Our boat is gone," he said in despair, more to himself than to Sobek.

The marid stared at Ali, another of those long, assessing looks that seemed to open him up and rearrange his insides. "Where do you mean to go?"

"Ta Ntry," Ali replied, his head spinning. "My mother's homeland. It is to the south, along the sea—"

"I know where Ta Ntry is." Sobek sounded snappish now and restless. He swung his head back and forth, looking more like a crocodile. "Will she be safe there?"

"Safer than with Qandisha."

"Then I will take you our way. There is a place where my waters meet the sea, where your kind often visits." Sobek made a beckoning motion. "Come."

Our way? Apprehension trickled down Ali's spine, but Sobek was already turning around, strutting toward the river like a general surveying conquered territory.

A trick, this could be a trick. "Why?" Ali called out. "Why would you help us?"

Sobek stopped at the water's edge, sharp lines blacker than

black against the moonlit sand and shadow-wreathed scrub of the opposite bank. He looked like a void cut in space, one that would drag in and devour anything that drew too close.

"I do not *help*." The marid sounded thoroughly irked, the Nile rippling with his mood. "I make exchanges, and one was to preserve her life." He jutted a snoutlike chin at Nahri.

It was not a comforting answer. Ali gazed again at the empty desert and then glanced at the woman in his arms. She too had once followed a mysterious magical being offering safety—and had her life upended as a result.

But they could not stay here, and the prospect of being whisked to Ta Ntry, to the richly lush coast his mother had spun bedtime stories about, to a place where Ali might find family and safety, was tantalizing.

Almost as tantalizing as facing off against his brother's murderer.

Do not be reckless. Ali rose to his feet. Nahri felt too light, her skin covered in blood and mud, her dress torn. He trembled with the knowledge of how close he'd come to losing her.

He swallowed the lump rising in his throat. "May I request an . . . exchange?" he asked, his pulse jumping.

The marid gazed at him. "Speak."

"She had a black bag with her, filled with medical tools. Metal things. I do not see it floating—"

Before Ali could finish the request, Nahri's bag was being held incongruously in the marid's webbed hands. It was dripping water but otherwise looked fine. "This?"

Ali nodded, trying to hide his fear. "And your price?"

Sobek tilted his head, considering. "Information. You will speak to me while we journey. I will have questions. You will answer them truthfully."

Answers you couldn't find digging through my head? But Ali didn't say that. He just nodded grimly and took the bag. He could do this for the friend who'd saved him so many times.

"Understood," he said, looping the strap through his weapons belt, still thankfully secure at his waist.

"Then let us go." Sobek turned back around.

Ali took a deep breath and followed the marid into the Nile.

THE WATER WAS AT HIS CHEST WHEN THE WORLD turned over. Ali stumbled as starlight and black water vaulted overhead as though he were rolling down a hill. His next step was on firm, wet earth, the smell of rich vegetation—of *life*—so heavy in the air it made him dizzy. He glanced up and gasped.

Gone was the dark, muddy river. Or if not gone, transformed. The water arched around him like a tunnel, marshy roots and submerged trees stretching to hold up a glittering canopy of refracted celestial light, glimmering droplets, and dappled green lily pads. Fish and turtles swam past, the silvery whites of their bellies flickering like candles.

Ali stared in wonder at the extraordinary sight. "Beautiful" didn't come close to capturing the magic of the world around him. He might have been in a temple to the Nile itself, an illuminated mosque of water and stars. A long, narrow path stretched into the distance, warm, silty earth pebbled with shining river rocks and flecks of gold and white stone. And though he was breathing air, gentle currents of invisible mist teased his waist, billowing under his arms. Ali felt as though he could close his eyes and catch them, drift in peace along the languid Nile as it wound through desert villages and lush mountains . . .

Sobek's heavy hand clasped his shoulder. "Take care. If your mind wanders here, you will go with it."

Ali nodded, still bewitched. He gazed at the river path again, the glimmer of gold and silver-white tugging at his mind. "The river of salt and gold," he said, remembering. "You—you're the marid of the river of salt and gold. You're the one whose memory I saw in my dream, of Anahid raising the island and—"

Sobek released his shoulder so fast that Ali tripped. "Yes," he said in a blunt way that left no space for questions. "You can breathe and swim in our manner?"

Thrown by the change in topic, Ali stammered an answer. "Yes. I mean, I cannot drown if that's what you're asking."

"Then it would be easiest if we swam." The marid's eyes flashed to Nahri. "I could turn her into a fish, and she could accompany us."

Ali instantly stepped back, hugging Nahri closer. "I don't want you to turn her into a fish."

Sobek's head swiveled on his neck. Again, Ali would swear he saw a hint of a long snout and serrated teeth.

"You fear I shall harm her." It wasn't a question.

"I saw your memory," Ali replied, trembling. "You swore vengeance against Anahid."

"She is not only Anahid's," Sobek countered, pointing at Nahri. The webbing between his fingers looked like an armored glove. "She is also born of the people of this land—*my* land, my waters—and my bond with them stretches back long before that daeva demoness set foot in our lake."

"Nahri's human family was from Egypt?" Ali suspected that would bring her comfort. When the marid nodded, he ventured further. "Does she have any relatives still here?"

"They are dead." The marid turned, the movement jerky; Ali half expected to see a crocodile tail hit the sand. "Come, if you insist on walking. These paths are meant to be swum and they are difficult to maintain in this manner."

Adjusting Nahri in his arms, Ali followed the marid. The *marid*. After all this time, it seemed impossible he should be at the side of one of the creatures. A hundred questions hovered on his lips, and yet Ali—who'd been desperate for answers about his possession, who was normally never one to turn away a source of information—found himself almost afraid to speak.

Sobek wasn't. "How many of you are left?"

Ali didn't understand the question. "It's just us," he said. "Nahri and I—"

The marid clicked his teeth in irritation. "How many of your *kin*? I have seen your sister spin water in your mind, and your mother keeps our tradition. How many others are there?"

New apprehension rose through Ali. "Why do you want to know about my family?"

"Because you requested a favor, and I granted it. Now answer me."

Lying in the powerful marid's realm with an unconscious Nahid in his arms seemed unwise, but Ali still skirted the question. "I'm not certain. I grew up in Daevabad and don't know my mother's relatives well."

"Have they always lived in Ta Ntry?"

"Yes," Ali answered before realizing that wasn't quite true. There was a reason his mother was queen, after all, her family well connected politically. "I mean, mostly. My mother told me our ancestors frequently traveled back and forth between Ta Ntry and Daevabad during the first centuries after the conquest. They were government ministers, advisors, that sort of thing. But since then many have returned to live in Ta Ntry."

"Ah," Sobek said quietly. "I see."

"See what?"

The marid ignored him. "Are any of them blessed like you?"

Blessed. Is that what Ali was? He thought back to that day in Issa's room, his worried mother begging the repulsed scholar for help. "Not as far as I know. Your kind are feared as monsters in Ta Ntry. I don't think there's anyone else like me."

"Your people have short memories."

Ali fought to keep up with Sobek's long stride, Nahri getting heavy in his aching arms. "What are you talking about? Does that mean they're not true, the stories about the marid?"

Now Sobek did glance back, his reptilian eyes gleaming. "I did not say that."

A chill swept Ali. *Are there stories like that about you?* he wanted to ask, but in a rare moment of self-preservation halted the question at his lips.

Trying to change the subject, he asked a different one. "The ifrit called you Sobek. Is that your name?"

"It is among the names mortals have given me."

"Mortals know of you?"

"Mortals *worshipped* me." Hunger again surged into Sobek's voice, the cold dispassion fleeing like a drawn tide. "They filled shining temples with my visage and built cities in my name. I am the reason this land is great."

Ali's mouth was dry. "And what did this cost them?"

"Brides." Ali gave him a shocked look, but Sobek didn't seem to notice, lost in a reverie that had changed the marid's entire misty expression. His face was all crocodile now, bloodlust in his yellow eyes and saliva glistening from his teeth. "Women, with that first flush of fertility, mortality . . . the power in such coupling, in their blood . . ." Sobek's voice turned wistful. "It is unlike anything else."

Ali swayed on his feet, but it was not exhaustion this time. The open craving and arrogance in Sobek's voice, the way he met Ali's eyes as though confiding a shared desire, it made Ali ill. And though he was trying to check his tongue in the presence of such a powerful creature, his heart could not let this stand.

"That's evil." He stared at Sobek. "Did you not think those women would rather have lived and had families of their own instead of being dishonored and drowned?"

"I did not always drown them." Sobek didn't seem bothered in the slightest by Ali's revulsion. "They were the ones who chose to settle on my riverbanks. And no matter what blood it cost, they always rejoiced when they saw my floods. I never had to take the unwilling—I couldn't. You know the laws between our races. I cannot kill a lesser being without their consent."

"And you still call it consent when you threatened families with famine and pretended to be the Creator?"

Sobek's gaze flickered over him, seeming to finally recognize Ali's disgust. A bit of the hunger left his expression, but if Ali feared anger, he needn't have: Sobek merely looked weary—and perhaps a little annoyed.

"You are of those who call themselves djinn, are you not?" the marid asked. "I assume then you share one of the faiths of the humans in this land, the faiths that displaced me. A rather ironic twist of fate for us both."

"What's that supposed to mean?"

"When your woman lay in your arms, your first words asked my price." Sobek snagged Ali's elbow, jerking him forward as the path behind them crashed down in a thundering waterfall. "In my experience, no man asks that unless part of him is willing to pay."

Ali recalled his wrenching despair when Nahri wouldn't wake up. He opened his mouth, but that was not a charge he could deny. "She is not my woman," he said instead.

The look Sobek gave him was withering. "I have been in your head." He turned back around, sparing Ali a response. "You are from a different time, mortal. A kinder one. You could not understand mine."

"But you were punished even in your time," Ali pointed out. "I saw your memory. Suleiman sent Anahid to punish the marid for abusing humans."

Fury rippled across Sobek's gray-green face, the fog churning at his feet. "Anahid went too far. She humiliated us, stole our lake, and forced my kin into servitude."

"So what happened? Did you help my ancestors take Daevabad from the Nahids? Was that supposed to be your revenge?"

"In part." Sobek raised his hand, snatching at the air, and a ribbon of gold mist froze in his fist like he'd pulled a rope tight. He jerked it over the three of them, and it was as if they'd entered a new world. The river was wilder here, crashing down boulders far above their heads and tumbling into the whirlpools of waterfalls.

Ali gaped in awe, but now that he had Sobek answering questions, he wasn't stopping. "But Manizheh and her . . . champion made the lake rise to attack my Citadel. That's marid magic. Why would your people help them now?"

Sobek hissed. "No marid would ever *help* a daeva by choice. If my cousins aided this Manizheh and the abomination at her side, it was because they had no choice."

"I don't understand."

Sobek tugged another current into his hand, a calm pool rippling over them. "It took us a long time to pry free of the Nahids. My people are proud, and we did not suffer their humiliations lightly. To bend ourselves to a daeva and be forced to erect a dry monstrosity of a city in our sacred lake—we rejoiced when the water finally tasted their flesh," he said, sending ice into Ali's blood. "I have been apart from my kin for a long time, but even I heard the rumors a descendant said to be Anahid's equal walked the land, and that she intended to partner with a warrior with even more magic and bring back the old ways of her family." Sobek's voice was filled with quiet remorse. "My cousins had just gotten their freedom. I suspect they were desperate to find a way to stop her."

"So they killed her warrior," Ali said, the pieces tumbling into place. There it was: the reason he'd been possessed. "Or made me do it, anyway."

"I suspect you were an opportunity they seized without much thought. My kin would have been looking for a way to get rid of him without directly staining their hands. To suddenly have a warrior like you in their waters—another daeva, or a djinn, or whatever nonsense you call yourself—who could wield the blade in their place? They must have thought it a blessing."

A blessing. There was that word again. "They tortured me," Ali replied, his voice hollow. "I had nothing to do with any of this."

"You were there, and you were useful." There was no cruelty in the statement. It was just that, a statement.

"But their plan didn't work," Ali pointed out. "Darayavahoush came back even more powerful. So what went wrong?"

Sobek halted without warning, and Ali nearly crashed into his scaly back. He turned around, staring as if he might break into Ali's mind again. God, did those eyes make his skin crawl. It was the gaze of a predator from another world, another age—the gulf between them insurmountable.

"Our exchange was not for your illumination," the marid finally replied. "It was for mine. Give me the girl a moment."

Ali tried to step back, but Sobek slipped Nahri from his arms as if a wave had stolen her.

"Be calm, you prickly creature," Sobek demanded as Ali tried to pull free of the ribbons of water wrapping his limbs, the visible exasperation out of place on the ancient being's face. "Seize the current to your left."

"*Seize the current?*" Ali repeated, baffled. "But I'm not marid."

"You still have hands, do you not? Seize it, or I shall toss your woman into it and offer you another challenge."

The marid moved as if to do so, and in a burst of panic, Ali obeyed. He threw his hand to the golden mists, grasping. He expected his fingers to close on nothing.

Instead it was as though he'd plunged his hand into a waterfall, freezing it with his touch. The power drove him to his knees, and Ali cried out, knives of pain raking down his arm. The ring scorched his heart.

Sobek was there the next moment, laying his free hand against Ali's brow. The pain was numbed to a dull ache. Ali opened his eyes.

"God be praised," he whispered. The world around them was suddenly even more wondrous, brighter, as though he'd stepped into a new level of existence. Ali could see a thousand currents, ten thousand, more possibilities and places than he'd ever imagined existed all spread out before him. Snowcapped mountains and tropical seas. Meandering northern streams and a cyclone-lashed shore. The placid fountain of a simple mudbrick courtyard and a puddle in a gray, rain-soaked city.

The one in your hand. Sobek's voice burst inside his mind. *Dive, little mortal.*

Acting on instinct, Ali let himself fall forward, dragging the current in his hand over them all. The moment he let go, all the paths vanished, and he tumbled to the white sand, breathing hard.

The marid magic lingered. Ali tingled with it, tendrils of water dancing up his arms. A pearly path of sand stretched before him, the fish that passed overhead dashing away. He could feel the raw power pouring off Sobek.

Nahri, though, was a different flavor. A tantalizing one. Salty blood and scalding magic. The kind that burned down the world and invited water to re-create anew. It was there, in her delicate veins and fragile skin that could be so easily pierced. So easily taken.

Ali gagged, and the awful hunger vanished—though he'd swear his teeth had briefly sharpened. "What did you do to me?"

"Nothing." The marid's eyes danced. "You still have it," he murmured, as if to himself. "A dozen generations removed, and it still persists."

Ali was still struggling to catch his breath, his palms braced on the sand. Beyond, a herd of hippopotamuses thundered past the gleam of the watery tunnel.

"How does all this *work*?" he asked, climbing to his feet. "The way you get inside my mind, the way we travel?"

Sobek beckoned him forward, and they kept walking. "It is a difficult thing to put into words. My kind do not communicate like yours. We join with one another and share what is in our minds, our souls. We are . . . we are like the water, yes? There may be many streams, but they all come from the same river." A dismissive tone entered his voice. "Not like daevas. You are all separate burning embers."

Ignoring the comment, Ali pressed on. "And the currents, all the paths I saw?"

"There is water everywhere. Not just lakes and rivers, but streams far below the surface and rain in the clouds. That is how we travel—or rather how those of us who are capable of travel do." Sobek seemed to be warming to the topic, more eager to explain this than the marid's violent history with the Nahids. "I am among the first generation of my people, so I can take this solid form, but most of my kin cannot be seen by mortal eyes. They exist as part of their birth water, possessing other small creatures in their domain when they wish."

"Not always when they wish," Ali said sharply. But there was something else, something he was missing . . . "Wait, can you travel to *any* water? Could you take us through the lake? Back to Daevabad?" he asked, hope rising in his chest.

The warmth vanished from Sobek's face. "No." He dumped Nahri back into Ali's arms and stormed forward.

Ali stumbled after him. "What do you mean, *no*? Because you can't or because you're unwilling?"

Sobek spun on him, baring his teeth. "Because I will not see the seal ring returned to that foul city. Not for anything. If there is any light in the catastrophe my cousin's heedlessness wrought, it is that Anahid's spell is finally broken. I pray that foul island and its fouler city follow suit and drown beneath the waves."

Ali reeled. "It is my home."

"Then how fortunate you have another." Sobek seized a new current, dragging it over them and stalking off.

Ali followed, unwilling to give up. "Then can I do it? Travel the currents myself?"

"*No.*" There was a new warning in the marid's voice. "You will never have full use of your powers with that ring in your heart, and you should be grateful for it." Sobek raised his hands, spreading them as though in prayer.

The watery ceiling collapsed, landing as light rain upon Ali's face.

The wondrous river tunnel was gone, the glimmering light, the gold-flecked path. Ali and Sobek stood in the knee-deep shallows of a winding, beachside creek. It was still night, but the stars and moon gave enough light to reveal that the desert had been replaced by a jungle of unfamiliar trees. Though he couldn't see the ocean, Ali heard the break of waves in the distance.

"Ta Ntry," Sobek announced. "Walk south. The coast and the forests are marked with the human ruins your kind like to haunt."

Ali was thrown by the abrupt change in scenery and found himself aching for a final glimpse of the Nile's enchanted underbelly, the radiant temple of water. Its vanishing echoed through him with a sorrow he couldn't explain.

He glanced down at Nahri. She hadn't so much as stirred in her charmed sleep, a damp curl plastered against her cheek.

What is your price? Ali was suddenly very glad he hadn't had to answer the question for himself. "You're the marid that cursed her appearance, aren't you?" he asked. "The one that made her look human and left her in Cairo."

"I am."

"Why?"

"Because her human kin paid my price, and it was the best way to protect her."

"She was a child, alone and frightened. That was no protection."

Sobek's eyes flashed. "I have saved her life twice and made a journey that might have killed you pass in a night. I have honored my exchange." He stepped back. "You should go."

"Wait!" Ali moved between Sobek and the deeper water. "Is there truly no way I could learn to travel the currents? To access the kind of water magic I had before I took the seal?"

"No." Sobek tried to step past him.

Ali blocked his path. "Then could another marid?" He thought fast. "Tiamat. The one who was birthed in the lake. Is this ocean not said to be her domain now? Could I—"

Sobek grabbed him, and any protest Ali might have made died on his lips.

"Tiamat would more likely rip your soul from your body and devour you, ring and all." Sobek stared into Ali's eyes with his black-and-yellow gaze, and Ali's heart skipped in fear. "I am granting you *mercy*, mortal. You have a place in your world. Return to it. Were you wise, you would forget what you know of marid. My people have your name, and you will not be able to fight them, not with Anahid's ring holding you back. Take your woman and flee to your deserts. It is safer."

He let go of Ali so abruptly Ali lost his balance, nearly dropping Nahri. By the time he recovered, Sobek was striding deeper into the creek, green clouds swirling around his lower half.

"Why?" Ali burst out, suddenly fearing that he'd missed something, that Sobek was twisting him in a way that would become clear too late. "You say you don't help us, you only work in exchanges. Why grant me your mercy or your advice?"

Sobek paused. His youthful humanoid form was almost gone. "Alizayd al Qahtani," he said, speaking Ali's name aloud for the first time. "I will remember you." The last bit of his visage slipped away under a crocodilian mask.

And then without another word, he vanished beneath the water.

16

DARA

It was silent in Daevabad's Grand Temple at this darkest hour of the night. For a people who honored the ascent and descent of the sun, marking the first and last glimpse of its burning orb with quiet gratitude to their Creator, this time farthest from its presence was meant for being safe and asleep with their loved ones, a fire altar burning to keep the demons out.

But Dara had no loved ones and was a demon himself, so here he was.

The first night he'd come, he'd been drawn to the earliest shrines: to the Nahids who'd united the tribes to build Daevabad and their Afshin protectors, figures from a world that seemed so much simpler, one in which heroes were just that, and their enemies as obviously wicked. His gaze traced their statues with envy and longing. How he wished that could have been his society.

And yet even Dara had a limit for useless brooding, and so though he found himself returning, slipping through the Temple gate and along the moonlit garden paths smelling so sweetly of jasmine, he did so with a purpose: sweeping the floor of ashes and dusting the shrines. He did so without magic, for it was not permitted in the Temple, and it felt better to perform this service with his hands, the smallest penance he could.

Dara was doing so, running a broom of dried rushes along the marble foundation of Anahid's enormous central altar, when the sound of soft steps caught his ear. He recognized the weary intake of air and the shuffling gait with the expanded senses his form now gave him, senses that had a predatory instinct he hated.

"I wondered when you would catch me," he greeted Kartir quietly, tidying the accumulated pile of dust without turning around.

"I thought to let the acolytes responsible for cleaning enjoy another morning of extra sleep," Kartir replied. "But it struck me that a man sneaking in to serve the shrines in the middle of the night might be in need of counsel."

"Is it that obvious?"

The priest's voice was gentle. "It has been apparent for a very long time, Darayavahoush."

Dara's grip tightened on the broom. "You are the only one apart from Manizheh who calls me that anymore."

"You are Darayavahoush to your Creator. Afshin is a title that need not define you here."

Dara finally turned around. "And my other title? Do you think the Creator knows that one? Surely They must; prayers for justice from a thousand lips must weep it." His voice turned bitter. "It was almost finally granted."

Kartir moved forward. "I heard. How are you feeling? There was word you were injured. Word you haven't been so . . . visible."

That was one way of putting it. Manizheh had been as good as her promise, pulling Dara from most of his official duties and replacing him with the warriors he'd trained. Dara could no longer offer guidance when it came to running Daevabad. Instead, he was given assignments by so-called cooler heads, expected to obey and keep his mouth firmly shut.

There is honor in being a weapon. He ground his teeth. "You might say I've fallen from favor."

"You and I both, to be honest," Kartir replied. "Banu Manizheh has made clear she desires my retirement more than my advice. But you saved the life of a fellow Daeva, did you not? The young woman?"

"Irtemiz." The presence of his protege at training had been a sliver of good news, even if, with her broken arm and leg, all she could do was shout corrections at his recruits from a chair.

But Dara's mood had already dimmed. That night at the hospital had broken something in him. Hunted like an animal, he saw clearly how the rest of the world viewed him.

"I probably took three dozen lives to save hers," Dara said. "Maybe more. Not that it matters, right? They were sand flies and dirt-bloods. Unnatural creations; soulless abominations whose very existence threatens ours, and their fanatical supporters."

"Do you believe that's what they are?"

Tears burned in Dara's eyes, the wetness sizzling again his hot skin. "I used to. I used to believe it all, Kartir. I had to."

Kartir's expression betrayed no judgment. "Why did you have to?"

Dara took a deep breath and then they were out, the words that expressed the most hidden fear of his heart finally spoken aloud. "Because it had to be true, Kartir. Because if the shafit were people, innocent mothers and fathers and children, and I did to them the things I did . . ." He exhaled. "Then I am damned. I am a monster, worse than the vilest ifrit, and I—I do not want to be that. I was just trying to serve my tribe. I was *eighteen* when the Nahids sent me to Qui-zi. I worshipped them, trusted them, and they *lied.*" He raised his hands, taking in the

Temple. "What is any of this supposed to mean if it makes room for such an atrocity?"

"I think it a mistake to judge the Creator by the misdeeds of mortals," Kartir replied. "I believe the Nahids are blessed. I believe they are meant to guide us, but that doesn't mean they're not flawed. It doesn't mean they don't fall prey to their own fears and desires. I love the Nahids enough not to burden them with expectations of perfection. I cannot. I have seen a Temple-raised woman use her gifts to kill, while a human-raised one broke a taboo I thought sacred and saved lives."

Dara was close to losing the battle with his tears. "Then what do you do?"

"I think you start by listening to this"—Kartir tapped Dara's head—"and this"—he touched Dara's heart—"as much as you do the holy words of priests, books, and Nahids. Your heart and mind are bestowed by the Creator as well, you know."

"My heart and mind are telling me that I committed the ghastliest, most unforgivable of crimes. That I helped create a world that can only be fixed by more violence. That I—" Dara hesitated. Still this felt traitorous. "That I followed the wrong people." He glanced, imploring, at the priest. "What do I do with that kind of burden, Kartir? If there were any justice, I would be burning in hellfire. Instead, I keep being brought back to life." He gestured to his body. "My form? The ifrit live for millennia like this."

"Does that not seem a blessing?"

"A *blessing*?" Dara repeated, the hysterical edge in his voice echoing across the empty vastness. "It is a curse!"

Kartir removed the broom from Dara's hands—just in time, for it was starting to smolder. "Walk with me, Darayavahoush." The priest took his arm, leading him past the enormous, gleaming silver altar and into the back corridors of the Temple.

"If you will permit me," Kartir said as they approached a pair of brass doors at the end of the hall, "all I am hearing from you is 'I this, I that.' Have you not considered that your suffering and redemption might be less important than making things up to your victims?"

The words struck deep, leaving Dara thrown for a response. "There is no making that up. You can't bring back the dead."

"You can stop making *more* dead. You are the bravest man I know, and you run now from ghosts? Sit with this burden, Dara. You may find doing so is easier than holding it over your head and waiting for it to crush you."

Kartir opened the door. Inside was a small circular room lined with glass shelves. At its center stood a crude, almost primitive fire altar, little more than a beaten brass bowl in which cedar burned brightly. It threw firelight across the room, reflecting on the glittering glass shelves and the soft velvet cushions they displayed.

And on the emerald ornaments that were everywhere.

Dara recoiled so fast he crashed into the door frame. Slave vessels—rings, lamps, bracelets, and collars. Dozens.

Kartir squeezed his arm. "Breathe, Darayavahoush. They cannot hurt you. They sleep."

Dara shook his head, trying not to rip his arm free and tear out of the room. "I do not want to be here."

"Neither do they. But I think you need a reminder of the position you're in, a reminder, frankly, that you've sided with the creatures responsible for this. These souls are fortunate; there are at least a dozen more, judging from the relics we have recovered, still out in the human world."

Dara forced himself to relax. In the hush of the room, he would swear he heard slumbered breathing.

Kartir let him go. "This is where I brought Banu Nahri on her first day. She came here afterward—not infrequently. She has a good heart. I pray to the Creator that she's safe wherever she is."

He paused. "I did not ever think to see the two of you on opposite sides."

Nor did I. Dara leaned against the door frame. "I am not capable of fixing this," he said. "I am not a prophet, not a priest. I am a murderer."

"Again with the 'I,'" Kartir rebuked him. "Tell me, Darayavahoush, what good will you be doing, burning in this hellfire you're aching to join? Will that help your victims? You *have* been blessed; you have been granted the power, the privilege, the *time*— all these centuries you don't want—to fix things. And when you finally do face our Creator, do you want to say you spent them wallowing in guilt?" Kartir's expression grew fierce. "Or would you rather say you spent every extra breath fighting for a more just world?"

"This is an easy thing to preach from the Temple. You do not see the threats we do from the palace or bear the responsibilities of protecting tens of thousands of frightened people ready to tear one another apart."

"You're right. I don't. But neither do you," Kartir countered. "Not alone. If Manizheh wants to rule Daevabad, she should be *listening* to Daevabad—not just the select Daevas who agree with her. She needs to make peace with the djinn and be seen as a unifier, as someone capable of mercy and reason."

Dara rubbed his temples, his own slave ring knocking against his skull. It made his stomach churn, recalling the moment he'd considering removing it to kill himself in the hospital.

But he'd survived, once more against the odds.

Could he change? Could Manizheh? Because heartbreakingly, Dara did see hints of the leader she might have been if Ghassan had not brutalized her. She was exceedingly brilliant, measured, level headed, and thoughtful. It was not her powers or name alone that had led people to follow her in the wilderness.

But it would not be easy to sway her.

It will be even harder to sway the djinn. He felt his face fall. "I would not even know where to start with the djinn. Which of them would possibly want to deal with, let alone trust, us?"

Kartir gave him an even look. "If I recall, you have a djinn with plenty of experience navigating tribal politics currently languishing in the dungeon."

Dara instantly scowled. "Muntadhir would never work with us. He would happily see the entire palace—himself included—crumble into the lake if it meant Manizheh and I went down with it."

"You don't know that. Muntadhir has his weaknesses, yes, but I always got the impression he truly cared about Daevabad and had a genuine affection for our tribe. And it might look good for you to suggest such an outreach," Kartir added. "Pragmatic and careful. If you want Banu Manizheh to listen to you, you must show that your opinions are worth their weight."

"If I let the emir out of his chains, he is going to try to kill me."

Kartir clapped him on the back. "A blessing, then, that accomplishing such a feat is so difficult."

17

NAHRI

It really was beautiful.

Nahri stared at the ocean. It was the first time she'd ever seen the sea, and it was dazzling, painted so beautifully with the rich colors of approaching dawn that it looked as though the Creator had personally blessed it, the water stretching to meet a hazy horizon. A gull cried as gentle waves caressed the soft beach, the surf rushing forward and pulling back in a steadying, hypnotizing motion.

"Please say something."

It was the second time Ali had begged her to speak since she'd woken to his stammered explanations of sunken boats and mysterious marid. He was a wreck at her side, reduced to only a ragged waist cloth and his weapons belt, mud clinging to his skin and beard. She imagined she looked the same, her dress ruined and scratches covering her skin. Numb, Nahri traced spirals in the sand, disturbing a line of shells and drying seagrass.

"Nahri—"

"Is any of our food left? The coins I exchanged the last gems for?" Her voice came out in a scratchy whisper, her throat smarting from the muddy river water that had poured down it and just as painfully been forced back up.

Ali hesitated. There was worry in that pause, a man wondering how to break bad news.

"I'm sorry," he said haltingly. "The boat sank so fast. By the time I got you out of the river, everything that wasn't already gone was on fire. The marid said it would be safer if we left immediately. He said if Qandisha returned with Darayavahoush, he couldn't protect us."

Nahri twitched at Dara's name. She could still taste the Nile on her tongue and remember with wrenching clarity the moment she'd lost the battle to keep her mouth shut. How poetic, both of them drowned by the same ifrit.

Both of them dragged back to life and forced to fight anew.

A salty breeze blew a lock of messy hair across her face. The ocean wind and swaying palms, the rise and fall of the waves like a slumbering liquid behemoth, it was splendid beyond words, as though she and Ali had actually died last night and been whisked away to a sliver of Paradise. A shame they hadn't. Maybe in Paradise, Nahri would have been allowed to finally rest.

"It'll be okay," Ali rushed to say, clearly trying to make her feel better. "There are coconuts if you're thirsty. I didn't see anything else to eat, but Sobek said if we walked south, we would find ruins there that djinn like to—"

Nahri burst into laughter.

It was a wild laugh, followed by another, and then Nahri couldn't stop, giggling so hard that tears came to her eyes and she struggled for air.

She wiped the wetness away. "I'm sorry, it's just . . . I mean, it's funny, isn't it? Do you know how many times I've had to do this?

Forget healing; my specialty should be having my life destroyed and then being forced to rebuild from nothing." Nahri thought of their little boat, now on the bottom of the Nile, along with Yaqub's precious tools and all the supplies she'd bartered and stolen. The previous days came back to her, idling in the shade of crumbling temples and the long, peaceful hours of sailing past green fields and sun-drenched villages.

She should have known it couldn't last.

"I'm so tired," she said, her voice cracking. "Everything I build gets broken. My life in Cairo. My dreams for Daevabad. I give everything—*everything*—I have only for someone to come along and smash it. It's all for nothing. *Nothing*."

The last word ripped from her in a choked sob, and then Ali was there, reaching for her hand.

"It's not for nothing, Nahri," he insisted. "We can still put things right."

She yanked away. "Don't. Don't talk like that. Don't *look* at me like that," she said, wrapping her arms around herself and rocking back and forth. "I don't need your pity. I don't need anything."

"*Nahri*." Undeterred, Ali knelt closer, wiping away the tears blurring her eyes. "You pulled me from my grief when I would have stayed and died with Muntadhir. You've saved my life more times than I can count." He stroked back the hair sticking to her damp cheeks, his voice gentle as he said, "There's no one else here, my friend. You don't need to keep up this front."

Nahri wanted to protest. To slap his hand away and withdraw to her usual distance. To put on her mask.

Instead, it all crashed down. She wasn't sure which of them moved first, but then Ali was hugging her, and she was clinging to him, burying her face in the warmth of his neck.

"I thought you were dead," she wept. "I thought *I* was dead. I thought I'd failed everyone, and I couldn't do anything. I couldn't even fight back. There were too many of them."

Ali pulled her closer. "It's okay," he whispered. "Qandisha is gone. Her ghouls are gone. She has no idea where we are."

"She'll find us. She was *waiting* for us." Fresh despair swept over Nahri. "She has magic we don't understand. They all do. The ifrit, Manizheh, Dara . . . and I have nothing. I don't have my abilities. And my mother . . ." God, Nahri couldn't even say the words, for what Manizheh had done was worse. It was magic without magic, and more powerful for it. She'd made Nahri feel worthless. Foolish. Her mother had looked right through her supposed cleverness and read her better than Nahri had ever read a mark, fashioning all her fears and ambitions into a blade of calculated words that knocked Nahri right off her feet.

"I can't do this," she choked out. "I can't." Nahri was strong, she was a fighter, but she did not have it in her to pick herself up yet again; to survive this new setback and fight for a future that seemed doomed either way.

Ali pulled back just enough to meet her gaze. For a moment, the warm gray of his eyes seemed to swim with a darker mist, but then it was gone.

"I'll take you back to Egypt," he promised. "I'll find a way. Qandisha thinks you're dead. That's the story I'll carry with me to Daevabad and Ta Ntry. You can return to Yaqub and build the life you want without a bunch of magical creatures ruining it. You deserve to."

His words went straight to her heart. Nahri could see it, the way out, the escape from all this. She could envision herself in thirty years with her own apprentices, surrounded by the neighborhood children she'd delivered as babes, the fantastic city of Daevabad—the land of djinn and magical courts—fading to legend.

It would just mean turning her back on everyone else she loved. And then Nahri would be the one breaking what she'd built.

The sun crested the ocean's horizon, turning the undulating

sea into a wild burst of fiery color. Scorching yellow and wine-dark crimson, burnt orange and warm copper. It reminded her of Daevabad's lake on the morning of the Navasatem procession. Of laughing and smiling with her people as they lit lanterns and sang verses to the Creator to celebrate the founding of their home.

How did Anahid do it? Her descendants might have gone astray—that seemed to happen to all revolutionaries—but still, how had Anahid pulled the tribes together from the ravages of Suleiman's curse, protected them from the predations of the ifrit, and built a dazzling city? Built an entire *civilization*? Had she been made of greater stuff than Nahri? Or had she hidden her bone-shaking doubt, forced a confident smile, and carried on while continually praying she wasn't making a mistake?

Nahri could feel the weight of Ali's expectant gaze. Taking a deep breath, she curled her fingers around his and then lifted his hand to her cheek.

"Thank you," she said softly. "But I need you to help me with something else."

Ali had gone still, so close their breath mingled together on the warm air. "With what?"

"I want to conjure a fire."

THE SUN WAS HIGH ON THE HORIZON BY THE TIME they were done digging a small pool at the tide break, their clothes freshly damp with seawater. Nahri carefully floated a cinnamon-colored scalloped shell in the pool, where it glimmered in the orange light.

She did what she could in terms of ablutions, rinsing her arms and feet in the ocean's spray, cupping her hands to let water trickle down her face and through her snarled hair. The salt and sand dried on her skin, smelling fresh, the aroma of a new start.

Nahri beckoned Ali closer and then laid a hand over his heart. "Lift the seal."

He complied, and it immediately fell away. They were getting better at this. She conjured a pair of flames in her other hand and used them to light one of the driftwood twigs they'd gathered. Then she let go of him, regret twinging through her as her magic fell away.

"Can I . . . can I sit with you?" Ali asked. "I don't want to intrude or if it's not allowed . . ."

Nahri blinked in surprise. "I wouldn't have thought you wanted to."

Ali gazed back at her, the ocean reflecting in his eyes. "I want to."

"Then sit." She patted the damp sand next to her. Nahri pressed the smoldering stick to the dried tuft of grass she'd stuck in the shell, and it burst into flame. Holding the stick in one hand, she bowed her head, praying quietly in Divasti.

It felt good to go through the ritual, better than she would have imagined. Nahri hadn't prayed since she left Daevabad. She hadn't actually prayed since the dawn of Navasatem when she'd lit oil lamps at Nisreen's side. Nahri had always had a mixed relationship with her faith, mostly because it felt more like a duty than any true belief. She might be the Banu Nahida, but often she'd felt like a fraud, yearning to share the sincere devotion so many of the Daevas around her enjoyed. She wanted their certainty in a higher power, a meaning to the cruelly chaotic violence that plagued their world.

Do Manizheh and Dara pray? Was her mother even now leading dawn ceremonies at the Daeva temple and marking the brow of her loyal Afshin? Nahri knew Dara had once been devout—he'd killed people because he'd been told that was what the Creator required.

And for a long time, that thought alone would have been enough to shake Nahri's faith. How could she share these rituals, these words, with those who would slaughter innocents in the same Creator's name? But as she gazed at her crude fire altar and the sunlight-streaked sea, some of her doubts settled.

Manizheh was a murderer, plain and simple. Her mother could say otherwise all she liked; *she* was the one who had betrayed their role. For whatever had happened between their peoples, Anahid had built her city for all the tribes. She'd been a healer, a unifier, a woman blessed with miraculous powers by the Divine itself.

Manizheh did not own that. No one did. Anahid's legacy and faith were things Nahri had equal claim on and could also be strengthened by.

She touched the smoldering stick to her brow to mark her skin with ash. Ali wordlessly lowered his head, and Nahri did the same for him. They sat in silence for a moment as the kindling burned and the sun pulled away from the waves.

"What do they mean?" he asked. "The prayers?"

Nahri flushed. "You'd be better off asking a priest. The prayers are similar to yours, at least from what I remember hearing when I used to beg for alms outside mosques as a child." She stuck the driftwood in the sand, letting the smoke perfume her skin.

"And the rituals? The fire altar?"

"The rituals remind us to tend the altar and keep the flames burning." She bit her lip. "I told Kartir once it seemed like a clever way to remind people to pray, since the fire would otherwise go out, and he told me I was a cynic. Even so, I like the ritual of the motions; they set me at peace. I like the continuity—that Anahid might have done these same things so long ago. That the Daevas have maintained them. That we have survived worse. When I first arrived in Daevabad, Nisreen told me I should take assurance from the flames that survived the night, because there would always be darkness. But as long as you kept a light burning, it would be okay."

"That's beautiful," Ali said softly. "I never knew that. I probably should have. I should have taken the time to learn what so many people in my city kept sacred."

"I imagine the Citadel thought it wiser to teach their soldiers that we were lecherous fire worshippers, not people. Made it easier to hurt us."

"That doesn't excuse my ignorance." Ali stared at his hands. "I've hurt Daevas, and I've hurt shafit. I've said things and done things that have gotten people killed. I've killed them myself." He lifted his gaze to study the smoldering grass on the floating shell. "We have a verse like that—like what Nisreen said. We say God is the light of the heavens and the earth, that it's a light as steady and protected as a lamp behind glass and shines as brightly as a star. That it is always there to guide us."

His last words, spoken with a hitch, echoed the growing decision in Nahri's mind. She picked up a chunk of driftwood, breaking it up to still the trembling in her hands, and then carefully set one of the tiny pieces upon the kindling. It caught, fire licking through the dry wood.

"I'm not going back to Egypt, Ali," she started. "I can't. The way Qandisha was talking, I think the ifrit had their own aims in allying with Manizheh. There are too many coincidences. Seemingly no one knew Dara was enslaved, and somehow my mother ends up with his ring and the company of the ifrit who enslaved him? And they're happy to help her, their mortal enemy?"

Ali had betrayed no surprise when she said she wasn't going back to Egypt—perhaps he really was starting to read her—but looked unconvinced at her other words. "Your mother was clever enough to outwit my *father*. Do you really think she'd fall for an ifrit scheme?"

"I think the ifrit were scheming for millennia before we were born. And yes, I think Manizheh might have been so hungry for power and revenge that she didn't care about the costs. Or perhaps she thought she could outwit them as well. Either way . . ." Nahri's throat constricted in fear, her body far more reasonable that her stupid, suicidal heart. "I can't sit this out. Daevabad is my home. *Our* home." She laced her fingers through his again. "The Qahtanis and the Nahids got us here. I think it should be an al Qahtani and a Nahid who fix it. Or more likely die trying in some horrible fashion."

He squeezed her hand. "I'm going to pretend I didn't hear that last part. But—oh!" Ali dropped her hand. "I nearly forgot!" He rose to his feet and loped off.

"Forgot what?" Nahri called.

But he was already returning. "I hung it on a tree to dry out."

Nahri recognized the black bag in his hands. "My instruments!" she exclaimed in delight. She jumped up and pulled the bag from him, quickly examining it. All seemed in order, and she breathed a sigh of relief, the sight of the tools lightening the mantle of despair heavy upon her. "Oh, Ali . . . thank you!" she said, throwing her arms around his neck. "How in God's name did you find this?"

"I . . ." She seemed to have caught him off guard. Then Nahri was suddenly very aware of his shirtless state. She blushed, stepping back, and Ali continued. "Sobek—the marid found it for me. I asked him to retrieve it."

"You asked a *marid* to fetch my bag?" Nahri shuddered. "You frighten me sometimes. But thank you. And thank you as well for all that back on the beach," she added, her cheeks going warmer with embarrassment. "You're a good friend. Probably the best one I've ever had." She hardened her voice. "But if you tell anyone I cried, I'll kill you."

Ali looked like he was trying not to smile. "Consider me properly threatened."

"Good. Let's go, then. We've wasted enough time, and I'd like to know what happened last night that left you on a first-name basis with a marid."

"It's a long story."

"Ali, nothing about this trip has gone well. You know we have a long walk."

NAHRI STEPPED OVER THE ROTTING REMAINS OF A fallen palm tree, pushing a sweat-soaked tendril of hair from her face. Leery of walking on the open beach, they'd stuck to the edge of the forest. "So he *was* a crocodile or just looked like one?"

Ahead, Ali cut through a net of green vines. "He seemed like something in between," he answered. "Like he was both at once. The more I tried to look at him, the harder it became to distinguish."

"And he knew of me?"

"He claimed he was the marid who cursed your appearance. He said it was part of a pact with your human kin, meant to protect you."

"My *human* kin?" Nahri stopped in her tracks. "I have family in Egypt? Did he tell you anything else?"

Ali glanced back, apologetic. "He said they were dead. I'm sorry, Nahri. He refused to tell me anything more. That's why he put you to sleep. He said it was best you didn't remember."

I had family in Egypt. I am *Egyptian—truly.* It was a bittersweet revelation, because deep in her heart, Nahri feared she'd never see Egypt again. And yet it only threw another knot into the tangled tapestry of her past. Her mother was a Daevabad-raised Banu Nahida whose every movement had been watched. Nahri had supposedly been born in Daevastana, on the road between Daevabad and Zariaspa. Where in that story was there room for an Egyptian father, a shafit? And how had Nahri been returned to his homeland as a child?

"Every time I learn something new, it just dredges up more questions." Nahri kicked a desiccated coconut. "I hate it. I hate puzzles. You can't come up with a plan if you don't have all the pieces."

"For what it's worth, he confirmed some of what we thought about the marid's involvement in the city's fall. He accused Anahid of stealing the lake and using Suleiman's seal to force his kin into servitude—that's why they helped my ancestors overthrow the Nahid Council. When they heard rumors a powerful new Nahid had arisen and intended to take the seal and Daevabad back, they became determined to stop her."

With the sun well risen, the day was sweltering, but a cold sweat broke out on Nahri's back. "So that's why the marid killed Dara. Because they feared Manizheh would use him to conquer Daevabad." Of course, it was a connection to the Nahids that doomed Dara once again.

Ali slashed at a branch. "It's also why they took me. Sobek said they would have been wary of killing a daeva directly, so they conspired to make sure it was one of Dara's own people who wielded the blade. But it wasn't enough, and now the marid owe him some sort of blood debt for killing a lesser being. They can't harm him and have no choice but to help him."

"You also couldn't harm him."

Ali seemed to go slightly still, but then he was pressing forward again, waving a mosquito away from his face. "Well, I still have the marid's magic on me. Maybe that's why."

"Maybe," Nahri echoed softly. "Did he tell you anything else?"

"No, but what he showed me, the way we traveled, my God, it

was incredible. Like the river itself was suspended above us. All the fish and the gold glittering in the sand, the stars reflecting in the water." Admiration filled Ali's voice. "He showed me how they chase currents, and it was as if you could glimpse the entire world through all its different waters."

"How very lovely for the people who tortured you."

"Trust me, I haven't forgotten that part. And there was plenty about him that *wasn't* lovely. The things Sobek talked about doing to humans—" Ali shuddered. "God forbid, I can't even say them aloud."

Things too atrocious to say aloud sounded more like the magical world Nahri knew. She gave the ocean, sparkling through the trees, an uneasy look, half expecting sea creatures to emerge from its depths. "I'm surprised he showed you all this. I'm surprised he *saved* us."

Ali hacked through another vine. "Well, like I said, he promised your family he'd keep you safe."

"I guess." But Nahri still felt like they were missing another piece. She kept walking, stepping carefully over the broken twigs covering the sandy ground. Her feet hurt, and the growing number of mosquito bites covering her bare skin itched like mad. They'd been traveling all morning, and the hot sun pierced the leafy canopy, the shade little relief.

Ahead Ali was marching like a damned automaton, his sword rising and falling. Dressed only in his waist cloth, he looked like he might have been plucked from the stone carvings they'd seen of clashing kings and divine warriors, his body all lithe muscle and supernatural grace. The slats of sunlight coming through the jungle striped his bare skin, illuminating gashes and bite marks from the ghouls' attack. Lifting the seal earlier had begun to heal them, but not entirely. For all that he looked like a divine warrior, Ali was still very mortal.

I almost lost him last night. Even thinking it made her stomach lurch—and *that,* in turn made Nahri even more anxious. To say their friendship had a tumultuous history was an understatement, but it wasn't until she admitted it out loud on the beach that Nahri really realized the depth of what had grown between them. She *didn't* have anyone else like Ali, her occasionally still infuriating, overly idealistic ancestral enemy who'd become the best friend— the partner she'd been ready to spend the rest of her days with back in Egypt.

You shouldn't be thinking like that, she chided herself. By the Most High, hadn't Nahri learned what happened when she got attached to people? Even saying something like that in her head seemed to be tempting fate.

They fell into silence as the temperature climbed and the sun rose higher. Finally, when Nahri was nearing exhaustion, the ground began to rise in a rocky hill—or rather not a hill, but some sort of crumbling brick foundation swallowed by weeds, roots sprawling over silvery stones. A wide creek twisted around it, the rich brown water coloring the azure currents where it met the ocean.

"Looks like a ruin," Ali commented. "Sobek did say that's where the djinn he knew of liked to congregate."

They waded through the creek. Though it only went up to her knees, Nahri shivered. She suspected it was going to take her a long time to regain her comfort with water after last night. They stopped at the foundation wall, its height twice hers. It stretched to the water's edge, melting away in the gloom of jungle.

"Climb or go around?"

Nahri wrung out the bottom of her dress. "Is nap not an option?" When Ali narrowed his eyes, she sighed. "Climb, I suppose."

"I'll help you," he offered, sheathing his weapons and taking her medical bag.

They climbed, emerging in a thick knot of scrubby greenery that scratched her skin. Nahri started to beat it away, but then Ali tugged her down.

"Company," he warned softly. "Look."

Following his gaze, she peered through the leaves. A massive ship lay badly beached on the foundation wall, trees smashed beneath its bulk as if it had dropped from the sky. The hull was painted in meandering stripes of warm beige and olive green, as though to blend in with the landscape. Its front third jutted over the creek, silvery sails tied up.

"That's a sandship," Ali said under his breath.

"Are you sure?" Nahri asked, studying the boat. "Maybe it's human."

"Not with those sails. Look, you can see the tide line halfway up the foundation wall. The water doesn't go high enough to beach it like that. And, well, there's them," he added as two rather obviously djinn sailors came around the hull, both with the distinctive crimson-streaked black hair of the Sahrayn—and what seemed like an excess of weapons gleaming from their waists and arms.

Her heart beat faster. "I guess we go make friends."

Ali grabbed her wrist. "No." Alarm colored his voice. "That boat should be flying Ayaanle colors, no matter the crew's heritage, to be permitted in these waters. The Ayaanle and Sahrayn are as much enemies as they are allies; they've bickered over their border for years. The only thing that keeps them from all-out war are those ships. The Ayaanle need them to trade goods, and the Sahrayn need the money they earn transporting those goods. There are a dozen treaties and taxes governing what flags—"

Nahri shushed him, deciding a history of intertribal trade was not what Ali was trying to tell her. "Meaning what?"

"Meaning we go around."

Silently cursing, Nahri followed his lead, retreating down the wall.

They hadn't touched the ground when a voice spoke up behind her.

"Stay right there, crocodile."

Nahri froze. The voice was speaking Djinnistani with an accent she couldn't pin. Careful not to move, she glanced down from the corner of her eye.

Three men, their faces covered, were waiting for them at the bottom of the wall. The first held a crossbow and was clearly Sahrayn, if the bright hue of his metal-toned eyes was anything to judge by. Another was small, carrying a scythe-ended staff, while the third man was massive, carrying a similarly sized mace and a sword at his waist. They were dressed in motley clothes: torn pants, a stolen Geziri belt, and Ayaanle turbans.

At her side, Ali had stilled. His face was only half turned, Suleiman's mark not yet visible to the others.

The djinn holding the crossbow spoke again, his words directed at Ali. "Drop the weapons, Ayaanle. I do apologize for ruining whatever forbidden entertainments you had planned with your pretty human friend, but if you don't hand over your sword, I'm going to put holes in both of you."

Nahri didn't even see Ali let go of the tree.

One moment he was at her side, and the next, he'd launched himself at the djinn holding the crossbow, sending the man crashing to the ground, ripping the weapon from his hands, and smashing him across the face with it in a single fluid motion.

The man with the mace was backing up, his wide eyes darting between the zulfiqar in Ali's hands and the mark now visible on his face. He let out a stream of what Nahri was fairly certain she would have understood as expletives had her linguistic powers been working.

The other djinn had already whistled, hefting his bladed staff in the air to swing at Ali's head. Nahri cried out in warning, but

Ali was already ducking, rolling to his feet to emerge behind the man with the mace. He brought the hilt of his zulfiqar down on the man's skull, sending him sprawling.

And Nahri was suddenly back on the roof of the palace as Ali cut through Daevas, on the burning boat as Dara cut through djinn. It was obvious these people meant the two of them harm, but Nahri had a sudden and irrational urge to grab the zulfiqar from Ali's hands, to keep the man who'd held her as she fell apart on the beach from taking another life.

Ali's last opponent was more skilled than his fellows, however, dancing away as he defended himself against Ali's whirling strikes. There was mad delight in his kohl-lined copper-brown eyes—shafit eyes—as though he was enjoying the challenge.

Not for long, though, because Ali's next strike cleanly lopped off the metal head of the other warrior's staff. Ali shoved an elbow in the man's face, provoking a loud crack, and then swept his legs out. The djinn fell hard, his headcloth rolling away.

Nahri gasped. It wasn't a man Ali had been fighting, but rather a young woman, her red-black braids tumbling free. Blood streamed from her nose as she crawled back on her elbows, looking at Ali with wide, frightened eyes.

"Please don't kill me!" she begged.

Ali lowered the zulfiqar, but his face remained hard as he stalked after her. "Who are you?"

"Traders!" she cried. "Merchants from Takedda. Please, my prince!"

"Rather well armed to be merchants in a foreign land," Ali scoffed. "Try again."

She abruptly smiled, triumph washing away her frightened facade. "You're right. We're not merchants. We're pirates." She licked her teeth and inclined her head toward the foundation wall. "They are too."

Nahri glanced up.

Over a dozen armed djinn stared back at her, crossbows drawn.

A Sahrayn man, wearing a long dagger on his forearm, stepped forward. "It seems we've won the hunt," he said with a leer. "Daevabad's missing royals are ours."

18

ALI

Ali strained against the chains wrapping his limbs, the iron shackles burning his wrists. "Cowards," he hissed as a pirate added yet another loop around his legs. "You outnumber me twenty to one and are still so afraid you weigh me down in iron? What kind of man are you?"

The man pulled the additional chain tighter. "The kind who doesn't want to die."

As the man stepped back, Ali spotted Nahri. The pirates had forced them onto the beached sandship, lowering their weapons only when the "Daevabadi royals" were shackled. Nahri wasn't wearing the blanket of chains he was, but fury surged in Ali's heart at the sight of her bound ankles. "Maybe next time, I'll just kill you."

"And that's why you're staying like this until we get to Daevabad."

"So here's the prince responsible for stripping our magic."

The Sahrayn pirate who'd gleefully announced "winning" them strode forward, his sandals clicking on the wooden deck. A few steps behind was the shafit girl Ali had fought. The man bowed in Nahri's direction. "And, of course, our blessed Banu Nahida. May the fires burn brightly for you, my lady."

No matter what humble roots Nahri claimed in Egypt, the imperious look she leveled on the pirate was all Nahid. "And you are?"

"Your savior!" He touched his heart. "Call me al Mudhib."

Ali eyed him. Judging from the lines on his sun-beaten face, al Mudhib had to be at least a century and a half old. His beard was entirely silver—and bright as the metal itself, an unnatural hue. He was broadly built and richly dressed in a sleeveless linen tunic accented with colorful silk embroidery depicting fighting snakes. Corded muscle and burns covered his exposed arms, and a turban in a flowing fabric like liquid gold wrapped around his head.

The weapon at his waist was Muntadhir's khanjar.

Ali glared. "That's my brother's blade."

Al Mudhib shrugged. "I can't imagine he has much need for it now, being ash and all."

"Ali." Nahri's voice cut a warning before Ali could test his chains. She turned back to the pirate. "You call yourself my savior, and yet you've shackled me to your boat."

"A precaution," al Mudhib explained. "You see, we're all a bit confused finding you so cozy with your kidnapper."

"Her *kidnapper*?" Ali repeated. "What the hell are you talking about?"

"Haven't you heard?" Al Mudhib's eyes danced with mirth. "Our new ruler, may God—sorry, the *Creator*," he amended, using the Divasti word, "bless her reign, sent her Afshin charging out with the awful story. That instead of accepting Manizheh's mercy, the treacherous Qahtani prince kidnapped her daughter, stole Suleiman's seal, and fled to his marid masters." Al Mudhib gave Nahri a wide, toothy grin. "Your mother is so very upset. She's warned that no one shall have their magic restored until her daughter and wretched captor are returned to Daevabad. And the one doing that returning? Ah, they are to be well rewarded."

They say I did what? Oh, but Ali was feeling murderous. Maybe Sobek had rubbed off on him. Because the thought of drowning al Mudhib beneath the Nile was suddenly terribly tempting.

Ali held his tongue, however, letting Nahri reply. "And you believe that story?" she asked.

"Some of it." Al Mudhib gestured to the downed ship. "You may notice my crashed boat. Clearly something ripped away our magic, and the Ayaanle villages we've been raiding have been consistent in their stories of Navasatem tourists sent fleeing home. Unless you have another explanation?"

"I do. My mother is a lying murderer who broke magic herself, killed thousands, and will give you over to the ifrit to be enslaved as your 'reward.'"

If the cocky pirate was taken aback by Nahri's fiery words, it was only for a moment. He shot an amused look at the shafit girl at his side. "Nobles. What did I tell you? No family loyalty."

The girl didn't smile. Her ears were a human round beneath curly red-black hair gathered in braids that fell to her waist, tied off with leather bands and decorated with cowrie shells and glass coins. A pattern of inky blue dotted triangles was tattooed across her brow and chin. Besides her bloody nose, a nasty gash marked one check.

She crossed her arms. "I don't like this." For the first time, Ali noticed a trace of familiarity in her accent. "We should take them to Shefala," she declared, sending his heart soaring. "The queen's family is there and would probably pay as handsomely as the Daevas. We could be there and gone in a week and wash our hands of this whole business."

"*Yes,*" Ali urged, wishing he could hug her. "That is exactly what you should do. My family has enough gold to pay whatever ransom you desire." He wasn't normally one to boast of his family's wealth, but he'd personally shower these two with coins if it kept him and Nahri safe.

"Enough gold to buy back my magic?" al Mudhib retorted. "You claim Manizheh is lying? Fine. Lift that seal on your face, give me a taste of my abilities, and I will consider taking you to Shefala."

Ali hesitated, not wanting to reveal how powerless he was. "I'm not going to do that. For all I know, if I give you your magic, you'll snap your fingers and have this ship halfway to Daevabad. But if you bring us to Shefala, I promise—"

"Your promise doesn't carry weight anymore, al Qahtani. I'm a sailor, and I can see which way the wind is blowing. Your family has lost this round, and *hers* is ascendant. I don't only want gold. I want to sail the dunes of my homeland again, and I'll need magic for that—magic I suspect you're not actually capable of returning to me."

"Captain." The shafit girl's voice was thick with warning. "It will take us months to get to Daevabad without magic. We'll be on the ocean for half of it, with a man they say is an ally of the marid. The crew is already whispering—"

"The *crew* will do as it's told," al Mudhib ordered, the humor gone from his voice. "As will you, Daevabadi. I've been sailing this ocean a hundred years and never seen a hint of any marid. Don't tell me you're frightened of a bunch of Ayaanle fairy tales after only a few seasons on their coast."

Daevabadi. No wonder the girl's accent was recognizable. But a Daevabadi shafit? Did that mean she'd escaped? Ali had never met a shafit who'd successfully fled the city they were bound to by law.

Nahri spoke up again. "You're making a mistake."

"We'll see." Al Mudhib turned back to the shafit girl. "We've been tarrying here too long anyway. It's time to get the ship down, even if we need to break it into pieces and reassemble them on the shore. Tell your fellows to get started." He jerked a thumb at Nahri and Ali. "And watch these two. If the prince starts whispering with his gilded Ayaanle tongue, feel free to cut it out."

"And the Nahid?"

Al Mudhib looked supremely unworried. "Keep the princess fed and make sure none of the men get her alone. I don't mean to deliver a half-starved royal weeping in her veil to the fire-worshipping lunatics running Daevabad."

He strode off without another word.

Ali swore. "Pirates. Of all the people we could have run into."

The shafit girl had watched al Mudhib leave, and Ali didn't miss the relief that passed over her face when he was gone. "My captain told me to take your tongue if you talk too much," she reminded him.

"I am going to take his head, so he can damn well say what he likes."

She turned to regard him, a playful smile on her lips. "I'd heard Geziris were hot-tempered."

Ali didn't rise to the insult. He could see how badly he'd injured her and felt guilty despite the circumstances. "I'm sorry about your face."

"Sorry you didn't kill me, you mean."

"I wasn't fighting to kill." He lifted his shackles. "But I *was* outnumbered."

"You were indeed." Curiosity lit in her eyes. "They teach you how to fight like that at the Citadel?"

"They did. And I take it you've seen it, if you're Daevabadi. When were you last home?"

"A long time ago." Her eyes dimmed. "Let me get you both some food. And please don't do anything that would require us to kill you. This is the most excitement we've had in weeks."

"Terrorizing and stealing from the local Ayaanle isn't entertaining?"

She tapped her round ears. "*I* haven't terrorized any Ayaanle, prince. Al Mudhib doesn't let those of us with human blood out of his sight. He staked a boy to the beach last week and let the tide drown him for trying to run out on his indenture. *Yes*," she added when Ali failed to mask his shock. "So you can keep your judgment to yourself."

She strode off, and Ali waited until she was gone to speak again. "So. Apparently I kidnapped you."

"Of course." Rancor laced Nahri's voice. "Even the lies Dara and Manizheh spin make me into someone who needs to be saved." She slumped back against the deck, exhaustion creasing her face. "I'm not being delivered to them in chains. I'll throw myself into the sea first."

"It's not going to come to that," Ali insisted. When Nahri's expression only grew more doomed, he went on. "Come now. Where is the woman who once braggingly picked a lock in Daevabad's library?" He rattled his chains. "I'd think you delighted by the challenge."

"Have you an actual plan or just wild fantasies that will end with our deaths?"

"Something in between." Ali tried to study their surroundings without being too obvious. The prow of the sandship jutted over the cliff, the rest of it settled in its bed of broken trees. The creek was a good distance below, even the high-tide line at least a body length away. And though the ocean wasn't far, the creek wasn't deep enough to carry such a large boat.

At least not now, it wasn't.

"Ali . . ." Nahri's voice was low. "Why do you look like you're considering something very reckless?"

God, they really had been spending too much time in each other's company. "It would need to be tonight," he said softly. "Before they start breaking the ship down." He gazed at the sprawling sandship and their chains. "And we'd need help."

"Help to do what?" Nahri prodded. "Al Qahtani, talk."

He inclined his head to the glistening ocean. "Sail to Shefala."

Her gaze darted between the creek and the ocean, following his path, and alarm crossed her face. "No. You shouldn't even be using this marid magic anymore. It's too dangerous."

Ali didn't disagree. Between Sobek's cryptic warning and his own unease, he didn't like this line of thinking any more than Nahri did. But the prospect of being delivered to Manizheh in irons was worse. And they were close, so close, to his family. To resources and safety that they wouldn't find trapped at sea with al Mudhib and his men.

"Do you have a better suggestion?" he asked.

Nahri seemed grim. "Are you even capable of something like that?"

"It's going to hurt, I won't lie." It was going to do a lot more than hurt—throwing off the ghouls with his marid magic had taken but a fraction of the effort freeing the ship would require, and that pain had nearly caused Ali to black out. "But maybe if you're by my side, we can lift the seal, and you can use your abilities to keep my heart from exploding."

"Nothing you just said made me feel any more confident."

"Still waiting for a better idea."

She took a deep breath, and then exhaled. "Fine. But you're going to need to get that girl on our side when she returns."

Nahri's response threw him. "*Me?* You're the more convincing one."

"Yes, but I'm not the half-naked prince she couldn't take her eyes off."

Ali abruptly tried to cover his chest, an impossible task in chains. "*I broke her nose.*"

"Danger can be appealing." Nahri's expression grew shrewder. "Keep talking when she comes back. Flirt. Find out what she meant about shafit being indentured. There was anger there—it might work."

Ali fought rising panic. Risking his life using marid magic to provoke an insurrection among pirates was one thing. Flirting was another. "I don't know how to do that."

Exasperation tightened her face. "*Try.* Do that thing where you act all earnest and talk about justice. It's endearing." Nahri straightened up. "She's coming back."

Flustered, Ali kept his mouth shut when the shafit girl returned. She carried a battered tin bowl, a ceramic canteen, and a net containing small vivid yellow fruits resembling tiny apples.

"Food for our royal captives," she announced, offering the bowl to Nahri.

Nahri eyed it with hungry regret. "Is that meat?"

The girl shrugged. "Turtle, maybe. I don't ask, I just eat. We're not all fancy people here."

Nahri shook her head. "I can't eat it. I'm Daeva. I don't eat meat."

"Then if you'd like to survive on fruit alone, be my guest." The girl tossed a handful of fruit and the canteen into Nahri's lap. "Drink." She offered the bowl to Ali. "You?"

His stomach growled, but Ali demurred out of solidarity. "Fruit is fine, thank you." He swallowed nervously. "May I ask your name?"

A little surprise entered her copper-brown eyes. "Fiza."

When Ali didn't respond, Nahri threw the canteen at him with what seemed unnecessary force before she turned to Fiza.

"You'll need to clean that cut on your face. And it's deep. It could probably use a stitch or two."

Fiza snorted. "I've seen that bag of yours, Nahid, and half the tools could cut my throat. I'll take my chances with a scar." She was dressed simply in a length of linen wound around her torso; Ali could see her stomach when she moved to depart. She looked strong but thin. Hungry.

"Stay," Ali insisted, nodding at the bowl. "Eat that quickly, and no one will know it wasn't us."

She shot him a guarded look. "I don't need mercy from a dead man."

Flirting was going well. Ali racked his brain, trying to think of something else to say.

Do what Dhiru would do. Summoning his courage, Ali smiled as broadly as he could, trying to draw on whatever charm he might have picked up from his brother. "Then grant me your own mercy. This dead man could use some company."

An amused glint entered her expression. "You are being rather obvious, prince."

"I'm desperate. And you don't need to call me prince. Alizayd is fine."

Fiza narrowed her eyes and then dropped, perching on a broken log like a seabird. "All right." She brought the bowl to her mouth, slurping back the soup. "At least give me a good story to take back to my companions. Has the Scourge truly returned? People say he flies on a shedu and split the Gozan like the Prophet Musa."

Ali didn't miss Nahri's flinch. Hating what he knew he had to do, he scoffed. "He is a man half dead. He and Manizheh won through trickery and are hardly the all-powerful lords your captain is so frightened of."

"Then why did *you* run from him?" Fiza laughed. "Did they find you in bed together?" she teased, tossing her head at Nahri.

"Because let me tell you, there have been a great number of creative additions to this tale Manizheh has concocted of you stealing her daughter."

"Of course not," Ali stammered. "She's married to my brother."

"Does that matter?" Fiza drank more of the soup. "When I was a kid, people said the nobles in Daevabad all cheated and slept with each other."

"Not all of us." Ali tried to pull the conversation in a more useful direction. "So . . . when do you think you'll start breaking down the ship?"

"Why?" Fiza asked, her eyes wide with feigned innocence. "Are you *planning something*?"

"Would you be interested if I was?"

Beyond Fiza's shoulder, Nahri threw up her hands in visible frustration.

Ali changed tactics, preferring honesty. "Help us," he implored. "Please. You know your captain is being a fool. Take us to Shefala, and my kinsmen will weigh you down in enough gold to escape all this."

"That took less time than I thought it would." Fiza put down the soup, the remnant sloshing about. "There's no running, Alizayd. You should get that out of your head. You're outnumbered, the forest is too sparse to hide in, and I'm definitely not helping you."

"I don't plan to run. All I ask is that you make sure the hull is sound until the next high tide and that anyone you trust is onboard."

"High tide?" she repeated. "If you're imagining the boat floating off the next time the water rises, let me be the first to puncture that dream. The creek goes barely halfway up the cliff."

"Tonight it's coming higher."

"Implying you cause the sea to rise doesn't make me want to

trust you. What's to say I don't report all this to al Mudhib, watch as he cuts out your tongue, and then break down the hull myself?"

Nahri took over. "Because you know he's wrong. Come on— one conversation with your captain, and *I'm* ready to mutiny. You're a good fighter; you seem clever. Why serve him?"

The other woman glanced quickly over her shoulder and then with a swift, discreet motion, swept her braids behind her head and pulled down her collar. Stretching across her jugular was what looked like a dull gray tattoo of a snake.

"It's an iron alloy," she explained, barely above a whisper. "Al Mudhib is—was—a metal mage. He bewitches the liquid metal to dig under our skin. It subdues our magic and can't be removed without killing us."

Nahri had paled. "He's done that to all the shafit here?"

Fiza nodded, adjusting her collar. "Ten years indenture, and he lets you go with enough silver to start a new life. It hurts, but trust me when I say there are worse options for shafit. I'm five years in," she added more fiercely. "And you're asking me to throw that away and risk my life for a pair of purebloods?"

Ali didn't know what to say. Every time he thought he'd heard the worst of what the shafit were subjected to, the bar was lowered yet again.

But Nahri had only grown more determined. "*I'll* get it out of you. I'm a surgeon, a Nahid healer. When I get my magic back, I'll get that abominable thing out of you and anyone else who comes with us."

"And why should I trust some exiled Daeva? Your people aren't exactly known for looking fondly on mine."

"Maybe because I don't enslave shafit with poisoned metal scraps!" Nahri hissed. "Would you rather spend six months traveling to a war zone? My mother is likely to kill all of you, especially if she doesn't want whatever information we might have shared getting out. And even if she doesn't kill you, you'll still belong to al Mudhib."

"Or you could be free in a night," Ali offered. "Rich in a week. If magic comes back, Nahri gets that brand out of your neck. If we fail and magic never returns, you can still take your gold, your ship, and live in the human world."

"Or I get a knife to the gut when we get caught twiddling our thumbs on a stuck boat going nowhere. Because like I said, *the tide doesn't—*"

Ali made the soup in her bowl shoot into the air.

The movement was small and quick, not enough to be noticed by anyone except them, but Fiza shoved backward, her eyes going wide.

"I can do it," he declared. "And I will." Ali lowered his voice. "You're Daevabadi, and, Fiza, what happened to our home is bad. If we're returned to Manizheh, if she gets Suleiman's seal, there may be no fighting back." He looked at her earnestly. "Please. If you still have loved ones there . . ."

"Fiza!" The shafit girl stilled, and Ali glanced up to see one of the pirates scowling their way from where he was lounging next to a spitted haunch of meat smoking over a low fire. "Al Mudhib isn't feeding you to whore around. Go get some more wood for the fire."

Fiza's eyes flashed. Ali saw her gaze briefly flicker to the camp of idle men and then over to the shafit servants scrubbing pots and making rope. She glanced at the ocean, her expression shifting.

Then she threw back her head and laughed.

"Can you blame me?" Without warning, she dropped onto Ali, straddling his waist. "I've never seen a real prince before." Fiza pressed against him, running her nails down his chest.

Ali jumped as her fingers slid lower. "Whoa, wait—"

A thin metal object slid under his belt. "Should be all you need if the two of you are as skilled as you believe yourselves to be," Fiza whispered in his ear, her breath hot against his neck. She laughed again, louder this time, and then slapped his cheek. "Maybe I'll come back for you after midnight, pretty man. They say you're touched by the marid. Be curious to see what the tide may bring."

She was gone the next moment, sliding from his lap to tend to the man who'd called her.

Leaving only Nahri staring at him, her black gaze as even and inscrutable as ever.

"I told you," she said. "The earnest, soulful thing."

Mortified, Ali didn't trust himself to speak. Unbidden, the thought came that he might not have minded that encounter with a different—more specific—woman in Fiza's place.

Pull yourself together. "I hope you remember how to pick a lock."

"What?"

Ali shifted, trying to maneuver to examine whatever Fiza had slipped him. "We have our accomplice."

NIGHT FELL THICK AND FAST ON THE NTARAN COAST, the ocean glowing in the light of a bright moon. It was mesmerizing, the sparkling water glittering and shattering as it rose and fell, and Ali found himself struggling not to stare, his own breathing in time with the sea.

"The tide is running high," he murmured.

"I know. I thought you'd have a visitor by now." Nahri sniffed, a feigned snobbishness—for with nightfall had come one of al Mudhib's guards to watch over them. "That shafit woman certainly sounded like she had plans for you."

I thought so too. From his spot on the deck, Ali had watched the pirates camp down for the night in a ring of tents set around a weak fire. Fiza had made a big show earlier of arguing with another shafit worker over the best way to break down the ship, insisting on taking apart an existing cabin and using it to build tracks to slide the pieces down the cliff before they touched the hull.

But if she'd made any headway in convincing her fellows to mutiny, Ali couldn't tell, and it worried him. She'd given him a metal spike that Nahri had already discreetly used to pick her locks, but there was no doing the same to the half dozen the pirates had used on Ali. In the meantime, plenty of the crew had found reasons to drop by, gawking and making remarks so crude about the bound Daevabadi royals that it was everything Ali could do not to summon the sea right there and then to drown them.

He closed his eyes. Ali could sense the creek had risen with the tide, but it still wasn't anywhere near enough water to carry the sandship off the cliff. Apprehension churned through him. Ali had wielded marid magic that powerful only once—when he'd submitted to it back on the beach in Daevabad. Now? With Suleiman's seal in his heart?

The strains of drunken, *extremely* off-key singing came to him, and Ali straightened up, catching sight of a familiar figure weaving—well, staggering—in their direction, a bottle dangling from one hand.

"Is that Fiza?" he asked, his spirits falling. That was not how he hoped their accomplice would arrive.

The shafit pirate stumbled onto the boat, crashing heavily against one side. "You're not dead yet!" she said by way of greeting, giggling as she crossed the deck.

Al Mudhib's guard stepped between them. "You're drunk, dirt-blood. Go sleep it off."

Fiza pouted, taking another swig of her bottle. She waved her hand in the vague direction of Ali. "Oh no. We have an *appointment*."

The guard grabbed her arm. "It makes no difference to me whether you leave on your own or I toss you off." A nastier note entered his voice. "Besides, you've denied the rest of us. Why should the crocodile get a taste?"

Fiza smiled sweetly. "You're right. You should get a taste."

She smashed the wine bottle into his mouth.

The guard didn't even have a chance to shout before Nahri, freed of her shackles, launched herself at his knees. He tripped, going down hard as the women pinned him, and then Fiza hit him with the bottle again and knocked him out.

"Always an asshole," she muttered, sitting back on her heels. She reached under the robe she was wearing, pulling out al Mudhib's pistol, Ali's zulfiqar, and Nahri's medical bag. "There," she said, dumping it all on the ground. "Presents for everyone."

Ali gaped. "How did you—"

One of the tents burst into flames.

There were shouts of surprise as the few men still awake jumped to their feet and ran to the tent. But then a second tent caught fire. A third and a fourth, the wild flames lighting up the night and illuminating the half dozen figures racing toward the ship.

"Up, up, up!" Fiza cried, waving to the rest of the shafit crew. She whirled on Ali and Nahri, both of whom were frozen in shock. "Come on, purebloods, be useful for once in your pampered lives!" Fiza's mutineers were already cutting the ropes and kicking away the boards binding the ship to its cradle of broken trees.

Nahri cursed but lunged to Ali's side. "No sense of discretion," she said, sounding scandalized as she fumbled with his locks. "For God's sake, we could have at least *tried* to sneak out of here."

A blast of gunfire made them both jump, Nahri nearly stabbing him with the pick. She swore again, breaking into the last lock and then helping Ali unwind his chains.

Another pistol shot, this time coming from the opposite direction and slamming into the sandship's mast, sending wooden splinters everywhere.

"*Would you two hurry?*" Fiza yelled, taking shelter behind a barrel as she fired back.

Ali climbed to his feet and kicked away the last shackles. With al Mudhib's men closing in, and crossbow bolts and bullets flying past, he didn't have time to indulge in his earlier doubts. Instead he raised his hands, staring at the shifting mass of salt water. It had been teasing at his consciousness all night. Remembering how difficult it had been to get the much smaller Nile to cooperate, when Ali called, he did so firmly.

COME.

The ocean, it turned out, was a lot more eager to play.

Beyond the shouts of the pirates and the crackle of the burning tents, the sounds of the waves crashing on the beach suddenly changed. There was a whisper, growing to a roar as the jungle bordering the creek was devoured, the trees smashed. None of which was visible—not yet. Instead, the destruction could only be heard, the noise getting louder and louder.

And then from the starlit dark, where there had been only a meandering beachside stream, came a rushing wave of water that would have breached the walls of Daevabad itself.

It was an incredible sight—well, it would have been incredible, had summoning it not felt like ripping Ali's heart in two.

Fiza gasped. "God preserve me . . ." She jumped to the middle of the deck, shouting at the shafit who'd followed her. "Everyone, hold on!"

Nahri grabbed Ali. Always prepared, she'd already tethered herself to the mast. She laid one hand on Ali's heart and the other on his shoulder, bracing him.

"I've got you, my friend," she assured him. "Lift the seal."

But it was already lifting; like last time, the ring in his heart responded more to Nahri's touch than any command Ali could give it. She sent a swell of cool relief surging through his body, and the pain immediately lessened.

Just in time, for the swollen creek had crashed over the cliff, lapping toward the boat in ravenous, frothy swells. As though he were the sea itself, Ali tasted the oily wooden hull and the bricks of the foundation wall. The ship bobbed like a toy on the rising wave.

Another shot glanced off the bow; al Mudhib was still out there somewhere.

You should drown him. You should drown them all. Al Mudhib and his thugs were murderers and thieves, worthless scum who'd preyed upon Ayaanle villagers and forced shafit like Fiza into servitude. They deserved to die. And it would be so easy. A bare flick of Ali's hand, and they'd be gone, devoured.

Waves lashed the boat, and Ali slipped, falling from Nahri's grasp and hurtling across the deck. He smashed into the opposite railing, and the pain in his chest returned with a vengeance, white hot and twisting through his heart.

DROWN THEM. Ali gripped the railing and hauled himself back to his feet. Desperate for a distraction from the murderous urges swirling in his mind, he threw himself into controlling the marid magic.

The sea, he commanded, pressing a fist against the agony in his chest. *Bring us to the sea.*

The boat shot forward like a released arrow. The new crew cried out in alarm, cursing and praying.

"Ali!" Nahri scrambled back to his side, reaching for him as a gray fog dashed across his vision. Her hands scorched his skin, and Ali jerked away, the ship moving with him and leveling more trees.

"I'm fine." And oddly enough . . . he was. The pain was gutting, yes, but it suddenly felt distant, like it was happening to someone else. Ali stepped forward, watching in wonder as they rushed toward the ocean. His legs seemed to have a mind of their own, steadying him as they careened around the bends of the wild, swollen creek.

Devour it. Ali grinned with mad delight as floods raced forward to consume the beach. Blood filled his mouth, dripping past his lips as the magic in his veins boiled and surged through him, dashing against the hard alien intrusion in his chest.

The ship burst from the forest, dashing through the inlet. And then . . . Ali sighed in pleasure, tasting the salt of the ocean as it overpowered the freshwater creek. Water raced over his skin in a welcoming embrace, fingers of it running through his hair and down his throat like a lover's caress.

But why was Ali up here, in this bobbing toy of dead trees and oily pitch, when the ocean was so close?

Come. This time the command wasn't his. As if in a dream, Ali turned, reaching for the wooden rail that separated him from the water.

"Ali, what are you doing?" He was dimly aware of a voice speaking his name. Nahri, one part of his mind told him.

Daeva, another part accused. The scent of their fiery essence soured the wet air. They were everywhere, surrounding him in a place they had no business being.

So leave them. Fling yourself into the sea and join us. Ali lifted a leg over the railing.

"Ali, no!" The daeva called Nahri threw herself at him, grabbing him around the chest. "Fiza, help me!"

Ali tried to wrench free. "Don't touch me," he hissed, the words coming out in a slither of foreign syllables.

"What's wrong with him?" another daeva cried, a woman. "What's wrong with his *eyes?*"

"Ali, please." The first daeva was begging now, trying to pry his hands from the railing. "Let it go. Let the marid magic go!"

They succeeded in dragging him back only a few steps before Ali shook them off. Foolish mortals, what did they know? Why stay here when the churning, heaving water beckoned so strongly? His blood ached for it, *he* ached for it.

He was dimly aware of the daeva running at him again, an oar in her hand.

"Ali, I'm really sorry," she said as she put herself between him and the ocean. She lifted the oar . . .

And smashed it into his skull.

19

DARA

Had Dara not been expecting Muntadhir, he would never have guessed the bedraggled man with wild eyes and overgrown hair was the same emir he'd first met lounging in the throne room. Though Dara had seen men in far worse shape after weeks of imprisonment, it was still a startling reminder of their change in fortunes. Muntadhir was thin, his skin pale from a month without light, and his stained waist cloth revealed an angry red scar from the zulfiqar strike that should have killed him. Bruises and scratches covered his limbs; a welt protruded on his cheek. As he shuffled down the garden path, his wrists and ankles shackled and a guard at each elbow, Dara could already smell him.

But even beaten and filthy, Muntadhir's expression was fiery when he met Dara's gaze. He drew up, glaring, and then spat at Dara's feet.

"Scourge."

"Al Qahtani." Dara glanced at the soldiers. "Leave us."

He waited until his men were gone and then stood. He'd arranged to meet Muntadhir in a private nook of the inner gardens. Roses climbed the pale stone wall, and water danced in the tiled fountain, a peaceful scene at odds with the tension between the men.

Dara stopped before Muntadhir. "I am going to remove your shackles. I trust you are not going to do anything foolish."

Rage burned in the emir's dirty face, but he said nothing, remaining still as Dara struck off the irons at his wrists and ankles. The skin underneath was blistered and raw. Dara stepped back with relief, resisting the urge to cover his nose.

Muntadhir shot a skittish look across the small courtyard. "What do you want?"

"To talk." Dara gestured to the basin of water he'd brought for washing and then pulled the top off a silver platter of spiced rice, greens, and dried fruit. "You must be hungry."

Muntadhir's gray eyes locked on the food, but he didn't move. "Is this a trick?"

"No. I wanted to talk and figured it would be easier if you did not smell of rot or were delirious with starvation." When the emir stayed put, Dara rolled his eyes. "For the love of the Creator, would you drop this whole 'noble suffering thing' your people so adore? You are supposed to be the agreeable one."

Still glaring, Muntadhir stepped forward and began gingerly washing his face and hands with the water. The movement drew Dara's attention to the small hole in his earlobe—the place his copper relic should have been.

He's probably one of the few people in the palace without one. With a pair of ifrit now wandering freely, everyone seemed to have taken to wearing their relics, as though their very presence might protect them from the horror of being enslaved. Save Manizheh, Dara had not seen a Daeva in days without an amulet—relic hidden inside—hanging from their neck.

Muntadhir let out a pained hiss as he rinsed his blistering skin, moving like an old man.

"You need some salve."

"Ah, yes, salve. I'll be sure to get some on the way back to my cell. I believe it's next to the decaying corpses."

Well, at least he was feeling sharper. Dara held his tongue, watching as Muntadhir finished washing up and then seated himself beside the tray, already looking haughtier. He eyed the food skeptically.

"Are you too snobbish to eat Daeva cuisine?"

"I rather like Daeva cuisine," Muntadhir countered. "I'm just wondering if it's poisoned."

"Poison is not my style."

"No, I suppose your style is torturing a dying man with threats to his younger siblings."

Dara stared at him. "I can put you back in your cell."

"And miss possibly poisoned food and your magnetic presence?" Muntadhir reached for the platter, rolling a small ball of the rice and popping it into his mouth. He made a face after he swallowed. "Underspiced. The kitchen staff must not be fond of you."

Dara snapped his fingers. Muntadhir jumped, but Dara had only conjured a cup of wine, bringing it to his lips in the same motion.

The emir watched with open jealousy. "Why do you still have your magic?"

"The Creator has blessed me."

"I doubt that very much." Muntadhir probably had mites in his clothes and was clearly starving, but he ate like the nobleman he was, every move precise and elegant. It threw Dara back into his memories of that last night in Daevabad. Muntadhir, drunk, with a courtesan in his lap, mocking his future marriage to the Banu Nahida.

Unable to stop himself, Dara opened his mouth. "You did not deserve her."

The words came out hard, and Muntadhir stilled, his hand halfway to his mouth, as if he expected to be struck again.

Then he relaxed, giving Dara a dirty look. "Neither did you."

"Did you hurt her?"

A hint of genuine anger blossomed in the emir's face. "I never raised a hand to her. I've never raised a hand to any woman. I'm not you, Scourge."

"No, you just forced her to marry you."

Muntadhir glowered. "I'm sure the thought of me dragging Nahri by the hair to my bed was very comforting to you as you were stepping past the bodies of Geziri children, but that's not how things were between us."

Dara knew he had no right to ask, but he could not go any further with this man if he had even once taken advantage of her. "Then how were things between you?"

"It was a political marriage between two deeply incompatible people, but she was my wife. I tried to protect her, to build something between us that might have been good for Daevabad. And I think she did the same with me."

"Did you love her?"

Muntadhir stared at him in exasperation. "How are you so old and yet so naive? No, I didn't love her. I *cared* for her—in fifty years, if she and my father didn't kill each other first, if we'd had a child, maybe things would have been different."

"And Jamshid?"

The other man flinched. He hid it well, but Dara still noticed. Muntadhir's true weakness.

Muntadhir shoved the food away. "Conjure another cup of wine or put me back in my cell. Discussing my romantic entanglements with you is almost enough to make me wish the zulfiqar had done its job."

Checking his temper, Dara conjured another cup and pushed it in Muntadhir's direction, the amber liquid sloshing over the rim.

Muntadhir tasted it, his nose wrinkling in displeasure. "Date wine. Overly sweet and utterly common. You really never did spend much time in the palace, did you?"

"I find politics loathsome."

"Do you?" Muntadhir waved about the courtyard. "And what do you think all this is if not politics? I find that those who look on politics with contempt are usually the first to be dragged down by them."

Dara drained his cup and set it down, not having any desire to get pulled in by riddles. "I saw your sister."

Muntadhir coughed, spitting out his wine. "What?" The mask slipped, worry filling his face. "Where? Has Manizheh—"

"No. Not yet, anyway. I saw Zaynab at the hospital, fighting at the side of a warrior woman of your tribe."

Muntadhir was gripping his cup so hard Dara could see the whites of his knuckles. "Did you hurt her?"

"No. Nor, for that matter, did I tell Manizheh she was there."

"Waiting to see how this conversation went?"

"I'm not telling you this to threaten her, al Qahtani. I'm telling you so you know you have a reason to live." When Muntadhir's only response was more arrogant staring, as though Dara were a speck of dirt on his shoe, Dara continued. "Our conquest . . . it has not exactly gone to plan."

Muntadhir feigned shock, his eyes wide. "You don't say."

Dara sucked his teeth, resisting the urge to boil the emir's wine. "We have made overtures to the other tribes, but none have responded positively." He thought back to the reports he'd been given—true to her word, Manizheh had not allowed him back to court, and he was now forced to rely on secondhand accounts. "The Sahrayn keep attempting to escape on boats they cobble together, Tukharistani bandits have been climbing the walls to steal from Daeva orchards, and the Agnivanshi hung two traders over the midan after they were caught selling grain to the palace. The Geziris and shafit have armed themselves with human weapons and are pushing for open civil war."

Muntadhir pursed his lips. "And the Ayaanle?"

"No one has heard anything from the Ayaanle."

"Then that should concern you more than the rest."

Dara waited, but when Muntadhir didn't explain, he threw up his hands. "That is it?"

Muntadhir gave him an incredulous look. "You could not have broken Daevabad more if you'd literally picked the city up and shaken it. This place is a pile of kindling, and my father spent his entire reign stamping out smoke before it could become flame, only for you and Manizheh to come and dump an ocean of oil over it and light a thousand bonfires. And that was *before* magic vanished. What did you expect?"

"That you might help me fix it."

The emir drew himself up, all humor vanishing. "I'm not going to help you. Kaveh and Manizheh murdered my father and a thousand other Geziris. Your *plan*, whose failure you're mourning, was intended to annihilate my people. I found you trying to *enslave my brother*. Everything went sideways, and now I am to assist you? Never. If I have found a glimmer of pleasure in all this, it is the assurance that you will destroy yourselves just as spectacularly."

Fire burned through his blood, and Dara struggled to check it. Immediately he thought of Zaynab—Muntadhir wore his fear for his sister so openly that it was an easy threat.

But he'd promised Kartir—he'd promised *himself*—that he would find another way.

He eyed the other man. "You are supposed to be the pragmatic one, are you not? If you truly love this city, help me. *Please*," Dara added when the emir snorted. "Djinn, I know you hate me.

You've every right to. But trust that I know too well what happens when cities fall, and Daevabad—*our* Daevabad—is on the brink. This needn't end with us all slaughtering one another. Help me save your people."

"*You're* the greatest threat to my people." But when Dara gave him a pleading look, Muntadhir let out an irritated sound of defeat. "God, I wish you'd just strangled me. Taking my chances with the afterlife would have been better than this."

Dara's spirits fell. "It is nice."

Muntadhir gave him a bewildered look. "Are you speaking from personal experience?" When Dara opened his mouth, Muntadhir held up a hand. "Never mind, I don't want to know." He rose to his feet, taking a long sip of his wine. "These overtures to the other tribes . . . tell me about them."

"I burned a section of land in each quarter, and warned them to submit and send tribute immediately."

"*That* was your overture?"

"Ah, yes, because your father was such a peaceful man."

"My father made sure his rewards were more inviting than his threats—and he had centuries of stability and a standing army to back them up, not just a mad Afshin and an even madder Nahid with ifrit friends. You need to make joining your side at least *somewhat* tempting. Most people just want safety for their families, food on the table, and a roof overhead. Give them that, and they'll look away from plenty. Give them nothing but violence, and they'll join with the idealists calling for your head."

Dara stared at him. "You really are your father's son."

Muntadhir shrugged, but Dara did not miss the tremble of his hands—the words had struck no matter how he pretended otherwise. "So, you've thoroughly isolated and bullied the other tribes. How do things stand with the Daevas?"

"The Daevas are on our side, of course."

"Oh?"

"Granted, Kartir and some of the priests are not pleased by the violence nor the presence of the ifrit, and I have not had much success recruiting new soldiers—"

"I'm going to stop you there." Muntadhir gave Dara a shrewd look, the pearly scar dividing his brow where he'd been scourged glinting in the sun. "The Daevas in this city aren't fools. They're survivors, and you are an outsider who has visited violence upon them twice."

Dara bristled. "I'm no outsider. I have been fighting for my people since—"

"You are an *outsider*," Muntadhir said firmly. "You are foreign to this century, Manizheh is foreign to the struggles of daily life in the quarter, and Kaveh grew up on a country estate where he likely saw a djinn once a year. You are all outsiders to *Daevabad's* Daevas, and you rushed in to save them—I assume without actually consulting any of them, yes? You want my advice? Make sure you have the support of your own people before reaching out to the other tribes. That was how we ruled."

"Your brother mounted a successful insurrection among the Geziris the same night we attacked."

"Which is why he stood a very good chance of taking my father down. It is those we are closest to who have an opportunity to observe our weaknesses best, and I take it your Manizheh has surrounded herself with Daevas."

Regardless of how strained his relationship with Manizheh was, a protective instinct raced down Dara's spine. "What do you suggest?"

"Reach out to your tribe's nobles. The Daeva noble houses are among the oldest and most respected in our world. More important—for now—is that they control most of the arable land outside the city walls and at least half the trade."

Dara grimaced. Kaveh had also said something about the Daeva nobles, hadn't he? "We seized much of the land outside the city right after the conquest. We wanted to secure the harvest, should trade with the outside world not resume quickly."

"Does 'seized' imply no payment was exchanged?"

"We are working on it."

"Work faster," Muntadhir warned. "Those houses are the backbone of this city. Many survived not only the fall of the Nahids, but all the civil wars and squabbles that have plagued us since. They'll still be standing when neither the Nahids nor Qahtanis are."

Dara didn't like the sound of any of that, and he didn't like thinking his people so easily divided and greedy for riches. "Kaveh is from a noble house. Surely he already knows this."

Muntadhir gave him a patronizing smile. "I would take comfort in your ignorance if it didn't affect my people. Kaveh is from the countryside; his family could be in Daevabad another eight centuries, and they still would not be viewed as equals among the nobles I'm talking about. They like that he earned them additional concessions and court positions while he was grand wazir, but they mocked his accent behind his back and would have died of shame before allowing their daughters to marry his son."

"That son is the same man you profess to love," Dara pointed out. "Are you so dishonorable that you mocked his name behind his back?"

Muntadhir grinned widely. "Oh no, Afshin. I drew my khanjar and threatened to open all their throats the first time they attempted to mock him in my presence. But then I smiled and sent them all home with gold, and strangely, Jamshid found himself receiving more invitations." He shrugged. "I knew my part, and I played it well. There will always be people who crave the attention of princes and you can go as far with wine, conversation, and glamour as you can with weapons. Putting aside the fact that we'd all stab each other in the back if our fortunes changed, I found their company quite enjoyable. Some very talented poets in the bunch."

Dara opened and closed his mouth, suddenly feeling rather provincial himself. Never again would he take for granted the simple ease of sitting around a cookfire with fellow soldiers. "And these honey-mouthed snobs with more coin than tribal loyalty are your . . . friends?"

"You could use that word," Muntadhir said, sounding almost cheerful. The topic of murderous court intrigue seemed to energize him. "The kind of tribal loyalty of which you are so fond has its limits. Manizheh was more feared and greeted with awe than loved by the Daevas when she lived here. You are *definitely* feared. Kaveh has good political instincts, but he just proved he's a disloyal traitor who plotted the massacre of children. Not to mention that the rest of the city openly hates you and is probably planning your demise. Why would families clever enough to have navigated centuries of occupation publicly support you? Far better to wait until you inevitably implode and then deal with whoever rises from the dust."

Dara indeed felt ready to implode. "Then how do we get the nobles on our side?"

Muntadhir twirled the cup in his hand. "I watched you turn into fire and survive being crushed by a ceiling. Surely you can conjure grape wine."

Checking his temper, Dara grabbed the cup out of Muntadhir's hands. A moment later, dark crimson swirled inside. "Here you are, Majesty," he said sarcastically.

The emir tasted it and smiled. "That's delicious! Maybe you should abandon this life. Leave the war, go open a tavern in the mountains—"

"Al Qahtani, you are trying me," Dara said through his teeth. *"How do we get the nobles on our side?"*

The mirth left the other man's face. "There is one more promise you must make if you want my help. Swear not to hurt my siblings."

Dara scowled. "I will not hurt your sister, but Alizayd is another matter. He allied with the marid to slaughter my men. If your brother comes before me again, I will kill him."

"*You* allied with the marid to bring down the Citadel and slaughter virtually everyone he knew, you insufferable hypocrite." Muntadhir's eyes narrowed. "Swear not to hurt my siblings. Swear on Nahri's life. Those are my terms."

Cursing inwardly, Dara touched his heart. "*Fine.* I will not harm them, I swear on Nahri."

"Good." Muntadhir took another long sip of wine. "You should throw a feast."

"A feast?" Dara spat. "I am to stay my hand from cutting down a hated enemy because you told me to hold a *party*?"

"You asked for my advice, and I know the nobles well. They want to be made to feel important, and they'll want to see signs of stability. Convince them you can rule, that you have a plan for peace, a way to bring magic back, and you may be surprised by the quiet methods they have of reaching out to their counterparts in the other tribes."

A feast for the rich fools who'd paid lip service to Ghassan all these years. Dara fumed. That was not the Daevabad he'd dreamed of returning to.

But the Daevabad he'd dreamed of was long gone—if it had ever existed.

Still, he pressed on. "Nahri had allies among these people?" He couldn't imagine the acid-tongued former slum dweller having the patience for these kinds of festivities.

"No," Muntadhir replied. "Nahri was *actually* beloved by her people. Because she teased their children in the Temple gardens, listened to their gripes in the infirmary, and used her dowry to fund weddings for the poor. She was not inclined to flatter nobles, and because I wasn't inclined to see her power eclipse mine, I didn't advise her to."

"A very happy couple you must have made. You know, when you weren't sleeping with her brother."

If the rebuke landed, Dara couldn't tell; the words seemed to slide past Muntadhir like water. He must have had a lot of experience in letting them do so, Dara realized. The court life Muntadhir spoke of sounded as deadly as a battlefield, and yet he'd navigated it for decades, holding tight to a lover he would never have been able to openly declare, checking an ambitious brother whose fervent allies would have happily seen Muntadhir strangled in his sleep, and dealing with a tyrant of a father.

A dangerous man. Muntadhir might not wield a zulfiqar like his brother, but Dara briefly wished it was Alizayd in his place. An armed duel, Dara could fight, but in this realm, he was not Muntadhir's equal.

The former emir seemed to be studying Dara in the same way. "Manizheh is going to have to embrace me as her son-in-law. At least publicly. It will look like she's attempting to preserve something of the old order and making a true outreach to the djinn."

"And if Nahri does not wish to remain married to you?"

"One problem at a time, Afshin." Muntadhir gestured to his rags. "Though on that note, you'll need to clean me up. I can hardly visit my dear mother looking like this."

"That may present its own difficulty."

"Meaning?"

"Meaning this has been mostly hypothetical. I've been demoted and Banu Manizheh doesn't wish to see me."

Muntadhir sighed. "You're really going to make me work for this, aren't you?" He set down his wine. "Let's get started, then."

20

NAHRI

In the dim light of the ship's tiny cabin, Nahri pressed her fingers against the pulse in Ali's wrist.

"Your heart sounds okay," she murmured, moving her examination up to study the bruised knot on his temple where she'd hit him with the oar. "How's the bump?"

Ali's groggy eyes rolled up to meet her gaze. "Well, there's no longer two of you."

Guilt rushed over her. "I'm sorry. I didn't know what else to do. You were fighting us, and I was so worried that if you went overboard—"

He touched her wrist. "It's all right. Really." It looked like Ali was trying to smile, but then he winced, the movement clearly pulling at the sizable swollen egg still rising on his face. "I'll take getting knocked out over being lured into the sea by mysterious voices any day."

Nahri went to move her hand to his heart. "Do you want me to try and heal—"

"No." His fingers instantly tightened on her wrist. "Don't heal me. I don't think we should be doing any healing magic while we're still at sea. Not after the way Sobek spoke about the Nahids. I don't want any new marid learning about you, especially not while we're floating in their realm."

She sat back. "So you do think it was the marid who possessed you last night?"

"I think it was the marid, but I'm not sure they possessed me." Ali shivered, water beading on his brow. "When the marid took me on the lake, when Sobek rooted through my memories, I knew what was happening. I could feel their *intrusion*. Last night wasn't that. I was myself the entire time. I *wanted* to throw myself in the ocean. I *wanted* to drown al Mudhib and his men. To devour them," he whispered, sounding sick. "When I looked at you, it was like you were a stranger." He met her gaze, and the open fear in his eyes sent ice flooding through every inch of her body. "I don't know what that means, Nahri."

She had never seen him sound so afraid—and she and Ali had faced a *lot* together. Nahri suddenly saw him falling to his knees as Manizheh tortured him, heard him crying out as he vanished beneath a mob of ravenous ghouls.

She took a sharp breath against the dread barreling through her chest. "It means no more marid magic. Not at sea and not when we get back to shore. Don't use it again. Not ever."

Ali sighed. "We're at war, and it's the only power I have."

"It doesn't matter."

"It *does* matter. We have an entire city to—"

"*It doesn't matter.* You don't want any more marid learning about me? Well, I don't want any more luring you to your death. We'll find another way to fight, okay?" Still seeing reluctance in his expression, Nahri added more urgently. *"Please."* She leaned forward, pulling a blanket she'd borrowed from the crew over Ali's body and tucking it in place around his shoulders. "I don't want to lose you. I can't."

The fervor in her response seemed to take Ali aback. This close, Nahri could feel the steamy heat rising from his skin beneath the thin blanket. He tried to smile again. "You really never are letting me out of your debt, are you?"

It was clearly a joke, but Nahri felt like she'd just been kicked in the heart. The sight of him attempting to smile, sick and weak, made her feel helpless.

It made her feel something she was not ready to, like she'd unknowingly taken a couple steps on a path Nahri realized only now was unsteady, with no way to go back.

No. Don't do this. Not again. Not now.

Nahri shot to her feet. "I'm going to see if I can't steep some willow bark," she said, forcing a strained professionalism into her voice. Work, her most favored distancing technique. "It will help with your pain. No, don't talk—" she added, raising a hand when Ali opened his mouth. "Just rest. Doctor's orders."

Then she slipped out of the cabin, shut the door, and leaned against it, closing her eyes. It was fine. Everything was fine. Her heart was a goddamned unreliable traitor, but that was fine too— Nahri was well experienced at ignoring its foolish, irrational impulses. She opened her eyes, hoping the sight of the bright, sunlit sea might help clear her head.

Everything was not fine.

The water was unnaturally still, a flat plain of pale glass that reflected broken slivers of sky. Broken, because as far as the eye could see, clumps of seaweed choked the tropical water, gnarled mats of rotting vegetation that had ensnarled cracked shells, rotting crabs, and the bleached skeletons of fanged fish.

Nahri inhaled, smelling death on the salty air. She didn't

know much about the sea, but she suspected, deep in her bones, this wasn't normal.

A surge of protectiveness burned through her, laced with anger. Good. Nahri knew anger. She trusted anger, preferred it.

"I'll kill you," she warned under her breath, glaring at the ocean. Maybe it was time she leaned into the fire and brimstone part of her Nahid heritage. "Come for him again, and I'll kill you all."

"Well, isn't that just the kind of level headedness I like to hear from people on my ship." Nahri glanced up to see Fiza perched on the roof of the tiny cabin, a smoking pipe in hand. "How's your lover?"

"He's not my lover," Nahri insisted, hating the heat in her voice. "Were you spying on us?"

"It's not spying if it's my ship." Fiza grinned. "My ship. What a glorious turn of phrase."

"Better hope the crew is more loyal to you than it was to al Mudhib."

"I could make it my life's goal, and I'd still never be as much of a bastard as al Mudhib, so I expect I'll be all right. But yes, I am spying on you, so why don't you make things easier and join me up here where it will be harder for you to dodge my questions."

You have no idea how capable I am of dodging questions. "I have to prepare some medicine for Ali."

"If he hasn't died yet, he can wait a few more minutes."

Nahri glowered but climbed up. Save for the seaweed carpet of death, the top of the sandship offered a stunning view. The sails might not have shimmered with magic, but the massive canopies of amber and gold were beautiful against the wind. To her far right, the coast was a ribbon of pearly white beaches and lush green palms.

Nahri lifted her face to the sun's heat. "This is nice."

"It is," Fiza agreed pleasantly. "I enjoy flying over the desert, but there's something special about the sea. How fortunate we are to be in the company of someone who can compel it to race up a creek and seize a boat."

"Maybe it was a lucky high tide."

"Luck is a fairy tale we use to make people feel better about the world being unfair as shit. Is he dangerous?"

"Why would you ask that?"

Fiza gave her a pointed look. "Because I've sailed with Ayaanle and know they've got legends about the demons that live in the waters of this land, legends that rarely end happily."

"The creative yarns of bored sailors."

"Daeva, I am enjoying your company more than I imagined I would someone raised to despise my blood, but if you avoid my question again, I'm going to throw you overboard. Which, you might remember, your prince tried to do to himself last night until you knocked him out with an oar. So I'll ask again: is he dangerous?"

I don't know. Ali's haunted confession and doomed eyes came back to her, and this time, there was no denying the rush of tenderness and worry that stole into Nahri's heart.

She skirted the question. "He's not dangerous. Not to you and your crew. He's given you his word about Shefala, and he won't go back on that. He's a good man."

"A good man who's sworn to the marid?" Fiza gave Nahri a skeptical look. "Sailor, remember? I know the old stories about people making blood sacrifices to them in exchange for power. There's little room for good men in those tales."

"Ali would never do something like that," Nahri insisted. "And you don't need to worry about it either way. Just get us to Shefala, and then you can take your gold and wash your hands of us."

"Forgetting something?" Fiza dragged down her shirt collar, revealing the iron snake beneath her skin. "You won't be rid of us that quickly. I want this out."

The sight of the brand made Nahri shudder. "Did you really choose to have that put it?"

"Yes."

"Why?" she couldn't help but ask.

"Because crewing on a sandship for a decade sounded better than where I was."

"Daevabad?"

Fiza shook her head. "No. I wasn't living in Daevabad by then. I was stolen from the city when I was a kid."

Nahri started. "*Stolen?*"

"Yes, stolen. And you needn't sound so surprised. Maybe in the palace, you're ignorant of it, but it happens to shafit all the time. Purebloods kidnap babies to pass off as their own kids. They grab older ones, claiming to be relatives and then forcing them into servitude. Most stay in Daevabad. I was . . . an exception. For reasons that are my own."

Nahri found herself struggling for words. She had known these things happened in Daevabad, but hearing it out of the mouth of a woman who'd chosen to have iron put in her neck as an alternative to a worse fate was a stark slap of reality.

"I'm sorry, Fiza," she said finally. "Truly."

"So am I." Fiza shrugged. "So were they, eventually. They ran afoul of al Mudhib's crew, and I turned on them the first moment I could."

She'd pulled her collar back up, but Nahri found herself still staring at Fiza's throat. "I'll get that brand out of you, I promise. I'll find a way, magic or not." She hesitated. "And if Ali and I make it to Daevabad, you're welcome to come with us. If you have family—"

Fiza flinched. "I don't know about that yet." She drew her knees up to her chest, looking younger. "But I don't need some Nahid's pity. I know what your people think about 'dirt-bloods.'"

"It's not what I think."

"Why? Because you grew up in the human world? Because you're supposedly cursed to look like us?" Fiza snorted, taking a drag of her pipe. "I've heard your story."

Nahri's throat was suddenly thick. "You don't know my story."

"Ah, yes. Poor little rich girl. Plucked off the streets by the Scourge and taken to Daevabad. What was harder, becoming a princess or marrying a handsome emir?"

"I'm not a princess, I'm a Nahid healer," Nahri snapped. "*And a shafit, for that matter.*"

Fiza dropped her pipe. It fell off the roof, rolling down the deck.

She didn't seem to notice. "Bullshit. The Daevas don't go near humans."

"Why *in the name of God* would I lie about something like that?" Nahri had finally let go of the secret she'd held tight for six years, and now Fiza didn't even believe her? "Do you know what my people would do if they learned the truth?"

The pirate gaped. "Wait, you're telling the truth? You've got human blood? And no one knows?"

You fool, what are you doing? But strangely enough, Nahri felt relieved, almost dizzy with this small release. "Ali knows."

"Pillow talk?"

"You're not the only one who can shove someone overboard."

"Well, don't you have some pointy edges?" Fiza whistled. "A Nahid shafit. Damn, how scandalous."

Nahri's head began to pound. "Yes," she said weakly, going from dizzy to nauseous. "I'm aware."

"So why are you telling *me*? You know I'm a criminal, yes? We sell scandalous information."

Why *was* Nahri telling Fiza? She'd just given Ali a lecture on safety and now here she was, spilling her most dangerous secret to an even more dangerous person.

"I don't know," she muttered. "I think I find you a kindred spirit." Then she shrugged, considering. "Though I guess you're a good test for coming clean with others."

"Why's that?"

"Because no one would believe a criminal if I said you were lying."

Fiza smacked her shoulder. "You were the one who picked the locks, weren't you?" When Nahri offered a wry grin, Fiza laughed. "I'd be tempted to offer you a place on my crew if I wasn't worried you'd turn on me the second the wind shifted."

"And I might be tempted to take you up on the offer if my mother wasn't slaughtering innocents in Daevabad. But I have to go back. It's the right thing to do."

"What the hell is the right thing to do?"

"Believe me, you don't want to find out."

21

DARA

Creator forgive him, Muntadhir al Qahtani might have been right.

Dara dodged a pack of excited children as they raced one another across the throne room, shaking brass noisemakers and swinging sparklers. Following them was a troupe of entertainers—acrobats walking on their hands or on stilts and dark-eyed beauties whirling, their braids snapping across the air. Men in brilliant silks, wearing enough jewelry to pay for Dara's threadbare army, were laughing uproariously in gathered groups, jade cups of expensive wine splashing beaded cushions.

The throne room in which his life had been knocked off course was unrecognizable, its solemn air of history giving way to a spectacular feast that Dara suspected would soon not be fit for the pious ladies who'd already set up a formidable wall of stern-eyed elders between their pretty, marriageable daughters and any lovelorn young men. In one corner, a storyteller was regaling an

enthralled group of wide-eyed youngsters with glamorous puppets set against painted backdrops. Seeing a wooden archer with
green coin eyes, Dara grimaced and turned away.

Still, it was the kind of scene he had dreamed of for centuries.
Daeva music filled the air, songs whose lyrics and rhythms had
changed from his time but were still recognizable, and a banquet
to feed hundreds had been laid out, copper platters and carved
quartz bowls upon a bright aquamarine cloth that ran the entire
length of the eastern wall. An atmosphere of wild relief gripped
the crowd.

*Of course they're relieved. The rich are once again dancing and feasting while
the rest of the city starves in fear.* For though Dara could not help but
enjoy this small sign of celebration, he suspected the laughing
Daeva nobles around him had once bowed to Ghassan with the
same smiles they now presented to Banu Manizheh. This was not
a holiday for the common people of his tribe: it was a very pretty
bribe—designed by Muntadhir, of all people—to convince the
nobles who had sidled up to the Qahtanis for generations that
they should instead throw their support to the Banu Nahida.

The absence of magic was unsettling as well. Though Dara
had done what he could—conjuring jewel-bright lanterns to float
overhead and butter-soft roses that climbed the walls and con-
tinuously blossomed, their perfumed petals showering the floor
and guests—there should have been more, and it was eerie to see
something so essential to his people stripped from them.

Suleiman's eye, this is why people call you brooding.

Forcing a more pleasant expression onto his face, Dara
abruptly helped himself to the blue glass bottle of wine nearest
him, feeling a sudden desire to get drunk and not particularly
caring that it clearly belonged to a circle of pearl-draped noblemen, whose protesting mouths snapped shut the moment they
looked up from their game of dice to see who'd stolen their wine.

Taking a long swig, Dara turned away to study Manizheh,

dressed in ceremonial garments and sitting upon the sparkling shedu throne, Kaveh at her side. A long line of people waited to greet them.

The sight of her sent more apprehension creeping over him. Manizheh had consented to his working with Muntadhir—seeming surprised but pleasantly so—but she had yet to invite him back to court, and seeing her now, a perfect portrait of the noble and sacred Nahids, Dara wondered if she ever would. Their years together in the sparse mountain camp, surviving brutal winters and dreaming of a less bloody conquest, suddenly seemed very far away. Dara had seen Manizheh at her worst; forget his insubordination, he must be an unwelcome reminder of the true cost of all this spectacle. The weapon that, if she was wise, Manizheh would keep stashed away until needed.

But Dara didn't want to only be a weapon anymore. So, the wine buzzing pleasantly in his veins, he decided to join her. Ignoring the queuing nobles, he strode up, prostrating himself on the carpet. "May the fires burn brightly for you, my lady."

"And for you, Afshin," Manizheh said, her voice warm. "Please rise."

He did so, catching Kaveh look askance at the wine bottle Dara was doing a poor job of concealing in the folds of his tunic.

The grand wazir raised his eyebrows. "You really have taken to partnering with Muntadhir."

"Oh, let him be, Kaveh," Manizheh chided. "I have no doubt our Afshin has already patrolled this place himself a dozen times." Dara caught what might have been a smile through the shimmering cloth of her veil. "And we could all use a break for a night."

It was the kindest thing she'd said to him in weeks, and despite everything, a light blossomed in Dara's heart. "Thank you, my lady," he said reverently. "I pray you are enjoying yourself as well."

Manizheh motioned for the servants to hold the line of waiting guests and then turned back to him. "It is a singular experience to provide a warm welcome to people I know kissed the hands of the kings who locked me away. But it's nice to hear laughter in the palace again." Her gaze fell on the children surrounding the storyteller. "Perhaps we may still wrest some good from all this."

Despite her optimistic word, her voice was melancholy. Manizheh had obviously nursed her own quiet dreams of returning to Daevabad, of arriving as a savior and being reunited with her children, instead of struggling to hold a broken, bloody city.

Dara ventured carefully. "Has there been any further word of your children?"

Manizheh's expression fell, and glancing at her, Kaveh answered. "Just the same rumors about Wajed and Jamshid—all of which contradict one another. Some people say the Tukharistanis have given Wajed safe passage, others that he's recruiting troops in Am Gezira or has boarded a stolen human boat for Ta Ntry." He shook his head, reaching out to squeeze Manizheh's hand. "It's impossible to say which is true. And of Nahri and Alizayd, nothing at all."

"It is still very early," Dara offered, trying to hold on to hope himself. Manizheh nodded silently, but he didn't miss the worry in her eyes.

Or the rather open display of affection between her and Kaveh. Manizheh didn't seem to care what people might think about their unmarried Banu Nahida sharing a bed with the grand wazir, and it slightly concerned him. Dara wasn't a politician, but even he knew it might have been more pragmatic for Manizheh to form a marriage alliance with someone not already in her camp.

There was also not a chance in hell he was saying that—not when he'd just started to return to her good graces.

"No smiles from the triumphant conquerors?"

Dara twitched at Muntadhir's mocking voice behind him but held his tongue as he turned around.

He was instantly glad he'd done so, for Muntadhir wasn't alone—he stood with three Daeva companions. They were all richly dressed, but the emir stood out. The only Geziri in the room, he'd dressed the part in a robe so black it looked as though a starless night had arranged itself around his shoulders, and a brilliant blue-and-copper turban pinned at a rakish angle with a pearl ornament. A patterned silk sash was tied at his waist, a khanjar tucked beneath.

"I don't recall saying you could have a weapon," Dara warned.

Muntadhir gave him a dangerous smile and turned to Manizheh, touching his heart and brow so politely one would never have imagined they'd faced off in a dungeon only weeks ago. "Peace be upon you, Banu Manizheh. If I may approach, I'd like to introduce you to a few of my companions."

Manizheh's greeting to the son of the king she'd killed was no less gracious. "If they are the companions you say have been in talks with the other tribes, by all means . . ." Manizheh motioned the group forward. "May the fires burn brightly for you, gentlemen."

The men brought their fingers together in smooth unison, bowing as Muntadhir introduced them. "Tamer e-Vaigas, Sourush Aratta, and Arta Hagmatanur . . . I'm sure you know well your Banu Manizheh e-Nahid and Darayavahoush e-Afshin."

Vaigas. Dara blinked in surprise. A familiar name. "I had a Vaigas in my command. One of my closest advisors," he added, remembering his long-dead friend. "Bizvan. He was a demon with a spear. Clever tactician as well."

Tamer's face shone with awe. "I'm his descendant," he gushed. "I heard growing up that he'd fought at your side in the rebellion but thought it might just be a story."

"Not a story at all." Dara grinned, happy to learn Bizvan had survived long enough to sire children—even if it was troubling to learn his descendants had flocked to the Qahtani's side. Dara clapped the young man's shoulder, nearly knocking him over. "Why have you not joined my army? You come from good fighting stock!"

A look of sheer terror crossed Tamer's visage before he let out a forced laugh. "Maybe a thousand years ago. Bizvan's spear hangs on the wall of our guest room. We're merchants now." He turned back to Manizheh. "Which is what brings me here tonight. My family has deep ties with some of the leading Agnivanshi traders; Sourush and Arta"—he nodded to the other Daevas—"with the Tukharistanis. Those trapped in the city are beginning to reach out. They're afraid to do so publicly, but I believe there's hope."

"Then I am even happier to meet you." Manizheh gestured to the cushions below her. "Sit." She glanced at Dara, a knowing look in her eyes. "Why don't you celebrate with your men? Watching nobles bow doesn't strike me as the way you'd like to spend your evening."

Oh, thank the Creator. Dara brought his hands together in blessing. "Your mercy is appreciated."

He was barely out of eyesight when he took another glug from the wine bottle. "They're using his spear as wall decor," he muttered to himself, his desire to get drunk growing deeper with each haughty fake laugh he heard from the rich snobs around him. Suleiman's eye, where were his fellows?

He finally found them in a sunken iwan near the back of the throne room, lounging on pillows and appearing to already be in the state of intoxication Dara hoped to achieve.

"Afshin!" Gushtap shot up unsteadily. "We're not on duty, I swear."

"Good, neither am I." Dara tossed his wine bottle to Gushtap before dropping to an adjacent cushion. "Relax," he added, trying to assuage the nervous expressions of his warriors. "We could all use a night off, and I have had enough of the fancy people back there."

Irtemiz offered a wan smile. "I had a man actually gasp when I said I was an archer." She clutched at an invisible strand of pearls. "*But how can you draw a bow? Does your form not impede you?*" She rolled her eyes. "I told him if he didn't take his eyes off my *form*, I would shove an arrow up his ass."

That was probably language Dara should curtail, but alas, Manizheh had given away his responsibilities. "You can have one of mine," he replied, taking his wine back from Gushtap. "How are you feeling, by the way? The leg and arm healing?"

"Banu Manizheh says it'll take time, but at least I'm alive. Thanks to you," she added, emotion thickening her voice. "I owe you more than I can ever repay, Afshin. I can't imagine the Geziris had a pleasant fate in mind for me if you hadn't shown up."

"You don't owe me anything," Dara insisted. He looked at them all, the warriors he'd trained in the frozen forests of northern Daevastana when he wasn't certain they'd ever get to Daevabad. As terribly wrong as the invasion had gone, it had eased the division between his first crop of soldiers and himself. There was a trust, the camaraderie of having bonded and grieved together. "You are my brothers and sisters, understand? This is what we do for each other."

Irtemiz smiled and raised her cup. "To the Nahids."

Dara raised his bottle. "To the Daevas," he corrected, feeling rebellious. He drank down the rest of the wine, his head finally starting to swim.

"May we join you?"

He glanced up. A pair of dancers had separated from the main troupe to approach his knot of drunken warriors, gliding forward on a wave of perfume and tinkling bells.

"Suleiman's eye," Gushtap whispered, his black eyes going wide. Dara couldn't blame him: the dancers were quite the sight—so stunning that it was hard to believe they weren't using magic to enhance their full-lipped smiles and thick inky-black braids. Enough gold to provision a dozen brides draped their necks and wrists, sapphires winking from their ears.

Unlike Gushtap, a farmer's son barely past his first quarter century, Dara had enough familiarity with Daevabadi dancers to know the women would likely be disappointed by his band's paltry offerings. However, he greeted them politely.

"May the fires burn brightly for you, my ladies. You are welcome to our company and our wine, but I fear we cannot match the financial appreciation of the men out there."

Gushtap gave him a look that bordered on treason.

But Dara's words didn't seem to deter the dancers. The first woman, wearing a dazzling collar of ruby roses, stepped forward.

"I have danced for gold aplenty," she replied, her gaze locking on his. "But never for the saviors of my tribe."

A little drunk, Dara spoke perhaps too honestly. "Is that what we are?"

"It's what you're calling yourselves, no?"

Charmed by the challenge in her eyes—as well as the pleading in Gushtap's—Dara inclined his head, gesturing toward the long-necked lute the other woman carried. "Then we would be honored."

Dara had seen enough dancing in his life to know the woman was exquisitely skilled the moment she started spinning. She moved with such precision and elegance that it was impossible to look away, and though he'd said yes more as a favor to his men, Dara found himself spellbound and slightly emotional as she sang, her bejeweled fingers tracing whirling patterns in the air that seemed to illuminate the gentle curve of a lover's cheek and the fall of tears. Her voice was lovely, the lyrics what they always were: love and loss and crushing heartbreak.

"Thank you," he said sincerely when she finished. "That was beautiful. It must take a lifetime to learn to perform like that."

"No less time than I assume it takes to master archery," she replied with a teasing smile. "Though the effect is more pleasant."

"Not when the songs are always so sad. Should love not be happier?"

She laughed, a pleasant, tinkling laugh that, combined with the wine, stirred a bit of heat in Dara.

"Poets don't write songs about that kind of love. Tragedy makes for a better tale." She held his gaze, boldness entering her expression. "Though were you to take me on a tour of the palace, I might sing you a sweeter one."

There was no mere stirring now. A bolt raced down his spine, the kind of ache he hadn't felt for a *very* long time. Dara might have been brought back to life twice, but both times had been in new forms, bodies that never quite felt his. His urges had been infrequent—and the awful suspicion that he'd likely been used and abused by human masters in such a way for centuries left him with little desire.

You desired Nahri. Badly, if he was to be honest. After being alone for so many years, the sudden presence of a beautiful woman with flashing black eyes and an acerbic tongue—who obviously hadn't given a damn what Dara thought about her bathing in rivers and sleeping beside him—had shocked him out of his routine, and he'd wanted her, weaving fantasies at night that left him occasionally embarrassed to meet her eye the next morning.

But now he and Nahri were on opposite sides, having both made their choice.

And Dara wasn't wallowing in his guilt tonight. He gazed at the beautiful dancer, and a moment of drunken recklessness consumed him. He embraced it, relishing the chance to briefly feel mortal again.

He grabbed her outstretched hand. "I would be delighted."

If Dara had any doubts about the dancer's true intentions, they were gone the moment the two of them slipped into the corridor. It was empty, the only sounds the distant feast and their labored breathing. She dragged him to her, her mouth and hands moving with professional speed, making him dizzy with lust. He didn't have time to be nervous, his body falling back into the familiar rhythm.

"Your room?" she gasped as he kissed her throat.

"Too far." Dara pulled her into the shadows and then took her against the wall, shoving her skirts past her hips. The transgression sent a thrill through him. Had an Afshin soldier been caught with a dancing girl in the hallowed halls of the Nahid palace in his day, they would have been whipped. It had been so long since he'd allowed himself even a hint of pleasure, let alone something so heedless and impulsive, and Dara moved faster as she cried out, tightening her legs around his waist.

She sighed when they were done, pressing her brow against his. "Sweeter, yes?"

Dara drew a shaky breath, his body still trembling. "Yes." He eased her back to the ground. "Thank you."

"Thank me?" She laughed. "Whatever for, you beautiful, tragic man? I'm the envy of half of Daevabad right now."

"For letting me feel normal," he murmured. "However briefly."

She smiled, brushing down her skirts. "Then you're welcome. I look forward to scandalizing my granddaughters one day with tales of the night I made the great Darayavahoush feel normal."

He leaned back against the wall, adjusting his own clothes,

a bit scandalized himself at how carried away he'd just gotten. In mere moments, she looked untouched and he marveled at the skill. "What's it like working for Muntadhir?" Dara asked knowingly.

She hesitated only a moment and then winked. "Never dull, that's for certain."

"I am honored he sent such a talented acquaintance my way. And glad the promised sweetness was not an iron blade between my ribs."

The dancer turned over a few of the floral gems he'd upset around her neck. "He has the same flaw as many men in his class, however."

"And what's that?"

"The tendency to underestimate women. Especially common ones." She met his eyes again, a new fierceness in her gaze. "A failure to recognize we can be patriots, no matter the coins in our hands."

"If this is a warning, you chose a very interesting way to pass it along."

"I figured I might as well enjoy the process. But no, I do not have a warning, Darayavahoush. I wish I did. All I can tell you is that he's a dangerous man. A *very* dangerous one. He is handsome and charming and loves so openly and generously that people miss it. But he is every bit his father's son, and if the emir wins through convincing what Ghassan won by fear, trust me when I say the consequences will be just as deadly."

Any lingering ardor vanished. "Muntadhir seems to care about Daevabad. Surely he would not ruin what little stability we are building."

She stepped forward, cradling his face. "I pray you are right." She ran a thumb over Dara's bottom lip, sorrow creasing her expression. "They will sing a thousand songs about you."

"Sad ones?"

"They are the best." She turned away. "May the fires burn brightly for you, Darayavahoush e-Afshin."

Trying to shake off the gloom already reclaiming him, Dara called out, "You didn't tell me your name."

"No, I didn't." She glanced back. "We common women are wise enough to enjoy a taste of heat without staying to be burned."

She walked away without another word and Dara watched her go, suddenly certain he'd never see her again. He ran his fingers through his hair. Well, that was not quite how he imagined this evening going.

He turned over her words regarding Muntadhir. That the calculating emir couldn't be trusted was not new information, but Dara did believe he had Daevabad's best interests at heart, and none of them wanted an intracity civil war between the tribes. Still, perhaps now that he'd made his introductions to the Daeva nobles, it was time to cut Muntadhir out.

Dara's head swam. Creator, this was not what he wanted to think about now. The wine buzzing in his veins, his body still tingling . . . Dara didn't feel like already reassuming the mantle of the brooding Afshin, the Scourge responsible for ending and protecting so many lives. He was tempted to rejoin his men but knew they'd have a better time if their commander was not among them. And yet he wasn't ready to retire to the small, sad room he'd claimed near the stables.

He pushed away from the wall. The pale stone of the empty corridor winding away in the distance, patterned with moonlight from the marble screens, looked inviting, and Dara suddenly had the desire to walk. He snapped his fingers, conjuring a cup of familiar date wine, and took a sip, savoring its sweetness. To hell with Muntadhir's snobbery. This was far better than that expensive grape swill the emir favored.

Dara walked and drank, trying not to stagger too much. His steps rang out on the floor as he trailed his fingers over faded frescoes and ruined plaster. Ahead a shadowed entryway beckoned, and he stopped, struck by the odd location—half tucked away and surrounded by far grander doors. He touched the cool marble of the arch.

This must have had magic before everything went to hell. A simple conjurement would conceal this entry quite well or give it the appearance of a dull, boring door—the kind that became harder to see the longer you looked.

Intrigued and having nothing better to do, Dara stepped through.

DARA WALKED FOR WHAT FELT LIKE AT LEAST AN HOUR, conjuring a handful of flames to lead him through a maze of abandoned corridors and crumbling stone steps. The pathways were long neglected, the dust thick enough that had someone come through, their footsteps would have remained. He swatted aside dozens of cobwebs, the movement sending rats skittering.

When the air turned foul, the stone mossy and slick, Dara began to question his judgment. He'd stopped drinking, figuring if he got lost down here, date wine was not going to help him. But his people were feasting and celebrating above him, he might still be able to track down that very accommodating dancer, and instead he was choosing to follow a hunch through moldy basement passages in a haunted palace? Those were not the actions of a sane man.

The corridor ended in a pair of low, grimy doors, the lintel barely coming to his shoulders. Lifting his handful of flames, Dara knelt to examine the doors. There were no knobs or pulls, but he could make out the glimmer of a round copper panel about the size of his hand.

A blood seal. The Geziris were fond of them. Perhaps it

hadn't been Nahids who'd built this mysterious place, but rather Qahtanis.

He kicked the doors in. The diminutive entrance was deceptive, for Dara could tell the moment he entered that the chamber was immense, swallowing his handful of flames in gloom. An unpleasant tang hung in the air, and Dara wrinkled his nose as he sent his flames spinning out in dozens of fiery balls. They danced along the ceiling, illumination spreading in uneven waves.

His eyes went wide. "Creator have mercy," he whispered.

The cavern was full of the dead.

Elaborate stone sarcophagi and crude wooden boxes. Coffins that could have fit four and tiny ones meant for children. Some looked well preserved while others were crumbling into dust, revealing blackened shards of bone.

Dara's stomach churned. All djinn and Daeva burned their dead within days of their passing, the one tradition they all still held from their earliest ancestors. They were creatures of fire, meant to return to the flames which birthed them. What reason could the Qahtanis possibly have had for building some secret crypt? Was this a sign of forbidden magic, the kind of blood enchantments the ifrit practiced?

Leave. Leave this place now and seal it up. Dara was suddenly, terribly certain that whatever was here, it was meant to stay buried.

But part of him was still the Afshin first, unable to walk away from a secret his enemies had clearly tried to hide.

His dread growing, Dara approached a low desk beside a rack of lead-sealed scrolls. The scrolls themselves got him nowhere—Dara couldn't read his own language, let alone Geziriyya. Tossing a scroll aside, he knelt to examine the desk, discovering a row of small drawers. He jiggled one free, snapping the soft wooden runner.

Inside was a single item: a smooth copper box. Dara picked

it up with a frown, noticing the faint etchings of another blood seal, broken now as all djinn magic was.

Dara held the box for a long moment, his heart racing. And then he opened it.

It took a moment for his mind and his eyes to meet. For the battered brass amulet—the kind his tribe wore to preserve its relics—to register as personally familiar. For Dara to remember the dent in one side was from a dagger strike, the scratches from a simurgh's talons.

To remember ripping this very same amulet from his neck fourteen hundred years ago when he realized he was not going to escape the ifrit who'd come for him on a moon-lit, blood-drenched battlefield.

Dara dropped the box. It fell softly upon the dank earth, and every conjured flame flickered out.

MUNTADHIR STUMBLED, FALLING TO HIS KNEES BE-fore Dara hauled him back up by his collar. Manizheh and Kaveh followed at their heels, tense and silent. They'd exchanged few words since Dara had reappeared in the throne room as the party wound down, covered in dust and striding for Muntadhir as if there was no one else in the world. They hadn't needed to say much.

The way Muntadhir's face drained of color upon hearing the word "crypt" was enough.

The emir hadn't spoken either, breathing too fast and too loud as Dara dragged him through the musty passageway. They'd reached the end now, and Dara shoved him through the doors, flinging fire into the torches lining the walls.

"Explain," he demanded.

Manizheh entered, Kaveh at her side.

The grand wazir gasped, recoiling from the nearest tomb. "Are these bodies?"

"Ask the emir." Dara threw one of the scrolls at Muntadhir's feet. "These records are in Geziriyya. And while we're at it"—he lifted his relic in the air, tempted to smash it into the other man's skull—"I'd like to know how *my relic* ended up in Zaydi al Qahtani's possession."

"What?" Manizheh strode across the room. She snatched the amulet from Dara's hand.

A thousand emotions seemed to pass over her face, her expression settling on anguish. "They had it," she whispered. "All this time, all those years . . ."

"Talk, al Qahtani," Dara demanded. "What do you know of this?"

Muntadhir was trembling. "No more than you." When Dara snarled, he dropped to his knees again. "I swear to God! Look around; this place is older than my father. Than *his* father. We had nothing to do with it. I don't know how my ancestors got your relic!"

"I can imagine how." Dara clenched his fists, trying to contain the fire aching to break free. "Qandisha knew where I was. She knew my name. Zaydi must have brokered a deal with them. The coward knew he couldn't defeat me on the battlefield, so he sold me out to the ifrit."

The emir was still staring at him, despair and doom written into his face as if Muntadhir knew all too well how this was going to end for him. And still a hint of defiance blazed in his broken voice. "I'm glad he did."

Kaveh rushed between them, putting himself in front of Muntadhir before Dara could charge. "No," he warned. "Calm yourself, Afshin."

"Calm myself? They sold me into slavery!"

"You don't know that." Kaveh put a hand on his shoulder. "Look around. He's not lying about the age of this place. And even if Zaydi did . . ." His voice lowered. "It wasn't Muntadhir. He's proving useful—you yourself said so."

Manizheh hadn't spoken again, instead walking into the forest of coffins and sarcophagi. She ran her fingers over a dusty stone slab. "These are Nahids, aren't they?"

Dara froze, shocked at the suggestion, but Muntadhir's expression was already crumbling.

"Yes," he whispered.

She stroked the tomb, as though touching the arm of a loved one. "All of us?"

Shame swept over Muntadhir's face. "From what my father knew—yes. Since the war."

"I see." Grief edged her voice. "Where is my brother?"

"He's not here. My father had Rustam and you—whoever he thought was you—cremated at the Grand Temple. He said when he first became king, he wanted to have all the bodies burned and blessed, but . . ."

"Oh, I'm sure he did. So my parents, my grandmother . . ." Manizheh glanced up, catching the pair of small coffins. "Children. We were defeated. You kept us locked in the infirmary like useful pets. You killed the ones who were too defiant, disappeared the pretty ones who caught a royal eye. And after all that, not even in death could we be granted peace." She motioned to the scrolls. "Are these records, or did no one bother to note their names?"

"They're records," Muntadhir stammered. "They're in Geziriyya, but I can't read them."

"We'll find someone who can."

Dara gazed upon the hundreds of dead. His Blessed Nahids, reduced to rotting in their shrouds.

"*Why?*" he asked. "Why did your people do this?"

"I told you I don't know." Muntadhir's voice quaked in angry fear. "Maybe they were afraid. Maybe they were right to be. Look at *you*. You should be dead twice over; you have access to powers not even you understand—and all because of her." Muntadhir gestured rudely at Manizheh. "Maybe they liked the occasional reassurance that you were all dead."

Manizheh closed her hands into fists, and for a moment Dara thought she was going to punch Muntadhir.

But then she inhaled, shutting her eyes. "Kaveh, get him out of my sight. Find a scribe who can read Geziriyya and one of our priests. People who can be discreet. I'm not ready to share this news."

Kaveh hesitated, clearly not liking the murderous look Dara was giving Muntadhir, but then he came to his senses and rushed the emir away.

When they were gone, Manizheh opened her eyes, gazing at the entombed remains of her relatives. She was still holding his relic.

Dara had to fight the wild urge to grab it away. His *relic*. If he opened it, would the curl of baby hair his mother tucked inside with a prayer still be there? Could he touch something she had once touched so many centuries ago?

But Dara's distant past wasn't the most pressing one. Not now. "Banu Manizheh," he said softly, "how did you bring me back?"

Manizheh stilled. "What are you talking about?"

Dara met her gaze. His anger was gone, and now he was just tired. "I know how slaves are freed and brought back to life. You would have needed my relic."

"I only needed a bit of your mortal remains, and Qandisha showed me where you died."

"I am not talking about that, and you know it. I am talking about the first time." His voice rose. "You and I have been dancing around this for six years. So now I am asking. How did you bring me back?"

Manizheh gave him a wary look. "This isn't a story you want to hear. If I've held back certain details, it was out of kindness."

Another time Dara might have believed that. He might have even found it compassionate.

No longer. "I have followed you and killed for you and asked for nothing in return." He was trembling. "I walk around you all, but I am not one of you. I'm not like other freed djinn. I can't remember my years as a slave, centuries—*centuries*—of my own life. I want to know why. I want to know *how*. You owe me that."

Manizheh held his gaze. Torchlight reflected in her eyes, but her expression otherwise gave nothing away.

Which was why Dara was shocked when she set down his relic, sat upon the desk, and began.

"We found your ring when we were children. The three of us: Kaveh, Rustam, and I. We'd discovered the ruins of a human caravan while exploring. We were very young, and it was very exciting—the closest any of us had gotten to humans, even if all that was left were bones and a few rotted possessions. The bodies had been scattered, dismembered. And on one severed hand there was a ring."

Dara was already uneasy, a caravan of murdered humans perhaps a too apt start to this tale. "My ring?"

"Your ring. The magic coming off it . . . any Nahid would know it was a slave vessel. There's a way to glimpse some of the dreams of the slave trapped inside, and when I peered inside yours, I recognized right away who you were. Your rage, your despair, the memories of Qui-zi and warring against Zaydi al Qahtani—you could be no other than the great Darayavahoush, the last of the Afshins."

She already looked lost in her memories, but more alarm spiked through Dara at her words. "And you didn't think it was too much of a coincidence that the last of the Nahids stumbled across the last of the Afshins?"

"We were children, Darayavahoush. It sounded like a fairy tale. The adults around us were all so cowed by the djinn, so defeated. So we brought the ring to Daevabad, hidden in our clothes, and tried to learn the truth of what had happened to you."

"Did none of my followers leave accounts?"

Manizheh shook her head. "If your followers knew, they didn't talk. Those who weren't executed after your rebellion fell apart were brought back to Daevabad and richly rewarded."

Ah, yes, the Daeva noble houses with their familiar names. Stung, Dara pressed on. "So if there was no record of me being enslaved, no hope of a relic . . ."

"It meant we needed to find another way. So Rustam and I tried everything. For years. Decades. Any new magic we came upon—enchantments and potions and conjurements. Wild experiments that would have horrified our ancestors."

Dara felt ill. "Experiments?"

"We were desperate. It felt like a cruel joke. To be so close to someone who could save us and not be able to bridge that last gap. I watched my people crushed, my brother beaten, Ghassan pressuring me to marry him, and I'd close my eyes and see this ancient warrior, a man who'd known the mightiest of my ancestors, rising from the ash to set it all right."

Dara scrubbed a hand through his hair, finding it hard to judge her. "So which . . . experiment," he said, repeating the word with poorly concealed distaste, "was the one that finally worked?"

She rose from the desk. "We'd been reading a lot about the history of our family, the origins of our magic, all the miraculous things our blood—our very lives—were said to be capable of." Manizheh brushed her thumb over his amulet. "There are stories of Nahids dying in battle and their lifeblood resurrecting all who'd fallen around them."

"Fairy tales, Banu Nahida. Like you said."

"Perhaps." She ran her finger against the edge of the brass. "But then I became pregnant a second time. I couldn't do it again—I couldn't strip another Nahid child of her abilities and abandon her in Zariaspa to never again see my face. Rustam agreed, or so I thought. We left Daevabad, but I'd hidden the pregnancy well and was far along on the journey. Too far along."

Manizheh fell silent. She looked crushed, more than Dara had ever seen her. "We were so broken, Afshin. Our spirits, our hopes. I had no doubt Ghassan would hunt me down. That when he realized I'd given away what he so openly desired, he would make me pay. Rustam knew that too. I think . . . I think in a way he was trying to protect me. To protect us all."

Sick fear swirled into Dara's heart. "What happened?"

Manizheh stared at her hands. "She was born. I knew it was obvious, but I was so tired, and when Rustam said he would handle things . . . I didn't realize what he meant." She took a deep breath. "When I woke up, he was preparing to use Nahri to bring you back."

Shock froze his tongue. Dara knew little about Manizheh's brother, but the scant amount he'd heard of a quiet man who'd liked to paint and had a talent for turning the plants he grew himself into pharmaceuticals did not add up to . . . that.

"Use her?" he whispered. "You mean, he meant to sacrifice her life to bring me back? His own niece? A *child*?"

"A shafit child."

Dara blinked. *Shafit?* "But you said Nahri was pureblooded. That her appearance was a curse . . ."

"And it is. But if it was the marid who cursed her, they had plenty to work with." She exhaled. "I continued the lie when Kaveh told me. She's my daughter, and I wanted to protect her.

I knew—especially now, when she's lied and deceived us—that if such information leaked, the Daevas would believe Nahri's betrayal was because she was shafit and turn on her. It fits the worst of what people believe about the mixed-bloods."

Dara was speechless. And yet there was another part of this that made no sense. "But who?" he asked, perhaps tactlessly. "You do not seem the type to—" He flushed. "I mean, the only shafit in the palace would have been . . ."

"Servants," Manizheh finished. "A Nahid child—with abilities so strong I could sense them in pregnancy—and a shafit servant as a father. It would be beyond a scandal, Rustam said. A disgrace so outrageous it might have cost us the support of other Daevas when we needed it most. At least this way, she could serve her family. Her tribe. And it would be painless."

"But a *baby*?"

Manizheh pinned him with her dark eyes, her expression suddenly frostier. "Were there no babes still at breast in Qui-zi?"

It was a cruel, if justified, question. "Are you saying you *agreed* with him?"

"Of course I didn't agree with him! We fought about it, and when it became clear that Rustam wouldn't stop, we . . . battled. In ways I didn't think our people were still capable of. He cursed me, I'm not entirely sure how. A blast, an explosion. I woke hours later. What Kaveh would find—the scorched landscape, the broken bodies—that was what I returned to. My daughter was gone, the ring was gone. And Rustam . . ." Her voice grew hollow with old grief. "It was too late. I couldn't save him."

Dara abruptly sat down. "Suleiman's eye."

"Suleiman had nothing to do with it. In the end, that was what we were reduced to. The last Nahids scrabbling in the dust over whether or not to murder a baby. How pleased the djinn would have been to finally see our ruin."

The anguish in Manizheh's confession tugged hard at his

soul. It was easier to resent the coolly aloof woman who'd ordered him to be a weapon and then dismissed him when he disobeyed. Dara could relate to someone who'd spent their life fighting tooth and nail for their freedom, for their people, only to lose it all at the end.

"You've not told anyone else this, have you?" he asked softly.

"How could I? It would confirm the worst prejudices of the djinn, and I knew the price Ghassan would demand to pardon me." Manizheh's voice grew fierce again. "I'd take my own life before I let him touch me."

"Does Kaveh know?"

Her face fell. "No. He all but worshipped us. I couldn't destroy his faith like that." She hesitated. "But . . ."

"But, what?"

"Aeshma knows."

Dara would not have been more surprised if she'd said the ifrit had gone out to dance in the midan. "*Aeshma?*"

"He showed up shortly after I found Rustam's body. He said the intensity of the battle, of the magic and the blood, drew his attention. And he knew me. Knew my name, what people said about my abilities . . . he said he'd been hoping to meet me one day."

"*Why?*"

"Is it not obvious?" Manizheh asked. "He wants to be like *you*, Afshin. The ifrit have been waiting for a Nahid powerful enough to free them from Suleiman's curse. There are only a handful left, and they're nearing the end of their lives. They want peace and a last taste of their old magic."

Dara stared at her. "Don't tell me you believed him. Banu Manizheh, for all you know, he'd been waiting for you to fall into a trap like that. He and Qandisha might have been the ones who put my ring in your path!"

"They probably were. And I didn't care. I couldn't go back to Daevabad. My brother was dead. I was certain my daughter was as well. The ring—*you*, my only hope—was gone, and I wanted to be free, no matter the cost. Even if it meant striking a deal with an ifrit—*lying* to an ifrit—because in truth, I had no idea how to remove Suleiman's curse. I didn't think it could be done."

Manizheh set down his relic, pacing away. The bottom of her chador had turned gray with dust, streaks of it like grasping fingers reaching up from the ground of the crypt.

"But you found me again," Dara said, trying to keep the bitterness from his voice. He had the feeling that somehow he was always destined to wind up in Manizheh's hands. "Or my ring, anyway."

"Nisreen recovered your ring." Sadness crossed Manizheh's expression. "She never told Kaveh how. I wish I had the story. I wish I could speak with her and thank her for everything. She was so loyal and worked so hard for all this. She should have seen it. She shouldn't have spent her last moments in pain because of some shafit savage."

Dara didn't know what to say. Nisreen was only the latest in a long line of people whose brutal deaths he mourned, and coming up with the proper words to assuage another's grief was beginning to leave him numb. "I take it you didn't need my relic once you had my ring and Qandisha to tell you where she left my body to rot."

"I still wasn't sure it would work. You should have died when Alizayd severed your hand; a freed slave's vessel cannot be separated from their conjured body. Whether it's because you were brought back with Nahid blood or something else, I don't know. But from the moment I held your ring, I knew you were still there. Your presence burned so strongly. I had your ring and I had your mortal remains. And when I woke you up, you were this."

The meaning of the wonder in her voice and the way she trailed off took a moment to register.

"Wait . . ." Dara's tone was shaky. "Surely you're not suggesting you didn't *mean* to make me like this?" He let his skin briefly turn to flame. "That you weren't trying to bring me back in this form?"

"I freed you the way I would free any ifrit slave. When you opened your eyes, when the fire failed to leave your skin, I thought it was a miracle." Manizheh laughed hoarsely, no humor in the sound. "A sign from the Creator, believe it or not."

Dara's mind spun. "I-I don't understand."

"That makes two of us." An almost desperate anger, a mad desire to be understood, seemed to have stolen over his usually so composed Banu Nahida. "*Don't* you understand, Afshin? I saw the shock in Aeshma's face when I brought you back. I knew how the story would carry, the power it would give me to lay claim to resurrecting the great guardian of the Daevas in such a way."

"You lied." The moment the words left his lips, Dara knew how naive they sounded. Manizheh had always made clear how far she would go to take back Daevabad. But this was different. Personal. It was *his* body and soul, shattered and re-formed. Snatched from the edge of Paradise and twisted again and again, into a tool—a weapon—to serve others.

Heat pooled in his hands, ribbons of smokeless fire wrapping about his arms. And suddenly Dara knew he was never going to have answers. Not about his memories. Not about his future. He was an experiment, a mess, and not even the Nahid who'd brought him back to life understood how.

"You were right," he said quietly. "I did not want that story."

"Then perhaps next time you should listen to me." Manizheh was breathing fast, pacing, and when she spoke again, it seemed to be as much to herself as to Dara. "And it's in the past now, anyway. It doesn't matter."

"No, I suppose not. Weapons are not permitted feelings."

Her eyes flashed. "Don't speak to me about feelings. Not here." Manizheh motioned to the decaying coffins of her relatives scattered on the filthy ground. "Not when my children are missing, and our city's at war." She picked up his relic and slipped it into her pocket. "You're not the only one with regrets, Dara. This isn't how I wanted to see the Nahids—the Daevas—rise.

"But I won't bow. Not again."

22

ALI

Ali jumped from the ship, splashing into the clear shallows of the inlet. "Looks welcoming," he remarked, glancing at the dense forest and impenetrable brush.

Nahri was giving the jungle an openly doubtful appraisal. "This is the land of golden streets and coral castles?"

Fiza leapt down. "You're in the human world, Daevabadis. Djinn here have to be discreet."

"Are those bones in the trees?"

"Yes!" Fiza cackled, trudging ahead. "Looks like a zahhak. Very creative. Come along, fancy people," she called over her shoulder, freeing the knife she wore on her arm. "I'm assuming most of the magical traps the Ayaanle set aren't working, but you should probably stay close."

"Of course there would be traps," Nahri muttered, taking Ali's hand and climbing down.

Ali said nothing but stuck to her side as two more crewmen

followed. The inlet narrowed as they ventured deeper into the jungle, becoming little more than a wide, lazy stream. With birds and monkeys chittering in the lush canopy and the smell of ocean air, it might have made for a pleasant scene . . . if not for the skulls, teeth, and rusting metal implements hanging in the trees. It was almost ridiculous—the exact scenario he imagined resulted from a bunch of paranoid djinn merchants gathering in a committee to decide what would best scare away curious humans.

"'Plague ahead,'" Ali read from a large stone cairn. "'Proceed, and you will most certainly die in painful fashion.'" The awkwardly phrased warning was written in a half dozen different languages. "Why don't they just fill the forests with wild karkadann?"

"It's probably been tried," Fiza replied. "The Ayaanle always have to overdo it. Back in Qart Sahar, we just go camp out in ruins once a century and scream and bang drums all night. Keeps the humans away for decades."

"Lovely," Nahri commented. "You know there's a human tale about a fisherman who traps a djinn in a bottle and tosses it out to sea? With every day I spend in the magical world, I like that story more."

They left the creek and kept walking, the forest closing in around them until Ali glanced back and could no longer see the sea. Its loss left him feeling unmoored, like he'd been cut off from a vital link. Ali had not dared use his marid magic since his near miss with a midnight ocean plunge, but he longed for it with a craving he couldn't explain. Every night since, he'd dreamed of the wondrous Nile path he'd walked with Sobek and the silky voice that had urged him to join with the sea. More than once, he'd woken up pressed against the ship's railing, reaching for the ocean.

His hand brushed his belt. The place where Muntadhir's khanjar should have hung was empty. Fiza hadn't been able to steal it before they'd left, and the thought of his brother's dagger, the one Muntadhir had put into his hands, in the possession of the filthy slaver made Ali want to drown the whole world.

Stop. Focus on Ta Ntry. Not the marid, not Muntadhir. Ali forced himself to look upon the sun-dappled jungle. His mother's stories came to mind, the nostalgic tales she told of playing by a creek under banyan trees. In another life, Ali might have grown up here, this land as familiar to him as Daevabad.

"You okay?" Nahri asked.

Ali glanced down in surprise, catching her studying him. "Just pondering our reception," he muttered, switching to Arabic. "I hope my mother is here."

"Even if she isn't, won't you have your grandfather? Cousins and the like?"

"I've never met my grandfather, and last I heard, he hasn't been well. As for the rest, I've kept my mother's family at a distance. To come to them for help now, as a prince on the run . . ." Ali fingered the torn, stained tunic he was wearing, loaned from one of the crew. "It feels deceptive and humiliating."

Nahri reached out to squeeze his hand, and the press of her fingers made him warm all over. "I believe deceptive and humiliating are the norm for our families. Besides, you're arriving with a bunch of shafit pirates and a scheming Banu Nahida. You'll be the most welcome face in the bunch."

Ali started to smile, but then movement between the trees caught his eye—the glimmer of metal, not anything natural.

He pulled his hand from Nahri's, edging between her and their unseen arrival. "Fiza," he called in a low voice. "We have company."

The pirate immediately halted, reaching for the pistol Ali had been unable to convince her to leave back at the ship.

"Touch the gun and die," a man, still hidden, warned in Ntaran-accented Djinnistani. "Drop your weapons, all of you."

Ali paused. Dressed in borrowed clothes, his hair and beard overgrown, he knew he looked more pirate than prince, but there would be no hiding his identity once he drew his zulfiqar.

"We come in peace," he greeted the man, saying the Ntaran words as clearly as he could and praying his accent wasn't too childish. "We're here to see Queen Hatset."

"The queen has little time for the scum raiding our coasts and even less for those who can't follow orders. Your weapons. Now."

Fiza muttered something in Sahrayn that Ali suspected was a return insult, but the man's warning had filled him with relief. His mother *was* here.

So Ali drew his zulfiqar, letting the sun glint on the copper blade before laying it on the ground, then motioning for Fiza and her men to follow suit. "I guarantee you she'll want to see us."

Ali's hand had barely left the hilt when an Ayaanle warrior emerged from the trees as though stepping through a slit in the air. His golden gaze went wide as it traced Ali from his zulfiqar to his gray eyes to Suleiman's mark on his cheek. He looked at Nahri, and he swore, calling back to the trees.

"It's the prince," he declared. "And if I'm not mistaken, the Nahid girl."

His words were followed by three more Ayaanle warriors stepping out from the forest in unison. Each was taller than the next, dressed in softly shimmering cloth rippling with the exact colors of the greenery around them. They were ridiculously well armed, with throwing knives and sickle-swords, crossbows and slender axes.

Fiza made a small sound between appreciation and alarm. "Well, if they don't kill us, maybe a couple will join my crew."

One of the warriors stepped closer, a woman—no less muscled than the men and wearing even more knives. "They could be imposters," she suggested. "Spies or assassins sent by Manizheh and her Afshin."

"I can probably tell if the prince is an imposter."

The voice was familiar, coming from behind them, and Ali spun to face the man who emerged from the trees.

"*Musa?*" He gaped, recognizing the distant cousin he'd met in Am Gezira—the one who'd played a part in his sister's scheme to return Ali to Daevabad. His cousin was armed far more lightly than the soldiers, his sickle-sword looking more like an accessory.

"Ah, you remember me. I should hope so, considering the fighters you sent from your village chased me all the way to the Sea of Reeds."

"You sabotaged our well. You're lucky they didn't drag you back and force you to eat the salt you dumped upon us."

Musa smirked. "Oh, good, you're just as charming as I remember." He glanced at the soldiers. "You can lower your weapons. This is definitely my cousin."

THEY FOLLOWED MUSA THROUGH THE FOREST, MOVING so swiftly that Ali struggled to keep his bearings—which he suspected was the point. The Ayaanle originally intended to blindfold the others, and he'd had to talk them down, shushing Fiza when she described in graphic detail what the djinn could do to themselves instead. Exasperated, Musa had finally agreed, and when the shafit pirate snorted in triumph, Ali's cousin pointed out that this meant they would more likely be killed without being released.

It made for a tense walk.

Worse, Nahri had yet to say a word, unnervingly and uncharacteristically silent at his side. Her expression gave nothing away, the guarded mask Ali remembered from the palace. After so many weeks traveling together, he was taken aback to see it now, and he found himself resisting the urge to take her hand lest she bolt, vanishing into the greenery around them, probably finding a way to take Musa's gold cuff and lapis earrings with her.

They came upon the town rather suddenly. Ali had been expecting cleared land and forbidding walls, a mighty fortress to match Ta Ntry's wealth. But Shefala was not that at all. Nestled in the ruins of an older human settlement, the djinn town seemed to bloom naturally from the earth and human past. What might have been the foundation of an ancient hilltop fort had been dug out and opened to shelter a marketplace, and large, airy homes had been built around the trees, utilizing recovered bricks, thatch, and coral walls. There were no straight, paved streets, but rather sandy paths that wound naturally around shade trees and freestanding gardens. A pleasant setting for the thriving merchant port Shefala was said to be.

Except it was virtually empty.

A plaza of teak benches with room for hundreds now sheltered only two women weaving on hand looms. Besides a fruit seller dozing in front of an open-air mosque and a handful of Agnivanshi traders, Ali saw no one. Granted, Musa was keeping them on an outer path that skirted the town's edge, perhaps in an effort to keep news of Ali and Nahri contained, but the sounds Ali would have expected of a bustling entrepôt—chatter in a half dozen different languages, the banging of tools and shouts of children—were nowhere to be heard.

Nahri finally spoke. "Where is everyone?" she asked as they passed a fishpond beneath the canopy of a massive baobab tree.

"Gone or in the castle," Musa explained. "For now, anyway. When word came of what happened to Daevabad, Queen Hatset ordered most of the women, children, and old folks away. We have some holdouts, as well as merchants and sailors from the other tribes who were passing through on magical means and got stuck. But the queen said she'd be better prepared to take a stand against Manizheh if she knew a thousand innocents couldn't be wiped out in response."

That sounds like Amma. Shefala's stone castle came into view then, and Ali had to resist the urge to break into a run. Though traveling here had been his idea, part of Ali hadn't allowed himself to envision seeing his mother, not wanting to be crushed if his plan fell apart.

He admired the castle as they drew nearer. Though far smaller than Daevabad's palace, the castle was lovely, its lime-plastered coral walls shining in the sun. The human ruins had been incorporated wherever possible, an old minaret turned into a wind tower, a broken wall given over to flowers. It conveyed age with warmth, whereas Daevabad had seemed brutal, a palace stolen multiple times.

Musa stopped them at a set of grand doors, carved in a pattern of scrollwork and set with bronze ornaments. "I will take them to the majlis," he told the female warrior. "Please tell the queen she has guests." He lowered his voice, but Ali heard him add softly, "Would you see how my grandfather is doing as well?"

My grandfather. Ali followed Musa, gawking at everything and feeling out of place.

The majlis was elegant and majestic, a place fit for entertaining royalty, with high windows of ebony wood; checkered marble walls in dark silver and glittering white; and soft, imported Daeva rugs. Agnivanshi tapestries depicting musicians and dancers hung from the walls, and a white jade and carnelian screen from Tukharistan sectioned off cushioned sofas surrounding a tiled fountain that looked like it had been plucked from Qart Sahar. Fine ceremonial weapons were displayed above a carved ivory platform: a zulfiqar and an Ayaanle shield in a place of prominence.

Fiza and her men had gone immediately for the fruit and

sweets left for guests, but Nahri hadn't joined them, eyeing the room like she was expecting a rukh to jump out and eat her.

"Are you all right?" Ali asked.

"Fine," she muttered. "Noting the symbolism."

"The symbolism?"

She gestured to the crossed Ayaanle and Geziri weapons behind the raised stage of seat cushions. "The Geziri and Ayaanle, allied and powerful . . ." Her finger lowered to point at the Daeva rug. "My people underfoot."

Ali tried to give her what he hoped was a reassuring smile. "Maybe they just liked the carpet?"

"You look displeased, Daeva," Musa said. He'd followed them into the majlis. "Is something wrong?"

Nahri's eyes flashed. "Yes. You've now referred to me as the 'Nahid girl' and 'Daeva' when I'm confident you know both my name and my title. So are you just being rude, or is this an Ayaanle custom I'm misinterpreting?"

"You'll forgive me. We don't have an established tradition for welcoming the daughters of mass murderers."

Ali's temper snapped. "Is there a tradition for getting punched in the majlis? Because between sabatoging my village's well and insulting my friend—"

"Alu?"

Thoughts of brawling with his cousin fled Ali's mind. Hatset stood at the door in widow's ash gray, her adornments gone.

"Is it really you?" his mother whispered. Her golden eyes had locked on his, but she didn't move. She looked as worried as Ali did that this might all be a mirage.

"*Amma.*" The choked word left his lips, and then Ali was across the room.

Hatset grabbed him as he fell at her feet. "Oh, baba," she wept, pulling him into an embrace. "I was so worried."

Ali hugged her close. She felt thinner, frail in a way she never had before. "I'm okay, Amma. God be praised, I'm okay." Gently taking her arm, he led his mother to one of the couches, giving Fiza a grateful look as the pirate motioned for her men to fall back.

Hatset had yet to let him go, only releasing Ali long enough to take his face in her hands. She lightly touched the bruise still marring his temple and traced the seal on his cheek.

Sorrow filled her eyes. "I would be lying if I said I didn't hope to see Suleiman's mark on you one day, but God, not at such a cost."

"I know." Ali fought to keep the emotion from his voice, his throat thick. He was not on a lonely riverbank with Nahri where he could openly grieve—he was a politically compromised prince in a foreign court that, though familiar, had its own interests, and there were a lot of people watching him. "But those we have lost are with God now. All we can do is ensure they get justice."

Hatset gazed at him, and he caught a glimpse of both pride and sadness in her eyes. "But of course, Alizayd." She straightened up, steel entering her voice as she glanced over Ali's shoulder. "Banu Nahri, welcome to Shefala."

"Thank you," Nahri deadpanned. "I've always wanted to travel."

"Amma," Ali spoke quickly. "Nahri and I were blessed to make the acquaintance of Captain Fiza and her crew"—he inclined his head toward the shafit pirate—"to whom we owe our lives. Could rooms be prepared for them to rest? Cousin, you appear to be doing nothing. Can you make welcome our guests?"

Musa gave him an incredulous look. "Oh, is it 'our' already?"

"Yes," Hatset said firmly. "Captain Fiza, I am honored to meet you. Please be assured you and your crew will be shown every welcome—and reward for aiding my son." She glanced at Musa, her gaze a bit more chiding. "Please, nephew, if you wouldn't mind seeing to our guests."

Musa bowed his head. "Of course, my queen."

His cousin and the sailors filed out of the room, leaving Ali alone with Nahri and his mother. The sound of the door closing echoed through the vast space.

His mother immediately pulled Ali back into a hug, clutching him tight. "Thanks be to God," she said, kissing his head. "I thought for certain you were dead. I feared Manizheh murdered you both and was spreading this lunatic story to buy herself time."

Ali released her. "Has there been any more news of Daevabad? Anything from Zaynab?"

Hatset paused. "No. Not yet." She cleared her throat. "But I did send a message to Manizheh."

Nahri drew up. "What kind of message?"

"I will absolutely see him," a man insisted outside the majlis door. "He is my prince, we are at *war,* and I don't need the permission of some trumped-up—"

Ali shot to his feet. "Is that *Wajed?*"

"Yes," Hatset said. "He came to Shefala when he heard Daevabad fell. He apparently believed me the next authority—not that he's always been acting that way," she grumbled. "Come in, Qaid!"

Wajed entered with what looked like barely controlled haste, two Geziri soldiers nipping at his heels.

"*Zaydi,*" the old warrior greeted him, relief in his voice. "Thank God."

Nahri flew up before Ali could respond. "Thank no one," she snapped. "What have you done with Jamshid?"

THE WARRIORS ACCOMPANYING WAJED HAD THEIR weapons drawn before Jamshid's name had even left Nahri's lips.

"Stop!" Ali rushed between them. "Lower your weapons!"

"I've done nothing to Jamshid," Wajed spat out, scowling at Nahri with undisguised hostility. "He's here, alive and confined below."

"Jamshid e-Pramukh is here?" Ali asked, keeping himself between Nahri and the Geziri soldiers. The soldiers might have dropped their weapons, but Nahri still looked murderous. "*How?*"

"He was in my custody the night of the attack," Wajed explained. "Your father ordered me to arrest Nahri and the Pramukh men after the Navasatem attack. I was to deliver Nahri and Kaveh to the palace and take Jamshid to one of our strongholds in Am Gezira. He's been with me since."

"Why?" Ali looked wildly between Wajed and Nahri, each of whom was glaring daggers at the other. "Why would my father arrest three Daevas for the attack on their parade? He knew they had nothing to do with it. He was already preparing to punish the shafit!"

"That's not why he arrested us." Nahri still sounded heated, but there was a new hesitation in her voice.

Ali was growing more baffled by the moment. "Then why did he arrest you?"

Nahri's dark eyes met his, an apology in them. "Because of you, Ali. Ghassan was going to use me to end your rebellion. He planned to charge me as your co-conspirator and threaten to have me executed if you didn't surrender."

Ali reeled, lost for words, but Wajed was already responding.

"That's a lie," the Qaid declared, sounding appalled. "The king would never have treated a woman under his protection in such a way!"

"Yes, he would," Ali whispered, hating the truth of it. "If he thought I was a true risk to his throne, to Daevabad's stability, there is nothing my father wouldn't have done."

Hatset had stayed quiet, observing their fight from a distance, but she spoke up now. "Why were the Pramukh men involved?"

Wajed still seemed aggrieved. "I don't know."

"I wasn't asking you." Hatset's gaze fixed on Nahri. "I'm talking to the Banu Nahida. Why were Kaveh and Jamshid involved?"

"I didn't ask," Nahri said through her teeth. "You'll forgive me for not thinking to pry into your evil husband's convoluted plots while he was threatening to kill me."

Hatset was undeterred. "So you have no thoughts, none at all, as to why Ghassan believed Jamshid valuable?"

Ali interceded. "We're not doing whatever this is. I owe my life to Nahri ten times over. She is my ally and my friend, and we did not come here so she could be attacked and interrogated the moment she stepped through the door."

"I'm not attacking her," Hatset said calmly. "I already know why Ghassan believed Jamshid so valuable. I am merely curious if Banu Nahri does as well."

Banu Nahri looked like she was about to stab everyone in the room. "Why don't you enlighten me," she said, her voice as cool and lethal as Manizheh's had been on the palace roof back in Daevabad.

Ali touched her wrist. This had been the exact kind of reception she'd feared. "Nahri—"

"It's fine. Your mother *clearly* has some things she'd like to say to me."

The men in the room may have been the armed ones, but they had nothing on the battle brewing between the two women. Even Wajed had stepped back, looking newly apprehensive.

Hatset nodded at the soldiers. "Would you leave us?"

With a glance at Wajed and Ali, the guards complied. Only when the door was shut did his mother speak again.

"Shortly after Manizheh supposedly died, a Daeva noble from the hinterland arrived. An inconsequential man, from a family that was more farmer than sophisticate, but one that had served the Nahids for centuries—the Pramukhs. When Ghassan heard he was in the city, he invited the noble to court out of sympathy—he'd been a friend to Manizheh and Rustam, you see, the unfortunate person who'd discovered their bodies when they were slain."

A chill went down Ali's back. He'd heard the stories growing up of the blood-soaked, smoldering plain in Daevastana where the last Nahids had supposedly been slaughtered by the ifrit. "Kaveh."

"But not just Kaveh," Hatset continued. "Jamshid too. I occasionally attended court in those days, and I still remember the way the color drained from your father's face when Kaveh formally presented himself and his son, a little boy who barely reached his waist. Ghassan shot to his feet, furious, and charged out. I immediately followed, the worried wife, to overhear my husband ranting to his Qaid about the 'ungrateful whore'—how the Nahid he'd desired had used the leave he'd granted her to rut with a country noble and how the man had to be a fool to turn up in his city. About how he planned to kill the boy and make Kaveh watch before throwing both their bodies in the lake."

Wajed spoke up. "We . . . intervened," he said delicately. "The king didn't tell us how he knew the truth of Jamshid's parentage, but it was clear Kaveh didn't realize he'd been found out."

"And Jamshid was an innocent. A child," Hatset said. "One who apparently had no healing abilities, but who knew what the future might hold? Manizheh's blood—his *mother's* blood—was strong, and the rest of the Nahids were dead. We could bring this one into the fold and make him loyal. Valuable."

Valuable. Ali's stomach dropped at the word. "Jamshid," he breathed. "You're saying that Jamshid is Manizheh's *son*?" He spun on Nahri, expecting to see her looking equally shocked. "But that would make him . . ."

"My brother," Nahri finished. "And I thank you, my queen, for that *illuminating* story. Tell me, at the point when the pair of you had to counsel Ghassan against slaughtering innocent children, did you ever stop to contemplate the consequences of serving such a tyrant? Or was violence in Daevabad acceptable until it affected your people?"

Wajed went red. "If you think to justify the slaughter of thousands of Geziris—"

"Enough." Ali swayed on his feet, but when he spoke, he made sure the command was clear. "You will take us to Jamshid. Now."

23

NAHRI

The corridor that led to Jamshid's cell was clean and simple: lime-washed walls with high narrow windows. It didn't look like the blood-soaked torture chamber that Daevabad's dungeon was rumored to be, but it was still a prison, and Nahri's anger—white-hot since the majlis—howled inside her like an animal. Had she her magic, Nahri thought she might be capable of the things Manizheh had done, breaking bones from across the room and seizing control of people's limbs. There had to be an outlet for rage like this, a release so it wouldn't devour her from within.

You naive little girl. Her mother's words on the palace roof came back in a rush, mingling with the suspicion in Musa's eyes, the open hate in Wajed's, and Hatset's awful story. Nahri couldn't condone what Manizheh had done to the Geziris, but she suddenly feared that putting herself in the hands of the djinn had been a terrible mistake.

At her side, Ali moved closer, his shoulder brushing hers.

"You knew," he said, speaking softly in Arabic so they wouldn't be overheard. "You knew about Jamshid."

Her reply was curt. "Yes."

He sighed. "I wish you had told me. There weren't supposed to be any more secrets between us, and I feel like we just fell into a trap."

"And that's *my* fault? I came here to make peace, not get set upon by your mother and Wajed. Did you not hear what they said about Jamshid? My brother's entire life is a lie because of your father!"

"I *know*, Nahri. I know, all right?" And indeed, she saw only frustrated sympathy in Ali's gray eyes. "But that's why you and I need to be united—*against* the rest of them if necessary." He touched her hand. "I meant everything I said to you in Cairo and back on the beach. I am your partner in this, your friend. I'm not going to betray you."

"And if you're not enough?" The question burst from her, giving voice to her fear. "They've already locked up one Daeva. What if we can't convince them that this fight is against Manizheh, not my entire tribe?"

Ali's expression grew fierce. "Jamshid is getting out of that cell today. They either let him out, or you and I break him out, we join Fiza's crew, and the three of us try our hand at piracy."

His words didn't vanquish her anger, but Nahri felt a little fear ebb away at the promise of a backup plan, even a ridiculous one. "Fine," she muttered, giving his hand a squeeze before letting it go.

They kept walking, following Wajed down a twisting staircase that ended in a hall of earth-packed walls. A single window let in a dusty ray of light, illuminating a row of wooden doors. All were open save one, which sported a new, human-looking metal lock and a heavy beam barring the entrance. Two soldiers sat on mats just outside, playing some sort of card game.

They shot to their feet when Ali entered, their eyes going wider as they took in Nahri at his side.

"Your Highness," one stammered, falling into an awkward bow. "Forgive us," he added, kicking the cards into the corner. "We didn't realize—"

"There is nothing to forgive. Is this where Jamshid e-Pramukh is being kept?" Ali asked, nodding at the locked door.

"Yes, my prince," the other djinn said nervously. His gaze darted to Nahri. "But he's made a mess of the place. I can prepare a different cell for her if—"

"No," Ali cut in, silencing the other man as if he felt Nahri's temper spiking again. "We won't be locking up any more Daevas as of today." He held out his palm. "The key, please."

Wajed had clearly been checking his tongue since their fight in the majlis, but he spoke up now. "My prince, I'm not certain that's wise. Pramukh has already tried to escape twice."

"And once he's free, he won't have to attempt a third. The key. Now."

The Ayaanle soldier obeyed, pulling a key from his pocket and handing it to Ali, who promptly gave it to Nahri.

"Thank you," Ali said politely. "Your assistance is appreciated. Qaid, would you and these men please go speak to my mother about finding rooms for our Daeva guests?"

Wajed looked like he would rather have shoved Nahri into a cell, but she knew enough about royal protocol to know he wouldn't question a Qahtani in front of his men. "Of course, my prince," he said, his voice cool.

Nahri waited until they left and then quickly fit the key into the lock.

Ali helped her with the crossbeam. "Do you want me to leave?" he asked.

I don't know. Now that she was facing the prospect of speaking to the man she knew was her brother, Nahri felt uncertain. She and

Jamshid were friends, yes, but it wasn't a relationship that time and their respective positions had let deepen. She had been his Banu Nahida first.

And he had belonged to Muntadhir. How was Nahri, never the most empathetic of people if she was honest, going to find the words to shatter his world? It didn't sound like Hatset or Wajed had bothered to keep Jamshid in the loop. Was she supposed to just walk in and announce he was a Nahid and that his parents had been behind the invasion that murdered the man he loved?

She shivered. "No, not yet." She didn't imagine Ali would be helpful—Jamshid didn't seem to like him—but she could use the support. She opened the door.

It took her eyes a moment to adjust to the gloomy light. Like the corridor, Jamshid's cell had a small window, barred and no bigger than a man's head. A single oil lamp burned in one corner, the eastern corner, her heart aching as she realized the cup of water and a half-burnt twig beside it were an attempt at a fire altar. A messy floor desk was piled with paper and books, half-stacked in toppled piles.

Jamshid himself was curled upon a sleeping pallet, facing the wall. He hadn't stirred when they opened the door, and for a moment, Nahri panicked, fearing she was too late before she spotted the rise of his chest.

"Jamshid?" she called.

A single tremor raced down his body, and he rolled over.

Dazed black eyes locked on hers. "Nahri?" Jamshid sat up, swaying like he was drunk. Then he lurched forward. *"Nahri!"*

She rushed to catch him, pulling him into a hug. "Thought you could use some company."

Jamshid clutched her tight. "Oh, thank the Creator. I was so worried about you." He released her. "Are you okay? How did you get here? They said everyone in the palace was killed!"

"I'm okay," she managed. Her brother, on the other hand,

looked awful, his face thin and pale, his beard overgrown, and his black hair hanging in tangled waves. "Are you all right? Have they been mistreating you?"

Jamshid scowled. "They flap their mouths but haven't laid hands on me. They're too afraid of—" He abruptly stopped talking, his attention shifting behind her. "*Alizayd?*"

Ali awkwardly cleared his throat. "Hello."

Wild optimism lit Jamshid's gaze. "If you're alive, does that mean . . . is Muntadhir here as well?" he asked frantically. "Did he make it out with you?"

Nahri's heart dropped. "No. I'm sorry, Jamshid. Muntadhir . . . he didn't make it out."

She could see the hope literally vanish from her brother's eyes. Jamshid swallowed loudly, looking like he was trying to pull on his courtier's facade. "I see." He turned back to Ali. "Then why are you here?"

Ali hadn't moved from the doorway. "What?" he whispered.

"I asked *why are you here,* al Qahtani? Because protecting Muntadhir was your job, your entire life's duty, and if you're standing here, I can only assume you failed or betrayed him. So which is it?"

Ali rocked back on his heels, the accusation richoceting around the cell. Weeks of healing seemed to unwind from his face in the blink of an eye. "I didn't betray him. I would never."

"Then you're a coward."

"*Jamshid.*" Nahri stepped between them. "He's not a coward. And it's not his fault. Muntadhir chose to protect his family and his kingdom the best way he knew. It was one of the bravest things I've ever seen, and I won't hear anyone dishonor it."

But her words didn't seem to reach her brother. Jamshid was starting to shake, fresh grief ripping across his face. "He shouldn't have had to make that choice. He wasn't the one *trained* to."

Ali stepped closer, looking like he was aching to make this right. "Jamshid, I'm sorry. I truly am. I know how close—"

"Oh, do you know how close?" Jamshid let out a hysterical laugh. "Because I distinctly remember having to hide how *close* we were because of men like you."

Nahri tried to intervene again. "Jamshid—"

"No," he cut in, his voice breaking. "I have spent my life shutting my mouth while the djinn crush my people. While they crush me, my father, my neighbors—*you*. Their lies and their politics have made a cage of my life, and now I want you to see who this man really is. This prince I tried to befriend only to have him turn around and order me to throw another man in the lake." He glared at Ali. "I *loved* your brother, understand? He was the love of my life."

Ali opened his mouth. He didn't look angry—he looked astonished, as though still trying to connect the dots.

And then it fell into place.

"But that's not possible," Ali stammered. "Muntadhir wasn't . . . I mean, there were so many women—"

Jamshid bellowed in outrage, lunging for a slipper on the floor and hurling it at Ali's head. The prince ducked, and Nahri moved between them again, deciding today's effort at uniting her allies was over.

"Ali, go. I've got this."

He made a strangled sound of assent, his eyes still wide as he reached for the door, backing out of the cell as if he'd stumbled upon a cobra.

The moment Ali was gone, the rage left Jamshid's face, and he collapsed, falling into a crouch on the dirt floor.

"I'm sorry," he choked out. "I'm sorry. I shouldn't have said that in front of you. But when you both walked in, I thought . . ." He sucked for air. "I thought maybe there was a chance." He fell forward into his hands, his shoulders trembling as he sobbed. "Creator, Muntadhir, how could you? *How could you?*"

Nahri watched him, frozen in shock. This grieving man who looked like he hadn't bothered even combing his fingers through his overgrown hair in days wasn't the Jamshid she knew, the quietly dutiful nobleman whose words and behavior had always been so precise. He suddenly felt like a stranger—like someone who'd just hurt her *actual* friend—and for a moment Nahri was terribly uncertain.

He's not a stranger. He's your brother. But "brother" was a foreign term to Nahri—she didn't know what that kind of relationship was supposed to look like. The siblings she'd spent the most time with were the Qahtanis—and if she'd occasionally envied the protective closeness between Zaynab and her brothers, the rest of the royal family's explosive drama had made her feel better about supposedly being an orphan.

Try, just try. Nahri knelt at his side, laying a hand on his shoulder. "You don't need to apologize to me, Jamshid. Just breathe."

"I can't." He wiped his eyes. "Muntadhir . . . he used to tell me how terrified he was as a kid of Manizheh. Darayavahoush despised him. What kind of end was that for him?"

"A brave one. He made me give him Dara's bow so he could shoot him with it." Nahri hesitated, searching for anything that might give Jamshid some comfort. "A quick one. He took a mortal blow during the battle. He knew he wasn't going to survive and feared he would only slow us down." That was a half-truth, but now decidedly did not seem the time for the details of Muntadhir's death.

Jamshid took a ragged breath and then straightened up. Nahri had to fight not to flinch. This close, his resemblance to Manizheh was unmistakable, the ghost of their mother's face in her brother's elegant winged brows and long-lashed eyes.

The shame that engulfed his expression, however, was all

Jamshid. "What I said to Alizayd about Muntadhir and me . . .
I'm sorry. I shouldn't have said that in front of you. We never—I
mean, after you married . . ."

Nahri took his hand. "Again, you don't have to apologize. I
already knew, and things were never going to be like that between
him and me. But you should know—before we escaped, Muntadhir asked me to tell you that he loved you. And that he was sorry
he hadn't stood up for you sooner."

Jamshid squeezed his eyes shut. "I used to tell him he was
selfish. Creator, I wish he'd stayed that way in the end and gotten
himself out. But Daevabad always came first," he said bitterly.

A mantra you might be adopting soon, Baga Nahid. Nahri hugged her
knees. "What have Hatset and Wajed told you?"

"I know the city fell and magic vanished. Scouts caught up
with us while we were still in Am Gezira, fleeing on stolen horses
like demons were after them. They said Banu Manizheh and the
Afshin were back from the dead, and that my father helped them
kill the king and all the Geziris in the palace."

Nahri's heart beat fast. "So they didn't say anything about . . .
you?"

"About *me*? No. I mean, they've been threatening me and
making pretty damn clear what they think about Daevas, but
otherwise they seem content to let me go mad alone down here."
Jamshid drew back, narrowing his eyes. "Why? You look worried.
Is there something else?"

You might say that. "Jamshid," Nahri began, "after the Navasatem
attack, you wanted to speak to me. Your wounds were gone, you
spoke to Razu in an extinct dialect of Tukharistani . . ."

He rubbed his head. "That seems like a thousand years ago,"
he confessed. "I don't know, maybe the Nahid magic you summoned to stop the Rumi fire finally healed me."

"It wasn't just me summoning Nahid magic." When Jamshid
only gave her a more confused look, Nahri continued. "You've

told me before that you know very little about your mother except that she was supposedly a servant, someone scandalous from a lower class. That she died when you were a baby, and your father never spoke about her." She met his eyes. "Jamshid, your mother wasn't from a lower class. She was from . . . as high as they go in our tribe. And she's not dead."

Jamshid stared at her. There was another moment or two of bewilderment in his expression and then shock—denial—coursed across his face. *"You can't be saying . . ."*

"I'm saying it. Manizheh is your mother. Ghassan confronted your father when we were arrested, and Kaveh confirmed it. You're a Nahid, Banu Manizheh's son."

"I'm not." Jamshid jumped up, pacing away. "I *can't* be," he insisted, pressing his hands to his temples. "I—I'm normal! I don't have any healing abilities. By the Creator, I dropped out of the *priesthood.* I'm definitely not one of Suleiman's chosen!"

"To be fair," she tried, "I do believe the priests are meant to honor us, not the other way around."

Jamshid's eyes only went wider.

Nahri rose as well. "Jamshid, trust that I know how hard this is to hear—you're talking to a woman who didn't believe in anything magical only six years ago. But I wouldn't be telling you this if it wasn't true. Ghassan implied Manizheh must have done something to mask your abilities, but he knew the moment he saw you as a child." She touched her cheek. "We have Suleiman's seal marked on our faces. Only the ring-bearer can see it, but it's there. Ghassan knew all this time. Hatset and Wajed as well."

Jamshid jerked back. "Does Alizayd know?"

"They just told him."

"Of course." He looked devastated. "So, Ghassan and Hatset. Wajed and Ali." He clenched his hands into fists. "Do you think Muntadhir—"

"No." Nahri had no proof, but everything in her heart denied it. "I don't think he knew."

"I don't understand this." Jamshid tugged at his beard, looking very close to pulling it out. "My father spoke of the Nahids with reverence, with grief. He gave not a damn hint away. They were like legends until I met . . ." His wide eyes met hers. "You," he whispered. "Oh."

Nahri flushed, feel oddly exposed. "Yes, I guess this makes us siblings. But it's fine if that's not the kind of relationship you want to have."

Jamshid stepped closer, reaching for her hand. "*Of course* that's the kind of relationship I want to have. You being my sister would be the best thing that's happened to me in years."

The sincerity in his voice only made her blush more. "It would be nice not to be the only non-murdering Nahid." It was as close as Nahri could get to acknowledging her emotions.

Jamshid paled. "Yes, I suppose we'll have to talk about that. About her." He glanced up. "Is my father . . . ?"

"No." She fell silent. Jamshid waited, looking expectant.

Tell him. For God's sake, Nahri had told Fiza—a pirate who would happily sell her out—that she was a shafit. Surely she could tell her own brother. Jamshid was kind. He was good, and she knew he was trying to do better when it came to the shafit.

But he was also a Daeva first, raised with the prejudices of most of their tribe. And Creator forgive her, Nahri did not think she could deal with his reaction right now.

"No," she said again. "I don't know who my father is, but it isn't Kaveh."

"It doesn't matter." Jamshid gave her a genuine smile. "It's going to be a little weird thinking of someone I admired as a high and mighty Nahid as my little sister." His expression fell. "Though it makes me want to grab you and run even more."

"There's no need to run." That felt like more of a lie than she liked. "Not right now, anyway. I chose to come here. I know you don't trust Ali, but I do, and we're going to need allies."

"His mother kept me locked in a cell for a month, Nahri. They're not my allies."

"Neither is *our* mother. You weren't in Daevabad, Jamshid. You didn't see how vicious her conquest was. She unleashed a poison capable of murdering every Geziri in the city. It killed scores in the palace—kids and scholars and servants. Innocents. I'm not on her side."

"So you're on the Qahtanis'?"

"No. I'm on Daevabad's. I want to fix this and maybe one day see a world where it's normal to pick sides based on what's right rather than on whose family we belong to."

Jamshid sighed. "And here I thought you were a realist."

"I am. Please. You stood by me in the Temple when I said I was going to work with shafit. I'm asking you to do so again."

He paced away. "This is so much more dangerous than the Temple, Nahri. The priests would have merely sanctioned you. I'm pretty sure half this castle wants to kill us."

"All the more reason to convince them not to."

He still seemed skeptical but let out a resigned grunt. "Why don't you tell me how you and Sheikh Fire-Sword ended up here, and I'll see how I feel about allies."

24

ALI

Ali stumbled from the cell, his mind whirling with Jamshid's accusations. Not quite certain where he was going, only that he had to get away—to give the Nahid siblings space; to give *himself* space from the man who had just reached into the guilty recesses of his heart and dragged the broken pieces into the light—he crossed to the stairs. All he wanted to do was get out of this sunken chamber of earth and stone.

Instead, he walked directly into Wajed.

The Qaid crossed his arms, looking at Ali as though they were back in the Citadel and he was about to deliver a scolding. It made Ali heartsick. Though it had been weeks, he still remembered standing in his mentor's stolen office in the Citadel and knowing Wajed would never forgive him for the rebellion. Wajed was Geziri to the core and utterly loyal to Ghassan, his king and friend since boyhood.

Ali was not, though he knew it would be useful for him to

pull on that tie now. "I realize we got . . . waylaid in the majlis, but I thank you for coming to Ta Ntry and seeing to my mother's safety." He touched his heart. "My family will always be grateful for your loyalty."

Wajed narrowed his eyes. "I could hear that Daeva screaming at you. If your first instinct is to come out here, thank me for my service, and then politely sack me, I'm going to tell your mother you've lost your mind."

The personal route they would go, then. "I haven't lost my mind, uncle. Nor do I want to sack you. I *need* you, Wajed. You were right—we're at war, but our enemy isn't down there," Ali said, gesturing to the cells. "Nahri has saved my life twice over from Darayavahoush and Manizheh. Jamshid was Muntadhir's dearest . . . companion," he said, faltering slightly. "And surely the warrior who taught me strategy sees the benefit in Manizheh's children being on our side."

"I see the benefit in them being hostages."

"Then I see the benefit in finding a new Qaid. I would rather not," Ali said, not missing the emotion storming across Wajed's face at the ultimatum. "But the Nahids are my allies, and I will not allow them to be threatened."

"Your father tried to make allies out of the Nahids. Look where that got him."

"My father tried to *force* them into being allies. That's not what I'm doing. Uncle, I know part of you must hate me for that night. But I do not regret disobeying him. I loved my father. I am sorry, sorrier than I will ever be able to express, that we did not part in peace, but more than that, I am sorry that he died with such sins on his soul. His final command would have slaughtered hundreds of innocents. He died threatening a woman under his roof, his own daughter-in-law. If you disagree with my actions and wish to leave my service, I'll understand. But I don't intend to follow his path."

Wajed pressed his mouth into a thin line. "You are like a son to me, Zaydi. You are a Qahtani, and you will have my service as your father did before you. But you must understand how angry our people are." He leaned closer. "Trust me when I say I'm not the only one who will look upon this alliance with doubt. Nearly every person in this castle lost someone to Manizheh or has a loved one trapped in Daevabad. You're very popular with our people, which I'm sure you know, having *used* your popularity to convince the Citadel and Geziri Quarter to riot," he added, a little acidly. "Be careful with that support."

Ali nodded. "I will. Right now, though, I need to find my mother. If I ask you to stay here . . ."

Wajed rolled his eyes. "Your Nahids won't come to any harm. I'll even apologize—yes?—and call them by their fancy titles."

"I knew I could count on you." Ali smiled before turning away.

But the brief lift in his spirits at winning over Wajed vanished as he kept walking.

He shouldn't have had to make that choice. It was the same thing that had been swirling in Ali's head since his brother first took the zulfiqar strike Darayavahoush had meant for Ali. Because Jamshid was right. It should have been Ali.

Instead, Muntadhir was dead, and Ali wore the seal, and he didn't think he would ever stop carrying that guilt.

A pair of servants passed, a soldier saluting. Ali barely managed a response. Protocol hadn't been something he'd thought about in weeks, and he didn't trust himself not to make an error. Instead, he stepped into the first alcove he saw, grateful to find that it twisted into a small, empty balcony. It was an otherwise lovely day, and just beyond the jungle, Ali caught a glint of the sea, the bright sun reflected against the water.

And then the other part of Jamshid's shouting came back to him.

Your brother was the love of my life.

Ali suddenly felt very, very foolish—a hundred whispers and comments and looks that had blown past him returning and making obvious in hindsight what he'd missed. But he didn't understand *why*—why would Muntadhir have gone to such lengths to keep his relationship with Jamshid a secret from Ali? It wasn't as if his brother had bothered to hide anything else. The drinking, the women, his lackluster attitude toward prayer, toward any element of their faith—a litany of sins.

And is that what you consider this? A sin? Was Ali even one to judge? He spent half his nights dreaming about his brother's wife and had the blood of innocents on his hands. What had Muntadhir done in comparison? Fallen in love with someone forbidden? All Ali could do at this point was relate.

But that hadn't been the worst of Jamshid's accusations. God, that night on the roof . . . There had been a time when Ali thought about that night every day. Now he could scarcely remember his would-be assassin's name.

Hanno. Hanno, the shafit shapeshifter from the Tanzeem. He'd had a daughter kidnapped and killed by purebloods, and it all came back to Ali in pieces. The grief in the other man's eyes, the blood, the pain, the curt order Ali had growled to Jamshid before passing out—*get rid of him.* Ali must have seemed like a monster.

He must have seemed exactly like Ghassan.

Was that how it started, Abba? Had his father felt like this as a young king, so scared and uncertain how to rule that he'd simply crushed anything he feared might hurt him? The act that Ghassan had put on in the court, the act Muntadhir had had to perfect his whole life—when saddled with that kind of responsibility, how else did you respond if you knew a mistake would doom everyone you cared for?

Your brother was the love of my life. Jamshid's words came again, but it was Muntadhir whom Ali saw in his mind. How much of himself had his brother had to hide behind his broken grin?

Ali leaned against the wall, embracing the shadow. For a moment, he wished for a proper imam, for someone who knew the Book and whose faith had not been shaken, to tell him what to do next.

A slippered step drew his attention. Ali instantly reached for his zulfiqar—and then dropped his hand.

"You found my hiding spot." Hatset stepped into the sunshine, smiling gently at him. "I've been coming here since I was a girl. There used to be an enormous vine you could climb to better see the ocean, but my mother had it cut down when I fell and nearly broke my neck." Her smile faded. "I am torn between clutching you to my heart and smacking you in the head, Alubaba. I thought you'd be here at least a day before I felt that way."

"I did not bring Nahri to Ta Ntry to be set upon by angry djinn," Ali retorted, assuming it was his rudeness on her behalf that irked Hatset. "She has reasons for her secrets."

"And we have reasons to distrust Nahids." Hatset gave him an astute look. "Did you enjoy your time with the new Baga Nahid?"

Ali didn't bother lying. His mother always seemed to know everything anyway. "I think our relationship needs some work." But then he paused. His mother *did* always seem to know everything. "Muntadhir and Jamshid . . . were they—"

"Yes. They were quiet about it, but most of us knew."

"Abba knew?"

"Yes." She sounded grim. "I suspect he encouraged their relationship—on Jamshid's end, anyway. I'm sure he got a measure of satisfaction at watching how far Manizheh's son would go to protect his own."

Ali's stomach flipped. "Muntadhir never told me. We were once so close. It makes me sick that he would have feared my reaction. That maybe he was right too."

"You were very young when it started, Alizayd. *Very* sheltered at the Citadel—which, as your mother, admittedly I did not mind. You don't know what your relationship with Muntadhir would have been like later in life."

"Because it was going so well." Ali shook his head. "I feel like I failed him, Amma. Failed Zaynab. Failed Lubayd and all my brothers at the Citadel. Am *actively* failing you and Nahri and everyone else." He leaned over the balcony. "Maybe it would have been better if our roles had been reversed. If I had died in Daevabad, and Dhiru—"

"Don't." Hatset stroked his back. "Don't go down that path, Alu. God put you here for a reason, and you haven't lost yet. You're also not alone. Come get cleaned up, have something to eat, and rest. Plotting your next move can wait until tomorrow."

Ali glanced sideways at her. "Extend the offer to Nahri and Jamshid, and I promise I'll even sleep in a bed."

"Always the negotiator."

"Does that mean I've convinced you?"

"I will release Jamshid, but both he and Nahri are going to be under heavy guard—as much for their own safety as ours. And you'll be granting *me* additional concessions."

He feigned a shiver. "What?"

"One, you're getting a tutor. At least an hour a day in Ntaran until you stop speaking it like a child. And two, you will then *use* that Ntaran to be polite and respectful to your family here. You can't just look to the Geziris anymore, Alizayd. You're going to need the Ayaanle. Let the past with Musa rest."

Ali offered an exaggerated bow, touching his heart. "I'll be the picture of diplomacy, I promise. Can I meet my grandfather?"

Sadness swept over his mother's face. "Not today, but hopefully soon. His health has taken a turn for the worse. When he's lucid, he seems to be living in his own world of ten years ago. I'm trying to keep him from learning about the invasion, but . . ."

Her voice hitched. "He always asks after you and Zaynab. It's been . . . it's been very hard not to react."

Ali hugged her. "I'm sorry, Amma." Small wonder his always indomitable mother looked worn out. "It's going to be all right, God willing. And we're going to get Zaynab back. She's smart, she's a survivor, and she has one of the most skilled warriors I've ever met at her side."

"I pray you're right." Hatset held him close. "I really do."

25

NAHRI

Whatever Ali said to his mother must have worked, for by the evening, Nahri and Jamshid had been set up in adjoining suites fit for, well, the exiled and long-lost royalty they apparently were. The rooms weren't as luxurious as those in Daevabad's palace, but rather had a restrained, natural elegance Nahri appreciated more, with tall ceilings of carved plaster held up by slender wooden columns. One wall was entirely given over to open windows and a balcony, bringing the smell of the sea indoors.

More important personally to her, she'd finally had a chance to *bathe*, scraping off enough muck to require multiple changes of fire-warmed water. It felt achingly good to be clean and have her stomach full—for she'd returned to their suites to find a newly groomed Jamshid had already sampled everything from the enormous platter they'd been given, stolen one of the serving knives, and was waiting to see if he died from poison before letting Nahri touch any of the food. When Nahri delicately questioned his washed but still very overgrown hair and beard, he matter-of-factly explained that no djinn was coming near him with a razor.

He was finally asleep in the next room. Nahri should have been as well; God knew she needed it. But her mind hadn't stopped racing, and the enormous teak bed—solid and covered in soft, patterned quilts—was too different from the myriad places she'd slept in the past few weeks.

It was also too quiet with Ali still gone. She hadn't seen him since he'd left Jamshid's cell, not that she should be surprised—he had his own reunions with his people and accommodations for Fiza's crew to sort out—but it left Nahri feeling adrift. She'd anticipated being at Ali's side when they had their first proper meal in weeks, arguing about whether the coffee or tea they'd been respectively craving was the superior beverage.

And she was worried about him. Nahri couldn't judge Jamshid for his grief-stricken accusations, but she also knew how deeply Ali still blamed himself for his brother's death. The look on his face when Jamshid had called him a coward . . .

Which was why, when a gentle knock sounded on her door, Nahri crossed the room with an embarrassing swiftness. She chided herself, and then opened the door with an affected aloofness.

She scowled. It wasn't Ali.

Queen Hatset gave her a knowing smile. "Peace be upon you, Banu Nahida," she said in Djinnistani.

"May the fires burn brightly for you," Nahri returned in Divasti.

Hatset tilted her head. "I apologize if you were expecting someone else. I just wanted to stop by and make sure you and your brother were settled. The rooms are suitable?"

"They're lovely. I only wish such hospitality had been extended to Jamshid earlier."

"And I wish his parents had not brutally murdered the father of my children and thousands of our subjects." The line was delivered crisply, but Nahri didn't miss the flicker of anger in the other woman's eyes. "I assure you it was best that Jamshid be kept locked away."

"Yes, you've all made quite clear what you think of Daevas."

"I apologize for that. But sometimes it's wisest to let people show you who they are. Wajed is a dangerous man. A man who served my husband loyally, who loves my son—but were I in your position, I would want to know how such a man viewed me. How everyone viewed me. You did not survive Daevabad by sticking your head in the sand."

"I have never—for even a moment—forgotten how people view me." Nahri was too upset to entirely slip behind her mask, but she checked what rancor she could. "And were I in *your* position, I'd view not being able to assure the safety of my guests as a weakness."

Hatset gave her an incredulous smile. "Well, haven't you loosened your tongue. I remember a far more careful Banu Nahida."

"I left my country, Hatset. Did Ali tell you that? I left my home and a peaceful life to come here with your son in the hopes of fixing things. In hopes of saving you all. I won't be threatened."

"If only it were that easy, child." Hatset beckoned. "Walk with me."

Nahri paused, sorely tempted to retrieve the serving knife Jamshid had taken. Instead, she settled for grabbing her shayla. "Where's Ali?" she asked, winding the shawl around her head and shoulders as they left the room.

"Sleeping," Hatset replied. "Rather against his wishes, but there's little resisting sleep when opium has been slipped into your food."

Nahri stared at her, shocked. "You drugged your son?"

"He needed rest."

"*He needed rest . . .* How much experience do you have with opium? It's a powerful drug. If you got the dosage wrong—"

Hatset let out an exasperated sound. "I did not pluck you from your bed to get a medical lecture. He's my son. I would never hurt him."

"In my experience, Hatset, parents in our world are capable of doing a great deal of hurt to their children."

The djinn queen gave her a long, considering look. "Fair point, Banu Nahri. But you needn't worry. Ali is fine, I assure you." She paused. "You care for him truly, don't you?"

Ali holding her so carefully on the beach, brushing the tears from her cheeks. *There is no one else here, my friend. You don't need to keep up this front.*

Nahri, however, did exactly that. "He's not bad."

"You are an exceedingly frustrating person to talk to."

"It's a point of pride." Nahri changed the subject as Hatset led her down another empty corridor. Aside from a gray-striped cat stalking a spider, there were no other signs of life in the quiet castle. "Your nephew mentioned that you sent people away. Is that true?"

"As many as I could convince. The Afshin sent people fleeing to their provinces with warnings of fire and retribution. If Manizheh came for Jamshid and burned this place to the ground, I didn't intend for all of us to be killed." Regret filled the queen's voice. "A shame. This castle should be filled with the laughter of children, and I would have liked to see my son greeted by all his cousins and aunts. But it wasn't worth the risk."

The sincerity in the statement undid some of Nahri's anger. Hatset had always been harder to hate than Ghassan—Nahri could relate too well to a woman for whom politics and family had left limited options.

They entered the castle's courtyard. It was half garden, half ruin, and utterly beautiful. Mirrored stepping stones lined the sandy path, reflecting the full moon with silvery pools of light. A rushing stream divided the courtyard, pale trees stretching to climb through the latticed ceiling.

"This is incredible," Nahri said admiringly. "I feel like I'm walking through the forest."

"You should see it when the magic works." Hatset trailed her fingers along a fern. "My father always says this is how djinn should live. On the edge and among the wilderness, closer in spirit to our ancestors than in 'messy human cities.' He never did think much of Daevabad." Longing filled her voice. "I had a far gentler childhood than my own children, and I could never help but wonder how they might have blossomed here. How at ease Zaynab might be if she wasn't confined to a harem full of politicking noblewomen. The kind of scholar Ali could grow into if he'd never had to pick up a zulfiqar."

"They wouldn't be themselves," Nahri replied, almost without thinking. She couldn't imagine Ali and Zaynab divorced of their royal identity.

"Perhaps not," Hatset mused.

"Was it your choice to leave?" Nahri asked. Hatset seemed like she was in a talkative mood, and Nahri was never one to turn away information—but she was also genuinely curious.

The queen shrugged. "I'm not sure people like you and I have true choices. Ghassan was looking for a new wife and made clear he'd be open to a spouse from Ta Ntry. The merchant families convened, and I was at the top of the list. It sounded like an adventure, a chance to support my tribe. He was a handsome, clever king, and deeply charismatic. I arrived wary, only to find he'd had my entire wing enchanted to look like a Ntaran castle."

Nahri glanced at her, surprised by the sorrow in the older woman's expression. "You loved him."

"I think we loved each other as much as we could. His loyalty was to Daevabad first and mine to Ta Ntry. Then when our children were born, I had no idea how fiercely I'd love *them* and how desperate I'd be to protect them from political fates that now seem unbearable." She shook her head. "And I could not forgive him for banishing Ali. I think I could have excused Ghassan a great many awful things, but sending our son to die—he stomped out himself the part of my heart he'd once claimed."

Nahri flinched. She knew how that felt.

Hatset was studying her. "Here, now I have spilled the details of my marriage, so you must do the same. I know you did not love Muntadhir, but do you think you could have one day ruled at his side?"

Nahri considered the question. A few weeks ago, she would have ducked it—this wasn't the first time Hatset had tried to pry into her marriage. Muntadhir and Ali had been rivals, and Muntadhir's alliance with the Daevas through his Nahid wife had been one of his strongest hands.

But that had all crashed down, and she found herself answering with more honesty than she usually did. "I don't know. I was willing to sacrifice a lot for my people, but I don't think I could have stood at Muntadhir's side if he'd turned into his father. And if he'd managed to change and *stand up* to his father, I think one of the first things he would have done was divorce me. We were terribly matched."

Hatset offered a grim smile. "A diplomatic statement. Prickliness aside, I do respect you, Banu Nahida. You have an admirable pragmatism, a willingness to hold contrary ideas in your head. I expected Manizheh's daughter to be clever—but your wisdom, that I did not prepare for."

"I am glad to be a surprise," Nahri said drily. "Did you know her? My mother, I mean."

"Not well, though I'm not sure anyone save her brother knew her well. Ghassan and I were only married a few years when she vanished, and I avoided her at court."

"Because of Ghassan?"

"No, not because of my husband's infatuation." Hatset turned to look Nahri in the face. "Because she scared me, Banu Nahri, and I am not a woman who frightens easily. I still remember Ghassan bringing me to the infirmary to meet 'his esteemed Nahids,' as he called them. It made my skin crawl—they were so obviously prisoners, and it shocked me that my husband couldn't see that. Rustam was so jumpy in his presence that he couldn't hold a cup steady."

Yet you were willing to make us prisoners again. But Nahri didn't say that. "And Manizheh?"

"I'd heard the Daevas whisper that she was a goddess. I dismissed it as fire-worshipper superstition," Hatset said, a note of apology in her voice. "But it was an apt description, and Manizheh knew it. You could see the rage, the resentment boiling behind her eyes, that inferior creatures such as we would dare to contain her. I remember thinking that I had no doubt if the winds of politics ever changed, she would not suffer a moment's hesitation in killing us all." Regret crossed her face. "And in a small way, I cannot blame her."

Neither can I. Nahri despised the violence her mother had wrought, but she couldn't blame her for striking back. Manizheh had gotten to Nahri that night on the roof, tugging hard at the part of her that wanted to stop bowing. That wanted to stop being afraid.

Nahri had denied her. And now she was surrounded by people she didn't trust, with no clear path forward.

Hatset was staring at her as though she could read Nahri's mind. "They won," she said. "At least for now. Your mother sits on the throne, your Afshin stands at her side, and the Daevas reign supreme over the wreckage of the Citadel and the ruin of the Qahtanis. So how does the consummate survivor—a woman who submits to the marriage bed of her enemy, who denounces the Afshin she is said to have loved—end up here instead of with them, Suleiman's seal on the brow of my son?"

"I would hope most people who saw what I did at the palace would stand against her." Nahri shivered, remembering the screams of Ghassan's guards as they clawed at their heads. "The poison my mother conjured was awful, and most of the Geziris it killed were completely innocent. Servants and scribes and normal people who just had the bad luck to get caught in the games of the powerful on the wrong night. Children." She paused, seeing the little boys in their bloody festival clothes again. Nahri didn't imagine she'd ever forget them. "It's a con," she said, freshly angry.

"A *con*?"

"It's supposed to be the mark of a wise leader, right? The willingness to make sacrifices for a greater good? But nobody ever asks those 'sacrifices' if *they're* willing—they get no say in whether or not their kids die for some supposed greater good. And I come from people like that," she said, recalling Yaqub's jaded description of Egypt's latest war. "From a country that's been fought over by foreigners for centuries. We die, and we bleed, and it's a debt the powerful never repay." Nahri trembled. "I don't want to be part of that."

Hatset looked at her for a very long moment. It was an assessing sort of stare. When the queen spoke again, it sounded like she'd come to some sort of decision. "As I said, wise."

"Or foolish. Because I don't know how we're supposed to fight someone who's always going to be more willing to exact violence."

"You outwit them." Hatset turned away. "Come. There is someone you should see."

Nahri was thrown by the comment. "There is?"

"You are not our only recently arrived visitor from Daevabad."

Bewildered, Nahri followed Hatset as she strode off, heading for a small corridor tucked behind a large library—the library

Ali had mentioned. Nahri longed to peek inside but settled for a glimpse of bookshelves soaring to a distant ceiling and beautiful windows of vibrantly colored glass.

Hatset nodded to the Ayaanle woman she'd seen in soldier's dress earlier and exchanged a few words of Ntaran before the guard opened the door, revealing a cozy room filled with candles. A small, elderly man was wrapped in blankets and sitting before a steaming bowl. He looked up as they arrived, his green eyes exhausted.

Nahri gasped. "Ustadh Issa."

NAHRI WAS AT ISSA'S SIDE THE NEXT MOMENT, HER healer's instincts kicking in. He looked terribly frail, his brilliant green eyes dim and the glimmer gone from his smoky black skin. She had had no idea how the freed slaves might have reacted once magic was stripped—their bodies were conjurements themselves, and truthfully, Nahri had been almost too frightened to contemplate the consequences.

But it seemed the Creator had granted her this one mercy. She took Issa's hand; it felt too light. "Are you all right?" she asked hurriedly.

He let out a hacking cough. "No," he wheezed. "I hate traveling." His bleary gaze focused on her. "Oh! But you are not dead. That is very good."

"I like it," Nahri replied, helping him sit up. "How did you get out of Daevabad?"

"The Afshin aided me. Razu made some sort of deal with him, appealing to his fellowship as a former slave."

Nahri opened and closed her mouth. *Dara* had helped Issa escape? Had he acted without Manizheh's knowing?

She shut down the thought before it dared spark even an ember of hope. No, Nahri was not going to lose herself in the madness of wondering if there was still goodness in Dara.

Hatset spoke. "I've kept Issa's identity a secret thus far; people think he's a cousin. I wanted to let him recover. And then with your and Alizayd's arrival, I wanted to be careful in deciding what information should come out."

Nahri's heart dropped. "Is it worse? The vapor, the rest of the Geziris—"

"They survived," Hatset assured Nahri quickly, although her tone indicated she was anything but comforted herself. "Zaynab escaped the palace, thank God, and was able to warn the Geziri Quarter in time for people to get rid of their relics. She and Ali's warrior woman are safe for now, as safe as they can be. Issa says the shafit and Geziri neighborhoods have effectively barricaded themselves off, along with the other tribal districts."

Barricaded themselves off? "Wait, do you mean Manizheh doesn't control the city?"

Ustadh Issa let out a mournful sound. "No one controls anything. It's chaos. Anarchy." He raised a trembling finger. "Such civil strife is the greatest danger to society!"

Nahri straightened up like a shot. "Ali needs to hear this."

"There's one more thing." Hatset met Nahri's gaze. "Issa says Muntadhir is still alive."

Worries over Daevabad's security situation fled Nahri's mind. "That's not possible," she whispered. "He was struck with the zul-fiqar. I saw its poison spreading with my own eyes." She whirled on Issa. "How do you know this? Have you seen him?"

The scholar shook his head. "No, but others have. Banu Man-izheh sent a note to the princess saying she'd kill him if Zaynab didn't surrender."

Nahri was buzzing with new information. Daevabad hadn't yet entirely fallen—though she wasn't sure being on the brink of a civil war was much better. Muntadhir was possibly still alive, a prisoner in the palace.

And yet even as a bit of relief flooded through her, so did

a strange foreboding, like waking from a dream into the harsh reality of day. So quickly all Nahri's chains were coming back. Another foreign city and deadly political court. Jamshid, the brother Nahri needed to protect, a weakness that others could use against her.

And now the husband she'd never wanted, a good man whose honorable death she'd truly mourned, might still be alive. It all fell heavily on her shoulders, a mantle of yet more responsibility.

Nahri took a deep breath, trying to focus. "I need to tell Ali and Jamshid." She couldn't believe Hatset hadn't done so already.

Hatset laid a hand on her wrist. "That's not a good idea."

"And why in God's name is it not—"

The queen was already pulling her out of the room. "Excuse us, Ustadh," she said to Issa, before shutting the door and leaving herself and Nahri alone in the narrow corridor. "Banu Nahri, you know my son. How do *you* think Alizayd will react when he learns Muntadhir is alive and being held prisoner by Manizheh? When he learns his sister is struggling to stay out of her clutches and the city is in open civil war?"

He's going to go summon a marid and beg it to drop him off in Daevabad's lake. But Nahri shook her arm free. "He's not as rash as he once was. And this is good news! If Manizheh's control of the city is weak, we might actually stand a chance of taking it back!"

The queen shook her head. "Neither of you should be thinking about Daevabad yet, let alone the ludicrous prospect of warring with Manizheh and her Afshin. Our *world* is in chaos, not just a single city, and people want nothing more than to get their magic back—the magic Manizheh is promising to return to whoever hands you and Ali over to her. The two of you need to stay in Shefala, long enough to establish an independent court with its own army. A court attractive and stable enough that the other tribes will want to ally with the two of you, not submit in fear to her."

Under different circumstances, Nahri would have seen the pragmatism in Hatset's suggestion.

But these weren't those circumstances. "We don't have that kind of time, Hatset. I wish we did. But I know how badly my mother wants Suleiman's seal. The moment she finds out we're here, she's going to send Dara—"

"She can't send him. Issa says the Afshin appears to be the only one left with magic. Manizheh must be relying on him to hold Daevabad." Hatset's voice grew more fervent. "Child, it buys you both time. A degree of safety."

But Daevabad doesn't have time. Issa's words ran through Nahri's head again. How long could the city survive, isolated and cut off, with the tribal quarters at one another's throats? How quickly would people run out of food, out of patience? If anything, Nahri was filled with a new urgency to return.

"I can't abandon Daevabad," she said. "My people are there, my friends, my allies at the hospital." She considered the second part of Hatset's suggestion and found it uncharacteristically impractical. "And to establish a court in *Ta Ntry*? You were just telling me how much the djinn here distrust Daevas. Why would they ever accept some Banu Nahida ruling over them?"

"Because of the other reason I don't want Ali to learn about Muntadhir yet. You won't just be the Banu Nahida here. You'll be the queen. Ali's queen."

Nahri's mind abruptly went blank.

"Forgive me," she stammered, feeling like they'd leapt past several critical steps in this conversation. "But we're not . . . I mean, *he's* not—"

"King? No, not yet—but he will be. And once Ali declares his kingship, he will marry you, preserving the alliance between our families and tribes."

Hatset said it all so plainly that Nahri almost felt foolish for being stunned, as if the queen was merely planning what they were having for lunch.

"Just to be clear," Nahri started again, "you want me to lie to Jamshid and Ali about Muntadhir—a man they love—being alive and then abandon my people and home to a mass-murdering tyrant, all so I can force my rule on a foreign land whose djinn would then *really* have a reason to hate me?"

"If that's what you're taking from 'make a pragmatic political alliance'—with a man who happens to be utterly smitten with you—instead of going to die in Daevabad in an unwinnable war, then yes."

Nahri stared at her. If she'd thought she was struggling with her emotions earlier, Hatset might as well have sauntered in, gathered all Nahri's feelings, stuffed them in a barrel, and then blown it up with human explosives.

Stay focused, be calm. This was like any negotiation, and now was the time to wear her opponent down and find flaws in their offer.

But it wasn't a deal they were negotiating, it was Nahri's life and her future. Which was why Nahri—who was normally more careful—chose the wrong part to argue first.

"Your son isn't smitten with me. Ali has never said anything, done anything—"

"And he won't," Hatset said. "He's devout, Nahri. He follows the rules, and he's not going to overstep. But surely you know why Ghassan chose you, of all people, to use against him."

Nahri had no response to that. Ghassan had been as good as she was when it came to reading a mark.

And then Nahri suddenly saw—through new eyes—the longing in Ali's face when she spoke about them having a life together in Cairo. His nervousness when she touched him. His shy grin as they sailed down the Nile and talked about everything and nothing.

She saw herself. How Nahri felt . . . better in his presence. Like she could breathe. Like a more open, more honorable version of herself, the Nahri she might have been in a world that hadn't tried so hard to crush her. Before she could stop herself, Nahri went to a very dangerous place. A place where it was Ali, and not Muntadhir, on their wedding night, Ali burning her marriage mask.

But it wasn't a vast royal apartment she saw or matching thrones in Shefala's majlis. It was a book-stuffed bedroom over a tea-scented apothecary closed for the night. A modest home filled with laughter and ease, a place where Nahri wouldn't need to perform. A person with whom she didn't need to wear a mask.

Stop. A rush of energy punched through her like it had back on the ship, an instinct of self-preservation. That was not the kind of future Hatset was offering.

That was not the kind of future Nahri would ever have.

Because the queen's words were untangling. How fiercely she loved her children. How reckless she knew her son could be in pursuit of doing the right thing. How her dead husband, another cunning ruler, had planned to bring Ali down with a single letter written in Nahri's hand.

"You're not interested in making me queen," Nahri finally said. "You're interested in ending this war before it truly begins, and you want to use me to keep Ali in Ta Ntry where he's safe."

The silence that fell in the corridor was deafening. Ah. Nahri could always tell when she'd called a mark true.

Hatset clasped her hands together, a very imperial gesture. "Do you know what it's like to wait for news that your child is dead? To wonder if every letter, every visitor hesitating on your doorstep, is going to be the one to shatter your world? Because I've gone through that twice now, Banu Nahri. So you will forgive me for not wanting to watch my son rush into a war he cannot win against the only person who's ever truly frightened me."

"You don't know that we can't win," Nahri said vehemently. "And what about your *other* child? Have you forgotten—"

"There is not a *second in the day* I forget where Zaynab is." True fury—the kind Nahri had never heard from the always calm queen—scorched in Hatset's voice. "Ali killing himself in Daevabad won't bring her home."

That was not ground on which Nahri was going to win. She changed course. "You can't truly be asking me to continue lying to Ali and Jamshid about Muntadhir. That's a cruelty beyond you."

"So tell them both and divorce Muntadhir," Hatset replied, launching into what must have been her backup plan with a speed Nahri envied. "There's not a sheikh in Ta Ntry who would deny you a divorce. You could be married in a matter of months."

"I don't want to be married in a matter of months!"

"Then you're a fool," Hatset charged. "You're the one who brought up Zaynab, so now you're going to hear what I would tell my daughter if she was in your position: women like us don't get to stay independent. You've journeyed alone with a man twice now. People talk, and they say vicious things. They've been *saying* vicious things about you and both of these men for a long time. You need to make your loyalty clear."

It was Nahri's turn to be angry. "I *have* made my loyalty clear." She was furious now, and she leaned into it. Fury was familiar. "I'm loyal to Daevabad and its people. I've been forced into a marriage once and seen the resentment it breeds. I won't do it again, especially not with a man who I—"

"A man who you what? A man who you betrayed your own mother to save? Who has you smiling like a schoolgirl when you open your bedroom door? Ah, yes, a terrible fate to marry a kind young king who loves you and stay a few years in a peaceful castle on the sea. Far better to destroy yourself out of pride and end up a prisoner in another gilded cage back in Daevabad."

The words were delivered with more frustration than malice. Nahri believed Hatset: this probably was the advice she would have given Zaynab. That made it worse, this passing of a barbed baton between women who, no matter how clever, how powerful, would always be known by the men to whom they were attached.

Nahri turned away. At the end of the corridor, a wide window opened on the midnight forest, revealing a glimmer of the sea shining beyond the tangle of black trees. Nahri paced toward it, wanting to put space between herself and the queen. She pressed her palms on the stone sill. It was cold and rough beneath her hands, solid.

Hatset was waiting for an answer. Nahri could feel her eyes on her back. Nahri did know about the whispers in the castle. She knew what people said about her and Dara. What they said about her and Ali.

To hell with them all.

"I'll give you until tomorrow to tell Ali about Issa," Nahri said, still staring out the window. "I pray you do. Because it's going to break his heart if he finds out you lied about Muntadhir, and Ali doesn't deserve that."

Hatset sighed. "You're making a mistake."

"I would rather make a mistake than have my choices stripped away." Nahri tried to sound firm, as if it didn't feel like she was also snuffing out something in her heart, something small and fragile and new. "I won't marry him. Not like this. And I will never abandon Daevabad." She drew her shayla close before turning back in the direction of her rooms. "Talk to your son, my queen. I've made my decision."

26

ALI

Ali was a groggy mess by the time he finally woke up the next morning. He groaned into his pillow; silk sheets tangled around his body.

Wait . . . a pillow? Silk sheets? A *mattress*?

Ta Ntry. He inhaled, smelling myrrh along with the ocean's tang on the fresh air. Ali rolled onto his back, rubbing his eyes. He felt unusually foggy-headed, sleep clinging determinedly to him as he tried to recall what had led to his being in this bed. The last thing he remembered was eating dinner with his mother and then being escorted to a dim room that some people—God, Ali had been so tired he couldn't even remember their faces—assured him was his.

He squinted in the darkness now. It was a pleasant room, three large windows lit with the deep purple of approaching dawn. Water for washing had been left beside a crisp pale blue robe with an unnecessary amount of maroon embroidery on the sleeves and collar, cut in Ayaanle fashion. A matching cap rested beside it.

Sluggishly rising to his feet—what was wrong with him this morning?—Ali made his way to the tin basin, mumbling a prayer of intention. His reflection rippled in the water.

As did a pair of flat black eyes, round as plates.

Ali recoiled. He shoved the basin away, and water sloshed out, splashing to the floor.

What in God's name was that? After a moment—and now fully awake—he edged closer again, peering over the basin.

There was nothing. His heart pounding, Ali dipped his hand in the cool water, running his fingers along the basin's smooth bottom. He wanted so desperately to believe that the sharklike eyes might have been a figment of his imagination, a sleepy remnant of a dream.

Except this was Ali's life, and being spied upon by some unseen water spirit seemed more likely.

There was also nothing he could do if indeed one of Sobek's curious cousins had just stolen a peek at him. Instead, Ali finished his ablutions and dressed. A prayer mat had been left on an embossed wooden chest, but with a glance at the sky, Ali estimated he had enough time to walk to the village's open mosque. He knew it would feel good to pray underneath the vanishing stars and in the quiet company of those who also preferred to perform fajr at the mosque.

A soldier just outside Ali's door jumped to attention when he opened it.

"Prince Alizayd," the guard greeted him, touching his heart and brow in the Geziri salute. "Peace be upon you."

"And upon you peace," Ali said. He frowned, studying the man's lowered gaze. "Wait . . . Sameer?" He laughed, clapping the other man's shoulder. "Is it really you?"

The guard smiled bashfully. "I wasn't sure you would remember me."

"Of course I remember you! I remember everyone in my cadet class—especially the boys who warned me that others had slipped a baby crocodile under my blanket. How are you? How did you get all the way out here?"

"I am well, praise God. I was transferred to Dadan after I finished training at the Citadel," Sameer explained, naming one of the northernmost garrisons in Am Gezira. "The Qaid came through on his way to Ta Ntry and ordered us all to accompany him."

Well, that accounted for the dozens of Geziri warriors milling about. "I'm glad to see you," Ali replied. "It's good to know others from our class survived."

Sameer's expression grew somber. "I still can't believe what happened to the Citadel." He flushed. "Forgive me, I know you were there—"

"It's fine. I know I'm not the only person who lost friends that night." But Ali changed the subject, trying to stay ahead of his emotions. "I'm headed to the masjid for fajr if you'd like to join me."

Happy surprise filled Sameer's eyes. "I would be honored, Your Highness—I mean, Your Majesty," he corrected. "I apologize; the men and I weren't certain which to use."

Taken aback, Ali realized that neither was he. The kingly title probably shouldn't have been a surprise—he was the last Qahtani prince and already bore Suleiman's seal on his face. There was a ceremony, of course, to make it official: a simple one in the custom of his practical tribe. The officers, the nobles, essentially anyone in a position of authority would pledge their loyalty to his rule in a public place, offering wooden tokens with their names while the sheikhs and leaders of various villages and clans would send contracts upon wooden slates or bark paper. Ali would have burned them a month after his coronation, in a fire conjured by his own hands—a fire he would have pledged to enter himself if he ever broke his people's trust.

As ridiculous as it seemed, Ali hadn't thought much about his political future. He'd been focused on getting to Ta Ntry, consumed by the catastrophic fall of his home and family. Oaths and ceremonies and titles—all that seemed a world away, belonging to a father who'd been larger than life and to a gleaming seat of jewels. Ali couldn't imagine sitting on the shedu throne or making anyone bow before him. He was an exiled prince on the run with no possessions save his zulfiqar, surviving on the grace of others.

Realizing Sameer was still waiting for a response, Ali said what felt honest. "'Brother' is fine. I'm not one for titles, and I think we're all in this mess together. Now let's go. We don't want to be late."

SHEFALA WAS LOVELY IN THE QUIET DAWN, THE CASTLE mostly empty. A mossy stone path led away from its coral walls and through a wooded glen of chirping birds and towering old trees, their silvery trunks so wide it would have taken two people holding hands to encircle them. Movement past the thick scrub caught Ali's eyes, and he let out a delighted sound as he spotted a pair of giraffes in the grassy field beyond, eating from a towering mimosa tree.

The mosque was elegantly sparse—reed mats and woolen carpets set on the cleared ground between enormous columns carved from baobab trees. A wooden lattice had been constructed overhead, perhaps to carry a roof during the rainy season.

A larger crowd than Ali would have expected was already gathered there, the men and women on opposite sides. The majority were Ayaanle and Geziris, but Ali also saw some of Fiza's shafit crew, a half dozen Sahrayn, and a handful of the merchants and travelers from the other tribes who'd been visiting Ta Ntry when word came of Daevabad's fall.

Ali entered, and a shift went through the worshippers, who murmured salaams and blessings. He offered a weak smile, uneasy at being a distraction, but trying to return as many of the greetings as possible before taking a spot in the back next to a white-haired Ayaanle man who'd been propped up against cushions.

The old man gave him a startled look, one eye blurred by a cataract, and then laughed. "What are you doing next to me, prince? We've been waiting for you to come lead the prayer!"

Blood rushed into Ali's face. "I'm honored, but that's really unnecessary. I wouldn't want to displace—"

"Oh, just do it." Fiza had entered the mosque, a turban wrapped around her hair. She grinned at the old man. "His recitation is very lovely."

Ali looked at her in surprise. "Thank you?"

Fiza laughed. "You don't need to look so shocked. Criminals occasionally need God too—we've got more things that require forgiving."

Ali glanced over the expectant faces. The last time he'd led prayer for a group this size had been back in Bir Nabat, and the memory stirred his heart. He'd been so content there, his restlessness satisfied by the good work he could do for the people who'd protected him. It was the kind of respect one had to earn, not the kind gained by fancy titles and jeweled thrones.

He smiled at the waiting congregants. "As long as some of you will chat with me afterward, I would be honored."

ALI STAYED AT THE MOSQUE UNTIL THE LAST PERSON left, leading prayer and then sitting and catching up with the djinn who'd attended. He listened more than he talked, drinking rounds of coffee and tea as Geziri soldiers spoke in grief-stricken voices about their murdered companions at the Citadel and foreign traders worried about being so far from home during a war. Nearly everyone had loved ones in Daevabad, more than one person breaking down in tears as they recalled sending an excited brother or daughter off to Navasatem. Ali heard stories of how panicked everyone had been when magic failed, their lives upended in a day as they wondered if the Almighty had come to punish them again.

They were heavy tales, and Ali perhaps should have felt weighed down by them, engulfed by the same dread that had overwhelmed him yesterday at the thought of such responsibility.

But he didn't feel overwhelmed. Instead, by the time Ali was ready to return to the castle, he felt . . . grounded. He and Nahri weren't doing this alone. They had people—good people, smart people, brave people—fighting alongside them.

He stopped at the door, smiling at the old man. Ali hadn't missed how intently the elder had been watching him. "Would you like me to take you back to the castle, Grandfather?"

His grandfather gave him a mischievous grin. "What gave it away?"

"A number of things, not least of which is the family resemblance."

The old man's eyes twinkled. Ali didn't doubt his mother's words regarding his grandfather's health and mental state, but Seif Shefala shone with cleverness. "Bah, I doubt I was ever as spry and handsome as you."

Ali laughed and offered his arm, helping his grandfather into a well-cushioned wheeled seat. "I'm sure you were even more dashing. But why didn't you introduce yourself earlier?"

"I find I can get a more accurate measure of a man when he's not aware he's being appraised."

"And have I passed muster?"

"That depends on whether or not you can sneak me back into the castle without your mother noticing. Since when are daughters allowed to shut their parents away?"

Ali began wheeling the chair back toward the castle. "She's always been overprotective."

The town was waking up, the aroma of brewing coffee and sleepy whispers coming from the homes around them. Again, Ali was struck by a surreal sense of belonging, the knowledge that this place had hosted those of his blood for centuries and, but for a few quirks in his fate, might have been his home.

Daevabad is your home. "I feel as though I should thank you," he said to his grandfather. "For all the support you've shown me through the years."

"You mean, the money I've filled your Treasury vaults with since you were a babe?" His grandfather cackled. "No thanks needed, my boy. The politely irate letters your father sent in return were their own reward. Nothing as prickly as wounded Geziri honor."

They entered the castle. The sweet song of birds and the dappled sunlight on the old bricks in the courtyard made Ali feel like he'd stumbled upon a forgotten ruin. He had no doubt the castle looked mesmerizing with its magic, bustling and lively when filled with people, but seeing it like this made him feel closer to his ancestors, to the men and women who would have wandered wide-eyed through the human world, creating new lives for themselves.

"This place is incredible," Ali said admiringly. "I love the way the buildings incorporate what the humans left behind. Do you know anything about the ones who used to live here?"

"Only that the humans were long gone by the time my great-great-grandfather arrived." Regret peppered Seif's voice. "They must have been a clever bunch. We still find old tools and pieces of these lovely pots with a glaze no one can re-create. But the first generation of our family to return to Ta Ntry after the war was cagey about their roots, and I suspect that extended to the past of their new home too."

"I didn't know that."

"Haven't you ever wondered why we don't have a proper surname, using Shefala instead? That's a Djinnistani custom. Not that it was uncommon among the Ayaanle who came back to Ta Ntry after serving the Qahtanis. I'm guessing in the chaos of war and revolution, there were plenty of people who reinvented themselves." His grandfather rolled his eyes. "There are a lot of snobbish old families who never left this coast and sniff down upon us now, but I like to think it means our ancestors were wily."

Ali thought of that. How much of his life, all their lives and their histories, unraveled the more it was examined? The stories he'd grown up on were just that—stories, with more complicated roots and vastly different interpretations than he could possibly have imagined. It was unsettling, the world and truth he knew getting constantly shaken up.

But it also seemed to bring the past nearer and make it real. Six years ago, people like Zaydi al Qahtani had been legends from another age. Perfect, their feats unparalleled. Now Ali could see the messiness behind the myth, the hero who'd saved the shafit but also made terrible mistakes.

"Abu Hatset . . ." A young Ayaanle woman appeared in an arched doorway. "You're going to get me in trouble." She bowed politely to Ali. "Would you mind if I take our fugitive back to his bed where he's *supposed* to be resting?"

"Of course." Ali glanced at his grandfather. "This was a delight. May I visit you again?"

"I would be offended if you didn't." Seif's voice grew conspiratorial. "Bring those date fritters the cook makes, the ones in rose syrup. Your mother is a tyrant when it comes to my sugar intake."

Biting back a smile, Ali touched his heart. "I'll see what I can do."

Right now, though, he had another destination in mind.

Nerves swept through him as he headed toward the rooms set aside for the Nahid siblings—not just because he was eager to see Nahri, but also because he had no idea what to say to Jamshid that wouldn't result in getting another slipper flung at his head. Ali was still struggling to find peace with the other man's accusations, and he'd never been the most diplomatic with his words. Making small talk with his brother's angry former lover—whom Ali had once forced to kill a man—seemed beyond his skill set.

A pair of well-armed guards stood in front of the finely carved teak door. The Geziri man saluted; the Ayaanle one bowed.

"Peace be upon you," Ali greeted them. "Is the Banu Nahida here?"

"Yes, my prince," the Ayaanle man responded. "She and her brother are taking breakfast."

"Excellent." Ali pulled free two of the many dirhams his mother had given him last night, handing one to each. "Please know your service is much appreciated," he said, motioning for them to leave. Ali expected a lot more yelling on Jamshid's end and didn't want anyone barging in to "save" him. "If you don't mind, could you see if any Daeva visitors have left a fire altar the Nahids could use?"

Once they were gone, Ali took a deep breath. Seeing Nahri's smile in his mind, he smoothed down his robe and ran his fingers over his beard before silently cursing himself and knocking on the door. He started to call her name and then stopped, remembering their surroundings. Did he risk speaking so freely to her in front of others? Should he ask for Jamshid instead? Use his Nahid title?

And oh, God, did it look like he'd just bribed his private entry into *Nahri's bedroom*?

The door opened while Ali's mouth was still open in indecision. Jamshid stared back at him, a serving knife poorly concealed behind his back.

"May the fires burn brightly for you!" Ali said in Divasti, in a voice he instantly knew was too loud, his accent atrocious.

Jamshid's hostile expression didn't waver.

Ali tried again. "I wanted to come by and make sure your accommodations were suitable. How did you sleep? The bed, it was comfortable?"

Now Jamshid's expression shifted to one of faint contempt and incredulity. "Nahri, your . . ." Jamshid's gaze traveled up and down Ali with what seemed like every ounce of new Nahid imperiousness he possessed. ". . . companion is here."

"Yes, I heard." The door was pulled from Jamshid's hand to reveal Nahri.

Ali's heart did an extremely unhelpful dance, as all the confidence he'd gathered this morning vanished. Nahri was dressed in a bold block-patterned tunic the color of a stormy sea and striped pants. He'd caught her in the middle of braiding her hair, and her sleeve had ridden up, revealing the delicate expanse of her inner wrist.

God forgive him, he wanted to touch her. Instead, Ali instantly dropped his gaze. "Sabah el-hayr," he greeted her, fighting the embarrassed heat rising in his cheeks.

"Sabah el-noor," she replied. "I wondered if I would see you this morning."

Ali glanced up in surprise at her tone. "Should I have not come?"

"No, that's not what I meant." But Nahri looked as though there was something she wasn't saying. "Come. Take some tea with us."

Uneasy, Ali stepped inside the room, not unaware of Jamshid's still-disgruntled expression. "Is everything all right?" he asked her.

"Of course." But the Nahri who Ali knew would not say "of course" to a question like that in their circumstances. She would have launched into a sarcastic litany of grievances. "Have you spoken to your mother this morning?" she asked.

His mother? Ali's suspicions instantly blossomed. "No, why? Did she say something to you?"

Nahri's hand paused on the curtain she was pulling back. In the pale morning light, she suddenly looked very tired. "No. She came by last night to make sure we were settled in, but that was it."

"Are you *sure* that was it?"

"Yes." She offered a tight smile that didn't touch her eyes. "Come."

With every additional moment of strained politeness, Ali was growing more convinced something was wrong. But knowing how guarded Nahri could be, he held his tongue, simply following her to a small balcony overlooking the forest. Cushions surrounded a low table set with fruit, pastries, tea, and juice.

Nahri motioned for him to sit, and Ali did. Then, more like herself, she snapped her fingers at her brother. "Oh no, Jamshid. Don't you slink off. You're joining us too." She fell onto one of the cushions and reached for a cup of tea. "You know, for all the lecturing I've heard about how emotional women supposedly are, we have nothing on the men I've known."

Jamshid sat, glowering.

Ali fidgeted for a moment and then decided to just let it out.

"I'm sorry." He met the other man's gaze. "I'm so sorry for that night, Jamshid. I was worried about getting caught, about my father learning the assassin was shafit and doing something awful, but that doesn't excuse what I did to you. I can't take it back, and I understand if you don't trust me. I also know how rudely I once spoke of your faith and your people; I know that even before Nahri arrived in Daevabad, your tribe was right to look upon me with suspicion. But I'm sorry."

There was a moment of silence, tension rising in the air,

and then Jamshid spoke, his eyes not leaving Ali's. "And what of Muntadhir and me?"

Muntadhir. His brother's name was like a wound; Ali feared it would never stop hurting. In his mind's eye, he saw his grinning older brother, always so charming, and wondered just how much it had hurt to hold that facade. It broke Ali's heart that he'd had to.

"Muntadhir saved my life," he said, noticing Nahri drop her gaze. "I will regret to the end of my days how we spent our last months together, and that my behavior meant he had to hide so much from me. But I am incredibly grateful he had someone like you at his side with whom he could share some happiness."

At that, he finally saw Jamshid's cool visage crack. "You have a politician's gilded tongue," Jamshid replied, but there was no heat in the insult as he quickly wiped his eyes. "I still don't like you. I'm only agreeing to work with you because Nahri has asked. You have a *very* long way to go to earn my trust."

"I pray I can one day," Ali said sincerely, pouring a cup of tea. "Perhaps this can be a new beginning for us."

Something quirked in Jamshid's expression, but there was a knock at the door, and then a steward entered.

"The queen would like to see you, my prince. The Banu Nahida and Baga Nahid as well."

God, did his mother have his every move watched? Ali had been here only minutes. "We'll be right there," he said with a resigned sigh.

Nahri rose to her feet. "Let me get my cloak."

Jamshid was pouring a drink. He pushed the cup toward Ali. "Tamarind juice before we leave," he said politely. "I know how fond you are of it."

Ali scowled. "I was fond of it before someone tried to poison . . ." He trailed off, noting the challenge in Jamshid's eyes. "Oh, you bas—"

Jamshid tsked, nodding at Nahri's retreating back. "We would not wish to upset her." He raised his own cup, smiling dangerously. "To fresh starts." He leaned forward, lowering his voice. "Betray my sister—hurt her in any way—and there will be no one around to interfere the next time you're poisoned."

Not trusting himself to respond, Ali simply grunted. Nahri returned, a hooded cloak pulled over her clothes and messy braid.

"Let's go." She sounded like they were headed to a funeral.

Ali let Jamshid get ahead of them in the corridor and then turned back to Nahri. "Are you sure everything is okay?" he asked again. "Should I not have said—"

"No," she cut in quickly. "What you said was perfect."

"Then what's wrong?" Ali pressed. "You seem so sad."

Nahri stopped, taking a deep breath as if to steady herself. "There's nothing wrong. But you shouldn't do that here," she added, pulling away.

Mortified, Ali realized he had unconsciously reached for her hand.

He instantly stepped back. "I'm sorry. I didn't mean—"

"It's fine. It's just we're not running around Cairo by ourselves anymore." A flush darkened Nahri's cheeks. "People talk. I wouldn't want them to get the wrong impression."

"No," Ali said hoarsely. "Of course not."

"Good." Nahri stared at him for another moment, and no matter what she claimed, Ali would swear he saw a flicker of regret in her eyes before she glanced away. "I should catch up with Jamshid."

Ali nodded, only following when the siblings were far ahead. He kept his distance, trying to pretend that he was fine and normal and there wasn't a whirling contraption of blades tearing through his chest where his heart used to be. Nahri was right. Ali shouldn't have touched her; he shouldn't be touching any woman who wasn't his wife.

You could ask if she'd like to be your wife.

The ridiculous thought galloped unwelcome into his head, followed by utter panic, as though down the hall Nahri might somehow read his mind. By God, had the marid messed with him so much that Ali had lost all sense?

She is beyond you, and she always will be. Nahri had been loved by the Afshin, a man so handsome his enemies wrote poetry praising his beauty, and married to Muntadhir, Daevabad's renowned breaker of hearts. Did Ali really think the brilliant, beautiful Banu Nahida would ever be interested in a scarred Geziri virgin with a propensity for saying exactly the wrong thing?

No. She wouldn't be. Which meant Ali was going to keep his mouth shut and see what his mother wanted without further contemplating blowing up his dearest friendship and most importance political alliance.

Hatset was waiting for them outside the library. "Good morning to you all." She smiled at Ali. "I hear you had an early start politicking at the mosque today."

"If by politicking, you mean genuinely talking to people about their lives and praying together, yes," he replied. "It was nice."

"I'm glad to hear it." His mother's smile wavered, and she took his hand. "Alu, there is someone here you need to see. I didn't want to overwhelm you yesterday, but—"

"Who?" Ali asked. Hatset looked unsettled, and he knew it took a lot to do that.

"Ustadh Issa."

"*Issa?*"

When she said nothing more, Ali moved for the library, still in disbelief. But he no sooner pushed open the door than the elderly scholar was there, draped in a homespun blanket and surrounded by books, his giant emerald eyes blinking like a bat's.

"Ustadh Issa . . . my God," Ali stammered. "Peace be upon

you." He crossed the long room in seconds. "When did you get here?"

Issa's eyes darted to Hatset before he replied. "Just recently. The journey exhausted me, and I requested a few days to recover."

"But you were in Daevabad," Ali said, reeling. "How did you escape?"

"It seems you have the Tukharistani woman, Razu, to thank," his mother explained. "She convinced the Afshin that Issa was distressed, and that it would be a kindness to let a fellow slave leave a city ifrit had invaded."

Ali had no problem believing anyone would think Issa distressed, but he was shocked to learn the Afshin had helped him. "Do you have any news?" he begged. "My sister, the other Geziris—"

Hatset answered again. "Zaynab is alive. She was able to warn the other Geziris, and those in the quarter survived. They've apparently joined with the shafit district and barricaded themselves off from the rest of the city." She paused. "They're not the only ones who survived, baba. Issa says Muntadhir is alive."

Ali stared at her, the words impossible.

Jamshid reacted first, his head snapping up. "What?"

"Muntadhir is alive," Hatset repeated. "Issa said he's being held prisoner in the palace."

"Oh, my God." Ali abruptly sat down, feeling like his legs had been cut out from underneath him. Tears pricked his eyes. "Are you sure? Are you really sure?"

"No," Issa said, sounding indignant. When Ali spun on him, he continued. "There is no such thing as certainty in this situation, young man. The emir is surrounded by deeply volatile enemies. They may have killed him since I left. Lady Manizheh was already threatening to do so if the Geziris and your sister did not surrender."

"They won't kill him." It was Nahri, exchanging an oddly loaded glance with his mother. "Not yet. Muntadhir is too valuable, and Manizheh isn't a fool."

"We need to save him," Jamshid declared.

"We need to save lots of people," Nahri corrected. "You're a Nahid now, Jamshid. All of Daevabad is your responsibility."

Jamshid looked mutinous, but Ali's astonishment had already dissipated, news of his brother and his city jolting him into action. He strode over to a desk, snatching a piece of parchment and a charcoal pencil. "Issa, I need you to tell me everything you know."

The scholar made a sour face. "It's going to be a lot. Razu and Elashia made me memorize all sorts of things before I left, about food and security and other such nonsense." He let out a scandalized sound. "Razu put maps in the lining of my *loincloth*."

Ali stilled, his blood rushing in his ears. This was no mere return of a "distressed" old man. Razu had intentionally passed them valuable information.

Jamshid exhaled loudly, his eyes widening as he met Ali's gaze. An identical thrill was on his face—Ali knew the former captain realized what a lucky victory this was.

"I can't believe Dara let you leave," Jamshid breathed. "He led the damn rebellion against Zaydi al Qahtani. How could he make such a mistake?"

"Razu can be very convincing," Nahri said softly. "And maybe Dara was trying to show some mercy."

Ali held his tongue on the prospect of the Afshin and "mercy," opting to pace instead. If he could have, he would have picked Issa up, turned him upside down, and shaken out all he knew. "You said the Geziris and shafit neighborhoods had managed to hold the Daevas off—do you know about the other tribes?"

"Everyone was on their own when I left," Issa explained.

"Your sister was in talks with the Ayaanle and Tukharistanis but wasn't having much luck. It is utter chaos, and no one trusts anyone else."

Ali's heart dropped. "So Manizheh doesn't control the city? Surely they brought additional soldiers, security."

"Oh no, not at all," Issa replied. "Razu said to tell you reports say that the Afshin has less than a dozen men. There are rumors he is training more, but Manizheh only controls the Daeva Quarter for now."

Jamshid gaped. "How did they overthrow your family with only a dozen warriors?"

Ali didn't answer. Dara had had more than a dozen soldiers, of course, but it didn't seem the right moment to tell Jamshid that Ali had personally killed that number with marid magic alone. He glanced at Nahri, but she was stone-faced and quiet. Why wasn't she reacting to any of this? To Issa's return? To word of the Afshin? To news of . . .

Muntadhir. Oh.

Well, Ali supposed it was good he'd held his tongue about his feelings for her.

War. Think about war. It's simpler. He returned to Jamshid's question. "They planned to annihilate the Royal Guard and the entire Geziri population. Manizheh is the most powerful Nahid healer in generations. Add two ifrit and whatever the hell the Afshin is now, and they probably thought it was enough to hold the city. And honestly, had Manizheh taken the seal and magic not fallen, I could see the other tribes surrendering. No one would have wanted to follow the example of the Geziris."

His words chilled the room for a moment, but then Jamshid spoke up again. "What do you mean, what Dara *is*?"

Nahri twisted the hem of her scarf in one hand. "Dara said Manizheh freed him from Suleiman's curse. He has the powers of an original daeva now."

Jamshid paled. "You didn't tell me that."

"It's been a difficult few weeks, all right?" Nahri replied. "You'll excuse me for not wanting to think about how my old Afshin turns into fire to set giant smoke monsters on his enemies."

"Oh." Jamshid looked even greener. "That's an unfortunate development."

"Tell me about it." Ali glanced at Issa. "Ustadh, my ancestors brought back a lot of the Nahids' old texts. They should be in the archives. I'm hoping we can find a way to defeat him."

"*Defeat* him?" Hatset interrupted. "Yesterday your only allies were a band of pirates and a Nahid fugitive. Don't you think it's a bit soon to be planning offensive measures?'

"I'm not going anywhere today. We'll talk to Issa, find out everything we can, and then evaluate our next move."

"Your position isn't strong enough to be evaluating any moves; you're lucky you haven't been *dragged* back to Daevabad. Don't you know there's a bounty on your head?"

"I've been living with a bounty on my head for a very long time, Amma," Ali said gently. "And I fear Daevabad doesn't have time for me to get comfortable here. If the city is truly embroiled in a civil war, if Manizheh has cut it off from the rest of the world . . ." He ran the estimates in his head. "We were preparing for Navasatem crowds, but we were expecting supplies throughout the month. People will be starving, and soon."

"Then let Manizheh and her Afshin deal with it. She wished to rule."

Ali stared at his mother in astonishment. "Zaynab is there."

Hatset's eyes flashed. "Believe me, I know. But right now, I need you to stop and *think*. To consider what is best for all of us, not just those in Daevabad."

Ali strongly suspected he was not going to like where this was going. "Meaning?"

"Meaning our *world* has been fractured, Alizayd, not just

Daevabad. When magic fell, people were hysterical: abandoning their jobs and packing into the mosques, expecting some new Suleiman to sweep in and rip us from our homes and lives. Frightened, leaderless mobs of people do rash things." Hatset hesitated. "But there's also a chance to build something new. Someplace secure. We need a new king, a new government. And not one centered around a man in a jail cell."

Jamshid shot to his feet before Ali could react. "Absolutely not. That is Muntadhir's position."

"Alizayd is as eligible for the throne as his brother. He always has been," Hatset insisted, glaring so fiercely that Jamshid shut up. She stepped closer to Ali, her expression urgent. "So take it, my son. Declare yourself king. You'll have the backing of our tribes and can establish a court in Ta Ntry, where you'll be safe."

"A court in Ta Ntry where you'll never see Daevabad again." Nahri sounded no less fierce than his mother. "You might as well speak freely, Hatset. You don't think we can beat Manizheh, and you don't want us to try."

"I don't want you to *die*. The two of you have no idea how weak your position is. You think a band of pirates would have laid hands on Ghassan? Mocked him and chained him up?" His mother turned back to Ali. "Do you understand, Alu? You need to establish yourself as a leader to be followed. A leader to be *feared*. Because if you don't rule these people as king, you're going to be given as a gift to their new queen in Daevabad."

Ali opened and closed his mouth, fighting for a response. Her words . . . this was not the mother he knew.

"Amma, you told me that Abba's mistake was being so afraid of his people that he crushed them. Now you're counseling me to do the same?"

"Yes." Hatset didn't even hesitate. "I want you to *live*," she said fervently. "And if you need to borrow from your father to restore order, so be it. When things are more stable, you can lessen your grip."

And that's how it starts. King. A court in Ta Ntry where Ali would watch Daevabad fall apart from afar, letting its bloody, starving instability serve as a warning to allies he'd cajole and blackmail into compliance. Served by soldiers he'd conscript.

That wasn't the kind of leader he wanted to be.

Then what kind of leader do you want to be?

Again Ali saw his father on the shedu throne, only the latest in a long line of Qahtani kings who had slowly abandoned the ideals of the revolution that had once driven them. Kings who had brutalized Daevabad as much as any Nahid. And then it suddenly became clearer, a decision he realized had been a long time coming.

"I'm sorry, Amma." Ali spoke softly, because he knew he was about to break his mother's heart. "But there's not going to be another Qahtani king."

Hatset stared at him in disbelief. "Excuse me?" Her gold eyes went wide with fury. "If these two have convinced you to put us all under Nahid rule again . . ."

"They haven't. I don't want to be under Nahid rule, though I will not speak over Nahri and Jamshid," Ali said, glancing at Nahri. She was watching him carefully, her expression guarded. "Our people do need a new government and an organized response to Manizheh. What they don't need is another tyrant."

"Oh, for God's sake, Alizayd." The anger left Hatset's face, replaced in a fell swoop by vexation. "This is not the time for your idealism."

"Yes, it is," Nahri declared. Ali gaped at her, but she pressed on. "The people aren't ready to be in charge? Because we've ruled them so well, have we? Ghassan was preparing to massacre an entire shafit neighborhood, and Manizheh just murdered thousands. I'd say the Qahtanis and the Nahids have lost the right to tell anyone they know better." She crossed her arms. "I agree with him. None of us should be on that throne."

Ali gazed at her, something blazing inside him.

No one else seemed pleased. Jamshid was staring at his sister, visibly aghast, and now even Issa got involved, wagging a finger in the air.

"What the two of you are advocating for is no less than revolution. Anarchy! Such a thing is forbidden, Alizayd al Qahtani. Our faith prioritizes order. *Stability*—"

"Our faith prioritizes justice," Ali argued. "It tells us to stand for justice, no matter what. We are to be a community that calls for *what is right*, that stands as witness."

"We already did!" Issa said, indignant. "My grandfather fought in Zaydi's war. He labored his entire life to free the shafit and make the tribes equal, and here you are tossing away his legacy without a care. And for what? Perfection? That is for Paradise, not this life."

Ali shook his head. He felt closer to his ancestor than he ever had; not to the legend, but to the flesh-and-blood man who had fought so hard, who had grieved his slaughtered family, and who in that anguish had made mistakes Ali never wanted to repeat. "I'm not tossing away Zaydi's legacy. I'm completing it."

"You're being a reckless fool," Hatset said brusquely. "One who's going to get himself and everyone around him killed."

"I'm not being reckless, Amma. You want me to listen? I have been. I've been trying to listen, to truly listen, to as many people as possible. And they want a voice in their lives and freedom for their children. Do you know the best thing I did for the shafit? *I got out of their way.* I got them the money and opportunities they should have always had and then watched *them* build it all. I don't believe in kings. Not anymore. And if I did, I would still be undeserving of the throne. I have the blood of innocents on my hands and don't speak the language of a third of the city's people. I come from a family that has let them down. No more."

"So you'll what? Assemble a committee?" Hatset demanded. "Because I can tell you: ask people to vote between two starry-eyed nobles with vague, pretty words about freedom and a Banu Nahida who gruesomely murders her opponents, and you'll find Nahri in another cage and the Afshin carving out your heart."

It was a frightening image. And yet it wasn't enough. This didn't feel reckless. It felt just. Too many kings before him had sworn to one day be better, to give their people freedom when they earned it. Ali would not. They were facing terrible odds, and he wasn't going to order people to their deaths without them having some say in it.

He'd just have to convince them not to do the same to him. "I'm not going to take a vote on our lives, Amma. But I won't claim the throne. And I'll make clear when assembling whatever resistance we can that we're all in this together. And that we're fighting for a different kind of Daevabad."

"Then you won't win." But Hatset must have heard the resolution in his words, because she was looking at him now like he was a ghost. "I have twice been weighed down with the grief of not knowing whether to mourn you." She stepped back. "If you finally make me do so, Alizayd, I will not forgive you. Not in this life or the next." She beckoned to Issa. "Come, Ustadh."

She slammed the door when she left, and Ali recoiled, her vow cutting him to the core.

"Sit, my friend," Nahri said quietly. "I can see the blood leaving your face."

"Okay," Ali murmured, obeying.

The next family feud was not his.

Jamshid was pacing back and forth, looking at his sister as if she'd just suggested they befriend a karkadann. "Nahri, I've made clear to you that I'm on your side, but are you *sure* about this? Daevabad has always been ruled by a Nahid or a Qahtani. Our people don't know anything else."

"I think our people are more capable than you give them

credit for. But yes." She glanced at Ali, sounding a little nervous. "This feels right. On the *extremely* small chance we recover the city, I think we owe it to Daevabad to put things as right as we can and then let the city take it from there. Personally, the only place I want to rule is my hospital."

"We just have to win a war first," Ali said bleakly.

Jamshid shook his head. "If you want to convince people not to sell you out to my mother, you'll stop calling it a war."

Ali gave him a baffled stare. "It felt pretty warlike, Pramukh. Soldiers fighting, palaces falling."

"But our *peoples* are not at war. Not entirely." Jamshid looked at them. "May *I* be a politician for a moment, since clearly neither of you is inclined?" When Nahri rolled her eyes and Ali made a sour face, he continued. "You need to discredit them. Don't call it a war, because 'war' implies there's leadership and strategy on the other side. Call them criminals instead. Call them monsters. Make the thought of a world under their rule so *personally* threatening that people feel the only thing they can do is fight."

There was silence for a long moment. "That's not actually a bad idea," Ali finally said.

Jamshid threw him an annoyed glare. "Glad to surprise you."

"Can you do that, though?" It was Nahri, looking at her brother. "I've crossed our mother already, but you haven't, Jamshid. And it's going to be both your parents you're standing up to. The ones you're calling monsters."

"They won't be the only ones in Daevabad we're calling monsters," Jamshid warned.

Nahri's eyes flashed before her expression closed in on itself. "He let Issa go." She didn't need to say Darayavahoush's name—it was clear who they were talking about. "Maybe he's not as loyal to Manizheh as we think. Maybe he could be an asset."

Ali forced himself to stay silent. Darayavahoush might not have succeeded in killing Muntadhir, but he'd stood at Manizheh's side as she planned to massacre Daevabad's Geziri population. Ali was no innocent and knew plenty of them had blood on their hands, but the Afshin had cities' worth.

And yet he loves her. Ali didn't have to speak Divasti to know Darayavahoush had been pleading with Nahri just before she brought the ceiling down on his head. Indeed, the first time the Afshin had tried to steal her away, it had been to stop Nahri from marrying Muntadhir. It might be a controlling, terrible kind of love, but it was there. And it was dangerous.

Perhaps a reminder to you as well, then, to keep your heart from ruling your head.

Thankfully, Jamshid replied. "We have no way to find out, Nahri, and it's too risky to proceed on the assumption Dara is anything but loyal to Manizheh. If what Issa says is true, it's the Afshin holding that city for her. He needs to be removed."

Removed. How careful a word. "The books," Ali reminded them just as carefully. "There might be information about magic vanishing, about whatever Darayavahoush is now, and about how to stop him."

Nahri rose to her feet. "Then I guess it's decided." There was a new edge in her voice. "Come on, Jamshid. Let's go search through our family's stolen books for a way to murder our Afshin yet again."

Ali stood to follow her. "Nahri—"

"It's fine." But Nahri didn't look fine. She looked like she was clinging to her last brittle veneer of control. "It was always going to be like this."

"Then let me at least—"

"No. This part, Ali?" Nahri pushed past him. "I think it's better we're on our own."

27

DARA

Dara stalked down the line of sparring men. "No," he said impatiently, cutting between one pair. "Your shield is not doing you any good down by your knees. Raise it up and then actually *hold* your sword. What sort of grip is this? A bird could knock it out of your hand."

The young man's face went red. "Forgive me, Afshin."

"I do not wish to forgive you. I wish for you to listen and do as I tell you before you get someone killed."

Irtemiz made her way over, her cane tapping on the arena sand. "Why don't I work with these two for a while?" she offered diplomatically. "And it's been a long, brutal day in this sun. Maybe they deserve a break?"

"They can have a break when they show some improvement." Dara glowered at his newest and least favorite batch of recruits. At Kaveh's suggestion, each of the Daeva noble houses had given a youth to military training. In theory, it was a good idea. Daeva military officers had always been pulled from the nobility. They were positions of great honor, ones that would entwine the nobles more closely into Manizheh's regime, making clear their livelihood depended on her.

But Dara doubted these young men and "great honor" would ever meet. They were merchant brats, and if a few seemed eager, the rest did not.

Irtemiz spoke again, her voice raised in false cheer. "Afshin, could I speak to you a moment about our new arms? The blacksmiths guild sent over an updated design."

"A moment," he grumbled, following her to the shaded pavilion.

Irtemiz collapsed into a cushioned bench. "Why don't you have something to drink?" she suggested, pulling over a pitcher of apricot juice.

"I am not thirsty. Where are these designs?"

She gave him a sheepish smile. "They've not actually been delivered yet. I just wanted to give the men a break."

"That is insubordination."

"I know, and I'm hoping you can forgive it." Irtemiz paused. "May I speak as a friend?"

Dara let out a disgruntled sound. "Your generation has no sense of decorum, but fine, out with it."

"You haven't seemed like yourself since the feast. You barely speak to us, you're pushing these men too hard . . ."

Dara flinched. Irtemiz wasn't wrong. The brief levity he'd felt at the feast—celebrating with his men, his dalliance with the dancer—had been erased by what he'd learned in the crypt. Worse, it felt like a punishment. Dara had dared to enjoy himself and flirt with the feeling of being normal and instead learned he was nothing of the sort. He'd been enslaved on the order of Zaydi al Qahtani and resurrected as an experiment, an abomination cobbled together by ifrit schemes, marid blood debts, and two Nahids blowing each other apart over whether to murder a baby.

It all had indeed left him in a fouler mood than usual. "If I am tense, it is because of this so-called peace summit," he lied, mentioning the meeting Manizheh was planning with the handful of djinn representatives her new Daeva allies had managed to intrigue. "I have to include at least a few of these fool boys in my security detail to please their fancy families, and they are useless."

Irtemiz didn't look convinced. "You had far more patience with us when we trained."

"You wanted to learn. It makes all the difference."

A steward emerged from the shadowed archway leading back into the palace. "Afshin, the Banu Nahida wishes to speak to you."

"I will be right there." Dara was still doing what he could to get back into Manizheh's good graces, determined to recover his place in court. Rising, he nodded to Irtemiz's leg. "How are you healing?"

"I believe the term is 'leisurely.'"

"If we went very slowly, would you feel up to getting back on a horse?"

Her eyes lit up. "That would be fantastic."

"Good. See to these brats, and then after the summit, perhaps we can take a loop of the outer walls. It has been too long since I checked them."

"Only for security purposes, I assume. Not because it could be in any way construed as an enjoyable activity?"

Dara feigned a scowl. "Go wag your tongue at the boy about to stab himself," he said, nodding at one of the recruits. "Let me see what the Banu Nahida wants."

DARA FOUND MANIZHEH IN THE GARDEN—CHIEFLY BE-cause he followed the sounds of her shouting, an act so unlike her that he ran through the underbrush, nearly knocking over a gardener in the process.

"—I will kill her. I will kill her if she hurts him. I will catch her children, make the blood in their veins boil them alive while she watches, and then I will kill her!"

He rushed around the bend. Manizheh and Kaveh were alone in a small glen encased by rose trellises, the peaceful scene at odds with her furious pacing. She had a broken scroll in one hand and was shaking it so hard Dara was surprised it hadn't ripped in two.

"Banu Manizheh?" he ventured. "Is everything all right?"

She whirled on him. "No. Ghassan's crocodile wife has my son and is threatening to kill him if I harm her children. No, forgive me, 'to take twice as long doing whatever is done to Zaynab or Alizayd' while perpetuating the same on Jamshid,'" she said, reading the letter aloud. "I will cut out her heart."

Dara jerked back. "The queen has Jamshid?"

Kaveh nodded, giving Manizheh a nervous look. "It seems Wajed made his way to Ta Ntry." He pointed at the tree where a scaled pigeon was roosting. "We received a message this morning."

Manizheh tore the letter in half. "I want Zaynab al Qahtani. This week. Tomorrow, even. If she's not going to respond to my threats against her brother, then I want you to offer her weight in gold and free passage out of the city to anyone who turns her over. To their families. I will give them horses, supplies, enough to make a comfortable life anywhere."

Dara hesitated. He still hadn't told Manizheh he'd seen Zaynab at the hospital. "I can send the message, my lady, but we've already offered plenty of incentives. According to rumor, she's the one who warned the rest of the Geziris to remove their relics. They're not going to betray her. She's likely surrounded by loyal, well-trained warriors at all times."

"Everyone has a price," Manizheh argued. "Maybe you should

start demolishing their little city block by block and see how long it takes until someone wants to get out."

Kaveh cleared his throat. "My lady, a third of Daevabad is behind those walls. We agreed we were going to try and reach out—"

"We *have* reached out. And for what? It's been nearly two months, and all we have to show for it is a half dozen merchants more interested in gold than peace. Meanwhile, there are shafit marksmen shooting any Daeva who tries to enter the midan. They are *laughing* at us. Laughing while they no doubt make more Rumi fire and bullets. Aeshma tells me he sees their forges burning all night."

"I would not listen to anything Aeshma says," Dara warned. Not that Manizheh would heed him. The ifrit was such a consistent presence at her side lately that Dara was surprised not to see Aeshma there now.

"And no one is laughing," Kaveh assured her. "You just need to be a bit more patient."

"I am weary of patience." Bitterness creased Manizheh's face. "Was Ghassan patient? The djinn tribes should be grateful for the mercy I've shown them. If they'd defied *him* like this, he would have slaughtered them. And when it comes to the Geziris and the shafit, we're being naive. We're never going to have peace with them. We might as well accept that and do what's necessary to protect ourselves before they strike first."

Her words landed heavily in the tense air. They were not surprising—they were indeed what Dara suspected all three of them had quietly thought at one time or another.

But that night at the hospital had changed him. Dara could not look at the other side of the city and see only shadows and weapons. There were people, tens of thousands of them. Families and children and soldiers as weary of war as he was. Elashia and Razu.

"If you believe what is necessary is another massacre, you will need another Afshin," he declared. "What happened to the palace Geziris was the last time. I won't participate in another slaughter. And if you send the ifrit in, you will lose all credibility as our ruler."

Manizheh's eyes blazed. "Then perhaps I'll send in the soldiers you have trained."

"Then *they* would be the ones slaughtered. They'd be outnumbered and surrounded."

"So instead you'd have us sit back and wait to be attacked? And you wonder why I question your counsel?"

"Manu." Using a name Dara had not heard before, Kaveh reached out to take Manizheh's hands. His voice was gentle. "Do not let this news shake you from your course. I know how worried you are about Jamshid. I am too. But trust me; it's better he is in Hatset's hands, regardless of her threats. Wajed might have killed him; Hatset will negotiate. I have no doubt she would trade her daughter for Jamshid if given the option."

"Except we still don't have her daughter." Manizheh continued ripping up the letter, letting the pieces fall to the ground, and then glared at Dara. "Can you assist with *that* or will it offend your new conscience?"

Dara checked his temper. He was supposed to be finding ways to convince Manizheh to avoid bloodshed, not getting tossed out of her presence entirely. And perhaps finding Zaynab would do some good. Their enemies would lose their leader, and if the princess could be traded for Jamshid . . . Maybe with her son safely at her side, Banu Manizheh would be more merciful and patient with her subjects.

Dara bowed his head. "Will there be any Ayaanle attending our meeting?"

Kaveh nodded. "An ivory trader by the name of Amani ta Buzo. She's one of Tamer's business associates."

"The man who keeps his ancestor's spear as a wall ornament?"

"The very one."

"Then I will try to speak with her," Dara promised. "Perhaps she might have some thoughts on luring Zaynab out."

"See?" Kaveh said, sounding like he was trying to cheer Manizheh up. "Progress." Dara saw him squeeze her hand. "We're going to get our son back," he said fiercely. "I promise."

Manizheh's gaze looked very faraway. "I wish I had your confidence."

Dara wordlessly stepped away as Kaveh brought Manizheh's hand to his lips. "We will all be together again, my love. I know it."

THE DAY OF THE PEACE SUMMIT WAS NOT A PLEASANT one. Daevabad's weather had always been erratic, but with no magic, it had gone into utter free fall—torrential rains bursting from cloudless skies, followed by afternoons of blistering heat. It was wreaking havoc on their crops, farmers losing the battle to protect their orchards and fields. Today Dara had woken to a cold fog that smelled like rot, the sky growing more and more mercurial until it finally opened, pelting with sleet those unfortunate enough to be outside. Despite the accumulating ice, a swarm of crickets had *also* descended, unexpected vermin being another side effect of the loss of Suleiman's seal.

"An excellent omen," Muntadhir said drily at Dara's side. The emir was in a great mood, clearly thrilled to be outside the palace walls for the first time in weeks. He crunched a cricket into the ice under his heel and then glanced sideways. "Tell me—in your more unsettling form, do you think you'd sizzle in the rain? That would be most entertaining. Like oil in a skillet."

"Al Qahtani, I am not above gagging you and stuffing you back in the carriage." Dara gave the sleet a look of distaste. Cold rain. Why did it have to be *cold rain*? "I do not even know why you are here."

"The sight of him will set the djinn at ease." It was Tamer speaking now. "My acquaintances are nervous. They fear being abducted the moment they set foot in our quarter. I've told them the emir is working with us, but seeing him here is better."

Muntadhir grinned. "And without even a leash!"

"That can still be arranged," Dara muttered. They were underneath a canopied pergola, but water still beaded down his skin, offending something deep inside him.

"Any sign of our guests?" Kaveh asked, joining them.

Dara nodded in welcome. "Not yet."

Muntadhir's mocking smile vanished at the sight of the grand wazir, replaced by open hostility. Dara guessed personally murdering his father was not something even the wily emir could move past. "Kaveh, I didn't think to see you here. Did Manizheh let you out of her bed early?"

"Watch yourself, al Qahtani," Dara warned.

"It's all right, Afshin," Kaveh replied, not taking his gaze off Muntadhir. "I lost what little respect I had for Muntadhir's opinion a long time ago." He lifted his chin. "Six years ago, to be precise. When you were too cowardly to stand up for my son after he saved your life."

"Oh, look, the djinn!" Dara said enthusiastically, moving between Kaveh and Muntadhir and pointing with as much excitement as he could muster at the two small groups approaching from the direction of the Tukharistani and Agnivanshi quarters. They were huddled under wet parasols and surrounded by Daeva soldiers. Dara had insisted on meeting the envoys first, before bringing them deeper in Daeva territory, let alone anywhere near Manizheh.

Tamer coughed. "It may be best if you don't do *that*," he said delicately. "They're already frightened of you."

Dara followed his gaze to see that, as usual, he was resting his hand on the hilt of his knife. He grunted, glancing again at Muntadhir, who was still glaring at Kaveh, but dropped his hand.

He surveyed their new arrivals—a single representative each from the Ayaanle, Tukharistani, and Agnivanshi tribes. They'd had no luck with the Sahrayn and hadn't bothered reaching out to the Geziri and shafit confederation of vengeance. The djinn representatives each had their own personal guards, and every eye—gold and tin and tawny sand—was on Dara.

At his side, Tamer bowed. "Greetings, my friends. And thank you for joining us. I pray today takes us all on a new path." He paused. "I am not sure my companions need an introduction, but may you be pleased to meet Darayavahoush e-Afshin, Grand Wazir Kaveh e-Pramukh, and Emir Muntadhir al Qahtani."

Muntadhir swept in. "Ah, Tamer, you speak as though we're all strangers and did not pull Naqtas from the lap of a singing girl with a reputation for leaving her patrons tied to the bed with their jewelry missing." He winked at an extremely straitlaced-looking Agnivanshi man who instantly flushed. "Peace be upon you all, my friends."

"May the fires burn brightly for you," Dara added, forcing a smile that seemed to provoke even more fear. Two of the djinn edged back.

"For you as well, Afshin," It was an older Ayaanle woman who'd spoken, in flawless Divasti. "You'll forgive me, Emir, for we haven't met. The laps of singing girls are not my natural environment."

Muntadhir's voice took on the slightest chill. "Amani ta Buzo, I assume."

"You assume correctly. Though I would not have thought my family illustrious enough to be known by the emir."

"Oh, have no worries of illustriousness, my lady." Muntadhir smiled, the expression dagger sharp. "I only know of your family's name because I've heard my stepmother referring to it as belonging to a pack of vipers."

Amani returned his smile. "And yet now the queen is gone, and you and I are at the side of your father's murderers. Perhaps neither of us should be so judgmental."

Dara intervened. "Let's not make our guests wait in the rain. Gushtap, you have searched the men for weapons?"

"Yes, Afshin. Those wearing weapons have already handed them over; however . . ." Gushtap lowered his voice. "There is an issue."

"I take it he's referring to my gift for the Banu Nahida," Amani explained, pointing to a large teak trunk two of her men were carrying. "You might as well take a peek, Afshin. You can have first pick."

Apprehensive, Dara motioned for the trunk to be opened. The earthy smell of iron hit his nose, and then he narrowed his eyes.

The trunk was entirely packed with weapons. Ivory-handled iron daggers and straight knives, short steel swords and throwing blades.

"*This* is your gift to Banu Manizheh?" he asked.

"I figured she'd appreciate the practical application. You'll be moving on the Geziri Quarter soon enough, won't you?"

Muntadhir's eyes flashed, and Dara made several quick decisions, trusting only himself to deal with the giant trunk of weapons, the prickly emir, and the arms-trading old woman. "Both of you are coming with me," he ordered, pointing to Amani and the emir. "As is that trunk."

Tamer gave him a nervous look. "It might be wise if I go with you as well, Afshin."

A diplomat could only help. "That sounds like a plan," Dara agreed.

"May my brother join us?" Tamer pointed to the knot of recruits loading the waiting carriages. "We have an extra seat."

Dara made a sound of assent, his gaze still on Amani and Muntadhir. They'd climbed into the carriage and were conversing in extremely angry-sounding, rapid-fire Djinnistani.

Kaveh turned to follow them.

Dara stopped him. "I don't think you and Muntadhir should be confined together in any small spaces." He pointed in the direction of Gushtap's carriage. "Trust when I say you'll find better company with my man."

Kaveh glanced skeptically at Muntadhir and Amani. "You can handle them?"

"I'm told I'm very frightening. Go. I will see you at the palace."

Tamer's brother ended up being one of the young men Dara had berated during training, and as the carriage door shut and Muntadhir started looking even more rebellious, Dara found himself regretting not taking a more experienced warrior. He sat on the box of weapons, fully meaning to divest the emir of a limb if he made any sudden movements.

Amani peeked out the window. "Such a gloomy day. I was curious to see how the Daevas were adjusting to the loss of magic. I see you have horses pulling your carriages now."

"Perhaps you might tell us how the Ayaanle are faring," Tamer suggested pleasantly.

"You mean, have we exhausted our food stores, and are we ready to fall at the feet of your Banu Nahida begging for help? No, not yet, Tamer."

"But I take it you wish to be the first in line once power shifts," Muntadhir accused. "Even offering up weapons to help that shift occur a bit faster."

Amani leaned back. "I must say I did expect more from a Qahtani prince. Oh, I know they say you are a drunk and a wastrel, but where is that fierce Geziri honor? I'd have thought you'd throw yourself on your own zulfiqar before aiding the people who murdered your father. Oh, forgive me," she corrected. "You were not the one who knew how to wield a zulfiqar."

At that Muntadhir flinched, murder simmering in his eyes. But he held his tongue when Dara threw him a look of warning and drew up, staring out the curtained window like they were all beneath him.

The carriage continued, rain beating steadily upon the canopy. Dara wrinkled his nose, fanning a hand in front of his face to alleviate the iron tang of the weapons that had grown thick in the close air. At the motion of his hand, Tamer's young brother—whose name Dara didn't remember—jumped.

And I am to make warriors of such men? Exasperated, Dara leaned back to glance through the curtain. He could see one of the other three carriages ahead, but otherwise the gray, misty street was empty. They were traveling along the avenue that led past Daevabad's finest estates—the homes of people like the Vaigas brothers—and none save an unfortunate servant dared go out in such unpleasant weather.

He studied the thick walls protecting the villas around them. A jagged crack ran down the paved road, but that was the only sign of Daevabad's decay. Wet roses and lush vines climbed the buildings, marble and brass accents marking their wealth.

Perhaps Dara should have taken solace in their existence, proof that his Daevas had survived worse. But he didn't. Instead, he now wondered at the cost, at the compromises that had been made to ensure the quiet power of the people who lived here.

A crack drew his attention, the noise not entirely dissimilar to the horse's clopping hooves, but enough to make him frown. There was a muffled cry from the carriage ahead.

Dara jerked up. That sounded like Kaveh. "Stop the horses!" he ordered. "Tell the men—"

A sharp pinch in his leg, like the bite of a particularly nasty bug. Bewildered, Dara glanced down to see some sort of small glass and metal tube sticking out of his thigh. It looked like a tool that might have been found in the infirmary, and Dara was so utterly baffled he only noticed a half second too late that it was filled with a dark liquid that sparkled with metal fragments.

And that Tamer's brother—the useless one whose name Dara hadn't bothered trying to recall—was holding it, pressing down on a plunger before Dara could stop him.

Dara ripped the instrument from his leg, grabbed the boy, and broke his neck before the others could even cry out. He shot to his feet, fire burning down his skin as he let his magic consume him.

And then it *stopped.* Dara collapsed as the carriage crashed to a halt, his leg giving out.

"*Tur!*" Tamer wailed, reaching for his brother. "No!"

Pain scorched through Dara's thigh, coming in waves from the spot where the boy had injected him. He was aware of screams coming from the other carriages, of Gushtap shouting his name before being cut off, but Dara couldn't focus. Silver stars were blossoming before his eyes, a horrible, paralyzing burn creeping through his body. He spasmed, writhing on the floor and trying to get his hand to obey him. The knife at his waist—if he could just . . .

A sandaled foot stomped hard on his wrist, and then Muntadhir was leaning over him, the emir's ruthless expression coming in broken pieces as he ripped the knife from Dara's hand. Distantly he heard another clap, a flash of light coming against the dark interior.

And then a white-hot burst of pain as Muntadhir plunged the knife into Dara's stomach.

"You were right, Lady ta Buzo," Muntadhir said, his voice flat. "I would never work with the people who killed my father."

From the corner of his eye, Dara watched Muntadhir flick open the teak chest. "I thank you for these," he added, running a hand over the weapons. "I'm glad to know we can still rely on the Ayaanle."

Amani bowed. "But of course, my emir." All traces of their enmity—of the stupid act Dara had fallen for—were gone. "Is there anything else you need?"

"Afshin!"

Kaveh. But Dara couldn't respond. He was frozen; whatever poison he'd been injected with made it feel as though he were watching all this from the prison of his own eyes.

"No, my lady," Muntadhir replied. "One of my men will take you back to your quarter. You should hurry."

Amani was gone the next moment, vanishing out the carriage. The wind snatched the door, pulling it wide open. Frozen rain pattered on Dara's face.

"Afshin!"

Dara managed to shift his head enough to see Kaveh. The grand wazir was surrounded by the other Daeva nobles. He looked terrified, his hands outstretched as if to ward them off. Gushtap was dead, his throat opened on the muddy street.

Muntadhir shoved the trunk of weapons out of the carriage. Dara heard it smash on the street, a cheer going up from the men.

He reached frantically for his magic, for his body, for *anything,* but the iron coursing through his blood had left him immobilized. Racked with pain, his body and mind disjointed, Dara could only witness the mob of noblemen fighting for weapons, Kaveh being dragged, bellowing in rage. And then other sounds. Awful, guttural rips and howls.

"Jamshid," Dara croaked. "His father. Don't—don't . . ." *Don't let him die like this.*

Muntadhir whirled on him, but the emotion on the emir's face wasn't the cruel vengeance Dara expected, but lost, dazed grief. The look of a man who'd been broken more thoroughly than Dara had realized and could no longer hide it.

"Jamshid is dead," Muntadhir whispered. "Ali is dead. Nahri is dead. We are all of us dead, because of you." He raised the short sword in his hands, leveling the point at Dara's heart.

There was a crack of thunder . . . and the entire carriage blew apart.

Dara saw flashing light, fire, and then hit the ground hard and saw nothing at all.

NAHRI

Nahri shoved the book in front of her aside. "Useless. This might as well be in Geziriyya."

Jamshid grabbed the text before it went tumbling to the ground. "Careful! That's two-thousand-year-old family history you're tossing around."

"It's two-thousand-year-old scribble to me." Nahri rubbed her temples, her head beginning to pound. "Every time I think I'm getting better at this . . ."

"You *are* getting better," Jamshid assured her. "By the Creator, Nahri, give yourself more than a couple of days to learn how to read an ancient dialect of Divasti known only to scholars."

"And former Temple acolytes," she grumbled. "*You* certainly don't seem to be having any problems."

"Queen Hatset did say she could put a call out for linguists."

"The only thing Hatset wants to find in these books is a way to magically compel Ali to stay in Ta Ntry forever. And I wouldn't trust Nahid secrets to any djinn she hires. No, this is on you and me alone."

"So me alone."

"You know, you've gotten very rude now that you know you're fallen royalty." Nahri lay back on her cushion to admire the carved coral ceiling above her. It was stunning, a masterpiece of geometry and art that spread out in intricate diamonds and whorls. Everything in Shefala's library was similarly beautiful. Though smaller than the vast cavern of books back in Daevabad's palace, the library was well stocked and elegant with soaring mahogany shelves and curved floor desks that allowed for small nooks of privacy beside the long windows. On sunny days, light streamed in, but with the approaching monsoon, the sky had darkened, and Nahri and Jamshid had resorted to well-guarded oil lamps. Banked fires kept the damp chill away, and save for their voices, the place was silent as a tomb.

Tomb might have been an accurate word, because it was difficult not to feel trapped. Jamshid and Nahri were guarded day and night, delivered to the library after a sunrise breakfast and staying through the evening. It was ostensibly their choice to spend every minute scouring the Nahid texts for ways to take down Manizheh and Dara, but it still felt too much like Daevabad. Nahri hated needing guards, but she feared the stares—both curious and hostile—of the castle's soldiers more.

Then perhaps you should protect yourself and marry the prince they all adore.

It was not the first time the thought had occurred to her. Hatset's offer had buried itself under Nahri's skin as it had most certainly been meant to. And Nahri hated it. She couldn't look at Ali, whose company she badly missed, without worrying about the whispers it would provoke. Without wondering whether Hatset had suggested such a marriage to *him*, and if he found himself just as torn between duty and politics and useless, messy feelings.

"Oh . . . oh, this is interesting," Jamshid said, excitement rising in his voice.

Happy to be pulled from her thoughts, Nahri sat up. "Does it tell us how to immobilize overly powerful Afshin warriors and restore magic to the entire djinn world?"

Jamshid's face fell. He'd long abandoned his serious scholar pose of sitting at the desk and was now lying on his stomach, propped up on bent elbows. "Well, no. But it mentions that the Nahids were beginning to have trouble controlling the marid and traveling through the lake." He frowned. "It says the marid asked to be released, but that doesn't make sense. We weren't controlling them. The stories say they helped Anahid build the city and brought tribute, but . . ."

"Dear brother, if there is anything I have learned since summoning a daeva, it's that those in power have a rather biased view of how they treat the people who 'bring' them tribute."

"Fair point." Jamshid glanced up with a grin. "I like when you call me that. Awful, *awful* extenuating circumstances aside, I'm glad to have learned of at least one secret relative." He sighed. "Though the fight I'm going to have with my father when I see him again . . ."

You will answer for the choice you just made. Not tonight. Not to me . . . but you will answer. Kaveh's words played in Nahri's memory—the threat he'd voiced after she refused to lure Ali to his death to save Jamshid.

Her throat caught. "I'm sure."

Jamshid glanced down at his book and then blanched. "Suleiman's eye . . . apparently they stopped traveling through the lake because Nahids who tried ended up washing up on the beach with their body parts rearranged—sometimes still *alive*. It says the water was entirely cursed shortly after, and that was the last time anyone heard from the marid." He turned the page. "Oh. There's a drawing. How . . . thorough."

Nahri held her tongue. *Another secret.* She hadn't spoken to Ali about the marid since they arrived in Ta Ntry—mostly because she was avoiding him, but she wasn't spilling his most dangerous secret, not even to her brother.

She changed the subject. "I wonder if that's how we ended up in Egypt. If I unknowingly transported Ali and myself using the lake's magic."

"It might have been, if Egypt was on your mind," Jamshid said distractedly. He turned another page, handling the delicate parchment as though it were the wing of a butterfly. "I still can't believe these books have been here all this time. When I think of the good they could have done back in Daevabad, actually being read and studied in the Grand Temple instead of being locked up to gather dust . . ." He shook his head, bitterness creasing his face. "What *else* doesn't our tribe know about its history and culture because our enemies robbed us of our heritage?"

"Probably a lot."

Jamshid sat up, quickly glancing at the door. "Then can I ask you something?" When Nahri nodded, he continued. "Are you sure, really sure, that we're going down the right path?"

"Jamshid, we've discussed this. And you agreed—"

"I didn't. I said that I'd listen, and I'm trying, Nahri. I'm really trying. But every day we're locked in here like prisoners, and I read about our stolen past . . ." He turned to her, his eyes seeking understanding. "You are the cleverest person I know, and I trust you. But when I look at our guards, I see Ghassan's thugs. I see soldiers who broke into Daeva homes and beat Daeva men when they were drunk and didn't like the look of someone passing them on the street."

"And do you not think they feel the same? That some of them look at *us* and see the 'fire worshippers' who murdered their friends in the Citadel? This was never going to be easy."

"I know, but . . ." Jamshid ran his hands over his face. "My whole life, I never imagined there could be anything different. The Daevas had been crushed by the Qahtanis for centuries before I was born. It would continue for centuries after. It was inevitable. Even Muntadhir—the man I loved, who I prayed might be kinder—was getting pulled into it. And now?" he whispered. "It's under Daeva rule again. Like it was in the glory age of these books. It feels like maybe we're fools to consider undoing that."

A chill raced down Nahri's back. "It wasn't a glory age for everyone, Jamshid. You speak as though there are only djinn and Daevas in Daevabad. What about the shafit? How do you think *they* feel about a Nahid ruling over them, about the Scourge of Qui-zi returning?"

"It's not like the last few Qahtani kings treated them much better."

"Yes, but a central tenet of their religion didn't teach that they were vermin."

Now her brother looked openly annoyed. "That's not what our texts teach. I'm not going to pretend we don't have bigots willing to twist our faith, that there are plenty of Daevas who look down upon the shafit, but Creator, sometimes . . ."

"Sometimes what? *What?*" Nahri demanded when he trailed off.

"Sometimes you sound just as angry as them, okay?" Jamshid seemed embarrassed but continued. "And I understand, I do. I know you grew up in the human world, and you're close to Subha—"

"You understand nothing."

Jamshid blinked, looking taken aback by the fury Nahri couldn't keep out of her voice. But not for long. "Then maybe you could *tell* me? It feels like you're keeping all these secrets, like you still don't trust me."

I don't. And that made Nahri feel awful. But she could barely breathe right now. She didn't have it in her to personally walk her brother through dismantling whatever prejudices he still held toward the shafit, while managing everything else tearing up her life.

"I think I'm done for the day," she announced. "I'm not feeling well."

"I . . . all right." Jamshid sighed. It was obvious they both knew she was lying. "Why don't I stay here and keep reading so I don't bother you?"

Nahri gritted her teeth, fighting back a sarcastic response. *You wanted a family.* Now she had one, thorns and all. "Fine. Then I'll see you at dinner."

29

ALI

Ali examined the silver coins in his palm. "And these are the coins you were given?" he asked the shafit carpenter in front of him.

"The very ones, my prince." The carpenter gestured angrily at a pair of djinn across from him: a Sahrayn ship captain and his Ayaanle trading partner. "My people and I worked from dawn until dusk on their sandship, and the bastards still cheated me."

Ali chipped a coin with his nail, a few silver flakes breaking off to reveal the copper beneath. "Paint?" he asked, giving the traders an annoyed look. "Really?"

The Ayaanle merchant crossed his arms. "Copper is the rate for shafit laborers anyway."

"Wages don't vary based on your nonsense ideas about blood. Not in Shefala." Ali put the coins back in the small cloth sack. "Where is the rest of the money you owe them?"

The merchant glowered. "We don't have it right now."

"Alas, then you don't have a ship either." Ali glanced at Fiza, who stood beside him. "Captain . . . surely there are ways to ensure a ship doesn't leave our coast until its debts are paid?"

She grinned wickedly. "I can think of a few."

"Then it's settled. The ship stays here until you've paid your workers, with an additional dirham for every day the pair of you delay." Ali glanced at the carpenter. "Does that sound fair?"

The carpenter still looked upset but nodded. "Yes. Thank you, Prince Alizayd."

"I'm happy to help."

He and Fiza left, winding through the forest of boats dragged up on the sand for repairs. Their variety was a marvel to behold: sandships and luminescent mirrored glass skiffs sitting alongside human dhows with intricately carved wooden prows and a small dugout loaded with fishing nets. The beach was the most crowded Ali had seen; it was an overcast day, and he supposed people were taking advantage of the cool weather to work and prepare their boats for the coming monsoon rains.

"So how many meetings left today?" Fiza asked conversationally. "Fifty? Sixty?"

"I've stopped counting," Ali replied. Word had spread like wildfire that he and Nahri were in Shefala looking for allies interested in taking back and building a new kind of Daevabad. But for every new arrival who seemed earnest, there was another digging for money, a future post, or score-settling, and it was as maddening as it was time-consuming. Their people were at war, tens of thousands at the mercy of Manizheh and Dara, and yet here Ali was, spending hours settling unrelated squabbles just to get this clan or another to join his side.

Then declare yourself king and command them, his mother's voice whispered in his head. Though Ali hadn't exactly jumped up on the minbar and announced the dissolution of the nobility—despite what Hatset thought, he *was* taking this slow—he'd made clear no one would be forced to fight. He was careful to speak of what they were pulling together as a rescue mission instead of just another war of conquest; a mission to save their kin, restore their magic, and shape a new kind of future for Daevabad. He'd kept to his mornings at the mosque, trying to gently lay out some of his ideas and make sure he was accessible to those who wanted to speak with him.

It turned out there were many people who wanted to speak to him. *Many.* And though Fiza and Wajed were helping Ali as much as they could, his grandfather's mind wandered, and Ali and his mother had remained in a testy détente since their argument in the library. Hatset was offering material support and shelter—and providing the public perception that all was well between them—but she wouldn't speak with him until he promised to declare himself king. "You want my counsel?" she'd asked. "I have given it. Stop acting like a starry-eyed fool and be the man your name implies."

As for Nahri, they'd barely spoken. She spent all her time in the library with Jamshid and seemed exhausted and distant when he did track her down. "I'm just tired," she insisted when Ali had finally broken the other evening and begged to know what he had done wrong. "*You* try spending all day attempting to decipher ancient texts while being glared at by soldiers."

He and Fiza emerged from the thicket of boats, climbing the sandy slope that led back to the town. With every step Ali took away from the ocean, he could feel it entreating him back, making him yearn for the touch of the surf twining around his ankles, the promised ease of floating in the warm, buoyant water and letting his muscles unwind.

Not a chance. Ali hadn't set as much as a toe in the sea since arriving in Shefala, and he had no intention of doing so anytime soon.

"It's going to rain," Fiza said, tugging him from his thoughts. She was looking at the gray sky with open displeasure. "I hate the monsoon. That much water should not fall from the sky."

But Ali's attention was still on the boats crowding the beach. "I wish I had a navy," he mused.

"Excuse me, you wish you had a what?"

"A navy. Or perhaps that's not the right word." Ali's crash course in sailing down the Nile aside, he knew little about ships. "A fleet, then, like the one Zaydi was said to have brought to Daevabad's lake. With ships and djinn from all over the magical world."

"And how long did it take Zaydi to assemble such a fleet?"

"Decades," Ali admitted. "But still, could you imagine such a thing?"

"Alizayd, I'm learning your grasp on reality isn't the firmest, but you do know there's no way to simply conjure up a hundred ships, sail them to dozens of different djinn ports, convince people to follow you, and then arrive in a landlocked lake, yes?"

He shrugged. "Oh, I don't know. I once convinced the most fearsome, cunning pirate on the Ntaran coast to mutiny."

Fiza broke off a twig and threw it at his head. "You didn't convince me of anything. I took advantage of your desperation."

"What if I put you in charge? You could be an admiral."

"The only thing more unlikely than you getting your hands on a fleet is thinking you'd get that many djinn to take orders from a shafit criminal."

Ali clucked his tongue. "You underestimate yourself. Your crew greatly admires you, and you've got an excellent mind for details and management—"

Fiza groaned. "Was another man complimenting me so, I'd think he was trying to get in my bed, but you're worse—you're trying to properly recruit me now, aren't you?"

"Is it working?"

"No." They passed under a pair of shade trees. It really did suddenly seem so much darker, slivers of bruise-colored sky visible beyond the leafy canopy. As if to mock Fiza's earlier comment, it began to drizzle. "I'm only here because your mother's kitchens are incredible, and Nahri still needs to find a way to get this out of my neck." She yanked down her collar, revealing the metal snake below her skin.

Ali didn't buy Fiza's indifference. "Every time I see that brand, it makes me angry. It must make you furious." He turned to address her properly. "Fiza, I know someone like me has little right to ask you to risk your life, but—"

A spike of pain cracked his skull.

Ali gasped, falling to his knees. He reached for his head, and his fingers came away wet—but with rainwater, not blood. It felt like he'd been hit with a hammer, every beat of his heart sending a new ache thudding through his temple.

"Aye, are you all right?" Fiza asked.

Ali winced. "I think something hit me." He touched the spot again. Though it felt like he'd been struck across the brow, oddly enough the pain now felt . . . deeper, throbbing in waves beneath his skull.

"I don't see anything." When Ali didn't reply, she knelt at his side. "You don't look right. Should I get Nahri?"

"I . . ." But Ali was having trouble putting words together. He was shivering now, sweat breaking out across his face as the rain began to fall harder. The pain in his head was lessening, replaced by a drumming buzz underneath his damp skin. Each raindrop seemed to ping against something inside him, as though Ali were the surface of a pond, the light patter rippling across him.

I had a pain in my head like this once—moments before the lake rose to swallow the Citadel. "Fiza," he whispered, "we need to get those people off the beach."

Without warning, the rain turned drenching. The wind

howled, tearing at Ali's robe and pulling him in the direction of the sea. Below he could hear sailors cursing and running to secure ropes and tools.

Fiza hauled him to his feet, ignoring his protests. "Forget the beach. I'm taking you to your Nahid."

But they'd only just gone around the bend when it became very clear the direction of the castle offered no refuge.

The western sky was a cauldron, storm clouds churning and boiling like foam on an unwatched pot. The land was going darker by the moment, as though someone had upset a great well of black ink across the horizon.

"The monsoon rains," Ali asked, "are they supposed to look like that?"

Fiza had paled. "No." She turned around and then abruptly let go of him. "Your eyes . . ." Horror swept her expression. "There's something wrong with them."

"My eyes?" On instinct, Ali went to touch his face, but the sight of his hands stopped him. Tendrils of water were dancing over his fingers. It looked like the kind of marid magic Ali himself used to summon.

But Ali wasn't doing this.

No. Oh, no. "Fiza," he said, dread washing over him. *Run.*

But Ali didn't get to finish the word. A presence burst into his head, both alien and terribly familiar. It seized him, *stole* him, and then without willing his limbs to move, Ali grabbed Fiza by the arm and smashed her against the nearest tree.

She crumpled to the ground, blood running down her face and mingling with the rain.

"YOU BETTER NOT BE DEAD," THE MARID WARNED, speaking through Ali's mouth and eyeing the mortal girl lying still in the grass. "My people grow weary of these debts." They tossed a leafy branch over the girl's body to better conceal her. One could never take too many precautions.

The marid closed the eyes of the djinn they'd taken, ignoring the whispers of the wind trying to tempt them back to the clouds. They'd been sent to investigate *other* whispers, the sightings of worried creek sprites and gossiping ocean swells.

And so they did, plunging into the djinn's memories.

It didn't take long. Not when the first vision of Sobek was the river lord charging out of the Nile to protect two mortals who should have meant nothing. Not when the notoriously cold crocodile so determinedly coached one of the mortals through seizing a current and then warned him to flee, genuine alarm in his ancient, brutal visage.

"Oh, cousin," the monsoon marid murmured as they bit down on the djinn's lip, tasting his blood. "What have you done?"

30

NAHRI

Nahri berated herself as she made her way back to her room.

You naive little fool. Did you really think that because you call him "brother" now, all differences between you would be erased? Jamshid was a Daeva noble who'd spent a decade in the Temple and believed up until a few months ago that simply speaking with a shafit was forbidden. He was Kaveh's son—God only knew what kind of things he'd grown up hearing.

What he still quietly believed.

If you continue lying to him, he's not going to be inclined to think well of you or the shafit either. Nahri stomped up the stairs. She was so very tired of secrets.

The corridor was dark when she emerged from the stairwell, rain lashing the open balustrade and the sky thick with purpling clouds. A pair of women were chatting excitedly in Ntaran by the windows, looking out at the storm, but they fell abruptly silent when they spotted Nahri and hurried away.

Loneliness sliced through her. *I want to go home.* But both of her homes were very far away, neither offering a safe or easy return.

Her room was dark when she entered, cold and unguarded—Nahri was not expected back yet, and the lamps hadn't been lit. The only light came from the makeshift fire altar she and Jamshid had cobbled together in one corner, glowing steadily against the wild storm outside . . . as well as the storm *inside*. The balcony door had blown open, and half the room was drenched, with more waves of rain batting through.

"Didn't have to deal with monsoons in Cairo," Nahri muttered, crossing to assess the damage. She unpinned the cowrie shell clip holding her shayla in place, tossing the silk scarf to a dry spot on the bed and shaking out her hair. The delicate scarf was a recent gift from Hatset, probably a reminder of what *else* Nahri could get if she agreed to marry Ali and set up a kingdom in Ta Ntry. But if Hatset thought Nahri too principled to take fancy gifts without following through on the attached strings, well, that was her mistake.

Nahri froze at the foot of her bed. She wasn't alone.

"*Ali?*" she asked, shocked to see Ali standing on her balcony in the pouring rain. He had his back to her and was soaked to the bone, his hands spread on the railing like he was surveying some sort of kingdom of the drowned. "What are you doing here? What are you doing *there*?"

He didn't turn around. "I wanted to see you and got caught in the rain. I figured that I might as well enjoy it."

"You're going to drown standing up."

Ali's eyes were still closed, but he turned just enough that Nahri could see the side of his mouth curve in a grin. "Always so worried about me."

"Someone has to be. You court death with far too much persistence."

"Considering how you've been avoiding me, I'm surprised to hear you mind such courtship."

Nahri flinched. The remark was more acerbic than usual, but also deserved—she had been avoiding him.

"I'm sorry," she apologized. "It's complicated." She looked at Ali again, still standing in the rain. "But it's good to see you," she admitted, some of her loneliness lifting. "Don't let it go to your head, but, Creator forgive me, I think I've actually missed your company."

"Then join me."

"No, thank you. I've had enough of water for several life-times."

Ali lifted his hands as if to embrace the storm, tilting his face to the sky. "Come on, Banu Nahida," he teased. "Live a little." His eyes were still shut, and the rain had soaked through his white dishdasha, making it cling to the broad line of his shoulders and the planes of his back. Ali's head and feet were bare, water streaming over his closely shaved hair and glistening as it coursed down the nape of his neck.

He looked beautiful, standing there against the storm-churned sky. He *was* beautiful—that was something she'd thought even from the first day they'd met and she'd wanted to shove him in the canal. But it had been a distant fact, the same way she might admire a lovely sunset.

Nahri wasn't thinking about Ali like a sunset right now. She had a very sudden desire to touch him, to trace the path of the rain running down his body and see what he did in response.

He's smitten with you. Damn Hatset and her poisonous, lingering words. But linger they had, going to a part of herself Nahri had buried when she signed her betrothal contract long ago, binding her life to a fiancé who'd spat at her feet.

What *might* it be like to be with a person who was smitten with her?

For Muntadhir certainly hadn't been, even if his hatred had faded by the time they were finally married. They'd slept together, and Nahri had enjoyed it—she would challenge anyone upon whom her husband turned his well-practiced talents to remain indifferent—but it had been transactional. There was nothing of the sweet fumblings about which she'd overheard blushing new brides whisper, or the laughing, scandalous advice of older married women. Muntadhir had been in Nahri's bed because his family had defeated hers, and his father wanted a Nahid grandchild.

And that had been enough to smother any inklings she'd had of desire or affection. But now Ghassan was dead, and Nahri was no longer a prisoner in Daevabad. And in the dark hush of the room—with only Ali and the storm for company—she suddenly wondered how it might feel to let it all crash down. To take the initiative she'd been both too proud and too vulnerable to seize with the husband she'd always known didn't really want her. To explore and to touch and to shake with mirrored longing.

Stop. Nahri was still a prisoner after all, married to Muntadhir, under Hatset's thumb, and surrounded by enemies. She had only one person who she trusted, and she could not conceive of a more spectacular way to blow that up than to indulge in her current line of thinking.

Even so, she walked over to the balcony, stopping at the doors and sticking a hand out just far enough to catch a couple of drops. "There. I've joined you."

Ali didn't seem to notice her sarcasm. "These rains travel so far," he mused. "Over the mountains and plains, the islands, and the great ocean of Tiamat. Can you imagine taking that journey year after year, for millennia? Eons? All the things you would see. My, you might even fly to Daevabad's lake on those clouds."

"I can't say I can put myself in the mind of a traveling raindrop, no."

Ali swished a hand over the wet railing, sending a spray of water to the garden below. "Imagine it being disrupted, then. A routine you'd kept since the dawn of time suddenly denied the sweet embrace that once ended it."

The sweet embrace? "Ali, forgive the question, but have you been drinking?"

The sound of his laughter mingled with the rain lashing against the castle walls. "Maybe I'm trying to loosen up."

Without warning, he grabbed her wrist, pulling her to his side. Nahri yelped in outrage, instantly soaked to her skin. The balcony had flooded, water rushing over her slippers.

"This is supposed to be enjoyable?" she yelled over the sound of the pouring rain, blinking madly. "I can barely see!"

"So close your eyes."

The wind whipped through her wet hair, and Nahri gave the ground an uneasy look. Rain rushed by in gushing torrents of red-brown mud. It wasn't that far a drop, but a fall would hurt, and the balcony's railing was low.

"I don't want to close my eyes. We're high up, and it's slippery. I don't need to trip and go flying—"

"I won't let you trip." Ali's hands circled her waist, pulling her close. "Trust that I want you here."

Every inappropriate thought Nahri had had in the bedroom came surging back. She could feel the heat of his hands through her soaked dress, her heart hammering against her chest. Startled, she glanced up, looking to see some sort of explanation in his face.

Nothing. Ali's eyes were still closed, the same oddly playful—and deeply out of character—smile on his rain-dotted lips. He looked more at ease than Nahri had ever seen him.

He looked inviting.

He's not the only one who's ever looked inviting. Six years ago, Nahri had kissed a handsome warrior just beyond the pouring rain on a whim, giving in to a wave of desire. And what resulted between them had nearly destroyed her.

"We should go back inside," Nahri blurted out. "And then leave. My bedroom, I mean. We should leave my bedroom. People will talk."

A pout twisted his face, and now Nahri really did wonder if someone had spiked his drink—Alizayd al Qahtani did not *pout*.

"I do not wish to leave." He leaned down to whisper in her ear, his breath warm on her neck. "I am very content here with you."

Alarm sparked through her. As undeniably pleasant as the unspooling of heat was in her belly, there was something clearly wrong with her friend. "I don't think we should . . ." Nahri tried to disentangle herself.

Ali's grip tightened.

If something seemed wrong before, the fact that he didn't let her go sent warning bells ringing in her mind. This was not the man she knew. "Ali, let me go."

He laughed, but there was no warmth in the sound now. "No, I do not think I will." He dropped his head and then finally opened his eyes.

They were a churning mirror of the storm-dark monsoon sky. Nahri instantly tried to jerk away. "Marid," she whispered.

Ali let out a giggle that was almost childish. "Oh, but I had you!" He held Nahri out, his wild eyes taking her in. "My, you are *lovely*. Sobek's exact type. Whatever agreement he had with your kin must have been very strong for him not to have snapped you right up," he said, clicking his teeth.

"Let me go," she demanded, trying to wrench free. "What have you done to Ali?"

He rolled his eyes. "Your Ali is fine. Well, no, he is not. He is screaming and begging me not to hurt you." Ali—whatever was in Ali—suddenly paused, cocking his head as if listening to a hidden voice. "What an unnecessarily vicious threat, mortal." He shoved a hand in Nahri's hair, yanking her close again. "He really is besotted with you, you know. He has wanted this for so long, aching to touch you, to taste you—" He pushed her away. "The irony is rich enough for one of the stories your people like to spin."

Nahri fell hard to the floor, splashing against the flooded stone. "Let him go."

Ali grinned, but it wasn't his smile. It was malevolent and twisted, and it shattered her to see it on his face. "Give me your name, daughter of Anahid, and I'll be gone from him in the next breath. Take me to your Daevabad, let me sink its filthy streets below the water, and I'll return you both to Cairo, wipe your memories of magic, and let you live as happy little mortals in your apothecary. It's what you really want, isn't it?" His voice rose in a high-pitched copy of hers. "*We could have a life here together, Ali. A good one.*"

More fury than shame boiled in her. Nahri shoved herself back to her feet. "Who are you?" she demanded.

Indigo-colored swells blossomed and faded in his eyes, reflecting the roiling clouds. "I am the marid of the monsoon," he explained, touching his fingers in a mocking attempt at the Daeva blessing. "An early monsoon this season, for I am also the most loyal servant of Tiamat, and she has sent me to discover just who has been causing our people so many problems."

It was raining so hard that Nahri must have missed the sound of the door opening, but suddenly she heard Jamshid's muffled voice, calling from the bedroom.

"Nahri? Nahri, listen, I know you probably don't want to talk to me, but—"

Ali was at her side in a flash. He seized her arm, pressed a knife—one of Fiza's—to her throat, and then stepped with her into the bedroom.

Her brother froze.

"Shut your mouth," the marid said coldly. "Close the door and come in, or I'll cut her throat."

Jamshid kicked the door shut and then stalked over, his gaze burning. "I'm going to kill you."

Nahri tried to object. "It's not—"

The marid clapped a hand over her mouth. "You'll forgive your sister," he said. "Poor girl's had such a difficult past few months."

Jamshid glared. "What do you want, al Qahtani?"

The knife pressed closer to her throat. "I want you to kill yourself."

Jamshid's eyes went wide. "Excuse me?"

"Kill yourself. Take a running dive off the balcony, and I'll let her go. You were willing to die for my brother. Certainly you'd make the same sacrifice for your sister."

Jamshid shook his head, looking more horrified now than angry. "You've lost your mind."

"No, I've lost my home and seen my kin enslaved." The marid abruptly released her, raising Ali's arms as if to admire them. "And an old cousin has done something *very* foolish in a half-hearted attempt at mercy."

Nahri scrambled away. "There's a marid possessing him."

Jamshid grabbed her. "A *marid*?"

Ali clucked his tongue. "She's been keeping a lot of secrets from you." His alien gaze turned to her. "Shall we tell him the other one?"

No. "Please," she begged.

His expression grew vicious. "We begged too, once, but your ancestors did not care." He tilted his head. "Well, some of your ancestors. The human ones had nothing to do with it—they were likely living their simple lives along your Nile, worshipping Sobek."

"Who the hell is *Sobek*?" Jamshid sounded utterly baffled. "And what human ones? What are you talking about?"

Ali grinned at Nahri as though they were in on some great joke together. "I suppose you were the one to get your mother's cleverness." He turned back to Jamshid, slowing his speech like he might have been talking to a child. "Your sister is a . . . what is the word your people use? 'Dirt-blood' sounds so cruel."

Jamshid's gaze darted to hers. "Wait . . . you're *shafit*?" And then Nahri saw it, her brother connecting the dots—the regret, the pity Nahri had never wanted to watch fill his eyes. "Oh, Nahri . . ."

The marid was cackling. "Surprise!"

But if the marid had thought to divide them with that revelation, he'd clearly picked the wrong brother. Jamshid pushed her firmly behind him in the direction of the door. "Nahri, run. I'll handle this."

"*Run?*" The marid sounded disappointed. "I was really hoping for far more of a fight. Anahid would have ripped me from this body by now and sent me fleeing into the clouds. A shame you broke her magic."

The goading in his voice was the last straw. "Surely you didn't disrupt your ten-thousand-year-old voyage across the ocean just to toy with a bunch of mortals," Nahri accused. "So why don't you just tell us what you want?"

"I want you dead," the marid replied, and in Ali's sincere voice, the words cut even deeper. "I want every one of you who carries fire in their veins dead, and I want your city destroyed. Alas, my people cannot seem to accomplish those goals without making it worse for ourselves."

"Maybe you're not as clever as you think."

The marid abruptly turned the knife inward, pressing the point against Ali's throat. Nahri tried to lurch for him, but Jamshid held her back.

"And maybe I am. Careful, Nahid," the marid warned. "You forget I see what he has lived through. I know how to hurt you."

"Is that the point of this, then? To hurt us?"

"Oh no. I was sent to investigate the strange happenings in the waters of this land and why it was my cousin Sobek refused our summons." The marid dragged the knife down Ali's neck. A thin line of glistening blood traced the blade's path—it was killing Nahri not to grab it out of his hands. "Torturing two Nahids is mere enjoyment."

He smashed the hilt of the knife into Ali's face. Blood burst from his nose.

"Help!" the marid bellowed. "*Guards!*"

Any hope that the soldiers who constantly shadowed Jamshid had decided to take a coffee break vanished the moment the doors burst inward, two armed men charging in.

The guards' eyes went wide, darting between Nahri, standing disheveled with her hair loose near the bed, a bleeding Ali, and a visibly enraged Daeva brother.

"Prince Alizayd!"

Ali pointed wildly at Jamshid. "The fire worshipper attacked me. I want him dead!"

Nahri lunged forward. "That's not true!"

"Kill him!" the marid shrieked. "Kill—" And then Ali let out a strangled cry, falling to his knees. A squall-colored mist burst from his skin, and then a hint of familiar gray dashed across his eyes.

"*Nahri,*" Ali said, choking out her name. "The river," he gasped. "The creek. S-Sobek. Get So—" His words turned into a bloodcurdling scream, his back arching as the mist dashed back into his body.

When Ali looked at her again, it was with the hate-filled gaze of the monsoon marid.

Thunder crashed in Nahri's ears, a gust of wind bursting

into the room and drenching them all. The rain pelted her, hard enough to hurt. The guards cried out, Jamshid moved to protect her . . .

But Nahri wasn't wasting another minute.

She ran, knocking aside her brother's hand and dodging the marid when he lunged for her. Nahri didn't stop running until she was on the balcony, and then she jumped over the railing and launched herself into the air.

NAHRI CRASHED TO THE GROUND. THOUGH LEAPING out of mansions was not a new experience, it had been years, and she bumbled the landing, crumpling painfully on one ankle in the slippery mud.

But with the marid roaring behind her, a howl that sounded nothing like her friend, she pushed on, jumping to her feet and fleeing into the forest. Branches and vines tore at her face, her slippers instantly shredded.

The sounds of pursuing feet came from behind her, barely audible against her ragged breathing. Ali made no other noise, and Nahri suddenly felt horribly hunted and outmatched, like a doomed gazelle fleeing a lion. Just ahead was the swollen creek, rushing red with mud and rain. She sprinted for it.

The marid caught her. They crashed to the flooded bank, Ali landing on top of her.

"Oh no, Nahid," the marid said. "This we do together. For I too am rather eager to see Sobek." He pulled free the knife. "So if you don't mind . . ."

He dragged the blade down her palm, breaking the skin. Nahri held back a cry of pain, refusing to give the marid the satisfaction as he yanked her bleeding hand away from her chest, shoving it underwater.

"*SOBEK!*" He spat the blood flowing from Ali's nose into the creek. "Your mortals call!"

There was no response. The rain lashed Nahri's face, the marid holding her so hard it hurt. She tried to wrench away, and his hand went to her throat, pushing her head closer to the surging water. The creek tugged viciously at her hair.

"What do you think would make him come faster?" the marid purred. "If I drowned you or if I shoved a blade through the heart of his little hatchling?"

"Nahri!" Jamshid had caught up, rushing from the castle gardens to join her.

Everything went very cold.

Below her, the creek chilled, flattened, and then stilled so completely that it might have been an untouched lake deep below the earth. The monsoon marid loosened his grip enough that Nahri scrambled free, crawling backward across the scrubby bank as something stirred in the mists billowing above the creek. She saw the outline of a reptilian head, dark scales, and glowing eyes.

A kind of primal terror Nahri had never known—not when glimpsing her first hint of the supernatural in a Cairo cemetery, not when facing down a fiery ifrit—rushed through her as the largest crocodile she had ever seen rose up before them. More mist shrouded it, circulating as if in devotion, and then the crocodile shifted, taking on the appearance of a youth with green skin and eerie dappled yellow-and-black eyes.

The creature—Sobek, Nahri realized, remembering what Ali had told her about the Nile marid—appraised each of them in turn, his head and neck darting like a snake selecting a meal.

His gaze settled on Ali, and he charged.

Ali barely swayed when Sobek thrust his hands at his chest. Instead, the squall burst again from his back with a hiss and the smell of fresh rain, and then Ali collapsed at Sobek's feet.

But the monsoon marid didn't leave. Thunder shook the ground, lightning splitting the sky as the rain condensed, shifting and darting like a wave to loom over Sobek and Ali. It wasn't the river monster the Gozan had turned into, but it was still intimidating.

It had nothing on Sobek, however. Nahri squinted, trying to get the image of the Nile marid to stay solid in her mind, but it was impossible. He carried himself with a speed and lethal grace that made Dara look slow, a low rumbling growl coming from his throat that caused every hair on the back of her neck to stand on end. The air smelled of blood, of mud on sunbaked scales.

Jamshid had made it to her side. "Suleiman's eye," he gasped, staring at the pair of dueling marid.

Ali rose to his knees. He retched murky water and then, with a wail, staggered to his feet and rushed the monsoon marid. His knife sliced uselessly through the rainy form.

Cruel laughter filled the air. No, not the air. Nahri's *head,* like a voice inside her mind. And then words as well, in hissing syllables that pieced themselves together.

Your spawn has your temper, Sobek. A pity you did not teach him to protect himself.

Sobek grabbed Ali by the arm and shoved him back, knocking him into the brush. "He is not your concern. Return to the clouds."

More thunder cracked the sky. Nahri jumped, Jamshid's grip tightening on her arm.

He is our concern, you arrogant fool! You consumed his memories; you know what has happened. We are in debt to the Nahids' champion because of your mistake!

"It was not I who chose to test the boundaries by killing one daeva with another," Sobek hissed. "That was a reckless decision. Had they taken the time to consider his blood—"

You swore they were dead! You promised the Blessed One herself it was done!

"And it *was* done. Tiamat knows. She feasted on the memory!"

Ali climbed back to his feet, putting his hands out as if to steady himself. He was a bloody wreck, his soaked clothes hanging in rags, his nose swollen. "What's going on, Sobek?"

Take him, the monsoon marid demanded. *You should have taken him the moment you realized what he was. Give him to Tiamat, beg for mercy, and pray the gift of Anahid's ring saves your soul.*

"No," Sobek insisted. "He has fulfilled his ancestor's bargain. He has taken the ring from the Nahids and their city."

He desires to give it right back!

Nahri wrenched free of Jamshid. She'd had enough of being spoken over by two sniping water demons.

"Your people aren't supposed to interfere with mine," she reminded them, stepping between Ali and the two marid. "Remember? This is *definitely* interfering, and at this point, I'm ready to take my chances calling that Nahid champion you're all so frightened of. Leave."

It was a lie, but both marid drew back—well, the cloud undulated.

But then the monsoon marid rushed forward, an icy, wet chill brushing over her skin. *You bluff. You think yourself clever, and yet you've turned on your own blood to protect an instrument meant to destroy you.*

"That is *enough,*" Sobek declared. "Tiamat's envoy will be leaving now." He returned his glare to the monsoon marid. "I will handle this."

You have handled nothing. Our patience is gone, Sobek. You and your daeva pet are to submit yourself to Tiamat by the next risen tide.

The Nile marid growled. "She does not command me."

The other marid rippled through the air as though laughing. *River lord, do you believe the Blessed One would have sent me to beg? You and your hatchling* will *submit yourselves, or she will come personally to this land and pluck him away.*

Sobek immediately stilled, his entire demeanor changing.

"She would not. There are tens of thousands of mortals on this coast. We are not permitted to hurt—"

The cold laughter again. *But we are, don't you see? He is ours, and we are permitted to hurt him. It is his decision whether to remain among so very many potential victims.*

Ali rocked back on his feet. "What does that mean?"

But the monsoon marid's foggy presence was already rising. *I have delivered our message. Were you wise, Sobek, you would heed it. Give yourselves to Tiamat by the next risen tide, or see this land devoured.*

In the next second, the monsoon marid was gone. The sky lightened by a fraction, but the rain stayed steady, pattering on the leaves and ground around them.

Ali's face was ashen. "They . . . they cannot do that. Surely they cannot do that."

Sobek moved for him. "You will come with me."

Nahri stepped between them. "No, he won't. What does that *mean*, that Tiamat will devour the land?"

Sobek's eyes pinned hers, and it took everything Nahri had in her not to crumble. Yet she couldn't look away from his petrifying, beautiful face. She wanted to move closer as much as she wanted to flee, suddenly seeing herself dragged beneath muddy water, feeling teeth break through her flesh.

"It *means* that if he is here, a wave higher than your Pyramids is going drown this entire coast by morning." Sobek spun on Ali with a snarl. "I tried to warn you. I told you to run to your deserts, to avoid my kind!"

"You told me I had a place in my world and should return to it," Ali shot back, sounding just as enraged. "That's not a warning. Had you said, 'attracting their attention will result in an ocean demon killing tens of thousands,' maybe I would have acted differently!"

Tens of thousands. By God. Nahri stared at the arguing pair, trying to wrap her head around the enormity of the threat. She probably should have told Ali to shut up, to stop fighting with the literal lord of the Nile as if this were some family feud.

A family feud.

"Why did it call him kin?" Nahri demanded, praying she was wrong. Praying the instincts that usually served her so well were wildly off the mark.

Ali stopped yelling at Sobek, glancing at her like she'd lost her mind. "What?"

Sobek growled, flashing dagger-sharp teeth. "This does not concern you, Nahid."

No. Oh no. But Nahri could see it, the puzzle piece that had been missing falling into place with the others she already knew. The water that had healed Ali's stab wounds long before the marid on Daevabad's lake ever touched him. The marid's careful plans to kill Dara with another daeva falling apart, creating the weapon they feared—the weapon they couldn't touch.

The weapon Ali hadn't been able to touch.

Sobek's hatchling, Sobek's spawn. The words the monsoon marid had flung at Ali hadn't just been insults.

Ali was looking between them. "What? What is it?"

Nahri couldn't speak. Her mouth was dry, her mind shouting a conclusion that should have been impossible. One that could fracture their world and devastate the man before her, the man she'd tried so hard to protect.

And yet they had promised to be honest with each other.

"You're marid," she whispered. She didn't know how else to say it because she could not put words like "family" and "kin" between the Ali she knew and the fog-shrouded crocodile wraith glaring at her. "You're *his.*"

The slow ripple of horror across Ali's face was a terrible thing to witness.

"I'm not," Ali stammered. "That's impossible. That's *ridiculous*." But his voice broke with emotion—Nahri could see him putting together the same pieces she had. "I have ancestors. Djinn ancestors! Sobek . . ." He whirled on the silent marid. "Tell her that's impossible."

The Nile marid shifted in the mists, the glistening scales vanishing beneath his skin and leaving him looking slightly less reptilian. When he finally spoke, his voice had softened to the quiet murmur of a gentle stream, water still relentless enough to cave in its banks and destroy its own foundation.

"I have seen much violence in the mortal lands I divide," he began. "I have watched how they fight, how they plot. How a walled city seen to be safe might be compromised." His unearthly eyes blinked, the irises flickering. "I could not directly attack Anahid and her ilk. So I created a breach."

"A breach?" Ali had gone gray.

Sobek hissed. "You have seen my memories, Alizayd al Qahtani. You know how Anahid stole our lake and forced our people into servitude. I narrowly escaped, but I found new daevas in the lands along my river as well. They were transformed; frail, frightened things trying to make sense of their new world. Closer to humans, to the mortal brides I was used to.

"I took a woman of these new daevas. One who was not afraid to enter my waters, who was clever enough to see the promise in such a pact. And then I raised your kin—*my* kin—from the dust to become one of the most powerful clans in their land. I taught them how to swim the currents and summon palaces from the sea. All I asked was loyalty. And discretion."

"I don't believe you." Nahri saw tears glistening in Ali's eyes. "My ancestors wouldn't have done that; they wouldn't have lived as some clan of marid spies for generations."

"They did not know the extent of their purpose. I told them merely to keep secret what they were and pass word down to future generations that one day I would require a service in return for the centuries of blessings. So I waited. I watched the Nahids weaken, and when an opportunity arose, I took it."

"Zaydi's war." Nahri felt sick. "So the marid did help him take Daevabad. *You* helped him."

Sobek gave her a cold look. "I have not gone near our lake since Anahid desecrated it. My descendant went in my place, bringing an entire army through the currents. *That* is what your family was capable of when it obeyed me," he said to Ali, his tone growing bitter. "Not that it mattered. The daevas always lie, and my kin among them were no better. I made clear the Nahids were to be annihilated and that I needed Anahid's ring to be returned to my waters. They failed on both accounts."

Nahri untangled his appalling words, hearing the deal beneath the surface. "You knew," she accused him. "Didn't you? You knew what would happen if the ring was removed from Daevabad?"

"That foul city only exists because of Anahid's magic. Your *world* exists because of it. Yes, I knew."

"The price," Ali said softly. He looked like he was going to throw up again. "Zaydi said the Ayaanle had paid a terrible price for their alliance with the marid. My ancestors didn't give you the ring, they gave it to him."

Nahri stared back at Sobek, dread creeping over her. "What did you do?"

The marid looked more crocodilian now, but there was a flicker of something very old and haunted in his eyes. "I loved them in the ways that I could. But they disobeyed. They were my responsibility, and they carried strains of my magic. A thing you should understand, Nahid, with your rules about Suleiman's code."

"That's why you asked me those questions when we met," Ali said. "Why you were surprised to learn of me." Horror rose in his voice. "What did you do to my ancestors?"

"I devoured them. All that I could find."

Nahri could not stifle her gasp, but at her side, Ali did not shake. He took a single deep breath and then stepped back, putting Nahri and Jamshid behind him.

"This ocean is the abode of Tiamat, yes?" he asked.

Sobek clearly wasn't as thrown as Nahri by the abrupt question. "Yes."

"Then leave."

The marid paused for a long moment. "You are upset. That is understandable. But you and I were both given a warning, and Tiamat will not care about your anger."

"I will deal with Tiamat on my own." Ali raised his knife, and now his voice did tremble. "You said I fulfilled my ancestors' pact, so *leave*. I do not ever wish to see you again."

If that landed, Nahri couldn't tell. But Sobek retreated toward the water.

He turned to her. "The next risen tide is shortly after dawn. For the debt I owe your human kin, I will tell you this. Flee west, daughter of Anahid."

"West?" Nahri repeated faintly.

"You will not be spared Tiamat's wrath. None of you will. Not if he is here."

Then Sobek vanished beneath the water's surface, leaving nothing but ripples. Ripples and the three of them, the unrelenting rain, and a threat that suddenly made Daevabad feel very far away.

31

DARA

Consciousness pulled at Dara in the form of crackling flames and foul, acrid smoke.

Blistering hot spikes jabbed his back, his legs, his skull, miring him in pain. A worse torture throbbed in his right arm, his wrist bound and wrapped in what felt like his own iron-studded scourge.

The attack on the carriage. Muntadhir's betrayal and Kaveh's gutting cries. Dara tried to free himself, finding his limbs constrained, chains rattling from his wrists and ankles. The attempt left him panting for air, his body so weak it felt like a stranger's.

"Ah, look who finally wakes."

Dara blinked, his vision blurry with ash.

Vizaresh loomed over him. "You're very irritating to watch over, did you know that? All this shrieking in your sleep and calling for your sister. *'Tamima! Tamima!'*"

Dara lunged against the chains holding him and then gasped

as a wave of pain left him breathless. He fell back against the smoldering surface to which he'd been bound.

Vizaresh slowly circled him, fiery eyes raking his body. "Careful, Afshin. Your Banu Nahida has gone through *such* efforts to revive you. It would be disrespectful to undo all her hard work. Especially now, when she needs you so dearly."

Dara was still struggling to breathe, but he clung to the ifrit's words like a drowning man. "She's alive?"

"She survived." The ifrit licked his teeth, revealing a glimpse of glistening fangs. "Such disloyal, flighty things, your Daevas. Running from this ruler to that ruler—"

"Where is she?" Dara demanded. "What have you done with her?"

Vizaresh's eyes lit up, incredulity crossing his face. "Oh, you poor man, you still don't see it, do you? *I* am not the one you should be worried about. Nor would I do anything to cross your Manizheh. At this point, I just enjoy watching her."

Dara wanted to strangle him with his riddles. "Where is Aeshma?"

"At her side, as always. I believe the phrase is 'helping her reach her true potential.'"

Dara writhed against his confines, a bit of strength returning. "Let me out of these chains."

Vizaresh snorted. "You'll never be out of chains. Not now." He left Dara's view, but when he returned, it was with a hammer. "I warned you the first time you took to the winds. You shouldn't have wasted your rebirth on these mortals and their wars."

Alarm spiked through Dara even as Vizaresh began striking off the chains. "What does that mean?" he demanded, wrenching his left hand free. "*WHAT DOES THAT—*"

Dara froze. His ring was gone.

He sprang up, all thoughts of Manizheh and Aeshma vanishing. "My ring," he whispered, staring in dread at his hand. The other mark of ifrit slavery was there: the winding tattoo recording the lives of the human masters he'd taken. But the glowing emerald and battered band, the ring whose previous loss meant his instant death, was nowhere to be seen.

Dara lunged at the ifrit, who was probably regretting his decision to free him. The sudden movement made his head spin, and he clutched at Vizaresh's collar. Creator, what had happened to him? Dara had never felt this fractured, like the pathways between his mind and body had been broken and badly pieced back together.

"Where is my ring?" he wheezed, wrapping his hands around the ifrit's throat.

Vizaresh writhed, spitting fire. "Gone," he choked out, nodding at Dara's right wrist. "You've that now."

Dropping him, Dara glanced down. He recoiled at the contraption embedded in his wrist. A brass sheath like an archer's bracer bordered by raw scar tissue and seeping, gold-flecked black blood. Set in the center was his relic, the amulet hammered out and flattened.

What is that? What has been done to me?

Sick with dread, Dara forced himself to look around. They were in the palace infirmary, but it had been emptied save for him and Vizaresh. Tools he couldn't recognize, scorched rags, and broken apothecary bottles littered the worktables as though someone had gone into a frenzy.

Dara shoved aside his broken chains. He'd been strapped to a low metal table set over a smoldering fire, and the smoke smelled wrong. He searched for what might have fed the flames, but there were no charred pieces of wood, or any oil. Instead, frayed bits of crumbling linen drifted through the air. Dara swept a hand through the ash lying thick in his lap, examining the crumbling remains. Tiny black shards peppered the pale dust.

Bone.

He reeled. "What is this?" There was so much ash. So much. "What did she do?"

Vizaresh had backed away and was massaging his throat. "You were all but dead by the time Aeshma and I brought you back. One of your traitors injected you with iron solution. A brilliantly ghastly idea, to be honest. It's still in you. Manizheh said there was no way to extract it from your blood without her magic. So she needed another way to save you." His gaze met Dara's, vicious and knowing. "How fortunate she was in possession of her dead kin. You know what they say about the power of the Nahid—"

Dara cried out, heaving away the bone fragments in his hands and trying to scramble out of the burning pit. He stumbled to his knees and sent up more clouds of ash. It was on his tongue, in his eyes, clinging to his skin.

The Nahid bodies from the crypt, oh, Creator. Men and women and children, all who'd died under the Qahtanis' thumb. His blessed Nahids, denied the peace of death to rot under the lake and then only burned so their sacred flame could bring back an abomination—him. Dara lurched from the ash, landing on the cold tile and retching a molten substance that scorched the floor.

Vizaresh was laughing. "Oh, Afshin, don't despair! At least she survived. Such a nasty business, coups. I've seen my slaves dragged into more than I can count, and they're always so much more violent than originally planned. When they're not successful, however?" The ifrit's eyes glittered. "Nothing quite as vicious as vengeance from those who almost lost power."

Dara clutched for a stool, trying to climb to his feet. "Where is she?"

"In the arena. It was the only place big enough."

The only place big *enough?* Dara moved forward, the entire room swaying. Desperate, he called for his magic, but it came to him in jerky, uneven waves. Fire swept over him in patches, only one hand turning to flame, the pain vanishing down his left side but not his right.

Creator, what is wrong with me? Dara made it to the infirmary door and fumbled as if drunk for the handle.

"You should have flown, Afshin," Vizaresh said again. "The Nahids do not deserve your loyalty. No one in their world does. Were you a wiser man, you would have seen that before destroying yourself for them."

"I am part of the reason for their world being the way it is. I will not abandon them." Dara pulled open the door.

And then he prayed he was not too late to save his Banu Nahida.

THE PALACE WAS EERIE, SILENT AND EMPTY, THOUGH the bright sun streaming through the stone balustrades indicated it was midday. Dara's heart raced, his breath echoing raggedly in the dusty corridors. Where were all the stewards? The servants and soldiers and scribes? The dozens of people who should have been milling about and hustling between appointments, all involved in the anxious running of a new, haphazard government attempting to stave off civil war and mass starvation?

Manizheh is alive, Vizaresh had said. His Banu Nahida had survived. Dara tried to banish all other thoughts as he rushed forward. They could fix this. He could still fix whatever this was.

The stench of blood hit him when he was still very, very far from the arena.

By the time Dara was staggering through a back passage, the miasma of rot and released bowels was so thick on the air that it choked him. It was the smell of a battlefield, bringing him back to the worst memories of his life. But there should have been no battlefield in the arena, in this palace—in the heart of the Daeva Quarter that Dara had done everything to protect. How could the djinn have broken in? How many people had they killed?

At the sound of a woman's scream, he broke into an uneven run. Finding the door ahead locked, he kicked it down with a grunt.

Dara had two arrows pointed at him in an instant. And yet the sight brought him relief—their bows were held by his warriors.

"Afshin," one of the men, Piroz, breathed. "Thank the Creator." He was shaking.

Dara gripped his shoulder. "What is going on? I just woke up in the infirmary; the palace is empty—"

Another scream came from the arena.

Dara stepped forward, but the second Daeva soldier moved to block him.

"Forgive me, Afshin," he said. "But the lady asked that she not be interrupted."

"*Interrupted?*"

The soldiers exchanged an uncertain look. Piroz spoke. "She . . . she is punishing the traitors."

The way he said that sent ice flooding into Dara's veins. "Stand aside."

"But we have orders to—"

At that, Dara shoved the soldiers apart and strode through. "I do not die," he warned. "If you shoot me in the back with weapons I taught you to use, remember that."

There was broken sobbing as he pushed through the last door. "Forgive me, my lady. I confess, I confess!"

"I do not want your confession." Manizheh's voice was colder than he'd ever heard it. "I've made clear what I require from you. Give your name, and I will spare your child."

Dara rushed into the arena.

He fell to his knees.

Bodies were everywhere. Dozens, hundreds. Men and women of all ages, and if he spotted no children, there were enough youths who skirted the edge. All were Daeva, many still wearing ash marks, their glassy black eyes opened to the sky. Some had their throats slashed, but more had puncture wounds to their hearts, their clothes soaked in blood that ran out into the sand, as thick and copious as the Geziri blood that had flowed across the palace gardens not long ago.

But Daeva blood wasn't supposed to spill like this again. That had been the focus, *the entire point*, of their war. Dara wavered on his knees, gazing across the sand.

Just in time to witness the woman kneeling at Manizheh's feet plunge a dagger into her own chest.

Dara let out a soundless cry, aghast and not understanding. The royal viewing platform had been stripped to its marble surface, and Manizheh, her head bare and her hair in loose, tangled waves, stood in the ceremonial gown he'd seen her in the day of the failed meeting with the djinn envoys. It was now entirely black with blood. She watched dispassionately as the woman crumpled to the ground.

From the shadows behind Manizheh, Aeshma emerged. The ifrit pulled the blade from the dead woman and kicked her with his foot off the platform and onto the tangle of bodies splayed across the sand. As he straightened up, his gaze met Dara's.

A look Dara had never seen from the mocking, haughty ifrit leader crossed Aeshma's face. It was . . . hunger. The anticipation of something more ancient and longed for than Dara could even imagine. As if Aeshma could scent the despair and horror radiating off Dara and wanted to taste it, to rip his teeth into them all.

And then it was gone. Aeshma handed the dagger back to Manizheh.

She stroked her fingers through the blood coating the blade, a twisted caress. She shivered, her lips briefly parting.

Aeshma spoke. "Your Afshin has joined us." It sounded like a warning.

Dara rose shakily from the ground, gazing in horror at the gory sand that stretched between them. He could not bear to cross it. "What have you done?"

She wiped the flat part of the dagger on her hand. "It seems Muntadhir was right about the fickle loyalties of the Daeva noble houses." Manizheh met his gaze, and the haunted vacantness in her eyes chilled Dara to the core. "So now there are no more Daeva noble houses."

He swayed on his feet. "Not all these people betrayed you."

"No, but their kin did. A lesson needed to be taught."

Dara's gaze fell back to the ground. A young woman lay curled on her side, a hand still pressed to her torn throat. She looked younger than Nahri had been when Dara found her in Egypt.

"Don't." Manizheh's voice was brittle. "You did worse at Qui-zi. You did worse during your rebellion against Zaydi al Qahtani. They wanted to put *Muntadhir* on the throne. He would have killed every Daeva who even thought about giving us support." She gestured wildly with the knife. "We tried another way. We tried mercy and kindness and were betrayed in return. *This* is all anyone understands."

Dara stared at her, but he could not summon the rage of their earlier fights. Because even as his faith in the Nahids finally, fully shattered, his heart broke for her. For the brilliant healer who should have been making advances in her field and saving lives instead of becoming a ruthless killer. For the woman who was clever and brave and who might have been a good leader in another world. Who should have seen her children grow up in safety and taken pride in the people they'd become.

He wanted to weep for her, for all of them. "My lady . . ."

"They killed Kaveh. *Our* people, Dara. They tore him apart in the street like animals." Her voice broke in raw grief, her blood-shot eyes wet.

Kaveh. Dara felt like his legs had been cut out from underneath him. He and the grand wazir had argued plenty, but Kaveh had been Jamshid's father and a determined, ruthless advocate for their tribe.

And the Daevas had killed him for it. Dara could not imagine a more destabilizing loss for Manizheh.

She shook her head. "The men put their hands on me, thought to *bind* me, saying surely I understood. That no one wanted to hurt *me*—I was their blessed Nahid, but it was time for men who knew better to step in. For a *Qahtani* to step in," she said, spitting the name. "They would have succeeded if it hadn't been for Aeshma."

"I am sorry." Dara didn't know what else to say.

"I'm sure you are." She stared at him. "They knew. They knew *exactly* how to take you out, and it was because of your actions in the hospital."

Dara tried to move forward, stepping over the bodies. "Banu Manizheh . . ."

"No." The rebuke was a slap in the face. "Afshin, I care for you. But I do not need your misplaced guilt right now."

Guilt. She thinks it's guilt I feel right now?

The door to the back of the platform opened, and his heart dropped further. Irtemiz and one of his newer recruits had a bound and gagged Muntadhir between them. The emir had been beaten; bruises and bloody gashes covered his bare, dirty skin; and his beard was hacked away.

But defiance burned in his eyes even as they shoved him to his knees in front of Manizheh. He glared up at her with open hatred.

We never had a chance with him, Dara realized. The dancer back at the feast who'd tried to warn him about Muntadhir had been right. They had killed his people and his father, so Muntadhir had struck back, planning their destruction the best way he knew how and smiling the entire time.

A new dread stole over Dara. "The djinn representatives . . ."

"Gone," Manizheh replied. "They fled to their quarters like rats before the ifrit could catch them. They were in on it. All of them. Do you understand now, Afshin? There is no one we can trust. Not the Daeva nobles. Not the djinn. Not anyone who's ever paid even lip service to Ghassan. They are poisoned. They are *infected*." She reached down, grabbing Muntadhir by his hair. "And *you* are the disease. Look upon your allies, al Qahtani. Pleased to have more blood on your hands?"

Muntadhir gazed wordlessly upon the dead.

Dara watched more rage burn through Manizheh at the emir's haughty silence. "Nothing? We really are pawns to you, aren't we? Seduce one, marry another. Kill us, torture us, crush us, and then when we finally fight back, turn us against one another." She ripped the cloth from his mouth. "Your companions are all dead. Every single Daeva who enjoyed your company. Every single one *rumored* to have enjoyed your company. No regrets?"

Muntadhir looked up at her. "I regret not watching you weep as you tried to find all Kaveh's pieces."

Dara would swear the palace itself trembled with her anger.

"Ghassan's son until the end," she hissed. "A selfish, venomous snake." Manizheh nodded at the soldiers. "Hold him still. The sand fly thinks tears a weakness, so surely he won't mind if I relieve him of the ability to have them."

Some of Muntadhir's courage seemed to leave at that. He writhed against the soldiers, and Dara did not miss the cruel triumph with which Irtemiz grabbed Muntadhir's face, clapping a hand over his mouth. Irtemiz's desire for vengeance didn't surprise Dara—it was a desire he knew damn well he'd stoked during their years in the wilderness. A desire that would only have grown when she watched her friends and her lover die at the hands of Muntadhir's brother, and when she'd been threatened with death in the hospital.

But Dara averted his gaze. He didn't need to watch. Munta-dhir's scream was loud enough from behind Irtemiz's hand.

Manizheh stepped back, and they dropped him. Muntadhir fell to his knees with an agonized wail in Geziriyya, blood pour-ing from where his left eye should have been.

"I shall leave you the other for now," Manizheh said coldly. "For I want you to look upon your sister when I catch her. I want her death to be the last thing you see."

At that, Dara spoke up again. "Banu Manizheh, if you kill the princess, her mother—"

"I have taken care of Hatset and her message. I have taken care of it all." She gazed at him. "You should go, Afshin. I do not think you are entirely recovered."

She lifted a hand. And then, with a beckoning motion, she did something she should not have been able to do.

Manizheh used magic.

The door behind him flew open with a bang, and a gust of wind hit him in the chest, a firm push. Dara stumbled back, shocked and betrayed.

"Forgive me, Afshin. But I'm doing things my way now."

32

ALI

His mother's gaze might have been a thousand miles away. "I don't believe it. It's not possible. It's *not*."

Jamshid had been pacing the same route along the carpet for so long that it was beginning to make Ali dizzy. "And I'm sure Tiamat will hold off from drowning us all because we declared it impossible."

"Then *you* go give yourself to her, Baga Nahid." Hatset glared at Jamshid. "It was Anahid who stole her lake, Nahids who forced the marid to serve them. Why should my family, my *son*—who has done nothing to any of them—pay the price?"

Ali stayed silent. He hadn't spoken since denying Sobek at the river, letting the Nahid siblings fill Hatset, Wajed, and Issa in on what had transpired. He didn't know what to add that wouldn't shatter his mother further or make the man he called uncle look as though he hadn't just aged a hundred years. Ali was supposed to be the reckless optimist, the idealist who never gave up.

But there was no fixing this.

So he said nothing. Instead, he stared at his stinging hands, which were cracked and dry. Ali had scrubbed his skin until it bled upon his return to the castle, scouring away every last bit of moisture, every physical reminder of the monsoon marid that he could.

Not that it mattered. Ali couldn't undo what had happened or what he'd learned.

It's not possible. Ali found himself repeating his mother's desperate words. He'd come to terms with the fact that his father had been ready to turn into a butcher, a man he was required to stand against. But this, oh, God. Sobek was beyond even that. He was a creature from another age, another element. A world that had required blood and rites, which Ali's had rightfully stomped out.

Those couldn't be his roots.

The door to his room opened, and Nahri slipped through the sliver of light. Ali dropped his gaze to the floor; he couldn't look at her.

"Fiza is all right. She took a nasty bump to the head, but she'll be fine." Nahri hesitated. "But she said she was leaving."

Ali closed his eyes. Everything they'd knit together was falling apart.

Jamshid's voice grew even more alarmed. "What about her ship? Her crew?"

"I didn't ask," Nahri said. Ali could sense from her voice that she was studying him. "But people know something's up. Apparently as the tide's been going out, it's been leaving lumps of gristle and blood and rotting fish on the sand."

Dead silence met that until Jamshid broke it. "Maybe we should *all* be going with Fiza."

"We don't have enough ships to evacuate even half the people here," Wajed pointed out. "And by the next tide? All we'd do is put ourselves on the ocean when it smashes into the coast. If the marid meant their threat, the timing was deliberate. Not to mention the rest of the djinn and humans on the coast won't have any warning at all."

Ali finally spoke. "Then I need to go. There is no other way."

His mother whirled on him. "I will lock you in a cell if you say that again." Denial and grief warred in her voice. "You're not going anywhere, Alu. This is preposterous. Our family hasn't had anything to do with the marid in centuries, no matter what involvement this Sobek claims he had with our ancestors. And I won't lose you," she said, her hand trembling as she waved a finger in his face. "Not again."

Guilt twisted through him. How could Ali do this to the mother who'd fought so hard to save his life? Whose husband had been murdered and whose daughter was surrounded by enemies?

Then again, how could he not?

Issa spoke. The scholar had been unusually quiet and deliberative as his mother and Jamshid argued, but Ali recognized his careful cough as the sound of a man with bad news.

"If Tiamat has demanded it, the prince may need to go. She is not just a marid. She is beyond our comprehension," Issa explained. "Stories of her predate Suleiman and speak of her as the great ocean itself, an abyss of chaos and creation. She very well could be the mother of the marid, having birthed them millennia ago when the world was still new."

"A collection of blasphemous legends," Hatset scoffed. "Primitive tales from an age of ignorance."

"Respectfully, my queen, I would not speak so blithely. It is not blasphemous to say this world is vast, that much of its history remains shrouded. There are things God set beyond our understanding. We don't have many of her tales, but Tiamat must have inspired a great deal of fear to be remembered and spoken of the way she was, so many centuries after she was active."

"Then where has she been?" Hatset challenged. "If she's so powerful, why does she let Darayavahoush terrorize her people? Why did she let the Nahids take Daevabad and force her children into servitude? Why is she only coming for us now?"

Issa sounded helpless. "I don't know, my lady. I don't think any of us can see into the mind of such a creature. Perhaps she's been sleeping under the sea, such mortal concerns below her. She may desire the seal, or she may simply want Alizayd and it as curiosities, the way marid were said to consume ships and villages in the era before Suleiman."

What did it mean to be consumed as a curiosity? Ali wondered. To give himself to Tiamat? Would she settle for killing him and sating herself on his blood? Or would it be worse—could she trap away his soul, devour it so he would be erased from existence, never to see Paradise or his family again?

Don't think like that. You're a believer in a more merciful God than that. But still, Ali wrapped his arms around his knees, trying not to rock back and forth.

"We can't take the chance that she won't come," Jamshid said. "You two weren't there. You didn't see how powerful these things were. How *angry*. Suleiman's eye, Sobek sounded like Anahid had freshly cheated him. He's spent ten generations plotting his revenge!"

Ali lifted his gaze, staring at the stormy sky past the open window. His room was higher than Nahri's. If he were a braver man, perhaps he would have thrown himself through the window and made the choice easier for his loved ones.

A sharp pain came from his arm, and Ali glanced down to see blood. He'd been digging his nails so deeply into the skin that he'd broken it, drawing four curved furrows.

"Then *I* will go." It was his mother again, her voice decisive. "I've got this marid blood in me as well, don't I? I will go to Tiamat and reason with her."

Oh, Amma. Ali wanted to weep for her. *I'm sorry, I'm so sorry.* But his voice was steady when he spoke—she'd wanted him to be a king, and he could go bravely into this for her.

"You can't. You cannot swim and breathe like they do. I can. And I'm the one they want," Ali said, skirting what he needed to do next. "The marid made clear they can attack while I take refuge in this land."

"I need you all to leave." Nahri's command rang out, professional and allowing no room for protest. When Hatset drew up tall, looking like she was about to object, Nahri stayed composed. "Your son is still injured, my queen. I understand we have limited time and must make some important decisions, but the rest of you can go argue while I take care of Ali."

Gratitude welled in him, followed by a wave of shame. God, the things the monsoon marid had made him say to Nahri, the way he had touched her . . .

Looking eager to escape, Issa bolted, but Ali's mother crossed to where he was sitting on the bed and gave him a hug. "It's going to be okay, Alu. I promise. We'll find a way around this."

Ali forced himself to look into her eyes. He already knew the only way around this was through it. "Of course, Amma." He held her close another moment, trying to set in his memory the smell of her perfume and the feel of her in his arms.

He did not imagine being able to hug his mother again.

She kissed the top of his head before departing. Jamshid and Nahri were whispering furiously in Divasti.

"Wajed," Ali called, beckoning the Qaid over. He switched to Geziriyya—this was not something he wanted anyone else to hear. "I'm going to need a boat. We'll need to be discreet. If my mother thinks—"

"I will get you out." Wajed sounded devastated, but they were soldiers first, and both knew protecting the people of this coast took priority over their own safety. "If this is what you have decided, my prince, it will be done."

Ali gripped the other man's hand. "Thank you, uncle."

Jamshid joined them. "I'm sorry," he said. "It's not personal."

"I know it's not. You don't need to apologize."

The Daeva man looked like he had more to say. "I'll look in the books for mentions of Tiamat. Maybe there's something there."

Ali could not even feign a hopeful smile. "Maybe."

Jamshid and Wajed closed the door behind them, leaving Ali and Nahri alone.

There was a long moment of silence. The rain had finally abated, the night song of chirping insects and dripping leaves the only sound. Ali wondered if this was the last time he'd hear it.

Nahri spoke first, her voice quiet. "This reminds me of our second encounter. When I thought you were drowning in the canal, and then you wouldn't let me look at the books in your bedroom without a chaperone."

Ali stared at the floor. That day seemed like a lifetime ago. "I remember being pretty unbearable back then. I'm lucky you didn't shove me in the canal."

"I was tempted." Nahri sat on the bed beside him. "Please look at me, my friend."

He shook his head, fighting tears. "I can't."

"Ali." Nahri touched his cheek, lifting his chin to face her. Her dark eyes were soft. "What was it you told me on the beach? It's just you and me right now."

Her fingers brushed the line of his beard, and then Ali broke. "I want to climb out of my skin," he burst out. "I can still feel that thing in my head, in my body. I'm *one* of them. My very family is the product of some evil marid's scheme. I have his blood, his magic running through my veins. Power he built stealing brides and devouring children." He squeezed his eyes shut, resisting the urge to throw up. "I . . . that can't be what I really am. I'm a believer," he whispered. "How can I be descended from some demon?"

"You're not descended from a demon, Ali, for God's sake." Nahri sighed. "I'm not going to justify what Sobek did to my family or his djinn descendants, but neither am I going to pretend he's the only one who's wanted vengeance. But you're not him. You've got your mother's blood, your grandfather's. You're descended from those of your ancestors who stood *up* to Sobek, the ones who chose to save the rest of us and paid the ultimate price."

I devoured them. Ali's stomach turned over. "He killed his own children. How could he do that and then save my life? Show me his magic? God, Nahri, I all but begged him to teach me more. I *ached* to see the currents again."

Nahri shifted beside him, pressing one of his hands between hers. "When I first learned what the Nahids had done to the shafit, I wanted to climb out of *my* skin. I had imagined them as these noble healers, and learning some were monsters, that they would have killed me as a child—that they *had* killed children . . . I told Dara I was glad the djinn invaded. I think I even told him that I was glad the Nahids were dead. But it's not that simple." She took his face in her hands again. "You and I are not the worst of our ancestors. They don't own us. They don't own our heritage. Manizheh uses Nahid magic to kill; I use it to heal. Just because Sobek has used magic for evil doesn't mean that's what it is when you use it."

Ali looked into her worried eyes. Nahri was so close that their heads were almost touching, and when he inhaled, he could smell the cedar incense that clung to her skin. "It's a shame you hate politics," he murmured. "You'd be a very good queen."

"Yes, but then you'd be advocating for people to overthrow me and turn my throne into a table for some sort of godforsaken governing council." Nahri gave him a broken smile, her gaze glimmering with unshed tears. "I prefer being on the same side."

That shattered Ali again. "I wanted to do it with you," he choked out. "To go back to Daevabad and fix things. The hospital. The government. All our foolish ideas. I wanted a future."

Nahri pulled him into her arms, and it was everything Ali could do not to weep. To scream. He didn't want to die. Not like this. Not now, when his people and family needed him most.

Nahri released him, wiping her eyes. "Let me heal you. Please. I'll feel less useless."

Ali managed a nod, slipping the sheet he'd wrapped around his shoulders low enough that Nahri could reach his heart.

But he wasn't prepared for the press of her fingers. Not now, when his emotions were a mess and the monsoon marid had already called out his feelings for her. Ali shivered, fighting a jump when her hand trembled.

She cleared her throat. "Drop the seal."

Ali obeyed, wincing as the familiar jab of pain came. But relief followed, the throbbing ache in his swollen nose extinguishing. Nahri's other hand traced the gash the marid had torn in his wrist, the skin healing as her fingers brushed over it. Longing ripped through him, the fiercest he'd ever felt. The skin she'd touched felt scorched. *Ali* felt scorched.

Nahri dropped her hand from his heart, the magic falling. But she was still gripping Ali's wrist, and her cheeks were flushed when she met his gaze.

"Better?" she whispered, her voice halting.

Ali closed the space between them and kissed her.

His lips had no sooner grazed hers—and *oh,* her mouth was so soft, warm and welcoming and glorious—than his wits returned, and panic crashed over him.

He jerked back. "Oh my God, I'm sorry. I don't know what—"

"Don't stop." Nahri slid a hand behind his neck and dragged him back.

Ali's apology died on his tongue, and then from his mind altogether as Nahri kissed him deep and slow and with agonizing deliberation. She parted her lips, pulling him closer, and Ali groaned against her mouth, unable to check himself. The noise should have stopped him, shamed him. Reminded him that this was forbidden.

But Ali's entire world had just been smashed, he was going to die before the next sunset, and God forgive him, he wanted this.

Stop, a voice in his head commanded as Nahri slid into his lap. *Stop,* as Ali finally grew brave enough to touch the black curls that tumbled around her face, to wrap his fingers around one and kiss its softness. This was wrong, it was so wrong.

Then they were falling onto his bed, overtaken by grief and madness. Nahri straddled his waist, and Ali traced her cheeks, her jaw, pulling her mouth back to his. Her hair was like a dark, fuzzy curtain around them, the press of her soft body and the taste of salt on her lips . . . he had no idea he could feel like this, no idea *anything* could feel this good.

She pulled the blanket away from him completely, and Ali caught his breath at the shock of cool air on his bare skin.

Nahri instantly broke away, meeting his gaze. She was breathing fast, uncertainty and desire warring in her dark eyes. "Do you want me to stop?"

There was only one answer he could give. She was Muntadhir's wife. *My brother's wife.*

Ali stared back at her. "No."

The look on her face—Ali shook. Nahri pinned him to the

bed, her fingers sliding through his own, and then she continued, following the pattern of his scars and exploring the rise of
his chest. Her touch was feather-light, and yet it burned him,
setting his body ablaze with each caress, each press of her mouth
to his bare shoulder, his collar, his stomach. Ali wasn't as bold,
not daring to touch her anywhere beneath her dress. But Nahri
sighed as he held her close, kissing her wrists, her ear, the hollow
of her throat. He had no idea what he was doing, but the sound of
her pleasure drove him on.

Once. God, please let me have this just once. Ali had obeyed the rules
his entire life, surely, he could have this moment, one moment
with the woman he loved before he destroyed everything between
them.

Then you'll destroy her. Because even dizzy with desire, Ali knew
all too well what was to come.

"Nahri." He gasped her name as she tightened her legs around
his waist, the rock of her hips sending him into a frenzy. Ali was
not going to be able to stop himself if they went much further.
"Wait. I can't . . . I can't do this to you."

She stroked his beard, kissing the underside of his jaw. "You
can. Really, I promise."

"I can't."

Nahri must have heard the change in his voice. She drew
back, guarded. "Why?"

Because we're not married. Because you're my brother's wife. Reasons that
were so much simpler than the one tearing through his heart.
Reasons that yesterday would have been enough to make what they
were doing unthinkable and now seemed almost petty in comparison.

"Because I need you to cut the seal out of my heart."

Nahri recoiled, staring at him with wild eyes. *"What?"*

Clever Nahri, always two steps ahead of him: how did she

not see what seemed so horribly obvious? "I can't go to Tiamat with Suleiman's seal in my heart," Ali explained, feeling sick. "We can't let the marid have it. You heard what Sobek said. That's been their goal all along—to seize the seal and steal our magic. To see Daevabad itself sink beneath the lake. You need to take the seal from me. Tonight."

Nahri was already shaking her head. "I can't. I *won't*. It will kill you."

"Then you can dump my body on a boat and float it out into her ocean. They're the ones who like to bend the rules," he said, unable to check the bitterness in his voice. "Let them have a taste of their own medicine."

Nahri was staring at him with a look of utter hurt, the black hair he'd mussed hanging in waves around her shoulders. "How can you ask me that? *Now?*" she added, angry heat building in her voice as she gestured to their still very inappropriate positions. She shoved away from him, shooting up from the bed and leaving cold the space her body had occupied. "Creator, it's like you're in a competition with yourself over picking the worst time to say something."

Ali pushed up, reaching for her hands. Any reserve of self-denial he'd built up had been ripped away with their first kiss; he didn't want to ever stop touching her.

"Because I don't know what else to do! I don't want to die, Nahri, I don't," he confessed in a rush, cradling her hands in his. "I want to live and go back to Daevabad. But I'll be damned if some marid uses me to take the rest of you down. At least with you"—Ali swallowed, his mouth going dry—"there's a chance I might survive. I saw the way you operated on that boy."

"He wasn't you!" Nahri yanked her hands from his. "I'm not a surgeon, Ali, I'm a Nahid. I cut into people only when I have magic to heal them!"

Forgive me, please forgive me. "Then I'm going to ask Jamshid." Nahri spun on him and Ali pressed on. "I'll tell him everything about the seal. You know he'll do it. But he's probably not experienced enough to keep me alive."

Nahri glared at him, looking freshly betrayed. "Would you do it?"

"I don't understand."

"Could you do it to me if the situation were reversed? Or did your father read you correctly that night?" Nahri lifted her chin. "Look me in the eye, Alizayd, and tell me the truth. You promised no more lies. If saving Daevabad had meant likely killing me, would you have done it? Could you take a blade to *my* heart and hope for the best?"

Ali stared back at her, shame slicing through him.

But he had promised not to lie. "No."

"Then how can you ask it of me?"

"Because you're *better* than me," he said. "Because if you wanted it, you would be a good queen. Because you're the strongest person I've ever met, and you're clever." Ali inhaled. "And because if *you* can look at this and see another way, I'll trust you, I will. But if not, then, Nahri, I need you to be the Banu Nahida. Because in a couple of hours, Daevabad's mortal enemy is going to have me, and Anahid's ring can't be in my heart when she does."

Nahri stared at him, a dozen emotions passing across her face. Her black eyes glimmered, wet with the tears she so rarely let fall.

Ali wanted to throw himself at her feet. To beg her to save him and beg for forgiveness. To tell her he loved her and tell her to run back to Cairo and be free of yet another responsibility.

And then the emotions left her face, one by one, like a series of candles flickering out, leaving nothing to read, nothing to seize. The face of the woman who had stared down his father and deceived her mother. The Banu Nahida he'd watched pray at the seaside and pick herself up once more.

"I will need to get my tools." Her voice had chilled. "And go speak to Jamshid—I'll need his assistance." Nahri stepped away, her entire demeanor changed, and Ali felt a wall crash down between them. "Prepare yourself."

33

NAHRI

Nahri tapped on the sketch before her. "Go through it again."

Across from her, Jamshid was ashen. He'd been getting paler since Nahri ordered him to her room, briskly told him the whole truth of Suleiman's seal, and then unrolled Yaqub's tools, announcing he was about to take part in some unplanned chest surgery.

"Again?" he repeated faintly. "We've talked it out ten times."

"Were it possible, I'd have us *practice* twenty times. Again."

"All right," Jamshid muttered, visibly nervous. "We have Ali drop the seal while we're touching him, and then I manage his pain while you work."

"How?"

"By dulling the nerves like you showed me," he answered. Ali was gone now, making final preparations, but they had quickly practiced that part, letting Jamshid get familiar with how his magic would feel. "And by talking to him, keeping him calm and awake so he can maintain his link with the seal while you carve into his heart."

"While I make an incision in the outer membrane," Nahri corrected, pointing to the sketch she'd made while examining Ali earlier. "The ring is right beneath it. I suspect our magic will fail the moment I remove the ring, and if that happens, Ali's going to be in a lot of pain. It will be enough to knock him out, but you should ready yourself for his reaction."

"And then you're planning to suture the incision, correct? Do you think that will be enough to save him?"

I don't know. Nahri was skilled, and she suspected that free of Suleiman's ring, the marid strength swimming in Ali's blood would help his recovery—it had when he'd been stabbed by an assassin back in Daevabad. But they were so firmly in the realm of the unknown that it seemed foolish to pretend this plan was anything more than hope.

"It might not be," she replied. "Which is why we're going to do something else as well: you're going to take the seal."

Jamshid started. "What?"

"You're going to take the seal," Nahri repeated, hating everything about this. "Because I'm not certain I can. Back in Daevabad, Manizheh claimed doing so would kill me since I'm shafit. That's why I gave it to Ali."

He stared back at her, looking uncertain. "So what the monsoon marid said—"

"Is true, yes. I have human blood, and it's very much not the time to discuss it. Manizheh might have been lying, but I'm not going to risk it. Not now. If there's even a slight chance that taking the ring will give you healing abilities, we're going to do it."

"It doesn't feel right," Jamshid protested. "I just found out I'm a Nahid. I have no experience with the magic, and you've been serving our tribe for years as Banu Nahida."

That line of objection made her feel slightly better—Nahri

didn't think her heart could take it if her brother's first instinct was to agree with their mother that shafit were weak. "I know. And if we were doing this in circumstances that did not involve Ali's open chest, I'd entertain the possibility. But we're not."

Jamshid paled even more. "Creator help us."

"And here you thought you'd left the priesthood behind." Nahri looked over the space she'd prepared: a waist-high table covered with clean cloth; her surgical instruments freshly scoured and laid out; suture supplies, boiled water, and linen. Every oil lamp and candle they had was blazing, filling the room with light, and a tin tub of water rested nearby so Ali could use his marid abilities.

The door to her room opened softly. Ali stepped through, and Nahri's heart crashed to the floor. She could still feel his hands in her hair and how badly he'd been shaking when their lips finally touched. Nahri hadn't known she could have that effect on him.

She hadn't known until Ali all but begged her to kill him, the effect he had on her.

He's your patient, she reminded herself. Right now, Nahri was a doctor first, and they would both be better for the boundary. "Did you speak to Wajed?" she asked.

Ali nodded, keeping his eyes from meeting hers. "Yes. He'll get me to Tiamat if I can't," he said, dancing around what they both knew he really meant. "He swore to keep you both safe."

"Do you believe him?" Jamshid asked.

"Yes." Now Ali did glance up, his gray eyes soft with exasperation. "I believe the man who raised me will honor my dying wish."

Nahri gripped the table's edge. "No one's dying. Are you ready to begin?"

Ali stared at the table like a man looking down at an executioner. "Of course." His fingers hovered over a large serrated instrument. "What is this for?"

Nahri felt sick. "It's a bone saw. I need to remove part of one of your ribs."

"Oh," he said weakly. "I would have thought I needed those."

"If I get my magic back, I'll reattach the bone. If not, you can live without it."

Ali swayed slightly. "I see." He took a deep breath as if to steady himself, his gaze darting to hers. It looked like he had a hundred more things to say, and Nahri felt the same. Words hovered at her lips, things she wanted him to know, emotions she couldn't articulate.

"Take off your shirt," she said instead. "And lie down."

He obeyed. Jamshid placed a drape over Ali's chest. "Keep your eyes on me," he said. "She doesn't need the distraction, and you *definitely* don't want to see what she's doing. We can talk about your brother, if you like, and the hundreds of signs you missed."

"So you plan to mock me as I bleed to death?" Ali asked as Nahri scrubbed his chest with disinfectant. "That sounds like a terrible bedside manner."

"Whatever it takes to keep you awake and focused," Jamshid said cheerfully. But when he glanced at Nahri, his expression was serious. "Ready?"

No. "Yes," she replied, pressing her fingers over his heart. Jamshid did the same. "Your turn, Ali."

Out of the corner of her eye, she saw him drop his hand to hover just above the water. He whispered a prayer in Arabic, and then a tendril of water dashed from the tub. The seal fell, and Nahri's magic flooded back into her, raw and wild and warm. At her side, Jamshid gasped.

Ali was breathing fast, his heart racing. "Can you . . . the pain," he wheezed.

"Jamshid—"

"I've got it." Jamshid squeezed his eyes shut in concentration, and Nahri felt a cool wave pass through Ali, numbing his nerves. Despite the circumstances, part of her marveled. It was incredible working with another Nahid like this, as though they were sharing part of themselves.

"I'm starting," she said in Divasti. "Keep him awake and calm."

"Will do, little sister."

Letting Jamshid hold the healing magic, Nahri broke contact to pick up her tools. As feared, her powers fell instantly away, but for this part, she wouldn't need them. Still, she paused with the scalpel. It felt so incredibly wrong to cut into Ali.

And yet Nahri had no choice. Because, like he'd said, she was the Banu Nahida.

Ali twitched as she sank the scalpel into his skin, but she had to hand it to Jamshid; he was doing a good job of keeping the prince oblivious to what was going on below his neck.

"So let me tell you all the ways in which you have terrible form as a rider," Jamshid began conversationally. "Because it really is distressing to watch, and Muntadhir never had the heart to tell you. He actually hoped *I* would tell you, in exchange for you teaching me how to wield a zulfiqar . . ."

Nahri let their conversation fade into the background. There was only the job in front of her. Skin and muscle that needed to be carefully cut and clamped back. Blood to be packed with gauze. It wasn't her doomed friend she was opening up, the man she'd been kissing only hours earlier. It was simply parts, a biological mechanism with a foreign object that needed excising.

It was only when she started on the bone saw that she felt the others waver. Jamshid's voice hitched, and Ali trembled beneath her.

"Al Qahtani," Jamshid said soothingly, "look at me, all right? Keep your eyes open so I know you're awake."

Ali's response was too muttered to hear. Nahri worked faster, the chalky smell of bone dust filling her nose. She cut free the rib, setting it aside. And then she stared in awe at his heart.

Jamshid let out a small sound of surprise. "Is it supposed to look like that?" he whispered in Divasti.

"No," she breathed. "Not quite." For Nahri had seen hearts in her work. Djinn hearts were larger than human ones and a rich, dazzling purple. Ali's was large as well but swirled with bright golden brown and silver-toned blue. Had the marid possession done that?

Focus, Nahri. The scalpel in one hand, she laid her other one against his pulsing heart and her magic returned even faster. Stronger. The muscles throbbed; the ring was ready to burst through.

It wants you, Ali had said once. Nahri had found that ridiculous, and yet it was hard to shake the feeling now. With magic burning through her veins, it seemed such an easy matter to pluck the ring from his heart and heal him right up.

One step at a time. Closing her eyes to tease out the different levels of the membrane protecting his heart, Nahri saw the ring in her mind's eye, nestled in the walls of undulating tissue.

"I'm opening the heart now," she warned Jamshid. "Get ready."

Ever so gently, she cut through the membrane, teasing it back with the edge of her scalpel. Bright amber fluid flowed out, and then it was there, Suleiman's ring, the gold band and black pearl gleaming wetly.

Creator, if you have ever listened to my prayer, I beg you now. Nahri took a deep breath. "Ali, this might hurt, but it will only be for a moment, I promise you."

He was breathing fast, his heart pumping in response. "Go."

Nahri hooked the ring with her scalpel and pulled it free.

Her magic, Jamshid's magic, everything instantly fell. The water splashed down from Ali's fingers, and then he screamed, a raw, wrenching howl as his entire body spasmed. His hands flew toward his open chest, and Nahri grabbed them before he could hurt himself, dropping her scalpel and the seal ring to the ground in her haste.

Ali's eyes were already rolling up, the lids fluttering shut as he slumped back against the table. But the movement had jarred his chest, the trickle of blood giving way to thicker gushes.

She fought panic, quickly stanching the blood with gauze and reaching for her suture supplies. "Jamshid, get that damn thing on your finger." It seemed like the passing of Suleiman's seal to a Nahid for the first time in centuries should have been marked by something a bit more ceremonious than the last Baga Nahid scrambling on the floor while his sister desperately pinched shut a heart membrane, but the time for that was lost. Jamshid bumped the table, cursing as he crawled after the rolling ring. He did as she asked, though, grabbing and shoving it on his finger without a second's pause.

Ali's heart was slowing. Nahri bent over his bloody chest, carefully pulling through her first suture. If she could just close the incision . . . "Jamshid, what's happening?" she called over her shoulder.

"Nothing! It's—it's just staying on my finger. It's not vanishing like you said it would."

"What?" Her own heart dropped. "Can you feel your magic?"

"No, I don't feel—"

Every flame in the room soared higher. Jamshid cried out, and Nahri risked a glance back to see him fall to his knees.

"Suleiman's eye, this burns." He raised his hands, fire swirling through them. "I can't control this."

"I need you to try." Nahri added a second stitch. Why in God's name was Ali's heart still slowing? The bleeding was under control, and it was only the outer membrane she'd pierced. "Can you use Nahid magic?" she asked, switching to Arabic. "Can you understand me?"

"Aywa," Jamshid responded automatically and then gasped. "Oh, that's strange."

Ali's heart gave a gentle push beneath her fingers. Still holding the membrane closed, Nahri drew her needle through a third suture. *Ali, please hang on.* "Test your healing abilities on yourself."

"But there's nothing wrong with me."

"Then *make* something wrong with you. We're in a room full of knives!"

Jamshid muttered something rude but then plucked up another of her razor-sharp medical tools. He pierced his skin, drawing a deep cut on his forearm.

It healed instantly.

Her brother's eyes went wide. "Oh."

"Now get over here."

Jamshid staggered to her side. "I feel like I just ate a firebird and washed it down with a dozen bottles of wine," he said, clutching his head. "I . . . everything is so *loud*. The hearts of everyone in the castle, your breathing . . . I feel like my brain is going to explode."

"Just breathe." Nahri finished her stitch and then glanced up to see Jamshid squeezing his eyes shut, his face creased with pain. "Jamshid? Take a deep breath, all right, and try to shut the rest of it out. I know it's overwhelming, but we don't have much time."

He managed a nod. With a quick prayer, Nahri removed one of her hands from Ali's chest and reached out to take Jamshid's. Like he said, the ring was still there, bloody and glittering from his pinky. Nahri pressed her thumb against the band.

She felt nothing but the metal. There wasn't even a hint of her magic sparking to life.

Ali's heart shuddered against her other hand, the faintest pulse yet, driving her to another decision. "Jamshid, I need you to heal him. I still can't use my magic."

His eyes shot open. "But your sutures . . ."

"It's not working. I'll walk you through the healing magic, I promise. But we need to be fast." Her voice cracked in fear. "Jamshid, I can't lose him. Please."

"Tell me what to do."

"Place your hands on his heart. *Gently,*" she added, guiding his fingers. "And try to open your mind. Tell me what you see."

Jamshid was trembling. "I don't know. I feel like I'm seeing ten things at once. There's his heart in front of me, but there's also liquid beneath and movement and buzzing—"

"Concentrate on his heart. His pulse is failing. Tell me what's going on with the blood."

Jamshid shut his eyes again. "It's coming through here," he whispered, gesturing to the right side of Ali's heart. "Then going out to—to something billowing open and shut . . ."

"His lungs," Nahri explained. "What then?"

"It pumps back through here." Jamshid's finger moved across Ali's heart, hovering just over the membrane she'd stitched closed. "And then . . ." He frowned. "It slows. There's some sort of block, a clot."

"Can you dissolve it?" she urged. "Visualize it falling apart, and then command it to heal. It's like any other magic; you need to focus. You can even say the words aloud."

He swallowed loudly. "I'll try." He shifted his hands. "Heal," he whispered in Divasti. Ash beaded from his furrowed brow. "*Heal* . . . I think it's working—"

Ali's heart abruptly shuddered and swelled, and then the membrane Nahri had carefully sutured shut burst apart with a spray of black blood that drenched them both.

"No!" Jamshid cried, reaching with both hands for Ali's heart. "Creator, no! I didn't mean to do that!"

Blood was gushing from Ali's chest with each pulse, filling the cavity and obscuring his heart as it poured over the table.

"Nahri, I don't know what to do!"

Nahri stared at the bloody table, her brother's shouts suddenly distant. But it wasn't a patient she was looking at, a body that needed fixing and one where she could divide her head and her heart.

It was Ali. The obnoxious young prince she'd fought with on her first day in Daevabad and the man who'd held her as she wept on the beach and made her feel like she could be open in a way she was with no one else. It was the Geziri elder in the infirmary, the first patient Nahri had killed. It was Nisreen, dying in her arms. Muntadhir, the zulfiqar poison leaving her useless.

Manizheh's words washed over her. *You cannot take the seal. Possessing it will kill you. You simply aren't strong enough.*

Nahri grabbed Jamshid's hand, slipped the seal ring from his finger, and shoved it over her thumb.

She had barely drawn a breath when the world burst into flame around her. Pain and power—raw and unbridled, as if she'd stuck her hands in a bolt of lightning—ripped through her and Nahri fell to her knees, choking as she tried to scream. The ring scorched her skin, so hot Nahri was certain she was about to combust, to be ash in the next moment. Black dots blossomed against her vision, and then everything flooded in. The stomach gurgles of a hungry guard across the palace squirmed in her belly, her temples thudding in time with a woman in the village having a headache.

Nahri couldn't breathe. She clutched the floor, the boards warping and smoking at her touch. Her heart felt like it was about to explode.

No. Nahri refused to let Manizheh be right. To let every so-called pureblood in Daevabad who had ever snubbed a shafit as lesser be right. To allow the worst of her ancestors—the ones who would have killed her as a child—have their prejudices confirmed. That magic was dangerous in the hands of the shafit. That they were reckless and weak, people to be wiped out or controlled.

Nahri was not weak.

She grabbed the edge of the wet table, sucking in air, and

then hauled herself to her feet. She plunged her hands back into Ali's chest. More practiced than Jamshid, Nahri found his heart immediately, the ruptured valve standing out like the last ember of a charred piece of wood.

Heal, she commanded it.

Darkness engulfed her, a clammy chill crawling over her skin like she was being seized by unseen tendrils of ice. Nahri fought the instinct to let go, the taste of salt filling her mouth.

Not salt. Blood. She coughed, the spray that came from her lips as black as bitumen.

"Nahri!"

She was dimly aware of Jamshid calling her name, but it seemed from a great distance. *Heal,* she urged again, pulling at the frayed tissue and gushing blood. *HEAL.*

The room vanished, a memory that wasn't hers stealing her away. Nahri floated in a midnight blue lake, her eyes just above the surface as she watched rocks and sand erupt from the water, swirling beneath a young woman in a faded chador and muddy dress. An island, growing larger and larger as the woman made her way down a forming path. She knelt to run her fingers through the dust, a gold-and-pearl ring glittering from one hand.

The woman glanced up, her black eyes pinning Nahri.

Anahid smiled.

"Nahri, let go!"

The vision shattered, replaced with an equally unbelievable sight: Ali's heart healing before her eyes, the membrane knitting back together and smoothing without a scar. His rib regrowing, nearly spearing her hand as Nahri jerked it away. Tissue, muscle, and skin raced to cover it, and then Ali seized, his eyes shooting open.

"Oh my God," he gasped, sitting up. "What happened?" He let out a strangled sound as his fingers brushed the rib fragment beside him. "Ah!"

Nahri didn't answer. She'd fallen with her brother to the floor, both of them weeping.

JAMSHID POKED AT THE RING ON NAHRI'S FINGER. "I thought it would be bigger. And somewhat grander."

"You've spent far too much time with Muntadhir if you're not impressed by the millennia-old ring, once worn by a prophet, that literally shaped our world."

"Oh, I'm plenty awed, trust me. Baffled but awed." A note of worry entered his voice. "How are you feeling?"

Nahri opened and closed her fist. The ring was still hot against her skin but no longer searing. "The room has stopped spinning. And I'm no longer suffering the headache of a woman in town or feeling the urge to vomit alongside a guard two floors below, so that's a mercy." She snapped her fingers, a conjured flame bursting between them. "It's my magic, but it doesn't feel more powerful than usual. Not like it did when I first put the ring on."

"Can you sense anything of the seal? I don't see the mark on your face."

"Maybe that's because the ring is still on my finger." Nahri tapped it against her knee. "I don't understand. I don't understand any of this at all."

"That makes two of us." Jamshid sighed. "Though you're clearly the right Nahid to be wearing it." He sounded ashamed. "Nahri, about before, I'm so sorry."

"There's nothing to be sorry about. You were asked to do something you couldn't possibly know how to do. And I pushed you. If anyone should apologize, it should be me."

Jamshid didn't look convinced. "I feel like such a failure. I could have killed him. I *would* have killed him if you hadn't been there."

Nahri knew that feeling. She also remembered the woman

who'd picked her back up after all her mistakes and accidents, who'd taught her everything she knew about healing. "This wasn't your fault. But even if it was, that's okay—you're going to make mistakes. Honestly, if you end up doing this work for decades, let alone centuries, you're almost certainly going to kill someone." Her stomach twisted. "I know I have. But that's a fear you'll have to manage if you want to help the many, *many* more people you'll help." She touched his hand. "Give yourself time, big brother. This takes patience and practice."

"But we don't have time."

"For this we do. On the slim possibility we survive everything and take back our city, I am setting the Daevas straight and going back to my hospital. And if it's what you want—what you *want*, not what you think you should do—I will teach you how to be a healer. I promise."

"I'd like that." Jamshid glanced past her shoulder. "I know we have a lot more to discuss, but I'll give you two a minute."

Nahri followed his gaze to see Ali standing at the door. He'd cleaned himself up, trading his blood-soaked waist cloth for a traveler's robe. A pale blue turban wound around his head and neck in the Ayaanle fashion, a bag was slung over one shoulder, and his zulfiqar and a new iron knife were sheathed at his belt.

"The tide will be coming in soon," he said. "I think I should go."

The blunt reminder that they'd done all this only for Ali to still have to surrender himself to some demonic colossus at the bottom of the sea set despair sweeping through Nahri again. She rose to her feet, trying to force some professional distance into her voice. "How are you feeling?"

A little relief entered Ali's expression as he rubbed the spot above his heart. "Like the world's worst thorn was removed."

Jamshid squeezed Nahri's hand. "I'll come find you after."

But Ali caught Jamshid's wrist as he attempted to pass. "Thank you, Baga Nahid."

Jamshid bit his lip, looking like he was contemplating a sarcastic response, but then he simply nodded. "You're welcome. And good luck, Alizayd." He left, closing the door behind him.

Ali eyed the table they'd only half cleaned up. "That looks like a *lot* more blood than was expected."

Nahri paused, not wanting to delve back into the terror she'd felt watching him die before her eyes. "It got a little complicated."

He drifted nearer but stayed out of arm's reach. "I knew it wanted you," he said, nodding to the ring on her thumb. His lips quirked in amusement, but in his expression Nahri saw poorly concealed grief at the good-bye they both knew he'd returned to say. "How many times have you saved me now?"

"I told you that you'd never get out of my debt."

"May I confess something?" Ali gazed at her in open sorrow. "I never really wanted to be out of your debt."

The floor seemed to move beneath her. "Ali—"

"Wait. Please. Please just let me say this." When Nahri exhaled, letting her silence stretch out, Ali continued. "I don't regret kissing you. I know it was wrong. I won't do it again. Yet I cannot make myself regret it. But the way we started, how I stopped—I didn't want you to think that . . . that it was impulsive. That I didn't want it." He dropped his gaze. "That I haven't wanted it for a very long time."

Nahri was going to cry. She was going to scream. This still didn't seem real; his fate monumentally unfair and almost too awful to truly contemplate. Yet Nahri checked the anguish threatening to tear her apart. He didn't need anything else to worry about. "I don't regret it either, Ali."

He glanced up, looking close to tears as well. "I'm glad," he whispered. "And I'm sorry. I'm sorry I couldn't do things the proper way by you. Sorry that we couldn't . . ." He trailed off, stumbling on the words.

Nahri should have offered them. But she couldn't. Because

if Nahri said those words, she knew he was never going to come back. She knew what happened when she dared to have hopes and dreams.

They got broken.

Instead she took two steps forward and flung her arms around his neck. She didn't kiss him—she would respect the line Ali had drawn—but she clutched him close, not missing the cool wetness on her cheek. She couldn't have said which of them was crying.

"Come back," she begged. "Cut a deal with Tiamat. Flatter her sea snakes, or throw yourself on Sobek's mercy. Don't be stupid or reckless or proud. Give her what she wants, Ali, and come back to me."

He was trembling. "I'll try."

Nahri broke away, giving him a fierce look. "No, promise me. Promise me you'll come back."

Ali stared down at her. She expected him to say there was no way he could honor such an impossible promise. That he'd already given to Nahri the one thing they knew Tiamat desired.

"I promise," he whispered.

There was a knock on the door. "Zaydi," Wajed called. The old warrior sounded heartsick. "It's time."

Ali stepped back, but his fingers stayed tangled in Nahri's for a moment longer. "About Daevabad . . ."

"We've got it," she said with the most confident smile she could muster—she was still the better liar. She squeezed his hand. "Jamshid and your mother and I. Don't worry about us."

"There was never a more capable group." Ali brushed his thumb over the ring on her finger and then released her hands. "May the fires burn brightly for you, my friend."

Tears pricked her eyes. "Go with God, Ali," she returned in Arabic. "Peace be upon you."

34

ALI

Though the rain had finally broken, the beach was so misty and humid that Ali was soaked before he spotted the ship Wajed had prepared, driven up on the sand. The tide lapped around the sewn hull, wild and ravenous. There were no stars, no moon, just monsoon clouds glowing faintly with the celestial light they concealed. The ocean, typically so gentle, lashed with spray as storm-churned waves beat against the beach.

Promise me you'll come back. Nahri's plea ran through his mind, her eyes wet with tears. Ali could still feel her lips on his, her touch driving him to madness. He was struggling not to. He'd made the most earnest apology he could muster during his last prayer while also being honest with himself and his Creator—there was little point in lying to the One who knew his heart either way.

But Ali feared he might have lied to Nahri. Because he didn't see a way back from this.

With the ring gone, he could barely check the marid magic

rushing through him. Whispers raced through his mind, the damp wind tugging him forward on ribbons of moisture. The wet sand sucked at his sandals, but Ali tried not to look at it. Like others had warned, the tide had carried with it rotting seaweed, decaying fish, and what smelled horribly, impossibly, like djinn blood.

Come, the ocean seemed to beckon, to mock. Ali swore he heard laughter and gripped his zulfiqar in response, aching to hold something familiar as he and Wajed came around the boat.

His mother was waiting. Ali froze, but neither Wajed nor Hatset seemed surprised to see each other.

Hatset crossed her arms. "Did you really think he wouldn't tell me?"

"Yes," Ali replied, shooting Wajed a look. "What happened to Geziri solidarity?"

"She's more frightening than you."

"And I'm not here to stop you, baba," his mother assured him. "Everything in my blood screams at me to, but I know I can't. However, I couldn't live with myself if I didn't help."

"We filled the hold," Wajed explained. "All of us. Jamshid and that nutty scholar tried to come up with offerings that might please Tiamat. Gold and incense and silks and ivory."

Guilt and gratitude rolled over Ali. "You didn't have to empty half the treasury for me," he protested. "You might need that for the war."

Hatset hugged him. "There is nothing I wouldn't give for you. I am so sorry for the words I spoke before, but I won't burden you with my regrets or my grief, my love. Just know how utterly honored and proud I am to call you my son."

"It is I who am blessed to have such a mother." Ali stepped back, quickly wiping his eyes. "Qaid, you will protect my family?"

Wajed touched his heart and brow in the Geziri salute. "To my dying breath, my king." He gave Ali a small, sad smile. "I had to call you that at least once."

"Then let me do the kingly thing and leave before my emotions get the better of me." Ali stepped into the surf, the sea licking at his legs, and climbed the hull. "If God wills it, I will return." Under his breath, he added, "—I promise."

And then Ali fixed his eyes on the horizon. This time when he called to the water, he didn't have to flinch. The ocean rose around him, the boat bobbing madly, and pulled him out to sea. It happened so fast that Ali didn't even get a chance to look at his mother again, a curtain of fog rushing between them. In moments, there was nothing but water surrounding him—the clouds threatening another downpour and Tiamat's sea, dark as indigo.

Sail east, Issa had told him. *As far as you can. It is the deepest heart of the ocean where she is said to rest.*

But "sail east" was advice easier given than enacted in the dark of a monsoon night with the tide and waves shoving his boat every which way. This wasn't the languid Nile—the river whose lord Ali now knew he descended from—and the ocean fought him when he reached for the currents, attempting to coax the water into carrying the boat along. He tried to steady the rudder, nearly getting the wind knocked out of him when a wave pitched the boat hard. The rain picked up again, the wind howling past his ears as the ship groaned and creaked, planks protesting.

It was so loud that Ali didn't think much of it when he heard a squeak on the wood, his arms full of the sail he was attempting to adjust.

Until a voice spoke up behind him. "You're doing that wrong."

Ali stilled and then slowly turned around.

To see Fiza standing at the entrance to the hold with her pistol pointed at his head.

"NO, DON'T DROP IT," FIZA WARNED WHEN ALI MOVED to let go of the sail. "I'd rather see your hands on that than on your weapons. And don't try *anything* magical. If you, the ocean, the fog, or so much as a stray drop of rain make any strange moves, you're going to get a bullet in your brain, and there's no Nahid around to save you."

"Fiza, you really should not be here."

"And why's that?" She let out a laugh, but it sounded forced. "I've got a ship, more treasure than I can spend in ten lifetimes, and my enemy at the end of a gun. For a pirate, I'd say I'm doing well."

My enemy. The blood-stained bandage wrapped around her head caught his attention. "I'm sorry for hurting you," Ali said softly. "I didn't mean—"

"Yes, Nahri told me. Some evil marid got in your head and made you do it. An even worse one wants to eat you up, or it will devour the whole coast. So what's this, then? Are you running? You're certainly carting enough riches to set up a nice new life somewhere the beach isn't bleeding and Afshins aren't after your head."

"You know I'm not running."

Fiza's hand trembled on the pistol. "Yesterday I would have believed that. I was starting to believe in you, in all these things you've been saying about a new Daevabad and equality for my people. I was getting ready to *follow* you, you bastard," she said, her voice breaking. "You made me think it might be possible. That if I went home, if I was some kind of hero, maybe all the other things I've done wouldn't matter."

She didn't elaborate, and he didn't ask. Despite her constant mocking and evasion, Ali had long had the impression that Fiza had survived much, much worse.

He so desperately didn't want to see her die now. "Fiza, you can't follow me. Not where I'm going. Nahri didn't lie, and I don't think the marid have any intention of letting me leave."

"So this was all for nothing, then? Nahri's and your big plans? You go get eaten by the ocean, and the murderers running Daevabad slaughter everyone I grew up with?"

With Nahri and his mother, Ali could put on a noble face. But he wasn't going to lie to another shafit he'd failed. Part of him hoped she'd just shoot him and get this all over with. "Seems like it. Take me east a bit farther, if you don't mind, and then throw my body over the side. Keep the ship and the treasure. Someone deserves to escape all this."

Ali dropped his hands from the sail.

Fiza didn't shoot him. Utter fury crossed her face—she certainly looked like she wanted to shoot him. But then she lowered the gun, shoving it back in her belt. "Pick that back up."

"What?"

"*Pick that back up,* you infuriating son of an ass. You haven't been going east, you've been going north. So I'm in charge now since you're too shitty a sailor to do anything right. I'll get you to your marid witch—and then, more importantly—I'll get you back."

Ali was speechless, certain he'd heard that wrong. "I don't understand."

"That makes two of us," Fiza muttered, pushing Ali out of the way so hard she nearly knocked him into the sea. "I'm *helping* you, prince. The right fucking thing to do and all that."

"There's no helping me," Ali argued. "I'm not getting out of this. All you'll do is get yourself killed, and I won't—"

"I didn't ask your permission. And I'm not doing this for you," she snapped. "I'm doing this because I want you to go back to Daevabad and make good on the promises you made my people. I won't let this all be for nothing."

"Fiza . . ." Ali let out an exasperated sound. "Tiamat is just as likely to swallow me, you, and the boat whole if you stay. *Please,*" he added when she ignored him to adjust the rudder. "I've gotten enough shafit killed."

"More reason to go back to Daevabad and see us free." Fiza did—something—and the ship immediately seemed less rocky. "My mother could still be there," she said, seeming to be talking to herself. "I think I'd like to see her again."

"The only thing we're going to see is the seabed."

Fiza flashed a glare that could have burned Ali to a crisp. "You know how you're always going on about how much you respect the shafit and want them to be equals? Shut your mouth and prove it. Respect my decision, stop arguing, and make yourself useful."

That did shut him up. Ali swallowed hard, then asked, "What can I do?"

She showed him, and for the next few hours Ali jumped at her commands, tacking and furling and a bunch of other things that made no sense but allowed the ship to sail through the storm as if by magic. It was exhausting work, but it kept his mind off what they were moving toward, and Ali would gladly have let the ropes burn his hands and the spray soak his skin for days if it meant delaying the inevitable.

Sooner than he expected, though, the wind died completely. The rain still lashed their faces, but otherwise there was no movement. It was impossible to see anything in the thick fog, as though they were floating in a black cloud rather than upon a vast sea.

"We must be pretty far out by now, yes?" Ali asked, his heart skipping. "Maybe she forgot about me."

Fiza looked uneasy. "They said nothing but 'give yourself to Tiamat by the next high tide'?"

"I wasn't really in the right frame of mind to ask questions."

"Because of the threat to Ta Ntry?"

"Because I found out I'm descended from a Nile marid who created my family in the hopes of destroying the djinn world."

Fiza spun to look at him. "Excuse me?"

"It's a long story."

The ship abruptly dropped.

They both lunged to grab on to the boat. Ali held his breath, expecting the motion to stop, assuming they'd just gone down the dip of a swell. Their boat had been rising and falling for hours with the natural motion of the waves.

But they didn't stop.

"Alizayd." Earlier Fiza had found a glass-enclosed oil lamp in the hold and lit it; the flickering flame now revealed her face had drained of color. "I don't think they forgot about you."

The wind returned, howling past as clouds of mist rushed away. A bolt of lightning, slow and lingering, splintered across the sky, casting jagged light over the ocean.

"Oh, God," Fiza whispered. "Oh, God."

They were indeed falling in time with a wave. With a whole *army* of waves. A wall of water surrounded them on all sides, higher than anything Ali had ever seen in his life, as though they'd been cast at the bottom of a mountain. More lightning, silent as death, flashed, illuminating the swelling waves as they reached a tipping point far above Ali's and Fiza's heads, the crests turning white. The wave edges touched, briefly enclosing the boat in a cocoon of water nearly as beautiful as the hidden passages of the Nile. More lightning flashed, glowing blue and green beyond the screen of water like an alien sky.

And then that oceanic sky crashed down.

35

DARA

For all that Daevabad was synonymous with the very idea of a city—bustling streets, towering buildings, and crowded markets— there was still wilderness to be found in the forests and rocky hills that hemmed the island's terraced fields and shepherds' pastures. Even after all these centuries, the land beyond the walls had remained Daeva. Their Geziri conquerors had never been able to replicate the knowledge Dara's tribe had perfected over generations, and risking Daevabad's nearest food source wasn't worth it, not when the Daeva landowners could simply be bribed or terrorized into submission.

Dara slipped through the scrubby forest now, as silent and invisible as the frightening wraith he might have been considered in the human world. He wasn't in the human world, however; he was on the island wherein he'd been born and which he feared was in more danger than ever. He passed fields devastated by hail and an orchard beset with locusts. Several farmhouses had burned; a broken mill left grain rotting on the ground.

He tripped over the landscape, his usual grace gone. If Dara had been boundless and powerful with Suleiman's curse removed—an original daeva free to shed his form and fly on the wind—being "healed" among the smoldering heap of Nahid corpses had shoved him back into a tight, barbed cage. Everything hurt. Moving hurt, breathing hurt. His powers were brittle, shaky things, as if neither his body nor his magic belonged to him, as if he were pulling strings to control a puppet he could not see.

There is something wrong with me, with all of this. For Dara couldn't get the sight of Manizheh surrounded by murdered Daevas, using magic she shouldn't have had, out of his head. He couldn't even bear to look at the relic she'd embedded in his wrist, the sick contraption of metal and blood. Dara had wrapped it in linen, but lines of speckled black gold still traced out across the left half of his body, the jagged lines of light pulsing with each ragged beat of his heart.

You should have fled, Afshin, Vizaresh had mocked. But Dara hadn't fled. He couldn't.

Now, though, he was headed toward an objective that felt even worse.

You are supposed to serve. To obey. A good Afshin could advise, they could argue, but they *obeyed.* That was their code.

But you do not only serve the Nahids. You serve the Daevas, and they need you too. Dara kept walking.

The crumbling structure where they'd arranged to meet looked like little more than a jumble of rocks. In Dara's day, it had been a celebrated pilgrimage spot: a cave in which a famed Nahid ascetic had prayed for survival from a famine only a few centuries after Anahid herself had died. It had been popular with couples hoping to conceive—a thing his people didn't do easily—and there had been all sorts of rituals associated with the place, from leaving a silver coin inside an infant's hat at the cave's base to simmering the small purple flowers that grew on the surrounding hills into a tea. Judging from the look of the cave, its significance had either been forgotten or failed to survive the Qahtani invasion—like so much of the world Dara had known.

A figure emerged from the shadows. "Stop."

Dara recognized the curt voice as belonging to the rude female warrior from Am Gezira and immediately scowled. "Where is my priest?" he demanded. "Where is Razu?"

"We're here." Razu stepped out from the cave, holding a small torch, Kartir behind her.

Dara stared at the three of them, fighting the wild urge to run in the other direction. *Traitor,* his mind berated him. It had been berating him since Dara had sneaked from the palace in the dead of the night to surprise the priest in his temple bedchamber. "She has done something terrible," he'd burst out before the startled old man had gotten a word in. Dara had not been able to say the phrase "blood magic" or put into words the true horror he feared, but his ramblings about Manizheh demanding the names of the murdered Daevas while Aeshma gloated—not to mention the sight of the vile contraption shackling his wrist—had been enough to make Kartir go pale.

"We need to talk to them, Darayavahoush," the priest had said after a long moment of silence. "This is beyond us now."

At the time, it had felt like the right decision, the scenes from the arena scoured in Dara's mind, and yet now this seemed like a rash mistake. Manizheh had just been betrayed by Daevas she believed she could trust, and now her Afshin was taking a secret meeting with her enemy?

Kartir must have seen the expression on his face. "It is all right, Darayavahoush," he said, his voice gentle. "All is as planned."

Planned. That only made Dara feel worse. No matter what

Manizheh had done, every bit of training and worship that had been carved into him was resisting this. Suspicion still gripped him as well, and Dara conjured his own torch, throwing brighter light on the djinn. Dressed in rags that looked stolen from various men, the Geziri warrior—Aqisa, Dara remembered, from his rampage at the hospital—was smirking, her crossbow aimed at his heart and a knife and sword at her waist. He glared at her, not missing that she appeared markedly thinner.

"Afshin," Razu prompted, a note of warning in her voice. "Kartir said you were coming in peace. The face you are making does not indicate peace."

"Neither does the crossbow aimed at me. I came to talk to your princess, so where is she?"

Aqisa tapped a pair of iron cuffs hanging from her belt. "You'll be putting these on before you see her."

"I will shove them down your throat."

Kartir let out a frustrated sigh. "Dara—"

"I have had enough of iron for several lifetimes," Dara said, hissing through his teeth. "Not to mention bondage. I am not putting those on. You either trust me or you don't."

"I don't." Aqisa cocked her head. "Tell me, what exactly is the difference between you and a ghoul? You both rise from the dead, make irritating moans that pass for speech—"

"That is enough, Aqisa."

The command was richly spoken, the new woman's voice calm and assured. And indeed, when Zaynab al Qahtani stepped out from the cave, she did so as though she might have entered a throne room rather than exited a hiding spot.

Dara straightened up. He'd gotten a glimpse of Zaynab at the hospital, but he took his time examining her now. Doing so perhaps should have filled him with shame—proper Daeva men did not stare at unrelated women. But Zaynab al Qahtani was their nearest enemy. While she stood free in Daevabad, ruling her own

united block of armed Geziris and shafit, she presented an alternative to Manizheh, a reminder that the city hadn't truly fallen.
Not yet.

So he looked at her. Zaynab hadn't given him much to read—
she was dressed in black from head to toe and had wrapped one
end of her headscarf across her face, concealing all but her luminous gray-gold gaze. Dara could see the resemblance to her
younger brother in the set of her high brow and large eyes, and
he wondered how else she might be similar to him. Did Zaynab
share Ali's fierce faith and refusal to compromise? Or had a life
in the palace tempered her, taught her the art of politics and
accommodation—not to mention lethal scheming—that Muntadhir had mastered?

Or perhaps she is something entirely different.

Either way, Dara intended to tread carefully. He would greet
her, but in his people's way. "May the fires burn brightly for you,
my lady," he said, bringing his fingers together in blessing.

"And for you," Zaynab replied, clearly taking her own moment to assess him in return. If she was frightened, and she
should have been, she hid it well.

"I would speak with you alone." Dara was thankful for the
priest's help in setting up the meeting, but this was not a conversation he wanted Kartir judging or the rude warrior interrupting.

"Absolutely not," Aqisa cut in. "Do you think we don't know
how badly your Nahid wants her?"

"If I was going to take her, I would have already." Indeed,
Dara was becoming more and more tempted to try. "A thing you
must have known when you agreed to meet."

Zaynab hadn't taken her eyes off him. "Aqisa, stay here."
When the other woman protested, she held up a hand. "Please."
She inclined her head toward the forest. "A walk?"

Dara bowed and then started off. He set a small globe of

conjured flames to dance overhead, illuminating a narrow black trail.

Zaynab followed him, and the forest soon swallowed them up. Once it did, her breath came faster, and this time Dara suspected it was due to fear rather than being winded by a stroll.

Be polite, he told himself. *But careful.* Zaynab had grown up politicking in the palace, and Dara had already learned the hard way from Muntadhir that he was no match in that realm. But neither threats nor diplomacy had worked thus far, so Dara needed to find another way if they were to avoid the catastrophe he feared was looming ahead.

"I was not certain you would come," he began, his steps silent on the soft earth. "Then again, bravery is one of the few attributes I have never been able to begrudge Geziris."

"Kartir gave me his word you meant me no harm. I trust him. He seems an honest man of God."

"How does a Qahtani princess come to know a Daeva cleric?"

"I met him in your Temple," Zaynab explained, glancing over when Dara's face lit in surprise. "Alizayd and I both."

Dara frowned. "But djinn are not permitted there."

"We visited as Nahri's guests. We went to show our support when she announced she'd be opening her hospital to shafit." Bitterness laced into Zaynab's voice. "She and Ali were trying something different, a small way to make peace before you destroyed any hope of that in our time."

"That peace was ended by the shafit attack on the Navasatem parade as much as it was by our conquest."

"I'm sure it's comforting for you to believe that. What a relief after you'd already plotted the slaughter of my people to learn you had a new justification to cling to."

The sharp words cut closer than he liked, and Dara found himself automatically reaching for his usual defense. "We needed no further justification. This is a Daeva city. It should be ruled by Daevas."

"Strange that, for a *Daeva* city, Anahid herself set quarters aside for each of the six tribes and made the only requirement for entry a mere drop of magical blood. It's almost as though she meant this to be a home for all and it's the rest of you who've twisted her legacy."

Dara regarded her. "With your tongue, you and Nahri must have either been the closest of companions or utter enemies."

Zaynab looked away. "I used to think the worst of her. I *feared* her—I'd heard stories about Manizheh growing up, and I didn't like how close her daughter was getting to my brothers. I thought Nahri plotted our destruction."

"Perhaps she did."

"Nahri wanted her people to survive. To thrive. If we needed to be destroyed for that, I think she'd have done it, but it didn't seem like vengeance was first in her mind." Zaynab glanced at him. "But I take it you're not sneaking out on Manizheh to discuss her daughter?"

Traitor, the voice whispered again. "No," Dara replied, not certain if he was answering Zaynab or his own doubts.

The princess stopped, gazing at him, the night song of insects filling the silence between them. The floating globe of flames did little to light up the thick darkness behind her, the silver of the trees standing against the soft black like stars in a vast, impenetrable sky.

Whatever she saw must have alarmed her. "Is it Muntadhir?" she asked in a whisper, fear filling her eyes.

"Muntadhir is alive for now. But she plans to kill him. To kill *you* and make him watch. Muntadhir plotted with some of the Daeva nobles to overthrow her. Kaveh was killed during the attempt and she blames your brother."

The mention of the coup attempt triggered no surprise in her expression—she clearly had her own sources. "Kaveh deserved it."

"Kaveh was torn apart by a mob in the street, and Manizheh is out for blood. We made a good faith effort toward your brother and his allies and were rewarded with betrayal. There will not be another." Dara steadied his voice. "Muntadhir is going to die, but you don't need to. He wouldn't *want* you to. This doesn't need to end in more violence, princess. Surrender. Convince your people to lay down their arms and open their gates."

"*That's* your message?" Zaynab was already shaking her head. "No."

"You would live," Dara said, struggling to stay calm. He wanted to shake her, to shake them all. "On my honor, I swear it. I will see you returned to your mother in Ta Ntry and let the rest of your tribe go back to Am Gezira."

"And those of us who don't live in Am Gezira?" She narrowed her eyes. "How can you not see that this city doesn't belong to you alone? There are thousands of djinn and shafit who call Daevabad home, who've only known Daevabad, who don't *want* to leave Daevabad. What happens to them?"

"They do what my people did for centuries and live under a foreign government. They call Manizheh queen and submit to our rule."

"The rule of a woman who plotted their deaths? Who killed their kin and executes her own people?"

"*Yes.*" Dara threw his hands in the air. "She is hardly the worst person to sit on that throne! Are you living in a fairy tale to imagine this ends another way? I can see you and your companion are thinner. I have heard reports of famine and sickness in your quarter—in *all* the quarters. The sky rains frogs and shards of ice. Our orchards are blighted, and the forests are rotting. You will starve. You will *fall,* one by one, leaving more dead. And when Manizheh's rage finally outweighs her patience and you are weak, we will take with force what you could have simply given."

Her eyes blazed. "We outnumber you. The other tribes are still holding their own—"

"She has magic."

Shock crossed Zaynab's face. "That's not possible. She would have used it on us by now."

Everything inside him coiled tight. The awful truth Dara so badly didn't want to admit, the only one that might make this girl see reason—even saying it seemed blasphemous.

"It is recent," he finally said. "I myself do not fully understand how—she does not take me into her confidence. But I have seen her use magic. A type of magic. After the executions of the Daeva traitors and in the presence of ifrit."

Zaynab stared at him. Her face might have been veiled, but he could see her eyes widen in the kind of instinctual fear one couldn't hide. "What are you saying, Afshin?"

"That you are out of time." Dara brought his hands up again in the Daeva blessing. "And I am asking—I am *begging* you to surrender. I do not wish to see more death, princess. Kaveh was not just her grand wazir. He was the love of her life, her closest companion since childhood, and she had to pick pieces of him up in the street. She is not going to show mercy."

Zaynab stepped back, panic sweeping her face. Good. Dara wanted it there, wanted to stoke it until she saw sense.

"We removed our relics," she whispered. "Her poison won't—"

"She will find something else. Do you not understand, al Qahtani? You have *lost.* Save yourself and what is left of your people before their blood is on your hands."

"My hands?" Anger spiked her words. "What about *your* hands? You claim you don't wish to see more death, you come here whispering of blood magic, painting a picture of a tyrant mad with vengeance, yet if you wanted, you could end this war in a day with a single, well-aimed thrust."

The true meaning of Zaynab's words took a moment to land, and when it did, fury roared through Dara's soul. "You think I would *hurt* her?" he asked, appalled. "I am her Afshin, she is my Nahid. If she has erred, it is only because your father—"

"My father is dead," Zaynab cut in. "I'm not going to deny he treated her with violence or that his rule left wounds, but he is gone. And handing Daevabad over to a monster because 'otherwise she'll kill us all' is not a solution."

A monster. How easy it was for this girl who'd lived barely a few decades to declare such a thing. She hadn't seen her people suffer for centuries. She hadn't broken her body and soul trying to set things right, only to see her efforts implode.

And yet . . .

And yet. The murdered Daevas giving up their names and Aeshma's coldly triumphant smile. The punch of magic that sent Dara flying from the arena.

I'm sorry, Afshin. But I'm doing things my way now.

Zaynab was still looking at him, and Dara broke away from her stare with a hiss, fixing his gaze on the midnight forest. A tremor of fire crackled through his fingers.

And what would you do? What *could* Dara do? For the thought alone of hurting Manizheh was unconscionable. She had lost her partner, her children, her magic. She'd tried to reach out to the djinn and nearly had her throne yanked out from underneath her by the Daevas she'd wanted to save.

"You wouldn't have come here without Manizheh's knowledge if you trusted her," Zaynab said, her voice more urgent. "Razu thinks there's still some good in you. Please help us."

Manizheh's hand on his cheek, lifting Dara's face while he wept at the Gozan and giving him the only hope he'd had since

Daevabad's fall. Watching her as she cared for and inspired her followers in Daevastana, knitting together a ragged band of struggling survivors.

Dara clasped his hands behind his back. "I have given you my warning."

"And I've given you my response. We will not surrender to her. So let *me* pass along a warning. You want to avoid more bloodshed? Deal with the woman at the root of it." Zaynab turned on her heel. "We are done here."

DARA RETURNED TO THE PALACE UTTERLY DISPIRITED. Still healing—or not healing or whatever in creation was going on—he found the hike exhausted him, and by the time he was making his way to the small room he'd claimed near the stables, every part of his body ached.

He clutched his wrist to his chest as he walked. Suleiman's eye, the damned relic hurt, the weight of the metal tugging at his still-healing skin. Not for the first time did Dara contemplate simply cutting his wrist off and letting the consequences play out where they might. Hell could not be much worse than this.

Two warriors were waiting outside his door. One was Irtemiz, the other a new recruit, some sallow-faced youth whose name Dara could not recall.

He stopped, annoyed. "You are blocking me from my bed."

Irtemiz looked stressed. "Afshin, where have you been? We've been searching for you for hours."

Dara was suddenly very aware of the dead leaves clinging to his boots. "Walking."

The young man frowned. "It's the middle of the night."

"*And?*" Dara glared. "In my day, had I spoken to a superior officer like that, I would have been cleaning simurgh enclosures for a year."

"He doesn't mean any offense," Irtemiz explained quickly. "Banu Manizheh asked us to retrieve you."

Dara didn't like the sound of that. He hadn't spoken properly to Manizheh since she'd thrown him out of the arena and couldn't imagine a worse time to do so than right now, with his body exhausted and his emotions a mess after meeting Zaynab.

Nor could he deny her.

Giving a last longing look at the door—his bed really was comfortable, and the faint smell and sound of the horses below could have so easily lulled Dara into the fantasy that he was elsewhere—he grimaced. "Of course. I am here to serve. *Always,*" he added, not bothering to keep the sarcasm from his voice.

They led him to Manizheh's office—Ghassan's old one. It had surprised Dara at first when she took it, Manizheh going so far as to have the dead king's desk repaired so she could claim that as well. Dara had offered to use his magic to conjure her a new room, someplace light and airy, close to the infirmary or the gardens, but she'd refused.

"Ghassan took everything from me," she'd said at the time, running her fingers over the ivory filigree set in the polished wood of the restored desk. "It pleases me to take what I can from him."

Dara's mood soured even further when he entered the office. Manizheh wasn't alone—Vizaresh sat across from her. Odd. It was typically with Aeshma that Manizheh kept company, Vizaresh busy with Aeshma's orders or generally doing whatever evil nuisances like him did to fill their days.

"Afshin. Finally. I was beginning to fear something had happened." Manizheh's gaze went to the leaves on his clothes. "A walk in the woods?"

"I like the woods. There are no people there."

She sighed, glancing at his soldiers. "Would you leave us?"

They obeyed, shutting the door behind them. The air in the

room was stifling, and feeling a little light-headed, Dara nodded in the direction of the fastened curtains. "Do you mind if I open the window? There is a pleasant breeze coming off the garden."

"I do not wish to look upon the garden. It reminds me of my brother."

Dara winced. He had indeed heard her express that sentiment before and forgotten. "Forgive me."

"It's fine. Sit." Manizheh motioned to the cushion next to Vizaresh.

The ifrit gave him a wicked smile. "You look pale, Afshin. Is your latest resurrection not agreeing with you?"

"It is not," Dara replied with as much sincerity as he could muster. "It is doing this thing where I become irrational and unpredictable and stab the throats of whichever fiery being is closest. Speaking of, have I told you just how bright you look this evening?"

"That's enough," Manizheh said testily. "Vizaresh, would you mind leaving us as well?"

With an exaggerated bow, the ifrit obeyed.

But it did little to help the tension in the room. Dara pressed his hands against his legs, struggling for words. He had never felt this way about someone before—this mix of loyalty and dread, love and revulsion.

Being alone with Manizheh reminded him of who else should have been here, so he started with that. "I am so sorry, Banu Manizheh. I know I said it earlier, but I am so very sorry about Kaveh."

"I know you are." Her voice was quiet. "I am too. But his death was not in vain. It made things clearer."

"Clearer?"

"Yes." Manizheh actually smiled at him. "But I'm getting ahead of myself. How are you feeling? I was alarmed to learn you'd left the infirmary. I need to know where you are, Afshin, at all times. Your well-being is important to me."

Dara cleared his throat. "I am fine," he lied.

"Are you truly? You're not feeling different? Weak?" She reached out, touching the linen Dara had wrapped around the relic in his wrist. "I would have thought you'd have questions about this."

He fought the urge to yank his arm away. "I assumed you would tell me in time."

"Yes, of course. Indeed, it's one of the reasons I summoned you here. I want to fix things between us, Dara. Our families have been tied together too long for our partnership to be so strained. I would like us to speak honestly with each other."

"Then what happened in the arena?" The question burst from him. "I saw you use magic. And the Daeva woman who was on the platform . . ." Dara shuddered. "You demanded her name. You demanded she *kill* herself in your name." Manizheh's expression was still calm, eerily so, and frustration broke through in his voice. "Please explain. Tell me I am misinterpreting things." He was nearly begging now. "That kind of magic, it is not ours. It is wrong."

"Why? Because its knowledge comes from the ifrit?" She shook her head. "Those so-called nobles were traitors, and they were going to die either way. Why let the power in their blood drain into the sand, unused, when we needed it?"

Oh, Manizheh. It had been obvious in the arena but hearing her casually admit to something so ghastly broke Dara's heart all over again.

And then Zaynab's warning came back.

He felt a decision settle inside him. But not one that had anything to do with violence. Manizheh was still holding his wrist, which made it easier for Dara to do something he'd never done before.

He took her hands. "Banu Nahida, I think we should leave."

Manizheh blinked in surprise. "Leave? What are you talking about?"

"We should leave Daevabad. This week. We'll take supplies, all the Daevas who wish to accompany us, whatever is left of the Treasury. We'll return to the mountains and—"

She jerked her hands away. "Have you lost your mind? Why would we *leave* Daevabad? The entire point of the war was to retake it!"

"No, it was to save our people. To reunite your family. And on that note . . ." *Creator, it was so hard to say.* "Banu Manizheh, we have failed. The city is falling apart, and our people are turning on us. I do not see a way we can fix things."

"So you want to run just because a few traitors and djinn don't like having to bow their heads? Absolutely not!"

"Because it is turning you into a monster!" Dara tried to steady his voice, but it was impossible. "Banu Nahida, you and I had this conversation back at camp about the vapor. You did not listen to me then. I beg you to listen now. Let us return to Daevastana, to our roots. Let us build something real. Without blood magic, without the ifrit."

"And Daevabad?" Manizheh sounded disgusted. "The Daevas who don't follow us to the mountains? The ones who can't? My *children*? You would abandon them?"

"I would see them live," Dara replied, hating the truth in his next words. He did not dare name Kartir, but Zaynab had impressed him, and he strongly suspected the Daeva priest and the others of their tribe would be able to negotiate a manageable peace with the princess, provided that things did not get worse. "At this point, I think they'd be safer not being tied to us. And perhaps if they believe Daevabad is safe, Nahri and Alizayd will return with the seal."

"And Jamshid?" Her voice was more cutting now. "I know

he's not the Nahid you're infatuated with, but you might remember my son is currently a prisoner. And if you think Hatset is letting him go while I take a break to rebuild my strength, you've misplaced any tactical cleverness you once held." Manizheh stood up and paced away. "I've lost Kaveh. I will not lose Jamshid."

"Then we'll get him back. If you don't need me in Daevabad to hold the city, we could go to Ta Ntry and try to—"

"No."

It was a curt answer, the kind of command that once would have shut him up. Now it only made Dara angrier. He dug his fingers into his cushion, fighting the desire to tear it apart.

Manizheh had stopped at the shelves opposite the desk. "The workers found something in here, you know, when they were going through the damage."

The change in subject took him aback. "What?"

She was already retrieving a slender black case. She opened it and turned around.

Dara went cold, rising to his feet. "That's an Afshin arrow," he said, recognizing the scythelike ends only his family had been permitted to use. But this particular arrow's style of fletching . . . "That's one of *my* arrows. Suleiman's eye. That must be from the rebellion."

"I thought it might be." Manizheh ran her fingers along the arrow, and unease crawled over Dara at the possessiveness in the gesture. "I said I wanted to speak honestly with you, and you've clearly unburdened yourself. I would like to do the same. We are obviously and unfortunately at odds when it comes to our goals."

Her calm tone was maddening. "*Our goals?* You're murdering Daevas for blood magic and using the corpses of your relatives to heal me. We are not 'at odds.' You've gone too far, and I'm trying to bring you back!"

She closed the case and put it back on the shelf. Her other hand toyed with something around her neck. Jewelry, perhaps.

"You know, Rustam said the same thing." Manizheh pulled free the gold chain underneath her braid and with a sudden jerk on the pendant, broke it.

Bewildered, Dara saw too late what had been hanging from the necklace.

His ring.

He lunged forward, but Manizheh had already slipped it over her finger.

"Stop," she whispered.

Dara stopped so suddenly it was as if he'd slammed into a wall. Shock froze his tongue.

Manizheh's eyes were wider than he had ever seen them, her entire body trembling. "Don't move."

The words were no sooner out of her mouth than his entire body went numb, as though his limbs were encased in stone. Dara tried to scream, but it was like his body no longer obeyed his commands.

His body no longer obeyed his commands. His ring was on Manizheh's finger . . .

No, this couldn't be happening. It wasn't *possible.* Dara had to be dreaming, hallucinating. Not even Manizheh had that kind of power. Only the ifrit—

Manizheh hadn't moved either. She looked like she wasn't certain, but then suspicion stole over her face. "Where were you this evening? Tell me the truth. You may speak."

His mouth released from her control, Dara gritted his teeth, biting his tongue so hard he tasted blood. It didn't matter—there was the burn of magic, and then his lips were opening. "In the forest."

Her eyes narrowed. "With whom?"

He writhed against the unseen bonds holding him. "Zaynab al Qahtani and her warrior. The freed djinn Razu." He groaned, fighting to shut his mouth. *No, Creator, no.* "Kartir."

Fury flashed across her face. "You and that blasphemous priest met with Zaynab al Qahtani? You stood before the woman I've been begging you to find, the woman upon whose life my son's life depends, and you let her walk away?"

"I was trying to make peace." He couldn't stop speaking. "To convince her to surrender before you—"

"Before I what?"

"Before you used blood magic against her."

Manizheh's eyes glittered. "You told that sand fly princess I was using blood magic?" She seethed. "Is there anything else you've been keeping from me?"

"Yes." Dara gagged, the words coming so fast that he tripped over them. "I helped another freed djinn flee to Ta Ntry."

Manizheh paled—she obviously hadn't expected that. "Who? When?"

"An old man named Issa. Weeks ago."

Manizheh took two steps toward him, grabbed the knife from Dara's belt, and then smashed the hilt across his face.

"Traitor," she hissed. "So you too have been working against me?"

Despair and pain swept him. "I have been working *for* you. All I wanted to do was follow you. To follow the best version of you. To see our people thriving and free under good and honorable Nahid leaders." Dara hated the words as they were ripped from him. How naive they sounded.

How naive he'd been.

You let them destroy you. Time and time again, you loved them, and they destroyed you for it. Vizaresh's mocking warning and Aeshma's look of cruel triumph. They'd known all along where this had been heading. The ifrit hadn't just taught Manizheh blood magic.

They'd taught her the worst thing they knew.

He blinked back tears, part of him still refusing to let the true horror land. It would drive him mad. She couldn't have done this. Not really. The relic, the ring, this desperate mimic of ifrit cruelty. She couldn't mean it. Manizheh was a Nahid, *his* Nahid. This wasn't—

"On your knees," she commanded.

Dara crashed to the floor, his knees hitting the carpet. Blood ran into his eyes from where she'd hit him with his knife. "Please let me go." He was not above begging now, his voice trembling like a child's. "Please do not make me a slave. Not again. Do not take my freedom from me. We can fix this. I can fix this!"

A little of the rage left her face. "I actually believe you. I believe you want to fix this." Manizheh reached out, wiping the blood from his eyes with the edge of her sleeve. "I'm going to make it easier."

"Easier?"

"I know you didn't want the responsibility of more bloodshed. So now you won't have to carry it," Manizheh assured him. "I'll carry it. I'll make the decisions.

"You'll just be the weapon."

The full impact of what she'd done hit Dara like a pile of bricks. Once again, he tried to struggle. "No, my lady, please, you do not—"

She laid a finger on his lips. "I will wake you when you're needed. For now sleep, Afshin. You seem so very tired."

Dara was tumbling into darkness before she even finished speaking.

36

NAHRI

Nahri teased out the last tendril of iron from her patient's neck with the surgical hook in her right hand, her left clamped against the back of his skull. With a precise twist, she caught a loop in the iron fragment and then carefully pulled it out, letting the metal drop in the tin pan beneath her elbow.

Her patient, one of Fiza's fellows, tried to speak. "Is . . . that . . ." His words came out slurred, echoing the daze in his glazed eyes. Nahri had given him a potion that partially paralyzed his muscles to make the procedure safer.

"Almost done," she promised him. "And you're doing great. Let me just check something—" Nahri closed her eyes, letting her mind sink deeper into her healer's sight. In a moment, his neck seemed to open before her—muscles and ligaments both there and gone, bone and blood and tissue shifting into separate particles. All traces of the iron were finally eradicated—al Mudhib's foul brand removed.

With but a nudge of intent, the wound healed, and Nahri watched the torn flesh give way to healthy skin. After weeks without her magic, she'd been healing everyone who would let her, from burned cooks to soldiers wounded in training accidents. And not just because it was a relief to finally, properly have her abilities back.

But because staying busy was the only thing keeping her from jumping on a boat, sailing out to sea, and making some very unwise decisions involving fire and attempting to threaten an ancient marid queen.

She refocused, sensing a specter of the paralysis potion drifting through his blood. Nahri urged it to lessen its grip, though she'd already warned the man it would take another day to fully leave his body.

She let him go. "You are well and free, my friend. If you feel any pain or stiffness in your neck, come right back, but otherwise I think you'll be fine."

Her patient touched his throat, looking close to tears. "I never thought I'd get out of my indenture," he confessed, his words clearer now. "Al Mudhib always found new charges to add against my debt."

"Well, he can't do anything to you now. He's probably still waving a fist at the sky and cursing Fiza."

His face fell. "I hope the captain comes back. She certainly seemed confident of it—she told us she'd gut us if her ship got damaged, but . . ." He trailed off, perhaps unwilling to put his fears into words.

Nahri knew how that felt. She'd been astonished to learn Fiza had gone after Ali, torn between relief and gloom. Fiza seemed like the type who picked the right gambles, and God knew Nahri was desperate to see Ali survive. But it had also meant another person Nahri liked, a woman who had the makings of a friend, ripped away.

Jamshid peeked in. "May I borrow the Banu Nahida?"

Her patient bowed. "I was just leaving. Thank you again, Lady Nahri."

Jamshid let him stagger past and then entered the room, his eyes widening at the spread of tools and the makeshift apothecary Nahri had made from pilfered kitchen ingredients. "You set all this up fast," he said, sounding awed.

"I made a promise to Fiza's crew when they saved us that I'd get that brand out of their necks."

Shuddering, her brother dropped into the opposite cushion. "I still can't believe someone did that."

"And I wish I'd been surprised."

Jamshid sighed. "No, I guess you wouldn't be surprised. But promises aside, are you okay, Nahri? I don't think you've stopped working in days. I don't think you've *slept* in days."

"There's a lot to catch up on," Nahri said, defending herself. "I like healing people, and we could use all the goodwill here that we can muster. Believe me when I say the sentiment of 'don't kill the doctors' probably took our family a long way during the Qahtanis' reign."

"Lovely." He leaned his head back against the wall, peering down at her through half-closed eyes as though he knew to look at her directly would be unwanted. "And if I said it seemed like you sequestered yourself behind a wall of potions and scalpels to avoid both me and the having of emotions?"

"I'm fine." Nahri forced a placid smile. "Truly."

"You keep doing that. Making that face like I'm an enemy you have to guard yourself against. I'm not. I'm family, Nahri. You can *talk* to me instead of keeping all these secrets."

"Oh, can I?" She set down the hook, suddenly angry at the presumption in his words. "Because you've certainly never made me feel like I could talk about being shafit."

Jamshid took a deep breath. "I'm sorry. I truly am. I would never have said those things about the shafit if I—"

"I don't just want you not to say them." Nahri tried to steady the tremor in her voice. "I want you not to think them at all."

He winced in shame. "Fair. Look, I won't pretend I know how hard it must have been to be among our people and hear the things we say about shafit. I won't. But you're not the only one who's had to pretend to be different, who's had to smile politely when people with power insult the parts of you that you never get to wear openly. I wish you had trusted me. But more than that, I wish I had behaved in a way that would have encouraged you to trust me."

Nahri crossed her arms, trying to muster more anger as her eyes pricked again with tears. "Do you have to do that?" she asked. "Sound all reasonable and kind?"

"I have a lot of experience in loving frustrating people. I can outpatience you any day, little sister."

"If you make me cry, I'm going to stab you."

"Then I'm going to take this away," Jamshid said mildly, moving the tray of instruments. "Why don't you wash up? You can wring out a rag and pretend it's my neck while I talk."

Nahri glared but had to force it as she headed for the washbasin.

He continued. "I understand why you didn't tell me you were shafit. I might not like it, but I understand. But you *should* have told me about the marid, especially if you knew how entwined they were in all this. Do you have any idea how many references to Tiamat I'd read and set aside? We need to be able to trust each other if we're going to fight back."

If we're going to fight back. Only a small change in phrasing, and yet didn't that say it all? In many ways, Ali had been the glue holding this fragile alliance of djinn and Daeva and shafit together in Ta

Ntry, and his possible loss was a setback they were all still dancing around.

Everything I build gets broken. Nahri gripped the edge of the wash-basin. "I don't want to talk about this right now."

"Then I'll keep talking. Because I'm being a bit of a hypocrite. There's a secret I've kept from you."

"There is?"

Guilt swept over Jamshid's face. "It was me at the feast," he confessed. "I was the one who poisoned Ali."

Nahri's jaw dropped. "I don't believe it."

"I didn't mean to kill him." Jamshid flushed. "I wanted to scare him into leaving Daevabad. The poison was a formula from a scrap of old notes that a . . . friend from my Temple days and I discovered and messed around with when we were young and stupid. It never had that kind of effect when he brewed it."

"When you *were* young and stupid? Just to clarify, you mixed up a poison you learned from an old lover and gave it to a prince—to *Ghassan's son*—in public, and you think you were stupid when you were *young*?"

"I think I was a fool. A desperate, arrogant fool who got an innocent servant killed and who knows how many others beaten and terrorized during interrogations. And I'll answer for that on the day of my judgment. But I didn't think of any of that when I decided to do it, Nahri. All I saw was Muntadhir. I was convinced Ali came back to replace him. I was convinced he was dangerous. Muntadhir was falling apart, and I knew he didn't have it in him to protect himself. So I did. It was the worst thing I've ever done in my life, and I didn't blink an eye."

Nahri studied him with alarm. "I hope you don't plan on unburdening yourself to anyone else about this. Hatset and Wajed are looking for an excuse to toss you in a cell."

"I have no intention of returning to a cell in Ta Ntry or anywhere else," Jamshid declared. "I'm telling you because I want us to be honest with each other. And because I know how hard it is to think clearly when someone you love is in danger."

Nahri flinched. Jamshid had a courtier's tongue and he chose his words carefully.

When she spoke again, her voice was quiet. "Nisreen asked me once what my heart wanted. Do you know what I told her?"

Jamshid's eyes had filled with sorrow upon Nisreen's name. "What?"

"That I didn't know. That I feared even thinking about the things that would make me happy would destroy them. And it does," she whispered. Had she not finally kissed Ali only to send him to his doom? "Even just talking like this . . ."

"Talking like this what?" he asked.

I'm afraid to get close to you. Nahri lost everyone she loved, everything she wanted. How could she risk Jamshid as well?

But a knock on the door saved her from a reply. "Banu Nahida?" a muffled voice called.

Nahri gripped the washcloth. "Come in."

It was Musa. "Forgive me," he greeted her, barely checked worry in his expression. "But we have a visitor from Daevabad."

THE PAIR OF CREATURES ON THE BEACH MADE EVERY hair on the back of Nahri's neck rise from ten paces away. From a distance they might have been normal, healthy simurgh, the firebirds Daevas enjoyed racing.

Except nothing about these firebirds was normal. Their brilliant feathers, typically in dazzling shades of crimson, saffron, and gold, were dull, limned with ash and purple-hued boils. Flies buzzed over their glassy, vacant eyes, and foam dripped from their half-open beaks.

"They haven't moved." Musa sounded ill. Jamshid was gone,

dressing to meet their mysterious visitor. "At first, we thought we might have to corral them, but they haven't moved. They look half dead."

A group of djinn had gathered, whispering and pointing with obvious disquiet. They parted for Nahri, and she drew closer. The seal ring on her finger had been buzzing since she'd left the castle, and it grew painfully cold now.

A warning. Nahri studied the simurgh's eyes again, the bright teal blank and feverish. There was no spark, no movement, nothing indicating life within the creatures, and as Nahri stretched out a hand, trying to detect the beat of their hearts without having to touch them, her unease grew. There was a pulse, but barely, and not one that made her think of life.

"And you said someone was riding one?" she asked.

Musa nodded. "A Daeva man. He called himself Manizheh's envoy and asked after your brother."

An utter sense of wrongness swept her. "There's magic controlling these creatures, but not like anything I know."

"Maybe the Afshin did it? He still has his abilities, no?"

Nahri studied the firebirds, recalling the smoky beasts Dara had conjured back in the palace. They'd been terrifying, but wild, lashing out in a typhoon of destruction—alive in a way these pitiful decaying creatures weren't.

"I don't think this was Dara." Then her heart skipped. Two simurgh. One for the rider.

And one for whomever he'd come to fetch.

JAMSHID WAS WAITING IN A SCREENED BALCONY THAT overlooked the majlis, his silhouette visible against a field of carved diamonds, their tiny bursts of light like stars in the sky. He glanced back as Nahri approached, and she started at his appearance. God only knew where the Ayaanle had gotten Daeva clothes befitting . . . well, a Baga Nahid, but her brother had been dressed to impress in a blue and white linen robe patterned with leaping deer and a gold diadem crowning his wavy black hair. He was clean-shaven save for his mustache, and an ash mark split his brow.

All in all, he looked very regal, and Nahri realized he'd started carrying himself differently as well. Jamshid wasn't the quiet Daeva courtier who'd had to keep his head down lest he attract the wrath of the wrong djinn. He was the last Baga Nahid, a warrior, scholar, and healer-in-training.

Nahri nodded at the diadem, the gold stamped with a snarling shedu. "That was definitely stolen from our family during the conquest."

"A nice reminder, isn't it?" Jamshid jerked a thumb at the screen. "I know our visitor. He's Saman Pashanur, one of my father's closest friends. A large landowner with priestly roots."

"A trusted friend?"

Jamshid nodded. "Growing up, I heard him make plenty of treasonous remarks about the Qahtanis when he'd had too much wine."

Treasonous enough that he'd now be Manizheh's envoy? Peering through the screen, Nahri studied their new arrival. Saman was dressed in a traveling robe with a dusty scarf still draped over his cap. He was standing up and looked rather defiant, considering he was surrounded by armed djinn. Hatset sat on a low, cushioned divan on the platform above him.

"And he's looking for you?" Nahri asked.

"That's what he says. I get the impression he doesn't know you're here." Jamshid nodded at a black chest at the envoy's feet. "He claims he has a message but won't say anything else until he sees me."

"A message in a box. That sounds promising." Nahri glanced at her brother, his expression difficult to read in the dim light. "He's going to want to know if you're a prisoner."

"Well, then we'll have that in common. You'll stay here?"

"For now." She gave him what she hoped was a reassuring nod, and he left.

But a pang of loneliness struck her the moment he was gone. Ali should have been here, frowning the way he did when trying to puzzle things out and undoubtedly finding a way to make being trapped together in a small, dark chamber more awkward.

A mix of grief and helplessness surged through her—God, but Nahri hated this awful not knowing. Had Tiamat taken him already and killed him? Or was Ali even now being tortured for having given away Suleiman's ring?

Don't do this. Not now. Nahri leaned against the screen, pressing her fingers into the cutouts, hoping touching something solid might ground her.

There was visible relief in the Daeva envoy's eyes when Jamshid entered the room. "*Jamshid,*" Saman greeted him. "Thank the Creator. I was starting to get worried."

Hatset cut in. "So familiar with your Baga Nahid," she said archly. "Don't your people remove tongues for that?"

Saman stiffened. "I don't know what you're talking about."

Jamshid drew nearer, and then in a bold move that made Nahri smile, her brother took a stool, set it next to the queen, and sat.

"We can speak honestly," he began. "I know who I am, Saman, and if Manizheh sent you after me, I suspect you do as well. I wish my father had been honest with me so that I didn't have to learn the truth from strangers in a foreign land."

Saman lowered his gaze. "Apologies, my lord. For what it's worth, I did not know until recently." He glanced up again, genuine concern in his eyes. "Are you well, Baga Nahid? Have they hurt you?"

Jamshid inclined his head, gesturing to the room of armed soldiers. "I've been better, but I'm unharmed. How is the city? My father? My . . . mother?"

Saman brought his hands up in blessing. "It would be best if we spoke of those things in private."

"Which is not going to happen," Hatset pointed out. "Come. You've seen him, so now we shall have some answers. Why has Manizheh sent you?"

"Because she received your threat regarding her son," Saman replied. "It came at a poor time—she'd been trying to make peace with the djinn, only to be betrayed once again. Baga Jamshid," he said more softly, "I am very sorry to inform you that your father is dead."

Jamshid rocked back on his stool. "What? *How?*"

"He was killed during a peace summit the Banu Nahida had graciously organized. Unknown to us, Emir Muntadhir had been poisoning the Daeva houses against her, offering all manner of riches. It is to my lasting shame that some of our people gave in to the temptation. They murdered the grand wazir as he fought to return to her."

Jamshid sucked for air, blinking rapidly. "Oh, Baba," he whispered. He bit his lip, his gaze dropping to the floor as if to hide the whirl of emotions in his face.

Nahri was gripping the screen so hard it hurt. She wanted to drag him away. She wasn't going to pretend to mourn Kaveh, but the sight of her brother trying to hide his grief in public—before djinn he considered enemies—broke her heart.

Hatset was still composed. "Where is the emir now?"

"Awaiting execution with his sister."

Jamshid jerked up, fresh shock blossoming across his face. At Hatset's side, even Wajed let out a short gasp.

Hatset, though, Hatset was steel, her golden eyes narrowing as though the other man were an insect. A lying insect barely worth her time. "Sources have assured me that my daughter is not in Manizheh's custody."

"Your sources are out-of-date." Saman spread his hands.

"I am but a messenger, Lady Hatset, and I was commanded to pass on a warning. The fates of Ghassan's treacherous sons are decided, but our Banu Nahida wishes to extend to you one last mercy. Return Baga Jamshid unharmed within five days, and she will spare your daughter."

"*Five days?*" It was Wajed now. "You can't get to Daevabad in five days."

"I can do it in three," Saman corrected. "Banu Manizheh has been blessed with great magic. *New* magic, unlike anything her predecessors have known. The simurgh I traveled with are but a small part. Baga Jamshid will return with me, and your daughter will be granted clemency."

"So that means they're both still alive?" Jamshid had recovered, his expression urgent. "Muntadhir and Zaynab?"

The ambassador gave him a careful look. "For now, Baga Nahid. But our lady is grieving and rightfully angry, and there is no one in Daevabad to speak for them."

Nahri pressed her lips in a thin line, hearing the words he didn't say. Clearly the ambassador wasn't a fool. Jamshid wasn't acting like some cowed prisoner, and his relationship with Muntadhir was public knowledge. Manizheh wanted to tempt him. To leave open the possibility that if Jamshid returned to her, he could beg for Muntadhir's life.

Hatset was glaring at the envoy with naked hate. She nodded rudely at the chest. "And the other part of your message?"

Saman crossed to the chest. "The Banu Nahida has heard rumors you may be welcoming a pair of refugees soon. This displeases her. Surely you'd agree that we are stronger as a united people. I know she is helping my tribe to see that.

"So she wishes to make clear what happens to Daevas who don't obey."

He opened the chest, kicking it over to spill the contents.

Dozens—scores—of blood-spattered brass amulets fell to the ground.

Relics. *Daeva* relics.

Nahri was suddenly done with watching from behind a screen.

She shoved open the door, ignoring the soldier who moved to help her. Nahri was not dressed to impress—she was in the plain cotton gown and striped leggings she'd worn all day, splotches of dried blood splashed across her chest and mud staining the bottom of her trousers. The humidity had left her hair wild, curls escaping the scarf she'd tied at the back of her neck.

But Nahri didn't need fancy clothes to announce who she was, not when she could literally sense the blood that drained from Saman's face when she walked into the majlis with every bit of arrogance she possessed. "Why don't you explain to me *exactly* what was done to these Daevas who supposedly disobeyed?"

Saman stared at her, blinking rapidly. "Banu Nahri," he stammered. "I . . . may the fires burn brightly for you. Forgive me, I did not expect—"

"To see me. Yes, obviously." Nahri pointed to the relics. "*Explain.*"

"As I told the Baga Nahid, the—the situation has grown more dire." Saman's practiced words came out a little less steady now, the man clearly rattled by her unexpected presence. "Banu Manizheh wished our tribe to know the price of letting the djinn divide it."

"And that price is being given to the *ifrit*? Is that what you're implying? Because Manizheh has lost the right to call herself anything but a traitor if she gave another Daeva to the ifrit."

Saman's eyes darted up at the word "traitor," heat entering his expression. A true believer, then. "And what would one call allying with the man who stole Suleiman's seal?"

Nahri held up her hand and conjured a pair of flames, Sulei-man's ring gleaming in their light. "Misinformation."

The shock that blossomed across the man's face was almost worth the whole experience. "That's—that's not what we were told."

"Then your sources are out-of-date," Nahri said, coldly re-peating his words. "I will give you one more chance to explain what happened to the Daevas these relics belonged to."

He buckled. "They were executed for treason, that's all I know. And though they would have deserved it, I am certain the Banu Nahida would have never done anything as foul as giving them to the ifrit."

"Then you're a naive fool. How many?"

"How many what?"

Nahri took another step in his direction, and he recoiled. "How many Daevas did she execute? Our people, Saman. How many relics did you bring?"

His heart was racing so fast Nahri thought it might give out. "I don't kn—"

"Then count."

Saman was visibly shaking. But he obeyed, reaching for a handful of amulets. His lips moved wordlessly.

"Out loud," Nahri commanded. "Come—you arrived boast-ing of how wonderful Manizheh is and presented her gift with such flourish. Surely you're not ashamed to delve into it, to hold each one and call aloud the Daeva she killed."

The majlis was as silent as a tomb. Saman glanced around, but no one was saving him here, and Nahri's expression must have been lethal enough to make him swiftly return to counting.

"One, two . . ." The clink of the relics echoed across the vast chamber. "Three, four . . ."

It took several minutes for him to get through them all, and by the time Saman pronounced "two hundred and sixty-four," Nahri's rage had condensed, white-hot in her chest.

"Two hundred and sixty-four," she repeated. "Tell me, ambassador, for I'm a bit new at politics, but I'm fairly certain if nearly three hundred people had been plotting a coup, Manizheh would have gotten wind of it earlier."

Saman flushed but anger swept his face. He obviously didn't enjoy being humiliated by a young woman in a court full of djinn. "I trust she did what was necessary."

"I'm certain you do. Consider her message passed on." She glanced at Wajed. "Qaid, the cells below the castle haven't flooded yet, have they?"

He was glaring at the ambassador with open hostility. "Not entirely."

"Good. Please take this man to one of them. See that he is fed and cared for." She inclined her head at Saman. "Do those pitiful creatures Manizheh pulled from the grave need anything, or can they just continue decaying on the beach?"

Saman glowered at her. "They wait to return to Banu Manizheh." He glanced at Jamshid and Hatset. "I suggest you heed her warning, Lady Hatset. There won't be another one."

Hatset's eyes flashed. "And I suggest you leave before *our* Banu Nahida stabs you."

The ambassador didn't struggle when the soldiers grabbed him, but he planted his feet at the door. "Baga Nahid, please," he begged, turning to Jamshid. "You are a sensible man. Go home. Take your sister. There may still be mercy."

Jamshid's gaze darted to hers, but he said nothing as Saman was dragged out. With a nod, Hatset dismissed the rest of the soldiers.

The queen's bravado lasted only until the three of them were alone, and then she leaned back against her cushion and let out a shaky breath. "Zaynab," she whispered.

Jamshid had shot to his feet. "I'm going back. I'll talk to our mother, make her see reason. Surely this is an exaggeration. No Daeva would give another to be enslaved by the ifrit."

Nahri walked over to the chest of relics. She picked one up, examining it in the shafts of light shining through the windows. Daevas wore their relics in amulets around the neck, and though the amulets were always brass, they came in a wild assortment of forms. The one she'd picked up was decorated with raised half-moons encircled by tiny inlaid rubies. Blood had dried in the grooves.

Who did you belong to? Was it one of the Daevas who'd stood up and bowed before Nahri when Ghassan humiliated her in the throne room? Or maybe one of the shy youths she'd teased in the Temple garden? A priest who'd dug through the dusty archives to retrieve her family's books or the men who'd pressed home-made sweets on her when they'd visited the infirmary? Perhaps it had been a noblewoman who'd worn this amulet, one of the ones who'd kept Nahri silent company during her wedding, forming a quiet but firm line between their Banu Nahida and the gossiping djinn?

Maybe these relics had belonged to scheming nobles. Or maybe they'd been patriots, or something in between. Either way, when Nahri looked at these relics, she didn't see bloody pieces of brass. She saw people. *Her* people, flawed and broken and bigoted in their own way, but still hers.

And Manizheh had butchered them. To send a message.

Dara, please say you had no part in this. Nahri was dimly aware of Jamshid and Hatset arguing, but it wasn't Shefala's majlis that Nahri saw right now. It was Daevabad the day she first arrived, the mysterious island of magic growing nearer as the ferry cut through the lake. The ziggurats and temples, minarets and towers, all looming over the walls upon which her ancestors had carved their visage.

Welcome to Daevabad, Banu Nahida. How proud and excited Dara had been that day. Nahri realized only later how nervous he must also have been—that in his own way, he'd taken a shaky step on a bridge to peace they both learned too late hadn't been steady enough for him.

Nahri replaced the relic and closed the chest. "Jamshid, you can't go back."

He stopped in mid-fight with the queen. "Why not?"

"He certainly can," Hatset insisted. "If he doesn't, Zaynab might die."

Nahri softened her voice. "You said yourself that it was unlikely Manizheh had her. This is probably a bluff."

"I don't care. Not this time." A piece of Hatset's carefully composed expression cracked. "I have lost my husband to Manizheh and my son to the marid. I will not lose my daughter. If Manizheh is bluffing, she has called me true."

"And I might be able to sway her," Jamshid persisted. "Convince her to let Muntadhir and Zaynab—"

"Will you both just *listen* for a moment?" Nahri pleaded. "You think Manizheh doing this means she has the upper hand, that we are outmatched. But it doesn't. It means she's *desperate*. This isn't the act of the woman I met on the roof of the palace. She's killing Daevas she should be wooing. She's lost her partner. She's *breaking*. And if we give in now, she's never going to stop. She needs to be removed, not rewarded."

"And how do you suggest we do that?" Hatset asked. "You took Suleiman's ring from my son, but you haven't been able to restore anyone's magic. Jamshid has yet to find the miracle you were hoping would be in the Nahid texts. And Alizayd . . ." Trembling, the queen gripped the edge of her divan. "There is no one else with his standing who could pull together the shafit, djinn, and Royal Guard. We've been avoiding what his loss means, and now it is here. We have no viable path toward retaking Daevabad."

"So we submit to a woman who makes Ghassan look like a saint? That's your solution?"

"We *survive*," Hatset said. "We try and make sure our children, our families, and as many people as possible live through this, and hope there may come another day to fight." She gave Nahri a baffled look. "I would think you of all people would understand this."

Nahri did understand, but she wasn't that person. Not anymore. Not everyone had a powerful relative arranging for them to survive or the luxury of deciding not to fight.

"I'll go," Jamshid said again, more quietly. "Let me talk to our mother, Nahri. I have experience with Daevabad's politics. If I can't—"

"Queen Hatset!" The doors burst open, an Ayaanle steward falling to her knees. "Forgive me, my lady. But it's your father."

NAHRI FINISHED HER EXAMINATION, BRUSHING HER fingers over Seif's frail wrist and urging the bones underneath his paper-thin skin to knit back together.

"Why was he in the north tower?" Hatset demanded. "I warned you that he was having one of his spells. You need to keep a better eye on him when he's like this!"

Musa let out a frustrated sound. "We're trying, Auntie, but you know how he is, and he always finds a way out. He's been muttering about angels, saying he hears them whispering around the castle."

Nahri shifted on her heels, gently moving the old man's skinny hip back into place. The break there was simpler than the one in his wrist, but there was only so much she could do to heal it. The vagaries of aging—atrophying bones and fading organs—could not be removed with the laying on of Nahid hands, perhaps the Creator's quiet pushback against their abilities. Immortality was not supposed to be theirs to grant.

She eased a small pillow beneath him to alleviate the pressure. "You're going to need to find a way to keep him in bed." This wasn't the first time Nahri had met Seif Shefala, a charming, sly old man who'd managed to win her over even if his mind remained a decade in the past. "I'm sorry, my queen, but I don't think he'll be able to walk again, even short distances. And his wrist . . ."

Hatset looked shattered. "He was transcribing his great-grandmother's poems. The oral history of our family. It was the only thing that would bring him back to himself."

Musa touched Hatset's hand. "He can dictate to us when he's feeling better. We'll record them. And we'll make sure one of the family is at his side."

Nahri heard the unspoken *until the end*. Because even with the best care, she wasn't sure Hatset's father would see another monsoon. And though she'd heard enough to know he'd lived a long, full life, that wouldn't make his passing any less devastating for his loved ones.

"Thank you, nephew," Hatset said softly. "Would you mind calling a meeting with the rest of the family? We should talk."

Musa left, and then it was just the three of them. By the time Nahri had finished healing Seif, the old man was starting to stir, a grimace passing over his face.

She rose to her feet. "I'm going to prepare a potion for his swelling. It will help with the pain when I'm not with him."

"Thank you," Hatset replied, her gaze on her father. "Banu Nahida," she called when Nahri was at the door.

Nahri glanced back, and the weary, haunted expression on the queen's face stopped her cold. She'd never seen Hatset look so defeated.

"Issa offered to give the funeral prayers for Alizayd this morning." The queen didn't look at Nahri as she spoke. "I don't think he realized how I would react. I think he was genuinely trying to be kind."

"Ali's not dead." The words rushed out of Nahri, a fierce denial. "He's coming back."

Hatset glanced at her, and for the first time Nahri saw a true hint of desperation in the queen's aching gold eyes. "Your people believe you are blessed. Do you know his fate somehow? For certain?"

Nahri couldn't lie to her. Not to a daughter whose father was dying. A mother who'd done everything to keep her children safe, only to have them ripped away by monsters. "No." Her own voice broke. "But I made him swear it, and I think he's afraid of me."

Hatset gave her an anguished, heartbroken smile. "He definitely is." She paused, some of the emotion leaving her face. "You may stay in Ta Ntry, Banu Nahri. For what you've done for my family, for my father, for my son, you will always have a place in my home."

Nahri probably should have been grateful, but she knew a catch when she heard it. "And Jamshid?"

"Jamshid is going back to Daevabad. I've made my decision. He's made his decision." Hatset sounded almost sorry. "And if you try to stop him, I will have you locked in a cell."

I'd like to see you keep me there. But Nahri bowed her head. "I should get started on that medication."

Only when she was alone in the corridor did Nahri let her mask fall, pressing a fist to her mouth to keep herself from screaming.

My brother is going to die. Jamshid's story about poisoning Ali came back to her. *He's not going to be able to convince Manizheh to turn away from violence, so he's going to do something stupid and brave to try and stop her, and then he's going to die.* It didn't matter that Jamshid was Manizheh's son; Nahri had seen the limits of their mother's maternal affection.

Despair consumed her as Nahri hugged her arms against the chill in the corridor, turning everything she knew over in her mind, desperate to find a solution that did not involve losing yet another person she loved.

I should go drown those firebirds. She'd be putting them out of their misery *and* removing Jamshid's ability to leave. Nahri shivered again, her steamy breath clouding.

And then she stopped.

It should not be this cold in Shefala.

A finger of ice brushed her spine as Nahri glanced down the corridor. She was alone, and there was an unnatural stillness to the air, a quiet so intense it felt physical. Smothering. It was the middle of the afternoon—there should have been a whole cacophony of various noises, and yet the castle was so silent it felt like Nahri was its only inhabitant. She reached out with her magic, the sixth sense little denied.

There was nothing. No beating hearts beyond the walls, no coughs or billowing lungs. No *people.* Instead, a biting wind, like the breath of an errant cloud, swept over the nape of her neck.

Nahri broke, sprinting for her room. She yanked open the door, lunged through the entrance . . .

And stepped directly onto an icy cliff.

She took one look at the impossible landscape before her: snow-draped mountains and jagged black rocks set against a pale sky—where her *bed* should have been—and abruptly turned around, reaching for the door.

It was gone. All that was there now was a smooth expanse of ice, a gleaming wall that stretched in every direction.

Before Nahri could panic, her mind unable to process what in God's name had just happened, she was thrown into shadow. A creature had landed behind her, large enough to block the cloud-veiled sun. Nahri spun, slipping on the ice.

A shedu stared back at her.

37

ALI

Growing up, Ali had heard stories of hell that painted it as a misery of blazing fires and scorching winds. A place that would have been crowded and loud, with the souls of evildoers and their awful cries.

He was beginning to fear that was wrong. But there could be no term more apt than hell to describe the silent, empty realm beneath the sea in which he was trapped.

There was no day, no night. No *sky*. Only a heavy encroaching blackness that loomed overhead, so solid and foreboding that Ali couldn't look up without getting dizzy and feeling like he was about to be crushed. The only light came from the glow of the eerie teal water that flooded the ground, revealing the ruins of what appeared to have once been a city even larger than Daevabad—one seemingly destroyed and abandoned eons ago. A lost city, at the bottom of the world, in which Ali was the only inhabitant and time had no meaning.

He limped through yet another narrow pass, pushing past the towering, barnacle-encrusted walls. "Fiza!" he cried, his parched throat protesting. *"Fiza!"*

His voice echoed back, her name bouncing in fading waves. There was no response. There had been no response, no other *sound* since Ali woke up alone on the flooded sand, covered in bloody gashes, with one ankle badly twisted and what felt like a cracked rib stabbing him in the side. Some of the gashes had begun to heal—at least the ones that didn't pull open when he walked, turning the blood-crusted wounds into his only way of measuring time. With every breath and step, his ankle and rib protested, and yet Ali didn't stop walking, desperate to find a way out of this place. To give up would be to invite madness.

Maybe this is my punishment. Maybe Tiamat had taken one look at Ali, seen that he'd given away Suleiman's seal, and then tossed him here to suffer. And he would suffer. He was a djinn. It would take him weeks to starve to death, and it would be wretched.

The narrow pass widened, and Ali gasped as the water that had been sloshing around his ankles was suddenly at his throat. He submerged, getting a mouthful of salty liquid before he recovered enough to swim, new muscles aching in response. His zulfiqar floated in its sheath, banging against his hip. He had given up trying to keep the blade dry.

In the heavy silence, his every splash sounded thunderous as he passed stone reliefs of bizarre creatures: bulls with wings and the faces of bearded men, lion-headed warriors with maces and whips. And not just creatures, but faded scenes of gardens and warring armies, peculiar round ships and careful hunters. The reliefs had fascinated Ali at first, with their lines of undecipherable script and mysterious images. He'd wondered who'd carved them, if this city had belonged to the marid or to mortals.

Now he didn't care. All he wanted to do was escape. To drink water that didn't taste like the sea and enjoy a minute free of pain.

"Fiza," he yelled again. The thought of his friend tossed into this awful labyrinth, pushed him on. "Fiza!"

The pool ended in crumbling steps that led to a flat expanse of flooded ground, an arena perhaps, with the seats of an enormous amphitheater melting into the darkness. Ali staggered onto the sand and fell to his knees. The water was low enough here that he could lie down without it passing over his face, and dear God, did he need a rest.

Please let Fiza be alive, he begged. *Let us get out of here.*

Let this all matter.

Ali shivered in the damp chill, curling in on himself. He just wanted to be dry. Warm. He'd never felt more like a fire-blooded djinn than he did in this awful, lightless place of water and ruin. He ached to hold a flame, to whisper the word in his mind and see fire blossom between his fingers.

And then, as though his magic hadn't been stripped away when he'd been pushed into Daevabad's lake, heat sparked in his hand.

Ali scrambled up, staring in shock at the conjured flames dancing in his palm. His magic. His *djinn* magic; the abilities that had nourished him since he was a child, the ones that weren't tainted with his possession on the lake or some horrible family secret. He was on his feet the next second, pain be damned as he yanked his zulfiqar from its sheath.

"Brighten," he whispered.

The zulfiqar burst into flames. Glorious, swirling flames of gold and green that raced down the gleaming copper blade. The light exploded outward, attacking the smothering dark.

And illuminating the hundreds of armed warriors who'd been waiting for him.

Ali dropped into a fighting stance, but none of them moved. They were *statues,* he realized. Creations of stone and shell so lifelike it seemed impossible, garbed in the dress of a dizzying array of nations and times. Short tunics and pleated skirts, armor the likes of which he'd never seen, and a dozen varieties of helmets and shields. And while most of the statues stood at attention, lined up as though awaiting command, plenty more were sprawled on the ground with their stone hands raised as if to protect their heads, anguished expressions carved into their faces. Severed limbs littered the ground as though someone had taken a great hammer to them, smashing free legs and arms.

Ali prodded a stone torso with his foot. The artist had certainly taken great care to exactly depict spilled intestines.

Get out of here. Now. Gripping his zulfiqar, Ali carefully edged away, turning back the way he'd come.

Just in time to see, out of the corner of his eye, something large skitter away.

Ali spun, but it was already gone, vanishing into the darkness. He waited, but there was no sound save his pounding heart and uneven breathing. Whatever was out there beyond the black was silent. Waiting.

Watching. Ali pulled free the iron knife Wajed had given him. A weapon in each hand, he stayed light on his feet, pushing past the pain in his ankle.

He still wasn't ready.

A scaled tentacle lashed out, hitting Ali in the stomach and sending him flying. He'd only just landed in the sand, the wind knocked from his lungs, when he saw them—two demons lunging from the abyss. One was a sea scorpion the size of an elephant, with the horrifying upper half of a dead-eyed, purpling man. The second was equally monstrous: a horned viper with a spider's legs and batlike wings.

Ali rolled just in time to avoid the scorpion man's tail. Its stinger plunged into the flooded sand next to his head, the wicked, blade-sharp scythe dripping with poison.

He scrambled to his feet, narrowly avoiding a rake of the

viper's serrated legs, which would have ripped open his belly. The demons, monsters—whatever the hell they were—had taken Ali off guard.

But they would not catch him.

A blazing zulfiqar in his hand for the first time in months, Ali felt the despair and grief and utter *helplessness* that had gripped him since his city had fallen—since his father had banished him, since the marid had tortured him, since he'd awakened to the reality of living in a broken world in which his hands were tied in a thousand ways—fall away. The marid wanted a fight?

Fine.

Ali bellowed in rage, answering the viper's hiss and the scorpion man's awful moan, and threw himself at them.

He ducked the stinger again, then kicked the scorpion man in the chest, lashing out with his zulfiqar at the viper. It reared faster than his eye could track and then seized his injured ankle, dragging Ali to the sand.

This time the stinger didn't miss.

Ali screamed as it pierced his shoulder, the burning pain of the poison like being flayed with a thousand iron knives. But more in fury than fear, he struck out with his zulfiqar, slicing through the scorpion man's tail and severing the stinger, still embedded in his shoulder. The demon screeched as a spray of salty blood gushed from the wound.

Ali dropped the zulfiqar, ripped the stinger from his shoulder, and flung it at the viper's face before retrieving his weapon. His left arm was numb, and he tripped over his own feet, battling a wave of wooziness. The scorpion man was squealing, wheeling and bucking about like a half-crushed insect as blood spurted from his tail.

The horned viper came back, though, whipping around Ali's lower half and squeezing hard. Ali tried to wriggle free, gasping as the beast pressed the air out of him. His one working arm still free, he shoved the zulfiqar against the viper's scaled hide. It sparked and smoldered as the two of them howled in their death match.

"*STOP.*" The rumbling voice was familiar enough by now that a mix of relief and apprehension was rushing over Ali before he even saw Sobek charging across the flooded sand.

The scorpion man pulled at his snarled beard, chittering and wailing.

"He is not an invader," Sobek snapped. "He is kin." Sobek seized the scorpion man's tail, but instead of hurting him, a rush of water erupted from the Nile marid's hands, pouring down the monster's hide. In moments, his stinger was restored.

Sobek came for Ali next, untangling the horned viper trying to asphyxiate his descendant as though the beast were an inconvenient weed. There was something almost paternal about the annoyed exasperation with which he dragged Ali out of danger, and the reminder of the bond between them—the history Ali was still struggling to accept—made him want to throw up.

That could have also been the poison.

Sobek gripped his arm, sinking his claws into Ali's skin and sending a burst of coolness surging through his body. Ali fell to his knees, and his zulfiqar sputtered out, but relief was already coming—his injuries gone in a flash. The puncture the scorpion had punched into his flesh sizzled like boiling water and then healed, leaving a new scar. Ali touched it, his fingers meeting rough hide. The patch of skin Sobek had healed, about the size of Ali's hand, looked as though it had been replaced with Sobek's own scales.

He didn't have much time to consider it. The Nile marid had let go of Ali's arm only to seize him by the chin, yanking him back to his feet. Sobek's yellow eyes searched for the spot on Ali's temple where Suleiman's seal had been marked. It had started fading when Nahri took the ring, the few glimpses Ali had caught of his reflection in the water down here showing it was now gone for good.

Sobek's eyes narrowed to reptilian slits. "You fool. That ring was your only hope of salvation with Tiamat."

Ali wrested free of Sobek's hand. "It wasn't worth my people's magic or my city's safety."

The marid's expression twisted, snarling teeth layering with a disappointed grimace.

Then movement in the inky void shut them both up.

The ground shivered beneath Ali's feet, ripples dancing across the flooded sand. The stone warriors trembled, a pair tipping over and smashing together, then breaking apart in an explosion of tiny cowrie shells. Another glisten in the distance, the glimmer of a scaled fin like a whale breaching the sea's surface on a moonless night. The fin, only one, indicated an unfathomable size.

Ali straightened up, urging his zulfiqar to brighten once again. "My fire magic . . ."

"Suleiman's curse doesn't extend to this realm. You have the magic you were born with, fire and water together." Sobek's eyes met Ali's. "It will not be enough."

The darkness was condensing, churning. Shades of gray and midnight swirled into the black, rain falling from the unseen sky.

It's no sky, Ali realized. *It's the sea itself.* He *was* at the bottom of the world, in a fragile bubble of air and sand, beneath the crush of the ocean. The teal water was sloshing violently around his feet, tendrils licking up like hungry tongues. The ground gave a second great shake, as if the entire abandoned city had been caught in the current of a passing ship, and a towering marble column fell, knocking over a troop of stone soldiers like falling dominoes. There was another dart of fins, closer this time, and a gleaming, impossibly large curve of muscled flank.

Any hostility he felt for Sobek vanished. "Sobek," he whispered. "What do I—"

"She likes to be entertained," the Nile marid cut in, his voice urgent. He'd grabbed Ali's wrist again, so hard that it hurt, holding him firmly at his side. "She thrives on chaos and passion and will take it at your expense if it strikes her whim. Make sure it does not."

How do I do that? Ali wanted to ask. But he couldn't open his mouth anymore, couldn't make another sound. The darkness had split, crashing waves and storm clouds surrounding the ruined city like it was an island about to be devoured. Thunder boomed, shaking him to his bones as more rain lashed his face. The air smelled like blood, like salt, like the sweet scent of death. Lightning cracked across the oceanic horizon, illuminating a wild sprawl of sea creatures in the deep. Sharks and squids and eels, but also stranger things—armored fish, human-faced merpeople and sea dragons with multiple searching heads.

Ali didn't care about any of them. For swimming forth was a colossus that made the vast city he'd wandered for days seem small.

Tiamat.

THE MARID MOTHER CAME TO HIM IN INCREASINGLY fearsome pieces, too massive and too daunting to look at all at once. A spiked tail like a massive club and horselike forelegs that ended in talons. What might have been an udder, weeping waterfalls, and armored plates jutting from her back like hazy mountains, obscured by rainy gloom. Her serpentine belly could have contained five of Daevabad's palaces and was sheathed by brilliant scales that glistened like wet marble in a dazzling array of colors— the scales he'd seen covering the bottom of Daevabad's lake and the pathways of the Grand Temple. Another crack of lightning revealed barnacle- and coral-encrusted wings, like an entire section of the seabed had risen. Tentacles wriggled and stretched from seemingly everywhere.

And her face . . . Oh, God. Ali had to look up and up, to where clouds and the sun would have been, had he not been in this hellish unknown realm. Her face was almost too terrible to behold, a leering skull that mixed the worst features of a lion and a dragon. Bull ears jutted over eyes like swirling typhoons, and jagged teeth that could have bitten a chunk out of Shefala filled a muzzle framed with more tentacles.

Tiamat wriggled and stretched, then opened her mouth as if to yawn, and the resulting screeching roar, like the break of tidal waves and the death cries of seabirds, would have sent Ali back to his knees if Sobek hadn't been gripping his arm. Even so, Ali abruptly shut his eyes, a primal part of his brain unable to process what was before him and closing off in response.

Sobek's claws dug into his flesh. "Look upon her," the marid hissed in warning. "Control yourself. Make clear you come as kin, not as an offering."

Ali was shaking. He didn't feel like kin to anything down here. But he forced himself to obey, gazing again at her monstrous visage. A churning, rainy mist orbited around her head like a loyal moon—the monsoon marid, Ali recognized, Tiamat's messenger.

A voice boomed in his head, and Ali clapped his hands over his ears.

My children, Tiamat said lazily. Her voice was a drawl and a hiss and a pounding in his blood. *What trouble have you gotten yourselves into now?*

The monsoon marid spun faster. *Sobek! He has lied, disobeyed you once again!*

"I have done no such thing," the Nile marid growled.

No? Tiamat's tail lashed the ground, encircling the flooded plain they stood upon. *You were ordered to bring your kin to me once, and instead you devoured them yourself. Now my messenger says one survives, that he stands with a foot in each world and has endangered us all.*

"I acted in good faith when you ordered the annihilation of my daeva kin. You all know I did," Sobek said, glaring at the marid swarming the stormy water. "I am sure you have feasted upon the memory I gave you more than once. Any survivors in Daevabad would have been unseen to us all." He raised his voice in a crocodile's bellow. "You were fools to tangle with the daevas again! Their generation had forgotten us, had forgotten how Anahid the Conqueror used her ring against us. This new Nahid might have held it and never come for the waters. Instead, you acted rashly and empowered her champion!"

An eel-like creature with a turtle's face surged forth from the water. *An easy thing for a river lord safe in exile on the other side of the world to say.* It snapped its beak. *You have never borne the yoke of their servitude.*

There is a simple enough way to learn the truth, Tiamat declared, and the eel creature instantly bowed low. *Sobek may be cut off from the communing of waters, but his misplaced hatchling is not. We shall see and share.*

One of her tentacles shot out, snaking around Ali's leg and ripping him from Sobek's grip. He yelped in surprise, the flooded sand growing small in the distance as he was passed up Tiamat's vast body, overwhelmed by the blur of dazzling scales and the briny smell of rotting marine life.

The last tentacle deposited him onto a massive, webbed paw, its claws rising around Ali like lethal saplings. Tiamat drew him close to her gruesome face and grinned, revealing brackish teeth. This close he could see that great scars marred her body, perhaps the remnants of some long-ago battle.

Such fuss for something so small, she said by way of greeting. *I hope you are worth being awakened.*

She ripped into his mind.

Ali was driven to his knees, clutching his head as Tiamat wrenched open his life before his eyes. This was not Sobek or the monsoon marid idly flipping through memories like a bored student might study a book. This was everything at once, a blur of faces and laughter and pain. Climbing trees in the harem and weeping for his mother. The thrust of a dagger through his stomach on a cold night and Darayavahoush strangling him in the infirmary. The smell of blood, always blood. Anas's blood in the arena sand, shafit blood drying on Ali's face, Lubayd's blood spilling from his lips, copper-flecked blood dripping from his father's ear. Emotions. Passions. Lusts and hungers and things so long forgotten Ali wasn't entirely sure they were even his.

Sobek lunging from the Nile to save him from Qandisha and guiding him through the currents. The monsoon marid seizing him; Ali seizing Nahri. Nahri tumbling with him to the bed, her hands running down his body. Her hands cutting into his chest. The seal ring, wet with blood, on her thumb where it belonged . . .

Tiamat abruptly turned over her hand. Ali plummeted to the sand, landing hard on his back.

He gave it back. The amusement had vanished from her voice. *You let him leave your waters with it, and HE GAVE IT BACK.*

Ali gasped for air, catching his breath just in time for Tiamat to press her clawed paw against his chest, pinning him to the flooded ground. The salty water washed over his face.

Mortal, do you know what I would have given you for that ring? You wish to travel the currents? I would have devoured your enemies and seated you on a throne of their bones. I would have given you such power that you could have broken your world and re-formed it in the light you so desperately crave.

Sobek grunted, a low warning sound that would have made every hair on Ali's back stand on end if Tiamat hadn't been crushing him to death. The Nile marid was almost all crocodile now. "He has fulfilled his ancestor's pact. He is under my protection."

Tiamat made a sound that could have been her version of a snort—a horrible clacking coming from her monstrous mouth. *You and your pacts, Sobek.* She put more weight into her paw, and Ali writhed, certain his chest was about to collapse. *Have you ever seen how protective a crocodile can be over its eggs, mortal? How swiftly that can change?*

"He is *kin*," Sobek insisted. "He can see the currents and shape our magic. The blood debt that binds us from striking back at the Nahid's champion marks him as well."

Tiamat laughed but then released Ali. He rolled onto his side, choking and coughing.

Kin? Have you read his mind? He thinks of us as hell-bound demons and monsters. He despises you for what you did to his ancestors. He told the Nahid he wanted to crawl out of his skin when he learned you were part of him!

Sobek didn't flinch. "He is young. He will come to understand."

And is that what you wish, Sobek? That I give him back so you may have another daeva pet to keep company with in your lonely river? Why don't we see what your cousins think?

Tiamat shifted, shaking the ground, and then a burst of light rushed down her finned back and through the spine of her tail, glowing faintly beyond the curtain of blue water like signal fire along a mountain chain. More marid were emerging from the depths now, clustering closer.

Ali climbed to his feet, his body and mind aching. "What's going on?" he asked Sobek.

"They are communing." There was open longing in the Nile marid's expression. "She is sharing your memories among them."

The prospect of even more creatures gaining access to his innermost thoughts made Ali's stomach turn. "Do you not join them?"

"No."

Sobek's voice was cutting, but Ali pressed him. Deadly family history aside, the Nile marid was his only ally down here, and there was still so much Ali didn't know. "Why not?"

Sobek gave him a look so vicious that Ali stepped back. "Because I disobeyed her."

Ali didn't get a chance to question him further. Tiamat was already moving for them again. *My children remind me that you came with offerings. Shall we see what you have brought to buy your life?*

With a burst of water, Ali's ship appeared before them. Tiamat dragged a claw down its neck, splitting it like a hawk might rip open a rabbit. The hold burst, jewels and incense and precious resins spilling forth. One of her tentacles rooted through the piled treasure, tossing precious objects this way and that as though it weren't a life-altering fortune on the sand.

Trinkets, she dismissed them all, burying in a spray of mud a chest of gold that could have bought an army. *What good will sparkly baubles do in my realm? I was awakened from my sleep to deal with you, and all you've done is disappoint me.* She snatched at the chest of books.

"No, don't—" Ali spoke up, finally finding his voice before her.

Tiamat paused, and Ali glanced up to see a wild grin on her terrifying visage. *Is this something valuable to you?*

Flustered, Ali tried to explain. "They're not baubles. They're books. Precious ones we thought might honor you. Knowledge and stories and history. Entertainment," he blurted out, remembering Sobek's earlier advice.

Tiamat leered closer. *Then perhaps I shall spare you and it, and make you both part of my court. Drag you out to read, to* entertain *us all when the whim strikes.* One of her tentacles reached out, stroking the new patch of reptilian skin on his shoulder. *Down here, you should last a millennium or so if we keep replacing parts.*

Ali tried not to shudder. "I—"

The marid mother didn't let him finish. The tentacle slapped him roughly, and then her laughter boomed again, cruel and mocking. *But that is not what you want, Alizayd al Qahtani. You want to go home to your people and be a great hero. To grow old with your daeva family and the Nahid you love without ever thinking of the marid again.*

There was no denial he could make. Tiamat had seen into his mind, and Ali didn't think she'd appreciate him lying.

"Yes," he confessed.

A spray of water destroyed the chest of books, striking it so violently that pages and bindings went flying, their ink instantly coloring the water. The liquid rushed to him, winding up his legs.

So why have you not mentioned your most worthy offering?

Ali trembled, watching the ruined pages float away. The abrupt annihilation of something so priceless shook him to his core. "I have nothing else."

But you do.

And there, with another burst of water, was Fiza.

The shafit captain was unconscious, her braids and clothing in disarray. A nasty gash split her cheek, and one eye was blackened. But she was alive, her chest rising and falling with her breath.

Ali lunged forward. "Fiza!"

Give her to me in our way, Tiamat urged. *Cut her throat in my name, and she'll be reborn as one of my fighters,* she said, gesturing to the stone army. *Once a century I grant one freedom when we gather to watch them battle. A woman with a touch of daeva blood should be a fascinating addition.*

Ali recoiled. "Never."

Then perhaps I shall let the sea crush her and give you to my fighters. Though it hardly seems fair—a man with the power of fire and water against poor, bewitched humans.

There was a cruel eagerness in the way she said the words that sent apprehension dancing down his spine. Tiamat had seen inside his head. She knew Ali was not going to murder an innocent friend, let alone do it while chanting some sea demon's name.

So what was she after?

"Do it," Sobek warned. "You have nothing else to give her."

"I don't need your opinion on murder," Ali snapped back, struggling to keep the emotion from his voice. He had a sudden, almost violent need to have Nahri at his side. She would have been able to figure out what Tiamat wanted. Cutting a deal was what she had begged him to do.

Tiamat was laughing. *So ungrateful to your progenitor.*

Ali swallowed hard. "There must be some way we can help each other. I am allied with the Banu Nahida. Perhaps we can negotiate the return of the lake—"

Tiamat chuckled and then dropped to his level so fast that Ali jumped. Her gleaming skull was the size of a hill, her jagged teeth longer than he was tall.

Beyond, more marid were coming. They'd pressed forward at the mention of the lake, bright eyes flashing.

Tiamat didn't seem as intrigued. *Why barter with daeva over an old lake when I have the entire ocean? No, mortal, I was awakened to deal with you and Sobek, and so I shall. You wish to preserve the life of yourself and your friend and travel the currents to save your home. Sobek, you are alone, yearning to rejoin us. What if there was a way to settle all of this?*

At Ali's side, Sobek stilled. "You said my exile was permanent. That if I communed with another, you would stop the waters that feed my river and make me watch my land die."

And now I offer you a chance at forgiveness, to prove your affection for these creatures has faded.

"His *affection*?" Ali repeated. "He lured generations of my ancestors astray, and when they refused to betray their people, he devoured them!"

Tiamat grinned. *See what your spawn thinks of you, Sobek? They will never be grateful, never loyal.*

Sobek glared, perhaps his own temper catching. A marid whose natural form was a crocodile likely had a short one. "I warned you to run," he growled to Ali. "I might have carved that seal from your heart. I might have let the marid of the monsoon drive you insane."

Tiamat was licking her teeth. Chaos, she craved. Entertainment.

Surely in an age where the humans have forgotten us, we only need one lord of the river of salt and gold. Tiamat moved back from the arguing pair, knocking over the top level of a ziggurat to lounge upon the drowned city. She gazed at them with her ghastly eyes. *May the victor be rewarded with my grace.*

The victor. Ali glanced again at the field of stone soldiers. At the *arena*. Surely she wasn't suggesting . . .

Don't be reckless, Nahri had warned.

Ali made a motion of peace. "Wait, let's just—"

Sobek lunged at him.

ANY HOPES ALI MIGHT HAVE ENTERTAINED OF SOBEK'S mercy vanished the moment the Nile marid smashed into his chest. They fell to the ground, and Ali threw up his arms to protect his face. Sobek raked them with his claws, and then went for Ali's throat.

Tiamat was indeed going to get her entertainment.

He thrust his shoulder into the underside of Sobek's snout— the Nile marid was all crocodile now, and three times bigger than his unfortunate descendant—just as Sobek's jagged teeth grazed his neck. Ali reached out, seizing his jaws and fighting with both hands to keep the marid's mouth shut.

"Oh, *you're* angry?" Ali accused as they wrestled. "Bastard." He grunted. "Do you know how hard it is to be worse than my father?"

Sobek rolled in response, spinning and crushing Ali beneath the water. Tiamat was cackling beyond the splashing waves and grappling fighters.

I need my weapons. Ali didn't think he had much chance against Sobek either way, but he was definitely not going to defeat the millennia-old lord of the river of salt and gold with his bare hands.

Ali kicked out, sending the nearest stone warriors tumbling.

A man in a toga, a laurel wreath in his hair and a tortured expression on his face, toppled over Sobek with a thud, pinning his tail. Taking advantage of the moment of distraction, Ali dashed away.

He lunged for the ruined wall, but Sobek caught him. His teeth closed over Ali's ankle and yanked him back. Ali cried out in pain, but he was already reaching for his zulfiqar.

"Brighten!"

Flames burst down the blade, provoking hisses and whistles and clicks from the crowd of watching marid. Ali swung it at Sobek's head but kept the poisoned flames from making direct contact with him, still reluctant to kill his ancestor.

"Let me *go*. Sobek, please, for the love of—" Ali screamed as Sobek's jaws clamped tighter. The crocodile was pulling him into deeper water, thrashing and shaking him as though to rip his very leg off.

Oh, God, it hurt. It hurt so much, and yet the marid's viciousness was the reminder Ali needed. He would see no mercy here.

So he would show none in kind. Ali lashed out with his zulfiqar and scorched a blazing line of fire across Sobek's eyes.

The marid bellowed, letting go enough for Ali to pull his leg free and scramble backward on his elbows as blood blossomed from his savaged ankle, staining the teal water. Sobek was writhing on the sand. Blood poured from him as well, lines of poison snaking out from his ruined eyes in delicate, deadly tendrils.

And then they stopped. Ali watched, frozen with horror, as the zulfiqar's poison started to reverse, Sobek's eyes stitching back together . . .

Ali shot to his feet and fled.

His maimed leg burned in protest, pain shooting through his ankle each time his foot hit the ground. Ali ran anyway. He'd just had a taste of the brutal death Sobek intended to deliver to him, and Ali would run from it for as long as he could, putting as much distance as possible between the two of them.

Think, al Qahtani, think! Ali dashed up a set of stairs, vaulting over a stone wall. Beyond was a maze of smaller buildings, a warren of bare structures that must once have been tightly packed homes and workshops. Half ruined, it was more labyrinth now than anything else.

It would have to work. Still gripping his zulfiqar and knife, though keeping the flames doused for now, Ali fled among the buildings.

Darkness crept over him as he took the turns at random, going deeper into the city. How did one kill a creature like Sobek, an ancient predator who healed as fast as a Nahid—*better* than a Nahid? Someone more powerful than Ali would ever be?

Someone overly powerful. Someone so used to winning and crowing over lesser mortals that they underestimated them. Ali's long-ago fight with Darayavahoush came back to him—their first one, the sparring match Ali had very nearly won until he'd stepped back, unwilling to put a khanjar through the throat of his father's guest, and the Afshin had responded by hurling a wall of weapons at his head.

Ali wouldn't make that mistake again. He glanced around at the ruins, all soldier now, the warrior who'd been trained to outthink his enemies.

And by the time Sobek came through, silent as the grave, Ali was ready.

He watched from upon a broken roof, high enough that the breeze wouldn't carry his scent. Stripped down to his waist-wrap, Ali was cold, but he didn't allow himself to shiver, didn't allow himself to breathe as he tossed a broken brick into the room where he'd left his blood-soaked dishdasha—the scent he'd let the marid hunt. Sobek lunged into the room with a snarl.

Ali leapt from the roof and landed on his back.

The marid was fast, but Ali was prepared, slamming the crocodile's head down, looping his weapons belt around Sobek's snout and binding it shut. The marid bucked and twisted as Ali smashed the hilt of his zulfiqar into the back of his skull, but it was like beating a rock.

Sobek started to transform. Ali's strikes gained more purchase as Sobek shifted, blood bursting from his softer, more humanoid neck. But in his other form, the marid would have the hands he needed to rip the belt off his face, seize Ali, and strangle him to death. Ali had the advantage, but only for another moment.

Kill him. Kill him, you idealistic fool. Cut off his head, spear his heart. He would kill you. He's going to kill you!

Sobek fought, slipping around so that Ali was facing him. It was a unwise move. He'd be able to grab Ali once he got his hands free, but right now it exposed the pale underside of his throat.

KILL HIM! It was Tiamat, bloodlust in her voice.

His ancestor struggled to wrench himself free. Ali plunged his knife into one of Sobek's hands, pinning it to the ground, and the marid bellowed in pain.

Sobek deserved to die. He'd slaughtered innocents for centuries. His marid cousins had tortured Ali in the lake and stolen him away when his people needed him most. He saw again his mother's despair as she sent him to his doom. He heard Nahri begging him to find a way back.

What was Sobek in comparison? A monster. A *murderer*. A demon from an age of ignorance and brutality that Ali's had rightfully stomped out.

Tiamat was laughing. Beyond, the other marid waited, their alien gazes unreadable.

Sobek's eerie yellow eyes met his. Ali saw himself reflected in the black sliver of pupil—he looked young. Terrified.

The Nile marid stared at him. His arms had been transforming, his claws reaching for Ali's wrists . . .

And then, so slightly that only Ali would have noticed, Sobek stilled.

A trick. It had to be a trick. Ali was shaking, the hilt of his zulfiqar slick with blood. He could bring it down. One strike, and Tiamat would give him everything he needed to save his people. To be a hero. To get his revenge.

Ali howled in frustration. And then he threw his zulfiqar away, rolled off the ancestor he couldn't kill, and stood to face Tiamat.

She had already dropped down to snarl at him. *Weak little mortal! Does your fiery heart ache with affection? Do you miss your murdered father? Think Sobek will stand in his place?*

Ali glared at her, several responses rising to his tongue. He could declare that these murderous entertainments were evil. That he wouldn't kill a bound man. That Tiamat was a monster. A demon.

The crowd of marid were still watching. They'd seen the memories of the naive youth they probably assumed was about to stand up for righteousness and promptly be devoured.

And Ali had seen them. Wailing as Anahid bound them. Sacrificing their strength to send Sobek away so that he might find a way to save them all.

Ali fixed a cold gaze on Tiamat. "So is this what you've been doing all this time?" He gestured between himself and Sobek, then nodded at the stone army. "While your children have been chased from their sacred lake, forced to toil for Nahids, and submit to their champion's terrors, you've been playing with toys in the mud?"

Tiamat hissed, a rush of fetid air and saliva nearly knocking him out. *Maybe I'll toss you back to this so-called champion.*

"I would welcome it. Better to fight than cower down here." Ali turned to face the crowd of marid. "You all judge Sobek, and yet at least he *did* something! Where are the mighty marid I grew up fearing? You claim you could devour my land, build a throne from the bones of my enemies, and yet you shrink from this Afshin?"

A figure emerged, what looked like a drowned man reduced to shell-encrusted bone, with weeds wrapped around his skull. *You do not understand his power and his viciousness. He murdered one of my acolytes, an innocent human, just to get my attention. He boiled my lake, slaughtering its creatures, and threatened to do the same to all our waters!*

"So let's find a way to stop him. We should be *helping* one another rather than wasting time on these games. Would you give up your freedom to travel the world, to tend to your own streams and lakes in favor of staying here . . . with your mother," Ali added delicately, "forever?"

A visible shudder went through the group.

Tiamat lashed the ground with her tail, shaking them all. *You are fools to listen to him. He is daeva, heart and soul, and all they do is lie. He is more likely to throw himself at this champion's feet and lead him to your waters.* She jutted her head. *Ask Sobek what happened last time he trusted a daeva.*

Sobek had climbed back to his feet, shifting to his other form and tearing Ali's belt from his mouth. Ali wasn't sure what had happened back there, if Sobek had meant to give up, but his ancestor still looked very capable of murder.

His words, though, were measured. "My kinsman speaks truly. He is ally to the youngest Nahid, and I have protection ties to her family. If there was ever time to make a pact with them, it is now." Sobek paused. "Or perhaps I could visit my river's mouth and see if the great mother who swims in the northern sea wishes to help."

Tiamat started to growl, but Ali interceded. He might not be an unkillable warrior or capable of transforming into a crocodile, but stoking political dissent in the name of justice?

They were playing his game now.

"Let me and my friend return," he implored. "Sobek may accompany us and teach me how to swim the currents. I will get you your lake back and find a way to remove the daevas who threaten you. Come now," he added when Tiamat's eyes churned faster, "surely I am more use to your people up there than as a flicker of entertainment down here."

The marid were murmuring and chittering, the water growing tumultuous.

Sobek stepped closer. "We desire another way, Tiamat. I do not need to commune with my kin to see that. I will take him."

Tiamat had drawn up, sneering. *You will not. Not until he pays a price. You wish to speak for the marid, mortal? To be our voice when you are too frightened to confess the slightest connection? You speak to my children of their loss, a loss of which you know nothing?*

"I will listen to them," Ali promised. "I swear. I—"

That is not how we do things. Tiamat gazed down with her terrible visage. *You wish us to trust you, to open our sacred currents, though you intend to dwell with your daevas? Then I will make it so you never forget your obligation. So none will forget it.*

Apprehension darted down his back. "What do you mean?"

You will give your name to me truly. And then I will drain every last bit of fire from your blood.

Ali's stomach flipped. "I don't understand."

"It means she will take your fire magic." Sobek turned to face him. "*All* of it. You will belong more to us than the daevas."

Ali's mind abruptly went blank. *You will belong more to us than the daevas.* His gaze fell upon his zulfiqar, the thrill he'd felt at finally enflaming it going cold.

But it wasn't just his zulfiqar. It was *everything*. The flames he'd taught Nahri to conjure, the magic that allowed him to pass through Daevabad's veil, the heat in his hands he'd use to boil a cup of coffee. Half their traditions revolved around fire, their *world* revolved around fire magic. It's why losing it brought their society to a standstill.

And his would be gone.

Ali's mouth went dry. "Forever?"

"Yes," Sobek replied softly. "You must understand, it will affect everything about you. Your life. Your mind. Your appearance."

My appearance. It was stupid that such a thing made his heart skip in fear, but there it was. Ali saw how cleverly Tiamat had trapped him. She knew how he felt about the marid. Knew how his people felt about them. There would be no careful diplomacy, no masking the marid's involvement as Ali's ancestors had done—or even slowly revealing it when the dust settled, if indeed this won him their victory.

Come back to me, Nahri had made him promise. Ali closed his eyes, seeing the anguish on her face when he'd begged her to cut the seal from his heart. Seeing Fiza's defiance when she'd insisted on accompanying him. Muntadhir's grim determination when he stayed behind to fight, and the quiet bravery with which Anas had accepted martyrdom. All the prices others had paid.

Daevabad comes first. One of the few lessons his father had taught that Ali still honored.

Tiamat let out a scornful growl. *See how he chooses them? The daeva brat lectures us on courage and then—*

"Alizayd al Qahtani." The syllables fell from his mouth like someone else was speaking them. Tiamat blinked, the great marid mother actually looking surprised, and so he repeated the words more firmly. "My name is Alizayd al Qahtani."

Tiamat regarded him. He couldn't tell if she looked annoyed or pleased.

So be it, she declared.

Ali didn't even get a chance to conjure a last flame.

Her words had no sooner blossomed in his head than he was driven to the flooded sand. It felt like a pike had been thrust through his heart, one made of ice and metal barbs. It *twisted,* filling him with cold poison and sucking every hint of warmth away. Ali nearly bit through his tongue, trying not to scream as the pain spread in slow, agonizing waves.

He fell forward onto his palms. Molten fire danced from his hands, the warmest, most beautiful golden glow he'd ever seen. Like a caught ribbon, it reluctantly let itself be tugged away, drops clinging to his fingertips before they fell. Ali fought the wild urge to grab them, to gather the precious liquid draining into the sand. More ran down his cheeks, whether the blood Tiamat had claimed or tears, he did not know.

A deep, clammy coldness rushed through his body, claiming the space the five had occupied as the flavors of the air shifted. A hint of gray stole over his vision, and the black void was suddenly clearer. The scars the marid's possession had carved into his arms were glowing, the lines of tissue melting into swirling paths of brilliant, iridescent scales.

Ali shut his eyes—he didn't want to see this. Racked with pain, he was only barely aware of Tiamat speaking again.

Show him, Sobek. Show him what we are.

Sobek laid a hand on his skull. "Let them pass. If you fight, it will drive you mad."

Ali was gasping for air, his eyes still closed. "What will drive me—"

Sobek's memories poured into his head.

Ali cried out, water bursting from his skin. He tried to free himself, but the Nile marid was ready, holding him firmly in his arms.

"Let them pass," Sobek urged again. "Let yourself hear and taste, see and feel. It is a blessing. Accept it."

Let them pass. His mind laid open, raw and scoured, Ali had no choice. It was too late to turn back now.

Hear. The crashing of waterfalls and herons in flight. The singing of harvest songs in tongues no longer spoken and his name chanted in soft worship.

Taste. The iron earth of flooding fields and the blood of his prey.

See. The glimmering cap of a stone pyramid that touched the sky, a structure so striking that he rose from his river and felt the first touch of trepidation at what the humans could do. An empty plain that seemed to sprout into a city overnight.

Feel. His daeva child, his first, in his arms, strangely warm and wriggling. Then dozens, the affection with which the first greeted him fading to apprehensive reverence. His favored heir, the one who might finally promise deliverance, falling to his knees.

Forgive me, Grandfather, his heir begged. *I could not betray them.*

The sudden blow of Sobek's banishment, loneliness as he watched his temples fall and mortals forget his name, scratching out his image and taking bricks with his visage for floors. The silence of centuries with no communing, no worship, no pacts until he was so weak he could no longer shift out of his crocodile form, until he'd crawled into the weeds, starving.

The little human girl who'd found him, utterly fearless as she slipped through the sugarcane surrounding her riverside village and dropped a pigeon in front of his jaws, the first offering he'd been given in a thousand years.

"My grandma said we should be good to crocodiles," she'd announced, crouching across from him. Her words took him aback as much as her eyes. Big, bright, and brown, with a hint of the gold that had colored the eyes of his long-dead daeva kin.

A hint of magic.

Ali tried to return to himself and seize upon the memory, but instead he noticed that the water had been rising and was now creeping up his neck, lapping over his closed lips. Despite his promise, he wrestled against his ancestor's grip, filled with the awful premonition that whatever the marid had already done to him, this last part would be the worst and place him at a remove from his people he'd never escape.

You promised you'd return to her. You swore to always put Daevabad first. Weeping and praying to God that there would be something left of him after, Ali let his lips fall open. Salty water poured down his throat, invading every corner of him.

Along with the lives and memories of hundreds of marid.

Rain spirits who danced in the clouds to shatter themselves upon the ground, seeping deep into the earth to join aquifers. Shy stream guardians, darting through quiet ponds and underground springs with webbed hands and turtlelike beaks. Merpeople with shimmering skin and seaweed hair, caught in the nets of humans, hunted and speared. For every lethal marid—ones like Sobek and others who commanded sharks, who lived on the blood of the drowned and warred with the daevas—there seemed twenty gentle ones, protectors not hunters, content with seeing to the tiny aquatic creatures who called their realms home and urging their life-giving waters to sate the surrounding lands and make them flourish.

Ali suddenly knew what Sobek meant when he said the marid were connected. They were more than a family—they swam among one another's minds and memories, intensely bonded with their kin and their waters, one foot in the physical world and another in the collective where the currents churned. Not all currents were the same. There were certain nodes, great waters where the marid met and shared memories, cavorted and birthed. A cold northern sea ringed with ice, and the warm, salty darkness at the bottom of the earth where Ali was now. A humid tropical waterfall surrounded by jungle and a riverine cave lit by glowing quartz.

A mist-shrouded lake. Deep and serene, perhaps the most sacred place they had. Ali saw it *stolen,* felt the air burn with choking, foreign smoke and fill with the cries of those of his people who were now trapped, who labored to build a city of dry stone and were crushed underfoot. He saw generations of cruelty before the daevas began to weaken and forget, and the marid fled, one by one.

He saw a daeva warrior on a chilly beach smash in the head of a screaming human acolyte. Watched the body burn, the *lake* burn, as the fiery-eyed man promised devastation and death. Ali felt sheer existential terror on a level he never had as his people tried to avoid a fate that seemed inevitable.

They will burn our waters. They will make us slaves.

Ali witnessed, through the eyes of an elder who'd been trapped in the molten crust of the lake since the days of Anahid, a young daeva man thrown to the waters. He was already dying, arrows through his throat and chest. A warrior, a gray-eyed youth whose blood didn't have quite the same acrid taste as the rest of the daevas, but the marid elder didn't think to worry about that. *Here* was a chance to rid themselves of the doom that seemed inescapable, to rid themselves of the Nahid's champion who the peris whispered would destroy them all.

They seized it.

Sobek relaxed his grip, the torrent of memories fading as Ali drifted in the water.

"Do you understand now?" the Nile lord asked.

Yes, Ali replied. *I understand.*

38

DARA

"Wake up."

Dara's eyes shot open.

For a second, he didn't understand where he was, or why the blackness he'd been dragged from was so encompassing, as though his very existence had briefly ceased. There was movement, the floor beneath him rumbling as though being wheeled over an uneven road. Above was a narrow silk-draped ceiling, patterned like those found in the palace carriages. A throbbing ache spiked from the relic clamped around his wrist . . .

The relic. The *ring*. Dara jerked up, reaching for his knife.

"Lie down."

He collapsed, the back of his skull slamming into the carriage floor.

There was an impressed whistle—Aeshma's, he recognized— and then three people were leaning over his prone form, Manizheh and her two ifrit. Dara writhed against her control, twisting and clenching his hands, but he couldn't remove himself from the ground.

"You did it." Awe glittered in Aeshma's fiery eyes when he turned his attention to Dara. "Have a nice sleep, Afshin?"

Dara had never felt such a violent need to murder someone. He dug his fingers into the wood. "I will kill you. I will rip out your fucking throat—"

"Enough." At Manizheh's command, the words died in his mouth. Dara hissed, wriggling once more against the invisible bonds holding him.

Vizaresh examined Dara's cuff, tapping the relic and pressing a finger against the pulse in his wrist. Dara wanted to scream. He wanted to weep. To burn down the world and himself along with it. He thought he'd given everything to serve the Nahids, only to learn that there were still things they could take from him. The little freedom that remained. His agency. His very dignity as these vile creatures poked and prodded his body.

"He's still alive," Vizaresh said. "I thought we agreed you would kill him. The curse would have bonded better." He sounded more fascinated than disappointed, though, and Dara chided himself for not paying more attention to Vizaresh's obsession with new forms of magic. To the slave rings the ifrit wore around his neck. Of course he and Manizheh would have experimented together.

"He's still my Afshin. I'm not going to kill him." Manizheh looked on Dara with affection. "Indeed, I'm hoping at the end of all this, when our enemies are dead, and we finally have peace . . ." She smiled gently. "When you understand why I did this, I will grant you your freedom."

Dara was too desperate not to beg. "Banu Nahida, please."

"Be quiet and listen."

His mouth snapped shut.

The furrowed line in her brow relaxed. "Better. Now, you have put me in a difficult position by meeting with Ghassan's daughter. Not only did we miss an opportunity to arrest her, but the Creator only knows what stories she's been spreading of your disloyalty. I cannot have that, Afshin. I cannot have the djinn whispering that my own general takes meetings behind my back. I need all of Daevabad to know your loyalty is mine alone. I need them to know what happens when they defy me."

Dara struggled to peel himself off the floor, to scream. But all he could do was make a strangled sound of protest in the back of his throat.

A knife. A *knife*. If he could just get a knife, he could cut his throat. Puncture his lungs, his heart, slice off the relic. Anything to stop Manizheh from using him like this.

She had one—Dara's straight dagger now sheathed at her waist. With all the strength he could muster, he tried to reach for it, but his hand felt like it had been pinned by a boulder. He finally lifted his fingertips . . .

Vizaresh noticed. "He's fighting your control. You need to be more specific, Banu Nahida. Use the words."

Dara grunted, roaring in his head as Manizheh pursed her lips. *No*, he wanted to shout. *Please!*

"All right," she started slowly. "Afshin, I wish for you to publicly demonstrate your loyalty. You will neither speak against me, nor do anything to draw suspicion to your state."

The fight went out of him. Forcibly. Dara's hands unclenched against his will, his boots ceasing their knocking.

Manizheh continued. "I wish for you to destroy the Geziri, Ayaanle, and shafit districts block by block until Zaynab al Qahtani surrenders. I wish for you not to show mercy. You will not disobey me or allow yourself to come to harm. You will sow as much fear and discord as you did during your rebellion.

"You will be the Scourge."

Creator, kill me. I beg you. I BEG YOU. But Dara was already sitting up, magic washing over him in waves. His dirty robe transformed, giving way to the black-and-gray uniform he'd worn when they'd attacked the city. Scaled brass armor crawled over his chest and down his arms, climbing up his neck to sweep back in what he knew would be a perfect imitation of the helm he'd once worn. The weight of a sword and a mace at his waist, a bow and sheath on his back.

Then the polished wooden handle of a scourge landed in his hand, barbed lashes sprouting from it like a vile weed.

There was nothing Dara could do. If he had begun to chafe under his Afshin duty to obey, this—this *theft* of his body and tongue—was the cruelest response imaginable. He turned toward the carriage door and kicked it open like someone was pushing the levers of his legs.

They were in the Daeva Quarter, just behind the gate that led to the midan. The bars keeping it shut were open, revealing the stone wings of the shedu statues that framed it. Dara could still remember how they'd leapt to his aid the day he'd returned Nahri to Daevabad.

Nahri. *Oh, little thief, would that I had listened to you that night.* Would that Dara had bowed his head to her instead and never set this horror in motion.

His warriors were lined up, as armed as he was, and already on horseback. Uncertain black gazes darted to him, confusion in their faces. After all, had Dara not been cautioning patience? Making quietly clear to his inner circle that the djinn outnumbered them and that to go in would be a bloodbath?

He wanted to tell them to run. Instead, power building in his blood, Dara raised his scourge to the air.

"Today we end this!" he announced. "The djinn have returned our gesture of peace with deception and murder. They need to be taught a lesson. You will show no mercy and take no prisoners. We do not stop until they submit, lay down their arms, and hand over Zaynab al Qahtani."

As the words poured from him, Dara prayed to see disquiet among their faces. Hesitation.

There was none. He had trained them too well. They roared their approval.

"For the Nahids!" Noshrad cried, brandishing his sword.

"For Banu Manizheh!" Dara snapped his fingers, and magic surged to his hand, a hundred times faster and more powerful than it ever had before, as if he'd jumped into a rushing river and been swept away. One of his conjured winged horses appeared before him, dazzling with a spray of smoldering embers in its ebony mane, the four wings billowing like smoke. He launched himself onto its back.

Dara had no sooner appeared in the midan than gunshots rang out, followed by a barrage of arrows. It didn't matter. Manizheh had wished for him not to be harmed, and so the curse simply didn't allow it—the projectiles bursting into flames and falling as ash before him.

"Djinn!" he roared, rising in the air on his winged horse. "I come with a simple message. Submit. Lay down your weapons and hand over Zaynab al Qahtani, or we will destroy you. The longer you take, the more of you will die."

He didn't wait for a response. He couldn't. Manizheh's wish was tearing through him, energy wrapping around his limbs and crackling down his fingers. His relic seared his skin.

Dara closed his hands into fists, and half the midan came down.

The three great gates, gates that had stood for centuries even when he was a boy—the stark Geziri archway, the studded pyramids with the proud Ayaanle standards, and the tiled columns leading to the warren of shops and shafit homes—crumbled into dust, the copper wall that connected them shattering. The wall came down with such violence that the buildings nestled against it were ripped apart, furniture and bricks and beams crashing down. It didn't take much effort—the city had been slowly dying, rotting from the inside since its magical heart was torn out. But to see something once so mighty, so old, obliterated in seconds . . .

We were supposed to be the saviors of Daevabad.

Instead, Dara gazed upon ruins. There were already screams rising from them. Children crying for their parents, the wails of the dying.

But Manizheh had ordered him to bring down the streets until Zaynab was caught. And so Dara raised his hands again, crying out in his mind as people ran to the buildings that had already collapsed, scrabbling at the heap in hopes of rescuing those trapped inside.

He rained down the next block directly on top of them.

That brought silence. For a moment. Dust rose from the rubble, hazy in the air. Dara motioned to his warriors and pressed forward.

He didn't have to speak. He'd given his orders and his soldiers, having spent the past weeks penned up in the Daeva Quarter as conspiracies and paranoia swirled, having just tended the funeral pyres of their comrades murdered in the failed coup, didn't need a reminder.

They threw themselves on the survivors, hacking at the djinn and shafit trying to dig through the rubble and firing arrows into the backs of those who fled. On horseback, they were faster, running down their victims.

Go away from this in your head. It was an old instinct, as though a past version of himself—a forgotten version, the Dara who'd survived centuries of ifrit enslavement—had quietly risen to hold his hand and see him through this latest horror so it wouldn't obliterate what was left of his soul.

But it was too late for that. Dara's horse landed on the road, and he lashed a man across the chest, getting what he knew would only be the first of many coats of blood on his scourge. He roared for his men to charge forward and then brought down another block of buildings. Bricks exploded outward, the roof of a long alley of shops crashing down on the crowd that had rushed to shelter there. Dara scourged another man. A woman. A boy. Blood was thick on his skin, the bodies piling up around him.

It wasn't enough. Zaynab al Qahtani was nowhere to be seen, and Manizheh's wish drove him to further destruction, further death. Dara returned to the sky to bring down a vast complex he recognized as a famed school in the Ayaanle Quarter and a public garden in the Geziri one. Then he headed for the old border between the Geziri and shafit neighborhoods.

The next block was Nahri's hospital.

No. Dara fought harder against the curse binding him, frantic for a way out. A way to delay. He couldn't harm himself; he couldn't *not* carry out the order.

So he sent his horse hurtling to the ground.

The cobblestones cracked under the heat and energy pouring off his body. It was as if he'd plummeted into the hell he deserved, nightmarish scenes of panicked mothers running with sobbing children and his soldiers locked in bloody, uneven combat with shafit civilians. There were blasts of gunfire and the punch of arrows. Homes were ablaze, the thick smoke a backdrop against the rise and fall of blades, the spray of blood.

The saviors of Daevabad.

Still Dara's feet carried him forth. His scourge was gone, ripped from his hand when it stuck too deeply into the back of a weeping man who'd fallen to his knees to beg for his life. Dara now held a mace in one hand, a dagger in the other.

But the djinn hadn't fallen apart completely. Not yet.

"Hold the hospital! Target the Scourge!"

Warriors threw themselves on him. Men mounted on horses, women flinging scalding Rumi fire. Yesterday he would have been dead a dozen times over, original daeva powers be damned.

Now, with the blood magic protecting him, Manizheh's curse de-fying nature itself, Dara stayed standing, cutting a path of death as he moved on the hospital that the woman he loved had worked so hard to rebuild. Tears pricked in his eyes, evaporating before they could be seen—he was not permitted to give any hint of the anguish ripping him apart.

Twenty paces from the hospital. Ten. Dara raised his hands. *Go away from this in your mind.* Energy sizzled through his fingers . . .

The great wooden doors burst open.

"Stop!"

Zaynab al Qahtani stood with a black flag in her hands.

It took a few moments for her cry to be carried. For the sight of her, unarmed save the flag, to freeze the djinn fighters where they stood. She took another step, and several people retreated, as though her very presence had forced them back. Razu was at her side, staring at Dara with naked hate and betrayal.

Gripping the flag as though it were a sword, Zaynab took an-other step toward him, her head held high. "We surrender," she said coldly. "We will lay down our arms if you stop." She dropped the flag. "Manizheh may have me."

Dara raised his own hand. "Stand down," he commanded his men. Not that he'd needed to. Zaynab had stilled them all.

Ah, but Manizheh's wish burned through him. It wanted more. *Humiliate her,* it demanded. *Make her cower.*

"Zaynab!" Aqisa charged out from the hospital doors.

Razu and a pair of Geziri soldiers moved to grab the warrior. They were ill-matched, Aqisa wrenching free as Zaynab glanced back.

"Fall back, my friend. We have no choice." But Zaynab's voice snapped across the air as she added something in what sounded like stilted Geziriyya.

Dara had borne much shame in his life but watching the

proud Qahtani princess approach with blazing eyes was a dishonor he knew he'd carry for the rest of his days. This wasn't how he was supposed to take Daevabad from the family that had ruined his.

They aren't the family that ruined yours. That family still rules you.

Zaynab stepped up to him. Like her younger brother, she was tall, and she evenly met Dara's height.

"Here I am," she declared. "May it please the wretched demon you call mistress."

Dara glared, even as he ached to fall at her feet and beg for forgiveness. "What did you tell your warrior?"

"To gut you."

The words were loud enough to carry. A few of his soldiers bristled, reaching again for their weapons.

Creator, kill me. Dara seized Zaynab al Qahtani, grabbing her roughly by the arm and yanking her forward. Manizheh's wish was urging him to do worse, to rip away her veil and drag her by the hair. Instead, he walked faster toward the midan through the neighborhoods he'd annihilated, trying to distract himself from the awful longing. It looked as if a great wheel had rolled through, pulverizing everything in its path and leaving only fire and blood-splashed rubble. And weeping. Always weeping.

Manizheh was waiting in the midan, framed by the ifrit. Dara had barely reached her when the wish finally overpowered him. He shoved Zaynab to her knees before the Banu Nahida. The princess didn't cry out, didn't flinch. Instead she gazed upon Manizheh with utter disgust.

The Banu Nahida gave her a condescending look. "Well, haven't you grown up." She inclined her head toward Dara. "Thank you, Afshin."

His chest abruptly expanded, the wish fulfilled. Dara took a shaky breath, and there it was. A sliver of freedom.

He grabbed his dagger, thrust it at his throat . . .

"Afshin, I wish for you to put that down," Manizheh said, the order curt but pleasant. "I wouldn't want you to harm yourself."

The dagger fell from his hands.

Zaynab's gaze darted to his. Whatever despair managed to slip through the obedient mask of his face must have been enough to trigger her suspicion, because she spun back on Manizheh.

Manizheh lifted her hand as though to beckon the carriage. It was a slight movement, but enough to let Dara's emerald ring briefly gleam in the dusty light.

Zaynab choked. "Oh my God."

Manizheh smiled, this time with triumph. "Come, girl. Your brother has been *so* anxious to see you."

39

NAHRI

Nahri yelped in surprise, stepping back and crashing into the wall behind her. The shedu was so close she could have touched it, and when it shook its head, the snow clinging to its silver-tinged mane fell upon her face.

"God preserve me," she whispered, her slippers sliding on the icy ground as she tried to retreat, wall be damned. Nahri thrust out a hand, conjuring a fistful of flames. But it wasn't much of a defense, and she suddenly found herself wondering if her mother hadn't been right to learn how to control limbs.

The shedu didn't seem impressed. It sat back on its haunches, regarding her with a catlike blend of curiosity and mild disdain. A very *large* cat, with muscles rippling under pale golden fur. Its eyes might have been stolen from the glistening ice around them, a silver so pale they seemed clear.

But its wings. Oh, its wings. If they'd been striking back on the banks of the Nile, they were utterly glorious now, the long, elegant feathers glittering in every color in creation, a jeweled rainbow reflecting the cascading prisms of ice and snow surrounding them.

Nahri and the shedu stared at each other for a very long moment, her ragged breathing the only sound. She didn't know if it was the same shedu that had come upon her and Ali in a sandstorm back in Egypt—she wasn't particularly experienced at distinguishing the faces of overly large, legendary flying cats—but the encounter hadn't left her feeling warm.

"Is this your doing?" she demanded, motioning to the snowy mountains surrounding them. It might have been madness to try and converse with the beast, but God knew she'd done stranger things since accidentally summoning a Daeva warrior.

The shedu shook out its wings and offered a lazy blink of its eerie eyes in response.

Nahri's temper—and fear—broke. "I'll wrestle you," she threatened, remembering Jamshid's long-ago story about how their earliest ancestors tamed the shedu. "Don't think I won't." It wasn't even a bluff. Wrestling a shedu at least promised a quicker end than freezing to death on whatever mysterious mountain she'd been transported to.

"They do not speak," a new voice cut in, its language a mix of warbles and chirps. "Though I do believe such a match would be quite entertaining."

Nahri jumped, glancing up.

A peri smiled back.

Identical to Khayzur in form, down to the talons clutching the rock and the birdlike lower half, this peri had the face of a young woman and brilliant pearl-colored wings. A fanlike crest of dark ivory feathers sprouted from her head like a halo.

The peri hopped down, taking advantage of Nahri's speechlessness to join the shedu, with which she exchanged a mischievous look. Then she nodded at the fire still twirling in Nahri's hand. "It is not an encounter with a daeva if they are not attempting to burn something in a quick-tempered rage."

Nahri felt both called out and defensive of her people. "I'm going to do a lot more than burn something if you don't return me to Ta Ntry."

Another playful expression danced over the peri's thin lips. Amusement, appraisal . . . things that indeed made Nahri want to set her on fire. "Are you not curious as to why we have invited you?"

"*Invited*? You kidnapped me!"

A tone of distress entered the creature's voice. "Oh no, we would never do such a thing. We could not, not to a lesser creature. Ours is an invitation. It is entirely your choice as to whether you climb upon my companion and fly to hear our proposal." The peri stroked the shedu's back. The winged lion arched under her hand and let out a grumbly sound of satisfaction. "Or you may stay here. Though be warned that the winds are treacherous at night, enough to strip a mortal's flesh from their bones."

That was Nahri's choice? "Return me to Ta Ntry," she demanded again. "If I die here, will it not be on your hands?"

The peri raised her wings in what might have been a shrug. "Would it truly be on our hands? We tried to warn you, and the weather, it is so unreliable . . ."

"Don't you control the winds?"

"Perhaps." The peri's pale eyes glittered. "But come, daughter of Anahid. I do believe we can help each other."

"I was told peris don't get involved with mortal affairs."

"And that is correct. Yet on occasion—a very rare occasion—we may point out possible corrections. Your choice, of course." With that, the peri spread her wings and took to the air, soaring off.

Nahri watched her go, pride and indecision warring inside her. But despite what the peri claimed, she had no real choice.

She turned to the shedu. "I'm a terrible rider," she warned. "And if you try to eat me, I'm going to give you ulcers."

The shedu might not have been able to speak, but Nahri would swear she saw understanding in its silver gaze before it folded its wings and knelt at her feet.

"Oh," she said. "Er, thanks." Feeling unnerved, she clambered onto its back. The lion was warm beneath her, its shaggy fur easing the chill from her bones. She gripped its mane. This was going to be so much worse than a horse.

"Go," she whispered.

The shedu leapt into the air.

Nahri's dignity lasted approximately the length of time it took her to suck in a breath for the scream that followed. She clutched the shedu's neck, burying her face in its mane and digging her knees into its side like a crab. The frigid air tore over her back, ripping away her scarf and making her wonder if freezing to death would really have been all that bad.

But after another moment of not falling and smashing on the ground, Nahri tried to relax. *You are the Banu Nahida,* she reminded herself. The "daughter of Anahid."

She would not show these creatures her fear.

Summoning every bit of courage she could, Nahri peeked up from the shedu's mane. They were rising higher, the mountain range shrinking to a stitched wound of rock and snow far below.

She struggled for air, feeling breathless as they ascended. The ring scorched against her finger, and her dizziness eased, but the air still felt too thin. They flew into a cloud bank, and Nahri shuddered at the brush of unseen hands and wings. There were whispers all around her, voices that didn't sound like any kind of creature she knew.

The clouds dissipated, and the shedu landed, the ground shrouded by mists. Nahri slipped from its back. One of its wings curved protectively around her. She could see nothing but swirling snow.

But she could *hear.* Flapping and rustling, like a library of books having their pages shaken out above her head. Nahri looked up.

There were a dozen flocks of peris flying above her. Scores. Perhaps hundreds, the creatures dipping and diving and soaring in formation. Avian bodies with silver scales flashed and cut through the clouds, here one moment, gone the next. Wings were winks of color: bright lime and peacock blue, burnt saffron and indigo night. Colorless eyes were everywhere, all focused on Nahri, pinning her down in a temple of ice and air.

Without warning, three landed. The one from the cliff with the pearl-colored wings and two more in shades of ruby and sapphire. They circled her, their long feathers—as long as Nahri was tall—dragging through the frost. A chittering erupted among them that, despite her magic, Nahri could not make out.

She crossed her arms, resisting the urge to hug herself. It was just so cold. Her thin robe was meant for Ta Ntry's heat, and Nahri's exposed hair, tossed in the icy gusts, had frozen in stiff curls. The ice spread over everything, tracing in wild swirls and fronds, light snow dusting her skin and catching in her eyelashes.

With the creatures stalking her like vultures, Nahri again found herself wishing for a weapon. Not that there was a point. She'd seen Khayzur use wind magic to bring down the marid-controlled Gozan when it was a watery serpent the size of a mountain. The djinn spoke of the peris with awe; they were creatures said to have flown to the heavens and listened to angels. To exist in a separate, unknowable realm.

And to supposedly never interfere with the lives of mortal, lesser creatures like djinn and humans. Khayzur had been killed, after all, for the "transgression" of saving Dara's and Nahri's lives.

None of which explained why they had snatched her out of a djinn stronghold in Ta Ntry. She looked around. They were surrounded by a seemingly endless expanse of white, towering walls that shifted and moved beyond the clouds.

The ruby peri clucked something to his fellows, sounding distinctly disapproving. If Khayzur had exuded warmth despite his strange appearance, this one seemed as coolly aloof as the air spirits were rumored to be, his colorless gaze and crimson mask arresting. His head bobbed and darted like an owl as he studied her.

"What?" she demanded in Divasti. "What are you staring at?"

The ruby peri seemed unruffled. "Banu Nahri e-Nahid," he replied plainly, as though the question were honest. "A daeva of part human heritage and the current bearer of the ring of Suleiman the Lawgiver."

All right, maybe not every peri had mastered sarcasm. "What do you want?" Nahri skittered back when he drew nearer, pressing against the shedu's warm flank. "Why have you taken me here?"

Her unease must have been obvious, for the sapphire peri spoke for the first time. "You are safe," they assured her gently. This peri looked older, their blue feathers tinged with silver and lines creasing their pale eyes. "We could not harm you even if we desired it. Your human blood protects you."

"A lie. You've already tried to harm me—you would have left me to die on a cliff. And it's not even the first time. You sent a rukh after Dara and me!"

"The rukh was sent to follow the Afshin after much discussion," the pearl peri corrected. "But they are wild creatures. Who can predict what happens when they are hungry?"

Rage boiled in Nahri again. "So sending a starving predator the size of a house across our path was permitted, while Khayzur's saving our lives was punished with death?"

"Yes," the peri declared, giving Nahri a careful look. "There had been whispers and warnings for years about a daeva who would upset the balance of the elemental races. Our people took counsel, and Khayzur betrayed it when he saved the Afshin the first time. He was warned. He knew the consequences."

"She is too young." It was the sapphire peri. "Too angry."

"Zaydi al Qahtani was not much older when his people were given the knowledge of their weapons," the ruby peri countered.

"And he took nearly as many lives as were saved," the other peri retorted. "We agreed then that mortals did not have the wisdom to receive our guidance."

Zaydi al Qahtani. "Wait." Nahri glanced between the arguing creatures. "The *peris* gave the Geziris their zulfiqars?"

"Indirectly," the sapphire one said swiftly. "Certain paths were crossed, and pieces left to complete. The final steps were not taken by us."

"So peris do interfere. But only when it suits you."

"We do not interfere," the ruby peri insisted. "We seek to avert the greatest harm, to listen to the warnings of the heavens when its laws are about to be broken."

"You *interfere,*" Nahri said, more vehemently. Arguing with these creatures while trapped in their realm was probably not the wisest move, but she was tired of being manipulated and deceived by people who believed themselves superior. At least Ghassan had been up front; these twisted half-truths, as if *Nahri* was the one being unreasonable, were almost worse.

The pearl peri looked amused. "I told you she had Anahid's tongue."

"I take it she too was given some of this 'guidance'?" Nahri asked.

"You wear it on your finger." The peri moved as if to reach for Nahri's hand, and Nahri jerked back. "But the seal ring's magic has not bonded to you, and it will not—not even if you bring it back to Daevabad. Anahid was a daeva who traveled the sands for millennia and was a companion to a prophet. She gave her life and heart for her city. That is not an enchantment you can fix without a similar exchange."

A similar exchange. Nahri heard the underlying message in those polite words. "You said your people had a proposal for me. So why don't you state it? Clearly, if that's even possible for you."

The ruby peri spoke again, bringing his hands together. "There are certain laws of creation. Of *balance*—a balance that benefits us all, peri and daeva, marid and human. Those laws have now been broken, twisted and degraded, again and again by one of your kin."

Nahri untangled the peri's words. "By Manizheh, you mean. You're a bit late with your outrage. She already attacked Daevabad and murdered thousands."

"The internecine squabbles of your people do not concern us," the peri replied, seeming annoyed by her interruption. "What the daevas wish to do to one another is their business—until it infects those whose blood flows with other elements. Until it threatens the balance."

"'Until it infects . . .'" Nahri repeated, ill at the choice of words. "Then that's what this is. Manizheh's gotten powerful enough to scare you, and you'd like another daeva to handle the unpleasant task of getting rid of her. Will I be getting a zulfiqar like Zaydi? Another seal ring? Or maybe just more nonsense riddles I'll need to puzzle out myself?"

"It is not Manizheh who is upsetting the balance. It is her servant."

Nahri's stomach dropped. *Her servant.* "Dara," she stammered. "You're asking me to get rid of . . . to kill *Dara*?"

"No," the pearl peri said. "*We* are not asking such a thing. We would never make that type of request. We are simply informing you of the cost of magic's return to your world and suggesting a way in which your burden might be eased."

"But Manizheh is the one responsible!"

"Manizheh is a full-blooded mortal daeva. Extremely powerful, yes. But still beneath us. Lesser. Were we to be involved in suggesting her demise . . ." The ruby peri gestured to the flocks swirling overhead. "We have agreed that the risk is too great. Her . . . creation," he said distastefully, "is an entirely different matter. He is an abomination, a monster she has cobbled together out of blood magic, murder, and a marid's debt. His removal has been deemed permissible."

Every careful word made Nahri more disgusted. It was what they'd wanted, what she and Jamshid had been searching for in their family's texts. But the idea of the peris, so smug and convinced of their own superiority, debating the assassination of mortals below—debating how to make it *permissible*—filled her with revulsion.

"So you do it," Nahri replied. "You're all high and mighty. Surely you can perform your own assassinations."

"We cannot," the sapphire peri objected. Of the three, this elder was gentlest, and their words were delivered in a way that seemed to plead for understanding. "It is against our nature."

"And he is in Daevabad," the pearl peri added. "We cannot enter the city. Since the veil has fallen, we can see into it. But we cannot enter."

Nahri clenched her hands into fists. "You could ask any daeva. Any djinn. Why me?"

The ruby peri swept a hand through the air, looking more fascinated by the snowflakes spinning in the wind than by the murder they were asking Nahri to carry out. "For many reasons. You can enter the city and get close to him. You need an act that will bond the seal to your heart. It is also believed your human blood will add an additional layer of protection that distances us. For a shafit to kill the Scourge, it would be justice."

"Let's not pretend you care about justice when it comes to the 'internecine squabbles of my people,'" Nahri shot back. "And I can't kill him. All your spying must be pointless if you haven't figured that out. I'm no warrior."

"But you are," the sapphire peri countered. "In the only war that truly counts."

"And you would be protected." The pearl peri gestured to the shedu. "We took the shedu from your family when they stepped off the righteous path but would permit them to serve again."

"There is also this." The ruby peri snatched at the air, snow and ice condensing in his hands to form a straight blade that gleamed like liquid mercury. "A weapon that strikes through any heart that beats fire." He tossed it to the ground before her feet. The hilt dazzled even in the snow-dimmed sky.

"You would be glorious," the sapphire peri whispered. "A daughter of Anahid with Suleiman's seal and a weapon of heaven, flying into Daevabad on the back of a shedu. Your people would follow you to the ends of the earth. No matter your human blood. No matter what revolutionary things you desired. You could transform your world."

Nahri tightened her fists, struggling to keep her face blank at the calculated offer. The peris really had been listening. They knew her wishes, her fears.

They knew she was the kind of person who would strike a deal.

So this was what it had come to, then. For all Nahri's efforts, she was still caught beneath the thumbs of more powerful brokers. A queen who would keep her as a vulnerable guest, a mother who would lock her away. Or a pawn, a well-rewarded weapon.

And it was still a wildly impossible goal. Kill Dara—*Dara,* a man who would have been worshipped as a war god in an earlier era. Even with a legendary mount and a celestial weapon, it seemed a ludicrous proposition.

But it's not.

Nahri remembered Dara in the palace corridor where it had all gone wrong, clutching her hands as he begged for understanding. *You weren't supposed to see it.* He had wanted so desperately to save her. He loved her.

It was his weakness. And it might be the only thing that made him an easy mark.

Nahri stared at the dagger, but no one moved. "You must take it for yourself," the ruby peri explained. "We cannot put it in your hands."

"Of course not. You wouldn't want to *interfere*." But Nahri knelt, picking up the dagger from the soft snow. The hilt was so cold that it stung her hands, and she found herself quietly checking her healing magic. The pain felt deserved.

You won't pick yourself up from this. Nahri had lost her mentor and her best friend. If she went back to Daevabad to murder her Afshin, the charismatic warrior who'd once stolen her heart—smiling and feigning affection as she plunged a dagger into his chest at the behest of these meddling creatures—it would break Nahri in a way she didn't think she'd recover from. If she survived, she'd have her brother, her Daevas. She might oversee the rebirth of her city.

But she'd have sold a part of her soul.

And that, apparently, was *exactly* the sacrifice she was being asked to make.

Nahri straightened up and slid the peri's dagger into the folds of her belt. She reached for the shedu, trying to take some assurance in the cozy heat of its fur. By the time she spoke again, she made sure her voice were steady.

"You should take me back to Ta Ntry now. There is not much time."

40

ALI

Fiza did not seem thrilled with Ali's transformation.

"Aghhh!" The pirate captain scrambled backward on the riverbank, drawing her pistol and pointing it in his face. "Demon! What did you do to him?"

Ali dodged the pistol. "Nothing! Fiza, it's me, I swear!"

She didn't lower the weapon, her hand shaking. "What the fuck is wrong with your eyes?" Her gaze darted to his arms, the silver-scaled lines dazzling in the early morning light as they traced wild patterns across his bare skin. "What is wrong with your *everything?*"

Ali paused. Sobek had taken them from Tiamat's realm back to the Nile, but it wasn't the winding desert river he and Nahri had sailed. Instead, they sat at the foot of a lush green plateau, the mighty river plunging over in a wall of waterfalls that stretched into the distance. Between the mist and the churning water, Ali hadn't gotten a good look at his reflection.

My eyes. His eyes had been an exact mirror of Ghassan's, the most visible sign of his Geziri heritage.

Gone now, apparently. "I had to make some choices. But forget all that. Are *you* okay?" he asked worriedly, nodding at her black eye. "It looks like you took a bad blow to the head."

"Yes, the ocean rising around us and punching me in the face left a mark." Fiza finally lowered the pistol and then groaned as seawater poured from it. "Damn, I was fond of that! Where are we? And what *happened*? The last thing I remember is the ship getting gobbled up."

Ali hesitated again, having no idea how to describe what had happened at the bottom of the sea without alarming Fiza further. Between getting chased by a massive scorpion-man, participating in a forced gladiatorial match with his literal pagan past, or having a thousand memories dumped into his brain as part of a pact with a colossal chaos spirit, he didn't know where to start.

So he just said, "I met Tiamat. We didn't really get along."

Fiza gave him an incredulous look. "You *didn't really get along*? That's not an encouraging statement, prince." She glanced around. "Where's the boat? Where's the *ocean*? Where's—" She screamed again, the pistol reappearing. "*What is that?*"

Sobek had rejoined them.

The Nile marid had emerged from the muddy water in his less frightening form, but he didn't need to be gnashing crocodile teeth to be unsettling—the green of his rough hide and dappled yellow-and-black eyes were enough.

Ali quickly stepped between them, lowering Fiza's hand. "This is Sobek. My . . . great-grandfather. In a way. He's not going to hurt you, I promise." He glanced at Sobek. "Right?"

Sobek's unearthly stare didn't waver. "I have already eaten."

Fiza closed her eyes. "I never again want to hear that shafit are the source of our world's problems. Never."

Sobek's gaze narrowed on Ali. "Are you ready?"

Ali's heart skipped, but he'd already paid Tiamat's price. He might as well claim the knowledge that had cost him so dearly. "Will you be okay here for a little while?" he asked Fiza.

"With him? No!"

"He's coming with me."

"Where are *you* going?"

"To deal with some family history."

THE GLADE SOBEK LED HIM TO WAS BEAUTIFUL, ONE of the loveliest places Ali had ever seen. Despite a waterfall that cascaded down a flower- and vine-covered cliff, the river was remarkably still, and there was a quiet to the air that seemed sacred. The lush scene could have been plucked from Paradise—a dragonfly lazily dipping over a water lily, a heron stalking the shallows, and a slender antelope drinking from the edge. The animals had all briefly frozen when Sobek appeared, the instinctual response of prey, before relaxing and continuing as if they weren't in the presence of a marid and a djinn who'd recently tried to kill each other.

"This is one of the places your ancestors would come pay their respects to me," Sobek murmured as they strode through the hip-deep water, lotus stems brushing against Ali's legs.

"Did they live here?" Ali asked, remembering what his grandfather had said about their family's early history being a blank slate.

"For a time. But they moved frequently, especially the first generations. Their water magic was impossible to hide then, and your world was chaos for centuries after Suleiman's punishment. My kin were careful." Bitterness edged into his voice. "Until they were not."

Ali tensed, but when Sobek submerged with a wave of his hand, Ali followed. The murky river was no trouble for his senses now; he could see clear as day, his ears picking up new underwater sounds he hadn't been privy to earlier. He swam faster, easily keeping pace with Sobek as they dove beneath the curtain of waterfalls to emerge in a hidden cave. It had been enlarged, with benches cut into the stone and pictograms carved into the walls.

Ali traced the image of a man with a crocodile's head. "Is this you?"

"Yes." Sobek laid a palm against the hand-drawn letters, and if his expression betrayed nothing, Ali could see wistfulness in the gesture. "It is our history. Their names, the deeds I did for them. Our pact."

Ali stared at the pictograms. "They mean nothing to me," he confessed, a great loss opening inside his chest. "They don't look like any Ayaanle script I know—they don't look like any script I've ever *seen*. Their language may have been forgotten." He could hear the ache in his voice. It shook him to think how thoroughly severed his family had been from its roots.

"That may have been intentional on the part of the survivors. Ignorance weakens the bond. It is more difficult to hold someone to a pact they had no part in making."

Ali felt sick all over again. "Why did you kill them?" He had to know. "Tiamat said she ordered them brought before her. So why did you kill them?"

Sobek had crossed to the rocky wall, moving stones from a cairn set against it. "Tiamat and I have long been rivals. We both hail from the original generation of our kind, and I was not always keen to pay her obeisance, especially when she abandoned the lake and turned her back on those of our people forced to toil for the Nahids." He pulled a bundle free.

"I don't understand," Ali said.

The marid returned, leaving a trail like a serpent across the damp sand. "You saw how she is. I was not going to give her my kin. She would have spent a thousand years slowly torturing them to death. It was more merciful—more swift—to handle them myself."

More merciful. "Could you not have *tried* to save them? Warned them to run to the desert, spared the children?"

"That is not our way." There was no malice in Sobek's voice. It was the simple truth of a creature from a time and place Ali didn't and would never understand. "They had a pact. They betrayed it."

They saved us and were destroyed for it. Ali tried to imagine what might have happened if his Ayaanle ancestor had taken Suleiman's seal away from Daevabad after the Nahid Council had been overthrown, magic vanishing with Zaydi's victory. People would have thought it God's revenge for rebelling against the Nahids, for daring to call for equality. The shafit probably would have been wiped out, the resulting civil war lasting centuries.

We do not cross the Ayaanle. Six words the only memory of a sacrifice that had decimated the half of his family Ali had grown up dismissing.

"What was his name?" he asked, his voice thick with emotion. "The name of my ancestor who betrayed you?"

There was a moment of silence before Sobek replied. "Armah." He pronounced the name with somber respect. "He was talented with my magic. The first in many generations to be able to travel the currents and share memories." Irritation slipped into his voice. "Apparently talented enough to keep me from realizing that he left a child or two in Daevabad."

Armah. Ali committed the name to memory. He would pray for his murdered and martyred ancestors later, and if he survived all this, he'd make sure the rest of his family and their next generations did so as well.

But first he would fight. "What is that?" he asked, nodding at the bundle Sobek held.

"His vestments. I made them myself. You are mortal still, and they will protect you when you travel the currents."

Ali took the vestments. A cross between clothing and armor, they looked like they were spun from crocodile hide and burnished to a pale green-gold. One was a flat, hooded helmet that trailed down the back and the other a sleeveless tunic, knee length and split down the middle.

He ran his fingers over the helmet and then noticed Sobek held something else—something more to Ali's taste. "Is that his blade?"

"Yes," Sobek grunted, handing it over.

Ali took it and admired the weapon: a long sickle-sword unlike anything he'd fought with before. The blade was iron and wickedly sharp, the hilt covered with polished bronze.

"You've preserved this," Ali realized. This sword had not been abandoned in a rocky cairn, untouched for centuries. "You say he betrayed you and deserved death, yet you've kept safe his vestments and weapon." He hesitated, then asked another question, one that had been spinning in his mind since their match. "Back in Tiamat's realm, you stopped fighting me. Why?"

Sobek gave him an even stare. "I am sure you are mistaken."

Ali held his ancestor's gaze. In the pale light of the cave, Sobek looked as frightening and mystical as ever, the falling water throwing undulating shadows across his stern face. He looked untouchable.

But he wasn't. Ali had seen Sobek's memories and felt those long, lonely centuries—a toll of time and miserable solitude Ali could barely wrap his head around. Perhaps keeping himself apart was how the Nile marid survived it.

They weren't the same. Ali would never forgive or forget what Sobek had done to his family. But he would let Sobek keep the boundaries of his affection private.

"Perhaps I am." Ali slipped into the armor. It fit like a second skin, cool against his body. "You'll teach me marid magic now? How to travel the currents?"

"That was the agreement. Where do you wish to go first?"

Ali ran his hands down the helmet. An utterly mad plan had been taking shape in his head, given new life by the marid memories Tiamat had poured into his brain.

"Is there a place where I can find shipwrecks?"

A HALF DOZEN ATTEMPTS AT TRAVELING THE CUR-rents later, the sea that stretched before them was shallow—at least compared to Tiamat's fathomless abode. Pale sand studded with vibrant waves of razor-sharp coral and dancing fronds dazzled Ali's eyes, jewel-bright fish flitting all about. Beyond was the surface, glimmering like liquid glass with sunlight.

Ali eyed the coral. *Dangerous for ships.* Beneath the water, he communicated to Sobek in the marid way, words swimming in his mind.

For centuries, Sobek agreed, spreading his hands to encompass the wrecks that surrounded them. *The marid of this sea is fat with the blood and memories of mortal sailors. She rules in a ruin far to the north with a court of sharks.*

Ali's skin pricked. *She will not mind our intrusion?*

She owes me a favor, a pact gone unclaimed. And she will not cross Tiamat.

Ali again studied the ships. Most had been reduced to broken beams and rotting, seaweed-covered hulls. There were the bones of small smugglers' canoes and elegant dhows, antique triremes and new galleons barely broken down. Lost cargo from across time and space was strewn across the sand: enormous stone amphorae and shattered porcelain vases, coins gone green with age and raw blocks of unpolished rock quartz.

You are certain this is possible? he asked Sobek again. Ali had told the marid his plan as Sobek coached him through handling the currents.

The magic is possible, yes. But you understand none of this will protect you from the Nahid's champion. No marid can stand against him.

I will not be alone, Ali replied. *This is only our first stop.*

You intend to go someplace other than Daevabad?

Ali smiled in the water. *I intend to go everywhere.*

He had promised Nahri he would return, and Ali would.

But first, he was going to get her an army.

41

NAHRI

The shedu landed lightly on the roof of Shefala's castle, the pearl-colored peri fluttering down beside them. It was dark, the moon and stars veiled by clouds, but even if it had been midday, Nahri suspected they wouldn't have been seen. The peris had literally plucked her from the castle's halls and taken her to a cathedral of ice and snow above the clouds. If they didn't want to be seen by djinn, they wouldn't be.

Must be nice to have power like that, to view problems that are life and death for us as mere errors to be "corrected." Nahri had sworn never to be a pawn again, and yet here she was, a peri blade in her belt, forced to serve another master in order to save the people she loved. She slipped off the shedu's back, aware of the peri's eyes on her.

"You should leave tonight," the air elemental chirped. "There is no time to waste."

"It that one of your 'suggestions' or an order?"

The peri bowed her head. "You are a mortal with human blood. I would never dare give such a lesser creature an order."

"If you call me a 'lesser creature' again, I'm going to stab you with this blade."

"Such fire." It sounded like the compliment one would give a toddler and, paired with the peri's condescending smile, indeed tempted Nahri to draw the dagger. "But that would be unwise. That blade is for the Afshin, no other." The peri's voice sharpened. "You must swear not to use it on Manizheh. She has been deemed impermissible."

"Not powerful enough for you?" When the peri's eyes narrowed in warning, Nahri rolled hers. "Fine, I swear. I won't use your blade on Manizheh."

"Good." The peri stepped back. "They only eat fruit, by the way."

"What?"

"Your shedu. He will need to be fed." Without another word, she vanished, flitting into the dark sky.

Nahri glanced at the shedu. "*Fruit?*"

He purred, a grumbly, grating sound, and then rubbed his head against her shoulder, nearly knocking Nahri from the roof.

She patted his head, scratching behind his ear. "Oh, all right. I guess you're not too bad." She tried to think, her mind spinning. After so many weeks of fretting and loss, the prospect of being in Daevabad by dawn seemed impossible. Dangerous. She needed a plan.

There is no plan. You fly to Daevabad, throw yourself weeping in Dara's arms, telling him you're sorry, telling him you love him—all the things he'd said to her in anguish the night of the attack—*until he lets down his guard.*

Then she would put a dagger through his heart.

I wonder if he'll crumble to dust again. If it will hurt, if he'll have enough time to look at me and realize what I've done. Nahri's fingers twitched in the shedu's mane, and he bumped her hand away.

He is Manizheh's weapon, she reminded herself. Dara had made his choice, and thousands had died for it.

She took a steadying breath. Food. Supplies. The cold distance and calm Nahri needed would come with preparation. It always did. Dara was just another mark. This was just another con.

Nahri glanced at the shedu. She wasn't certain how much the creature understood, but she supposed they were going to learn together. "Stay here and out of sight," she warned. "I'll be back."

She slipped into the castle through a broken rain shutter, landing lightly on her feet in a dark, empty corridor. Doing so made Nahri feel younger, as though she might be breaking into a mansion back in Cairo. She padded down the corridor, startling the guards outside her door.

"Banu Nahida!" The Geziri one gaped, looking between the closed door and her face. "Weren't you—"

"I had a meeting." Nahri pushed through the doors.

Jamshid was waiting for her.

Her brother looked like he'd been there awhile, notes and books spreading across the low table, but he rose from his couch the moment she entered.

"Nahri." Jamshid let out a relieved sigh. "There you are. I was starting to worry."

Nahri closed the door behind her, silently cursing. Jamshid was the last person she wanted to see right now. She had limited time and couldn't risk her overprotective brother getting even a whisper of what was going on. "Just checking on patients."

"Ever the devoted healer." Jamshid smiled, but the expression didn't touch his eyes. "We need to talk."

You have no idea. A wave of exhaustion washed over her, and Nahri glanced around, spotting a samovar. "Is that tea hot?"

"It was."

"Good enough." Nahri was aching for a cup and could always reheat it in her hands, one of the most genuinely blessed parts of having fire magic.

She crossed to the samovar. It had been crammed onto the same table as her accumulating pharmacy supplies, a tilting stack of tea cups sharing space with her mortar, pestle, and the assorted vials, tins, and herbs she'd gathered to make the paralysis serum for the shafit sailor. Nahri chided herself—she was normally careful about stowing away such dangerous medicines. She was lucky some unfortunate soul hadn't come through here, topped off their tea with a bit more than sugar, and ended up frozen on the floor.

Nahri stopped, staring at the vial of serum. There was just the smallest amount left. "Jamshid," she said softly, "would you mind taking down the storm shutters and dragging the couch onto the balcony? I could use some air."

"Certainly." Nahri heard him scrape back his chair. Always so eager to please. Her brother might never have the grasp of magical healing that she did, but he would be better at the bedside.

If he survived.

It took Jamshid several minutes to open the shutters and pull the couch out. Enough time for Nahri to prepare two cups of tea. Perhaps the veiling of the sky had been a peri trick, for when Nahri stepped out onto the balcony, she saw stars and a thin moon now, and through the trees, light reflecting on the ocean.

She dropped her gaze. This was the balcony upon which she'd stood with Ali, the monsoon churning in his eyes, and if Nahri never saw the ocean again, it would still be too soon. She handed Jamshid his cup of tea and then sat, taking a sip of her own.

Jamshid mirrored her motion but then made a face. "It's gone bitter."

Nahri smiled at him, her heart breaking. "Snob."

"Refined," he corrected, setting the cup back on the table. His expression turned serious. "Is the queen's father all right?"

"He took a pretty bad fall and broke his hip and his wrist. I've set the bones, but not even Nahid magic erases old age. I think for now we do what we can while preparing his family."

Jamshid sighed. "I don't have much warmth for the queen and her kin since they tossed me in a cell, but Seif seemed a kind man. How did Hatset take the news?"

"Like you'd expect a woman who's had her husband murdered, her son abducted, and her daughter threatened with imminent execution."

Jamshid leaned forward on his knees. "I need to go back to Daevabad. We don't have a choice."

"We might."

"Nahri, come on. We've discussed—"

"A peri came to me."

Her brother jerked upright, staring at her with stunned eyes. "I'm sorry, a what?"

"A peri came to me." Nahri set down her tea, trying to judge the minutes, and then, for one of the first times in her life, she told someone everything without prodding. From being plucked out of the hallway and soaring on the shedu to the vast chamber of snowy clouds and the peris' infuriating "guidance."

Jamshid didn't interrupt. He grew paler as she continued, but there was no despair, no shock—not even when she showed him the icy dagger and explained what was expected of her. He just listened.

A long moment of silence stretched between them when Nahri was done. Jamshid opened and closed his mouth, but it was the trembling in his hands Nahri looked for and the drop in his shoulders.

He finally spoke. "So there's a shedu on the roof?"

"Waiting for his fruit, yes."

"Suleiman's eye." Jamshid exhaled. "All right, I know this seems bad. But we've been searching for a way to take down Dara and Manizheh, right?"

Nahri was already shaking her head. "They said the dagger couldn't be used on Manizheh. Even if we succeed with Dara, Manizheh and her ifrit will still be there."

"And considering the things Saman was saying about her and those poor firebirds penned up on the beach—" He grimaced. "She must have some sort of magic."

The peris' vague words came back to Nahri. *She has taken a step we didn't anticipate.* The half-dead simurgh and the hundreds of slaughtered Daevas . . . what had Manizheh done to have finally frightened the peris into taking action? "I believe so, yes."

"Then we go back together," Jamshid said firmly, his decision obviously made. "We *fight* together. I can handle the Afshin. You shouldn't have to—" He reached out as if to touch her shoulder in assurance.

His hand quaked badly and then fell back to his lap.

"I'm sorry, big brother," Nahri said quietly. "But you won't be coming with me."

Jamshid attempted to push himself up from the couch. He had barely taken two staggering steps when he collapsed, his legs giving out.

"The tea . . ." His voice was already thicker. He looked at her wildly. "You *poisoned* me?"

"I'm sorry," she whispered. "But I mean, you did sort of give me the idea."

"My legs . . ." Jamshid's expression twisted with horror. And not just horror—with utter betrayal. "*No.*" He grasped for his legs, clearly struggling to drag them up. "How could you do this to me again?" he choked out.

Nahri had not known until that moment how truly deep guilt could cut. Her brother might never forgive her for this.

Tears blurred her vision. "I couldn't think of another way." She crossed the space between them to lift him off the floor. She wouldn't have him found like this. "It will wear off by tomorrow, I swear."

Jamshid grabbed her when she tried to pull away, tangling his hands in her shawl as his strength continued fading. "Don't," he panted. "*Please.* You'll be outnumbered. They'll kill you!"

"Then I'll take as many of them with me as I can." Nahri shoved her brother's hands away. "Please understand. I've lost everyone I've dared to love. I can't lose you. Not you. You're good, and you're kind and you're going to be a great healer . . ." Her voice broke at the anguish in Jamshid's expression. He was scrabbling for her skirts, her wrists, but Nahri stepped out of arm's reach. "If you get back to Daevabad, take the Nahid texts and go to Subha. You can teach each other."

"Please don't do this," Jamshid begged, tears rolling down his cheeks. "Nahri, you're not alone anymore. You don't have to do this all by yourself! We could wait." He tried again, clearly searching for any reason to delay her. "Alizayd might still come back!"

He'd picked the wrong thing to say. If Nahri had been clinging to her last shreds of hope and optimism, the peris' cynical deal might as well have snatched them from her fingers. She had been foolish to make Ali promise to return; she'd all but sealed his fate the moment she'd opened her heart to him.

"I don't think Ali's coming back, Jamshid."

"Nahri, don't," he cried, his voice growing weaker as she turned and walked away. "You're my sister. We can do this together. I don't need you to save me!"

I don't need you to save me.

Had those not been the words—the *exact* words—she had flung at Dara the night he'd stolen into her bedroom, intent on "rescuing" her from her decision to marry Muntadhir? The night everything had gone so spectacularly wrong?

You're doing to Jamshid exactly what Dara did to you. And Nahri was doing so just as violently, incapacitating her brother in a callous mirror of the way he'd suffered for years. It was as vicious as Dara putting a sword to Ali's neck and telling her to choose.

And Jamshid was a warrior. He was clever and brave. He could be an asset, a valuable ally. Nahri could see them flying back to Daevabad together, fighting side by side. She wouldn't have to be alone; she wouldn't have to confront this awful task alone.

But then the memories came to her. Dara crumbling to ash and the light leaving Nisreen's eyes. The slaughtered shafit in the workcamp and the murdered Daevas from the parade. Ali begging her to cut the seal from his heart, with the lips she'd just kissed.

Everything I build gets broken. Nahri stepped back from her brother as if she'd been burned.

"I'm sorry, Jamshid," she said as she reached for the door. "I really am."

PART III

42

NAHRI

When the sun was at its zenith, burning straight down upon the dusty plains that bordered the Gozan River, Nahri stepped out of the shade of her shedu's wing and got ready.

First went her shabby clothing: the wool robe she'd worn to protect herself from the chilly air high above the earth. Underneath Nahri was dressed in a sky-blue gown that fell to her shins, patterned with bronze sunbursts. Leggings in the same color were tucked into comfortable riding boots she could run in. She rewrapped her gold-and-green headscarf, taking care to pin the cotton so the wind wouldn't wrench it away. Nahri had chosen her clothes with care—colors reminiscent of the Nahids' imperial past, and cuts that would allow her to flee if this all blew up in her face.

She opened her bag, taking a sprig of the sweet basil she'd swiped from the castle kitchen back in Shefala. *For luck,* Nisreen had told her many years ago, twining a similar sprig in Nahri's braid before her first day in the infirmary.

I miss you, my friend. I wish your last moments had not been so violent, and I wish that you'd trusted me. Nahri didn't think she'd ever make peace with the knowledge that her beloved mentor had been a partner in Manizheh's conspiracy, but she also wasn't going to waste her life regretting other people's choices. Especially not when she had a city to save. Instead, Nahri tucked the basil sprig under her headscarf and moved on.

Her shedu was busy rustling through the basket of fruit she'd brought.

"There are no more apricots left, you picky creature." Despite the rebuke, Nahri reached out to ruffle his mane, scratching behind his ear when he pressed his nose into her chest with a happy grumble. "Maybe I should call you 'Mishmish' for how much you love them."

He tore apart the basket in response. Nahri caught a glimpse of a last apricot, stuck in the straw fiber, before the giant lion ate it, basket and all.

"I'll take that as a yes."

Steeling herself, Nahri reached deeper into her bag. There was just one more thing she needed.

The peri's dagger.

She removed it, the blade gleaming silver bright in the sunlight, so razor-sharp that the barest press of her finger drew blood. It had remained icy to the touch and shone wetly. Fairly small, it took little effort to flick the dagger from her belt and shove it upward, an easy motion for a former cutpurse who still liked her knives compact.

The size is probably deliberate. They've probably been watching, waiting for years for the right person, the right mark to take him down.

Nahri stared at the knife. A single thrust to the heart, the peri had said.

Dara's hands on her face, his green eyes pleading. *It's going to be okay,* he'd promised as they stood in the palace thick with slaughter. *She's going to set everything right.*

"We'll see about that," Nahri muttered, sliding the dagger into her belt. As ready as she suspected she'd ever be, she crossed back to her shedu. "Come on, Mishmish, it's time to go settle a family argument."

THEY FLEW LOW TO THE GROUND, NAHRI HOPING TO remain as discreet as possible while upon a massive magical lion with rainbow-colored wings. But perhaps she needn't have worried—for the sight before her was more than enough distraction for any unfortunate travelers. Where there had once been simply another dusty plain after the Gozan River, an illusion to hide the city, now jutted a massive ring of gloomy mountains, the deep forests a bizarre contrast to the rocky desert. It might have made for a marvel, two so very different worlds shoved up against each other.

But it was no marvel. For as Nahri drew nearer, she saw rot had overtaken the trees, their bark covered in bulging pustules and their leaves leached of color. Entire stands had fallen, crumbling into windswept dunes of ash. A jagged gash ripped through a hill covered in dying wildflowers; from its depths burst fingers of serrated rock like protruding knives. The stone was stained dark crimson, the exact shade of Nahri's blood.

An excellent omen. Just really promising all around. But Nahri pushed on. She'd made her choice, and so she flew over the fallen divide between her worlds.

A wave of heat stole over her, the ring scorching against her skin. Nahri clutched Mishmish, struggling to hang on as a burst of raw, jittery energy—as if she'd had way, *way* too many cups of tea—rushed through her body. She suddenly felt . . . connected, intertwined with the world below, as if it were a patient whose body she'd opened with her healer's sight to examine.

A very sick patient. Acting on instinct—or perhaps not even on instinct, but rather the world *itself* pulling her close, drawing what it needed as magic swirled in her hands, in her heart, dancing from her body in waves—Nahri held fast to Mishmish, feeling like they were being tossed about in a tumultuous, unseen sea.

Her patient began to heal.

The diseased trees beneath her sprouted new growth, their rotted bark falling away to reveal healthy wood. Buds and shiny new leaves unfurled, a sped-up spring. Color blossomed in waves as Nahri flew overhead, pale blue flowers and pink clover racing across the landscape, moss sheathing the jagged rocks in a curtain of softness. The magic raced ahead, a welcome mat of green unrolling before her.

"Oh, wow," she whispered. Nahri had no other words, only tears pricking her eyes.

She was home.

Her healing touch abruptly ended at the beach. The lake beyond stayed unaffected, its water churning with the violence of a tropical cyclone. Waves smashed against the shore, frothy whirlpools spinning with fallen tree branches and debris. If water could be angry, the marid's lake was furious, lashing out at everything it could. But it didn't hold Nahri's attention.

Nothing did, not when her city finally came into view.

Daevabad, in all its glory and infamy. The mighty brass walls embellished with the facades of its founders, her ancestors. The crush of ziggurats and minarets, temples and stupas; the dizzying array of clashing architecture and eras—each group, each voice leaving its defiant mark on the city of djinn. The shafit stolen from Persepolis and Timbuktu, the wandering scholars and warrior-poets from every corner of the world. The laborers who, when their work was left unacknowledged in official chronicles, had instead emblazoned their names in graffiti. The women who, after erecting universities and libraries and mosques, were kept silent because of "respectability," had stamped their presence on the cityscape itself.

Yet everything was a touch off. There were empty spaces where conjured buildings should have stood, ugly pockmarks on the skyline. The brass walls were tarnished, the edifices riddled with missing bricks and blackened mortar. Defying any weather pattern Nahri knew, somehow the eastern half of the island was draped in snow while the sun scorched the western side so fiercely that small fires smoldered in the scrubby hills. A hazy black cloud revealed itself to be a swarm of flies, and the ruined Citadel lay bare to the sky like a scar, its tower half drowned in the lake.

Like the mountains, Daevabad was sick. But there was no magic leaping from her hand now, and Nahri feared that whatever damage had befallen her city was going to need more than a single Nahid flitting through the air to fix it.

She took a deep breath as they approached the walls—she and Mishmish would be visible in seconds. *Creator, if you have ever listened to my prayer, help me save my home. Guide me like you guided Anahid.*

Make my hand steady when it needs to be.

Then Nahri and her shedu soared over the walls and into the city of Daevabad.

They flew directly into the Grand Bazaar. The crowded marketplace of djinn shoppers and arguing bargain hunters—the place she'd originally wandered through, wide-eyed and dazzled at Dara's side—was almost unrecognizable. Most of the shops were shuttered, and several had been ransacked. There were no browsing families now, only knots of people sticking to the shadows, blades sheathed at their waists.

Knots of people who *very* swiftly noticed the enormous flying lion. Alarmed cries rang out, followed by an awful metal racket, like someone had upended an entire rack of kitchen pans.

"The Scourge!" she heard someone wail. "He's back!"

"He's not!" Nahri shouted down at a group of men in tattered military uniforms. Oh, how lovely—one was loading a rifle.

But they must have heard her, for the tone of the shouting immediately changed.

"It's the Banu Nahida!" a woman cried. "Banu Nahri!"

Nahri's name carried on the wind, and the clanging went *wild*, people stepping into the street and leaning out of windows to gape upward. And while being cheered was certainly more encouraging than being shot, Nahri didn't slow down. Signs of decay and disease were everywhere, from buildings sheared in half to public water pumps submerged in fetid ponds. With relief, Nahri noted the hospital still stood, a small blessing. She urged Mishmish to fly over the hospital's roof and toward the midan.

Utter devastation met her eyes.

Nahri blinked, certain her mind was playing tricks. Because where there had once been blocks upon blocks, lively *inhabited* neighborhoods that stretched between the hospital and midan, there was now nothing but rubble—as though a great hammer had fallen from the sky to smash everything in its wake. The destruction wasn't confined to the shafit district either: a vast swath of carnage also stretched across the Ayaanle and Geziri quarters. Their three gates lay in ruins, half buried under the shattered remains of the midan wall.

She kept staring, as though the scene before her eyes would resolve. She wasn't naive. Nahri knew war, and she knew cruelty; her homeland had been occupied since her birth, and she'd fled through a palace filled with slaughtered djinn. But the enormity of what was before her very eyes . . . how did one process that? How did one make sense of entire neighborhoods, long-standing places with history and roots and community, simply being erased? Ground up. Homes and schools, tea shops and gardens;

the lives and stories they'd contained, the hard work and dreams that kept them standing.

All gone now. Pulverized.

She was shaking. *Where are the people?* Had they been warned? Or was it a graveyard she was flying over, thousands buried beneath the ruins?

And Nahri knew very suddenly why the peris had finally interfered. This was nothing like the sickness infecting the rest of Daevabad, a slow and steady rot. It wasn't the kind of devastation the ifrit could wreak. Or Manizheh.

This was the wanton destruction of the daevas of legend. The ones who had traveled the winds to bury caravans in the desert and devour human cities. The daevas it had taken a prophet to beat.

Dara had done this. And Nahri would kill him for it.

As if sensing her wrath, Mishmish roared, a bone-shaking sound that split the sky. Nahri almost hoped they heard it in the palace. She hoped they knew she was coming for them. That she was coming for vengeance.

With her own cry, she urged the shedu forward and cut through the sky.

They were flying faster now, but a quick glance at the Daeva Quarter and Temple revealed nothing out of the ordinary— whatever death Manizheh had visited on their tribe must have been done behind closed doors. The palace veered nearer. Archers were scrambling on the wall, but they didn't shoot, whether out of shock or uncertainty, Nahri didn't know and didn't care. Mishmish vaulted up and up, over the garden in which she'd spent countless hours grieving and healing; the massive library in which a prince had taught her to read and that they had then destroyed together; the throne room where Ghassan had attempted to humiliate her and was instead met with defiance from her tribe . . .

Then they were there at the top of the ziggurat, the palace Anahid had designed and built while wearing the ring now on Nahri's hand. Mishmish landed with a flourish, spreading his dazzling wings against the sun and roaring at the sky.

Their epic entrance wasn't a lonely one for long—it was probably the roaring—and it was only a minute or two before a pair of Daeva soldiers burst through the doors, their swords flashing.

The first paled so fast Nahri thought he might faint. "By the Creator," he choked. He held out his blade, the sword dipping madly. "Is that a—a . . ."

Nahri raised a fist, the magic of the palace leaping to her hand like an old friend. Her rage echoed in its old stones. It had always been there, simmering in the walls whose shadows had hidden her when she needed and ripped the rug out from under Ghassan's feet, but it had new life now. Daevabad's heart and soul had been gutted, and everything in it cried out to be saved. *Healed.* Flames burst from her palm, the ring gleaming in the firelight, and she inhaled, power rippling through her.

Nahri snapped her fingers, and the soldier's sword shattered.

He jumped, gasping and dropping the hilt. The second man hadn't even reached for his weapon; he was touching his ash mark and whispering prayers.

"Go," she commanded, offering mercy. "I am here for Manizheh, her Afshin, and the ifrit alone."

The first man stammered a response. "W-we have orders to protect—"

"Warrior, I am a Nahid standing before you, on a shedu, with Suleiman's seal. Trust me, your orders did not consider this. *Go.*"

"You should listen to her." A quiet voice spoke up. "I wish I had."

Nahri whirled around.

Dara.

THE AFSHIN HAD APPEARED WITHOUT A SOUND BE-
hind them, perhaps even more dazzling than Nahri, on a winged
horse of shifting smoke and flashing embers. He was dressed in
black, scaled brass armor covering his chest and wrists and
glittering in the sun. A matching helmet with a crest of vibrant
feathers crowned the ebony hair tumbling down his shoulders.

His horse landed lightly on the parapet and then fell apart in
a rain of cinders. Dara approached, looking every bit the beautiful Scourge of legend. He was carrying one now—the foul weapon
dangling from his belt along with a sword and a dagger, his bow
lying across his back. The helmet threw his face into shadow, but
his emerald eyes still shone fever bright, and when Dara moved
closer, it took everything Nahri had to not step back. Forget the
emotional entanglements between them—she was mad to think
she could take on such a man. Why had she even thought this was
possible? Because the peris gave her a fancy knife? Dara looked
like death itself.

And how did you kill death?

Mishmish growled, baring his teeth and curving one wing
around her. Dara stopped, glancing at the soldiers. "Leave us."

The two men vanished, tripping over each other in their
haste to get out the door.

Dara stared at her, his gaze tracing Suleiman's ring blazing from her smoldering hand to the shedu curled protectively
around her.

"You look glorious," he murmured. "The Creator has favored
you."

Nahri's heart was racing. "Probably means you should switch
sides."

Dara gave her a broken smile. Smoke curled from his collar, melting into the dark of his hair and making him as otherworldly as ever. "Were it that easy, my love."

"You don't get to call me that," she snapped, her voice shaking with anger. All thoughts of lulling Dara into a false intimacy, of throwing herself into his arms so she could shove the peri's dagger through his heart, had fled at the enormity of what he'd done. Not even Nahri could wear a mask after flying over street after street of ruined homes and untold dead.

"Was that your handiwork back there on the other side of the city?" she demanded. "Were a thousand Geziri dead not enough? Was Qui-zi not enough? You had to add another thousand? Five thousand? *TALK TO ME!*" Nahri screamed, her control shattering when he didn't respond.

Dara squeezed his eyes shut. He was trembling, his lips contorting as though he were fighting his own response.

But when he finally spoke, his voice was flat. "I am loyal to the blessed Banu Manizheh. Those were her orders."

"'Orders,'" Nahri repeated. "A good man would have defied those orders."

His eyes seemed to sparkle with unshed tears, but then the wetness was gone, vanishing as swiftly as it had come. "I am not a good man. I am a weapon."

A weapon. Dara had called himself that before, but not in this oddly muted way, his head lowered. This was not the hot-tempered Afshin she'd known, defending himself in the corridor. This was not the Afshin she wanted. *Needed.* Nahri almost needed Dara to shout back at her, to give some hint that there had been emotion and a heart that roiled within him.

"I went back, you know. To the cemetery where we first met." Fighting the hitch in her throat, Nahri plunged forward. "Was any of it ever real between us? Because I don't understand how the man I thought I knew . . . who I thought I—" She could not say the word as easily as he did. "How could you have done it, Dara? How could you have stood by her side as she did that to the Geziris? How could you have done the things they said you did at *Qui-zi*? Their women . . . is that what you really are?"

The name of the city he'd terrorized long ago seemed to break whatever spell of dispassion he'd been under, a hint of despair stealing into Dara's voice. "I . . . no. Qui-zi, their women—that part at least was a lie. My men never—"

Nahri recoiled. *That* was where Dara wanted to draw a line? "Oh, please. You really think no one in your batch of murderers went off mission between slaying shafit children and burying men alive?"

There was pleading desperation in his eyes now, as though he could speak more honestly about the past than his current duty to Manizheh. "You do not understand."

"Then tell me!"

Dara looked pained. "They . . . some of the women had lain with shafit. My men would not have touched them."

Nahri felt the floor move beneath her. "I hate you," she whispered. "I hate that I ever had feelings for you."

Still in his celestial finery, Dara dropped to his knees. The sight was incongruous. "I had to do it, Nahri. The people I believed were the Creator's messengers on earth looked me in the eye and *begged* me to. I was eighteen. They told me we would otherwise lose the war and our world would be ripped apart."

"And the people at Qui-zi? The mothers and children *you* ripped apart? Did they not beg you? *Tell me,*" Nahri demanded when he dropped his gaze in shame. "Tell me how you could look at people—at *anyone*—hear those cries and not break? Tell me how you could do it *again*. You're not eighteen anymore, Dara. You've got *centuries* on me, and do you know what I did when Manizheh asked me to join her? To view the massacre of innocents as an acceptable price for victory?

"*I turned her down.*"

But at her mother's name, Dara had rocked back on his heels, a vacant daze sweeping his features. "You should not have. Banu Manizheh is blessed, rightly guided, and I am loyal only to her." Again, the stilted, almost rehearsed-sounding words. "I cannot act against her. I cannot speak against her." He was staring at her, a glimmer of odd beseeching in the otherwise bleak set of his face. "Please understand."

"But I don't understand!"

Still on his knees, Dara shivered and then rose to his feet in an awkward fashion entirely unlike him, as if he was fighting his own body. He clenched his fists, embers falling from his lips. "I have orders to capture you."

"You take another step near me, and my shedu is going to have *orders* to eat you." The threat didn't take, because Dara was still moving toward her. Yet he was going slowly, like he might have been wading through churning water. He stepped into a ray of sunlight, the angle finally illuminating his visage beneath the helmet.

Nahri went cold.

Jagged lines of smoldering fire cracked across the left side of Dara's face like a lightning bolt, creeping down his neck to vanish under his collar. He was pale, too pale, a gray cast to his skin and deep shadows beneath his swollen, glassy eyes. He looked . . . *sick,* in a way that instantly reminded her of the cursed simurgh back on the beach.

But there was no vacant stillness in Dara's eyes. There was complete and total despair, hopelessness beyond anything she'd seen from him before.

Her throat caught. "What's wrong with you?"

Dara stared at her, pleading in his gaze. "I have orders to capture you," he repeated, seeming to choke on the words as if an unseen hand were strangling him. "You have betrayed your people and your family. But Banu Manizheh is ever compassionate." The overly formal words didn't match his devastated expression. "Surrender now and be granted mercy."

Nahri's mind spun. *This is not him.*

But what if it was? She'd read Dara wrong before and been nearly destroyed in return. What if he was playing on her weakness, on her affection?

What if Nahri was the mark?

He lurched forward, and Mishmish growled again. "Nahri, please," Dara implored. "Surrender. I cannot fight her. You cannot fight her. She—" His mouth snapped shut.

Then he shuddered, reaching for his scourge. It transformed in his hand, the iron barbs turning into shackles and chains. A *leash*.

"I am very sorry," he whispered. "But I have orders to bring you to her."

Nahri stared in horrified revulsion at the transformed scourge. But it was also the reminder she needed, jerking her loose from whatever this conversation was. She couldn't stay up here, not where the lake and sky were so visible.

That wasn't the plan.

She leveled her gaze on Dara, feeling the chill of the peri's dagger through her clothes. "I'm shafit, you know." The truth felt good, filling her with pride. "It's human blood flowing through here," she added, tapping her wrist. "Probably not dark enough to have passed your foul test at Qui-zi. But let me tell you, Afshin, I will bury you beneath the lake before that scourge touches me."

She would swear sorrow briefly lit his eyes. But then the flat mask of obedience again slipped over Dara's features, like a man pulled underwater, and he lunged.

Nahri was ready. With barely a thought, the palace magic

surged through her. She threw up her hands, and the stone floor rushed up like a wave, groaning and fracturing, to snare around Dara's legs.

She didn't expect it to hold. Nahri jumped on Mishmish as Dara twisted and roared, the stone already starting to crack. "The garden, go!"

They flew, dashing over the overgrown palace heart. An object whizzed past Nahri's ear with a metallic whistle, a glimmer of silver vanishing into the undergrowth. A second one tore by, and then a third whizzed past her calf with a lash of pain.

Arrows. He was shooting at her.

Mishmish yelped, swerving as he was hit in the wing. Another arrow dashed by, narrowly missing his throat and Nahri's arm. She whirled back, spotting Dara on the edge of the parapet. He drew back his bow again.

Nahri brought the roof down.

Dara disappeared in the explosion of wood and stone, swallowed by falling bricks. Nahri didn't bother watching. It wasn't going to kill him. Deep in her bones, she knew he was going to keep coming for her until she put her dagger through his heart.

But with Mishmish hurt, this gave her time. "Land," she urged, waving toward the trees.

They crashed through the canopy, her shedu roaring in pain. Nahri rolled off his back, trying to get a look at his wing.

"It's okay," she said as Mishmish thrashed. Nahri grabbed his mane, trying to calm him down. "Let me help you!"

The shedu stilled, allowing her to take his wing, and Nahri sent a burst of magic to ease his pain. But the arrow was metal, the shaft unbreakable, and each bit of fletching still razor-sharp.

"I'm sorry, Mishmish," she whispered, trying to numb him as much as possible. Then she shoved the arrow through, yanking it out and dropping it on the ground. The shedu let out a birdlike shriek even as Nahri soothed him, pressing her hand against the wound and urging it to heal.

A warning shivered through her blood. And then a root dashed up from the soft earth underfoot. It wrapped around her ankle, and yanked her out of the path of an arrow that zipped over her head.

"Surrender!" Dara was atop a pile of debris that used to be a gazebo, another arrow drawn back. "Nahri, please!"

"No, I don't think so, *my love.*" He'd shot her shedu, so she'd hurt him in turn. And judging from the pain that sparked in his eyes, the words cut deep. Nahri called to the magic burning in her blood once again, and the tree nearest Dara swayed wildly before ricocheting back and knocking him to the ground.

She paid for it. In the next breath, the garden had burst into flames, a ring of fire surrounding her and Mishmish. From the billowing black smoke rushed twisting forms: a massive viper, a screeching rukh, a sharp-horned karkadann, and a fire-breathing zahhak.

Mishmish knocked her aside, putting himself between Nahri and the monsters. But her shedu was outmatched, unable to fight four at once, and even as he dragged down the viper, biting it clean in half, the zahhak tore at his golden flank. He roared in pain, narrowly avoiding the charging karkadann.

The rukh landed between them, hissing and snapping its sharp beak. Nahri scrambled back. Panicked, she called upon the palace magic for protection, but the giant bird simply dodged the tree swinging at it and then seized Mishmish with its talons.

"No, stop!" she cried.

"Surrender, and he is free." Dara was already back on his feet, stepping through the line of flames like a demon striding through hellfire. "Keep fighting, and my beasts will tear him apart."

Of all the things he had threatened her with . . . Nahri would rather have been shot and bound with the scourge.

"You would do that to me again?" she asked, her heart breaking. She would not have thought Dara could keep finding ways to accomplish that. "Was the first time not enough?"

"I must obey my orders."

"Oh, *fuck* your orders." And this time, Nahri launched herself at him.

It was a supremely foolish move, one that caught Dara unaware as expected—she had literally no chance of defeating the legendary Afshin in hand-to-hand combat—but it was enough to startle him, knocking him off-balance. They wrestled to the ground, Dara easily thwarting her feigned efforts to grab the sword at his waist.

"Nahri, *stop*," he said, sounding exasperated. "I do not wish to hurt you!"

"You won't," she hissed. "I've learned the garden is very protective."

And with that, the roots beneath her surged up and seized him by the arms.

Nahri rolled free, climbing to her knees. Mishmish had slipped from the rukh's grip but was still struggling to hold his own against Dara's conjured beasts, silver blood gushing from his wounds. Dara was swearing, trying to twist free as more roots wrapped around his body.

Do it. Now! It wasn't the plan, but Dara was at her mercy for a moment. His monsters were about to kill Mishmish. She had no choice.

Nahri drew the peri's dagger.

Dara's bright eyes went wide, locking on the icy blade. The roots holding him were already smoldering, cracking as new ones raced to replace them in a race Nahri knew she would eventually lose.

He'd saved her life in a Cairo cemetery. He'd jested and grinned and stolen her heart as they flew across the world on a journey plucked from a fable. He loved her.

She was shaking. "Let my shedu go."

Dara thrashed against the tightening vegetation. "I cannot disobey Banu Manizheh."

"*Stop saying that!*" Nahri gripped the dagger, the handle so cold it hurt. "Call off those beasts, or I'll kill you!"

He met her gaze. The emerald eyes that had once terrified her. The ones she'd watched crinkle when he smiled and grow soft with longing in a cave above the Gozan. The eyes of perhaps the first person she'd ever trusted in her life.

Dara looked at her—and then a dozen more conjured beasts rose from the smoke to surround Mishmish.

Nahri choked. "Why are you doing this to me?"

"Because I *cannot* disobey her," Dara repeated, tortured begging in his voice. "I cannot speak against her. Do you understand? Nahri, I need you to understand!"

Mishmish screeched in pain.

You made a deal. He made a choice.

Nahri closed the space between them and raised the dagger.

There was a crack of thunder, and then lightning burst before her eyes, striking the nearest tree, a towering cypress. Heat seared her face, the tree trunk splitting . . .

Nahri threw herself across Dara, calling on her magic as the cypress crashed to the ground. It turned to ash before it crushed her, falling like snow upon them both.

And in the few seconds she took to protect him, Dara tore himself free of the roots.

He knocked the dagger from Nahri's hand, sending it flying into the undergrowth. Then he grabbed her by the collar and lifted her to her feet.

Briefly blinded by the burst of light and the smoke from the burning tree, Nahri blinked, trying to clear her vision. She expected to see the mocking grins of ifrit before her, their fiery eyes bright with heartless amusement. They were the ones who used blood magic to travel upon bolts of lightning, after all.

It wasn't the ifrit.

Manizheh smiled gently. "Daughter," she greeted Nahri. "You've returned home."

MANIZHEH LOOKED LIKE THE QUEEN SHE WAS, DRESSED in a dark silver gown dashed through with crimson insets and embroidered with rubies and pale opals. Ink-dark gloves covered her hands, but her face was unveiled, a copper-colored chador flowing over her long black braid like liquid metal. The color took Nahri aback, the allusion to the vapor Manizheh had used to kill the Geziris so bold that Nahri at first thought it had to be a mistake.

But she suspected Manizheh was not the kind to make such mistakes. It was a reminder.

No, it was a point of pride.

Manizheh's gaze was calm and very nearly warm as it moved from a brawling Mishmish to Dara holding Nahri by the collar. It dropped to linger on the seal ring glittering from her daughter's hand before finally rising, her black eyes settling on Nahri's face. She'd swear her mother looked almost impressed.

"I must admit, this was not how I saw you returning." Manizheh returned her glance to Mishmish. "Though if you've exchanged Ghassan's son for a shedu, I'd say you made a good trade. Dara, would you call off your beasts? I'd rather not have the first shedu to visit Daevabad in millennia be savaged. You can let her go as well."

Dara dropped Nahri to the ground. In the same instant, the smoky monsters surrounding Mishmish fell apart, smoldering embers showering the grass. Nahri lunged for the bushes in which he'd tossed the dagger, but Dara was faster, snatching up the peri's blade before dutifully crossing to Manizheh's side.

"You wished her disarmed," he murmured, his voice again uncharacteristically muted. He handed over the peri's dagger. "This was all I saw."

Manizheh examined the blade, and Nahri watched her shiver as she ran her fingers down the icy length. "Have you ever seen anything like this?"

"No."

She glanced up, eyeing him carefully. "Tell me the truth, Afshin."

"*No.*" The word seemed to tear itself from Dara's mouth. "I know nothing about a blade like that."

"A shedu and a dagger as cold as ice." Manizheh turned back to Nahri. "Tell me, dear daughter, where did you ever come upon such things?"

Nahri brushed herself off, contemplating tackling Manizheh for the blade. "Luck."

"I doubt that very much. Another lie. Two you've told me now." Manizheh tilted her head. "But then you've always been good at that, haven't you? A thief, Dara tells me. Some sort of two-bit criminal."

Dara told her I was a thief. Betrayal resounded in her, but Nahri glared back. "I wasn't the only liar that night. A shafit couldn't take the seal without being killed?" She raised her hand, summoning a pair of flames and letting them dance through her fingers and around the ring. "Interesting."

"And yet despite it being on your hand and returned to Daevabad, our magic is still broken. A coincidence, I'm sure." Manizheh's gaze turned more appraising. "Did you kill Alizayd for it?"

Nahri had known in advance that was not a lie she'd be able to sell. "No. I removed it from his heart and healed him with my own hands. He is with the marid now, beyond your grasp."

"Is he?" If her mother was surprised, it didn't register. "A shame. Had you killed him, I might be more inclined to welcome you back."

"I'm not interested in your welcome. I came back because I received that foul present you sent to Ta Ntry. You've taken to murdering and enslaving our people now, have you?"

"I've taken to executing traitors. I have no choice; that's the only law this city recognizes. Believe it or not, I tried to reach out to the djinn. They responded with deception, as they always do—which you must know if you were there when my envoy arrived. Did he tell you about the coup your sand fly husband instigated? The way they murdered Kaveh?"

"Kaveh chose his path when he let that vapor free. Or you did, giving it to him."

That landed. "Kaveh was fighting for our people decades before you were even born," Manizheh snapped. She steadied her voice. "You're angry; I understand. But you're also very young, Nahri, and new to our world. I offered you mercy once, and you threw it in my face. Don't make that mistake again."

"I told you, I'm not looking for your mercy. I'm here to save our people."

"'Save our people.'" Manizheh pinched the bridge of her nose in an expression of pure frustration. "Do you hear yourself, child? Do you have any idea how naive you sound?"

Nahri bristled at the condescension in her mother's remark. "I'm no child."

"You are," Manizheh exploded. "An ignorant, self-righteous child who has no idea what she's talking about and is lucky to be alive. One who is *very* alone and exceedingly outmatched. But never mind all that. Where is your brother? He is the one my envoy was actually intended to escort back."

"I left him behind. Jamshid is safer in Ta Ntry than with you."

"*Safer?* Do you have any idea what Ghassan's wife threatened to do to him?"

Nahri shook her head. "Hatset won't hurt him. We made a deal."

Her mother didn't look reassured by that—indeed, she looked even angrier. "So you make deals with djinn but not your own family? Why is that? All I hear about you is your supposed pragmatism. How willing you were to work with the djinn and the shafit, with the Qahtanis. You went to Muntadhir's bed, called Ghassan father—"

"You think I had a *choice*?" Nahri raged at the judgment in her mother's voice. "I had no one and nothing! They were hanging Daevas from the palace walls!"

"Which is why I *killed* them! You think *you* didn't have a choice? Try living under your enemies for a century, Nahri, instead of five years. Watch your brother beaten for your defiance and have it be *Ghassan,* not Muntadhir, trying to touch you. Burn a mark into your newborn child's shoulder, stealing his heritage and abandoning him forever. Then you can lecture me about choice. I did not want this violence. It will haunt me to the end of my days, but I will be damned if it was for nothing."

Manizheh's calm was gone, the words bursting out of her as if they had been penned up for far too long. And what was worse was that Nahri understood.

But that didn't justify it.

"I saw what the two of you did out there," Nahri argued. "You've gone too far."

"And because you've somehow wrangled up a shedu and cut a gem from your prince's heart, you think you're capable of removing me?" Her mother's voice was sarcastic and annoyed, and it hurt, because despite everything, Nahri could hear the undercurrent of familiarity beneath it, a parent dealing with a wayward child.

But Manizheh wasn't done.

"Enough of this." She sighed. "Nahri, please. I will offer you this chance again, but only once. You're my daughter. You are, by all accounts, an extremely promising healer. Surrender. Call off your shedu and hand over the ring. You won't be free, but I will see to your comfort and your education, and you'll be permitted to return to the infirmary. Play your part, and you could have a life here, a family—the kind of opportunities I never had."

Dara had remained at Manizheh's side, a silent sentinel. His gaze was downcast, and in his dazzling uniform, he was the perfect picture of obedience.

And that was what Manizheh would make *her*—the daughter who'd gone astray but returned to the fold, living proof of Manizheh's beneficence. Nahri would be a healer again, quiet and dutiful, dragged out and decorated for festivals, expected to keep her mouth shut about whatever new atrocities her mother committed to keep the gilded illusion of their power.

It wasn't an opportunity Manizheh was offering, it was a nightmare.

"No," Nahri replied. "Never. You call me outmatched, and yet you have a single Afshin and a pair of unreliable ifrit. I have the seal, our magic, and the city itself."

"You have a broken ring, a bleeding shedu, and a handful of angry trees. But you clearly don't want to listen to me. Fine. Let's see if someone else can make you see reason. Darayavahoush—" Dara's head snapped toward Manizheh. "You had to be brought more forcibly back into line. Speak freely. Tell my daughter how that's been."

Dara . . . broke.

The consummate Afshin—so obedient, so strong—crumpled to the ground. He ripped away his helmet, revealing the jagged lines of light breaking over his face.

"*Nahri.*" Dara fell weeping at her feet, pressing his brow to the dirt as his entire body shook with sobs. "I am sorry. I am so sorry. I did not want to hurt you. She gave me no choice. She made me destroy the city," he blurted out, pushing himself up on his knees to look at her. His eyes were wild, tears streaming down his cheeks. "Please." He clutched at Nahri's dress. "Surrender. I cannot watch her kill you. I cannot—" He broke into louder sobs, his words incoherent, and then simply threw his arms around her knees, holding her tight.

Nahri was speechless. Lost for words—for *any* explanation as to what could have rendered the legendary warrior, the man who looked like death incarnate, into the shattered Afshin at her feet, she glanced up.

Manizheh met her gaze, raised her hand, and pulled free a black glove.

An emerald ring glittered on one of her fingers.

I cannot disobey her. I cannot speak against her.

No, that wasn't possible. It *wasn't.* Nahri grabbed Dara's hands, wrenching them away from her legs to search his fingers.

His ring was gone.

"No," she whispered. "Oh, Dara, no . . ." But in his miserable, wet green eyes Nahri saw the awful, impossible truth.

He tangled his fingers in hers, pressing them to his face. "I am sorry. I am so sorry." His skin scorched her knuckles. Still on his knees, she might have been a queen, a goddess Dara came to beg for intercession.

Nahri looked to her mother again. Her *mother.* "You enslaved him." Her voice was still hushed, the words too repulsive to say any louder.

"I *saved* him. He would have died of iron poisoning after the coup failed, had I not found a way to preserve his life. So I tied it to mine. Gave up my own blood and the remnants of our ancestors."

"On your own or with the assistance of the ifrit?" Manizheh's eyes flashed in response, but she had nothing on Nahri's anger now. "Call it what you will, you still enslaved him. Your own Afshin. With blood magic. *Ifrit* magic." Nahri was trembling. "He spent fourteen hundred years as their prisoner, and you—his *Nahid*—stole his freedom yet again. The Creator curse you," she breathed, having nothing else to say. There was no cutting remark now, no sarcastic refrain. It was a perversion of their family's role, of the relationship between the Nahids and the Afshins, deeper than anything Nahri had imagined possible.

"He betrayed his vows," Manizheh said. "He was straying from the path of loyalty. I set him back upon it in a way that empowers us both."

"In a way that empowers you both," Nahri repeated weakly. "What in God's name are you talking about?"

"In this—form"—Nahri didn't miss how Manizheh avoided the word "slave"—"Dara is even more powerful than he was before. He can level cities and take on entire armies." She smiled at Dara, still weeping into Nahri's hands. "And it's easier for him this way. He's already been through so much; his heart can't take what this last war requires. When we've finally won and enjoy peace, I will release him. He'll understand."

Nahri stared at her traumatized Afshin. So this was why the peris had sent her to kill him—the final act that had pushed them over the edge. *Manizheh's* act, for which Dara would suffer.

But the reminder of her bargain sent Nahri's mind spinning in a different direction. "And what kind of deal did you cut with the ifrit for this *assistance*?" she demanded. "Was it the souls of the Daevas you executed? Something else?"

Her mother's gaze dimmed. "A price I'd rather not pay. And one I won't need to, not if you stand at my side."

"Surrender." Dara said the word with defeat, with aching regret, but he said it. "Nahri, please, you don't want this." He pressed her fingers to the jagged line of fiery light cracking over his temple. "Surrender. You cannot defeat her. It will be easier."

Nahri briefly let herself cradle Dara's face in her hands, stroking back a lock of his hair. Not in a thousand years, even in the depths of her worst anger, had she wanted this for him.

"Oh, Afshin," she murmured. "You always did underestimate me."

"Nahri . . ."

But she'd already stepped away. This was between Nahri and her mother now.

"You remember those things you said to me on the roof?" Nahri asked. "About knowing how Ghassan had controlled me? About how much you were like me?" Manizheh gave her a wary look, and Nahri continued. "You were right, you know. You were exactly right. And for that I'm sorry. I'm sorry you and I didn't grow up in a time of peace, where we could have lived happily together. Where you could have raised Jamshid and me and taught us the Nahid sciences. I mourn, truly, the kind of relationship we could have had."

Manizheh's expression grew guarded. "Please think very carefully about what you're getting ready to say, daughter. There will not be another chance."

Nahri steeled herself, reaching for her magic. "Ghassan didn't break me." *Like he clearly cracked you,* she was tempted to add. "You won't either. I will never surrender to you. I would rather die than see you possess Suleiman's seal."

Genuine sorrow swept over Manizheh's face. "You have your father's spirit," she said softly. "It got him killed too." She turned to Dara. "Rip that ring off her finger right now."

Nahri didn't even have a chance to react to the words about her father before Dara rose shakily to his feet, taking a stunted step forward.

She backed away, quickly appraising her situation. Nahri had the seal ring and the palace magic, but Mishmish was badly injured, and Manizheh had the peri's blade. If she was smart, she'd use the palace magic to try and take Dara out, but watching him even now visibly fight the slave curse, ash beading off his skin . . .

"Afshin," Manizheh warned as Dara grunted. "I can alter the wish to have you remove her entire hand if the ring alone is too much trouble."

With a groan, Dara lunged for Nahri.

An arrow went straight through his wrist.

Dara gasped as it was followed by two more, arrows punching into his arm and chest and knocking him back.

"You were wrong, Mother," Nahri said. "I'm not alone."

Jamshid came soaring over the garden wall.

An enormous bow in hand, her brother made for an alarming sight on the ghoulish flying simurgh, but Nahri had never been so happy to see him.

She also didn't waste a moment—taking advantage of Manizheh and Dara's shock to dart past the wounded Afshin and through the burning trees to Mishmish's side. One of his wings was tattered, a gash across his flank deep enough to reveal bone. Nahri laid her hands on his bloody fur, commanding the wounds to heal. The laceration vanished, his wing stitching back together.

Jamshid landed, the stench from the half-dead simurgh hitting her hard. "Nahri!" He jumped from the ensorcelled firebird, sprinting to her side. "Are you all right?"

Nahri waved a hand in front of her face, coughing on the fumes. "Your timing couldn't be better."

Jamshid grinned back, a mix of fear and pride on his face. "See what happens when guilt gets the better of you?"

Nahri flushed, because that was indeed what had happened.

She hadn't been able to abandon Jamshid, not after he'd

thrown her own words back at her. She'd gotten close—but in the end, Nahri couldn't do it. Instead, she'd returned to where she'd drugged him, waited until the poison was out of his body, and then wept as she begged for forgiveness.

Jamshid had been furious, rightfully betrayed and hurt.

But then he'd helped her plot.

And now they were here. Nahri grabbed him by the shoulder. "Were you able to find—"

She shut her mouth. Dara was coming for her again.

Jamshid shoved Nahri behind him and drew his sword. "Stop where you are, Afshin!"

"He can't. He doesn't have a choice!" Nahri said in a rushed explanation. "Manizheh enslaved him."

"She exaggerates."

Their mother had joined them.

"Dara, stand down," Manizheh continued tersely, and Dara swayed, falling back. With Jamshid's arrows still sticking out of his back, he looked like a puppet with cut strings.

But the woman controlling those strings had eyes for only one person.

"It's you, isn't it?" Manizheh whispered, the ghost of hope in her voice. "*Jamshid.*"

Jamshid was gazing at their mother with a look of open, fragile wonder. "Yes," he said hoarsely.

Manizheh stepped closer, seeming to drink him in. A lifetime of longing flickered in her eyes, a wave of regret not even their mother, normally so careful, could conceal. "You were in their custody for so long . . . Are you all right? Have they hurt you?"

"I'm—I'm okay," Jamshid stammered out. "But my father . . ." Grief edged his voice. "Is what your messenger said true?"

"Yes," she said softly. "I'm so very sorry, my child. I wished you to be here when we returned him to the flames but didn't want to delay his soul's rites." She nodded at his sword—Jamshid hadn't lowered it. "You can put that down. I'm not going to hurt you. I would never hurt you."

Nahri opened her mouth, having a number of very rude responses to that, but Jamshid beat her to a reply.

"You *have* hurt me," he choked out. Something seemed to have broken inside him, words and emotions he must have locked away long ago. "You *left* me. You took my magic away, magic that might have healed me when I couldn't walk. You, Baba, you all lied. My entire *life* is a lie."

"I had no choice." Manizheh moved closer still, looking like she wanted nothing more than to touch him. "I knew you'd be freer and happier in Zariaspa than you could have ever been trapped in Daevabad as my son."

Jamshid was shaking. "I don't believe you." But even so, he'd slightly lowered his sword.

"I understand. And I'm sorry." Manizheh took a deep breath. "I can only imagine how many questions you have. How angry and frightened you both must be," she added, looking at Nahri as well. "I would even understand if you hate me. But I promise that I'll explain everything in time. We're together again now, and that's all that matters."

Nahri watched anguish roll over Jamshid's face. "It's not. I'm sorry. But there was a reason Nahri arrived here before me."

The earth began to tremble.

It was a slight movement initially, no more than a shudder. But then a second tremor came, enough to provoke a shower of smoldering leaves from the burning branches above. It must have rained recently, for the garden was pocked with puddles, and the one nearest began to ripple. The water rose and fell as though a great plunger were thrusting in and out.

"Banu Manizheh!" A very out-of-breath scout raced down the path. He skittered to a stop, looking hastily at Mishmish and the two young Nahids. But not even the presence of a shedu and Manizheh's estranged children stopped his warning.

"There's something wrong with the lake," he panted. "These mists—they appeared from nowhere. And the water is rising, the waves breaking over the walls."

Hope rushed through Nahri so fast it left her breathless.

Manizheh clearly didn't miss Nahri's reaction, her eyes narrowing at her children. "The top of the palace, Afshin," she ordered. *"Now."*

With a burst of magic smelling like decayed viscera, the garden beneath them abruptly rose as though the patch of grass had been carved out and shoved upward. Jamshid grabbed Nahri's arm to steady her. His simurgh didn't make it, tumbling into the rain of falling rocks and twisted roots, but Mishmish flew clear, flapping his wings to follow as they tumbled unceremoniously to the top of the palace ziggurat.

The sky was dimming, great walls of fog rising to veil the sun. Nahri rushed to the edge of the parapet, her heart in her throat.

Please, she prayed. *Let me have this.*

Vast clouds of mist blossomed across the surface of the lake, dancing over the dark water. Pale shapes swam just below—jagged spikes and great billowing fins. Curves that might have been sails and enormous bristling spears.

And then the boats began to emerge.

First there were just a handful. Then dozens. Scores. Calling them boats might have been a kindness, for they were more like the cobbled-together skeletons of hundreds of different shipwrecks with barnacle-encrusted booms and massive rusted anchors set as battering rams. More slipped out of the fog as Nahri watched, dhows and galleons, ancient triremes and the pleasure boats of forgotten sun kings. Banners flew from their masts, hastily painted with vibrant colors and sigils.

Tribal sigils. Nahri exhaled as Jamshid joined her. "So Fiza wasn't lying," she whispered.

"Fiza definitely wasn't lying."

He's building an army. The unbelievable words came back to Nahri, the words Fiza had shouted when she came soaring out of the sea on a skiff of teak and sandblasted glass, sailing so fast along an unnatural wave that it looked like she was flying, landing on Shefala's beach literally the morning Nahri and Jamshid had planned to leave for Daevabad. The shafit captain, dressed in clothes that looked like they had been taken from an Agnivanshi noble—and they had been, Nahri had learned: a noble *in* Agnivansha—had seemed like a hallucination, her words even madder. *"He's tied up in negotiations with some sand-dragon riders out in Tukharistan, but the prince is coming, I swear!"* Fiza had insisted.

Ali had apparently survived his submission to Tiamat.

But Fiza's breathless tale of flitting through rivers and streams, over vast oceans and underneath icy lakes in the blink of an eye to gather djinn from around the world, had not changed the ultimatum Manizheh's envoy had made: in three days, the Qahtani siblings would be executed if Jamshid was not returned to her.

Which meant he had three days to find Ali and his mysterious army and get them back to Daevabad before Nahri faced their enemy alone. It had been more than a gamble, it had been a fleeting shot in the dark, a prayer.

Nahri supposed then it wasn't always bad to have a little faith.

Yet her relief was edged with dread now. Because no matter Fiza's rushed words, this . . . this *fleet* of drowned ships was not what Nahri had expected. Sobek had made damn clear how he felt about mortals, and the marid did nothing for free; there was always a price.

What price had Ali paid for all this?

Then make it worth it. Because Nahri could see opportunity in the awe-inspiring sight below them. Maybe this didn't have to end in bloodshed.

She turned to face her mother. Manizheh's mask was back in place as she assessed the vast array of resurrected warships like it was a group of children armed with sticks, paddling canoes.

"You've already gotten your victory, Mother," Nahri said. "Ghassan is dead, and our people are free of Qahtani rule. So stand down. We're not here to quibble over the throne or the past. We're here, *all* of us," she emphasized, pointing to the tribal sigils, "united to save the one home we share. Jamshid and I—we'll take it from here. You know we'll look out for the Daevas. Let us. Stand down."

"Please, Mother," Jamshid said softly, the familiar word falling from his lips too as he reached out to touch Manizheh's hand. "We don't want to hurt you. We just want peace and for the fighting to stop. Surrender, I beg you."

Manizheh didn't look even slightly swayed. Instead she shot a look at Nahri. "You're the one who keeps harping on what Dara did to your djinn and shafit neighborhoods . . . surely you must realize all you've done is deliver everyone on those ships to their deaths? With but a few words, I can command him to annihilate your prince and his army."

Oh. No, Nahri hadn't quite realized that fact as immediately, not seeing the potential for mass murder as readily as her mother.

She thought fast. "I'm guessing that kind of devastation isn't too precise?"

Jamshid interrupted. "There doesn't need to be *any* devastation!"

Oh, big brother, you keep trying to love people who don't deserve you. And Nahri would know, because as Manizheh opened her mouth to give Dara his next command, and Mishmish flew by, Nahri was already moving to use Jamshid yet again.

"Stay with the ships," she hissed. "She won't risk you."

His eyes went wide. "Wait, what are you—"

"You're the better rider." Nahri shoved him off the wall.

Manizheh cried out, reaching for her son, but Jamshid had already landed on Mishmish's back. He swore, giving Nahri a look that promised the worst of sibling retribution, but then rolled, grabbing Mishmish's mane and soaring for the lake.

Manizheh didn't waste any time. "*Get him back, Dara.* Now!"

The Afshin was gone the next moment, on a conjured winged horse of smoke.

There was murder in Manizheh's eyes when she whirled on her daughter. Well, that was how it felt when someone called out your weaknesses. And it had been clear since the moment he landed in the garden that Jamshid occupied a far dearer spot in their mother's heart than Nahri. Her firstborn, her son. The child she shared with the man she had loved and lost.

No, there would be no orders to annihilate Ali's army while Jamshid was among them.

Nahri tried to pull on that tie again. "You're outnumbered, Manizheh. Don't make Jamshid watch you die. He's been through enough. Surrender."

"I'm not worried about him watching me die." Manizheh glanced back at the fog again, as though hoping to see her son, and then beckoned to the Daeva scout who'd had the bad luck to get dragged up along with them and had been cowering since delivering his news. "You—come forward and lend me your knife."

Trembling, the scout nonetheless complied, drawing near and handing Manizheh his knife. "Of course, my lady."

"What is your name?"

"Yexi."

"Yexi." Manizheh smiled. "Thank you."

She slit his throat.

Nahri cried out, rushing forward, but Manizheh had already shoved the blade deep, killing the scout before Nahri could get close enough to lay her hands on him. She grabbed her mother's shoulder.

Manizheh spun out and slashed Nahri across the cheek.

It was not a mortal wound. Indeed, Nahri had no sooner fallen back in shock than it was already healing, the sting fading. But though they were facing each other as enemies, though they'd just threatened each other plenty, there was something about actually being cut—intentionally hurt, by her own mother—that sent Nahri reeling. She touched her cheek, her fingers coming away bloody.

There was a trace of regret in Manizheh's eyes. "I truly did want things to be different between us." She was still holding the knife, now wet with Nahri's blood. More poured from the murdered scout, his lifeblood steaming and boiling as a column of sick haze rose from his body like a flare.

From the sky, two crashes of thunder returned it.

Nahri was backing away before the lightning even flashed, leaving two figures against the bright explosion.

This time it was the ifrit.

AESHMA GRINNED, LICKING HIS FANGS AS HE STROLLED nearer. The ifrit leader was decked out for battle in a battered bronze chest plate, his massive bloodstained mace resting on one shoulder and chains looped around the other. Behind him, Vizaresh looked no less malevolent, twirling an ax.

"I was wondering when you would call for us," Aeshma said in greeting. "Such exciting things happening below. You know, I could be wrong, but I do believe the marid have returned to avenge themselves on you."

"Those boats will be the grave of everyone upon them."

Manizheh turned to Vizaresh. "You told me you could make those slain on the lake rise, yes?"

"For a price."

"Your price awaits in the Grand Temple. There's a small pavilion on the third level facing the south. Behind that is the room you seek."

"And *my* price?" Aeshma asked sharply.

Manizheh handed over the knife, still wet with Nahri's blood. "Consider our pact complete. I want my enemies destroyed. Those on the lake. Those in the city. Those in the palace. Any who would dare stand against me."

Nahri was moving forward before her mother had even finished her genocidal demands. The room in the Grand Temple . . . she knew that room. Knew what was kept in the room. And Nahri would be damned if the ifrit were getting in there.

Aeshma struck the bloody knife against the chains he was holding and then turned to her with a wicked smile. "Banu Golbahar e-Nahid, won't you stand down?"

Nahri's hold on the palace magic vanished.

As though she'd drunk an entire carafe of wine, Nahri was suddenly unbalanced, her mind fuzzy and her body heavy. She tripped, trying to steady herself on the parapet.

"What . . ." Her tongue was thick in her mouth. "What did you call me?"

Aeshma was working the knife against the chains like a blacksmith's hammer, sparks flying. "Your true name," he replied. Blood flowed from the knife, coating the links, far more blood than could have possibly stained it. With every surge, Nahri felt weaker, as though it were being drawn from her very own veins. "Unlucky girl. The fewer people who know your true name, the more power it holds. A name that only one person knows and not even its bearer? Oh, the magic in *that*."

He snapped the chains. "I've been forging these for weeks, chanting your name—Golbahar! Golbahar!—adding all the bits you Daevabadis are too cloistered in your city to beware leaving out. A brush with a bit of hair, silk cut from the sheets of your marriage bed, the incense you would have touched in prayer . . . just needed one last spice," Aeshma added, chuckling as he tossed away the bloody knife.

Golbahar. *Golbahar.* Nahri felt like she'd just been thrown into a realm of dreams, a dozen voices whispering the name to her.

"Golbahar, finish your letters!"

"Golbahar—such a strange foreign name. That mother can't be trusted—"

"Gol-love, just ahead. The Nile, do you see it?"

She was vaguely aware of the ifrit moving for her. Nahri tried to fight back, but her movements were labored and then the chains were wrapping around her, robbing her of the rest of her senses. She collapsed, falling heavily to the cold stone. Her eyes fluttered, half-closing as drowsiness smothered her mind.

Manizheh was suddenly there, although blurry. "The seal ring is mine." She seized Nahri's hand, only to hiss in pain.

Aeshma's voice instantly darkened. "Can you not retrieve it?"

Her mother tried again, and now even Nahri felt the heat as she touched the gold band.

Manizheh jerked her hand back. "No. Try yourself."

Aeshma twisted Nahri's fingers, painfully hard, but the ifrit had no better luck. "The blood magic," he said grimly. "You've been as tainted with it as we are."

"What do you mean, *tainted*? She's supposed to use that ring to free us from Suleiman's curse!" Vizaresh sounded enraged. "That was what you promised us! Why we . . . *what is that blade at your waist?"*

Manizheh answered guardedly. "Nahri arrived with it. Do you know what it is?"

"I certainly do! It's—"

"It's a distraction." Aeshma cut in, snarling. "I don't care if it's the Creator's own knife. That's not what matters right now. Manizheh, you knew my price, and it wasn't just for your daughter. It was for freedom from Suleiman's curse."

"Aeshma," Vizaresh hissed. "We need to leave."

"So go," Manizheh said. "Take her and the ring. You're the ones who are so clever, aren't you? Figure out a way to put her in your thrall and get your own powers back."

"That was not our deal!"

"Consider the terms changed. Now go. I have an army to destroy."

Aeshma cursed. "Cowards and blood-poisoners. *Lying* blood-poisoners. As selfish and unreliable as your ancestor." Nahri saw his mace rise in the air.

Then it came down, and she saw nothing at all.

43

ALI

Ali stood on the prow of the small ship he and Fiza had originally sailed into the sea—the last one they'd brought up from the deep. It had taken some wrangling, since it was in Tiamat's realm, but in the end, the mother of chaos seemed to enjoy the outrageous plan he had in mind.

It's preposterous and will almost certainly result in many, many deaths.

Go with my blessing.

And now Ali was here, back in Daevabad—albeit a lot sooner than he'd intended.

Please be safe, my friend. Ali had not known his heart could experience the level of panic it had when Jamshid had flown up with Fiza on what appeared to be a half-dead simurgh, informing him that not only were his brother and sister due to be executed in two days, but that the woman he loved was flying back to Daevabad, alone on a shedu, with a magical ice dagger the peris had given her to kill the Afshin.

Nahri said she hoped they caught up in time.

And she calls me reckless . . . "All the boats are through?" Ali asked Fiza softly. He tried not to raise his voice unnecessarily around others, learning his appearance—his eyes now yellow and black like Sobek's, fog wreathing his ankles—was startling enough.

Fiza, God bless her, had stopped finding anything about his transformation intimidating and treated him with her normal base level of rudeness. "Yes, Your Wateriness," she said with a sarcastic bow. "God, I still don't understand why we have to be on the dullest boat. A hundred different ships—ships made of bone, ships that haven't been seen in a thousand years—and you stick us on a trumped-up felucca. This is torture for a sailor, you know that, yes?"

Ali raised a hand, steadying the lake. Though he stood on a solid deck, he still felt submerged, pushed and tossed in an unseen current. "We're relying on marid magic for all this," he pointed out. "And there's not going to be any marid magic if the Afshin spots me on a flashy ship of bones and murders me."

"He has two new Nahids and an entire army to deal with. You really think he's that focused on you?"

Ali paused. He was not an arrogant man, but their interactions had left him fairly certain that if Darayavahoush had a kill list, Ali occupied a prime position. "I think he'd take a lot of satisfaction from murdering me, yes."

"My prince," Wajed said, joining them. "The boats have all made it. Are you ready to take us to the beach?"

Ali nodded. They had little clue what else to do but meet up with the remains of the Royal Guard and then head to the palace—they needed all the men and firepower they could get. But Ali hated having no idea what he was walking into. Jamshid had rushed back to help his sister, adding only that they believed Manizheh might be using some sort of blood magic.

"Just wonderful omens all around," Ali muttered to himself,

glancing again at the fleet he'd organized. The mist might have been too thick for djinn eyes to pierce, but Ali saw with perfect clarity the scores of ships he'd reassembled and dragged from the abyss with Sobek's help. As impressive, if not more painstakingly gathered, was its crew: djinn from literally all over the world. Ali and Fiza had spent every waking moment dashing through the currents to chase down leads from the farthest western coasts of Qart Sahar to the islands beyond Agnivansha. They had burst from the water with a simple message.

Return to Daevabad and save your kin.

Under any other circumstances, Ali knew they would have been denied. They probably would have been chased off and killed, or he would have been kidnapped for the ransom Manizheh was offering. But the desperate times she'd had taken advantage of—the pilgrims from all over the world who'd been trapped in Daevabad and the loss of magic—were just as easy to turn against her. Manizheh and Dara were distant stories, effortlessly spun into monsters. Ali, stepping from the deep with magic pouring from his hands, impossible ships before their eyes, offered a far nearer solution. And though plenty of people had turned him down, out of fear, caution, or because he looked like a "marid abomination," he'd gathered enough fighters, supplies, and aid to make a difference.

Or so he hoped. Ali looked again at his army: sand-dragon riders from east Tukharistan who'd been living around a cold mountain lake and shafit riflemen from a hidden refuge in southern Agnivansha. Warriors from all over Am Gezira—he'd had no problem convincing his tribesmen, nearly all of whom had lost family and friends—and nearly an equal contingent from Ta Ntry.

Ali said a prayer under his breath and then finally answered Wajed. "We're—"

A blur of gold fur and brilliant wings dashed by overhead. Ali glanced up and gasped at the sight of a shedu zipping through the air in a daringly erratic pattern, like a dove fleeing a hawk.

But it wasn't Nahri riding the astonishing creature, it was Jamshid, back once more.

Jamshid glanced down, his gaze finding Ali's. "She's at the palace!" he yelled, turning around at the same moment to aim an arrow at whoever was pursuing him.

From the fog burst Ali's nightmare.

Darayavahoush was finally the demon Ali had always known him to be, swathed in scaly black armor and riding a winged horse of smoke and embers. Fiery light crackled across his furious face as he flew after Jamshid, but then he whirled around . . . glowing emerald eyes landing on Ali, a conjured bow flashed.

Wajed lunged between them and shoved Ali into the lake.

The Qaid's face brightened in pain, but Ali didn't even get a chance to shout his name before the cold water closed over his face. The lake tugged Ali deeper, and he fought a moment of panic, his memories of being dragged down during his possession returning.

But the pull of the lake was like a worried friend now. *Danger*, memories that weren't his warned. The surface was perilous, the fire-bloods who raced over it enemies.

No, they're my family. The watery grip on his ankle relented slightly, and Ali swam for the boat, calling for the mists above the surface to thicken even further. He waited a moment, searching the sky, then pulled himself out of the water and climbed back onboard.

Relief coursed through him. Wajed was sprawled on the deck, cursing and fighting the djinn attempting to help him with the arrow piercing his shoulder, but still very much alive.

Ali fell to his knees at his side. "Are you all right?"

"I'm fine," Wajed insisted, even while hissing in pain. "We need to get to the docks."

She's at the palace. Nahri. Ali traced the distance between the crumbling docks and the palace. They were on opposite sides of the city, and it would take time to get there—assuming they weren't bogged down by enemy forces in the Daeva Quarter.

"No, please!" A horrifying scream pierced the lake, bouncing around the fog like a ghostly echo passed from ship to ship.

Ali looked around but could see no source of the sound. "Fiza?"

"I don't know." Fiza drew her pistol—a new one she'd "found" in a rather disagreeable trading post on the coast of Qart Sahar—and searched the fog. Another wail reverberated across the deck, and he saw her shudder. "Do you smell that?"

He inhaled and gagged as the scent of scorched hair and rotten meat washed over him. "What *is* that?"

As if in response, there was a sizzle and then a hissing splash as a wet projectile flashed from the sky and hurtled into the lake. A second. The third globule landed on the deck, blood-dark and smoldering as it soaked into a pile of ropes.

The ropes burst into flames. Another foul splash set the sails of the nearest ship on fire. A man screamed, diseased pustules breaking out across his skin as one of the globules struck him.

And then it was chaos. People dashed for cover under anything they could, yelling and swearing as the fiery blood showered down.

Spurred into action, Ali let his marid powers consume him. Energy surged through his limbs, unrestrained and eager. Another time, trying to harness such a thing might have made him black out, but the armor Sobek had given him cushioned the blow, magic rippling through the scaled hide of Ali's helmet and vest.

They wanted to fight him with fiery *rain*? Ali raised his hands and emptied the clouds.

The torrential downpour that answered extinguished the flames, but Ali didn't dare let it stop, shifting his focus to keep calling down the rain even as he urged the lake to carry his fleet toward the docks. It wasn't easy; it felt like splitting his very mind in two, and Ali was so distracted by the effort that he didn't notice anything else amiss until Fiza shouted:

"Alizayd, look down!"

Ali obeyed—just in time to see the swollen white hand that had been creeping over the deck, half the flesh nibbled away, seize his ankle.

It yanked hard, and Ali slipped, grabbing the rigging to keep himself from being dragged back into the lake. But the wraith that had seized him was only the first. Before he could cry out, more figures burst from the water below them, landing on the deck with silent, deadly purpose.

"Dear God," Wajed breathed.

Ghouls. And not just any ghouls. For the tattered remains of the clothes clinging to their putrid flesh was familiar. *Very* familiar.

"My brothers," Ali whispered. "No. Oh, God . . ."

It was the slain troops of the Royal Guard, the soldiers who'd been drowned and murdered the night of Manizheh's first attack.

That's not possible. None of this should be possible. The sky should not rain fire, and murdered djinn did not become ghouls.

It was blood magic. Jamshid had been right.

With a roar, Ali yanked free his zulfiqar and sliced off the hand gripping his ankle. He didn't have time to contemplate all this. They needed to fight.

A shot rang out. Fiza frantically reloaded her pistol, the bullet having done nothing to slow the advancing ghoul. Ali rushed for her. Sick with grief, he nonetheless raised his zulfiqar and cut clean through the ghoul's neck. The creature stumbled . . .

And then it kept going.

That had not happened with the human ghouls.

Fiza screamed, shooting again as the now-headless corpse

reached for her. Out of options, Ali snatched up a belaying pin and knocked the reanimated body back into the lake.

It won them maybe a minute. The creature bobbed right back up like a cork, again coming for the ship.

Fiza stashed her pistol, and Ali tossed her the belaying pin, swapping his zulfiqar for the sickle-sword Sobek had given him. A cool surge of magic dashed down his arm when he touched it, a burst of water twining around his wrist.

"Zaydi!"

Wajed's cry was enough warning for Ali to dive out of the way, avoiding a lunging ghoul. He whirled back around, cutting the ghoul straight across the chest with the marid blade.

It stopped dead in its tracks. It moaned and swayed, and then, with a sick squishing sound, the fluids burst from the wound. Water and rotting sludge drained from the bloated corpse with such force that the entire body shuddered, leaving nothing but a wrung-out husk on the deck.

Ali was suddenly very glad he couldn't remember the last time he'd eaten. Around him, more than one man was retching. He stared at his sickle-sword.

His *marid*-gifted sword.

Then he sheathed it, running for the railing. "Keep knocking them back into the water!" he yelled.

"Where are you going?" Fiza cried.

"To get help!"

Ali launched himself back into the lake.

THE VIEW BENEATH THE SURFACE WAS NOT ENCOURaging.

The water was so thick with the dead that swimming past them felt like cutting through a school of fish—fish who avoided him, thankfully, lurching away like Ali was a shark in their midst. Ghouls were clambering onto one another's backs, digging what remained of their nails, their teeth—anything—to get onto the ships. The press of dead flesh reminded Ali of his time on the Nile, and he couldn't help but shiver at the memory of how close he'd come to being eaten alive.

It was not a fate he'd see befall the army he'd brought to Daevabad or his loved ones inside the city, even if it meant inviting some almost equally alarming-looking allies.

Sobek had told Ali how important Daevabad's lake was, but he could see it with his own eyes now. *Feel* it. Thousands of currents danced across the water in every direction, beams of pale gold rippling like dust twirling in the light. Ali reached out a hand and took hold of one.

Cousins, he begged. *I could use your help.*

At first nothing happened. Even below the water, Ali could hear his men screaming and dying. But gradually the light began to change, shifting in different parts of the lake as some of the currents abruptly snapped straight, like ribbons pulled tight. Then tunnels of water opened. A tropical green-blue from turbulent seas. Inky black from the deepest trenches. Languid brown from ponds and rivers. Crystal clear from streams. Icy white from turbulent rapids.

And from those tunnels came all kinds of marid.

All kinds of his kin.

They streamed through with the frantic, angry power of those who had seen their home invaded. Merpeople, carrying vicious spears. Half-otter half-crabs, chattering and snapping their pincers. Sharks and kraken and eels longer than a city block. They'd heard his call and were back in the lake they'd feared never to see again.

They didn't hesitate to attack the ghouls infesting their sacred water and, in doing so, save the lives of the djinn above the surface. Gratitude welled in him, but Ali didn't have to say anything. His emotions carried on the water, as did their relief and pleasure.

Then, from the bottom of the lake, the muddy bed itself seemed to stir. Tentacles snaked upward, encrusted in eons of debris. Bones and fishing hooks, crabs and the roots of drowned trees.

It was the lake marid that had possessed him.

Ali stilled in the water as the creature carefully approached, one of its tentacles brushing his arm. They exchanged no words; they both already knew each other, Tiamat having shared their worst memories. Ali's torture, the lake marid's dispossession and unfathomed loneliness.

Instead, Ali's mind filled with new visions. The cliffs beneath the palace and how fiercely the lake beat against the rocks there, enough to spray the walls. Images of midnight blue water rising and falling, great swells licking up mountains and flooding the valleys.

And he knew what he needed to do.

He brushed his hand against the lake marid. Leaving his new kin to deal with the ghouls, Ali swam back to the surface and headed for the nearest ship, a drowned galleon of coral and re-claimed wood. An Ayaanle sailor cried out in alarm when Ali rose to his feet on the deck, but no one attacked him, so he took that as an encouraging sign.

Ali stared again at the docks. He'd stopped the fleet when the ghouls attacked, not wanting to lead the undead into the city, but he pulled on the water now, feeling the lake marid below lend its strength. They needed to get to the palace.

But he had to stop thinking like a djinn. Ali didn't need a dock or dry streets—streets where his warriors might get set upon by enemies or pinned by the Afshin.

Ali could carve his own path.

Fixing his gaze on Daevabad's cliffs, he drove his fleet directly at them.

A great wave rose beneath the ships, and then they were rushing forward, soaring across the water. The palace sat high atop the cliffs overlooking the lake, but cliffs could be devoured, swallowed. Usually it took ages. Now it would take seconds. Ali drove the water higher and higher, the lake marid cackling in his head, his kin cheering.

He landed his navy on the palace walls themselves.

That took far more care, Ali falling to his knees as he settled the fleet around him, trying to set the boats in places where they would do the least amount of damage and pulling the water back *into* the lake, rather than dumping it into the city.

By the time it had receded, Ali was spent. He released his hold on the marid magic and then—empty stomach notwithstanding— threw up, collapsing into the arms of a very bewildered sailor.

His vision blurred and went black, Ali's efforts to remain conscious meeting with mixed success. He could hear running feet and more screams, bizarre beastly shrieks and the sound of blades hacking through flesh.

"Where is he?" Fiza. "Alizayd? *Alizayd!*"

"Over here!" the sailor holding him yelled.

A foot nudged his side. "Are you dead?" Fiza asked.

Ali spat blood. "Not yet."

"Good. Might want to open your eyes."

He opened his eyes—and immediately regretted doing so.

Blood beasts and dead-eyed simurgh soared across a black sky choked with smoke. Bursts of bloody fire rained down like ghastly shooting stars, and as Ali turned his head to glance below at the palace garden, he realized the animal shrieks he'd heard belonged to his father's menagerie—the karkadann used for state executions included—now loosed and trampling through the grounds.

Banu Manizheh was apparently not going down without a fight.

"Is my sickle-sword still in my belt?" Ali asked weakly.

"Yes."

"Can you put it in my hand?"

"Why, so you have a better chance of impaling yourself when you pass out again? Because you don't look ready to do anything else with it."

Despite Fiza's words, she helped Ali back to his feet and placed the hilt of Sobek's gift in his hand. As soon as the sword grazed his palm, Ali felt better—well, the world started spinning more slowly, anyway.

He gripped the ship's railing in his other hand, studying the deck splintered against the palace's exterior wall. Ali's head was pounding, and his heart felt ready to explode, his body still trying to recover from all the marid magic he'd just done. He couldn't remember the last time he'd eaten, and he hadn't slept in days.

But all that could come later. Daevabad came first.

"We made a pact, Fiza. You get me to Tiamat, and then we return to Daevabad and do right by your people." Ali shoved away from the wall and wiped his mouth. "The battle's just beginning."

44

NAHRI

Nahri was dreaming, swaying back and forth, her head an aching weight.

She ran through the sugarcane, free as a bird. A weed ripped at her ankle, but she ignored the sting of pain. The blood would be gone by the time her mother caught her.

"Golbahar! Gol, come back here right now!"

"—a lie all along, Aeshma! Decades, and for what? You promised us freedom!"

"I promised we would see Anahid's legacy destroyed, and we have. We just ripped through her very Temple! They have no magic, and they're tearing each other apart. The only thing that's going to be left of Daevabad and that race of weak-blooded traitors when Manizheh is done with them is ash."

"I never cared about Anahid and her legacy!" Vizaresh shouted. "I knew I should have listened to Sahkr. All you were ever interested in was your vengeance against the Nahids. You let them cast aside Qandisha, our companion for millennia. You let this dirt-blooded child live after murdering my brother. Where is the Aeshma who battled with prophets and sent storms of wrath against Tiamat?"

"We have Suleiman's seal now!" Aeshma shot back. "We have a Nahid. Her name. There is power in that. You saw what Manizheh did when she murdered her brother!"

The words washed over Nahri, half meaningless. She had never felt so weak, so bound, her mind and body wrapped in barbed wire. She caught an upside-down glimpse of burning gardens and a blood-filled fountain. The Grand Temple. A Daeva elder in priest's garb lay slaughtered on the path.

The shadows swallowed her again.

Her throat was sore, her voice nearly gone. It had been the screaming, she knew, but she couldn't say why she had been screaming. Couldn't say why, after hours in the river, her hair smelled like smoke, her eyes swollen from crying tears she couldn't remember. Instead she drifted down the Nile, her cheek pressed against scaly hide, her small fingers clutching a ridged back.

"Is that a child?"

"Oh, God—it's a little girl. Beat the water, get the crocodile away!"

An explosion brought Nahri briefly back to the present, bricks and brass raining down. There was a hole in the city wall where there shouldn't have been, the island's wilderness beckoning.

"—because it's not right! We followed you for years!"

"Will you not cease your *nagging*?" Aeshma snapped. "You want to have this argument *now*, when you're the one who jumped out of your skin when you saw the peri's blade and whimpered that we should flee to the clouds?"

The fishermen bundled her in a shawl, river mud still staining her face and clinging to her hair.

"It's okay, little one. It's okay." One of the men knelt across from her. "What happened, child? How did you get in the river?"

She stared at him. "I don't know."

He tried again. "Then what's your name?"

"I . . . I don't know." She started to cry. *"I want . . ."* But the word for what—who—she wanted wouldn't come, as though it had been snipped from her mind.

"Oh no, there's no need for tears." The fisherman wiped her cheeks. *"It's okay, little river girl. We'll take you back to Cairo and get it all sorted out, God willing. Ah, there it is. Bint el nahr. A title for a Nile princess."*

Bint el nahr.

Nahri.

The bonds around Nahri slipped just slightly.

"I don't understand why you're complaining. You got your prize, a bunch of new little pets. Go clap your hands as they sow mayhem, Vizaresh. Run away if following me is too frightening."

"Not without the rest of the vessels," Vizaresh hissed. "And not without the girl. You promised me she would die for Sahkr, and it is *I* who earned all this. I was the one who guided Manizheh's hand when she enslaved the Afshin. I was the one who commanded the ghouls. You would not be here without my magic!"

Nahri was dropped to the ground. She landed in a bed of leaves, rocky earth beneath her. It was dark, the sky churning with smoke, and the air thick with rot. Far off, there were screams and screeches and the bellow of dying unnatural animals.

Open your eyes, little Gol. Banu Golbahar e-Nahid, a proper Daeva name. Nahri fell back into her memories.

"She doesn't even have a real name, the little witch!" the boys yelled, chasing her down the street. *"Nahri, bah. Probably the cast-off from some whore."*

"Your *magic*? You mean, your handful of cheap tricks?" Aeshma snarled. "I have rewarded them enough, you little pest. You should be grateful I've given you *any* vessels. Honored I even included you in this to begin with. You are *nothing*, Vizaresh. You never have been. Where were your worshippers? Your feasts? You were never more than a murmured name, a creature of spells and shadowy bridges."

A warrior with wary green eyes, dragging a knife through the sand in one soot-covered hand.

"There is power in names. It's not something my people give so freely."

She scowled but decided to tell him the truth—for now. "My name is Nahri."

Nahri. My name is Nahri. Again, the chains slipped, and the world came more into focus. They were in the woods, on a path winding through the hills beyond the city walls. The distant screams were louder, blending with the crash of waves and the closer sound of crickets.

Magic was returning to her in pieces. Nahri lay in the grass where Aeshma had dropped her, vines reaching out to wind around her skin.

Nahri. My name *is Nahri.*

Her vision cleared as though someone had peeled away the last strip of gauze covering her eyes. Nahri saw the arguing ifrit as Aeshma returned for her. Vizaresh was still standing on the path, watching Aeshma's retreating back.

"I'm not nothing," he whispered under his breath. His fiery gaze was wild and boiling with spite. With resentment long buried. "I'm not nothing."

Aeshma snorted in derision. "You can chant that all you like. Not even you have the tricks to sell that spell. Now come—"

Vizaresh swung his ax and buried it in Aeshma's back.

"I'm not nothing," Vizaresh screeched, yanking the ax free with a sickening crunch.

Aeshma fell to his knees, spitting fire. His smug, sadistic smile had been wiped clean, replaced by genuine shock.

He scrabbled for his mace. "Traitor," he said. "You cowardly, traitorous worm . . ."

"Survivor," Vizaresh corrected. "One who intends to stay that way."

He swung the ax clean across Aeshma's throat and decapitated the other ifrit. Molten gold blood splashed across the path, splattering Nahri's feet.

Vizaresh was breathing fast. For a moment, he looked almost as stunned as Aeshma by what he'd done, but then he recovered and began rooting around the gory remains of the other ifrit's neck. He pulled free another chain—one made of gold like a bride might wear.

But there was far more than jewels hanging from it.

There were rings. Dozens of them. Anklets, bangles, and a handful of neck cuffs. All with one uniting feature.

Emeralds. The slave vessels from the Grand Temple, all of them. The vessels of the stolen souls who'd been resting quietly in the light of Anahid's original altar, awaiting a Nahid who could free them. That hadn't been Nahri, not yet. Before the invasion, she hadn't considered herself skilled enough to risk the extraordinarily advanced Nahid magic said to be necessary. But she'd visited the enslaved souls regularly, always leaving with the promise that when she was strong enough, she'd learn to wake them in the fires of rebirth, holding their hands as they took their first breath of freedom.

Now another Nahid had betrayed her promise and handed them over to the very creatures who'd enslaved them in the first place. Vizaresh ran his claws over the chain of stolen souls like a perverse twist on prayer beads, his eyes lighting with pleasure.

Then he noticed her.

"Well, look who's awake." His mouth curled in a smile, half giddy, half frantic—as if he still couldn't believe what he'd done to his companion, vacillating between regret and thrill. He was trembling madly, bouncing on his feet—a frame of mind that Nahri suspected did not bode well for her, his brother's murderer.

Sakhr was clearly on Vizaresh's mind as well. "I know who he is," the ifrit growled. "Your brother, Jamshid. A long time Manizheh held that secret, but we eventually pried it loose." He hefted his ax again. "I had hoped one day to kill him before you. What is it the humans say, an eye for an eye? I wanted *your* brother to suffer, to make his death as painful as a blood-poisoning."

There was genuine grief in his voice. Nahri remembered

Qandisha's anger back at the Nile and Vizaresh's own keening howl when he'd discovered Sakhr's body. She knew now that in some way Sahkr had acted in good faith back at the Gozan—he truly had been working with her mother.

And Nahri had killed him.

My name is Nahri. She breathed, and her voice returned to her. "I don't imagine you'll believe me, but part of me is truly sorry."

Vizaresh scoffed. "You're right, I don't believe you. You come from a line of liars. Liars and dirt-bloods, and even if your apology was sincere, I would not want it." He lifted the chain of vessels around his neck, caressing the rings again. "I think after I kill you, I'll drop a few of these in your human land and see what chaos they may bring. For now, shut your mouth, Golbahar, and do try to lie still."

But Nahri was done with lying still. As Vizaresh raised the ax again, she called to Daevabad's magic, to the seal, and to her own strength.

To the little girl who'd chosen her own name.

Her shackles and chains burst apart.

Vizaresh froze in midstep. "But your name . . ."

"I have another."

He recovered, swinging the ax anyway. Nahri ducked and then rolled to her feet. She raised her hands, calling again to her magic and preparing for his next attack. She was going to rip that foul chain off his neck.

This time, though, Nahri hadn't read her mark. Because Vizaresh took one look at her, roiling with unknown magic, another look at the seething city—blood falling from the sky and marid waves beating the walls—and then vanished in a bolt of bright lightning.

"No!" Nahri threw herself on the spot where the ifrit who'd declared himself a survivor had just been, but he was gone. Along with the dozens of souls he'd stolen.

And Nahri couldn't do a damn thing about it. Not when nearer catastrophes loomed. Jamshid being hunted by Dara. Howls from the lake she couldn't even comprehend. And, behind it all, her mother, who would pay any price, including enslaving her people and handing her daughter over to demons, to stay in power.

Nahri closed her fists. The seal ring held tight.

And then she turned back to Daevabad. It was time to end this.

NAHRI WAS NO STRANGER TO VIOLENCE. SHE'D watched the Navasatem parade turn to carnage and had survived her mentor dying badly in her arms. She'd fled through a palace filled with murdered djinn, and watched, helpless, as innocent scholars were swallowed by blood beasts. She'd flown over entire neighborhoods that had once been lively, bustling places and were now reduced to crushed tombs, untold dead beneath the rubble.

None of it had prepared her for Manizheh's last stand.

Fiery blood fell from the sky in clumps, its smoke illuminating twisting, terrible beasts both conjured and resurrected. Half-dead simurgh, rotting elephants and lions, and vacant-eyed karkadann ran wild through the palace, trampling fleeing servants and screaming soldiers. Ghouls stalked the corridors—the Daeva nobles Manizheh had massacred. Still dressed in blood-stained finery, their relics gone, they fell upon the living with no discrimination between Daevas and djinn. Nahri wasn't sure if her mother had intended such chaos or if the blood magic was out of her control. She suspected Manizheh didn't care. A victory would be a victory, no matter the cost.

But it wasn't all lost, not yet. A fierce rain poured down, water extinguishing some of the smoldering patches of blood, and Nahri raced through the outer gardens to see lake creatures—*marid*—climbing over the walls, crab-men and water snakes, attacking the ghouls and conjured beasts. With a great crash, the wooden doors smashed in, and a mixed troop of soldiers rushed through—a Daeva acolyte on horseback shouting to a group of similarly garbed youths and a Geziri warrior woman brandishing a zulfiqar.

"*Aqisa?*" Nahri shouted over the mob, recognizing Ali's companion.

Aqisa fought her way over, slicing the head off a ghoul, and Nahri raised her hands, calling for the palace magic to bring down a wall on the karkadann about to stampede through the djinn and Daeva warriors.

"Nahid." Aqisa clasped Nahri's wrist. "We thought you might need some reinforcements."

"You thought right. Have you seen Ali?" Nahri asked.

"No, though I'm guessing the giant crab creatures are courtesy of the man who used to summon springs in the desert?"

"I'm working on that assumption, yes."

A bloodcurdling scream came from inside the palace.

Aqisa gripped Nahri's shoulder, the humor vanishing from her face. "Manizheh has hundreds of people locked up in the dungeons who are going to be slaughtered if these ghouls get any farther."

"Then save them." Nahri nodded at the many knives Aqisa was wearing. "Can I take one of those?"

The other woman handed over a blade. "Where are you going?"

"To kill my mother."

The bleak, knowing look Aqisa gave her was torn between respect and doom. "I'll give you some men."

Nahri stuck the knife in her belt. "Thanks, but I'll have better luck sneaking up on them if I'm alone. If you find Ali, please keep him alive, okay?"

"I'll do my best. Go with God." Aqisa turned back to her warriors. "Draw up!"

Nahri had already let the palace shadows shroud her. Gripping the knife to steady herself, she closed her eyes, listening to her family's home speak to her like a sick patient, one infected by the foul perversion of magic staining its halls with fresh death.

It was easy enough to trace the source.

"Ah," she said softly. "Appropriate."

Then Nahri headed for the pavilion overlooking the lake where Ghassan al Qahtani had been killed.

THE LIBRARY NAHRI AND ALI HAD DRAGGED A WATER-fall through had yet to be repaired, the damaged section curtained off and its books removed. It was empty, the only light coming from a fire raging in another part of the palace and the scorching gushes of smoldering, diseased blood that continued to fall from the sky. Even so, Nahri crept carefully along the shadowed outskirts, slipping through the door that led to the winding staircase.

She could hear shouting from the roof before she got to the top.

"Then let me see her!" *Jamshid.* "Please! If Nahri and Muntadhir are safe, let me see them!"

Nahri opened the door a sliver, just enough to press her eye to the light now spilling in. She could see Mishmish, trapped under a net, and Jamshid in irons, pleading with their mother. Ice glimmered at Manizheh's waist—the peri's dagger, still in her belt.

"Banu Nahida, please!" It was Dara, unseen from Nahri's vantage point. "You need to control your magic. I cannot protect our people and fight at the same time!"

With a screech, a vicious, bloated locust—as large as a dog—landed on the parapet near Jamshid and Manizheh. Nahri saw Dara and another Daeva soldier lunge to protect them, Dara cutting the locust in half as his warrior drew its attention. A gash had torn through Dara's armor, exposing his chest and revealing more of the cracking lines of light. Screams in Divasti came from the garden the next moment, and Dara spun around, firing a blur of silver arrows downward before jumping back to the parapet to kick a marid in the shape of a giant purple lobster off the wall.

No matter what curse Manizheh had used to enslave her weapon, Dara looked ready to break. He was gasping for air, liquid fire seeping from the jagged lines crossing his body. Even so, he was still fast enough to leap from the parapet and knock his soldier out of the way of a globule of smoldering blood. Dragging the young man away, he yelled for Manizheh again. "Banu Nahida, stop this!"

Manizheh didn't seem to hear him, her attention on her distraught son alone. "The ifrit are keeping Nahri and Muntadhir secure in the dungeon," she insisted. "The way isn't safe right now, but I promise after the battle . . ."

"I don't believe you!"

A wise decision, brother. Nahri watched as Dara rushed across the pavilion to slay another marid and then, shouting orders to his warrior, thrust up his hands to keep a storm of bloody rain from lashing them.

He was distracted. So was Manizheh.

Nahri made her move. With every thief-honed instinct, with the protection of the palace, she slipped from the doorway, raised her knife, and rushed at her mother.

Jamshid's eyes went wide. He shouted no warning, but it was tell enough.

Manizheh whirled around, seizing Nahri's wrist as she tried to bring the knife down. But Nahri had not spent her time in the company of warriors for nothing. She kicked out Manizheh's legs, sending them both tumbling to the ground.

"Nahri, don't!" Jamshid cried. "She's still our mother!"

Jamshid was right, but that was a fact that didn't slow Nahri in the slightest. Not after the devastation Manizheh had visited upon Daevabad. Not after she'd enslaved Dara again, given Nahri to the ifrit, and sold out the poor souls who'd been resting in the Grand Temple. It didn't matter what blood they shared. Nahri's family was out there on the marid boats. They were working in the hospital and imprisoned in the dungeon.

And there was nothing she wouldn't do to save them.

But Nahri had underestimated how strongly her mother felt about her own goals.

Manizheh's grip tightened on Nahri's wrist, and then it was Nahri's turn to cry out, a burning pain scorching where her mother touched. As they wrestled for the knife, boils erupted across her skin, rolling out in waves from Manizheh's fingers. Then, with a strength she shouldn't have possessed, her mother threw her off. Nahri went flying, losing her grip on the knife and smashing the back of her skull against the stone of the parapet.

"You unworthy little brat," Manizheh snapped, climbing to her feet. "I have been nothing but patient with you. I've extended mercy multiple times, been willing to embrace you as my own, and now you think to put a knife in my back like a common street thug?"

"*Mercy?* You gave me to the ifrit!"

If Nahri had ever considered herself a talented liar, the scornful toss of Manizheh's head put her to shame. "Yes! To be held until after the battle since you clearly can't be trusted!"

"Liar!" Nahri clutched her wrist. The boils had stopped spreading, but the imprint of Manizheh's fingers could be seen in the burned flesh. "You gave them my name and told them to use me to free themselves from Suleiman's seal!"

Still bound in irons, Jamshid had lurched to Nahri's side. "Are you okay?" he asked, trying to check her wrist.

Resentment flashed in Manizheh's face. "Your affection is

wasted on her." Bitterness laced into her voice. "Our ancestors were right. The shafit *are* a disease. Their blood is tainted—*her* blood is tainted. And I will not see another Nahid brought down by a dirt-blooded liar."

Dara moved as if to interfere, but then another pair of Manizheh's hellish blood beasts descended—one a winged serpent and the other an oversize rotting vulture—and he turned back with a groan.

Which was fine. This was between Nahri and her mother.

"You black-hearted bitch," Nahri shouted. "It wasn't a shafit who told Vizaresh where to find the vessels in the Temple. It wasn't a shafit who enslaved Dara and used him to slaughter thousands."

Manizheh's eyes flared. "How *dare* you judge me? You know nothing of our world. You think your pathetic human existence was anything compared to the suffering the Daevas have endured? You think a few paltry years here makes you one of us?" Her voice hardened as she glanced back at Dara. "I've had enough. Afshin, I wish for you to—"

"No!" Jamshid shoved himself in front of Nahri. "Don't hurt her!" He sounded close to tears. "Mother, please. I don't want either of you to die. Nahri is my sister. She saw me through the darkest years of my life—"

"Before or after she pushed you off the wall in the hopes you'd land on a shedu? She's not worthy of your loyalty, Jamshid. And she's not your sister. That's a piece of protective fiction I'll end right now. She's Rustam's *mistake*," Manizheh hissed. "An error in judgment in the form of a wretched kitchen girl from Egypt. Another *thief.* One who couldn't keep her legs closed or her hands off things that didn't belong to her."

Nahri felt the entire palace shake. The complex was in chaos, fire and water raining from the choked sky, and beasts of various elements and states of death rampaging around them. Her people

were dying, Daevas and djinn and shafit all, the acrid air thick
with wails.

But everything suddenly seemed very distant.

"My mother was an Egyptian?" she whispered.

She wasn't the only one to react. Dara decapitated the serpent
and then spun around, still fighting back-to-back with the other
Daeva soldier.

"Rustam? She is *Rustam's* daughter? But you told me—"

"I told you to be silent," Manizheh commanded, and Dara's
mouth snapped shut. "Unless it has to do with keeping Daevabad
safe from the horde breaking through the walls, you will keep
your counsel to yourself, Afshin."

But Nahri was already putting the pieces together. Rustam,
the quiet shadow to Manizheh's bright star. The uncle she knew
so little of, whose orange grove she used to take shelter in.

Her father. Manizheh's *brother*. The accusations the ifrit had
been hurling as they argued . . .

"You—you killed Rustam," Nahri stammered out. "Aeshma
said you killed him."

Manizheh rolled her eyes. "So I've enslaved Daevas, given
Temple vessels to the ifrit, and murdered my own brother? Are
there any other wild accusations you'd like to make, or do you
need a few moments to think of your next lie?" She turned to her
son. "Jamshid, listen to me. I know you're a good man. I know
you love her as your sister. But she is shafit, and her loyalties will
always lie with the djinn first. She was just willing to murder the
woman she believed her own mother! She was willing to let you
be killed by Ghassan to save her djinn prince!"

Now it was Jamshid who stiffened. "What are you talking
about?"

"Did she not tell you?" Manizheh goaded. "Ghassan wanted
her to convince his lunatic son to lay down arms. He told Nahri

and your father that he'd kill you if she didn't agree. And faced with the choice of your brother or Alizayd, who did you choose to save, Nahri?"

The vulnerability in Jamshid's eyes tore at Nahri's heart. Manizheh had read him just as clearly—Nahri knew how fragile and new his sympathies toward the shafit were.

She knew he believed Ali a weakness for her.

Nahri swallowed. "Ghassan would have slaughtered half the city if the coup failed. Ali stood a good chance of taking him down, of getting rid of the man oppressing our people. *Jamshid*," she cried as he swore. "Please! I was just trying to put Daevabad first!"

Jamshid looked like he'd been punched. "I know. Your husband used to say the same."

Manizheh swept in. "He's still alive, my son. Leave her side, tell me what you know of the enemies invading, and I'll let Muntadhir live."

Jamshid was breathing fast, his hands in fists.

But Manizheh had underestimated her son.

"No," he said grimly. Jamshid stepped back, again putting himself between Nahri and Manizheh. "I stand with my *sister*. I stand with my people and my city. And it is clear you are an enemy to all three."

His words went straight to Nahri's heart. To the vulnerability and fear that had so long left her in knots when it came to her identity. She could have hugged him.

Except she was fairly certain he'd just doomed them both.

Manizheh stared at him. Flames flickered in her eyes, whether a reflection of the lethal rain she was using to scorch their home or something deeper, Nahri didn't know.

"You were all I wanted," Manizheh said. "I dreamed of seeing you again every night. When things were at their worst, I would close my eyes and envision you one day upon the throne, grandchildren at your feet. I imagined teaching you to heal." Her voice was eerily steady, and when she turned her attention back to Nahri, Manizheh's expression was still glowing, as though she were lost in that future that would never come. "I will make you suffer a hundred years for taking him from me."

At that, Dara stepped away from his warrior, looking like he was very done with the Nahid family feud.

It was a mistake. Because he'd no sooner left the young man's side—too far to help—when a smoldering globule of blood came hurtling from the sky.

It struck the soldier directly in the chest.

What happened next was almost too horrific for words. The foul sludge burned straight through the other man, leaving a diseased, pustule-ridden cavity where his chest had been. If there was any mercy, it was that the onslaught was quick. The soldier had time only for a short hair-raising wail before he was dead, another life cut short in a night that had already seen too many of them extinguished.

Dara cried out, rushing to his warrior. Manizheh glanced back, and Nahri shot free of Jamshid. She grabbed the knife Aqisa had given her and whirled on her murderous aunt.

Ah, but she'd forgotten how fast her Afshin was. There was a glimpse of his bow and a flit of silver. A whistle on the wind . . .

And then a punch of searing pain that knocked the breath from her lungs.

Dazed by the blow, Nahri looked numbly at Dara as she stumbled, not understanding right away that the bow still pointed in her direction and the silver shaft protruding from her chest were connected. They couldn't be.

Jamshid let out a bellow of outrage, but he hadn't taken two steps toward the Afshin when Dara snapped his fingers, instantly wrapping her brother in thick, binding tendrils of smoke.

"Enough," Dara said quietly, and the lethal command in his voice seemed to silence even Manizheh. He closed the eyes of his dead warrior, his gaze still on the man as he spoke again. "You could have surrendered, Nahri. She offered you a fair deal. A life. And instead you chose to bury our home in more death."

Nahri was speechless with pain and betrayal. He'd shot her. Dara had looked her in the face and put an arrow through her body.

And it hurt. It hurt so much. There was blood in her mouth when she spoke, trying to deny his words. "I didn't . . . that was blood magic. Manizheh—"

"*There are marid ships in the palace!*" The words exploded from him, and then Dara spun back on her, grief raging in his eyes. "We always wondered, you know, how Zaydi brought his army through the lake so quickly. All the survivors had the same story, ships rising through the mists like magic." He jabbed a finger at a ghastly dhow of bones and broken timbers beached on the opposite wall. "A ship like that brought the army that slaughtered your ancestors. The army that hunted and tortured and murdered my family. *My little sister.*" His voice broke. "And you brought them back here. You *fight* with them."

Manizheh spoke up. "Afshin . . ."

"No." Dara was trembling, his eyes wet with tears, but his tone was firm. "No. You told me I could speak when it came to defending our home, and I am. You're not the only one who gets to use Tamima's memory." He turned back to Nahri. "I *loved* you. I would have served you to the end of my days, and you chose a Qahtani."

Nahri had never truly been afraid of Dara until that moment as he slowly rose to his feet, uncurling like a cornered, beaten tiger. One about to maul his way through the world that had trapped him. She reached for the arrow. If she could just pull it free, she would heal. She could fight.

But Nahri had no sooner given it a tug than she nearly blacked out with pain. Her knees gave out, and she fell.

"I'm not your enemy," she tried to protest. "Dara, please . . ."

"If you led those creatures to my home, you most certainly are." Dara gave her a look so cold it stole what was left of Nahri's breath. "I remember, you know. I remember the night I told you of the war, of the djinn who massacred my family and your ancestors. I remember how you said you were *glad*."

She gasped. "I didn't mean it like that."

"I do not believe you. Because I know you. And you *are* a liar. A thief." He met her gaze. "A trickster and a dirt-blood who twists words only to land her mark. And I am done being deceived. I am done *listening* to a bunch of Nahids bicker over power while their city burns." Dara crossed to Manizheh.

And then he knelt at her feet.

"My lady," he started, "you and I have battled, and we have warred, but I have never doubted for a moment that you wanted to save your people. To give the Daevas the freedom we deserved and make a world in which your son could hold his head up high."

Manizheh flinched at that, her eyes going to Jamshid, who was visibly fighting the bonds holding him. "I've already lost him. She *took* him, poisoned him against me."

"You haven't lost him," Dara said firmly. "He just needs time. The peace that distance and time will bring. The peace that you brought us so close to before the djinn betrayed you. I would bring you that peace now. But I cannot protect us from your magic, navigate my curse, and fight all at the same time."

Her expression turned guarded. "What are you asking, Afshin?"

"Let me fight the way I know best." Dara reached behind him, plucking an arrow from his quill and holding it up. "You told me once I should be proud to be a weapon of the Nahids. You begged me to understand. I do. I wish I did not, but I do. You offered mercy, and they turned you down. *She* turned you down," he added, jerking his head back at Nahri. "You were correct. This only ends in violence. But then it will *end*. Let me be Daevabad's weapon. Let me give you peace."

Manizheh glanced again at Jamshid. "I didn't want it to happen like this," she said, her words so low Nahri barely heard them. They weren't for her, she knew. They were for Manizheh's Scourge, her partner in death and destruction.

"I know." Dara gave her a broken smile of bitter understanding. "I wish I could say it gets better."

Manizheh exhaled. "I just wanted him to be safe. I wanted to stop being afraid to lift my head."

"And he will be," Dara said softly. "Let me help you, like you dreamed I would when you were a child. Let me save the Daevas."

No. Nahri made a strangled sound of protest, more blood dripping from her mouth.

The sound must have caught Manizheh's attention, for her aunt briefly glanced away from her Afshin, to the niece she'd accused of betraying her. The woman Dara had loved, now bleeding on the dirty ground for having tried to attack her.

When Manizheh looked at Dara again, the doubt in her gaze was gone.

"Save the city, Afshin," Manizheh said softly. "Save our people."

Dara's eyes glimmered with new wetness. "Thank you, my lady." He drew back the arrow.

And then he plunged it through Manizheh's throat.

Nahri choked, not believing her own eyes.

But Dara was already reaching for the knife at his waist, his sorrow-filled gaze for Manizheh alone.

"I am sorry," he whispered as Manizheh rocked back, her hands going to her gushing throat. "I truly am."

He thrust the knife through the side of her chest, a clean blow straight to the lungs.

Manizheh didn't make a sound. She looked bewildered, her black eyes wide with pain.

Then she fell. The smoke holding Jamshid burst and he rushed over, just in time to catch Manizheh as she collapsed.

"Mother, wait . . . just wait." Jamshid was frantic, reaching to stem the wound.

And now Dara was coming for Nahri.

Still not comprehending what was going on, knowing only that someone who had hurt her was growing nearer, Nahri tried to crawl back and let out a guttural moan as the motion jarred the arrow still speared through her shoulder.

"Forgive me, little thief. I knew not of another way." Dara knelt at Nahri's side, placing one hand on her shoulder and the other on the arrow. "Close your eyes. It will be fast."

Entirely uncertain whether he meant to kill her or save her, Nahri gritted her teeth as Dara snapped off the silver fletching as though it were made of kindling. But she couldn't help the scream that tore from her mouth as he pulled the arrow out of her chest.

"I am sorry," he said again, his hushed words a mirror of what he'd just told Manizheh, bleeding to death in Jamshid's arms. "She was unraveling, and I saw an opportunity . . ."

". . . to trick her," Nahri finished, understanding the intent behind Dara's brutal denouncement. And what better way than by tearing down Manizheh's enemy and appealing to the most vicious things she believed? Tears rolled down Nahri's cheeks, not all due to physical pain. Her wound was already healing. "Okay." She didn't know what else to say.

"Nahri . . ." It was Jamshid, his panicked gaze darting to hers. "Nahri—I can't heal her! I don't know how."

Nahri didn't move. This was all too surreal. And yet there was one thing she still clung to. Nahri was a Nahid, and Daevabad was her responsibility.

She would not save its foe. "No," she said simply.

Her brother—her cousin—gave Nahri a look torn between anguish and understanding, and then Manizheh reached out with a shaking hand to touch his face. Jamshid turned back to her, still cradling her body, seeming to think if he prayed enough, he could save her.

But it had been some of the first advice Dara had given Nahri—the throat and lungs, a sure way to kill a daeva. And he was a weapon.

It was what he did best. Nahri could sense Manizheh's heart slowing, one lung already collapsed. Her hand fell from her son's face, leaving a smear of blood on his cheek.

Then she was gone, the most powerful of them since Anahid, dead at the hand of her Afshin.

Dara moved again, stumbling for Manizheh's body like a drunk. He took her hand. He did so gently, reverently, still bowing his head, but there was no denying the urgency with which he removed his ring from Manizheh's finger and then picked up one of the broken chunks of stone.

"Dara," Nahri started to speak, trying to find her words. "I don't think—"

He smashed the ring.

Once, twice, and then he howled, smashing it again and again with a cry that didn't sound like anything she knew, as if it were being ripped from him. Finally he dropped the rock, falling back against the parapet and gasping for breath.

But he wasn't done. Dara clawed at the contraption on his

wrist, ripping the wires out and wrenching the plates from his skin, blood and fire pouring from him in equal measure. When it was free, he flung it away with another wail, the shackle sailing toward the lake.

Trembling, Nahri forced herself to her feet. Blood was still falling from the sky, and when she looked down upon the palace's heart, she saw Manizheh's beasts and ghouls running even more rampant.

This wasn't over yet.

But then Dara let out a frightened hush of breath that stilled everything inside her.

His face was going paler by the moment, ash beading on his brow. The smoldering lines that snaked over his skin like lightning were snuffing out, turning a dull iron gray.

The next minute, she was at his side. Dara swayed, seeming to have a hard time focusing on her face. Golden blood gushed from his wrist, with more blossoming from an unseen wound on his thigh.

"Nahri," Dara murmured, "I think we have done this dying thing before."

Her heart broke all over again at his words. Nahri wanted to slap him and strangle him. She wanted to clutch him and save him.

Instead, Nahri swallowed hard. "What did Manizheh do to you? Dara—" She turned his cheek to face her when he started to drift off. "Talk to me," she begged. "Tell me how to fix you."

He blinked. "Iron," he whispered. "They poisoned me. I was dying, and she . . . and she . . ." Tears filled his eyes. "I killed my Nahid."

"You saved us. You did the right thing. The poison—what do you mean? How did they administer it?" She laid her other hand on his wrist, pulling for her healing magic.

It didn't come. Nahri tried again, and then yelped, an icy jolt of pain rushing through her hand.

The seal ring was freezing.

Frosty patterns traced over the black pearl, winding around the gold band. And not just the ring, but the very ground. The air. Her breath steamed as snow began to fall, and Dara's green eyes brightened in fevered wonder.

"Nahri." It was Jamshid. He'd laid his mother on the ground and closed her eyes. A storm of hurt raged in his expression, but the alarm with which he spoke Nahri's name cut through all that. "You made a deal with them."

"I don't care!" Nahri reached for Dara again.

This time, the punch of air was enough to knock her back.

You promised. Angry screeches in her head, icy pinpricks stabbing her skin. *You promised.*

The peris.

"Manizheh is already dead!" she yelled.

In response, a viciously cold wind spun across the pavilion, hurling bricks and debris. Hail the size of her fist plummeted through the sky, ricocheting around her.

Because it had never been about Manizheh, not truly. Or Daevabad. The peris themselves had confessed to not caring about the "squabbles" of her people. It was about Dara. The abomination, they'd called him. A daeva whose power threatened theirs.

They wanted him dead.

Dara touched the snow gathering on his face. "Peris," he said just as knowingly.

Jamshid pulled free the icy dagger from Manizheh's belt. "They aided us on the condition . . . on the condition we got rid of you," he confessed.

"Oh." A kind of weary despair, like he'd known all along how this was going to end, like he'd stopped even hoping, swept Dara's ashen face. "I suppose I should not have said all those things about burning down the wind."

Jamshid swallowed loudly. "I can do it. I'll be quick."

Dara shivered. "No, Baga Nahid, I cannot ask that of you. I—"

"Will you two shut up? I can't hear myself think!" Nahri snatched the peris' dagger out of Jamshid's hands and shot to her feet.

The wind tore at her clothes, whipping her face with stinging needles of ice. The peris' words from the mountain—the promise they'd made her swear—swirled in her head. As she had flown over Daevabad, this had all seemed so simple, so just. Dara was a killer. He needed to be brought to justice.

This was not justice, though. It was murder. And it wouldn't end at Dara. What was to keep the peris from "correcting" again? From sticking their beaks in her people's business and selecting yet another djinn to toy with?

She glanced out at the battling city. Nahri could hear death cries, the screams of those who were suffering for no good reason and the moans of ghouls and monsters. She tried to reach for the ring. With their powers restored, she knew the people below might have a fighting chance.

But nothing happened. Nahri felt no closer to granting anyone else magic. The peris had spoken of an act to bond the ring to herself, snobbishly declaring she was no Anahid.

In the distance, a tornado spun out of the sky, tearing across the terraced fields. Nahri stared at her broken home, made the plaything once again of overly powerful beings, and then she ran a finger down the icy edge of the peri's dagger.

It was so very sharp, immediately drawing a drop of blood. She stared at the dark crimson blood, at the color that unfairly defined so much.

Her lesser blood.

"Nahri . . ." Concern filled Jamshid's voice. "Nahri, what are you doing?"

Nahri looked again at her city. She gripped the dagger. "Calling a mark."

She plunged the icy blade toward her chest.

THERE WAS A SHRIEK ON THE AIR, A DOZEN BIRDLIKE voices crying out, and then taloned hands tugging at her. *No!* they shouted. *Do not!* Cold, invisible fingers grabbed hers mid-thrust.

Nahri's own quick hand still whipped forward—years of snatching purses keeping her reflexes sharp—dragging the peri with her as she shoved its blade into her heart.

The pain drove her to her knees, and then blood was gushing over her hands, pouring from her mouth. Suleiman's ring scorched on her hand, her magic going wild as her body frantically tried to save itself, tissue trying to close.

But there was no healing with the dagger in her heart.

Jamshid cried out, rushing toward her. "Nahri!"

With her dying strength, she called to the palace once more. The floor bucked up, tossing him away.

The sky changed, the clouds growing so thick it might have been a pit of gray she'd been tossed down into. The stone floor turned slick with snow and ice, wind lashing her face. Spots blossomed across Nahri's blurred vision, her mind fuzzy. But they were there—wings in dazzling jeweled colors. Angry, chirpy shouts, a great debate.

Save yourself!

A liar, she has deceived us!

This was not foreseen; this is not permissible!

The pearl peri appeared before her, her hand still pinned to Nahri's on the dagger. "Heal yourself!" she ordered. "We cannot have your blood on our hands!"

Oh, Creator, this hurt. It hurt so much. Nahri knew enough

about hearts to be able to keep a bit of blood pumping through her body, but she had only moments before she died.

So she gave herself enough strength to spit in the peri's face, more blood now than saliva, vividly crimson. "You *will* have my blood on your hands," she choked out. "My human and daeva blood. My lesser life. You will be in debt to my people for a thousand years."

The screeches started up again. God, these creatures were dramatic hypocrites. No wonder Khayzur had chosen to spend time in Dara's company.

She has ruined us! She has destroyed the balance!

"No." It was the sapphire peri, appearing at the edge of Nahri's darkening vision. A cloak of pale blue fog, like a dawn sky, draped their head. "She is waiting for our offer."

Nahri briefly closed her eyes, grimacing in pain. A half dozen sarcastic responses hovered on her tongue, but not even she was acerbic enough to waste the moments of life she had left spitting them out. "You will remove any debt I have to you—any debt my people have to you. I want our magic restored as it once was, and the veil set over my city to conceal it from humans . . ." She gasped for breath. The pain was fading, a numbness settling over her limbs. "And Daevabad . . . the marid, the island . . ."

Her speech left her. Blackness was closing in, the snowy sky her last sight. But Nahri could still feel the cool wind dancing over her cheeks, the even colder breath when the peri leaned in.

"We agree," the peri whispered. "But know this, daughter of Anahid . . . you have made an enemy today."

The peri drove the dagger deeper.

Nahri arched in pain, her body convulsing. But then the icy blade hit an object with enough force to stop it. Her mind already shut to the world outside, Nahri's abilities had turned inward, acute to every change in her body—the increasingly sluggish pulses in her brain, her last trickle of fresh blood circulating in her veins . . .

The bright, hot metal that had vanished from her finger to materialize in her heart and collide with the dagger.

Suleiman's ring.

The dagger shattered.

The icy fragments instantly melted, all but one that fused with the ring in a flash of sharp pain. The peris' cavern vanished, replaced by the sight of a crying Jamshid bent over her, his hands pressed against her bleeding chest.

"Nahri!" he begged, packing the wound. "Creator, no! Please!"

Jamshid. Nahri tried to say her brother's name, but she could barely breathe past the crushing weight in her chest. She inhaled, power rippling out from around her.

"Nahri?" Jamshid looked up from her wound, and then his eyes went very, very wide. *"Nahri?"*

She didn't respond. Nahri couldn't, overwhelmed by the world around her. It was like seeing with a new set of eyes, magic lapping from her in waves. Everyone and everything had opened up, a chaos of competing heartbeats and breaking bones. The palace itself, alive in a different sort of way, the stones heavy with age and accumulated power—the blood and work and sacrifice of centuries of Nahids. And not just Nahids. Nahri could sense the marids' presence as well—spikes of ancient strength in the scales of Tiamat laid upon the Temple garden, water magic alive and binding in the foundations and streams, in the bodies of tiny aquatic creatures crushed beneath the great building's feet. She could feel the pain of the lake, the island's dry presence an open wound.

She all but floated to her feet, glancing around and trying to get her bearings straight.

Dara. If the rest of the djinn and Daevas were bright lights,

Dara was a blazing torch, the connection Nahri felt between Suleiman's ring and the others completely absent. And yet she could see the iron killing him, the tiny particles spread through his blood like a deadly constellation.

She could see how easy it would be to remove them. To drag him back to life once more.

Dara stared at her, his eyes wide and wondrous even as he faded. "Creator be praised," he said. "Are you . . . are we . . . ?"

"Dead? No, not quite." Nahri knelt, taking his hand. It was light to the touch, ash flaking from his skin.

"I think I see it," he whispered. "The cedar grove. My sister . . ."

Grief crashed through Nahri. "Do you want to go to her? I can heal you, but I won't bring you back against your will. Not again."

Tears brimmed in Dara's eyes as he stared into a realm Nahri couldn't yet see. "I do not know." He blinked, returning his tormented gaze to her. "I do not deserve to choose."

Nahri was barely checking her own tears. She touched his face. "Your Banu Nahida is telling you to choose. You're free, Dara. Free to go. Free to stay," she said, her voice breaking.

Dara's eyes briefly slid past her shoulder again. Then he closed them, looking anguished as he took a deep breath. When he opened them again, he was focused only on Nahri.

"Save me," he begged her. "Please."

She'd been fully prepared to murder him barely an hour earlier, but now Nahri had to fight not to sob with relief. "Oh, thank God." She immediately positioned her hands, one over his heart and the other on his bleeding thigh.

Then she *pulled,* dragging the iron backward through his blood. It was something she'd never have been capable of before— something that would have killed another man.

But neither she nor Dara were normal, and so the iron came

rushing out in a metallic swarm, thick and vile on the air. Nahri snapped her fingers, and it flew off and disintegrated.

His flesh healed beneath her hand in a surge of fire. His body shifted to his other form, claws and fangs erupting from his fingers and lips. The emerald vanished in his eyes, replaced by a violent swirl of flame. The magic pouring off him was enough to knock her back.

Good. Nahri might need to use it. She staggered to her feet, power nearly ripping her apart. It was only growing stronger, the sensation of magic and heat aching to burst from her skin and stream from her fingers.

Because it wasn't hers alone. Nahri gripped the parapet, gazing out at her city. At her world, broken and bleeding.

Then she healed it, giving everything she could, everything she had to the people Suleiman had marked so long ago. To Jamshid, her fellow Nahid, gasping as his healing magic shot back through his own injuries. To Fiza and the other shafit, who felt no different to Nahri than the so-called purebloods battling at their side. To the Daevas in her quarter and the Sahrayn on the distant edge of the world. She dismantled the conjured beasts and the cruel blood magic controlling the ghouls as easily as blowing out a candle.

My home. Nahri beckoned, drawing back conjured buildings and tracing the patterns of orchards that had burned and fields struck with rot. A new warmth bubbled up in her soul as she tended to the gardens and forests, the sweet scent of orange blossoms filling her nose.

But as her hands moved and danced, Nahri saw something else.

The curse Sobek had cast upon her appearance clung to her skin in a shining dew. It would be simple to throw it off, to remove from herself the guise that had granted her a life in the human world.

I am who I am because of that human world. It wasn't the Banu Nahida who'd driven the peris to their knees, it was the con artist of
Cairo, and Nahri wouldn't cast her away. Instead, she turned her
attention outward, drawing the veil back over the mountains and
hiding their kingdom from the outer world like a mother tucking
in a child.

But Nahri wasn't done. She'd dealt harshly with the peris;
however, she knew now the marid deserved a fairer deal.

She reached out with her magic and spotted them immediately. There were only two people in Daevabad that Nahri hadn't
needed to restore power to, the two men whose paths had tangled
with hers even as they each went their own way, claimed by oppos-
ing factions and families, by the elements themselves. Water and
fire and earth. Held in check. Balanced.

Anahid had raised a city from the water. Now it was time for
her descendant to raise it even farther. Nahri reached for the city's
bedrock and shifted it as though resetting a spine. The ground
roiled beneath her feet.

She gritted her teeth, magic tearing through her. "Dara," she
managed. "The city, the buildings . . . keep them safe."

Dara didn't hesitate. Rejuvenated, he soared off on the next
wind.

Nahri reached for the embrace of the mountains, pulling
them close as if dragging a boat on a line. A very *large* boat. She
sensed the water of the lake rush up to attack . . .

. . . and then it stopped, peace settling over it.

Ali. She knew the familiar touch of his magic and could not
help but feel a similar calm as the water began to recede and change,
a wild river twisting around the city to bar it off from the lake as
the mountains closed between them. Nahri drove the mountains
higher, the new boundary between their peoples, their realms. The
lake vanished from sight, boats getting caught in new green hills
and rocky promontories as the water departed and the mists faded.

The sun kissed her face, and Nahri swayed, weary beyond measure. "Is the lake gone?" she asked, stars blossoming across her vision once again.

Jamshid let out a choked sound of disbelief. "I . . . yes. You put a *mountain* in front of it."

"Oh, good," Nahri slurred. "It worked." And then she fell into her brother's arms as darkness—denied multiple times now—finally stole her.

PART IV

45

DARA

It was remarkable that for a man of fourteen centuries, Dara was acutely certain he'd never been more uncomfortable in his life.

The hospital room was packed, the air stuffy and loaded with more tension than a room had any business containing. It was a group that should not have been together, but for the unconscious woman at its center holding them fast—and perhaps more importantly, keeping them peaceful. Because Dara suspected the only thing preventing him and the Qahtani prince from coming to blows was the fear of Nahri's wrath.

Alizayd chose that moment to look his way, his newly yellow-dappled eyes eerie and unreadable. Dara glared back, his arms crossed over his chest. He was not leaving. Not even if Razu, Kartir, and Jamshid had all tried taking him aside and suggesting a visit to the Nahid hospital at which he'd gone on a murder spree, in a section of the city he'd pulverized, was perhaps not the most diplomatic gesture to make.

Dara wasn't budging until Nahri opened her eyes.

Aqisa must have noticed the two men glaring at each other. She leaned closer to Alizayd, whispering in Geziriyya while caressing the handle of the knife at her waist.

But it was Subha who spoke. "I am *very* close to throwing you all out," the shafit doctor warned, handing a cold compress to Jamshid. "Don't think I won't." She threw a darker look Dara's way. "And don't think I'm impressed by your bluster. I still have my pistol—I know how to make you run."

Dara bristled, Aqisa laughed, and Zaynab coughed loudly, seeming to try and cover her companion's troublemaking.

"Aqisa, why don't we go check on my brother?" the princess suggested, grabbing the other woman's arm.

Jamshid glanced up. "Tell Muntadhir I'm coming to him next to check the bandage on his eye, and if he's fussed with it, I'm going to stick him in the eastern ward with the other children until he learns to follow directions."

"Will do." The Qahtani princess swept past Dara like he was a speck of dirt.

Aqisa, however, did stop. "Still hope to gut you one day," she said with a pleasant smile before following Zaynab.

Dara grunted in response, and Razu laid a hand on his shoulder. She and Elashia had planted themselves on either side of him, and Dara got the strong impression that if he made any sudden movements, he was going to find out just what kind of magic the women held.

But all other thoughts fled when Nahri stirred, mumbling in her sleep. Dara's heart lurched, and Razu tightened her grip on his shoulder.

Subha knelt at Nahri's side. "Banu Nahida?" she called softly. "Can you hear me?"

Nahri blinked slowly, clearly fighting the last vestiges of sleep. The sight made Dara ache, reminding him of the mornings on their journey so long ago. "Subha?" she croaked. "Is it really you?"

The doctor smiled. "Welcome back, my friend."

Nahri looked weary and more than a little confused. "I'm sorry about your headache. And one of you . . ." Her dazed black gaze traveled the room. "One of you is so nauseated I can't focus."

The shafit girl Dara hadn't been introduced to—the extremely disreputable-looking one who'd been waving a gun at Alizayd's side when they burst onto the roof after Nahri had passed out—flushed. "Sorry. I made some poor choices when celebrating our victory."

Faint surprise lit Nahri's face. "Did we win, then?" she asked, her voice strained.

"We won." Jamshid moved closer, bringing a cup to her lips. "Drink. You sound like a drunk frog."

Nahri scowled. "I didn't give you magic back so you could mock me." She took a sip of the water. "Speaking of water, the marid . . ."

"Are satisfied," Alizayd said. "*Very* satisfied. They're celebrating in the lake as we speak—or at least I think they're celebrating. They're a very weird lot." His voice softened. "You did it, Nahri. You saved the city."

Dara watched their gazes meet, the prince's strange eyes glowing. An expression Dara couldn't read flickered on Nahri's face, gone the next minute, replaced by a small, sad smile. "And you came back," she said.

There was something so fragile and raw in her voice that Dara stepped forward, uncaring about the many hostile glances immediately aimed his way.

"You should be resting," he announced. "All this talking, it will tax you." Suddenly aware he'd made himself known only to tell Nahri what to do yet again, Dara flushed. "I mean, if you want to rest. It is, of course, your choice," he added quickly, bringing his fingertips together in respect.

Ah, well, now everyone was simply staring at him like he was a fool.

But then the corner of Nahri's mouth lifted, quirking in what might have been a sarcastic smile and sending his heart tumbling end over end. "I am glad for your change in disposition," she said drily. She sat up, wincing and then glancing askance at her cup as the water in it abruptly boiled. "It's going to take some time to get used to this magic."

"It suits you," Dara said softly. "The magic. The seal. All of it."

Nahri met his gaze again, this time looking more uncertain. "Thanks."

Better uncertain than recoiling. But now that she was awake, the awful things he'd said to her came back. "You do not need to thank me. I should be at your feet for what happened on the roof. For the lies and shooting you—"

Alizayd whirled on him, and the temperature in the room dropped, a clammy chill sweeping the air. "You *shot* her?"

"Wasn't more than a scratch," Nahri lied, putting her hand on the prince's wrist. "I heal quickly. And it worked, Dara. That's all that matters."

But the damage had been done, the room so tense Dara felt even more violently out of place. He realized the others were already settling in—Fiza and Elashia adjusting Nahri's cushions, Subha taking her pulse, and Jamshid holding her simmering cup. Against the crush of blankets, Nahri was still holding Alizayd's wrist.

She belongs to them. And they to her. Dara bowed his head, feeling the weight of his choices and his centuries settle heavily over his shoulders. "I will not burden you further. I just wanted to make sure you were all right."

He stepped toward the door.

"Dara?"

He glanced back.

Nahri still looked guarded, but her voice was firm when she spoke. "I was glad to have saved your life. I'm glad that you chose to stay in this world."

He brought his hands up in blessing again, taking refuge in protocol as he bowed low. "May the fires burn brightly for you, Banu Nahida."

Razu left with him, pulling the door closed behind them. "I'll walk you out."

"I do not need a guide," Dara grumbled, fighting heartache. "I know this city better than all of you."

"Glad to see your spirit has remained intact, but think of this more as 'let's make sure he actually leaves.' Come."

He scowled but followed her down the darkened corridor. "Will she be okay here?"

"Of course." Razu sounded surprised by the question. "This is her hospital; people loved her here *before* she rescued the city from Manizheh and restored their magic."

The image of the packed room came to his mind again. "I did not realize the roots she'd put down in Daevabad. The family she created." It was the best word he knew to describe the crush of bickering, worried people who'd been hovering over Nahri. Daevas and djinn and shafit. From all the tribes. From different faiths.

Dara hadn't realized something like that was possible.

"Well, she is charming." Razu sounded wistful. "God, in another life, she and I could've cleaned out half the gambling halls in old Arshi."

"And in what century did Arshi fall?"

"The Creator only knows." Razu shrugged. "I try not to think about the passage of time. I'd go mad if I thought about my old life too often."

"Tell me about it," Dara muttered. "Still, you have a place here. A purpose. A life you have made and enjoy."

"Do you not think you can do the same?"

"I have not missed that you are taking me the long way out the back."

Razu's expression dimmed. "I thought it best we avoid running into, well, anyone. I believe you were under Manizheh's control when you attacked the quarters, but many don't. They believe it too convenient. They're angry and grieving and want to see someone punished."

Of course they do. It had been fourteen centuries since Qui-zi, and still he'd been known as the Scourge. How many centuries would this newest horror take to atone for?

"I should not have come to the hospital," Dara said, the realization making him ill. "I am sorry. You should not have to be guiding me about like this—I don't wish the hatred people have for me to hang on you."

"Oh, believe me, Afshin, I can handle myself."

They kept walking, emerging from a back door that led into the street. It was still early in the morning, and there weren't yet many people out.

Which meant not much blocked Dara's view of the devastated neighborhoods stretching from the hospital to the broken midan. The bodies had been removed, but dark stains, torn clothing, and abandoned shoes marked where they'd been killed, surrounded by the contents of smashed buildings—broken pots, filthy quilts, and shattered toys. The products of a lifetime, homes that had housed generations, destroyed in moments.

By him. In one corner, he'd started to conjure tents for shelters earlier before literally getting chased out. His victims didn't want his help.

And Dara didn't blame them. "I should have stood up to Manizheh sooner," he said bitterly. "Creator, a day earlier. An *hour.* So many people would still be alive."

"Afshin, if you're looking for absolution, you won't find it from me," Razu replied. "But I don't think any of us realized how far she'd fallen. Not in a thousand years would I have believed her capable of murdering other Daevas for blood magic, let alone enslaving her own Afshin."

That's not all she was capable of. In his bones, Dara knew the nobles weren't the only Daevas she'd killed: Manizheh had murdered her brother as well. The story she'd told of Rustam wanting to sacrifice his newborn niece—Dara would put money on those roles being reversed.

"I cannot even imagine how we fix all this," he confessed.

"Bit by bit. I find even the most impossible tasks seem less daunting from the inside. And we all have our own strengths, our roles to play."

Dara grimaced. "I suppose."

"Afshin, can I ask you something?" When he nodded, Razu ventured forth. "Do you love her? Truly love her?"

"I did not say you could ask me *that*." If Dara had doubted his feelings for Nahri would survive all their betrayals and battles, he'd known the moment she'd smiled at him from her hospital bed that he was besotted as ever.

"Yes," he answered after a time. "I love her. More than my life. I do not imagine I will ever love another in such a manner."

Razu gave him a sad smile. "Then make sure you follow your own words back there. She is young and brilliant, and despite everything, seems to have pulled through with soul intact." Her smile faded. "Make sure you are not her burden."

KARTIR SAT BACK ON THE CUSHIONED BENCH, DESPAIR in his face as he gestured to the scattered relics across the floor. "They're gone. Every single vessel we'd been keeping safe."

Dara knelt on the ground, picking up one of the relics. "How many?"

"Thirty-seven." Kartir's voice was hollow. "And that's only

from our records. I strongly suspect Manizheh gave the ifrit some of the 'traitors' she had arrested as well. She threatened us with that during interrogation. I would never have wanted to imagine such a thing, but men went missing, and . . ." He trailed off, looking very old. "Vizaresh travels on lightning. He could have scattered them across the world by now, and there's no way to trace them."

Dara kept picking up the relics. It didn't seem right for them to be on the floor. And yet the djinn and Daevas they belonged to were already possibly in a far worse state of affairs, waking to new human masters after the somber peace of the Temple. His memories of Manizheh's awful, gripping control came back to him, the way he'd been reduced to wailing in his head as his lips commanded destruction and his hand cut through innocents.

He swayed on his knees and reached out to steady himself on the bench. No one should have to go through that. "If they can't be traced, how were the vessels found in the first place?"

Kartir sighed. "Luck. On occasion, the ifrit would return one themselves, usually a victim who'd been particularly traumatized, to terrorize us further. But mostly it's luck. A djinn traveler hears a rumor of an oddly powerful human or an event with possibly magical roots. It's like looking for a particular grain of sand on the beach."

Creator have mercy. That went beyond luck—it sounded like an impossible task.

Dara set the collected relics aside and joined Kartir on the bench. "I still cannot believe she gave them to Vizaresh."

"She slaughtered scores of innocents for blood magic and had you destroy a fifth of the city. I'd think it would be easy to believe her capable of doing worse to victims who couldn't protest." Kartir rubbed his brow, his head uncharacteristically bare. "I keep wondering if I could have changed things. I'd known Manizheh since she was born, watched her grow up. Watched her be crushed," he said more softly. "I failed her. I should have counseled her better."

"She didn't need your counsel, my friend. She needed a different world." For no matter what Manizheh had done, part of Dara would always mourn her in a way he suspected no one else would, not even Jamshid. Dara had been in Manizheh's place—had seen his loved ones killed and his people crushed—and had believed, truly believed, that their cause was worth any amount of bloodshed.

He hadn't lied to her on the roof, even as he'd twisted his words to seize his freedom. Dara *had* understood Manizheh. He'd wanted peace for her.

He hoped wherever she was now, she found it.

"A different world," Kartir repeated faintly. "I pray we can create it. I do have faith, at least, that Banu Nahri and Baga Jamshid will be better."

"Do you think Nahri will take the throne with Muntadhir?"

The priest laughed. "They are already divorced. When I visited the Banu Nahida at the hospital this morning, I found them taking tea over the burning remains of their marriage contract, and it was the happiest I've ever seen them together. When I asked her about the throne, she told me she'd rather deal with vomiting patients than 'sit in a fancy chair I would just as soon pawn while listening to useless petitions.'"

"That sounds like her."

"I can't say I blame her. She's got enough work at the hospital and at least seems to enjoy that. She also told me that she and Alizayd have been in talks with the other tribes and the shafit about power sharing. Committees and reparations and all these other modern things."

Power sharing. Despite everything, Dara still bristled at the thought. Nahri had flown to Daevabad on a shedu and harnessed magic like Anahid herself to save the city, appearing like a goddess as she healed him with a snap of her hand. Dara could see her so easily upon the magnificent shedu throne, adorned in ceremonial finery. It was what she deserved, the only fate that seemed worthy of her glory.

But it is not what she wants. And that *is what she deserves.*

"I cannot imagine how it works," he said.

"A new government? Me neither. But give it time."

Dara had to force a smile. He might look the younger man, but he had a millennium on the priest and knew all too well the "time" that kind of change took. "Of course."

"Though speaking of time . . ." Kartir rose to his feet with a struggle, leaning heavily on his cane—it was clear imprisonment had taken a toll. "Our Baga Nahid awaits."

JAMSHID HAD WANTED HIS MOTHER'S LAST RITES CAR-ried out privately, and so Dara had built her pyre himself, letting Kartir lead the prayers. He'd stayed silent when Jamshid lit the shroud with fire conjured from his hands, watching as Kartir bowed a final time to Banu Manizheh and then quietly left.

"Do you want me to leave as well?" Dara had asked.

Jamshid hadn't looked away from the burning pyre, the flames reflected in his expressionless gaze. "No. She should have someone who knew her here."

So Dara had stayed at the side of a young man whose life he'd turned upside down, mourning a woman he wished so desperately he could have saved from herself.

After some time, Jamshid spoke again. "Was there any good in her?"

"Yes," Dara said honestly. "She was an incredible healer and cared deeply for her original followers. She loved your father. I genuinely believe she wanted better for her people and her city.

She just got very, very lost." Dara glanced at Jamshid. "And she loved you."

"She didn't know me."

"You were her son. She loved you."

Jamshid's gaze hadn't wavered. "I wish I'd had more time with her. I had so much I wanted to say. To her, to my father. A hundred accusations and questions. I'm so *angry*, and yet I'm heartbroken. And now—because I don't want to burden the people I love by mourning the murderers who ruined their lives—I have no one to talk to except you."

Slightly stung, Dara offered what he hoped was a reassuring pat on Jamshid's shoulder. "It is all right. I do owe you. For all the arrows in the back."

"It was enormously satisfying to shoot you."

"I am glad to keep finding new ways to serve the Nahids," Dara said mildly. "You still have your talent with the bow."

Jamshid shuddered. "I don't ever want to pick up a bow again. Not after the blood my parents spilled. I don't even know that I want to be called 'Baga Nahid.' That kind of responsibility . . ." Fear crept into his voice. "What if I fail?"

He is going to be a good leader. He and Nahri both. Overwhelmed by everything, Jamshid couldn't see it yet, but Dara could.

An odd sensation settled over him, and it took Dara a moment to realize it was peace. Considering the deeply traumatized state of the city, perhaps he shouldn't have felt such ease, but he did. His people were in good hands. Capable, compassionate hands. Ironic that after fighting to recover their throne for centuries, the pair of Nahids most worthy of it had the wisdom not to want it.

"What about you?" Jamshid asked, glancing at Dara for the first time. "I will not lie; I did not conceive of a way we took Daevabad back with you still alive."

"Thank you for your honesty," Dara replied, biting back his

sarcasm. Everyone was making very clear how they felt about his not being on a funeral pyre. He sighed. "I do not know what I will do next."

Jamshid was still looking at him. "I heard you and Nahri talking when she saved your life. Have you . . . have you truly seen what's *after*?"

Tamima's teasing smile and a quiet grove of cedars with a rug his mother had woven. He wasn't sure that was a place meant to be seen and shared with this world.

Dara hesitated and then spoke. "If what I have seen is true, it means there is peace for the worst of us. Rest for those who do not deserve it. It was beautiful. And it spoke to a mercy this world does not deserve."

Jamshid trembled. "I wonder if one day my parents may still see it." He glanced at the smoldering pyre and then at Dara again. "Were you not tempted?"

"Terribly so."

"So why didn't you go?"

Because I had not earned it.

The words popped into his head with almost startling clarity, taking Dara aback. Racked with pain, Manizheh dead at his hand—when Nahri appeared before him, fiery bright with Suleiman's seal blazing on her temple, she might have been an envoy from the Paradise whose judgment he feared. And when she asked what Dara wanted, the death he had craved and begged for . . .

He hadn't earned it. Not yet.

But with that revelation, more clarity. The slow settling of a decision that seemed almost obvious in retrospect.

Dara returned his gaze to Jamshid. "Because there is still something I need to do."

OF THE FORTY-TWO WARRIORS DARA HAD BROUGHT to Daevabad, eight were left, another loss for which Dara would do penance. Studying the wan, scarred faces of his paltry band made him only more aware of who was missing. Loyal Mardoniye, who'd fallen first while protecting Banu Manizheh, and Bahram, whom Dara had last spoken to when the blushing young man was trying to steal a few moments alone with Irtemiz. Gushtap, who'd always been grinning, and Laleh, one of Dara's quietest, who'd apparently been executed by Manizheh when it was discovered she'd helped some of the elderly noblewomen escape the arena.

They had all been so young. So earnest and full of life and promise.

Now they looked broken, despair in their slumped shoulders and angry mouths. Dara recognized that feeling—it was the same kind of grief and resentment that had once fueled him.

So he was going to do what he could to make sure it didn't end them. He'd found a quiet place in the Temple gardens for them to meet, a grove of shade trees surrounded by manicured rosebushes. They were not entirely concealed—there was the occasional curious face peeking through and the sound of pilgrims—but Dara suspected the sight of his group was sufficiently intimidating to scare off interlopers.

Nor did his warriors interrupt as Dara spoke; they were too well-trained. But there was no missing the growing horror and disbelief on their faces as he detailed what Manizheh had done, from executing the Daeva nobles for blood magic and enslaving him, to letting the ifrit sack the Temple for vessels and conjuring the devastating attack on the palace that had killed as many of their own people as djinn.

There was silence when he was done. Irtemiz was so pale that he almost wanted to check her pulse.

"But—but we followed her orders," Piroz finally replied. "She said all those people were guilty. Afshin, she had me dragging parents away from their children."

"I know," Dara said. "And I am so, so sorry for not having

stopped her sooner. You were my responsibility, and I failed to see what she had become until it was too late. I failed to teach you how to see it." He swallowed hard. "For a very long time, I thought my only role was to obey. To teach you all to obey. I was wrong."

"But she was a Nahid," Irtemiz protested. "One of Suleiman's blessed. She performed miracles!"

"She performed magic," Dara countered. "There was nothing miraculous about the way she murdered the Geziris or brought me back to life under her thrall."

"This is nonsense." Noshrad, the warrior Manizheh had replaced Dara with at court, shot to his feet. "There were already whispers you were going astray. Now the Nahid everyone knows you truly wanted is back, so how convenient that Banu Manizheh was corrupt." His face twisted in fury. "*You* killed her. Your own Banu Nahida. Were there any decency left in this city, you would be strung up from the Temple walls." He spat at Dara's feet. "I am finished with this conversation."

Irtemiz opened her mouth, looking upset, but Dara was already shaking his head. "Let him go." Noshrad wouldn't be the only angry Daeva. Manizheh's supporters had been dwindling, but she'd had plenty of true believers, Daevas who'd been thrilled to see their tribe rise and would not take kindly to Nahri's ideas of "power sharing." Dealing with them would be a priority for the people rebuilding the city.

But Dara was not going to be one of those people.

"Listen to me," he continued, taking a moment to look at each of them directly. "Because I am going to teach you a final lesson, one I wish had been taught to me. There is a time to fight, and you are all fierce warriors, students I am deeply proud of. But there is also a time to put down your weapons and make peace. A time to recognize that a new kind of fight has started, and it may be even harder. You may have to battle with words and with your very beliefs. But it is worth it. Your *lives* are worth it. Don't let them be made into fodder for those who will never be in the trenches. Make something of yourselves. Find happiness, and if you cannot find that here, make fresh starts in outer Daevastana."

Irtemiz spoke. "They will want to punish us, these new rulers. You don't think Muntadhir al Qahtani remembers the soldiers who held him as Manizheh cut out his eye?"

"I will take the blame for you. For all of you. I have already spoken to Baga Jamshid and Kartir. You will be safe."

"But then they will hate you."

"They have always hated me. I thrive on djinn hate." Dara smiled. "Now go. It is a lovely day, and there is rebuilding to do. Do not waste your time listening to the sermons of an old man."

They obeyed his last order with obvious reluctance, but they did leave. Dara watched them go, his heart feeling a twinge. No matter the circumstances, he had found companionship with his warriors. Training them had saved him and given him a purpose in the bleak first years in which he'd been brought back to life and was going mad with fear over Nahri. Dara loved them.

He was going to miss them terribly.

He closed his eyes, soaking in the chatter of Divasti and the smell of the fire altars. He wanted to remember this place, to imprint it upon his soul.

"What do you mean, your final lesson?"

He opened his eyes. Irtemiz had returned, her dark gaze filled with apprehension. Of course she had disobeyed. In a way, he had counted on it.

Dara took her hand. "My friend, I must beg a favor of you."

46

NAHRI

Nahri ran her hands down the little girl's shattered arm, dulling the nerves as she rebroke the parts of the bone that had healed incorrectly and then urged them to knit back together.

The Geziri girl watched with enormous gray eyes. "That's *so* neat," she enthused. She glanced back at her father. "Abba, look!"

Her father was slightly green. "I see." He turned to Nahri. "And she'll be okay after this?"

"As long as she rests for a couple of days." Nahri winked at the girl. "You're very brave. If you still think this is neat in a decade or so, come look me up, and maybe I'll take you on as a student."

"That would be amazing!"

She tugged one of the girl's braids. "I'll see if someone can't rustle up a couple of bandages for you to take home and practice with."

Nahri ducked out of the examination chamber, immediately on alert. She was light enough on her feet to avoid being trampled by the bustling crowd in the corridor, but only just barely. "Busy" didn't come close to describing the hospital. Between injured soldiers, civilians hurt in the city's destruction, and the general magical maladies that had gone untreated for weeks, the place was bursting at the seams. Subha had called in everyone she knew with the barest medical training, and Jamshid was getting a crash course in Nahid healing on the spot. But even so, it was chaos. Nahri had barely slept, barely eaten.

She didn't care. The hospital was the only place Nahri wanted to be. The work might have been grueling, but it was all that was required of her. She didn't have to think about politics or what had gone down during the brutal last fight with the woman she'd thought was her mother. She didn't have to have *feelings*. All Nahri had to do was fix people; her patients needed her so desperately that to even contemplate anything else would be selfish.

She headed for the apothecary. In the courtyard, Elashia was tending to a flock of children, having taken it upon herself to watch over the offspring of the hospital workers and patients. The kids were a brightly colored mess, laughing as they played with finger paints and squealing with delight as Elashia made their drawings come alive in squiggles of sea monsters and flying cats.

Nahri opened the apothecary door to cursing.

"Suleiman's eye," Jamshid wailed. "You're not supposed to be yellow! Why do you keep *turning yellow*?"

"Problems?" Nahri asked.

"Yes," Subha answered from the other side of the room, where, in true multitasker mastery, she was feeding her daughter and going over inventory rolls. "Your impatient apprentice thinks 'chopped' and 'minced' are interchangeable." She eyed the churning and indeed very yellow potion threatening to escape the glass vial Jamshid was holding as far away from him as possible. "Zahhak hide," she said dismissively. "You know what doesn't have a violent mind of its own? Human ingredients."

"And we bow to your superiority at every turn," Nahri said, touching her heart.

"I don't think you've voluntarily bowed to anyone in your life," Subha replied. "Especially not the way you've been brandishing your new powers. There really is no reason to heal bones from across the room. Surely sitting by the bedside is equally effective."

"It's more efficient."

"Damn it!" Jamshid dropped his flask in a metal bowl. "Now even the *bowl* is yellow."

Nahri crossed to his side and moved the tray of ingredients. "Why don't I work on potions for a bit, and you do a round in the surgical wing? Let me know if there are any emergencies."

Relief filled his face. "Have I told you that you're the best sister?"

Nahri's good mood faded a bit. "Cousin, actually."

"Sister," he insisted. "I don't care what blood says." Jamshid pressed a kiss on the top of her head and then left.

Subha sighed, setting her quill down on top of her papers. "We're running low on, well, everything. Alizayd had his ships bring as many medicinal herbs and supplies as they could carry, but we still need to find a way to get more, and soon."

"We will." Nahri took a moment to study the other doctor. Subha looked like she might have aged five years, stress lines around her eyes and new strands of silver in her hair. "When's the last time you went home and slept?"

"Before Navasatem."

Nahri sat across from her. "A wise woman once warned me that I wouldn't be helping my patients if I overexhausted myself."

"That woman had no idea what it would be like to run a hospital during a war." Subha rubbed her eyes and resettled her daughter in her lap.

"Why don't you let me take Chandra for a moment?"

The doctor gave her a skeptical look. "Much experience with babies?"

"I'm a woman of innumerable talents." Nahri set Chandra against her shoulder and rubbed the baby's back. She was warm, her soft weight unexpectedly pleasant.

"Don't be doing any Nahid tricks to summon up burps," Subha warned and stood, stretching her neck.

"Never." Nahri paused. "I'm sorry, by the way. For leaving you here all on your own."

"I didn't get the impression magically vanishing through the lake was a conscious choice."

"No, probably not. But still, it's hard not to feel guilty."

"You returned. You helped set things right. Though if we're speaking honestly, I have another question. I've heard the story going around about what Manizheh told you regarding your parents. Is it true?"

The question didn't surprise her. Nahri knew that rumor was circulating—she was letting it, taking advantage of the opportunity to declare her human heritage. "As far as I know, yes."

"So you're shafit." Subha gazed at her. "Did you know?"

That question Nahri was less prepared for, but she wasn't going to lie, not to Subha. "Yes. I didn't know the truth about my parents—I really did think I was Manizheh's daughter. But Ghassan told me years ago that I was a shafit, and I believed him."

Subha's face was unreadable. Not angry, not judging. Just waiting. "Why didn't you tell me?"

"Because I was afraid." It wasn't brave, but it was the truth. "I didn't tell anyone. I didn't think I could. I was terrified the Daevas would turn on me, and Ghassan would use it to destroy me."

"I see."

A new type of guilt snarled in Nahri, this one edged with shame. She had lived a difficult life in Daevabad under Ghassan, but it hadn't been a shafit life. She'd traded on her supposedly pureblood privilege to survive and knew it was a thing she'd be rightfully called to account for. "Do you hate me?"

"For keeping yourself alive in a foreign, hostile city of magic? No. I also don't speak for all the shafit. No one does. But make it right, Nahri. Don't let us stand alone again. That's better than any apology you could offer."

"I will," Nahri promised. "I swear—ouch!" she yelped when Chandra grabbed a handful of her hair. "Are you your mama's enforcer now?"

There was a knock at the door, and Razu stuck her head in. "Do you need saving, Banu Nahri?"

"Yes. I am thoroughly outmatched."

"No doubt." But Razu's tone turned serious. "Could we speak alone a moment?"

Subha was already taking her daughter back, expertly untangling Nahri's hair. "We'll talk more later."

Razu stayed quiet until the shafit doctor left and then entered the apothecary. "How are you feeling?" she asked. "Truthfully?"

Nahri managed a smile. "I'm exhausted and would like to no longer experience emotions, but besides that, I'm fine."

The older woman joined Nahri to lay a hand on her shoulder. "I couldn't help but hear some of your conversation as I approached. I'm sorry—I must confess that I suspected you might have been Rustam's. When we first met, I felt a shadow of the bond I'd had with him. I never had that with Manizheh, and it did make me wonder."

"Was he like her?" Nahri couldn't keep the fear from her voice.

Razu reached out, sweeping one of the curls Chandra had mussed out of Nahri's eyes. "No. Rustam never had the drive his sister had or her darkness. He was very kind and very skilled, but the Qahtanis had defeated him long ago, and I think he was just trying to survive." She gestured at the courtyard garden beyond the apothecary door. "He would have loved this place. He was incredibly talented with plants and pharmaceuticals. He'd be sitting outside, and flowers and vines would start crawling over him like pets."

"That happens to me sometimes," Nahri realized, fresh sorrow twisting through her. "God, there's just so much I'll never know."

Razu gave her a hug. "I'll help you piece together what I can. I have my stories, and I'm sure others do as well. Rustam didn't take many confidantes, but he was a well-liked man."

Nahri tried to smile. But in truth, it wasn't just her father she wanted to know about. She wanted desperately to know who her mother had been. To fill in the blank spaces in her mind and memory that had been wrenched open even further with Manizheh's cruel admission. Nahri wanted to know about the Egyptian who had come to Daevabad and crossed the path of a Baga Nahid. The woman who had defied death and Manizheh's wrath to return to her country and make a pact with the lord of the Nile himself.

Razu released her. "I haven't only come to talk about Rustam, however. I came with a message." Her bright green eyes met Nahri's. "The Afshin would like to see you."

DESPITE HAVING LIVED IN DAEVABAD FOR YEARS, Nahri had spent little time in the forests on the other side of the island. Besides well-guarded Daeva farms, the remaining wilderness was said to grow wild and unchecked. There were whispers that it was haunted, of course. That the fields of waist-high wildflowers and impenetrable woods were thick with the spirits of star-crossed lovers and wailing huntsmen, with the lost souls who'd fled to the forest and taken their lives rather than surrender to Zaydi al Qahtani's original forces.

Nahri wasn't sure she believed that, but it was remarkable

how quickly the sounds of the city vanished once she and Razu crossed through the ancient cedar doors that separated the Daeva Quarter from the woods. A well-worn road cut deep in the rocky soil, leading through a tunnel of greenery, but otherwise nature ran unchecked: vines crawling up the brass walls and the trees so thick their depths melted into darkness. Beyond, the mountains that had always been so distant now loomed close, Daevabad's island freshly nestled in their heart.

"Dara wanted to meet me *here*?" Nahri asked.

"I did."

She and Razu both jumped at Dara's voice, the Afshin suddenly on the road behind them as if he'd been there all along.

He must have seen the looks on their faces. "Forgive me. I did not mean to startle you."

Nahri stiffened. He was both the Dara she had known—his distinctly old-fashioned accent and the utterly unapologetic-sounding apology—and a stranger, the enemy general she had until just a few days ago been planning to kill. Though it was healed, her shoulder suddenly ached, a shadow of the wound his arrow had struck.

"That's all right." Nahri could hear the chill in her voice, the distance she was already trying to force between them, her body protecting itself from a future hurt.

Razu touched her wrist. "Would you like me to stay?" she asked in Tukharistani.

"No, I'm fine," Nahri insisted, feeling anything but.

Razu gave Dara a look of fierce warning and then departed. But the moment she was gone, the tension in the forest seemed to soar. It was the same wall that had reared up between them at the hospital—Nahri simply did not know how to feel about the man before her.

She stared at him, not missing that Dara was doing the same to her. Out of the splendid uniform he'd worn as Manizheh's slave, he was dressed plainly in a midnight-colored jacket that fell to his knees and baggy trousers tucked into dusty boots. His head was bare, his black curls hanging loose around his shoulders.

And yet there was something so alien about him. A feeling of otherness that Nahri had noticed back on the roof, but not given much thought to in the madness of restoring magic and moving an entire island.

"You're not marked by the curse," she said, realizing it aloud. "By Suleiman's curse, I mean."

An expression Nahri couldn't read swept Dara's face. "No, I suppose I am not. I feel restored to what I was when Manizheh resurrected me in the desert." He raised his hand, and it briefly shifted, his skin turning fiery and his fingers ending in claws before turning back. "An original daeva."

"With powers Suleiman considered too dangerous to allow to persist," Nahri added. "And I must say, I agree."

"Then I suppose it is only right you now bear his ring." Dara stepped closer, his emerald eyes trailing over her face. "How are you feeling?"

Like I'm being stabbed by an ice dagger again. "Fine," she lied. "Powerful." That wasn't a lie. "Capable of taking down an original daeva."

Dara blinked in surprise, and one corner of his mouth turned up in the bare lines of a smile. "Six years in Daevabad, and your tongue is no less sharp than when I found you scheming in a Cairo cemetery."

Nahri's heart shot into her throat. "You were the most infuriating, arrogant creature I'd ever encountered. You deserved every cutting remark."

"Fair." He took another step nearer, drinking her in. "But I hope you will not feel it is necessary to 'take me down.' At least not yet. I wished to speak with you."

"In the forest alone?"

"I thought it might be better if you were not seen with me. And it did not feel right to return to the hospital again. Not after . . ."

"I heard." Nahri knew all about Dara's attack on the hospital and the path of death he'd carved while trying to escape. She knew because she'd heard it from his victims themselves, many still in the hospital, including soldiers and civilians left crippled and children left without parents.

And that didn't even touch on the Geziris who'd died at the hands of Manizheh's poison. The soldiers and young cadets of the Royal Guard who'd been drowned, crushed, or devoured by ghouls the night of the attack. The *thousands* of innocent civilians who'd been killed when Manizheh had him pulverize the city.

Nahri glanced up at Dara's face—his earnest, uncertain, mesmerizingly beautiful face—and asked a question she hoped against hope had a different answer from the one she suspected.

"Were you . . . have you been under her control this whole time?"

"No," Dara answered simply.

She gazed at him. Alone in the forest, Dara seemed so much like the daeva who'd plucked her from Egypt. The exasperating, brooding warrior who had wanted so much for his people. For her. For both of them.

But he wasn't only that. He never would be. Nahri couldn't look at Dara and not see death and devastation. His anguished explanation about the women of Qui-zi . . . that would live in her forever.

"You rip me apart," she blurted out, the words slipping from the battle she was waging with her heart. "I've spent every day since the attack replaying your words in my head and trying to reconcile the man I knew with the merciless weapon you claimed to be. I was ready to *kill* you. And then you had to go and do the right thing."

Dara bit his lip, looking like he was close to both tears and a smile. "I am sorry. It does seem our time together has always been a source of much frustration for you."

"Not always, Dara. Not always."

He exhaled noisily and then looked away. They were both staying out of arm's reach as if by silent agreement, the shared fear that getting any closer would be to invite more pain.

After a moment, he gestured to a narrow path that wound through the tall grass. "Would you . . . would you walk with me?"

Nahri nodded silently, and they set off. Dara set the pace, seeming to glide gracefully over the uneven ground. It reminded her of their original journey, of passing through deserts and frozen plains, the long days upon their horses and barbed conversations under the stars. She'd always thought herself clever and experienced, but Nahri looked back now and realized how young she'd been. How naive about how haunted her companion truly had been.

So they walked. Through fields of pink clover and over rocky hills, along a meandering brook, and underneath the canopy of massive old cedar trees whose gnarled trunks would have taken five men to encircle. Nahri suspected much of this wilderness had originally overlooked the lake, but was hidden now by a belt of thickly forested mountains and Ali's new river, the boundary the marid wanted between their sacred waters and the djinn city. Either way, it was lovely, healthy and healed, and Nahri thought it might be time to pull down the city walls. The quiet peace and natural beauty of Shefala had impressed her, and it would be nice to let her people breathe fresh air and wander beneath the trees.

Dara spoke again, pulling Nahri from her thoughts. "When I was very young, we used to play with the Nahid children in these woods and scare ourselves silly with stories of ifrit and ghouls and all sort of beasts that would gobble us up. My cousins and I would gather fighting sticks while the Nahids healed our scrapes." His tone grew wistful. "It did not last, of course. I grew up hearing whispers from my father and uncles about the ways the Nahid Council was changing, but it took me centuries to understand."

"I suppose that's what happens when you're taught to worship your rulers."

"You were willing to sacrifice your life for Daevabad. You hold the power of a prophet in your heart, power you used to re-shape the land itself and restore magic to hundreds of thousands across the world. Do you not think yourself worthy of worship?"

"I think worship sounds exhausting. I've got enough responsibilities—I don't need expectations of perfection and divinity on top of them."

Dara regarded her, the light filtering through the canopy dappling his black hair. "Then what do you want, Nahri?"

What do you want? How many times now had Nahri been asked versions of that question? How many times had she demurred, fearing that to voice her dreams would be to destroy them?

So instead she envisioned them. She saw Daevabad rebuilt and thriving, the walls surrounding the city and dividing the tribal quarters tumbling down. The hospital filled with eager, brilliant students from all over the magical world, Subha's daughter grown enough to be doing schoolwork in the garden and quizzing Kartir and Razu on history. She saw Jamshid working hand in hand with a shafit surgeon, magic and human techniques compliment-ing each other in a perfected dance.

Nahri saw herself happy. Sitting in the Temple garden with chattering Daeva children and playing backgammon in a shafit café with Fiza. Ali grinning at her from across an unreasonable number of scrolls as, together, they rewrote the rules of their world.

"What I've always wanted," she finally answered. "I want to be a doctor. I want to fix people and fill my head with knowledge. And maybe find some riches and happiness along the way."

"You're beaming," Dara said. "I do not think I've ever seen you smile like that."

Heat filled her cheeks, and Nahri tried to reach for aloofness again. "I'm sure you disagree. You probably think I should take the throne and make everyone bow down before me."

"It does not matter what I think. It is your life." Dara's voice grew more halting. "I wish I had realized that earlier. I am sorry, sorrier than I can ever say, Nahri, that I tried to rob you of that choice. If I could go back . . . it breaks my heart to think of the different path we might have taken."

Nahri's throat constricted. She nodded, not trusting herself to speak. She was not in a place where she could look back and wonder what might have been—Nahri suspected she had as many years of healing to get through as Daevabad itself did. She had simply spent too much of her life being a survivor, picking up the pieces and moving steadily forward.

Maybe it was good the djinn lived longer than humans; Nahri had a feeling she would need those centuries.

They kept walking, still on opposite sides of the path but now not so far apart. The forest grew sparser, opening onto a lovely, flower-filled glen. Dragonflies zipped over the waist-high grass, bees dipping between the blossoms. A hoopoe bird hopped along a knobby tree branch at the edge of the woods, its black-and-orange crest catching her eye.

It wasn't the only thing that caught her eye. Nahri squinted, frowning as she studied the eastern corner of the glen. Though it was a clear, sun-drenched day, an odd haze—like the yellowed air after a sandstorm—hung over that part of the landscape, curtaining it off.

Dara must have noticed her staring. "The veil," he explained. "I discovered it earlier. The new threshold of your realm."

Nahri shivered. "I don't think I'll be crossing that anytime soon. Or possibly ever," she added, fighting a little grief at the realization. It meant she might never see Egypt again. Would almost certainly never see Yaqub again. "Not after the last time Suleiman's seal left the city."

"No," Dara agreed, his voice toneless. "I do not imagine you will."

Despite everything, Nahri could still read Dara well enough that apprehension swept her. "Dara, why did you bring me here?"

He swallowed, his bright eyes averted. "Shortly after dawn tomorrow, a Daeva warrior is going to call upon you. Her name is Irtemiz. She is—she is like a little sister to me," he said, tripping over his words. "She will have a story for you, a story I've asked her to spread."

Nahri stilled, not liking the sound of any of this. "What story?"

Dara glanced back at her, and the heartbreak in his eyes sent fear spiking through her before he even opened his mouth. "She is going to tell you that last night I got very drunk and even more brooding than usual. That in a fit of guilt, I swore to go after Vizaresh and the enslaved djinn and then crossed this veil before anyone could stop me."

Nahri blinked. Of all the things she'd thought Dara might say, that was not one of them. "I don't understand."

"I'm going after Vizaresh," he repeated. "I am going to hunt down the enslaved djinn he has stolen and return them to be freed. But I do not intend to stop there. I intend to hunt down *all* the enslaved djinn and Daevas in the human world. The ones who were lost and forgotten like I was. The ones we know about and the ones with no hope. I'm going to find their vessels and bring them home."

She fought for a response. "But *how*? The way people talk— that's impossible. Most of the vessels are rings; they're tiny. They could be anywhere in the world, and there's no way to track them."

"Then how fortunate I have millennia to discover a way."

Millennia . . . Nahri had not contemplated that aspect of Dara's new future, and the prospect tied her stomach into knots. "Dara, I know you feel guilty, but you don't have to do this. To swear yourself to some impossible quest because—"

"I know I do not have to. I want to." Dara held her gaze. "Nahri, I cannot go back and undo my mistakes, but I can find a way to do penance. To actually *use* this second chance I've been granted." He gave her a broken smile. "Or maybe at this point, my third or fourth chance."

"But you can't just leave," she objected. "The Daevas need you."

"The Daevas have *you*. They need nothing else for centuries. But they are not my only people, and there is no one better suited to go after the enslaved djinn. I have the time. I have the magic. I *very* much have the urge to hunt down ifrit. Vizaresh, Qandisha . . . they're still out there."

Nahri took a deep breath, not understanding the finality in his voice. "All right. But you can still come back and forth to Daevabad. It's not as though—"

"I cannot. Once I am past the veil, it will be like before. I will not be able to return. As you said, I do not bear Suleiman's curse."

And I cannot leave. The full weight of what Dara was trying to tell her nearly knocked Nahri off her feet.

Tears burned in her eyes. "So I'll never see you again."

"I think that likely. *Nahri*—" Dara closed the distance between them as Nahri promptly lost the battle with her tears, pulling her into his arms for the first time since the night they'd been ripped apart on the lake. "Nahri, please. Do not grieve," he whispered. "You are going to build a wonderful life here, the life you always wanted. Daevabad will be glorious for it, and it will be easier if it does not have me." Dara held her face, kissing the tears as they fell. "You have earned your happy ending, little thief. Let me do the same. Let me earn a place in the garden with my family."

Nahri choked back a sob. "But you'll be alone."

"Oh, Nahri . . ." Dara shuddered, but his voice stayed steady. "I will be all right. I won't have to hide as I once did. I can visit the places of my childhood, tell the Daevas out on the border to go pay a visit to their new Nahids." He broke away enough to look at her; his eyes were shining with his own unshed tears. "There is a whole world to explore. Kingdoms beyond our realm and so very many ifrit and peris to frighten. I am off to have adventures." He gave her a shattered half smile. "You're the one who has to stay behind with bureaucrats."

Nahri let out a weeping laugh. "Infuriating man. You don't get to make me laugh when you're breaking my heart."

"But then how would I see you smile one last time?" Dara slipped his fingers into hers, bringing them to his lips. "I will be all right, Nahri, I promise. And if Daevabad ever truly needs me—if you need me—my other vow remains. I will find a way back. I can go bully the marid again or perhaps your weird prince can take me through his waters."

"He would hate that."

"All the more appealing."

Nahri shut her eyes, grief charging over her. Falling back into their teasing—to his hands on her face and his lips on her fingers—only made this so much worse. There had to be a way around it.

You told him to choose. Back on the roof, Nahri had given Dara his freedom. She'd promised to honor his choice. Now he had made it.

Let me earn a place in the garden with my family. Nahri had no right to take that away from him. No one did.

She pulled Dara back into her arms, burying her head into his shoulder. She breathed in the smoky citrus of his skin and summoned every bit of strength she could. Another time Nahri would let herself grieve. She'd let herself mourn everything they could have become.

But right now, she would be the Banu Nahida he deserved. "I'll learn how to free them," she whispered in his ear, running her fingers through his hair a final time. "I swear to you, Afshin. Find our people, get them home, and I will free them."

Then Nahri forced herself to let him go. To unclench her fingers, untangle her arms, and stand tall.

Dara brushed the edge of her chador and then slowly, purposefully released it. "The cave alongside the Gozan. The cave where we . . ." His voice hitched. "It is well-protected from the elements. I will leave the vessels there as I find them. Send people to check every few years." He hesitated, looking like he didn't want to continue, and when he did, Nahri knew why. "Teach your children to do the same. Tell them to teach their children and the generations that come after."

Nahri swayed on her feet, seeing the centuries spill out before him. The millennia in which she would no longer be there. "I will. I swear."

Dara stepped back toward the veil, and Nahri instantly moved for him, realizing he meant to leave now.

"You don't have any supplies," she protested. "No weapons. How will you protect yourself?"

The half smile he gave her, amused and brokenhearted, would follow her to the end of her days. "I can become the wind. I think I can manage."

She wiped her eyes. "Still so arrogant."

"Still so rude." Dara's smile vanished. "May I ask you something?"

You can ask me anything if it means you stay another moment. But Nahri only nodded.

Fear lit his expression. "Back at the Euphrates, when I asked if you wanted to continue, and you took my hand . . . would you do it again? Should I have stopped, returned you to Cairo—"

Nahri instantly reached for his hand. "I would do it again, Dara. I would take your hand a thousand times over."

Dara brought her hand to his lips one last time, kissing her knuckles again. "Find your happiness, little thief. Steal it and do not ever let it go."

I won't. Nahri plucked a twig from the nearest tree and burned it in her hand. Dara wordlessly bowed, and she marked his brow with ash, fighting to keep her voice steady.

"May the fires burn brightly for you, Afshin."

Dara straightened up, holding her gaze another moment. She drank him in, memorizing his brilliant eyes and wine-dark hair. This was the man she would remember.

Then her Afshin stepped back and was gone.

Nahri waited a long moment, the noise of the forest—the hoopoe's song and rustle of leaves the only sounds.

There was a tickle at her wrist. A delicate vine, green with new growth, teased her fingers. As she watched, a jewel-bright purple flower unfurled its petals.

Nahri brought it to her face and burst into tears.

But she wasn't alone. Not in Daevabad. And she hadn't been weeping long when there was the heavy pad of a large beast, then a brilliant rainbow wing curling around her.

Nahri pressed her wet face into her shedu's silky mane. "Let's go home, Mishmish. I don't think he's coming back."

47

ALI

The lake was still once again.

Ali sat in the shallows of his river delta, submerged to his waist, his toes digging in the mud. The air was thick with fog, so moist it was hard to tell where the lake ended and the sky began. Sheets of misty rain drifted overhead. Though it was midday, the sun shining brightly overhead on the other side of the green mountains, here the light was muted to a pale glow.

He didn't mind. It was overwhelmingly peaceful, and Ali closed his eyes as he leaned against the boulder upon which Sobek lounged. The creatures of Ali's new domain, the minnows nibbling at his shins and the water snake twining around his waist, seemed to embrace him, the cool rush of mountain springs cascading over his lap.

Sobek released his wrist, and Ali blinked, dazed, as though awakening from a dream.

"See how much easier it is when you don't fight communing?"

the Nile marid remarked. "Tiamat will be pleased by these memories. You fought well."

Ali ran his hands over his face, returning to himself. Tiamat. Sobek. They were the reason he was here, reporting as the new envoy between his peoples. "It is satisfactory?" he asked groggily. "The Banu Nahida promises to respect the river as our border."

"It is satisfactory as long as the rest of her people do as well." Sobek stretched, uncurling like the crocodile he was. "You should make your river wider. I can send more of my children to settle its waters."

Ali had a very good idea what kind of children those were, and he was not ready to fill his river with djinn-eating crocodiles. "I thought we might try peace first."

"As you wish. Will you return to them now?"

He nodded. "My brother and sister wait for me. There is still much work to be done." Much work, of course, was an understatement. They had a war-torn city to put back together. They had an entire civilization to put back together. To potentially build wholly anew.

The marid let out a distinctly unimpressed snort. "Firebloods. You aim so low, Alizayd al Qahtani. You could be a proper river lord, and instead you will settle for paperwork and *numbers*." He sounded scandalized. "Wasting your life attempting to make peace between squabbling djinn in a dry stone city."

"I am sorry to be such a disappointment," Ali said drily. "I can return the armor and sword if you like."

Sobek bristled. "That will not be necessary. But know that Tiamat will expect you to return to her court and honor your pact, at least once every few years. It would be beneficial for you to visit me as well."

"Careful, Sobek. You very nearly sound fond of me."

"You know nothing of caring for a river. Someone must teach you." He gestured to the river Ali had dragged through the land when Nahri had moved the city. "These waters and the life that flow in them are your responsibility. When they thrive, you will. Neglected, you will both fall." He eyed Ali with the reptilian gaze they now shared. "You must understand, you will never have more than one foot in your djinn world again."

"I know the price I paid." Ali saw it in the eyes of every single person he encountered—from the shocked djinn around the world who needed Fiza to convince them he was still one of them to the whispers that followed him everywhere. No one had rebuked him—yet. He was one of the saviors of Daevabad, among friends and family.

But Ali knew the rebukes would come. He knew the whispers would occasionally be cutting. He'd be called a crocodile, a traitor, an abomination. His loyalty and his faith would be called into question. He knew too there would be times when it would be unbearable, when he would ache to call a flame into his hands and be a part of his people again, knowing it would never happen.

He still didn't regret it. He had helped free his city and knew too well others had paid worse prices—his Ayaanle ancestors, for one. And if he was honest, part of Ali felt at ease for the first time in his life, as if the trace of him rooted in Sobek had been acknowledged and settled.

Ali rose to his feet. "I should return."

"Yes, I suppose you should. Tell the fire-bloods we will drown them if they approach our lake."

"I'm not going to say that."

Sobek strode through the water at his side. "You should mate with the Nahid if you insist on staying here. Offspring between our peoples would better seal our new pact. They could visit me too."

And with that, Ali was abruptly done with his ancestor. "Oh, would you look at the sky," he remarked, gesturing to the featureless fog. "It's getting late. Why don't I continue alone?"

Sobek didn't seem to register Ali's dodge, looking lost in his own thoughts. "She wasn't much older than a child when first we met."

"Nahri?"

"Her mother."

Ali stopped walking. This was the first time Sobek had brought up Nahri's family on his own and definitely the first time he'd specifically mentioned her mother.

Knowing how guarded Sobek could be, Ali chose his words carefully. "So, what Manizheh told Nahri was true?" He had already shared his memories with Sobek, and the marid knew what Ali knew: that the story of Manizheh denouncing Nahri as her brother's "mistake," the daughter of a shafit mother, was spreading like wildfire.

"Yes." Sobek was silent a long moment. "Your Nahid took a great risk for peace with my people. Giving back the lake . . . it edges into a gift."

Ali sensed where this was going. "You would not wish to remain in her debt."

"No, I would not." He fixed his gaze on Ali. "The promise I made to her mother was to remove her memories so that she might start a new life. You are ally to her; I will leave it to your discretion if she has done so."

"Yes," Ali said in a rush. There was little he knew Nahri would want more. "Restore her memories. I will bring her immediately—"

"Your Nahid's memories are gone. But her mother struck a deal with me. Duriya," Sobek said, pronouncing the name with quiet reverence. "Her remembrances passed to me when she died. I can share them with you, and then you may do the same."

"But I've never done that kind of magic."

"It is not difficult." Sobek paused. The marid's face was rarely readable, shifting between humanoid and reptilian, but Ali would swear he saw a trace of sorrow. "They are not easy memories. They would be better coming from a friend."

Ali hesitated. In his mind's eye, he saw Nahri sitting beside him on the bank of the Nile, the river reflecting in her dark gaze as she spoke with palpable longing of the early years she couldn't remember.

He saw the woman she'd become, surrounded by people who loved her, the woman brave enough to challenge death itself to save them.

Ali held his hands out to Sobek. "Show me."

ALI'S HEAD WAS STILL SPINNING AS HE MADE HIS WAY upriver to where Zaynab and Muntadhir waited. It would have been faster to call upon the marid magic that would have transported him along the hidden currents beneath the water's surface. But Ali needed the walk to clear his mind of what he'd seen—not to mention contemplating how he was supposed to break this new history to the friend who'd just had her world shaken up again. He needed firm ground beneath his feet, a gradual return to the other realm that claimed him.

He heard them joking before he even came around the rocky river bend.

"—because it's not fair that you make everything look good," Zaynab was complaining. "You've been out of the dungeon less than a week. How do you already have some fancy embroidered eye patch?"

"Adoring fans, little sister. A whole network of them."

Then they were there before him, lounging on the mat Ali had carried out here and having clearly finished the food he'd brought from the kitchen. The siblings he'd thought he'd lost, the ones he'd missed and worried over so fiercely it took his breath away.

Muntadhir glanced up, grinning widely. "Zaydi! We feared you might never come back. We ate all the food just in case."

Zaynab elbowed their eldest brother. "Don't tease him. He already looks like he's going to start crying and kissing us again."

Ali was suddenly glad he'd walked back, because he had enough muddy river water clinging to his clothes to send it splashing over his brother and sister as he dropped between them, provoking yelps from both. "You know I could have been king in Ta Ntry instead of coming back for the two of you. A castle, riches . . ."

"Amma controlling your every move." Zaynab pulled over the basket. "I didn't actually let him finish the food."

"Bless you." His stomach grumbling, Ali plucked out a piece of flatbread rolled up tight with spiced lentils and cabbage.

His sister was still watching him, concern visible beneath her air of indifference. "Did everything go okay with the marid?"

"He pried a bit too deeply into plans for grandchildren, but otherwise we're fine." Ali said nothing about what Sobek had shown him; that was for Nahri alone. "As long as we respect the border, I think the peace will hold between our peoples." He took another bite. "He did suggest filling the river with crocodiles."

Zaynab shuddered. "I hope you know I'm not exploring this part of our heritage. *Ever.* I'm happy being a djinn, thank you very much." Her voice grew grimmer. "Do you think there's any chance they'll . . . let you go?" she ventured. "Return your fire magic or—"

"No," Ali said somberly. "But it's all right."

"Eh, I kind of think 'marid ambassador' looks good on you," Muntadhir observed. "You've got your own river, the silver marks add an air of mystery, and your eyes are terrifying. Should suit you well when you're negotiating the upheaval of our entire government."

"He's definitely going to auction off any family treasure he gets his hands on," Zaynab warned. "I hope you've put some away,

Dhiru. I know I have. I'll be observing this revolution of the people from the sidelines."

Ali scarfed down the rest of his food and lay back, shielding his eyes against the sun piercing through the leafy canopy. "I was hoping the two of you might *join* the revolution of the people, and then I could simply pay you salaries."

Zaynab was already shaking her head. "I love you, little brother, and I love my city, but as soon as things are calmer, I'm leaving."

"Wait, what?" Ali asked, taken aback. "Where are you going?"

"Everywhere?" His sister gave him an uncharacteristically shy smile. "I've never left Daevabad. I never thought I would leave, not unless it was for the palace of some foreign noble, a husband I'd be expected to play politics with." Zaynab toyed with the gold bangle on her wrist. "For a long time I was okay with that; I believed it the best way I could serve my family. But that world is gone, and overseeing the resistance in Daevabad . . . it was grueling. But it also taught me a lot. It taught me I want more."

Ali couldn't conceal his worry. "At least tell me you're not going alone."

"No, but thanks for thinking me incapable. Aqisa is coming with me. We'll go to Bir Nabat first. She wants to take Lubayd's ashes home."

"That's where he should rest," Ali said softly, grief rising in him at the mention of his murdered friend. "But I am going to miss you, ukhti. Terribly."

Zaynab squeezed his hand. "I'll be back, little brother. Someone responsible needs to make sure you're not mucking everything up."

Ali had left his weapons behind when he'd visited Sobek, but he sat up and reached for his zulfiqar now. "Take this."

Zaynab's gray-gold eyes went wide. "I can't take your zulfiqar!"

"It's not mine. It belongs to our family, and I'll never wield it the way I once did. Take it. Learn to summon its flames and go have some adventures, Zaynab."

Her fingers closed around the hilt. "Are you sure?"

"I am. Just as long as I can write and beg your counsel when I inevitably muck everything up."

His sister smiled. "Deal."

Ali turned to Muntadhir. "Don't tell me *you're* leaving to journey across the unknown too?"

Muntadhir shivered. "Oh, absolutely not. You will have to pry fully stocked kitchens, soft beds, and clean clothes from my bejeweled hands." He paused. "But I'm not going back to the palace either."

"You're not?" His brother and Daevabad's palace were utterly entwined in Ali's mind. "But you're the emir. I need your help."

"You'll have my help," Muntadhir assured him. "But not as emir." He looked like he was trying and failing to offer a jesting smile. "I mean, you *are* planning to abolish the monarchy, and I . . ." Muntadhir exhaled, suddenly frailer. "I can't go back there, akhi, I'm sorry. I can't go back to that place where she slaughtered my friends and poisoned my people. Where they—" A tremor rocked his brother's body, and he quickly wiped his right eye. "I know that's probably cowardly."

But Ali didn't think his brother a coward. In fact, after finding Muntadhir in the dungeon, Ali was pretty sure his brother was one of the bravest people he knew.

Ali had gone to the dungeon as soon as he knew Nahri was okay, surrounded by a ring of friends and Subha on her way. He hadn't gone alone—Jamshid had insisted on accompanying him, and as the two descended into the grim bowels of the palace dungeon, coming upon cells packed with Manizheh's rotting enemies, Ali had never been so grateful not to be alone. It was an awful scene—a testament to Manizheh's brutality as much as the pulverized neighborhoods above and the mass grave of half-burned Geziri remains they'd uncovered in the arena were.

There had been familiar faces among the prisoners, scholars and ministers and nobles Ali had known growing up, names for the rising list of the dead. And as he and Jamshid ventured deeper, Ali had started to lose what remained of his composure, begging God that he wasn't going to find the bodies of his murdered brother and sister.

He hadn't, a mercy Ali would be grateful for every day of his life. They'd discovered Zaynab first, locked away but unharmed—part of Manizheh apparently still pragmatic enough that she'd kept her most valuable hostage alive.

Zaynab had thrown herself into Ali's arms, clutching him so tight it hurt. "I knew you'd come back," she'd whispered. "I knew it."

Muntadhir had been a different story.

When they'd finally found his brother's cell and broken open the door, Ali had been convinced Muntadhir was dead. The smell of decay and bodily filth was so thick on the air, Ali could barely breathe. And when he'd spotted the emaciated man chained and slumped against the gray stone wall, it seemed impossible that it was his charming, seemingly untouchable older brother. Bruises, scars, and open weeping wounds had covered Muntadhir's grimy skin, a stained cloth barely clinging to his hips. His brother had collapsed as much as his shackles would allow him, his arms held over his head at a painful angle. His hair was overgrown, matted black curls plastered across his face.

At Ali's side, Jamshid had let out a low cry, and so Ali had ventured in first, trying to spare him as much pain as possible. Muntadhir hadn't reacted when Ali touched his neck, but Ali had been relieved to find a pulse. And when he had gently called his brother's name, Muntadhir had stirred, his chains rattling as he'd blinked open his lone eye.

And then he'd shrieked. He'd wailed that Ali was dead and had been replaced by a demon, jerking back from Jamshid's touch as well when his lover rushed across the cell. Muntadhir had started slamming his head into the wall, weeping and sobbing that the two men before him were a "Nahid trick."

Ali had been beside himself. He'd challenged Tiamat and traveled the currents of the world, but watching his big brother fall apart, he'd suddenly felt so small. So useless.

So Jamshid had stepped in.

The Baga Nahid had carefully taken Muntadhir's hands, healing him as he brushed his fingers along Muntadhir's dirt-caked skin and eased him out of the shackles. "It's me, Emir-joon," he'd assured him softly. "Just me, no tricks." He'd kissed the tips of Muntadhir's fingers. "You woke me like this after I'd been shot, do you remember? You said you were so afraid of hurting me that you knew not where else to touch."

At that Muntadhir had stopped fighting. Instead, he'd pressed his face into Jamshid's shoulder, crying even harder. "I thought you were dead," he'd sobbed. "I thought you were all dead."

And fancy eye patch and jesting smile aside, Ali still saw that man when he looked at Muntadhir now, his brother clearly trying to convince his younger siblings he was fine. Ali had learned the hard way how talented Muntadhir was at hiding his true self, even from those he loved.

Ali reached out now, gripping his brother's hand. "It's not cowardly, Dhiru. Not at all."

"I have money set aside," Zaynab said softly. "Enough to buy you a house in the Geziri Quarter."

"I'm not moving to the Geziri Quarter," Muntadhir replied.

"Jamshid . . . he said I could stay with him for a bit. He has the space, and we've always been close . . ." His brother seemed to stumble over the words, the story he must have practiced.

Oh, ahki . . . Ali bit his lip, aching to speak freely. But he didn't know if Jamshid had told Muntadhir that his little brother knew about their relationship, and Ali felt like he'd lost the right to pry. Instead, he'd work to earn Muntadhir's trust and let his brother choose when and how to share his confidences.

For now, Ali just squeezed his hand again. "That sounds like a great idea. I think it would be good for both of you."

Muntadhir gave him a slightly guarded look, but there was a glimmer of hope there. "Thanks, Zaydi." He leaned back on his elbows, the sunlight playing on his still pale face, and winked, a hint of mischief stealing into his expression. "Though you're being very rude in failing to congratulate me on my latest personal accomplishment."

"Which is?"

"Divorce." Muntadhir sighed, sounding dreamy. "Ah, the sweet feeling of freedom and the world's most ill-matched partnership going up in literal flames."

"Yes," Zaynab said sarcastically. "Because your marriage so clearly restrained you."

"You and Nahri are divorced?" Ali asked. "It is . . . official?"

Muntadhir grinned and glanced at Zaynab. "I'm telling you—at least three times."

Zaynab shook her head. "Just once. He's definitely rash enough to have done it, but there's no way he didn't immediately fall apart into a panic over sin."

Ali did indeed find himself fighting panic. "What are you two talking about?"

His sister's eyes twinkled. "How many times you've kissed Nahri."

Ali was suddenly glad he'd given up his fire magic, because otherwise he would have combusted into embarrassed flames.

"I . . . that's not—" he stammered. "I mean, it was a very emotional night."

Zaynab and Muntadhir burst into laughter.

"Once," Muntadhir agreed, laughing so hard he had to wipe a tear from his eye. "I owe you a dirham."

"You *bet* on whether or not I kissed your wife?" Ali was aghast. "What is wrong with the two of you?" When his brother and sister only cackled harder, he drew up. "I hate you. I hate you both."

Zaynab laid her head on his shoulder. "You love us."

Ali had to force a disgruntled sound. Because he did love them. And though they were mocking him and planning separate futures, he suddenly felt a spark of pure hope here in the quiet of the forest with his brother and sister, sitting between the river and the city—*his* river and *his* city—the worlds and people he would bring together. Ali had more work on his plate than ever before: a new government to establish and a ruined economy to fix. Alliances to knit back together and new family secrets to confide to his dearest of partners. A mother expecting a *very* long letter and a father to finally say funeral prayers for.

But right now, he simply sat, enjoying the sun on his face, the lake-fresh air, and the company of his family. "Alhamdulillah," he murmured. *God be praised.*

Muntadhir glanced up idly from where he was twisting a blade of grass. "What's that for?"

"Nothing. Everything." Ali smiled. "I am just so very grateful."

48

NAHRI

It took surprisingly little time to pack up the life she'd made at the palace.

Of the dozens of silk gowns and gold-embroidered chadors, Nahri took few. They were lovely, but she'd have little need for fine dresses and fancy clothes on the new path she'd set for herself. When it came to her jewelry, though, she took everything she could fit in a trunk. Nahri would never shed her memories of poverty, and while she was happy to contribute some of her belongings to the fund being established to rebuild Daevabad, she wasn't going to leave herself penniless, especially when her hospital had its own needs.

She picked through her books more carefully, fearing she'd have little free time to read for the foreseeable future. Medical texts got pulled out and packed away in a special trunk. Then Nahri straightened up, glancing around the room.

A row of small objects on the window ledge caught her eye: the little gifts the old Egyptian cook had given her with her meals. Nahri retrieved one, a small reed boat, and brushed away the dust with her thumb. She wondered if the old man had survived the attack on the palace. Maybe after she was finished packing, she'd go down to the kitchens and find out.

I should try and reach out to the other Egyptian shafit here. Now that Nahri was free to embrace her roots, it might be nice to spend some time with the rest of her exiled countryfolk. Maybe someone would be interested in returning to Cairo and bringing a very long letter to a very confused apothecarist.

Maybe someone knew of a young woman from their community who'd once caught the eye of a Baga Nahid.

But before Nahri left to go anywhere, there was one more thing she needed to retrieve. She returned to her bed and knelt on the floor.

She hesitated. She knew there was a good chance it wasn't here anymore. Though her room at the palace looked dusty and untouched, Nahri suspected it had been searched after Manizheh's invasion.

So when she ran her fingers under the crossbeams, it was with trepidation. Then her heart skipped, her hand landing on the linen-wrapped blade she'd slipped there nearly a year ago.

Dara's dagger.

Nahri pulled free the jeweled knife and unwrapped it. The polished iron glimmered in the dim light of her curtained room, the carnelians and lapis stones twinkling. She stared at the dagger, remembering the day Dara had taught her to throw it, his laugh tickling her ear. Grief rose up in her, but it had a different flavor now. A less bitter one.

I hope you earn your happy ending, Dara. I really do. Resheathing the dagger, Nahri set it next to the reed boat and the clothes she intended to bring back.

There was a soft knock. She glanced back.

Ali waited at the open door.

In the midmorning light, he seemed to stand apart, a quiet, roiling void. Ribbons of mist played around his feet, the yellow in his eyes glowing faintly, like a cat's gaze. The sun caught on what was visible of his scars, the silver molten and dazzling against his black skin.

He came back different. Fiza's parting words on the beach in Shefala, right before the pirate captain raced off with Jamshid, returned to Nahri. Nahri had been prepared, or at least, she'd tried to be, masking her shock as quickly as possible when she woke to see Ali at her side, the soft gray of his eyes replaced by Sobek's reptilian yellow-and-black. But his stilted words—for they'd barely seen each other since the battle and had yet to be alone— had only provoked more questions.

I am to be an ambassador between our peoples. They changed me so I could speak for them.

And indeed, half hidden in the shadows, Ali looked the part. A visitor from the deep, the envoy of a mysterious, unknowable world at the bottom of the sea.

He spoke softly, greeting her in the way she'd taught him. "Sabah el hayr."

"Sabah el noor," Nahri replied, rising to her feet.

Ali crossed and uncrossed his arms, as if he didn't know what to do with them. "I hope you don't mind me intruding. I heard you were here and figured I should come by. I know it's been a couple of days since we spoke."

"A week, actually," Nahri pointed out, trying to keep the emotion from her voice. "I was beginning to think you'd forgotten about us at the hospital."

He kept his gaze on the floor, toying with the tail of his turban. "I knew you'd be busy. I didn't want to bother you, and I thought—I thought I should give you some space."

Nahri inclined her head skeptically. "'Give me space'?"

"Yes."

"Alizayd al Qahtani, there is no way those are your words."

"It was Zaynab's suggestion." Ali's voice thickened with embarrassment. "She said I could be smothering."

And with that, he went from mysterious marid ambassador to the Ali she knew. A genuine smile tugged across Nahri's face, and she joined him at the door. "I don't need space from you, my friend," she said, pulling him into a hug.

Ali clutched her close. "Please don't ever stab yourself in the heart again," he begged, his words muffled against the top of her head.

"I'm hoping it was a once-in-a-lifetime event." Nahri pressed her brow to his chest. Ali felt cooler than usual, though not unpleasantly so. The smell of salt and silt was sharp on his skin, like she'd immersed herself in a stream on a chilly morning. The beat of his heart was different, slower and more drawn out.

He was changed. But it felt so good to be in his arms that Nahri didn't care. They had survived, and that was all that mattered. She let out a shudder, feeling some of the tension she'd been bottling up for days finally escape.

"Are you okay?" Ali murmured.

"No," she confessed. "But I think there's a chance I might be one day, so that's progress." Nahri took another deep breath, running her hand down the soft cotton covering his back, and then stepped away. "Come, stay with me awhile—oh, don't look at the door like that," she said, fighting a blush. Nahri *definitely* hadn't forgotten what happened the last time they were behind closed doors. "I'll leave it open so the devil can escape, all right?"

Ali looked mortified, but he didn't object as Nahri pulled him inside. "Your apartments seem to have come through the war in one piece," he said, seemingly just to be saying something.

"One of the few things that did. I can't even go into the infirmary here. Not after what Manizheh did in there. I feel like I can still smell the burned bodies of my ancestors." She sighed. "God, Ali, it's just all so much. There are so many people dead, so many lives ruined. What you said back in Cairo about it taking lifetimes to make peace—"

"Then let it take lifetimes. We'll give it a good foundation, the best we can."

Nahri rolled her eyes. "You always were a reckless optimist."

Ali clucked his tongue. "Oh no. You don't get to ever call me reckless again after threatening *peris* by puncturing your own heart."

"They annoyed me." Nahri said the words mildly, but then a hint of her old anger returned. "I won't be called inferior or lesser again. I won't have my people—*any* of them—be called that. Let alone by some meddlesome puffed-up pigeons."

"And do you think the puffed-up pigeons might return to make us regret that?"

You have made an enemy today, the peri had warned. "They didn't seem happy," Nahri admitted. "But I'm hoping their own convoluted rules about interfering keep them away until we're stronger."

"God willing." Uncertainty crept into his voice. "Regarding another overly powerful being, I hear we had an escape."

Nahri's stomach flipped. "Something like that."

Ali held her gaze; despite its new appearance, she could see a dozen questions in his eyes. "There are people demanding justice, Nahri. People who want to send soldiers after him."

"They would be wasting their time, and we all know it. No one's going to catch Dara if he doesn't want to be caught. I know people want justice," she said. "And I know we're going to be building a new government, a new world. But he's something that needed to be settled the old way, the Daeva way. Let Dara spend his millennia recovering the souls stolen by the ifrit. It's more useful than him wasting away in a dungeon."

Ali looked unconvinced. "He could raise an army and return."

He won't. Nahri had seen the resolve in Dara's good-bye—it had been just that, a farewell from a man who did not expect to see the woman he loved again. "Ali, you say you trust me," she said softly. "So trust me. He's gone."

He stared at her a moment longer but then managed a small nod. It wasn't much—Nahri knew the Geziris were within their rights to want vengeance. But their vengeance would be the result of prior vengeance. And the problem was, they weren't the only ones caught in that cycle.

It was indeed why peace was going to take lifetimes. And why, as much as it hurt, Nahri knew Dara had been right to leave. His presence would have been too divisive—too many Daevas protective of him, too many djinn and shafit rightfully furious to see Manizheh's weapon living freely among them. There might be a day when he could return—perhaps a distant generation would be removed enough from the war to know Dara as a hero first, as the Afshin who dedicated himself to rescuing enslaved souls, rather than the Scourge.

But Nahri feared that day was very far in the future.

Ali had reached up to rub a spot on his shoulder. His collar tugged away enough for Nahri to glimpse a section of scaled hide covering his skin.

"What's that?" she asked.

Ali dropped his hand, looking embarrassed. "One of Tiamat's children stung me."

"*Stung* you?"

"You don't want to know the details, believe me. Sobek healed it, but he left a mark."

"Can I see?" When Ali nodded, Nahri pushed aside his collar and traced the narrow path of the scaly scar, a ribbon of changed flesh. She didn't miss the quickened pulse of his heart as she touched him—or the effect that running her fingers over him again was having on *her*—but that was not a thing to delve into right now. "Is it permanent, what they did to you?"

"Yes. Tiamat drained the fire from my blood. She wanted to make sure I couldn't turn my back on them." Ali held her gaze, his glowing eyes filled with sorrow. "I don't think I'll be helping you conjure any more flames."

"You came back," she said fiercely. "That's all that matters." Nahri smoothed down his collar and then raised her arm, pulling back her sleeve to reveal the scar Manizheh had burned into her wrist. Despite her magic, it had not healed. "We match."

That brought a sad smile to his face. "I guess we do." Ali glanced past her shoulder and frowned. "Are you packing?"

"I am."

"Does that mean . . ." His face fell. "Are *you* leaving the palace too?" He sounded crushed but added, "I mean, not that I expected you to stay. I don't have any expectations of you. Us."

Nahri took his arm to stop his stammering. "Walk with me. I could use some fresh air."

She led him to the infirmary grounds, picking her way along the overgrown path. The garden had been poorly tended, weeds and grass snaring her healing plants, but it wasn't anything that couldn't be fixed. The orange grove was lush as ever, white flowers and bright fruit thick upon the trees.

Her father's orange grove. The resilience of the plants struck a new chord with her, as did the name he'd given her. Golbahar, a spring flower. It might not be the name Nahri had chosen, but she could still honor its meaning.

The promise of new life, unfurling after a winter of violence.

"I've found a house in the shafit district," she started. "It looks like it was abandoned even before the invasion, but it's got good bones and a little courtyard, and it's only a short walk from the hospital. The owner was willing to sell it to me for almost nothing, and I think . . . I think it would be good for me to live there."

"That sounds nice," Ali said. "Though I wish everyone I knew wasn't leaving." It sounded like he was trying to make a joke and failing. "It's going to be me, a haunted palace, and a bunch of bickering government officials and delegates trying not to kill one another."

"As if that's not your dream." Nahri pulled him into the orange grove, seating him next to her on the old swing. Ali looked warily at the roots sprawling over the ground. "Relax. You have an invitation this time. And I'm not leaving you. I'm going to help you, I promise. But I also want to start building something for myself," she said, feeling a little uncharacteristically shy. "My own home, the hospital, the kind of life I want."

"Then I'm happy for you," he said warmly. "Truly. I'm going to miss not seeing you every day, but I'm happy for you."

Nahri dropped her gaze. "I was actually hoping"—she nervously twisted the edge of her chador—"that you might visit me. Regularly. The books for the hospital . . . I was never any good with them," she added, fighting the heat in her cheeks.

"The books for the hospital?" Ali frowned and shook his head. "I can find you a much better accountant, trust me. There's so much you can do with charitable funding, and if you have a proper specialist—"

"I don't want a specialist!" Creator, this man's obliviousness was going to be the death of her. "I want to spend time with you. Time at my house being normal and not on the run from monsters or plotting revolutions. I want to see what it's like."

"Oh." Delayed understanding crossed Ali's expression. "*Oh*."

Her face was burning. "I'd make it worth your while. You check my books, and I'll teach you Divasti."

"You've saved my life multiple times, Nahri. You definitely wouldn't owe me anything for *checking your books*."

Nahri forced herself to meet his eyes, trying to summon up a very different type of courage than she was used to.

The courage to be vulnerable. "Ali, I thought I made it clear I don't intend to let you out of my debt."

She said nothing else. She couldn't. Even revealing this much of her heart was terrifying, and Nahri knew she wouldn't be capable of anything deeper, perhaps not for a long time. She'd simply had her dreams shattered too many times.

But she would lay down roots and see what grew. Nahri would steal her happiness like she'd promised Dara, but she'd do it on her terms, at her speed, and pray that this time what she built wouldn't get broken.

Ali stared back at her. And then he smiled, perhaps the brightest, happiest smile she'd ever seen from him.

"I suppose it would be the smart thing to do . . . politically," he conceded. "My Divasti really is terrible."

"It's abominable," Nahri said quickly. She fell silent, feeling both awkward and yet overwhelmingly pleased. And very aware of how quiet and isolated the orange grove was, the two of them secluded away in a nook of greenery.

That was, of course, the moment Ali chose to speak again. "You know how I have bad timing?"

Nahri groaned. "Ali, why? What now?"

"I don't know how to tell you this," he confessed. "I thought I should wait for the right time or let you grieve first." Ali reached for her hand. "But I know if I were you, I'd want to make that decision myself. And we promised—no lies between us."

Nahri's heart rose in her throat. "What is it?"

"I met with Sobek this morning." Ali held her gaze, his eyes soft. "He has your mother's memories. He showed me how I might share—"

"Yes," Nahri cut in. "Whatever they are, yes."

Ali hesitated. "They're rough, Nahri. And I've never done this before. I don't want to overwhelm you or hurt you . . ."

"I need to know. Please."

He took a deep breath. "Okay. Let me see both your hands." Nahri held out her free hand and he grasped it. "This part might sting a bit." He dug his nails into her palms.

Nahri gasped—and the garden vanished.

The memories came so fast and so thick that at first it was hard to separate them, Nahri only catching flashes before they were replaced by others. The smell of fresh bread and cuddling against a woman's warm chest. Climbing a tree to look at fields of waving sugarcane hugging the Nile. Bone-deep grief, wailing as a shrouded body was lowered into a grave.

A name. Duriya.

And then Nahri fell deep.

She was no longer the Banu Nahida, sitting in a magical garden at the side of a djinn prince. She was a little girl named Duriya, who lived alone with her widowed father in a Nile village.

Duriya raced between the sugarcane fields, jumping over the irrigation ditches and singing. She was alone as always—little girls with gold flickering in their eyes, who made cookfires flare when they got angry, had no friends—and so she spoke to the animals, telling them stories and confiding her secrets.

Then one day, one spoke back. The oldest crocodile she'd ever seen, half-starved on the riverbank. One whose eerie gaze had flickered with recognition at the gold in her eyes and the offer of salvation.

"Bring me blood," Sobek had begged. "I am so hungry."

So Duriya did. Pigeons and fish she stole from coops and nets, determined to keep her scaly pet alive. Both lonely in different ways, she spoke to him and he spoke to her. In exchange for blood, Sobek taught her small tricks, magic and mortal alike. How to conjure fire and urge wheat to blossom. The best plants for making salve and drawing out poison.

Such skills were useful in her small village. Duriya was clever, and she was dis-

creet. She might have made a happy life for herself there, if she found an adoring husband on the dim side.

But there were those who hunted humans who did magic, and when the Nile was at its lowest, Sobek too far to hear her cry for help, one of them found her.

The djinn bounty hunter had been merciless. There was money to be made in returning shafit—the word Duriya learned that would define the rest of her life—to some magical city with a foreign name on the other side of the world. The djinn had offered to spare her father if Duriya went willingly, making clear with his metal-toned eyes on her body what "willingly" meant. Tearfully, she had agreed, and then he had lied, seizing them both, and taking her anyway in the dark on the longest journey of her life.

Thus had been her introduction to her new world.

Daevabad. An overcrowded apartment in a crumbling section of the city with other shafit who spoke Arabic, who welcomed Duriya and her father and helped them find jobs in the palace. The palace itself, a thing from a fairy tale filled with equally beautiful and monstrous creatures. A king said to set vicious beasts upon his enemies and a pair of black-eyed siblings who broke bones from across the room. Frightened out of her wits, Duriya was relieved to find herself only responsible for serving the queen—a kind woman whose open love for her little son made Duriya think there was something possibly human about the creatures who'd destroyed her life.

But then the queen died, and Duriya was given to the Nahids.

A black-eyed man who veiled his face and prayed to a fire altar she couldn't understand. Who never spoke to her until he'd caught Duriya in the garden and called the jute plants she was growing to make molokhia for her homesick father a weed. The Baga Nahid had gone to tear them out, and, enraged, Duriya had struck him, lashing out with all her frustration at one of the most dangerous men in Daevabad.

He'd looked at her with astonished eyes, his veil torn and the gash she'd cut on his lip healing even as she watched.

But Rustam hadn't demanded her execution, nor had his even more frightening sister boiled her blood. Instead, he'd listened as Duriya tearfully explained why she wanted the jute, and then he touched the dark earth and made a dozen new stalks sprout.

She fell in love. It was foolish and dangerous, and back in her village, Duriya would never have been so bold. But she'd been desperate for a bit of happiness, and a sad-eyed fallen prince who was just as trapped as she was made an irresistible mark. Until her belly began to swell and her own cuts began to heal, the child growing inside her rich with magic.

Telling her father had gone badly. Telling Rustam had been worse. Duriya had not grasped the politics of the city she'd been imprisoned in. They were all djinn to her, and she hadn't understood Rustam's panicked pleas when he took her to his sister.

"Help me, Manu," he'd begged, and Manizheh had taken one look at Duriya's belly with her unreadable eyes and agreed. Again, Duriya had been smuggled away, not daring to tell her father lest the palace intrigue she'd gotten caught up in ensnare him as well.

Her daughter, born on the road and blinking up at Duriya with black eyes. Rustam holding her, a look of fragile wonder in his face as he kissed the top of the baby's head, touching her soft curls. She'd been a mix of both of them, too djinn to pass in the human world and yet visibly shafit.

"I want to take her home," he whispered, tracing a tiny peaked ear. "Back to Daevabad."

Duriya had been shocked. "But you said no one could know."

"Let people know. I don't care." Rustam, always so soft-spoken, was suddenly fierce. "I want to have a family in the city my ancestors built and teach my daughter our ways."

But Manizheh had had other ideas.

The burning plain full of broken bodies. Rustam, dazed and dying, having battled with magic Duriya hadn't known existed as he struggled to help her onto the last horse.

"Return to the human world," he'd begged, choking on his own blood as he took a last anguished look at their daughter. "Flee as fast as you can. But take this."

The emerald ring he and Manizheh had warred over. It had bonded to his finger, and blood erupted from his hand when Rustam finally ripped it off, as though the ring itself had been draining his life away.

"Get rid of it," he mumbled, ash beading on his brow.

"Come with us," Duriya had begged, adjusting the shrieking baby in her arms. "Please!"

Rustam shook his head. "Manizheh will return. I'll hold her off as long as I can. Go!"

A race across the burning grasslands. It would have killed Duriya, should have killed her, her body still recovering from labor.

But magic poured from the dark-eyed infant pressed to her chest, healing her mother unnaturally fast. When the emerald ring began to shiver, scorching her skin, Duriya had hurled it into a field, hating what the foul gem had cost her.

Duriya was done with magic. Instead, she used everything else she had to get back home. Her wits and her wiles and her body when she had no other choice. She stole, and she begged, and she conned until she stood once again on Egyptian soil.

She didn't go back to her village in the south. Instead, remembering what people said about the djinn not liking human cities, she found a town on the outskirts of mighty Cairo. Still on the Nile. Still close enough that she could kneel in the river's shallows, cut her arm, and watch the blood and tears billow on the muddy water.

"Old friend," she had wept, "I need a favor."

The years passed in a blur, Duriya finding work as a midwife and healer of sorts—piecing together what she'd seen in the infirmary and what she'd learned from Sobek. Little Golbahar, for she'd kept the name Rustam had granted their daughter, grew strong, her djinn appearance masked by Sobek. Duriya loved her fiercely, doing everything she could to keep Gol safe and hide what she could of her daughter's magic. When they curled up together at night, her daughter's knees pressed against her belly, her little chest rising and falling in sleep, Duriya had prayed to all she knew.

It hadn't been enough. Because Rustam had been right, and Manizheh eventually came for them.

The village hadn't stood a chance, destroyed in a storm of fire, its people screaming. Duriya had barely had enough time to grab Golbahar, race for the river, and call for its lord.

Sobek had not been encouraging. "They are Nahids, and our pact has been paid. The blood your request would require . . ."

Duriya didn't hesitate. She had known from the day they'd fled the burning plain that there was nothing she would not do for her child.

"I will get you your blood." Then she kissed Golbahar's head, told her she loved her, and shoved her daughter into the scaled hands of a monster.

When Manizheh arrived, she'd been furious. Duriya had never been more than a dirt-blooded nuisance, a lesser being barely worth her notice but for the Nahid child she had carried—and the ring Manizheh believed she had stolen. It didn't take much taunting to shove her over the edge.

It didn't take much to ensure Sobek got his blood.

The water was warm when Duriya finally fell, the Nile cradling her in a last embrace. She would swear clawed hands stroked her hair, but of course that was impossible. Sobek never showed such affection.

But he did whisper his promise as she died, as assuring as any prayer. "I will protect her. I will protect her always."

NAHRI WAS WEEPING BEFORE THE TOUCH OF THE RIVER faded. Her own memories were coming back in pieces. Gripping her mother's dress as Duriya jested with customers. Simple meals of beans and bread, of the sugary feteer her mother's father had taught her to make.

Of the words her mother had told her every night, simple ones, but ones no one had told Nahri since, not in language she still used to summon flames.

I love you, little one. I love you so much.

Ali was already reaching for her. Sobbing too hard to speak, Nahri threw herself in his arms and there, in the garden where her parents had met, finally mourned them.

IT WAS EVENING BY THE TIME NAHRI MADE HER WAY to the palace kitchens. She knew she looked like a wreck, her eyes red and puffy from crying. She knew as well that it would have been wiser to wait until tomorrow, until her grief had settled. Even Ali had tried to gently dissuade her, fearing the devastation that awaited if she was wrong. There had been a war, after all, and so many people had died—especially in the palace.

Nahri had gone anyway.

The kitchen staff was threadbare, reduced to a handful of shafit. But Nahri knew the moment she saw his stooped back and oil-splattered galabiyya. The old man from Egypt who'd quietly cooked meals from their shared homeland and slipped her small trinkets.

He glanced up from the dough he was kneading, and it was the face from her mother's memories, only more aged.

Nahri burst into tears. "Grandfather?"

"I KNEW THE FIRST SECOND I SAW YOU," HE WHISPERED. "You look so much like her, and when you smiled at me . . ." Her grandfather wiped his eyes with the edge of his scarf. "You have her smile. She used to smile so much back home."

The rest of the kitchen had cleared out, and the tea he had insisted on making for her sat untouched, the mint blackened. Nahri had no appetite for anything but his words.

"Why didn't you say anything?" she asked. "All this time . . ."

"I didn't dare. They were treating you like royalty; I couldn't take that away from you." He shook his head. "I'd spent a generation in this city. I knew all too well how they treated shafit, and it wasn't a life I would wish on my enemy, let alone my grand-daughter."

Nahri squeezed his hand. "I wish I had known. I wish I could have done something for you."

"I deserved every hardship. Duriya, she came to me about the pregnancy, and I—" Her grandfather briefly shut his eyes, pain crossing his face. "You grew up in our country, you know how things are. I was afraid and upset, but it's no excuse. I said things I'll never be able to take back, and then I lost her forever."

Nahri didn't know what to say. Her heart ached with the knowledge of her parents' fates. They had fought so hard to save her and to build lives for themselves in an impossible world, only to be cut down by Manizheh.

And yet she'd also seen enough to know they'd be proud of her. Nahri felt a yearning, intimate closeness with her mother, their lives almost mirrored. The lonely little girl set apart in the human world by magic, who'd been crushed in Daevabad. The woman who'd fought tooth and nail to get back to her homeland with an infant still at her breast. Nahri was a survivor, but she didn't think even she had as much strength as her mother.

I am as much Duriya as I am Rustam. Nahri had spent so much of her life focused on her Nahid heritage, and yet it was her mother, the smooth-talking shafit fighter who'd outwitted Manizheh in death to protect her child, whom Nahri had more in common with.

It gave her more peace than she would have imagined possible.

"We have each other now," Nahri said finally, still holding her grandfather's hand. "And we'll honor her memory."

For Nahri was going to bring forth a world in which her mother would have been free.

EPILOGUE

Six months after she first had tea with her grandfather, Nahri lounged on the shedu throne.

She sighed, pressing her back against the hammered gold and trailing her fingers over the priceless gems making up the wings and rising sun. The cushion was wondrously plump, and Nahri reclined, taking full enjoyment of the ludicrously expensive throne.

She tossed an apricot to Mishmish. The shedu, who seemed content to stay in Daevabad and follow her around instead of returning to the peris, caught it easily, swallowing the fruit in one gulp before returning to the nest he'd made by tearing up the carpet.

The doors to the throne room opened, revealing a man so bowed down with scrolls his tall frame was bent as he entered.

Nahri raised a palm. "Bow before me, djinn peasant. Hand over your gold, or I shall take your tongue."

Ali offered his scrolls. "Would you accept extensively detailed notes on the condition of the Treasury instead?"

"No, Ali. No one would. Everything about that sounds miserable."

"Alas." He nodded at the throne as he approached. "Don't tell me you're having second thoughts."

"If I was having second thoughts, I would have kicked you out of my house last night and gotten a proper amount of sleep instead of letting you yammer on about tax rates."

"Blame your grandfather's tea," he replied, setting down his scrolls and holding out his hand to help her down. Workers had been spending the past week starting to carefully crate up the throne so it could be taken to the Grand Temple and put on display. "It's like drinking lightning. I can't sleep for hours."

"I would never blame anything on him. He's a sweet old man who fills my house and the hospital with pastries at all hours of the day. There is a place reserved for him in Paradise."

"Undoubtedly." Ali smiled. "Are you coming down?"

Nahri stroked the jeweled arms a final time. "Yes. I just had to sit here at least once." She took his hand, clambering over the crate.

"Couldn't you sit on it at the Temple?"

"It's going to be mobbed by children day and night. Seems undignified to fight them for a seat."

She swung down, letting Ali catch her. Nahri didn't really need the help, but he looked rather dashing in a billowing silver-dark robe, and she allowed herself to enjoy the flutter in her stomach at the brief press of his hands before locking it down. She was getting better at doing so: allowing herself to savor pockets of happiness instead of worrying they'd be ripped away. Tea with her grandfather as he told stories about her mother's childhood. Venting over difficult patients with Subha and Jamshid and cracking horribly grim and inappropriate jokes. Playing the addictive human card game Fiza had introduced her and Razu to—with which the former pirate was steadily enriching herself at their expense.

Ali set her down and picked his scrolls back up. "Nervous?"

"A bit," Nahri admitted as they walked. "I'm the more 'conning everyone into compliance' than 'actually making genuine alliances and compromises' type."

"Bah, it's just like bargaining in the bazaar. But with actual life-and-death consequences. As long as we're diplomatic and patient, it will be fine, God willing. After all, what is it they say in Divasti?" he asked, reciting a very mangled and rather filthy verse in her language.

Nahri stopped, scandalized. "What did you say?"

"'A pleasant voice brings a snake out of its hole,'" Ali repeated, this time in Djinnistani. "Jamshid taught it to me." Nahri covered her mouth, failing to suppress a laugh. "Wait, *why*?"

She tried to be merciful. "That's not the exact way we say that phrase. The word he told you was 'snake.' There's another, more common meaning. For a man's, well . . ."

"Oh no." Ali looked horrified. "Nahri, I've been saying that to the Daeva delegates. I said it to the *priests*."

"Consider it a creative way to break the ice?" Ali groaned, and Nahri took his arm. "Next time, make sure you clear with me in advance any Divasti phrases Jamshid teaches you. Though I'm sure he and Muntadhir got quite the kick out of it."

"I am going to command all the liquid in the pipes running under their house to back up."

"Let me find a plumber who will give us a cut of the repair costs, and I'll help you."

Ali grinned. "Partners?"

They were at the doors to the old Royal Library. "Until the end," Nahri replied.

They entered the library, but it wasn't only books that greeted them. There was a crowd of people, already bickering. Djinn and shafit and Daeva. Representatives from all the tribes, from dozens of towns and all the provinces. From the Grand Temple and ulema, the craft guilds and the army.

To say they were a varied lot was an understatement. Not wanting to interfere, Nahri and Ali had given leeway to groups in choosing their delegates, and it seemed to have already backfired. For starters, no one was sitting. Instead, people were shouting in a dozen different languages over cushions surrounding an enormous table.

Ali gave the crowd an uncertain glance, looking a little overwhelmed. "An auspicious start to a new government."

But Nahri laughed. "Bargaining, you said?" She surveyed the crowd with the practiced air of a professional, smiling graciously as various arguing delegates glanced their way.

Nahri always smiled at her marks.

CAST OF CHARACTERS

THE ROYAL FAMILY

Daevabad is ruled by the Qahtani family, descendants of Zaydi al Qahtani, the Geziri warrior who led a rebellion to overthrow the Nahid Council and establish equality for the shafit centuries ago.

GHASSAN AL QAHTANI, king of the magical realm, defender of the faith

MUNTADHIR, Ghassan's eldest son from his Geziri first wife, the king's designated successor

HATSET, Ghassan's Ayaanle second wife and queen, hailing from a powerful family in Ta Ntry

ZAYNAB, Ghassan and Hatset's daughter, princess of Daevabad

ALIZAYD, Ghassan and Hatset's son, prince of Daevabad

Their Court and Royal Guard

WAJED, the Qaid and leader of the djinn army

ABU NUWAS, a Geziri officer

AQISA and LUBAYD, warriors and trackers from Bir Nabat, a village in Am Gezira

THE MOST HIGH AND BLESSED NAHIDS

The original rulers of Daevabad and descendants of Anahid, the Nahids were a family of extraordinary magical healers hailing from the Daeva tribe.

ANAHID, Suleiman's chosen and the original founder of Daevabad

RUSTAM, one of the last Nahid healers and a skilled botanist, murdered by the ifrit

MANIZHEH, Rustam's sister, one of the most powerful Nahid healers in centuries

JAMSHID, Manizheh's son with Kaveh, and a close confidant of Emir Muntadhir

NAHRI, a Nahid healer of uncertain parentage, left abandoned as a young child in the human land of Egypt

Their Supporters

DARAYAVAHOUSH, the last descendant of the Afshins, a Daeva military caste family that served at the right hand of the Nahid Council; known as the Scourge of Qui-zi for his violent acts during the war and later revolt against Zaydi al Qahtani

KAVEH E-PRAMUKH, the Daeva Grand Wazir

KARTIR, a Daeva high priest

NISREEN, Manizheh's and Rustam's former assistant and Nahri's current mentor

IRTEMIZ, NOSHRAD, GUSHTAP, PIROZ, MARDONIYE, and BAHRAM, soldiers

THE SHAFIT

People of mixed human and djinn heritage forced to live in Daevabad, their rights sharply curtailed.

SHEIKH ANAS, former leader of the Tanzeem and Ali's mentor, executed by the king for treason
SISTER FATUMAI, Tanzeem leader who oversaw the group's orphanage and charitable services
SUBHASHINI and PARIMAL SEN, shafit physicians

THE IFRIT

Daevas who refused to submit to Suleiman thousands of years ago and were subsequently cursed; the mortal enemies of the Nahids.

AESHMA, their leader
VIZARESH, the ifrit who first came for Nahri in Cairo
QANDISHA, the ifrit who enslaved and murdered Dara
SAHKR, Vizaresh's brother, slain by Nahri

THE FREED SLAVES OF THE IFRIT

Reviled and persecuted after Dara's rampage and death at Prince Alizayd's hand, only three formerly enslaved djinn remain in Daevabad, freed and resurrected by Nahid healers years ago.

RAZU, a gambler from Tukharistan
ELASHIA, an artist from Qart Sahar
ISSA, a scholar and historian from Ta Ntry

GLOSSARY

Beings of Fire

DAEVA: The ancient term for all fire elementals before the djinn rebellion, as well as the name of the tribe residing in Daevastana, of which Dara and Nahri are both part. Once shapeshifters who lived for millennia, the daevas had their magical abilities sharply curbed by the Prophet Suleiman as a punishment for harming humanity.

DJINN: A human word for "daeva." After Zaydi al Qahtani's rebellion, all his followers, and eventually all daevas, began using this term for their race.

IFRIT: The original daevas who defied Suleiman and were stripped of their abilities. Sworn enemies of the Nahid family, the ifrit revenge themselves by enslaving other djinn to cause chaos among humanity.

SIMURGH: Scaled firebirds that the djinn are fond of racing.

ZAHHAK: A large, flying, fire-breathing lizardlike beast.

Beings of Water

MARID: Extremely powerful water elementals. Near mythical to the djinn, the marid supposedly haven't been seen in centuries, though it's rumored the lake surrounding Daevabad was once theirs.

Beings of Air

PERI: Air elementals. More powerful than the djinn—and far more secretive—the peris keep resolutely to themselves.

RUKH: Enormous predatory firebirds that the peri can use for hunting.

SHEDU: Mythical winged lions, an emblem of the Nahid family.

Beings of Earth

GHOULS: The reanimated, cannibalistic corpses of humans who have made deals with the ifrit.

ISHTAS: A small, scaled creature obsessed with organization and footwear.

KARKADANN: A magical beast similar to an enormous rhinoceros with a horn as long as a man.

NASNAS: A venomous creature resembling a bisected human that prowls the deserts of Am Gezira and whose bite causes flesh to wither away.

Languages

DIVASTI: The language of the Daeva tribe.

DJINNISTANI: Daevabad's common tongue, a merchant creole the djinn and shafit use to speak to those outside their tribe.

GEZIRIYYA: The language of the Geziri tribe, which only members of their tribe can speak and understand.

NTARAN: The language of the Ayaanle tribe.

General Terminology

ABAYA: A loose, floor-length, full-sleeved dress worn by women.

ADHAN: The Islamic call to prayer.

AFSHIN: The name of the Daeva warrior family who once served the Nahid Council. Also used as a title.

AKHI: "My brother."

BAGA NAHID: The proper title for male healers of the Nahid family.

BANU NAHIDA: The proper title for female healers of the Nahid family.

CHADOR: An open cloak made from a semicircular cut of fabric, draped over the head and worn by Daeva women.

DIRHAM/DINAR: A type of currency used in Egypt.

DISHDASHA: A floor-length man's tunic, popular among the Geziri.

EMIR: The crown prince and designated heir to the Qahtani throne.

FAJR: The dawn hour/dawn prayer.

GALABIYYA: A traditional Egyptian garment, essentially a floor-length tunic.

GHUTRA: A male headdress.

HAMMAM: A bathhouse.

ISHA: The late evening hour/evening prayer.

MAGHRIB: The sunset hour/sunset prayer.

MIDAN: A plaza/city square.

MIHRAB: A wall niche indicating the direction of prayer.

MUEZZIN: The person who gives the call to prayer.

MUHTASIB: A market inspector.

NAVASATEM: A holiday held once a century to celebrate another generation of freedom from Suleiman's servitude. Originally a Daeva festival, Navasatem is a beloved tradition in Daevabad, attracting djinn from all over the world to take part in weeks of festivals, parades, and competitions.

QAID: The head of the Royal Guard, essentially the top military official in the djinn army.

RAKAT: A unit of prayer.

SHAFIT: People with mixed djinn and human blood.

SHAYLA: A type of women's headscarf.

SHEIKH: A religious educator/leader.

SULEIMAN'S SEAL: The seal ring Suleiman once used to control the djinn, given to the Nahids and later stolen by the Qahtanis. The bearer of Suleiman's ring can nullify any magic.

TALWAR: An Agnivanshi sword.

TANZEEM: A grassroots fundamentalist group in Daevabad dedicated to fighting for shafit rights and religious reform.

UKHTI: "My sister."

ULEMA: A legal body of religious scholars.

WAZIR: A government minister.

ZAR: A traditional ceremony meant to deal with djinn possession.

ZUHR: The noon hour/noon prayer.

ZULFIQAR: The forked copper blades of the Geziri tribe; when inflamed, their poisonous edges destroy even Nahid flesh, making them among the deadliest weapons in this world.

THE SIX TRIBES
OF THE DJINN

THE GEZIRI

Surrounded by water and caught behind the thick band of humanity in the Fertile Crescent, the djinn of Am Gezira awoke from Suleiman's curse to a far different world from their fireblooded cousins. Retreating to the depths of the Empty Quarter, to the dying cities of the Nabateans, and to the forbidding mountains of southern Arabia, the Geziri eventually learned to share the hardships of the land with their human neighbors, becoming fierce protectors of the shafit in the process. From this country of wandering poets and zulfiqar-wielding warriors came Zaydi al Qahtani, the rebel-turned-king who would seize Daevabad and Suleiman's seal from the Nahid family in a war that remade the magical world.

THE AYAANLE

Nestled between the rushing headwaters of the Nile River and the salty coast of Bet il Tiamat lies Ta Ntry, the fabled homeland of the mighty Ayaanle tribe. Rich in gold and salt—and far enough from Daevabad that its deadly politics are more game than risk— the Ayaanle are a people to envy. But behind their gleaming coral mansions and sophisticated salons lurks a history they've begun to forget . . . one that binds them in blood to their Geziri neighbors.

THE DAEVAS

Stretching from the Sea of Pearls across the plains of Persia and the mountains of gold-rich Bactria is mighty Daevastana—and just past its Gozan River lies Daevabad, the hidden city of brass. The ancient seat of the Nahid Council—the famed family of healers who once ruled the magical world—Daevastana is a coveted land, its civilization drawn from the ancient cities of Ur and Susa and the nomadic horsemen of the Saka. A proud people, the Daevas claimed the original name of the djinn race as their own . . . a slight that the other tribes never forget.

THE SAHRAYN

Sprawling from the shores of the Maghreb across the vast depths of the Sahara Desert is Qart Sahar—a land of fables and adventure even to the djinn. An enterprising people not particularly enamored of being ruled by foreigners, the Sahrayn know the mysteries of their country better than any others—the still lush rivers that flow in caves deep below the sand dunes and the ancient citadels of human civilizations lost to time and touched by forgotten magic. Skilled sailors, the Sahrayn travel upon ships of conjured smoke and sewn cord over sand and sea alike.

THE AGNIVANSHI

Stretching from the brick bones of old Harappa through the rich plains of the Deccan and misty marshes of the Sundarbans lies Agnivansha. Blessedly lush in every resource that could be dreamed of—and separated from their far more volatile neighbors by wide rivers and soaring mountains—Agnivansha is a peaceful land famed for its artisans and jewels . . . and its savvy in staying out of Daevabad's tumultuous politics.

THE TUKHARISTANIS

East of Daevabad, twisting through the peaks of the Karakorum Mountains and the vast sands of the Gobi, is Tukharistan. Trade is its lifeblood, and in the ruins of forgotten Silk Road kingdoms, the Tukharistanis make their homes. They travel unseen in caravans of smoke and silk along corridors marked by humans millennia ago, carrying with them things of myth: golden apples that cure any disease, jade keys that open worlds unseen, and perfumes that smell of paradise.

ACKNOWLEDGMENTS

Well. This has been a trip.

If you have made it this far, I would like to first thank you, dear reader. We are living in a glory age of fantasy fiction, and I know most of us have a towering pile of books we'd love to read. So thank you for picking up mine and taking a chance on a new author, a new world, and three increasingly large books. I hope you enjoyed your trip to Daevabad.

Enormous gratitude is owed as well to the book community. To the reviewers, the bloggers, the Instagrammers, the Discord, the Twitterati, the librarians, and everyone who passed the word, shared their fan art, their theories, and their love of the series. This was very much a "word of mouth" trilogy, and I am extremely grateful and honored to all the fans who kept it going. You're incredible, and I hope I didn't just completely break all your hearts. Thanks as well to all the wonderful writers I've befriended over the past few years, for your support and your advice, especially those who were kind enough to read my books, spread the word, and help out a newer colleague. You've given me an example to follow. To Cam, John, Cynthia, Fran, Roshani, Peter, and Shveta—I owe you all so very many baked goods.

Jen and Ben at ALA, thank you for guiding me through a very interesting few years! To David Pomerico, Pam Jaffee, Angela Craft, Kayleigh Webb, Mireya Chiriboga, Natasha Bardon, Jack Renninson, Jaime Witcombe, Ronnie Kutys, Mumtaz Mustafa, Mary Ann Petyak, Paula Szafranski, Victoria Mathews, Shelby Peak, Nancy Inglis, Liate Stehlik, Jennifer Hart, and everyone at HarperCollins who had a hand in putting together this trilogy, I am so, so grateful and honored to have worked with you. You have changed my life. Thank you as well to Alan Dingman for that showstopper of a final cover and to Priyanka Krishnan for getting this project off the ground.

I would never have made it through the past few years if not for the enormous support of my family. Mom and Dad, this one goes out to you, and I hope that I made you proud. Shamik, thank you for continuing to be my rock and reading approximately ninety versions of this book. Alia, my love and my greatest blessing, I could have never written the last chapter if you weren't in my life, and one day, I hope you know how much all the little drawings and notes you left on my desk kept me going.

Finally, it is no secret that we live in challenging times. There are days when it feels silly and selfish to spend my days crafting tales of monsters and magic. But I still believe, desperately, in the power of stories. If you take any message from this trilogy, I hope it is to choose what's right even when it seems hopeless—especially when it seems hopeless. Stand for justice, be a light, and remember what it is we were promised by the One who knows better.

With every hardship comes ease.

ABOUT THE AUTHOR

S. A. CHAKRABORTY is the author of the critically acclaimed and internationally bestselling Daevabad Trilogy. Her work has been nominated for the Locus, World Fantasy, Crawford, and Astounding awards. When not buried in books about thirteenth-century con artists and Abbasid political intrigue, she enjoys hiking, knitting, and re-creating unnecessarily complicated medieval meals. You can find her online at sachakraborty.com or on Twitter and Instagram at @SAChakrabooks, where she likes to talk about history, politics, and Islamic art.

She lives in New Jersey with her husband, daughter, and an ever-increasing number of cats.